IN THE SILENCE
OF TIME

Vol. 1

Kevin Corby Bowyer

Mysterious Strawberry

Cover design by: Joseph Loganbill

CONTENTS

PREFACE AND ACKNOWLEDGEMENTS

This book is based on characters introduced in my first novel, *The House on Boulby Cliff*. Readers of that book will recognise some of the names found here, particularly Kate, although she appears in the current volume only under her maiden name. *In the Silence of Time* and *The House on Boulby Cliff* occupy opposite ends of an ongoing narrative, although neither can be said to be a sequel, or prequel, of the other, and the reader can adopt either book as a starting point. The outline of the series is as follows, with *The House on Boulby Cliff* occupying both the first place and the last:

The House on Boulby Cliff
In the Silence of Time, Vol. 1
In the Silence of Time, Vol. 2
Close to the Silence
Splinters of Silence
In the Wake of Life, Vol. 1
In the Wake of Life, Vol. 2
These things, and us, are left behind
The House on Boulby Cliff

I won't say much here about the book's content – that's for you to find out. Many of the locations exist in this world; others don't. Glaisdale, Egton, Roxby, Easington, Ribchester are all real places, although some details have been modified, and precise locations tweaked just a little; lovely old Beggar's Bridge exists. Many of the pubs and inns named in the text are real, several of them still extant under the names used here. A few people are drawn from life: James Nares and Lancelot Blackburne both existed, the former as organist of York Minster, the latter as Bishop of Exeter and then Archbishop of York; and Robert Boyle is a name known to many.

I love my characters, each and every one of them. They keep me company, they haunt my thoughts, I see them all, share their hopes, their joys, their disappointments, and their sufferings. I guess every author feels something similar, especially when the story is such a long one and the souls who populate it have so much space in which to unfold. Now the time has come to cast them adrift for you, the reader, to find. It's a little frightening to allow them out into the light of day after holding them in my heart so intensely for so long.

A table of Principal Characters precedes the text of the book, but there are more tables at the end, including an alphabetical list of everyone, so you can keep track of people if you like, even the ones who only appear for a scene or two. Some will find these tables useful, others won't worry.

Many people offered advice and comment. I'd like to thank Moira Richardson, Sarah Beedle and Lisa Whistlecroft for their thoughts and wisdom on gardens and flora; Dick Williams for information on water pumps; and the huge number of friends on social media (particularly Dave Clarke) who offered advice and opinion on a multitude of subjects. I'm again indebted to Joseph Loganbill, who created the astonishing cover painting, and also to my daughter, Jeanne, who did the graphic design.

Lastly, I must thank my wife, Sandra, for reading the whole thing (twice!) and offering advice and reason. At the very last minute, she advised me to cut something out, and sitting here, writing this, I can see she was right. She's my reader and my censor. And she makes great cakes.

Needless to say, any errors that remain (and I'm sure there'll be a few) are all mine.

Kevin Corby Bowyer, Seamill, West Kilbride, Saturday
March 27, 2021

LIST OF PRINCIPAL CHARACTERS

The year of birth is given in each case to enable identification of peer groups.
The year of death is given in some instances where the disclosure does not undermine the unfolding of the story.

Catherine (Kate) Swithenbank – March 29, 1749. Principal character of this story; daughter of Alder and Nara Swithenbank; granddaughter of Hazel Priestly.

Hazel Priestly (née Sykes) – 1695. Daughter of John and Scarlet; wife of Oswin; mother of Adam, William and Nara; grandmother of Kate Swithenbank.

Nara Swithenbank (née Priestly) – May 18, 1733. Daughter of Oswin and Hazel; sister of Adam and William Priestly; wife of Alder Swithenbank; mother of Kate.

Alder Swithenbank – April 2, 1703. Labourer at Cappleman Farm; son of William and Heather; husband of Nara Priestly; father of Kate.

Meadow Reid – February 2, 1737. Daughter of Sigbert and Persephone.

Hugh Flesher – 1701. Owner of Cappleman Farm; son of Benjamin and Emmeline; father of Louise and Henry.

Cornelius East, Revd – September 12, 1700. Parson of Glaisdale.

Neil Levinson, Doctor – 1710. Medical practitioner at Easington from 1741.

Alexander Regan – January 10, 1735. Irishman; pig farmer; alehouse worker; shepherd.

Jacob Crowan – April 20, 1729. Headmaster of the Lookout; business partner of Edgar Foxley;

Knox Quinton – December 25, 1718. Jacob Crowan's assistant at the Lookout.

Stella Tenley (née Seagrove) – 1718. Headmistress at the Lookout.

Hollis Wayland, Doctor – June 27, 1729. Medical practitioner at the Lookout.

Clara Sutherland – April 27, 1738. Harp tutor at the Lookout.

Mabel Stanton – 1724. Member of the Lookout cleaning staff.

Speck Beckwith – July 7, 1719. Farmer at the Lookout.

Edgar Foxley – 1720. Business partner of Jacob Crowan and Margaret Siddon.

Valentine Parker-Sinden, Sir, Earl Horsforth – 1706. Nobleman and landowner; colleague of Edgar Foxley.

Anne (Bip) Pringle – 1749. Pupil at the Lookout.

Fuzzy Craw – September 28, 1747. Pupil at the Lookout.

Orla Stapleton (later Orla Clarke) – 1745. Pupil at the Lookout.

Vivianne (Viv) Stamper – April 15, 1743. Pupil at the Lookout.

PROLOGUE
An Island in the South Pacific
December 18, 1773

Crowan watched the boat carrying his horrified companions disappear out of sight along the coast.

He stood in the submarine silver-blue of the starry night,
the native canoe pulled up on the beach nearby, its cargo
of baskets containing the butchered remains of shipmates
he'd known. Some of the meat had been roasted. A few
bloody, hacked-off hands were recognisable by the tat-
toos they bore. The two native men who'd been on board
when Crowan and the others had intercepted the boat had
run away into the trees, leaving everything behind them.
Crowan hoped they would return. He intended to be ready.
The narrow shoreline was sticky with thick dark silt. He
knelt and smeared it on the exposed paleness of his face
and arms. Then he turned, scanned the direction in which
the two had fled, and made himself tight and small, squatting low. He knew they'd be able to see him there. They
were familiar with the terrain, probably had better night
vision than him, and were almost certainly more practised at stealthy attack. Despite his efforts at camouflage,
he'd be a sitting target. But he knew that Vivianne was
close. She wouldn't allow such a simple, pointless death.
He waited, his blade ready, listening intently for their approach.

Ten minutes passed. The gentle, regular wash of the ocean
lapped away the passage of the night. A soft breeze played
in the treetops. Birds punctured the velvet stillness with
their calls: the mysterious alto warbling of a morepork;
the sharp, knife-like thrusts of kiwis and keas; the mechan-

ical flicks and pops of a tui singing to the waxing moon.

The men came out of the woods like ghosts, totally silent, knives raised to strike. In a single movement, Crowan uncoiled and flung his blade into the chest of the closest one. The other turned to run, but Crowan was quicker. He caught the man from behind, tackled him to the ground and knelt savagely on his back, cracking ribs. The native's blade went flying, but Crowan reached out and grabbed the weapon. He pulled back the man's head and slit his throat in a single pull from left to right, then held him by the hair as his life gurgled away into the black mud.

The stillness of the night returned. Crowan stood and looked at the other man lying injured nearby, the knife protruding from his chest. He was attempting to sit up, panting, grasping the weapon's handle, wincing in pain. Crowan bent down and yanked the knife out of the dying man's body, causing him to cry out in agony. He fell back and stared up in terror at the tall, powerful Englishman.

Fate had presented an opportunity for Crowan to test his recently acquired property. He reached into his pocket, pulled out the little wooden pot and carefully removed the lid. There was just enough light for him to see the greasy substance inside. The helpless man on the ground was wearing some kind of animal skin around his loins. Crowan knelt and cut it off, pressed a corner of the garment into the ointment, and smeared the substance on his opponent's chest. The effect was as he'd remembered. In less than a minute all physical movement ceased, although the victim's horror-filled eyes indicated that full consciousness remained. He was paralysed.

Crowan calmly took up his razor-sharp blade once more and showed it to his victim. Then he began to cut...

1. CAPPLEMAN FARM
Wednesday April 22, 1733

The name, Cappleman Farm, was an old one. Geoffrey Capple-
man was the last occupant to bear it, and he had only a single
child, a daughter, Margaret. In 1626 Margaret married William
Flesher, and Cappleman Farm had been passed down in the
Flesher family ever since – from William to Timothy to the cur-
rent patriarch, Benjamin, who eventually handed over the run-
ning of the place to his son, Hugh.

Hugh Flesher and his parents lived in the fourteenth-century
manor house on the high ground in the estate's eastern end. The
building was a substantial timber-framed two-storied struc-
ture, its external plaster a dull orange. The front of the house
faced an enclosure containing stables and other outbuildings.
Extensive landscaped gardens, a knot garden and a pond lay to
the building's rear, and woods to the east higher up the slope.

Families grew up on Cappleman Farm, generations came and
passed, traditions were laid down, loves and rivalries were es-
tablished. It was a precious place for those who lived there – it
was their world.

Funeral of John Sykes, 1657-1733
The Address, by Cornelius East, Parson of Glaisdale

"Today we mourn the loss of a dear friend, one of the most
cherished members of our community, and a personal
friend of mine during the last nine years, ever since my
calling led me to you. I'm sad that I never knew John's wife,
Scarlet – mother of our own beloved Hazel…"

(Hazel Priestly, sitting in the front row, tearful and heavily
pregnant, felt her hand squeezed by her husband, Oswin.)

"…lost to him – and to all of us – fourteen years ago when

she was still in the prime of her life..."

(My mama, thought Hazel. Only forty-nine, and such a beauty.)

"John began working on the farm in 1675. He was one of the wisest men I've known. But the history of his family was a tragic one. His father was attacked in York, robbed and left to die in the street; his mother succumbed to a fever a year later. John, orphaned, wandered from place to place, taking itinerant work wherever he could get it. He told me he felt no sense of belonging until he found his way to Cappleman Farm and became part of our family. He met Scarlet Marshall here and fell in love. As we know, Scarlet's history too was a tragic one..."

(Certainly was, thought Hazel. Scarlet's own grandmother, Anne White, was hanged for witchcraft at Stowmarket in 1646 by Matthew Hopkins, before the very eyes of her five-year-old daughter Daisy.)

"John and Scarlet pledged themselves to each other in 1693, handfasted in the old way, the traditional way known in these parts since before the Church came. The ceremony was held in the meadow, with the river running by – a hot, sunny, happy day, so it's said. John was thirty-six, Scarlet twenty-three. He loved her dearly. It must have been memorable." He scanned the stalls. "Yes, looking out at you now, I can see nodding heads – the older folk here – some of you remember it."

Cornelius paused, bowed his head, and Hazel saw he was struggling to control his emotions. *Poor Cornelius. I think my dad was your best friend...*

The parson blinked the moisture from his eyes, looked up and went on. "Many times during these last years I sat with John in his garden while he shared his memories. He'd look far away into the sunset and tell me about his girl, his Scarlet. He held her in the eye of his mind. Their life together was a blessed one. John was always calm, always thoughtful, always loving. I never heard him raise his voice..."

(Neither did I, thought Hazel.)

"...I never heard him speak ill of anyone. I never saw him dismiss or belittle anyone. He was a fine man. Whenever we feel despondent, irritated, angry, uncharitable, ill-contented or forgotten, we should remember John. He was an example and a guiding light to us all."

Cornelius's address went on, but Hazel found it difficult to stay focused. The baby was kicking, and she needed the jakes. She was becoming anxious, sweaty, trying not to draw attention to herself, hoping she wouldn't wee on the floor.

The sermon came to an end, and there were a few prayers; then the church band began to play some dignified music for the exit of the funeral procession. The pallbearers lifted John's coffin, and the congregation stood. She and Oswin followed behind, he supporting her on his arm, their two sons, Adam and William (aged thirteen and nine), behind them. Then came Benjamin Flesher and his wife Emmeline, together with their son, Hugh, all dressed in their best black. John and Benjamin had enjoyed a good relationship, often sat together and toasted the sun as it went down, just how Parson Cornelius had described.

Two other local parsons followed: Hubert Cromwell, from Roxby, and old Egbert Trommel, parson of Easington. Egbert had never married. He always looked dusty, creased, and smelt a little odd.

Next came Doctor William Clover and his wife, Miriam, close friends of the Priestlys despite what some might have believed irreconcilable professional beliefs. Hazel Priestly had inherited the mantle of "wise woman" from her mother and was often called upon to ease maladies and supply salves, potions, oils and more, the techniques and recipes handed down through generations. She was asked to bless children from time to time and carried out various other functions. In many parts of the country, the practice of such an art was known to bring the "wise woman" into conflict with the local surgeon. Hazel felt fortunate in her relationship with Dr Clover, who treated her with respect and gave her his friendship.

Behind the doctor and his wife came the Swifts and the Buckleys. Seventeen-year-old Elys Buckley held hands with his young sweetheart Alicia Hebden (fourteen, but blooming into young womanhood, all rosy). The remainder of the congregation followed – Alicia's parents, then the other farmworkers and visitors: Alder Swithenbank, Tozer Robinson, Tozer's pretty, young wife Apple, Apple's elderly mother Fiona Barrow, and all the rest. About a hundred and fifty people in all.

It was a bright day, sunny, comfortably warm, but not overbearing. The people passed through the gate into the burial ground adjoining the main churchyard and gathered around the newly dug grave. Parson Cornelius waited for the crowd to become still, then read the committal while John's body was lowered into the earth beside that of his wife.

Benjamin Flesher waited a few seconds after Cornelius had given the final blessing, then called out, reminding everyone that all were welcome at the reception in the manor house.

Cappleman farm was large, and the big house was situated close to its eastern boundary, some distance from the church in the village of Glaisdale. Several carriages had been organised for those less able to undertake the journey on foot, and these began to fill as the crowd dispersed. Hazel received the greetings, kisses and good wishes of the people as they passed.

"Ready to go, dear?" asked Oswin, their two boys at his side.

"I need a pee, " she replied. Looking over Oswin's shoulder, she saw Benjamin Flesher approaching. "I'll burst..." she whispered.

Benjamin was not completely ignorant of the inconveniences of pregnancy and saw Hazel's discomfort in her face.

He waved and said, "We'll wait for you – there's no rush."

"Thank you, Benjamin." She hurried to the far side of the plot and through the gate into the adjacent field, currently lying fallow. Once out of sight, she lifted her skirt and her shift, squatted down as best she could with her back resting against the cool wall, closed her eyes and let go. "Oh, blessed relief..." she muttered, the flow darkening the earth between her shoes.

As she squeezed out the last few drops, Hazel opened her eyes and looked over the field. The cool breeze refreshed her, and the clouds, huge white barges, sailed across the sky with almost imperceptible slowness. The gentle chattering of birds punctuated the tranquillity, and a pair of large white butterflies played in the old Yew tree. A cuckoo called, far away, languid. Hazel allowed the gentle breath of the air to dry her flesh. The love of her father was close by. She felt his calm in the trees, in the wind.

"Bless you, pa," she murmured.

After a moment she drew herself up, tutted at the small splash on her stockings, smoothed her clothes and walked back through the gate.

Oswin watched, smiling as she approached. "Better?" Hazel inclined her head and gave him a big-eyed sideways grin. *The problems of motherhood begin long before birth*, she thought.

Benjamin waited at the reins of the carriage just beyond the churchyard wall. Emmeline waved as the Priestlys approached and moved over to make room for them in the open coach. "Up you come," she said to Hazel, and Hugh rose from his seat to take her hand as she stepped forward.

"Mind how you go," said Oswin, helping her up onto the running board and following her in, the boys behind.

"All aboard?" asked Benjamin, craning round to see. "Away we go then." He clicked the horses into action, and they set off.

The village common lay to the left of the road, the Red

Lion and the houses of the main street facing it. At the crossroads, they turned left and entered the farm, following the tree-lined southern edge of the common, the field used for extra pasture on the right. Soon the river Esk became visible, flowing in from the left and passing beneath the road. The common gave way to farmland at that point, and the water meadow appeared on their right, beyond the river. From that point, they began to pass people on foot, heading towards the manor house. Many raised their hats or their hands in greeting as the carriage passed by.

The farm labourers' dwellings came into view, the cottages scattered on either side of the road, making a little village clustered round a large wooden handpump. They drove on past barns, cattle sheds and other farm buildings, with yet more fields beyond. Vine Cottage lay at the eastern end of the meadow...

(A two-storied thatched house of uncertain age, Vine Cottage was largely timber-framed, with dark plaster, but extensive areas of stonework suggested that parts of the house were older than the main structure. One of these portions was around the front door, where the image of an ancient Green Man smiled above the lintel. The cottage drew its name from the leafy vines that flowed from his mouth. Another substantial patch of stonework rose to one side of the house, where a weather-worn sheela-na-gig lay in the wall on its side as if it had been reused from some earlier structure. The designation "Cottage" was said to predate the enlargement of the building some centuries previously.

Vine Cottage was the home of Hazel and Oswin Priestly and their two boys...)

... Vine Cottage lay at the eastern end of the meadow at the junction of two roads. Watermill Lane turned off to the right, tracing the course of the Esk, but the path to the big house lay straight ahead, following the road uphill, with more fields on either side. As they neared the manor house, they passed the homes of the Swifts and the Buckleys, next to each other on the north side of the track. Carriages were drawn up in the yards of the two houses, the horses already stabled...

(...Two substantial houses – handsome buildings, timber-framed with whitewashed plaster, and slated roofs. They were situated immediately to the west of the manor house. Erected in 1579, they were built on the site of two much older dwellings that had been destroyed by fire. The houses were occupied by two families who'd been in service to the Fleshers for generations: the Swifts and the Buckleys.
Douglas Buckley, middle-aged, grey, portly and dignified, fulfilled the role of butler to the Fleshers. Douglas's wife Maria worked as head cook. Their two children, Elys (seventeen) and Sally (fifteen) – both slender, brown-haired and freckly like their mother – fulfilled the functions of footman and maid.
Bernard Swift, head of the other family, acted as steward to Hugh Flesher, helping to run the estate, looking after its financial affairs. Bernard was twelve years younger than Douglas, more lightly built, blonde, with a receding hairline. Bernard's wife Florence was the assistant cook, second in command of the kitchen. They had a nine-year-old son, Richard, and their household was further augmented by Bernard's sixty-eight-year-old mother Lucinda, and Florence's fifty-four-year-old mother, Martha Wheatley. Lucinda was frail and rarely ventured outside the house, but Martha, still strong and full of enthusiasm despite her plumpness and long, unruly grey hair, could occasionally be found assisting Maria and Florence in the Fleshers' kitchen...)

Benjamin drove through the manor house gates and pulled up before the front door. Douglas Buckley, dressed in his best butler's black and white livery, watch chain gleaming, came out to greet them.

"Mrs Priestly," he said, kissing Hazel's cheek in welcome.

"Douglas," she returned, giving him a little hug.

Once inside the house, Benjamin took Hazel by the arm and steered her to a large wooden armchair with a red goose-feather cushion. She settled into it gratefully – the road through the farm was always bumpy, and she was acutely aware of the baby's weight.

Hazel was thirty-eight years old, Oswin forty-three. Their boy Adam had been born in 1720, William in 1724, and the child she was currently bearing had come as a surprise. She secretly hoped it would be a girl, although a third boy would be equally welcome. She had names prepared for either eventuality, both approved by her husband.

William brought her a plate of food; Adam, a china cup and dish of tea. "Thank you, my dears," she said. Chairs were drawn up to her right and left, and she was soon engaged in conversation.

Cornelius East, parson of Glaisdale since 1724, stood nearby with his teacup, his trim, expertly-sculpted black beard as immaculate as ever. Nine years previously his bishop had sent him from Oxford to this remote part of the rural north, with a warning about the familial line of so-called "wise women" associated with Glaisdale and the neighbouring hamlets. It was said to be a powerful tradition handed down from mother to daughter. The old Pagan religions were reported to linger with an unusual tenacity in the region despite the instruction of the Church and the threats of hell. The bishop had made it clear that Cornelius was expected to grub out the unwanted weeds and set the people firmly on the road to Christ Jesus. Cornelius, aged just twenty-four, had arrived in the village with a sense of trepidation. Although fuelled in his faith, he was equally aware that he'd been set the task of stamping out traditions that were ancient. He felt very much the incomer that he was.

Cornelius spent the first few days of his arrival worrying about how he should begin, conscious of the likelihood of resistance and swift failure. After a few days he decided that the best course of action was probably to face the dilemma head on, and asked his housekeeper where he might find the celebrated "wise-woman". She directed him to a house on the farm, little more than two miles from his church. Dressed in black and white clerical garb, frock coat, tricorn hat, and carrying his most impressive walking stick, he made his way to the house, heart pounding ever more fiercely with anxiety, and knocked on the door. He'd been expecting a warted, filthy old crone with straggly grey hair, who would cackle as she mocked him. But the door was opened by a beautiful blonde young woman with blue eyes, rosy cheeks and a wide happy smile, pregnant to almost full term with her second child.

"You must be our new parson! Welcome to the village. I'm Hazel." She took his hand and kissed him on both cheeks. The vision and the greeting were so utterly unexpected that he was hardly able to speak. He fell in love with her immediately. There was no question of any kind of hostility between them. In any case, it was clear to Cornelius that the only way to win the affections of these people, with their deep sense of history and tradition, was to embrace their way of life and make it part of his own, so he joined in with their festivals and celebrated together with them. In return, they attended his church. Everyone was happy.

And now here he was nine years later. Hazel was pregnant again and looked just as adorable, and not a day older, than when he'd first laid eyes on her. Her family had been a source of great support and encouragement to Cornelius, and his friendship with John was particularly precious in his memory. But he gave equal thanks for his closeness to Hazel and calm, kind Oswin.

Cornelius felt very deeply that the Lord God had smiled on

him the day he was sent to Glaisdale.

A brief aside concerning the circumstances
that brought about Apple Barrow

Harry Barrow and his older brother Robert arrived at the farm in 1675. They'd come from a farm near Berwick where they'd had a serious argument with their father's second wife and were looking for a new place to settle and begin afresh. Harry was only seventeen at the time, his brother two years older. Just a few months after their arrival, Robert fell in love with a girl at Houseman Farm, twelve miles to the southwest, having met her at a fair in Whitby. He moved away and left younger brother by himself, hoping that one day perhaps he too would find someone with whom he could share his life.

Harry enjoyed a couple of short-lived relationships with farm girls, but it took him seventeen years to find Fiona Lemon, the love of his life. Sadly for Harry, Fiona was already married to big strong Vincent Lemon, a loud, overbearing bully. Even so, the two new lovers embarked on a secret affair that lasted for thirteen years. They met whenever they could and kept their passion completely hidden, even from their closest friends. No-one ever found out about them.

When Vincent was killed in a brawl in Whitby in 1705, the coast was clear for them to emerge into the light and marry. They were handfasted in Cappleman meadow in 1706, old Daisy Marshall presiding – one of the last such ceremonies that she performed. Daisy was Scarlet Sykes's mother, Hazel Priestly's grandmother. She was also the daughter of Anne White, the famous witch hanged at Stowmarket by the Witchfinder General.

Fiona Barrow (née Lemon) had never before managed to conceive, either with Vincent or with Harry, so it came as a great surprise to everyone when she became pregnant in 1707, at the age of thirty-seven. Their one and only child, Apple, was born in May 1708. Harry was fifty by then – old enough to be his daughter's grandfather. Apple – pretty, blonde, lively, loving and popular – was the joy of their lives. One day, in the fruitiest, juiciest bloom of her girlhood, Apple met gangly, awkward Tozer Robinson...

Back to the funeral reception

Two labourers – best friends, Alder Swithenbank and twenty-eight-year-old Tozer Robinson – sat together drinking ale in the warm sunshine beyond the manor house's kitchen door, avoiding the bustle of the reception within.

"A sad day," said Alder.

"So it is," Tozer agreed. "At least the sun's shining."

Alder raised his flagon. "Here's to old John."

Tozer elevated his ale and agreed. "Old John. One of the best."

Tozer Robinson had arrived at Cappleman Farm in 1721, aged sixteen. He aspired to be a thatcher but was accident-prone and regularly fell off roofs, injuring himself. Benjamin Flesher invited him to stay on as a ploughman and general labourer, which he was happy enough to do. He was thin, awkward, with straw-coloured hair and an apologetic expression.

Alder, nearly two years older than Tozer, had appeared out of nowhere in 1724, when he'd been twenty-one years old. He was vague about his earlier life; his parents were "down south"; he'd worked "here and there". He was big and strong, muscly and powerful. Tozer, thin and gentle by comparison, admired Alder's build and felt pleased that the bigger man seemed to like him despite being his physical opposite. Tozer was also impressed that Alder was named after a tree. He decided that if he ever had any children of his own, they would all be named after trees, like Alder.

A few short months after Alder appeared on the farm,

Tozer noticed lovely Apple Barrow, sixteen years old, all ripe and soft. Perhaps some of Alder's masculinity rubbed off on Tozer, because Apple became pregnant with Tozer's child almost as soon as she disappeared into a hayloft with him. Apple's parents were none too pleased with Tozer, although they'd grown fond of him and his sunny sense of humour. Tozer promised to marry their precious daughter, their much-loved only child.

Willow Robinson was born in 1725, and Tozer wed Apple the year after. More tree-children followed: Hazel in 1729 (named in honour of Hazel Priestly, who blessed the child), and Cedar in 1731. Tozer liked to think that he and lovely Apple were planting a forest.

Alder Swithenbank had a secret: he was on the run from a string of furious parents, having already fathered at least eight children before he was twenty, the earliest when he was just fourteen. On arrival at Cappleman farm, he'd decided to settle down and try to keep his breeches on – and had managed the exercise with some success, although he was quite well known among the Whitby prostitutes. He was familiar with the clap and the itch, but had been lucky in avoiding the pox.

Old Egbert Trommel, parson of Easington, sat with Benjamin Flesher (at seventy, just five years Egbert's junior), Benjamin's wife Emmeline, and Hubert Cromwell. Hubert, a young man in his middle twenties, had become parson of the nearby village of Roxby in 1726. He was more than forty years younger than Egbert and was well used to hearing the old bachelor's ingrained opinions.

Egbert disapproved of country superstitions. He was courteous enough to Hazel but considered her "spells" (as he called them) to be against the teachings of the Church. He'd moved to Easington in 1722 in what he considered to be his retirement after a long life of ministry in Cambridge. He was a serious, intellectual, troubled man who rarely smiled. Since his late teenage years, he'd been aware that he found the company of men more appealing than that of women, and had gone on to lead a lonely life, celibate and aloof. He avoided any situation in which his feelings might become apparent. Consequently, he'd never had a companion, and his only real friends were his books.

Hugh Flesher sat with Bernard Swift and Doctor William Clover drinking mead while William's wife Miriam wandered in the garden inspecting the blooms. Hugh and Bernard discussed business. William listened politely, offering occasional comments, keeping half an eye on Hazel. William had delivered both Hazel's boys and expected to be called to the birth of her third child in the next few weeks.

Doctor Clover was popular and had managed his practice in Easington since 1708. He'd known Hazel's mother Scarlet very well and had enjoyed just as warm a friendship with her as he did with her daughter. There had never been any animosity or conflict between them. Scarlet sometimes sent her "patients" to see William; William sometime sent his patients to Scarlet – later to Hazel. He didn't dismiss the old ways, and like Parson Cornelius, was accepted into them by the people as a friend. He was a modest, quiet man. William and Miriam had married late in life, just four years previously. They'd both been fifty and accepted that it was too late to have a family of their own.

Maria Buckley, Florence Swift, Sally Buckley, and Apple Robinson worked hard in the kitchen below stairs, ensuring a steady supply of refreshments.

Meanwhile, upstairs in the house, Douglas Buckley, his teenage son Elys, and Elys's sweetheart, Alicia Hebden – all respectfully dressed in their best – kept the glasses and cups filled.

Monday May 18, 1733

It was a warm afternoon. The boys were outside, playing nearby with their friends. Oswin Priestly sat helpless before his hearth, too concerned about his wife to do anything or to think clearly. Doctor Clover had presented him with a glass of brandy and told him to sit still and wait.

Oswin listened for sounds from upstairs. There were occasional cries and shouts, probably all from Hazel, the words indecipherable. He thought he should be doing something but didn't know what. This swamp-like feeling of impotence was not new to him – he'd experienced the same sense of redundancy at the birth of his two sons – but the familiarity didn't make things any easier. The doctor had basically told him to stay out of the way unless called, and had then leapt up the stairs to join Hazel, already in labour, and the three women who'd been on standby to help: Maria Buckley, Florence Swift, and Tozer's wife, Apple. Hazel had sent Adam running for them much earlier, and they'd arrived, calm and efficient, aprons in place, carrying blankets and various bits and pieces. They'd prepared water in the bedroom, both cold and warm, and had more ready in the kitchen.

Oswin had desired a function of some kind. He'd asked Apple, "What should I do?" and she'd shrugged and replied, "Read a book?"

Hazel was lying on her back, knees spread, sweat draining in rivulets from her face and body. This birth seemed no easier than the previous two, and she whimpered, panted and groaned with the effort of it.

"It won't be long, Hazel. Just a while more. It's going really well. Makes me want another," said Apple, giving her shoulder a squeeze.

Hazel snorted. "That's funny! Every woman who's ever been here must think, *I'll never bloody do this again!*"

"Almost done, m'dear," said William Clover. "You're an established expert. The head's coming. Give it a nudge if you can."

Hazel took a deep breath and pushed down, crying out.

"Very good," said William. "You make it look easy. For the record – I feel no pain."

Hazel had always been fond of his sense of humour and even now couldn't help laughing.

Florence gave an excited cry. "Oh my! There's the hair!" She and Apple watched with amazed delight as the baby's head emerged.

William took hold of the child and said, "You're over the threshold, Hazel. Another shove and there'll be no going back for the wee thing."

Hazel pushed again, and the baby was suddenly there in his hands. The watching women gasped with delight. After the initial hesitancy it had happened so quickly.

"She's arrived," said the doctor. "You have a little lady. Well done!"

Hazel sighed with relief and lay back. William took a scoop of cold water and splashed it on the tiny girl, who flinched in shock and began to cry loudly. The child was not alone – Florence and Apple were also in tears – the bedroom thrummed with the sound of three sobbing females. Maria quickly cleaned the baby, wrapped her in a blanket and handed her to Hazel, the uncut cord trailing behind.

"Let's get the father," said William. He opened the door and found Oswin already standing outside on the landing.

"I was listening," he explained.

"Congratulations Oswin," said William. "Your wife's done it again." He stepped back and motioned the thankful father inside. Oswin sat on the edge of the bed, took his wife in his arms and tearfully looked at the new life. "My darlings!" he said.

"Oswin," said Hazel, streaked with sweat and tears. "You have a daughter." She looked at the tiny child and quietly said, "Nara."

"Nara Priestly," whispered Apple.

"Nara," said Florence.

William smiled, wiping his hands.

"Nara Priestly," said Maria. "That's a lovely name!"

2. THE RISE OF JACOB CROWAN
London, 1729-1747

Jacob Crowan had not always been evil.

He was born in 1729 to William and Ruby. William was a cobbler and rented the Ludgate Hill shop above which the family lived. The street was busy, with the west front of St Paul's Cathedral a few hundred yards uphill to the left. Jacob's father was a small, morose man who found little joy in life. His profession necessitated membership of the Cordwainers' Company, and he found himself constantly irritated by their restrictive rules of manufacture and trade. Nevertheless, he made a reasonable living and was known to be a good craftsman.

Ruby found him increasingly dull and left the family when her son was four years old. Jacob had only vague recollections of her and was never sure if his memories were genuine or invented to fill the empty space she left behind.

William Crowan remarried in 1737 when Jacob was eight. He'd met his glamorous, ginger-haired, fleshy new wife, Alison, in an alehouse on Lovat Lane. She was twenty years younger than him. Alison willingly learned his craft, assisting in the workshop and helping to keep the accounts straight. She seemed happy and smiled at Jacob a lot, though she never cuddled him. Jacob sensed that she found him a little disgusting for some reason. Perhaps he smelled or was ugly. He never really warmed to her as a mother, but his father appeared to be happier and even whistled now and then as he worked.

In the autumn of that year, Jacob was formally taken on as an apprentice in his father's business. He began to assist in the shop and set out to master the art of leatherworking.

John Noon and Margaret Southwell, both in their twenties, also worked in the shop. They were quiet, diligent workers who earned a modest wage and produced shoes fine enough in quality to gain William's approval. Margaret was married and lived with her husband on the other side of the river in Southwark, crossing London Bridge in the dimness between the overhanging houses each morning to get to work. John Noon was studious, unattached, and lodged in a rented room in Cheapside. In addition to his work in the shop, William employed him as Jacob's tutor.

Many of William's clients preferred to be fitted at home, so he made a weekly round with his tools and materials, John in tow. Alison took advantage of these regular absences. She would send Margaret out to purchase provisions, or charge her with some other task, and tell Jacob to go upstairs and study in his room until summoned. She would then lock the double doors leading to the living apartment and wait alone in the shop.

For the first two weeks of this repeated ritual, innocent Jacob thought nothing was amiss. But then he began to wonder what Alison was up to all alone and decided to find out. Mustering his courage, he crept down the stairs and stealthily made his way to the swing doors that gave access to the workshop. They were locked of course, and he couldn't get in, but he found that the pressure of his toe against the left door forced open a gap, a narrow slot through which he could spy.

There was a man in the workshop, standing very close to his stepmother, his hands on her waist. Jacob had a good view of the man's left side. He was well dressed, middle-aged and sported a splendid moustache. Jacob recognised him as one of his father's customers. He could just make out their voices, although they spoke quietly as if concerned about being overheard.

"Come on then, Your Worship. We don't have long," Alison said. "You'll want to inspect the evidence."

"Over you go then..." The man encouraged her with a wave of his hand.

Alison turned around and leant over the workbench, her top half disappearing from Jacob's view. The man then lifted her skirt and shift, and for a brief moment Jacob caught a glimpse of her exposed backside. The sight shocked him – he'd never seen it before. The man seemed to be fiddling with his own clothes, but the angle of vision available to the spy obscured most of the detail. Some kind of activity was taking place, the man apparently executing a species of subtle dance. They were speaking, but Jacob couldn't make out the words. The motion went on for a couple of minutes, accelerating towards its conclusion, their voices becoming increasingly urgent. Then the action ceased, there was a moment of stillness, and the man leaned forward and sighed. He remained immobile for a few seconds, then muttered something Jacob didn't understand and stepped back. Whatever had occurred, it appeared to have achieved its termination.

"Nice, Your Honour?" It was Alison's voice.

"It was delightful, as always. Thank you, Mrs Crowan."

Alison stood up and allowed her clothes to fall back into place. She reached up, and resting her hands on her friend's chest, offered him a brief kiss, which he accepted before dropping a couple of shiny gold coins onto the worktop.

"Why, thank you, My Lord," she said. "How thoughtful."

He chuckled gently. "Please madam – you're not in the dock. I shall visit you again if I may." He seemed to be fiddling with her through her clothes.

"You're most welcome." She was smiling at him. The man (Jacob still couldn't recall his name) turned, unlocked and opened the door to the street, and left. Alison strode towards the double doors at the rear of the shop, behind which Jacob was hiding. He turned and fled up the stairs as quickly as he could before the lock clicked open.

"Jacob! Studies over. Back to work, please."

Margaret returned to the shop just as Jacob reappeared from his "studies". Alison looked at him and smiled, but Jacob still had in his mind a vivid image of her buttocks and found it a struggle to come to terms with his newly widened awareness of the universe. He managed a polite greeting.

During the following weeks, it became ever more clear to Jacob that his mother was running some additional business in the shop. He spied on her as she entertained several visitors. A few of them appeared only once; others were satisfied customers who required a regular service. Despite repeated scrutiny, he was never able to see his stepmother's pego. There appeared to be quite a lot of hair in that general region, but no physical appendage resembling his own. Jacob wondered if this was a fundamental difference between boys and girls, and became determined to ascertain if it was indeed the case.

He had a few coins of his own, and on the rare occasions he was asked to go out and purchase things – fruit, vegetables, whatever may have been the requirement of the moment – he would cast his eye around for one or other of the poor street girls, and offer her a penny to show beneath her skirt. He felt no erotic urge at this stage – only an intense curiosity. And he quickly learned that his suspicions were correct. Jacob had a vague notion that his secret alleyway activities were probably wrong and that he would be in trouble if his father or stepmother found out.

There was a near disaster one day. He was returning to the shop with a basket of fruit from Spitalfields Market when he caught sight of what he took to be a suitable girl standing in the street. He said hello, and offering his usual reward of a penny, asked his question. He always accepted if any particular girl said no, and would apologise and walk away immediately. This girl just looked at him, her face impassive beneath her bonnet and curly hair, and gave no answer at all. He took her hand, led her into the adjacent narrow passageway and lifted her skirt. There was a cry from the street and her mother came running towards him. Jacob had no time to flee – the woman was on him in an instant and repeatedly boxed his ears.

"Filthy, filthy, filthy little toad!" She was out of control, striking him in outrage. Jacob thought she might actually kill him. He turned tail and sprinted away, leaving his fruit spilt on the ground. The woman ran after him but gave up, probably fearing to leave her daughter alone again.

Jacob, bruised and bloodied, returned to the shop and made up a story about being attacked by boys in the street. He was genuinely shocked at what had occurred – hadn't realised that his activities might be construed as harmful, and certainly hadn't anticipated such an aggressive reaction. He never went experimenting again. His remaining pennies stayed where they were.

The months went by, Jacob regularly spying on his stepmother. He could have told his father what was happening but was unsure if he would be believed. In any case, the result could well be a cooling of relations all round, and possibly Alison's expulsion.

As Jacob got older, his childish fascination developed into a more erotic response. He began to get strange sensations in his groin. Then catastrophe came.

One day, a few months after his twelfth birthday, he was watching Alison with a particularly large and powerful man. The energy involved, and the noises too, were unusually vigorous. His own piece seemed to be changing shape, and he became alarmed. He stepped away from the door and looked down at himself to investigate, but the quick release of the pressure of his foot caused the door to snap audibly back into place. There was a commotion in the shop, and seconds later Alison turned the key and caught him. She looked at Jacob with disbelief. Her client had adjusted his clothes and stormed out of the shop. Jacob heard the door bang.

"You dirty little turd!" she shouted. "You were spying on me!" She was immediately walloping him with both hands. Jacob ran up the stairs trying to defend himself, but she was after him. He shut himself in his room and leaned against the door. Alison banged on it and shouted, "Don't you dare spy on me again! And keep quiet about what you think you've seen, or you'll be very sorry."

She was gone. Jacob's heart was pounding.

His entertainment was over. From that day, Alison made a point of banishing him from the shop in Margaret's company every time she needed privacy.

He became increasingly irritated with her treatment of him and one day decided to confront Margaret with what he knew. They were walking together in Fleet Market, wandering between the open shop fronts. The market was not as busy as they often found it, although Margaret picked out two or three acquaintances with whom to exchange greetings.

"Margaret, why do I always have to come shopping with you? You always used to manage alone before."

"Your mother's the mistress. I do what I'm told – and so do you."

"She's not my mother."

"Your stepmother then."

He walked silently beside her for a few more seconds, passing through the archway under the clock, trying to make up his mind. Should he tell her or not? He decided he would.

"Do you know what she does? I mean when we're out of the shop?"

Margaret didn't answer immediately. Pigeons scurried away as the two emerged into the cobbled street on the far side of the clock tower. The tall, dark wall of Fleet

Prison was visible on the left beyond the shops. Rain suddenly began to spatter the ground, just a few drops at first, but then strong enough to force them to retreat under the tower.

"It's not my concern, Jacob."

"Men come…"

She turned on him. "Shut up." He looked at her, surprised. "I don't want to know."

That was unexpected. He never mentioned it to her again. Jacob began to wonder what Alison was doing with the money she made. Two guineas seemed to be the going rate. Suppose there was only one man each week, and there were on average thirty such encounters a year. In that case, she must have earned well over two hundred guineas since that first time he'd seen her – a substantial sum of money – yet she never seemed to buy herself anything special. Her clothes were adequate but inexpensive. Their standard of living had not risen, so her earnings were clearly not applied to the family. What was she doing with it? Was she gambling? Was she secretly supporting someone?

When Jacob was fourteen years old, his father began to pay him a wage. It felt strange to have money of his own beyond the few pathetic pennies in his room, but he knew straight away what he was going to do with it. He saved up a couple of guineas (it took four months) and went to look for a prostitute.

He'd managed a few preliminary forays into likely districts of the city and had a good idea where he might be successful. Covent Garden and Drury Lane were bustling with activity of all kinds, constantly awash with women looking for customers. Jacob had filled out well, lost his youthful, boyish appearance and probably appeared a suitable enough target for them. Several girls looked at him, and it was just a few minutes before one of them took him on.

"Looking for company, sir?" she asked.

"I am," he replied, a little timidly. Despite his extensive observation, studies and analysis of the sexual act, he was still nervous about actually taking part in it.

She introduced herself as "Polly", and Jacob estimated she was in her middle twenties. She was dressed in red silk, her cleavage emphasised by a very low décolletage and provocatively tight lacing, and her broad straw hat was decorated with a huge ostrich feather. She'd made a studied effort to conceal her smallpox scars beneath makeup, and Jacob found her more than presentable. He made no secret of the fact that he'd never done this before, and she seemed to warm further to his boyish honesty. She took him by the hand and led him to a narrow street nearby, in through a dark, ill-smelling corridor and up two flights of stairs. Her room seemed clean enough, even cosy. It was already lit by two oil lamps.

Polly undressed without hesitation while Jacob watched. Sensing his pleasure, she removed everything. It was the first time Jacob had seen a woman completely naked; he was excited, his heart beating very fast. She was waiting for him, so he took off his clothes as quickly as he could and stood silently before her. He wanted her opinion.

Looking down at himself, he asked, "Is it alright?"

She laughed, "Looks perfectly normal to me." Jacob was relieved.

Polly spread her arms, displaying herself. "Will I do, young sir?" she asked.

"I think you will," Jacob replied.

The copulation was accomplished extraordinarily quickly. On one level Jacob was very pleased and felt he'd passed some kind of milestone, but he was disappointed that it had all been over in seconds. He lay in her arms afterwards for no more than three minutes before she was up, washing and dressing.

"I'm sorry," he said.

"Why?" She seemed surprised.

"Isn't it meant to last longer than that?"

"It will next time," she said. "You'll see. You were perfectly fine. It all worked well."

He was getting his clothes on.

"Can I see you again?"

She laughed. "I'll be looking out for you!"

Polly waited by the door, clearly anxious to get to the next client. Jacob finished buttoning up his clothes, put on his shoes and walked over to her. She held out her hand, and Jacob dropped his coins into it.

"Oh *my!* Mr Generous! You can come again!" She kissed him on the cheek, opened the door and motioned him away. "Off you go," she said. "I'll come down in a minute."

And then he was back in the street. He was smiling, felt very different about himself. He was a man.

During the course of the next year, Jacob tried several times to find Polly again but was never able to do so. He hunted for her, asking the other girls he met, but they were unsure to whom precisely he was referring. One girl offered a possible answer.

"Polly. Do you mean Mary? Mary Blake? I think she used to call herself Polly now and then."

"Mary Blake?" he replied. "I don't know. She had smallpox scars."

The girl smiled at his naivety. "A lot of us have smallpox scars, dear."

"Middle twenties? Curly brown hair?" He gestured the curls with his finger.

"Could be almost anybody. If you mean Mary Blake, she got herself hitched up to a gentleman. It happens to the lucky ones. I don't know where she went. Anyway my love" (moving closer to him and becoming intimate), "I'm sure I'll do just as well..." The last phrase was a whisper, close to his ear.

None of the girls he questioned seemed to know where

Mary Blake had taken her clients, so none could tell him if Polly's room was indeed Mary's.

He waited outside her door on one occasion, but the girl who arrived, swarthy young man in tow, was not her. She didn't know who had previously rented the room.

As time went on, Jacob had sex with many different girls and discovered that a single guinea was often more than they expected. Repeated practice ensured his increasing proficiency in the art of "knocking", as Polly had told him it would.

Jacob liked strenuous exercise – running and climbing. He'd also developed a fondness for rowing, particularly on the Thames, hiring a boat a couple of times each week and pulling himself through the filthy water, dodging the sailing ships and other craft, shooting the rapids beneath London Bridge. The river's width and grandeur were only fully appreciable from the vantage point of a tiny, isolated, lonely boat.

Jacob found he could think with great clarity when his body was occupied in some exhausting activity, and he began to muse in some detail on a possible career in the flesh trade. His observation and analysis suggested it would be lucrative, and the social circles with which he'd acquainted himself provided suitable paths into the business. He'd developed no friendships with other boys; his only acquaintances, outside of his immediate family, were prostitutes.

Jacob became bolder and stronger with age – and more arrogant.

Friday lunchtimes in the shop were something of a ritual. William would pay everyone their wages for the week, then they would all sit down together and eat a simple meal, the business being closed for an hour. On this particular Friday, just after Jacob's fifteenth birthday, Alison looked at him across the table and said, "Jacob, what do you do with your money?"

Jacob glanced at her and shot straight back, "What do you do with yours?"

No one said anything. Alison ignored the question, cast her eyes down at the table, and continued eating. Margaret and John pretended not to have noticed the remark. William looked puzzled, shifted his eyes between his wife and his son. Nothing further was said.

Shortly after that confrontation, something happened that lent significant focus to Jacob's evolving life-plans. William and John were out on their usual rounds. Soon after they left, Alison glanced at Margaret, who needed no further prompting, understanding the dismissal straight away. She put on her hat and cape, took up her basket and waited for Jacob.

"Jacob will stay here today, Margaret," said Alison. "Can you manage alone?"

"Of course," she replied, opened the door and left.

As soon as the shop was closed, Alison went quickly to the back room, the doors banging behind her. Jacob wondered what was going on. She returned in a few seconds, carrying a pistol. The boy stepped back in surprise, his hands raised at chest level.

"Do you know what this is?" she asked.

Jacob nodded, eyebrows raised in astonishment. "I think so..."

"Ever used one?"

He shook his head. "No."

She took hold of the muzzle and handed it to him. "Take it." He did so. "Hold it up." Jacob pointed it at her. "Not at me! Idiot!" She knocked the gun aside. "Hold it out, like you mean it – as if you're used to it."

He stood straight, held the weapon at arm's length and looked along it.

"Look like a killer," said Alison quietly.

The gun felt good; the sleek wooden handle rose elegantly to the long barrel, encased in silver and leading to a flared muzzle. It was heavy. A large spring mechanism with a lever was mounted on top of the weapon, a flintlock. Alison stood next to him and pulled the lever back carefully until it locked into place.

"Now it's armed," she said. "If you point the gun at someone and pull the trigger you'll kill him." She released the mechanism. "Now, you do it. Arm the pistol." Jacob tried it a few times. It was easy enough.

"I might need your help today. Will you help me?"

Jacob nodded.

"Keep the gun ready and stay out of sight behind the door. If I call your name, you step into the shop with that thing pointed. Look mean, like a killer, but don't fire unless you have to. Understand?"

Jacob nodded again.

"Right." She took a deep breath.

He could see that she was nervous. "What's going on?"

"Just stay alert. Don't come in unless I shout for you. Go."

A moment later, Jacob was back in his old position behind the swing doors. They were not locked this time, and he could press open the left one wide enough to see clearly into the shop. Alison paced about, anxious, fidgeting.

In just a few minutes the shop door banged open and two large men appeared, both in their late fifties.

"Gentlemen," greeted Alison.

Neither of them replied. One of the men turned the key, securing their privacy, while the other began to unbutton his breeches.

Jacob was fascinated by what he saw. The action was slow, drawn-out, soulless and cold. One man sat and watched while the other went to the task. Occasionally they'd bark obscenities, encouraging each other. Jacob heard Alison's voice only once, but too quietly for him to make out the words. The man who was currently engaged responded by cuffing her across the face, swearing as he did so. After a while, the men changed places. The whole process took nearly half an hour.

Jacob watched, enthralled. He stood completely still, the weight of the gun in his hand, and impressed the whole scene into his mind forever. Many times in later life he would return to this afternoon, coldly reliving the events. The procedure was complete. The men were preparing to depart, and Alison had risen, rubbing her assaulted face. One of the men leant towards her and spat, "Whore...," his face twisted in contempt. She cowered back, frightened. The men turned their backs and walked towards the street door.

"Pay," she said. The man who'd previously slapped her now returned and hit her again. She fell to the floor. The man stepped forward and applied his boot to her ribs.

Alison doubled up in pain and gasped, "Jacob!"

He'd been waiting for her summons. Pistol readied, he strode forward through the double doors, quite prepared to fire and kill. The men were surprised, both retreating, hands raised. Jacob smiled, relishing the situation. He was the bringer of death. The sensation of power was intensely erotic. He *wanted* to kill them, but he was also aware that there was only one round in the pistol. If he fired, he'd drop one of them while the other ran to summon help. Nevertheless, there was an almost overwhelming urge to pull the trigger.

"Pay," he commanded. "Slowly. Give me a chance to put a hole in you, and I'll take it."

"Keep calm," one of them told him. "We don't want any trouble."

Each man dropped a handful of coins onto the table. Jacob caught the glint of silver and gold, but he shook his head, *no.* "It's not enough. Pay for the bruises too."

"Damn you!" said the closest man. Both emptied their

purses.

"Get out," said Jacob. "I'll kill you if I see either of you again."

One of them hawked and spat on the floor. Then they turned, opened the door and were gone, a cool breeze from the street running through the shop as they left.

Jacob lowered the weapon and Alison staggered to her feet. She hobbled painfully over to him and took the gun. Steadying herself against one of the worktops, she pointed the pistol at his head and pulled the trigger. Jacob threw up his hands, shocked, and cried, "It wasn't loaded!" He was astounded.

She was bent double with laughter, despite her pain. "Not loaded? *It doesn't work!*"

A moment later, Jacob was laughing with her. The release of the coiled tension increased the hilarity. They gradually calmed themselves, and Jacob noticed her bloodied face, starting to blacken with the inevitable bruises. "You're hurt."

She touched her lip, split with the blows, dripping red beads. "I'll be alright. I've had worse." She looked at him. "Thank you, Jacob."

He shook his head, gesturing *it was easy*.

They counted the coins. Six gold guineas, nine crowns, twelve half-crowns, twenty-one shillings, seventeen six-pences, sixteen threepences, thirteen pennies, eight half-pennies and three farthings. A considerable sum. She gave him a third of it.

"I was attacked in the shop," she said. "A man came in here looking for money. He knocked me about. You heard the commotion and drove him off. He was a beggar. Old clothes, filthy, about thirty. Understand?"

He nodded, *yes*.

"You were very good, Jacob."

"You need to get a real gun."

She was quiet, pressed her lips together, then asked, "Did

you watch?"

He nodded and made an affirmative noise in his throat.

Alison paused, inclined her head slightly and looked into his eyes in silence for a couple of seconds. Then she sat and waited for William and the others to return.

Jacob went to his room and dropped his earnings in the box where he kept his money. Now he fully understood the potential for moneymaking in prostitution. He would amass his fortune in it. His path was clear.

The following week, Jacob inspected various premises near Covent Garden, looking for a suitable location to lay his venture's foundation stone. There were several possibilities, but he was attracted to a large apartment in a house on Maiden Lane – partly because he was amused by the street name, but also because the rooms were large and well-lit. The landlady, a self-important middle-aged matron named Mrs Barge, asked his age, and he answered her question by handing her the first three months' rent in advance.

The rooms were partly furnished, but Jacob bought two additional beds, several lamps, a few tables, washbasins and various other items. He selected a space for his own occupation and set about drilling holes in the walls so that he could spy into the chambers on either side; then he decorated those rooms in such a way as to conceal his spyholes.

He'd been taking unscheduled days off work to achieve all this and dismissed his father's complaints by explaining that he was bored and preferred to go rowing. William became increasingly furious, but Jacob was unperturbed. He had a home of his own and would soon have a reliable income vastly superior to that offered by his father. Inevitably, after a month of this behaviour, William ejected his son from the business. "You're on your own. You'll get no help from me!"

Jacob had become Alison's guard; she didn't want to lose his services. They remained in touch, and he made himself available to watch over her more dangerous encounters. She felt safe under his eye and split her earnings with him, although genuinely dangerous situations were rare and usually dispersed with a single flourish of the gun barrel.

Jacob knew he would require genuine weapons to deal with any trouble at his own establishment, so he asked his female acquaintances in Covent Garden if they might suggest leads for the procurement of such things. They had a few ideas, and it proved remarkably easy to acquire what was needed; he commissioned a thief to steal on his behalf. Within days Jacob was the proud owner of a pair of fine flintlock pistols, together with a substantial supply of lead bullets and gunpowder. He also took possession of several knives and a military spadroon sword. The gathering of his arsenal almost exhausted his funds; he needed to get the business going as soon as possible. It was time to recruit his first girl – and he knew who that would be.

Alison was intrigued. Jacob was going to run his own little brothel; he was going to get rich. He offered her the opportunity to join forces with him – to move her activities from the cobbler's workshop to a dedicated room with its own bed and other facilities in a part of town where business was easy to come by. She found the invitation hilarious, irresistible, and said she'd inform her gentlemen of the new trysting place. She smiled at Jacob and gave him a little peck on the cheek. "How lovely of you to think of me."

New weapons are like new friends. The owner has to know them, has to become familiar with the way they talk, the way they're likely to respond.

On the grey Saturday and the still greyer Sunday before he opened for business, Jacob walked across London Bridge, out beyond Southwark to Lambeth Marsh. He found a remote spot and listened carefully to the conversation of his new colleagues. Their voices had a noble finality, and he relished the gravity of their handshakes.

It was challenging to shoot with much accuracy at a distance, but he found he could reliably kill bottles at moderate to close range.

The following Wednesday afternoon was the appointed time. Having given William warning that she would not be in the shop that afternoon (she was "meeting an old friend"), Alison packed a large basket with various items of clothing and accessories, and walked the mile to the house on Maiden Lane. The thought of being pimped by her stepson gave her a thrill; the twisted perversion of it delighted her – and the opportunity to earn more money brought closer her undisclosed dreams of a new life.

Jacob waited for Alison in his lair. He greeted her ("You look good...") and showed her his room, his spyholes (she peeped through one and caught her first glimpse of her new domain), his pistols and other weapons. It was impressive – thorough. Then he showed her to her bedroom. It was fresh and clean, with a good view of the street and the buildings opposite. There was a basin of fresh water and plenty of scents, soaps and oils.

"I'm meeting my man at Knole's coffee house at half past one," she said. "We'll be here by two. Does that suit you?"

"Anything you like," he agreed.

They talked about money. Jacob had to cover the apartment's rent and make a profit for both of them, so he suggested four guineas. Alison readily agreed, then asked him to leave the room so that she could change into something nice. She knew he'd be spying on her as she changed into her bright frilly clothes, but that just made her smile all the more.

She dressed, painted herself, made her way carefully down the stairs and out into the busy street. Several passing gentlemen turned their heads, some wished her "good day," and raised their hats in admiration.

Just before half past one she met her friend at the agreed spot, and they had a light lunch together. Then she brought him back to her room.

Jacob watched them. He recognised this particular man from his frequent visits to William's premises, so knew there was no danger. Alison's sessions in the shop had always been furtive, clandestine, but here she could be more relaxed. Everything was easy, and the exuberant noisiness of her gentleman's love-making was encouraging for Jacob to hear. In his mind's eye he saw the pile of golden guineas teetering up to the sky.

The man, having no reason to hurry, lay quietly for half an hour or so after his exertions, cradling Alison in his arms – a pleasure that would have been impossible in the shop. They both seemed to drift off to sleep, so Jacob left his spyhole, sat contentedly at the window, and drank a glass of ale. When he looked again, they were coupled for a second time, though with reduced energy. All was well. There was no need for him to watch.

About twenty minutes later he checked once more, and seeing that Alison was alone and dressing, he tapped on her door and walked in.

"How was it?" he asked.

"Very good," she said quietly, pecked a little kiss on his cheek and handed over two gold coins. "Four guineas. Two for me, two for you, yes?"

He nodded.

"I have another. It's alright? I'm meeting him at four o'clock."

Jacob was surprised, but delighted that Alison was embracing their venture with such enthusiasm.

The next assignation proved as successful as the first – and Alison had skilfully picked up a third client for the evening. It was a little like fishing. Jacob earned six guineas in a single day, about the same amount of money he would have made had he worked for his father an entire year.

He moved his remaining things out of his father's house and took up permanent residence in his own apartment on Maiden Lane. He searched out tutors in fencing and boxing and worked at gaining proficiency in both. A few of the Covent Garden prostitutes, tempted by his offer of increased earnings and a safe operating environment, agreed to work exclusively for him. He hired a local physician and arranged for a regular inspection of all his ladies, ensuring that they kept clean and avoided disease. Very soon he was earning a lot of money and had built up a respectable and fashionable patronage.

Mrs Barge soon realised what was going on and threatened to have him thrown out (*"There's already too much o' this kind o' thing round 'ere..."*). Jacob offered to triple the rent in return for her silence (and her absence) and found her only too pleased to accept (*"Very generous, sir. I can see you're a man of honour..."*). He raised the girls' fees to six guineas, which effectively limited the clientele to the higher levels of society.

In 1747, when Jacob was eighteen years old, Alison told him she was going away and taking William with her. It was another surprise, but now he finally knew what her money was for. Ever since she was a girl, she'd harboured a dream to live in Venice, a city that was for her an icon of luxury, a symbol of independence. She'd saved enough to purchase a house of her own and had the wealth to live there freely. She offered William the chance to join her.

"I'm leaving, William."

"What? Leaving? Leaving *me*? Why? Where will you go?"

"To Venice. I'm going to be an Italian lady."

"You're mad. How will you earn your keep?"

"I have my own money. I don't need anybody."

"What about me?"

"You can come too if you like."

"What will I do there?"

"Drink wine in the sun, and look at the boats and the painted women."

"...You're joking."

"No, I'm not. I've bought a house on the island."

Silence. He looked at her as if she were a visitor from ancient Egypt – alien, suddenly unknown.

"I'm going the day after tomorrow. Say yes or no."

"How did you get your money?"

"Ask no questions, William. That is my one condition."

"What about my business? I've worked all my life to make it a success."

"You make shoes for people who will always be better off than you."

It was true. He was a humble nobody and always would be; he knew it.

"You make good shoes," she said, nodding gently.

"I do."

"But do you care?"

He looked at the floor and thought for a moment, raised his eyebrows and said quietly, "No."

"Then, will you come with me?"

"...Yes." A pause. He nodded his head. "I will."

A few weeks before Christmas of that year, one of Jacob's girls brought a new man to Maiden Lane. He was expensively dressed, statuesque, with a confident air. Jacob watched him through the peep-hole as the girl began to undress. The man looked carefully round the room, glanced at the girl, gave a wave of his hand and said, "Thank you, that won't be necessary. Please dress yourself." He threw her a brief caricature of a smile.

Jacob was puzzled and continued to watch closely. The man, having identified the most likely spot where a spy might lurk, looked directly into Jacob's eye and said, "I am addressing Mr Jacob Crowan. I should very much like to see you." To the girl, he said, "Thank you, my dear, you may leave. I intend no disrespect – you are very becoming. For you." He dropped two guineas into her hand. The girl, embarrassed and confused, muttered, "Thank you very much, sir, I'm sure." She offered an awkward curtsey, stepped past him and through the door, just avoiding Jacob as he entered the room.

Jacob shut the door behind him, stood still, arms by his sides, and introduced himself in a quiet voice. "I'm Jacob."

The gentleman smiled and held out his hand, which the younger man took. "Edgar Foxley. Glad to make your acquaintance at last."

The name was familiar; Jacob had heard it on the lips of some of the girls, but he couldn't immediately find its context. His visitor enlightened him; "King's Place," he said and allowed time for the phrase sink in.

Jacob had it immediately. The address was close by – the location of one of the capital's most celebrated brothels.

"You're running an impressive establishment. Word has spread. By all accounts you're a good keeper, look after your nuns well, run a clean shop." Foxley paused briefly, then gave his proposition. "I'm here to offer you a partnership. We'd like you to work for us. A union of fine fleshdens. You'll bring your expertise into our fold – and we'll increase your earnings to the tune of ten."

3. CAPPLEMAN FARM
1735-1748

The tides of life washed gently at the shores of the community at Cappleman Farm. The flow of the seasons hid some figures from view and brought new ones in their place. Old loves faded, new passions rose, new joys, new sorrows, happiness, grief.

Egbert

One day in the autumn of 1735 a great revelation came to old Egbert Trommel as he sat in his privy. His bowels had become increasingly troublesome as the years passed and he sometimes had to sit at great length to relieve himself, although these extended periods at stool supplied him with time for deep reflection.

In the two years since the funeral of John Sykes he'd become increasingly close to his colleague Hubert Cromwell, parson in the nearby village of Roxby. Egbert was more than twice Hubert's age and held diametrically opposing opinions on many subjects, but a feeling had grown between the two men that had greater significance than any belief or set of values. It puzzled Egbert. Hubert had taken to visiting him, seeking permission to use Egbert's extensive library, and the older man had found great warmth and contentment in allowing access. Now and then Egbert would sit with him as he worked into the evening, the library hearth crackling. Occasionally he would feel a tear in his eye and didn't know why. Hubert would look up and smile at him, asking if there might be something he could fetch – tea perhaps, or a glass of wine. On one occasion, Egbert, sitting in intense reverie, vocalised Hubert's name...

"Hubert..." It was very quiet, no more than a whisper and its utterance surprised Egbert himself; Hubert perhaps not so much.

Hubert looked at him, eyebrows raised in question. "Egbert?"

"Oh, I'm... I'm sorry... I..." He shook his head. "I was drifting off to sleep. My apologies. Do go on reading."

Egbert felt deep embarrassment and decided to enliven himself with a brief walk in his garden, watching the wind playing in the trees, listening to the soft brush of leaves. The unseen creator was in the stillness – the certainty of it calmed Egbert. He himself was a single leaf in the tide of time.

But this day, sitting in his privy while Hubert wrote a sermon in his library, Egbert was struck with a completely new realisation. For him, it was like a message from Christ on the road to Damascus. He suddenly realised that for the first time in his life, he was happy.

1736-41. New lives and old

The year 1736 brought the final sapling to Tozer Robinson's little wood of tree-children, baby Holly joining Willow, Hazel and Cedar. He felt blessed, his heart singing every day with his love for Apple and their precious brood. The Robinson family was one of the most popular on the farm, and visitors were plentiful, bearing gifts for the happy youngsters.

Apple's mother, Fiona, had been weakening for some time. She lived long enough to meet the new child but died just a few months later and was buried next to her husband, Harry.

The arrival of baby Holly was not the only celebration of 1736; there was a marriage too. The family at the big house welcomed Hugh Flesher's new wife into its embrace. Amelia Barker, slender and elegant at the age of twenty-three, wed thirty-five-year-old Hugh at Glaisdale church that summer. It was a grand affair, old Benjamin and Emmeline dressed in their finery, sitting opposite Amelia's parents, themselves strikingly attired in the height of fashion, Amelia's father sporting an ebony walking stick of deepest, blackest black, topped with a large knob of solid gold with which the bright sun played all day. Hugh was desperately in love with his bride and could hardly wait to get her to himself. He'd grown a smart black beard and moustache for the occasion and looked handsome, sculpted, compact, virile. Amelia licked her teeth suggestively at him when she arrived at the altar. Hugh took her hand and widened his eyes, hardly able to contain his excitement. The house and grounds bustled and thrummed, with celebrations continuing well into the evening. Two children arrived in quick succession: Louise in 1737, Henry in 1739. Cornelius East presided at the baptisms of both, as he had at the wedding of their parents.

The next two years brought sadness. On Thursday, June 2nd, 1740, Douglas Buckley died suddenly of a heart attack at the age of sixty-four. He'd long been one of the most respected men on the farm, having served as butler to the Fleshers at the manor house for more than thirty years. He was survived by his wife Maria, nine years his junior and still a fine-looking woman. Many people fondly recalled the day that Douglas and Maria were married in 1714, a cloudy, overcast April Saturday. The wind had knocked off Douglas's hat, and a squad of men had to chase it as it blew across the field by the church.

In 1741 Hazel Priestly suffered a double blow. She awoke one August morning to find that her husband Oswin had died in his sleep. She knew it the moment she reached out and touched him. He was cold – he'd been dead most of the night. It happened without warning, and Hazel was heartbroken. Oswin had been only fifty-one. Doctor Clover, a family friend for thirty years, rode from Easington and confirmed the death. He offered his heartfelt condolences to Hazel and hugged her tearfully and tightly. Her two sons, Adam and William, comforted her as best they could, and eight-year-old Nara clung to her constantly, needing to both give and receive love and reassurance.

But the sadness did not end there. Little more than a month later, William Clover himself died. He'd been summoned to a birth at one of the more distant farms, drove his horse too hard in his determination to get there quickly, and had been thrown and killed. The baby was successfully delivered without him, and William's body lay in a ditch, undiscovered until the next day.

Neil

The community languished without a doctor for only a few weeks. An advertisement for the rural practice appeared in the press and was picked up by someone in Leeds who'd been dreaming of just such a posting.

Neil Levinson grew up in Wigton near Carlisle, where his father Angus ran a medical practice. Neil's grandfather William had also been a doctor, and it was assumed that the boy would follow in the family tradition. In due course he was sent to study medicine at the University of Glasgow and became accustomed to lively city life. He thought that a practice in a busy metropolis might suit him, so he took up work in Leeds at the completion of his studies, although he missed the quiet hills of the border country. The advertisement from Easington caught his eye and lodged in his thoughts; the opportunity to work in the villages and moors of North Yorkshire pulled at the strings of his soul, so he handed over the reins of his successful metropolitan practice and moved north, arriving in the village shortly before Christmas 1741.

Neil was tall, handsome, fair-haired, quick-witted, had a warm sense of humour and a fondness for cats; all qualities that endeared him to eligible young ladies, although he politely kept them at a distance and declined their occasional advances, treasuring his solitude. The community was a welcoming one, and things were peaceful enough at first.

Early one March morning he was woken by a loud knocking at his door. Bleary-eyed, and with nightcap still in place, he opened it to find sixteen-year-old Nicholas Miller jumping from foot to foot with worry. His mother had disappeared. She was prone to do scatty things and run off, but this time she was pregnant to full term, and he was concerned not only for his ma but also for the baby. Natty Miller was thirty-two (she'd given birth to Nicholas when she was very young) and was known as one of the Cappleman Farm peculiars. Her son Nicholas just managed to support her through his various small jobs – he was assistant warrener, although little was required to fulfil that function. They lived in a small cottage near the woods at the northwest edge of the farm. Natty's husband had run away before Nicholas's second birthday, and she kept secret the identity of her new baby's father. It was a mystery. Some joked that she'd been visited by an angel.

Doctor Levinson gathered his things and rode to Cappleman Farm, Nicholas following on his own horse. The house was empty – Natty was not at home. Neil questioned Nicholas, trying to gather some leads, but nothing of use came to mind. They called her name loudly for ten minutes or so, wandering about the immediate environs of the cottage. Given the child's imminent arrival, the doctor thought it best to draw together a search party. The farmworkers went from house to house gathering assistance, and the farm and surrounding area was scoured until midafternoon. At nearly three o'clock a rider came with news. Natty had been found in the millpond beyond Beggar's Bridge, a few miles from her home. It seemed she'd walked through the night to get there. The doctor said he'd ride straight over to confirm her death but then received the news that the woman was alive. She was lying on her back in the cold water and refusing to come out. Levinson was astonished but was told that this kind of behaviour was not entirely unexpected. He rode to Egton Mill as quickly as he could.

Many people had gathered on the bank of the millpond. Even the reclusive Hugo Ash, sole resident of the watermill, emerged from his hiding place to see what was going on. Natty was on her back in shallow water within a few steps of the bank, in labour though very cold. Neil sprang from his horse and ran down to the water's edge, the crowd parting for him.

"Natty, I'm Doctor Levinson. What on earth are you doing?"

"I'm 'avin' baby, doctor. What dost think I'm doin'? What do it look like?"

"Yes, but why here, in the pond?"

Natty told him that she'd had a dream in which a shining deity told her she must give birth in water, so she'd risen from her bed in the small hours and struggled across country to get here.

"But this water is very cold, Natty. I don't think it'll do the child any good. Besides, how clean is it?" He looked around at the muddy banks and the green tendrils and growths in the water.

"I'm 'avin' it 'ere," she insisted.

The doctor disagreed and requested four men to get into the water and forcibly remove her. It was not a good decision, and one of them came splashing out of the pond with wounded dignity and an eye that would become impressively swollen and blackened as the evening wore on.

"For God's sake, then! Let's get it done as quickly as we can." Neil spread blankets and other equipment on the bank, removed his jacket and knelt in the water between Natty's legs. Watched by a crowd of a hundred, he delivered Buffy

Miller within fifteen minutes. The shock of the cold water was so intense that the baby screamed instantly. It was a hard welcome to the world, but other hands reached out, took the child and wrapped her in the blankets, already warmed by thoughtful women at the water's edge. There was thunderous applause from the assembled multitude, and Doctor Levinson immediately acquired folk hero status.

Natty had been screaming blue murder at the birth but now struggled weakly to land and grasped the doctor's sleeve.

"See? I told yer. It were easy, weren't it?"

"Next time, Natty – tell me in advance, please."

Buffy Miller was known for the rest of her days as "Pond Girl". She was destined for an easy, happy life, but would eventually know the most profound sorrow of all.

1742. Lucinda Swift and Martha Wheatley

Lucinda and Martha never really got on. Lucinda, the older of the two, married Lawrence Swift in 1695 at the age of thirty. It came as something of a relief to her parents, who'd long thought they'd be left with her forever. Lucinda made up for her plainness through her aloof and dismissive attitude. She had a habit of disagreeing with people and giving the impression that she could do better than anyone else, whatever it was they might be doing. Whenever the house received a visitor – clergyman, nurse, cooper, candlestick maker, butcher, shepherd, surgeon, taxidermist, dentist, wig-maker, undertaker, whatever – Lucinda might well admit that she didn't have their particular skill, but managed to give them the impression that if she *did* have their particular skill she'd carry it out rather better than they themselves did, *that* was for sure.

When her son Bernard married Florence Wheatley in 1723, Lucinda made it known that she didn't think much of Florence's mother, Martha. Martha's husband had the audacity to be named almost identically to her own Lawrence. The one tiny saving grace was that the names were spelt differently. Laurence Wheatley was fifteen years younger than Lawrence Swift. Neither man liked to be called Larry, so when it was necessary to shout for one or the other it always had to be Lawrence Elder or Laurence Younger. It was not a satisfactory state of affairs at all, and Lucinda assured them that should it have been up to *her* to name them, she would have done a darned sight better job of it than their own parents had.

The two men looked at each other and shook their heads.

Grandson Richard was born in 1724, and all the grandparents doted on him. Lucinda and Martha set about making him clothes, always in competition with each other, always bickering. Lawrence, Laurence and Bernard drove the cart out to the Red Lion in Glaisdale whenever they could escape, leaving Florence to cast oil on the perpetual arguing.

Lucinda's husband died in 1726, Martha's in 1732. The house fell silent for a week or so after each bereavement, but the stillness was short-lived. The two elderly women lived to irritate each other. Their mutual prickliness animated them to the perpetual annoyance of those with whom they lived. The fighting only stopped when Martha was out of reach, helping in the Flesher's kitchen or assisting her daughter elsewhere. On all other occasions, the two sat together, in matching armchairs six feet apart, tearing verbal holes in each other like a pair of duellists using words for weapons.

The years went by, the blistering crustiness of the two remaining undiminished. They were the focus of one another's lives, each the target of the other. "Grannies, grannies, grannies!" Florence would cry in despair. Richard was fond of them both equally and gave them the same love and attention. But the two were like jealous dogs, each snarling inwardly when the object of their devotion showed affection to the other.

One day in spring 1742 Lucinda stopped in mid snipe, realising that Martha had offered no retaliatory bickering for several minutes. She looked across at her opponent's chair and realised that the woman was dead. There was an unexpected silence in the room. Lucinda blinked and sat still, watching a string of drool descend from the corpse's gaping mouth, like a slippery rope being let down to enable the escape of some tiny prisoner. Martha's eyes were open, unblinking. Florence, alerted by the lack of argument, pushed open the door and peered in.

"She's dead," said Lucinda, very quietly.

Lucinda took to her bed permanently after that, her partner taken from her. She lay quiet and looked at the ceiling, her skin greying day by day. Little more than a month later, she too gave up the ghost.

1743/44. Elys & Alicia – Richard & Emma

The year 1743 brought a long-awaited celebration to the farm. Elys Buckley married his childhood sweetheart, Alicia Hebden. He was twenty-seven, she twenty-four. People said they'd put it off for long enough, and perhaps they were right. (The two had been openly co-habiting for three years, and their intimate relationship predated that by a long time. Both remembered a warm September afternoon in a shadowy hayloft ten years earlier, the sun's gentle rays penetrating the dimness through gaps in the woodwork. He conjured up in his mind the vivid recollection, both tactile and visual, of the glowing smoothness of her skin. She recalled his passionate gentleness and the increasingly insistent promises of their kisses.) Their marriage was a joyful occasion, and the Fleshers provided a grand reception, with a huge cake ordered specially from the village bakery. It carried a big banner made entirely of sugar icing, that read *AT LAST!* in big red letters.

The Swifts, living next door to the Buckleys, were not to be outdone. Richard Swift, son of Bernard and Florence, married Emma Barnaby in 1744. Richard was just twenty years old and Emma, three years his senior, was already heavily pregnant. There was another celebration in the big house. This time the cake read, to Richard's mild embarrassment, *ALMOST TOO LATE!* Emma gave birth less than a month after the marriage. Amy Swift was baptised at Glaisdale two months later.

Benjamin

Benjamin Flesher died in November 1744. He was eighty-one, had become increasingly frail and was confined to bed in his last months. His funeral was attended by many Yorkshire farmers and landowners, who gave dignified and lengthy eulogies. Benjamin's wife Emmeline sat in the front row, together with Hugh and Amelia and their two young children, Louise and Henry. The Swifts and the Buckleys occupied the two pews behind them. Hazel Priestly sat nearby, Adam, William and nine-year-old Nara by her side. The manor house reception was a sombre event, with speeches, toasts and many reminiscences. Old Benjamin had been the father of the farm, and his passing felt like the end of an era.

Hubert Cromwell – James Kirby

The simple 13th-century church of St Nicholas, located at the end of the scattered village of Roxby, looked out across miles of open, windswept moor. Roxby Hall, an old manor house, had once stood nearby, but only a fragment of wall remained, standing sentinel, a marker to the past.

Hubert Cromwell, parson, preached about love from the pulpit of his church on Christmas Day that year. He spoke of a light shining in darkness and drew attention to the winter fields, the apparent inactivity of living things. He said that love could be found in the most unexpected places and encouraged his congregation to nurture it in themselves and in others, especially in situations where its presence might seem strange. "Love is the most important thing in the world", he said, "and at Christmastide its most powerful symbol is the tiny light of the Christ-child, shining in the dark, still night."

It was the last sermon he gave at Roxby, having decided to retire altogether from what had been his calling. Before the year was out, he'd moved into the parsonage at Easington to nurse his friend, old Egbert Trommel in his final years.

The church became inactive; for a few months, the township of Roxby was without a parson.

James Kirby arrived in June 1745, fresh from his studies at Durham, twenty-five years old and full of the Faith. It was his first posting. He was a fine keyboard player, and the strains of his harpsichord could soon be heard by anyone standing close enough to his open windows.

Walter – Beatrice - Grace

A week or so after James Kirby's arrival, Elys and Alicia Buckley welcomed into the world their baby son, Walter.

Two further children arrived in the staff houses before the decade was out. Beatrice was born to Richard and Emma Swift in 1746, a sister for two-year-old Amy. In 1747, shortly before Walter Buckley was two, Elys and Alicia celebrated the birth of their second child, Grace.

The dwellings abutting the manor house's perimeter wall overflowed with the cries of happy children.

Louise – Henry – Meadow

On the other side of the wall, in the grounds of the manor house, Louise and Henry Flesher often played together – tennis, tag, or whatever might be their favourite game. Louise was increasingly accompanied by her friend, Meadow Reid, her equal in age if not quite in social status. Meadow didn't live on the farm but wandered over from her parents' house in nearby Egton. Her father, Sigbert Reid, was a gentleman of independent means, considered something of an eccentric. He wrote plays and poetry and enjoyed some success in London and other centres of culture. Meadow's mother, Persephone, was a beauty who could, so it was said, occasionally be seen wandering naked along the nearby riverbanks in the early morning, singing to herself. They were not married but had lived together as man and wife for more than ten years. Now and then they threw unusual parties for their city friends. The word "orgy" was often applied to these events by curious local men who dared to prowl about and peep through the windows when they were in progress.

Meadow herself was a confident ten-year-old in 1747 and had become best friends with Louise Flesher in the preceding two years. Eight-year-old Henry was entranced by dark-haired, slender Meadow and told her that she would be his wife when they all grew up. Meadow laughed at him, thought him just a little boy, and took delight in teasing him. Louise recognised the cruel streak in Meadow but enjoyed watching as she tortured her little brother.

Tozer and Alder

Tozer Robinson and Alder Swithenbank walked together in the cool of the evening towards the Red Lion alehouse close to the church in Glaisdale. The breeze was picking up, the low sun cast long shadows. They'd spent the afternoon turning out the cattle after the winter.

"Tozer, my head's filled with something. I need to tell you about it."

Tozer glanced across at his tall, muscular companion as

they walked along. "What's that, Alder?"

"I saw something the other day. It's in me head all the time. I can't shake it out."

Tozer waited silently, but nothing more was forthcoming. Alder was clearly inviting his enquiry.

"What's that then, Alder? What sight was that?"

"I saw Nara Priestly. Up the river, by the warren."

Tozer looked at him, puzzled.

Alder returned his gaze and added, "Bare-arsed."

"Nothin' on?"

"In the skin." He turned his head away from Tozer and looked ahead, although his eyes were glazed as he recalled the image of Nara's body. "She was swimming with a few of the other young wenches – the water's deep enough there."

Tozer looked away. "You got a dirty mind, Alder."

"Maybe. You can't tell me you wouldn't have looked, though. She's somethin'..."

"Alder! She ain't fifteen yet! I only got eyes for Apple anyway."

His friend continued. "She saw me looking at her. Bold as brass she was, with her little tits and..."

"Alder! If Hazel heard what you were sayin'..."

"I tell you, Tozer, I could show 'er a thing or two, teach her a few tricks." He flexed his fingers, imagining the warm yield of her flesh. "I reckon she's a wriggler, a squeezer, tight..."

Tozer shook his head as if to say, *You're beyond help, my friend.*

The sun illuminated the clouds and painted the sky red as they neared the village. Nara Priestly filled Alder's thoughts – her brown hair, soft skin, her lips, her tongue... The fire of his lust pulled him relentlessly towards her.

4. CAPPLEMAN FARM
1748/9

It was the last week of June 1748 and the scything, the mowing, was underway, the meadow alive with the sweating bodies of farm labourers and their children. Cut grass lay drying in the heat, soon to be gathered in as hay. The sun beat down.

Alder sat quietly amid the activity, elbows on knees, eyes unfocused. Tozer, working hard nearby, had been aware of his companion's idleness for some time and knew that his friend's lack of activity was not due to fatigue. He stopped cutting, and propped himself on the handle of the scythe.

"What's up, Alder?"

Alder gave a small shake of his head but offered no explanation. Tozer wondered for a moment if he should sit and try to discover the source of the problem, but there was work to be done. He sighed, lifted the tool and got on with the job.

A few minutes later, Nara Priestly walked by barefoot behind them. Tozer caught sight of her as she approached. As Alder had said, she was a very pretty girl. She fixed her eyes on Alder as she passed, unsmiling.

"Alder," she greeted, ignoring Tozer altogether.

Alder looked up briefly. "Nara." Then she was gone, passing deeper into the meadow.

Tozer pursed his lips, thinking, *What's this then?* He braced himself and said, "Alder, you better tell me."

Alder sighed. "I've had her."

Tozer looked down and shook his head in mute disbelief. After a moment, he asked, "How old are you, Alder?"

"I'm forty-five, Tozer."

"And how old is she?"

"Fifteen..."

"Alder, you ever heard the phrase, *Don't get your meat where you get your spuds*?"

"I have, Tozer."

"You'll be in trouble. She told her ma?"

"Don't know. I don't think so."

Tozer was silent. He picked up his scythe and went back to work.

"I couldn't help meself, Tozer."

Tozer stopped again, set the scythe upright and leant on the shaft with both hands.

"Did you *make* 'er do it?"

"No! I'd never do that!"

"So, how'd it come about?"

"I watched her for weeks, up in the river. She swims up there with her friends."

"Always in the skin?..."

"Always in the skin. She knew I was there. She didn't hide. The other girls, they thought it was funny, but Nara – she *liked* me looking at her. Went on for weeks like that. Then one day she told me *come back tomorrow*. So I did. She was alone that day." He dropped his gaze to the ground.

Tozer said, "So you went back next day... and took her."

Alder said, "I'm ashamed of myself, Tozer."

"I bet you are," said Tozer, setting back to work. "Maybe you'll be lucky, if it was only the once."

"Six times," Alder replied without hesitation.

"Jesus!" Tozer muttered, nearly dropping his scythe.

"What shall I do, Tozer?"

Tozer thought, then said, "Wait. Wait and see what happens. Maybe she'll just forget you and find someone 'er own age."

"What about her ma?"

"Well Alder, you done Hazel no respect by what you done with 'er daughter, that's for sure."

"It weren't all my fault, Tozer."

"No? How d'you make that out?"

Alder paused. "I can't tell you."

Nara had stood before him in the wood next to the river, not five feet tall, stark naked, bold as brass, the warm sunlight filtering through the trees setting her skin aglow, dappled with leafy shadow; the soft splash of the river nearby. The image was impressed forever in his mind.

"Let's see you then," she'd said. So he'd stripped out of his clothes as she watched.

There'd been blood the first time, and she was a little frightened, not expecting the pain. Alder had encouraged their second attempt, and she'd certainly liked that...

Tozer said, "Get to work, Alder. Maybe nothing'll come of it. P'r'aps it'll all blow away in the wind."

Alder got up and began to scythe. It was sweaty work, but he put his back into it, trying to forget.

An hour later he paused, set the tool down and wiped his brow. He knew she was standing behind him, watching. His senses opened like a flower, and his need for her was instantly overwhelming. The shock of it flowed out of him and passed through Tozer, several yards to his right. The effect was like ripples produced by a stone dropped into a pond, and Tozer felt himself bobbing in the passage of the waves. It was an extraordinary, forceful, physical sensation. He opened his eyes wide in surprise and looked in his friend's direction. Alder was facing away from her, Nara standing about six feet to his rear and staring at his back. Alder turned and met her gaze.

"Now," she said. It was a command.

Alder, unsmiling and with eyes cast down, turned his head in Tozer's direction. A strange stillness descended on the meadow. The soft breeze ceased; the world seemed to hold its breath; the mowing halted, and all eyes followed the two as they walked out of the meadow, across the river, through the gate, and out of sight.

The child conceived that day would become one of the county's most celebrated legends.

Hazel Priestly was at work in the kitchen of Vine Cottage when her younger son William came running with the news that his sister and Alder Swithenbank had been seen walking together, hand in hand.

"What?"

"I just heard. About half an hour ago – they left the meadow together. Everyone saw."

"Thirty minutes ago? Why do I hear only now?"

"I was at the well with Adam, fixing the new rope. He said I should go and join the mowing. That's when I heard. I thought I'd better tell you."

Hazel was alarmed enough to wander more than a quarter of a mile along the road, the meadow on her left, farm buildings, houses and fields on her right, casting her eyes around, looking for some sign of her daughter. She went into the meadow and asked several people what they'd seen, but no one could tell her where the pair had gone.

If they were actually going to… (she could hardly bear to think it), they'd be looking for somewhere secluded. The woods at the north of the farm might be the most likely place, up beyond the warren, but the area was huge, and she'd never find them. Or possibly one of the barns, up in the lofts… Images formed in her head, driving her almost insane with anger and concern. Eventually, she realised that the deed was probably done already, and the best thing she could do was go home and wait.

Nara walked into the cottage at half past six. Hazel was sitting with an open book, although she was too distracted to make sense of the words. She tried to remain calm.

"Where have you been?"

"In the meadow."

"All day?"

Nara realised something was wrong. "No, I went walking with some friends."

"What friends?"

"Ma?"

Hazel felt her blood begin to boil. "You were with Alder Swithenbank."

Nara was caught. She didn't know what to say.

"Where did you go?"

Nara began to tremble.

Hazel repeated, voice rising, "Where DID YOU GO?" She rose from her seat.

"Into the barn behind the cowshed. Up in the loft."

Hazel caught Nara by the arms and shook her. "What did he do to you?"

"MA!" She protested. "You're hurting me!"

"WHAT DID HE DO?"

Nara began to cry. Hazel wanted to slap her but fought off the urge and restrained herself.

"Did he... Did he...?" She was appalled, could hardly bring herself to put the words together. "DID HE DO IT TO YOU? TELL ME!"

"YES! YES, HE DID!" Nara shouted, struggling, breaking away. "IT WAS NICE! I LOVED IT!"

There it was.

The reaction was on the tip of Hazel's tongue: *YOU LITTLE BOB-TAIL!* But she managed to contain the words and bit her mouth shut, shaking with emotion. She stepped back, tears in her eyes, hands raised, gasping for breath, looking to the side rather than at Nara. Her daughter was sobbing.

There was a moment of silence, then Hazel burst into tears and took Nara into her embrace. It was some time before either could speak. When Hazel had gained some control, she stepped back, held the girl at arm's length, and said, her voice catching, "He's more than old enough to be your father."

Nara's energy was gone. She could only shake her head, a few sobs still pulling at her chest, her face wet with tears.

"Stay here in the house till I get back. Will you do that please?"

Nara nodded her head, *yes*.

"Alright, love," said Hazel and kissed her daughter's forehead. "Everything'll be fine." Then she set out to find Alder.

Nara sat in stunned silence, alone in the house after her mother's confrontation, her thoughts scattered and confused like a swarm of surprised bees. After a while, she cupped her hands to her nose and breathed in. Alder's smell was still there – his skin, his sweat.

She'd been aware of him all her life. Alder was the biggest, strongest man on the farm and his figure was striking, even at a distance. The farm girls, shy and teasing, had always giggled in his presence. But the first day she'd caught him watching her in the river, Nara had known he was the one. She'd looked up and seen him there surrounded by the trees that bore his name: alders, with their roots in the water. He squatted amidst them, a tree amongst trees, and something whispered to her, *This tree...* Ever since then, it had been as if there was a presence nearby directing their two paths to ultimate union, beyond her control. Their first coupling had seemed like the fulfilment of a prophecy. And today she'd felt like an automaton, steered as if she were a vehicle, the soft voice in her mind whispering to her, *This day, it must be this day, now*. In the warm afternoon, at the apogee of her passion with Alder, the voice had become part of her, no longer external. It had come home, had taken root in her womb.

The sudden and unexpected opening of the door shocked Nara out of her dreaming. Adam and William stood there, staring at their little sister.

Adam's voice was disbelieving. "Nara. They're saying that

you and Alder..."

She couldn't immediately think of anything to say but glanced quickly from one to the other.

Adam was insistent. "He forced you, didn't he?"

She frowned, shook her head. "No!"

Adam again, impatiently: "Did Alder hump you, Nara?"

She was angry and stood up indignantly. "It wasn't like that!"

But they were gone, the door slammed.

Hazel knew where Alder lived. He had no home of his own but rented a small room in a cottage occupied by one of the labouring families. The building was situated to the rear of the cattle sheds, overlooking a field currently occupied by sheep. The way there was filthy, populated by cowpats and dirt from the animals' feet, but Hazel strode up the path and knocked. Bridie Lyle, Alder's landlady, opened the door and was surprised to see her standing there.

"Hello, Bridie."

"Hazel. How lovely to see you! Come in and have some cake."

"I won't if you don't mind, Bridie. I'm actually looking for Alder."

"Alder. I think he's in the meadow. He's been out all day with the others."

"Thank you, Bridie. I'll look there." She was about to leave but turned back and said, "Let's have the cake another day. That'll be nice."

Bridie smiled. "It *will* be nice. Bye-bye."

It was just a few minutes' walk from there to the meadow, where many folk were still hard at work. Hazel made her way in through the bottom gate and strode about, hunting. There was no sign of him. Miriam Exley, carrying her new baby Amos in a sling on her back, asked if Nara had returned home.

"Nara's home," said Hazel. "Thanks for asking, Miriam. It's

Alder I'm looking for."

"Is it trouble, Hazel?"

"We'll see," she replied. "But Nara's fine. Excuse me, I'm going to keep looking. Lovely to see you, Miriam."

She pressed on and eventually saw Tozer, engrossed in his task.

"Tozer," she greeted him.

He turned with a sigh, anticipating her question. "Mrs Priestly."

"You know why I'm here."

He frowned in regret and nodded his head. "I think so."

"So, where is he?"

"I don't know. He left a few hours ago..."

She interjected, "Yes, I know – with my daughter. She's at home now, so where's Alder?"

"Well, if he's not at 'ome..."

"He isn't."

"...he'll probably be in the Red Lion."

That meant continuing all the way to Glaisdale. Supposing she walked all that distance and he wasn't there after all? She toyed briefly with the idea of going home. Despite the gravity of the situation, perhaps it could wait...

But no, this needed to be sorted out tonight. She thanked Tozer and marched out of the meadow, turning left to follow the road through the farm and into the village. It was still warm. She paused briefly at the handpump to splash water on her face and take a drink.

Hazel was in good health and walked vigorously, calmly greeting people on the road. At eight o'clock she crossed the bridge over the Esk by the lower fields opposite the pasture, then followed the road by the common and turned right into Glaisdale, arriving at the alehouse almost fifteen minutes past the hour. She'd spent occasional evenings here in earlier years with Oswin and a few friends but hadn't visited since he'd died. She stood outside for a moment, listening to the buzz of conversation within, remembering him; then smoothed her clothing, tidied her hair and pushed open the door.

All conversation ceased as she entered the tavern. It was unusual for a woman, especially one as well-respected as Hazel, to appear unaccompanied in the taproom, but after the initial instant of surprise she was greeted warmly. "Mrs Priestly!" rang out from many individuals, or "Hazel!" from those who felt comfortable enough to use her first name in public. She raised her hand in acknowledgement and smiled as the general hubbub of voices resumed.

"Drink on the house, Hazel?" called the landlord, Jack Morris, from behind the bar.

Hazel waved her hands and called, "Next time – but thank you." Jack thumbed an acknowledgement, and Hazel cast her eyes around the room.

There he was, over to her right, not far away. His tankard was cradled in his hand, and he was watching her intently, consternation etched on his face. Two men sat across from him. Hazel focused her mind on Alder's companions as she approached the table, and they rose and left, greeting her as they did so. She smiled at them as they passed her by.

Alder was alone. Hazel sat down opposite him.

"Alder." She nodded hello.

"Mrs Priestly." It was difficult for him to meet her gaze.

"I'm not pleased with you."

Alder was a man of instinct, not of words. He didn't know what to say. Instead, he looked deeply into his ale and breathed firmly through his nose.

"What will you do next?" asked Hazel, staring hard at his lowered head.

"What *should* I do? Should I go? I'll go, Mrs Priestly, if you wish it."

"Are you sorry?"

There were a few seconds of silence before he answered. "I'm sorry to cause you any hurt or sorrow."

Hazel was quiet for a moment. She felt the anger returning, then said, "You thought my precious daughter was just a pretty little girl you could fuck."

The force of the word on Hazel's lips shocked Alder to his core. He looked up in surprise, hardly able to believe she'd said it.

"No! No, it wasn't like that!" He returned his gaze to the tabletop. "She's special."

Hazel said nothing for a few seconds; then, "You'll stay here on the farm, Alder. You won't try to run away. You'll remain here as if nothing happened, until we decide what's best. You won't see Nara again."

"Not see Nara... alright. I'll do as you say."

"Don't disappoint me, Alder."

He looked up at her and watched as Hazel, eyes fixed on his, rested her right elbow on the tabletop and inserted the middle finger of her right hand into his ale. It began to steam, then to boil. Alder's blood chilled. He looked around at the crowded bar. No-one was looking; no-one paid any attention to what was happening.

"They're not watching, Alder," said Hazel quietly, concentrating hard with her mind, enclosing herself and Alder in a bubble beyond the awareness of the others. These were gifts she rarely used but which she kept carefully in practice.

Half of Alder's ale had boiled away. Hazel removed her finger, unharmed. She stood up, ran her tongue around her teeth, watching him.

"I'll see you again, Alder."

He was too astonished to speak but followed her with his eyes as she left. He raised the tankard cautiously to his lips. The ale was too hot to drink.

Not wanting to re-encounter her on the walk home, he gave Hazel ten minutes before he rose and left the tavern.

Hazel cut across the village common on her way home.

She found the cool grass refreshing after her confrontation with Alder and relished the mild breeze of the dusk, the low sun casting her shadow far ahead as she walked.

Her chosen route meant that she missed her two sons on their way to make Alder pay for his mistake.

Adam and William saw him approaching. He was about ten minutes' walk from the Red Lion, just inside the farm's perimeter. They stood and waited for him to reach them.

"I know why you're here," said Alder. "I've just been speaking to your ma."

"Put your fists up, Alder," said Adam.

"I don't want to fight you boys," Alder replied.

But there was no stopping it. The two brothers had to protect the honour of their sister. They came at Alder with no further warning and laid into him. Alder fought back, reluctantly at first, then with increasing force. Soon there was a small crowd of onlookers shouting encouragement for one side or the other.

"Come on, boys!" "Knock 'em out, Alder!" "Get thy boot in!" "C'mon! Give 'im *proper* batterin'!"

(Hazel, re-joining the road at the bridge in the southeast corner of the common, heard the commotion far behind her, but thinking little of it continued towards home.)

The confrontation was prolonged and became increasingly bloody, all three participants beating their way to exhaustion. As the sun sank, their weakening punches and parries were rendered still less effective by their debilitated staggering. The crowd steadily lost interest, its members wandering away one by one. Eventually, all three men lay on their backs in the road, entirely depleted of energy. A single young boy, about nine years old, ambled by as they lay there. He slowed and looked down at them, puzzled, before trotting on into the farm.

The three combatants remained motionless in the mud of the lane, breathing in the cooling air. The sky had darkened, and the stars became ever more visible, the vast wheel of the cosmos rotating with infinite slowness overhead; the Milky Way splashed across the firmament, sprayed from the brush of the eternal artist, the seed of aeons and incomprehensible distance.

William, watching it all above him, felt an immense sense of calm, and could have lain there all night. But after a while he became concerned about the other men, rose painfully to his feet, walked over to Adam and helped him up from the ground. They stood in the road, wiping the blood from their faces and hands, the road's muck from their clothes, and looked at their opponent.

Alder, too, was contemplating the sky from his prone position. Even if he'd had the skill and vocabulary to enunciate what he felt, he probably could not have done so. He was recalling his interview in the tavern with Hazel, and the things that had occurred there. Gazing into the inky limitlessness above, he realised how precious Nara had become to him, how unique. It was a new sensation. He loved her, and felt his eyes filling with moisture at the revelation of it.

Adam appeared in his field of vision, holding out his hand; then William on the other side. Alder accepted the offered assistance, reached up and allowed the boys to pull him to his feet. They limped home together, each of them groaning, cursing their wounds. The brothers took Alder as far as his front door.

"Goodnight, Alder. Sleep well," said Adam.

Alder fumbled with the door. "Goodnight, boys. I'm sorry. I..." He shook his head, his thoughts in confusion. William patted him gently on the shoulder.

Then they were gone.

Alder clawed his way to bed and collapsed.

Hazel arrived home after dark and found Nara sitting uneasily before the empty parlour fire. She looked up at her mother, concerned, frowning in anticipation of bad news.

"I've spoken with Alder."

Nara raised her eyebrows and gave an almost imperceptible shake of her head, *And...?*

"He's agreed not to see you again."

"I don't believe it."

"We'll just sit and wait, see how things progress. Give it a few weeks. I know you're besotted with him. It'll probably pass."

"I'm pregnant."

Hazel was silent for a moment. She bit her lip, then said, "You can't possibly know that, Nara."

Nara didn't reply. Hazel glanced at her and found her daughter staring back with a small, incisive smile on her face. The expression said, *But you know I can.*

Hazel sighed. "I only want what's best for you. I do trust you, Nara. But please humour me for a while. I'm just your caring old ma who loves you."

Nara melted a little. "I know, ma. I know you are." Then, "I'm lucky to have a mother like you."

Hazel walked over to where Nara was sitting, knelt down, leaned forward and hugged her.

"Go to bed, love. We'll take things a day at a time."

Nearly an hour after Nara had retired, the door opened and the boys tumbled into the cottage, blackened and bloodied.

Hazel was aghast. "What on earth happened to you?"

William held up his hand. "Alder."

"You mean...?" began Hazel.

Adam stopped her. "Don't worry. Alder looks the same as us."

Hazel said, "You didn't need to do that," but then thought to herself, *Actually, you probably did...*

The brothers both collapsed into chairs.

"For goodness sake!" said Hazel, "Get yourselves cleaned

up."

But they were already almost asleep. Within a minute they were both snoring. Hazel shook her head and tutted, *Men!* before climbing the stairs to bed.

Nara heeded her mother's request and remained in the house, or close by, during the following weeks. It was not easy. She missed Alder – his strong arms, his bearhugs, his kisses – and wondered if he thought of her...

The farm was always busy in summer. Several times, as June turned to July, she watched the men drive the livestock along the lane on their way to market or to fresh pasture in the fields to the south. From the other side of the house she could see the work continuing in the meadow, the line of activity coming ever closer to the cottage as the grass fell. Nara peered very hard, trying to spot Alder, but the figures were as yet too distant. The cut grass remained on the ground for a few days, drying in the sun before it was gathered, so there were two lines of workers: those closer to her, who cut the fresh grass, and those further away, who gathered up the dried hay and piled it in the waggon ready to be taken to the barn. She tried standing by the stone wall at the far side of the cottage garden, looking out into the meadow from there. She was closer to the workers by about thirty yards, but the view at ground level was obscured by the tall meadow grass, and she could see almost nothing.

The task was nearing completion by the start of the second week of July. Nara stood at her bedroom window, scanning the field. The figures were closer now, and she could pick out more detail. She ran her eyes along the rows of people... then she saw him. Could Alder see her, framed by the window at this distance? She leaned out as far as she dare, raised her arm and waved vigorously. He wasn't looking – couldn't see her. Nara's best skirt was bright pink silk. She found it, took it to the window and waved it from side to side at arm's length in as big a gesture as she was able. That caught his attention. He stopped working, stood up straight and looked right at her.

She suddenly felt intensely happy. Her heart beat faster and harder, her breasts seemed to swell, there was a tingling sensation in her loins. She threw the skirt back into the room and sobbed with joy, waving to him vigorously with all her might. She blew him kisses and shouted, "I LOVE YOU!" Could he hear her? All work in the field had stopped; everyone was looking at Alder. He went down on his knees, put his hands to his lips and blew her a shower of kisses. The meadow broke into spontaneous applause, and the air was filled with cheering voices.

Nara suddenly became aware that her mother was standing in the garden, looking up at her. She was shaking her head from side to side – but smiling.

Hazel stood in her kitchen, thinking hard. She'd never seen Nara so happy. She went to the bottom of the stairs and called up. Her daughter came running down.

"Go to Alder," she said.

Nara threw her arms round her mother's neck and kissed her. "Thank you, ma!" She was already striding towards the front door.

"Nara…"

"Ma?"

Hazel sighed. "Be careful. Take care of yourself."

Nara was smiling so widely – Hazel responded with a happy wave, *Go on, away with you!*

Minutes later, Nara Priestly, barefoot and with heart full of sunlight, strode through the meadow's top gate, over the river, and down towards the people working in the field. They watched her approach, parting for her as she marched through them. There was Alder, smiling broadly, arms wide open, waiting. The crowd of people broke into uproar as the two came together, Nara jumping into his embrace, hugging him, crying, kissing. It was a spectacle that was retold for decades.

Hazel watched from Nara's bedroom window, sobbing with happiness at the sight of her daughter's elation.

Their relationship fully repaired, Hazel waited for Nara to tell her about any developments. Nara saw Alder every day and was clearly very happy, rosy and blushing, her eyes far away. All seemed well.

One morning towards the end of August, she woke feeling ill, staggered downstairs and sat opposite her mother in the kitchen. Hazel knew immediately. Nara turned bright pink, rose to her feet, and vomited on the floor in her haste to get outside. She dropped to her hands and knees in front of the mess and said, "Oh, God..."

"You were right," said Hazel, helping her daughter back to her chair.

Nara sat with her head in her hands as her mother cleared up the sick.

"You haven't bled, have you." It wasn't a question.

Nara shook her head. "No."

"Does Alder know?"

"I haven't told him."

"You probably should."

But Nara was on her feet, quickly opened the front door and vomited on the path. Hazel shook her head. "Oh dear, oh dear..."

There were footsteps on the stairs, and William appeared. He saw Hazel clearing up and heard Nara's retching.

"No..." he said.

Hazel nodded shallowly and made an affirmative noise in her throat.

William walked through the front door, greeting Nara as he walked past her. "Morning, sister. How are we today?"

Nara swore at him, and he marched off to work, laughing as he went.

Alder was at Hazel's door well within the hour, concerned, knocking persistently. Hazel, responding to the urgent battering, assumed it must be someone in need of attention for an injury or some similar emergency. Instead, she found Nara's mature sweetheart, fists clenched in worry.

"Hello, Alder."

"Is it true?" he blurted.

"Well, *that* news didn't take long to reach you..."

Nara, bleary-eyed and in her nightdress, appeared behind her mother. Alder got down on his knees and looked up at Hazel, hands clasped in supplication. He'd rehearsed his speech.

"I'm just a poor man, with no goods or money. But I do have my love to give, and my love is as big as the world..."

Nara stepped around Hazel and interrupted him. "Stop it, Alder." She took his hand and told him to get up. Then she faced Hazel. "He's special. I want him. It's alright?"

Hazel thought, *Would it make any difference if I said no?* She shrugged as if to say, *It's your life.*

Nara turned to Alder and said, "Alder, will you marry me? You better say yes."

Alder, taken by surprise, glanced at Hazel, then back at Nara before muttering, "Yes... I will, thank you very much."

"Kiss me then," she said, holding her arms out and closing her eyes. Alder put his arms around his future wife and set his lips on hers.

Hazel said, "Oh Nara, and you in your nightdress."

Alder broke away from his kiss and said, "Don't worry, Mrs Priestly. I'm used to seeing her in less than that."

Hazel walked away, rolling her eyes. "Oh, Alder!"

Nara pondered over when the marriage should take place. Should they wait until the child was born or start making plans straight away? Alder seemed happy with either choice. Nara knew the baby had been conceived in the afternoon of June 25th, putting the birth around March 25th. She didn't want to be heavily pregnant at her marriage ceremony, and didn't really want to wait until after the birth. Harvest Home was to be celebrated on September 27th, so she asked her mother if their handfasting might be included in the festivities. It was little more than a month away, but Hazel thought there was nothing to lose. The "damage" had been done, the child was coming, Nara and Alder seemed committed to each other, everybody knew about their relationship. She went up to the big house to consult Hugh Flesher.

The door was opened by Bernard Swift, who'd taken over the role of butler after Douglas Buckley's death. Hugh was out on the farm but expected back at any moment. In the meantime, Hazel was shown in to see old Emmeline, still in her mourning black four full years after Benjamin's death.

"Hazel," she greeted her guest. "How good to see you." She didn't rise, being rather frail now at the age of seventy.

"Emmeline," replied Hazel. The two had been on first name terms for many years.

Bernard remained standing at the door, awaiting instructions.

"We'll take tea, Bernard." She turned to Hazel and said, "You would like a cup, wouldn't you, my dear?"

"That would be lovely. Thank you."

Bernard left, closing the door behind him. Emmeline turned to her guest. "You have happy news."

"My word," replied Hazel. "I can't believe how fast news travels."

Emmeline laughed. "We're a very close community. But you know that very well. A grandchild on the way."

"Yes, but Nara is so young..."

"Perhaps, but she's fifteen, is she not? Above marriageable age."

"It seems only yesterday that I was nursing her."

"Children grow up so fast. It seems to me that Hugh was a child only a few short weeks ago, but now he's forty-seven and has charge of the farm. People call him *Squire*, as they used to with Ben." The door opened and Amelia entered the room, greeting Hazel as she approached. Emmeline continued, "And here's my daughter-in-law. Please join us, my dear. We're talking about children – and grandchildren."

Amelia reached out and took Hazel's hand. "You're going to be a grandmama!"

Hazel smiled. "I am; it's true." She inclined her head, eyebrows raised, and added, "although Nara's pregnancy is still very new."

"Congratulations!" said Amelia. "It's so exciting!"

"But I need to talk to you and Hugh about the wedding," Hazel went on.

There was a knock at the door. "Come," called Emmeline. The door opened, and Sally Buckley appeared with a tray of tea things. She nodded to Hazel. "Mrs Priestly."

Hazel responded, "Nice to see you, Sally. Give my love to your mother."

"Thank you, Mrs Priestly, I will. She's in the kitchen. And congratulations!"

"Oh my!" said Hazel. "Thank you!" She wondered if all this fuss was premature – Nara was only two months pregnant. Suppose she lost the baby? If it hadn't been for William's blabbing they could have hushed it up for another month or two. Ah well, wasn't there a saying about horses bolting and stable doors?

Sally left, closing the door. Hazel broached the subject about which she'd come. "We've been talking about the date of the handfasting."

Again, the door opened. Hugh entered the room and strode straight to Hazel, who rose.

"Hazel," he said warmly, took her arms, and kissed her

cheek.

"Hugh," said Hazel, re-seating herself as he sat down by his wife. "I'd like to talk about Nara's marriage if I may."

"Yes, of course!" said Hugh. "And many congratulations!"

Oh, my... thought Hazel. "I know it's very soon, but we're thinking about Harvest Home..."

"You mean, holding the ceremony at the festival?"

"Yes," said Hazel.

"What a wonderful idea! I can see it right now..." His imagination began to fire up. "The harvest, the celebration of a union, a new child on the farm... Wonderful! Let's do it!"

That had been very much easier than Hazel had feared.

"You'll have the old handfasting ceremony – in the meadow, I imagine? I hope the weather's good. You're welcome to use the house if it rains – or we could have one of the barns ready – that's probably easier, with all the dancing."

"I'm so glad you're happy with the idea..."

"I am delighted, Hazel." He glanced at Amelia and Emmeline. "...as we all must be." They nodded vigorously and voiced their unanimous approval.

"You'll conduct the ceremony yourself, of course?"

"I will," she said.

"What about witnesses? Isn't it traditional for there to be two? One for the man and one for the maid?"

"That's right," said Hazel, "but we haven't got so far as to think about witnesses yet."

She was always impressed with Hugh. He never did anything by halves. Whatever he did, it was well done – and his respect for the old ways meant that he was dearly loved in the community. Weddings often took place in the church, but many of the country folk still preferred the handfasting in the fields, and Hugh supported both traditions. Hazel's own family, stretching back for unknown generations, favoured the old ceremony, believed by many to predate the arrival of Christianity.

Amelia poured the tea, and they took up their cups. Hugh said, "I don't know if it's considered acceptable to toast with tea, but here's health to you, Hazel, and to Nara, Alder and the child."

"You are very kind," said Hazel, sipping.

Hugh set his cup down and looked at her. "Hazel, please tell me if this is presumptuous, but I'd like to be your daughter's witness, if she'll have me."

Hazel was astonished and couldn't help but show it. "Do I mind? No, it would be an honour... assuming that Nara hasn't already asked someone. But why would you want to do such a thing?"

Hugh sat back, his eyes glazed. "The thought of it. The autumn fields, the sun, the celebration of the crops, the promise of new life, the energy of young love... It appeals to the *earth* in me." He paused. "I'm sorry – I'm a bit of a romantic at times..."

"He is!" interrupted Amelia.

"My boy!" said Emmeline.

So it was settled, and the day came bright and sunny. Almost all the grain had been gathered into the barns. Only one waggon-load remained, and that stood ready while the two huge draft horses that would pull it were brought in from the road and attached. The Harvest Home, or Ingathering, was an age-old ritual. The country folk from all around the farm had decided that Alder, in honour of his wedding, should be the last reaper, the Lord of the Harvest, so it was his task to cut the final sheaf. A cheer went up as he did so. Then he climbed into the seat of the waggon and set off towards the barn. A crowd of farm folk accompanied him, all bedecked with flowers: dahlias, marigolds and more.

Nara, decorated with garlands of apples, pears, plums and damsons, and a crown of blueberries, raspberries, blackberries and rosehips, had been chosen as Harvest Queen and joined the procession in a waggon of her own, drawn by white horses. She was waiting on the road with her own acolytes and waved to Alder as he emerged from the field. "My love! Today's the day!"

Hugh, Amelia and Hazel waited at the barn and watched the steady cavalcade of revellers as it approached, greeting people as the waggons pulled up. Alder took the last sheaf and gave it to Hazel, who fashioned it into a doll while the remainder of the harvest was unloaded. She dressed the sheaf of corn in white cloth, decorated it with coloured ribbons and blessed it.

The weather was fine, so the feasting was to take place in the open air of the meadow. It had taken the combined efforts of three kitchens to produce all the food for the event. Maria, Sally and Alicia Buckley, and Florence and Emma Swift had masterminded it all, planned all the cooking and gathered together a squad of volunteers to help. There was roast beef, ham, baked fowl, baked hare, roast goose and autumn vegetables.

The drinks – supervised by Bernard Swift, Richard Swift, and Elys Buckley – included ale, cider and all kinds of fruit wine: Elderberry, primrose, parsnip, dandelion and currant, as well as mead – spiced and un-spiced.

When the work in the barn was complete and the last grain had been unloaded, the people made their way across the road to the meadow. Earlier in the day, Nicholas Miller had prepared a narrow hole in the earth, about four feet deep, awaiting the erection of the pole that would display the image of the corn mother. Hazel tied the corn-doll sheaf to the top of the pole in readiness. There was an expectant silence while she set the pole in the ground before turning to cry, "Behold! The Mother of the Corn!" The meadow erupted with a tremendous cheer, and the revelry began.

The feasting and dancing continued into the early evening, the music provided by musicians drawn from the bands of the local churches. Parson James Kirby, himself a skilled singer and organist, winced from time to time.

The dancing drew together unexpected partnerships: Hugh Flesher with Apple Robinson; Natty Miller with Parson Cornelius East; Hazel Priestly with Cedar Robinson, dashing and handsome at seventeen; Doctor Levinson with Amelia Flesher; Willow Robinson with Parson James Kirby. James was entranced by twenty-three-year-old Willow and asked to dance with her again and again. Willow was more than happy to oblige. Tozer couldn't help but notice, and pointed them out to Apple.

"Look at Willow."

"Oh my goodness me! I think she likes him…"

"I think… he likes her…"

When he'd arrived at Roxby three years previously, James Kirby had been opposed to the Pagan practices in which he was now willingly taking part, having intended to bring the *Word of the Lord* forcefully home to his flock. But in the fulness of time, he'd found himself drawn into the community and was now (although he hadn't quite realised it yet) dancing with the woman who would soon become his wife.

Meadow Reid and Louise Flesher, hiding from young Henry, ran amongst the crowds of people, trying to evade capture as they played tag. Buffy Miller, Amy Swift, seven-year-old Alan Flathers and the other youngsters were entrusted to the care of twelve-year-old Holly Robinson, who was bedecked with blonde pigtails and relished her position of authority. Buffy and Amy got on especially well and danced together for much of the evening. Little Amy was entranced by Buffy's nickname and improvised snippets of songs about the "Pond Girl".

Cornelius found Hazel and hugged her, saying how happy he was at the news of her grandchild, and wished Nara and Alder well. He brought best wishes from Hubert Cromwell, who regretted he was unable to attend; Egbert had be-

come increasingly frail and demanded his full-time attention (Hubert's sentiments of goodwill were not seconded
by Egbert, who remained staunchly against such "heathen"
festivities – by which he meant not just the handfasting
but the Harvest Home also).

The sun began to sink, and the sky took on an increasingly red hue. Hazel asked the musicians to pause, and
the dancing ceased. She was a little tired, and it was an
effort for her to speak loudly enough to reach everyone in
the field. She shouted, "Can everyone hear me?" There was
a general noise in the affirmative, although a few hands
were cupped to ears. "I'll do my best," shouted Hazel. A
few thumbs went up. She moved quickly to the highest
point of the meadow, the agreed location for the handfasting, and called, "The Lord of the Harvest, and the Harvest
Queen!" Alder and Nara appeared from a hidden spot down
by the Esk and walked hand-in-hand towards the crowd of
people. They were both dressed in white: she in a single
flowing robe; he in a simple tunic open at the neck, spot-
less breeches, shiny black shoes with silver buckles. The
crowd was silent as they passed through the field and made
their way to Hazel. Alder stood on the right, Nara on the
left, Hazel facing them. The two witnesses approached and
stood behind: Tozer Robinson, unnaturally well-dressed,
and Hugh Flesher in his brightest waistcoat, looking every
inch the gentleman farmer that he was. There was a light
breeze. "All ready?" Hazel whispered. Both nodded, Nara
smiling, Alder more solemn.

Hazel called out, "We're here to fasten Alder and Nara in
marriage." Her voice was already breaking with emotion,
and she realised this was going to be more difficult than
she'd imagined. Tears came to her eyes. She covered her
mouth with her left hand and tried to control her breathing. Fortunately, the ceremony was brief and simple, and
the couple had been practising their parts. With luck, they
wouldn't need prompting. "Now we hear their vows," she

called.

The two faced each other, and Alder took Nara's right hand. "I, Alder, take thee, Nara, to be my wedded wife, thee, and thee alone... and thereto..."

"You missed a bit!" hissed Nara. "...All that I am..."

"Sorry," he said, then raised his voice again. "...my wedded wife. All that I am, and all that I have, is thine from this day. I shall be true to thee, and thee alone till death parts us. I promise that it shall be so."

Nara took his right hand and repeated the simple vow: "I, Nara, take thee, Alder, to be my wedded husband. All that I am, and all that I have, is thine from this day. I shall be true to thee, and thee alone till death parts us. I promise that it shall be so."

Then they exchanged twists of straw; first Alder to Nara, which she tucked into her hair; then Nara to Alder, which he tucked into a buttonhole.

The sky had become crimson, the wind had grown stronger.

It was time to tie the knot. Hazel produced three lengths of ribbon, and the two knit their hands together in preparation, right to right, left to left, wrists crossed. Hazel lay the three bands around their wrists and hands, wrapped them over and around, and tied them loosely before standing back. The couple looked at each other. Alder said, "These hands will be your protection, always." Nara repeated the phrase. The two stepped apart, hands slipping free of each other but keeping hold of the ribbons as the knot tightened in the space between them. It was done. There was a thunderous cheer, and the field burst into applause.

Hazel could no longer contain herself. She was in floods of tears but managed to say between sobs, "Kiss your wife, Alder." That action elicited another cheer.

Nara said quietly, "Let's go home."

Alder looked at Hazel as if seeking permission.

Hazel said, "As you wish. She's yours."

March 29, 1749

Alder tapped on Hazel's bedroom door just after midnight. Nara was up and complaining of cramps and backache – symptoms that Hazel had told Alder to watch out for. She wiped the sleep from her eyes and accompanied him to Nara's bedroom, which he'd shared with her since their marriage. Nara was perched on the edge of the bed in obvious discomfort.

Hazel approached. "Let me see, dear," she said.

Nara, very big with child, crawled onto her back on the mattress, drew up her knees and spread her legs apart while Hazel pushed up her nightdress.

It was too much for Alder. "I'll wait downstairs," he said.

It was clear to Hazel that the labour was still in its early stages, so she reassured her daughter and went down to the kitchen to make tea. Alder sat there, fidgeting. Adam and William occupied two more chairs, having been disturbed by the noises and now too tense to sleep.

"You're up early," said Hazel.

"How is she?" asked William.

"As expected. You can go back to bed for a while if you want."

Soon they were all drinking tea, an expensive night-time luxury, but it was calming, and Nara, in particular, was grateful for it.

Hazel sat with her daughter and read before nodding off in the chair at about half past two.

At five o'clock, she was shaken awake. Nara was standing before her, dripping. Her waters had broken. "Ma?" she said. Hazel was alert in an instant and had Nara back on the bed. A quick inspection confirmed that things were moving on – Nara's cervix had begun to dilate. Hazel hurried down to the kitchen and found the three men asleep. She woke them and sent Alder running up the hill to the Buckleys and Swifts to fetch Maria and Florence. Adam rode to Easington for Doctor Levinson, who'd been expecting the event for several days.

Neil conferred with Hazel, then followed her upstairs to join Nara, Maria and Florence in the bedroom. Nara was fully dilated by half past seven, shortly after dawn, and Neil said she should begin pushing. It was painful, sweaty, and she was frightened, wanting it to be over. Hazel comforted her as best she could, mopping her brow and face.

Things became noisy as time wore on, the sounds carrying downstairs to the three concerned men. Alder was tense, and the brothers did their best to reassure him.

"Ma's delivered lots of babies all by herself," said Adam. "Today the doctor's there as well. Everything's as safe as it can be. It sounds worse than it is."

"Let's get some fresh air," said William. "Might do us good." They opened the front door and stepped outside with Alder into the cool of the morning. It was windy, and the sky was broiling with angry dark clouds. Nara's cries could be clearly heard through her wide-open bedroom window, the sound mingling with the increasing cacophony of the birds as they sang against the coming rain.

A few waggons passed by. One of the drivers leaned over and greeted the three men. "Nara's baby born yet?"

"Soon," shouted William.

The man pointed ahead as he began to move forward, and shouted, "There's a storm coming."

She flew with the storm clouds, filling them red, furiously riding the torrent towards the farm. If she'd had wings, they would have been vast, spread across the angry dome of the sky. If she'd had claws, they would have been terrifying, sharp, merciless talons. She was old, older than imagination, her story spun out through countless generations past. But she was coming to

an end – there would be only two more: this one – audacious,
provocative, daring, brilliant; then one more – the quiet one –
modest, kind. Then she'd wheel away, spinning quietly into the
eternal silence of the future...

Up in the bedroom, things were on course despite the agonised screams of the expectant mother. Neil said, "Nara, you're doing very well. We're nearly done. Deep breath and push. We can see the baby."

Nara pushed hard, shrieking, sobbing with the effort.

The open window was suddenly blasted with lightning, thunder crashing a second later. The women almost jumped out of their skin. It was as if something had come flying into the room from outside.

"Oh my word!" cried Florence, her hands at her face in fright.

The violent flash made Nara convulse, and the child's head was suddenly out – Neil had it in his hands.

The room darkened as the storm clouds rode over the farm, cancelling the dawn. The oil lamps dimmed as if they were cowering in fear against the gloom.

"Another push if you can!" shouted the doctor.

There was something elemental in the room. Maria and Florence felt the clutch of it. Hazel, watching the shadows, thought, *Someone's here.* There was a presence, hiding in the dark corners but watching every move. *Who are you?* thought Hazel fearfully. Nara was entirely consumed with the effort of giving birth. Her eyes were closed, and she was only partly aware of the atmosphere in the house.

Neil looked around uneasily. Something was happening – the room seemed to crackle with energy. There was another flash, and the sky roared. "My God!" he whispered. *"What is this...?"*

Nara took a huge breath, pushed with all her strength, and the child arrived in Levinson's hands. The heavens tore apart with thunder, and the room was filled with flashing white light.

Alder, Adam and William watched as the firmament split open; a furious finger of lightning exploded on one of the barns opposite the meadow, and bright flames began to consume the building.
Then the heavens opened, and a torrent of rain began to fall, relentless and dense.

The atmosphere in the bedroom had quietened. There'd been something at the birth with them – they all knew it, although none wanted to be the first to say so. But now the darkness had receded and the oil lamps, flaring bright again, shared the room with dull, rainy daylight. Water spattered loudly on the sill of the open window. The impression of the entity, presence, whatever it was, began to fade, and the baby became the centre of attention.
It had begun to cry loudly the second it was free of Nara's body. Neil handed the child to Hazel, who wiped it, wrapped it in a blanket and presented it to the exhausted new mother.
Hazel said, "Your daughter Nara."
Nara wept with joy and relief as she took the child.
Maria gazed at the baby in astonishment. "Look at her hair!" she said. "I've never seen such brilliant red hair in a new-born."
Hazel nodded. "It's Anne White's hair. My great grand-mother."
"Anne White?" said Florence.
"Stowmarket. She was hanged in the witch trials. My grandmother Daisy was there. I remember her talking about it."
Nara explored her daughter's face and tiny hands. The baby's eyes were open – she seemed to be looking intently at her mother. Nara whispered, "She has hazel eyes. Beautiful..."

Hazel said to Nara, "Say the child's name…"
Nara replied, "Catherine. Kate."

5. BALLINADEE, IRELAND
1750/51

"Xander!"

Alexander stood almost ankle deep in pig shit, shovel in hand, and caught his mother's shrieking voice over the squealing and grunting of the animals. He gestured *back shortly* to Patrick and Michael, propped his tool against the wall of the pen and strode the hundred yards to the hovel in which he and his mother lived.

Ellen was still able to see shapes as long as there was plenty of light, and the swaying motion of an approaching dark object suggested that her son was on his way. Alexander found her in a pool of vomit. He said nothing. He was used to it.

Ellen purchased her potcheen from the pedlars who brought the stuff door to door. She was a reliable customer and had been perpetually drunk ever since Alexander's father had walked out seven years previously. At that time Ellen Regan had been a presentable woman of thirty-one. Admittedly she hadn't been happy, having to tolerate the constant unfaithfulness of her husband Richard, but she had accepted her lot and immersed herself in the family pig business. It was exhausting and filthy but paid enough to keep them all in the house.

Richard Regan was a thoughtless, selfish man. He let his wife and son earn the money for him while he indulged himself in women and drink. He spent his days in the two inns of Ballinadee or walked to the nearby villages – south to Ballinspittle, west to Kilbrittain or north to pretty Kilmacsimon on the banks of the Bandon, and often stayed away from home for days at a time. He walked out of the house one sunny summer's day in 1743 and never came home again.

Ellen got on with the business, but as the days wore on into weeks, the weeks into months, she began to find comfort in the bottle. The potcheen pedlars made regular rounds of the villages, and Ellen, greeting one of them at the door one rainy day, thought, *why not?*

The first sip nearly choked her; it was a hideous concoction, and almost unbelievably strong. The vile fierceness of the taste became exaggerated in her memory overnight, so the next attempt was easier. *That's bad*, she thought, *but I can get used to it if I keep trying.*

So she'd kept practising – every day, for months, years. The booze ruined her. Ellen became fat, dirty, incapable of work, and almost blind. Now she relied entirely on her fifteen-year-old boy Alexander. He was in charge of the pigs now, and was also responsible for cleaning up his mother's mess.

Ellen was on her hands and knees just inside the back door of the house, swaying a little, unable to get up. Alexander cleaned his boots with water from the trough nearby and came over to her.

"Mam," he said, "you did it again."

"Sorry, son," she mumbled through her spittle.

He was used to it. Holding his breath against the smell of the sick, he helped her upright and walked her to the kitchen chair. He removed her stinking clothes, cleaned her up, and dressed her in her bathrobe – an operation he'd performed a hundred times and more. There was no humiliation left in it for either of them.

He squatted before her when the task was done, looking up at her shattered, worn features.

"Ma. Please stop the drinkin'. I'm workin' to make a better life for the two of us. One day you'll be happy again. I promise."

She ran her hand through his curly brown hair and shook

her head slowly, shallowly. *You shouldn't be here with me. I'm a dead weight to you.* But the words were not given voice. She might have cried, but her tears had been used up long ago.

Deep within his heart, Alexander knew his promises were false. He and his mother were condemned to a life of hopeless poverty. Managing the swine was a cyclical business. He kept about forty sows and two boars. The sows would gestate for nearly four months, then nurse their piglets for about three weeks. After that, Xander, Michael and Patrick would move the piglets to the big barn where they lived for about four months before being driven to market. Alexander was able to pay his workers, keep a roof over his head, buy basic provisions to keep them alive and finance the next round, identical to that which preceded it. There was never anything more – and no prospect of there ever being. Ellen knew it too. It was a hopeless, miserable existence, every day the same.

One gloomy February day in 1751, Alexander interrupted his tasks and walked back to the house to check on his mother, having heard nothing from her since he began work at sun-up. He found Ellen hanging from a beam in the kitchen ceiling, a chair kicked away and lying on its side nearby. She'd found a length of rope from somewhere and had managed to fashion the noose and fasten it to the kitchen beam despite her poor eyesight. A few drops of sticky darkness spotted the floor beneath her. One of her shoes had fallen; the other remained dangling on her toe. She was cold, her body motionless. She'd been dead for hours.

Patrick and Michael helped Alexander cut his mother down. They laid the body on the table, and Xander sent Michael to Kilmacsimon to fetch the surgeon. While he was gone, Xander walked to the church to inform the priest of his mother's death. The priest then sent a boy to fetch the undertaker, and Xander returned home to wash his mother's body.

It was a horrible task, but he managed to accomplish it by progressing steadily, keeping his mind closed as far as possible – and trying to avoid looking at her face. He called for Patrick's assistance only when it was necessary to turn the body over. With a little effort, they managed to dress her in clean clothes.

Shortly after the task was done, Michael returned from Kilmacsimon with a death certificate. The surgeon had been drunk and unwilling to come to Ballinadee to personally inspect the deceased, so had written out the document in absentia.

An hour or so later the undertaker arrived in his cart with a few coffins of varying sizes and a set of three trestles. They selected a box for Ellen and set her in the kitchen. Alexander asked for the lid to be screwed into place, thanked the undertaker and sent Michael and Patrick home. Then he fed the pigs.

Xander moved his things out of the house and prepared a place to sleep in the barn.

That night there was a gale, and the wind banged and howled around the old wooden building. In the small hours, he became convinced that he could hear Ellen's voice calling him from the house.

"Xander!"

He lay awake in the tumult, his ears straining to hear it again. Ten minutes, twenty. He began to nod off.

"Xander!"

The cry haunted him until the wind died down and the dawn light began to show.

He'd forgotten to take food from the house, so had to return before work began to find something to eat for breakfast.

There was the coffin, in the kitchen as it had been left the previous day. Xander opened the larder door and was suddenly sure that Ellen was standing behind him. His spine chilled, and his eyes began to tear. The house was very cold. If he turned he'd see her, face deathly white, eyes sightless, neck cracked at an odd angle...

"Xander."

He almost collapsed in fright, then realised it was Michael. "I'll be there shortly," he replied, gathered together the items he needed, and left.

The burial was set for three days later. Alexander, Patrick and Michael were the only mourners. Patrick and Michael had hardly known Ellen, had exchanged no more than a hundred words with her in the two years they'd worked at the pigs. They attended the funeral only because they felt it would be doing the right thing for Xander.

There was no wake, no gathering of any kind. After she'd been laid in the ground, Patrick and Michael shook Xander's hand and left him alone in the rain at the graveside.

He had nothing; nothing but the cap he held in his hand, a few clothes, a bunch of pigs and a miserable, empty hovel he no longer felt able to enter. He slept in the barn again that night. The rain beat relentlessly on the roof and dripped through the holes.

The next morning was cold, although the rain had stopped. Xander had made a decision, and as the sun came up, the kiss of its first rays painting the furrowed sheet of clouds a deep red, he determined that this would be the day everything changed. He waited for Patrick and Michael to arrive. Then, throwing them the keys to the house and pens, he told them everything was theirs – the pigs, the pens, the barn, the house and everything in it.

"Are you mad?" asked Michael.

"Probably," said Xander. "But what of it? You're welcome to this, fuckin' hell-hole, so it is." He raised a hand in farewell, turned his back, and left the village of his birth forever.

Alexander walked the six and a half miles across the bog to the walled town of Bandon, arriving in the afternoon. He carried a small sack containing all his belongings; there were a few coins in his pocket. He had a dream: he would find a job and begin a new life with great prospects, building himself a happy future.

On arrival in the town, he smartened himself up as best as he was able and went from shop to shop, inn to inn, unsuccessfully seeking employment. No one gave him a second glance. He became cold, had nowhere to go. He bought bread and cheese and ate a simple meal by the river, the chill biting ever more deeply into him. He had to find somewhere to pass the night. Perhaps tomorrow would bring more luck. He walked about the town looking into alleyways and gardens, seeking shelter. The sky began to darken. He was chilled to the bone and needed to get inside. Soon he'd be so cold that he wouldn't be able to move – and then…

He was on Kilbrogan Hill. To his right, he could see the edifice of Christ Church surrounded by its graveyard. In three minutes he was in the porch. The church was unlocked. He pushed open the door and made his way to a seat halfway down the nave. Others were there, praying as evening came down. Xander pretended to do the same.

At about seven o'clock, he looked about himself in the near darkness and found the building empty. He'd been pondering, deciding on a place to doss down for the night. Picking up two hassocks, he made his way to the east end of the building – to the altar. The narrow space on the floor behind it was cobwebby and dirty, but it was big enough for him to lie down. He arranged his hassocks as pillows and made himself as comfortable as he could.

A few minutes later, as he lay still, Alexander heard the latch click and the church door open. Someone had entered, and he could hear them walking purposefully about. He held his breath – made no sound – hoped he wouldn't be caught. His eyes closed, and exhausted as he was, sleep took him.

He awoke in pitch blackness, sweating, bursting to pee. For a moment he couldn't remember where he was. Then the events of the previous day came back to him. He listened hard. There was no sound at all in the church except the wind whipping about the building's exterior. He continued to lay still, not wanting to move, hoping his need would go away. Instead, it became more urgent – and there was an increasingly sharp pain in his bowels.

He rose to his feet. Nothing at all was visible – he may as well have been down a mine. He put his hands on the altar and moved out of his hideout, feeling his way as best he could. Using his memory of the church interior as a guide, he found the sanctuary wall and began to feel his way to the left. There was a complicated piece of stonework, probably a monument, then the featureless wall again... He was concentrating so intently on his hands that he completely forgot about the stone steps that led down to the nave. He lost his footing and fell, hands grasping, helplessly trying to break his fall, but he hit the floor hard.

"Shite!"

The darkness was shot through with sparks of agony. His right knee was on fire, and he doubled up, clutching at it. The pain cancelled the concentration he'd been using to hold control of his bladder, and he started to piss in his breeches. He cursed and began to unbutton them as quickly as possible but felt a surge of sticky heat between his buttocks as he fumbled with the fastenings. In desperation, he pulled down his clothes, knelt on the floor and submitted to the demands of his tortured entrails.

Xander sighed and remained motionless for a while, the stink filling his nostrils. He felt physically relieved but very weak, squatting in the blackness of the church. There was nothing to clean himself with, so he stood and pulled up his breeches, hoping they wouldn't soil too badly.

He felt clammy and began to shiver uncontrollably. Staggering forwards, he found the pews in the nave easily enough, opened one of the doors and collapsed onto the floor inside. Within seconds he was asleep.

Hours later he was shocked into consciousness by the clicking of a key in the church door. From his prone position, he saw that the interior of the building was glowing with dawn light. Footsteps approached and a shadow passed by him. A few seconds afterwards he heard somebody whispering. Xander listened hard and realised the man was praying. He raised himself a little and looked to the top of the nave. There was a figure in black, on his knees and facing the altar, mumbling quickly under his breath. As he watched, the man stopped in mid-flow, turned his head to the left. There was an audible sniff, then the figure rose and walked to the site of Xander's nocturnal accident. "Holy Jesus!" said the minister, "What the fuckin' hell is this?!"

Alexander sprinted for the exit, heart pounding, and the minister ran after him in furious pursuit. Xander clicked open the latch and ran through the porch out into the churchyard, but dizziness hit him as soon as he was in the open air. He tried to continue his escape but had to clutch at a tombstone to remain upright. His pursuer was on him, but Alexander had already passed out and collapsed.

Soft light; pink. He was warm. The fingers of his left hand were in contact with the edge of a mattress. He flexed them, exploring the material of the sheet on which he lay. He felt comfortable, safe.

Xander opened his eyes. He was in bed, daylight streaming into the room through a large window. A clock chimed ten.

He closed his eyes and went back to sleep.

Sometime later he woke again. A bearded face was looking down at him.

"Are you awake?" The voice was quiet, gentle.

Xander opened his mouth to say something, but no sound emerged.

"You've been ill."

Again, Alexander tried to speak but found himself unable to form any words.

"Do you drink tea? I'll get you some warm tea." The bearded face disappeared from view.

Alexander pushed himself up closer to the bedhead. He drew his hands out from beneath the bedclothes and looked at them. They were clean. He touched his face, his hair. Clean. He smelt his hands. Soap.

After a moment, the bearded man returned with a tray of things. Xander looked more closely at him. He was about forty, dressed in black. The tea made a rippling sound as he poured it.

"I'll let it cool a little," he said. "Do you remember where you are?"

"Where I am..." Xander managed, trying to think.

"You're in Bandon. I found you in the church."

He remembered. "Did I...?" He said. "I'm sorry."

"Don't worry," said the man. "You were quite ill – and exhausted, I think."

There was a short pause. "I'm Francis Byrne, minister at Christ Church. Do you have a name?"

"Xander. Alexander Regan."

Francis held out his hand and Xander took it. "I'm pleased to meet you, Xander. Try the tea."

Alexander had never drunk tea before. It was dark brown and bitter, but he found its warmth comforting. "It's good," he said. "Thank you."

"You're very welcome," Francis replied. "Do you feel up to

telling me what's happened to you?"

So Alexander told his story: Ballinadee, his parents, the pigs, abandonment, drink, death...

"And you came here looking for what – a new life?"

"What's left?" asked Alexander. "There *is* only new life – or nothing."

Francis thought before replying. "That's a very enlightened thing to say." He paused. "And you know – you're right."

Alexander shared Francis's house for the next few days, during which time they talked about what he might do next. The rudimentary level of Xander's reading and writing imposed certain limitations, and Francis had neither the time to teach him nor the funds with which to pay for lessons. The house was full of books, and Xander frustrated himself on several occasions by taking one down and painstakingly picking through a few words, shaking his head in exasperation.

Francis Byrne was well-known among the townsfolk, and he went about seeking unskilled labour for his temporary lodger. His enquiries were almost entirely unsuccessful, although one possibility presented itself.

"Would you care to work in a tavern, Alexander?"

"I'll take any honest work. Is it here in town?"

"It is. It'll be in the Kings Arms. I was in there yesterday..." Francis paused, furrowed his brow. "I can see how you're lookin' at me there, Xander. Even men of God have their weaknesses, you know! Anyway, they've just lost a kitchen boy. It'll be simple enough work, but they'll drive you hard, I'm sure."

"Thank you, Father. I've reason to be very grateful to you."

"Ach, it's nothin'." Silence for a moment. "It was Mrs Newce I was speakin' to. She's right enough, but you might find her husband Archie a bit of a challenge. Do as he says and don't get under his feet; that's my advice. I'm sure you'll manage."

So Alexander moved into a tiny attic room in the Kings Arms tavern.

Archibald and Mary Newce were both in their fifties. She smiled, he swore. Xander was set to work waiting at tables, serving at the bar, cleaning the place, and was master of the bucket and mop for cleaning up spillages, accidents and vomit. He was worked hard, took his meals in the kitchen and earned almost nothing. Many regulars got to know him by sight and remembered his name, although he didn't develop any real friendships.

Archie Newce never smiled but was civil enough when sober. He drank heavily in the later evening and spent most nights shouting at his wife, who took his abuse in silence. Xander tried to stay away from these regular confrontations. Now and then Francis Byrne visited the tavern and chatted with Xander at the bar. He'd take a drink or two and wish him well. He was the only person Xander considered to be a genuine friend.

In the summer, Archie Newce took on an extra helper – a pretty girl of sixteen, Xander's own age, named Bridget Kelly. She had long auburn hair, milky pale skin and freckles. She was shy, delicate, and Xander liked her very much. Bridget was never given the filthy jobs, never told to slop out the privies or clear up the sick, but Xander wasn't unhappy about that; he liked to think of her as being above such things. She spoke kindly to him, and they often worked together in the bar. Bridget helped Mary with the guest rooms, cleaning and changing the bedsheets. Occasionally Mary Newce sent Bridget or Xander out to the market, but Archie never allowed the pair to go in each other's company.

As summer wore into autumn, the two built up a rapport in the taproom. The customers, seeing one of them, would ask after the other as if they were a couple. Xander liked that. He suspected that Bridget knew he was growing fond of her. She smiled at him shyly now and then, blushing. Xander thought about her a lot, but they never found any time to talk at length. Archie seemed keen to keep them apart and growled at Xander whenever he sensed the two might be getting too close.

Bridget slept in the room over the coach house at the far side of the tavern courtyard. Xander spent weeks attempting to gather sufficient courage to visit her there at night after everyone had gone to bed, if only for company and conversation. He'd never asked her permission, fearing rejection, but he'd grown so fond of her that he had to move things on.

Late one crisp November night, long after twelve, he gathered all his courage together, crept downstairs and let himself out into the stable yard. He tiptoed stealthily across the open space and was about to try the latch to the coach house door when he heard footsteps descending the stairs on the other side. The door opened, and there stood Archie Newce.

Archie was startled at the sight of Xander's figure, motionless in the moonlight. He stopped in his tracks, peered and swore, seeing who it was. Then he let fly with his fists, and Xander went sprawling.

"You fuckin' little shite! You leave that girl alone! If I catch you prowlin' round her, I'll wring the fuckin' life out of you. Filt'y little arsehole!" He locked the coach-house door and kicked Xander hard before striding back to the main building.

Alexander staggered to his feet. He was horrified. Archie and Bridget? The thought was nauseating – it couldn't be true. He had to find out for sure and decided to confront her the next day. Xander hobbled back to his room and lay awake, picturing fat, filthy, coarse, greasy Archie and milky-white, frail, beautiful Bridget together. He was too appalled to sleep.

Next morning Alexander arrived early in the kitchen to prepare the breakfast things, as was his duty. Archie arrived a little later. He'd slept poorly, outraged at the memory of having been almost caught in the act, and his anger remained undiminished. He saw Xander, walked over to him, stared him in the eye, hawked and gobbed on the floor.

"Clean that up, yer little lickarse gobshite."

Xander looked right back at him and spat, "Clean it up yer fuckin' self, yer fat shit."

Archie was on him straight away, laying in with fists and feet. Mary, hearing the commotion, ran into the kitchen and tried to separate them. "Archie, for God's sake! What are you doing?"

"Fuck off, woman!" her husband replied, and slapped her across the face. Mary fell to the floor, and Bridget appeared in the doorway.

Xander, lips split and bloodied, called, "Jesus, Bridget! Are you fuckin' that bucket o' lard?"

Bridget threw her hands to her face in horror, and Archie set about Xander again. Mary pulled herself to her feet and glanced between Archie and Bridget. "Is it true, Archie?" she shouted.

"Will you fuck off, Mary! Get the fuck away!" He lashed at her again, but she was gone. Xander had collapsed to the floor and was trying to defend himself against Archie's continuous booting.

"Stop it!" cried Bridget. "For God's sake Archie. You'll kill the boy!"

A moment later, Mary came running with two bottles, one of which she smashed over the back of her husband's skull. Archie, dazed and surprised, ceased his kicking and turned to face his wife. His right hand tested the rear of his cranium and came away bloodied. "...what the fuck...?" he said. But before he could continue, Mary kicked him squarely and heftily between the legs. Archie collapsed in agony to his knees, cradling his pulped testicles. Mary took up the second bottle and swung it hard, smashing it to pieces on the side of his head. Archie collapsed sideways, unconscious.

There was complete silence for a few seconds, then Mary shouted, "There, yer fucker! There's something yer weren't expecting." She leaned forward and spat on his prone form. Xander pulled himself up and looked at Mrs Newce. She said, "G'warn. You better get out of here. Put your hand in the box and take some money. God knows you deserve it, boy."

Xander walked past her. Bridget was standing there, speechless. He stood in front of her for a moment, and their eyes met. His heart was broken. She knew it, and beginning to cry, mumbled, "Forgive me…"

He struggled up to his room and gathered together his few things, then returned to the bar and filled his pockets with coins. A moment later he was out in the street, never to return. Bridget watched as he walked away.

Francis Byrne was at home. He opened the door and found Alexander on the other side of it, physically and emotionally shattered. "What the hell happened?" he asked, and caught the boy as he fell.

Xander spent six days in Francis's house recovering from Archie's beating, trying to gather some semblance of his wits.

"So, have you decided what to do?"

"There's nothing for me here," replied the boy. "I'll be leaving tomorrow."

"And where will you go, Alexander?"

"I'll go to Dublin. Perhaps I'll find a life there."

"You're welcome to stay here for a while, you know. You're a fine boy. I'd be happy for you to stay."

"And you're a kind man, Father. You've shown me more kindness than anyone, and I'm very grateful for it, so I am, but I need to find my own life."

Francis looked at him quietly. "Stay till Christmas then, son."

"I'm away in the morning. No point in waiting."

Father Francis had grown fond of his young friend and felt his emotion rising. "Ach, Xander. You're a noble soul. I hope you'll take care of yourself."

"I will. Don't worry about me."

The minister nodded inwardly, acknowledging the boy's determination.

The next morning, dressed in a new coat, tricorn hat on his head and money in his pocket, Alexander Regan set out on foot for Dublin.

6. CAPPLEMAN FARM
1751

Holly Robinson, fifteen, dreamt of marrying a handsome prince. He would visit the farm one day, searching for a wife...

Word had preceded his coming, and a great crowd had gathered by the hand pump, awaiting his arrival. There was a cloud of dust in the distance as he approached, his golden coach drawn by six magnificent white horses. It pulled to a halt in front of the gathered multitude, and a footman climbed down from the box, wordlessly opened the carriage door, and there he was, immaculately dressed in regal colours, bejewelled and wearing a powdered wig, a fetching little black spot on his cheek.

"I have heard of a great beauty," he said. "Her legend has spread far and wide, and I have travelled a great distance to discover her. They say she lives on this farm, and I have come to seek her hand in marriage."

Shy Holly stepped back, concealing herself more deeply in the crowd, thinking, "Who is this great beauty the prince speaks of? Perhaps it's Louise, or Meadow..."

Holly looked down, too humble to be seen. But the crowd was parting, and she realised that the prince was standing right before her. She looked up and saw him there, smiling lovingly at her – the most handsome, dashing prince there ever was. Her heart fluttered. She curtsied and looked shyly away.

"It is you, my love," he said. "You are the most beautiful girl in the world, and I shall take you as my bride." He wrapped her in his strong arms and kissed her passionately while everyone cheered and shouted: "Congratulations, Your Majesty. We always knew she was the most beautiful girl, the most beautiful girl..."

The door opened, and Apple's head appeared. "Have you finished decorating that hat, Holly? The carriage is waiting."

The daydream dissolved. "Sorry, mum, I'll be right there."

Holly's sister Willow waited in the carriage with Apple, Tozer, Cedar and Hazel. The creation of Willow's wedding clothes had been a joint effort over several months, with Apple, Hazel, Holly and Nara Swithenbank all taking part, while little Kate ran around making them all laugh. The dress was made of a rich, cream silk brocade with a décolletage that would emphasise Willow's fine figure. She wore a bonnet of the same colour and design, and matching shoes with high heels. Apple had wanted to add a veil, but the idea had been voted down as being out of fashion.

James Kirby nervously waited in his church at Roxby, the nave already half full with his parishioners. The building had been beautifully decorated by members of his flock, who were thrilled to see their own parson wedded in the church during his tenure in the parish. James's father, mother and brother had travelled from Harrogate to be at the wedding and were sitting patiently in the front row.

He'd arranged for his harpsichord to be moved from the parsonage to the church, and his friend James Nares, organist of York Minster, agreed to entertain the congregation as it assembled. Nares's wife, Jane, sat next to him to turn pages.

The reception was to take place at nearby Borrowby Farm, in the barn (which had been converted to accommodate such events, and was often used for the purpose) and adjoining field. Peter Dore, the farm manager and one of James's parishioners, had agreed a special price for the use of his facilities. The venue was almost a mile's walk through the field behind the church, taking the track by the hedge, so Mr Dore had arranged the hire of a few carriages to convey by road those who were less able to make the short journey on foot.

James greeted the guests from Cappleman Farm as they arrived: The Fleshers – Emmeline, Hugh, Amelia, Louise and Henry; the Swifts – Bernard, Florence, Richard, Emma, little Amy and Beatrice; the Buckleys – Maria, Sally, Elys, Alicia, young Walter and Grace. And here was Hazel Priestly and her sons Adam and William; Alder and Nara Swithenbank and little Kate, all smiles and curls of red hair. Doctor Levinson from the neighbouring village of Easington.

Hubert Cromwell had again sent his apologies. Egbert, now aged ninety-three, was said to be on the point of death.

Cornelius East stood ready to conduct the ceremony. The church musicians waited at the rear to herald the bride and accompany the singing.

It seemed that Willow and her family were a little late. James stood at the church door with Cornelius and looked south in the direction of Cappleman Farm. It was a sunny August Saturday afternoon with a refreshing light breeze. An ideal day for a wedding.

Inside the church, the children were becoming impatient, and there was a low hum of chatter. James Nares shot a disapproving glance at the congregation from his position at the harpsichord, set just outside the sanctuary area. His wife sensed his irritation. "Don't fret, my dear; they'll be here shortly. I'm sure the wine will be worth waiting for."

James momentarily lost his way in the gigue he was playing but managed to cover the fault convincingly. "Wine?" he muttered, "It's something stronger I'll be wanting. Let me at the mead and you may see me smile again."

James Kirby waved a signal from the church door. The carriage was arriving. James Nares continued on to the end of the piece he was playing while Willow and her family prepared themselves outside. A moment later, Apple, Cedar, Hazel and Holly seated themselves in the left pew at the front of the church; James Nares and Jane withdrew to their allotted seats; Cornelius East took up position before the altar, and James Kirby stood proudly in front of him, waiting for his bride.

The church band struck up a march, and Tozer escorted his beautiful daughter along the aisle for her wedding. Apple dabbed her eyes but managed to keep her emotions mostly under control. Tozer, never able to hide his feelings, was more weepy, his handkerchief continually busy.

Willow arrived at the altar and smiled at the man who was to be her husband in a few moments. James looked at her, his heart filled with love – then glanced down at her breast and sighed.

My God, he thought. *How did I ever get so lucky?*

At that very moment, a little less than four miles away in the parsonage at Easington, Egbert Trommel lay dying in his bed. Hubert sat quietly with him, cradling his hand. Warm afternoon sunlight bathed the room, dust motes drifting in the rays.

Hubert had grown up in Exeter. His father, Samuel, long deceased, was a gentleman of independent means, and the family lived in a substantial house overlooking the cathedral. Sam Cromwell was known to be fond of women; and his wife, Faith, often had to steer him away from the housemaids. There were a few conquests, which she tolerated.

One of the most frequent visitors to the house was Lancelot Blackburne, who generally appeared with his wife, Catherine. Lancelot had a long association with the cathedral, appointed Dean in 1705 and Bishop twelve years later. At Sam's request, Lancelot became Hubert's godfather.

Lancelot was a fine storyteller and would regale young Hubert with unlikely tales of piracy, always with himself as the hero. He possessed an encyclopaedic knowledge of geography, particularly of the islands in the Caribbean Sea, and joked that he'd once kept a harem of many wives, winking at his own wife as he did so. *"One wife is not enough for a pirate..."*

Hubert's closest childhood friend was the son of his father's coachman. Clemmo was the same age as Hubert, and the two were often left alone to play together. As they grew towards their teenage years, they became fond of fishing and liked to walk out of town to their favourite streams and rivers. The days seemed to pass very quickly when they were together, and Hubert would sometimes tell Clemmo that he loved him.

One day, when both the boys were thirteen years old, Hubert asked his mother if it were possible for a man to marry another man. Faith looked at him in a curious way and asked him if he was thinking about anyone in particular. He told her about his fondness for Clemmo, and she replied that, no, it wasn't possible for such a thing to occur. Hubert thought nothing more about it that day, but he never saw Clemmo again – or Clemmo's father. They both disappeared from the house without explanation.

Sam Cromwell was determined that his son should receive a good education, so he advertised for a governess. The successful applicant, Miss Eliza Melbury, was young and pretty, although her charms had no particular attraction for Hubert. Sam seemed to enjoy her company, though. Whatever her association with Hubert's father may have been, Eliza was a fine teacher. In the fulness of time, Sam suggested that Hubert should be sent to Cambridge to study Theology. Lancelot Blackburne agreed, and the boy had no objection.

Hubert spent four years at Cambridge and made many friends, including several girls. The more perceptive ones understood why he wasn't physically interested in them. There were a few young men to whom he felt very close, but remembering Clemmo, he never allowed his casual friendships to become more than that. Consequently, he'd always felt a little isolated and beyond reach of companionship. He decided he needed to spend his life alone, so began to think of a clerical posting to a remote location.

In 1724 Lancelot Blackburne became Archbishop of York. The two had kept in touch, and Hubert wrote to him asking about possible jobs in Yorkshire. Lancelot replied by inviting him to work as his own secretary. Hubert was delighted. Two years later the parson of St Nicholas, Roxby died unexpectedly, and Lancelot suggested that Hubert might find his ideal spot there.

He arrived in the little township in September 1726 and instantly knew he was going to fit in. Cornelius East had been parson of Glaisdale for just two years. He'd shown Hubert round several of the local parishes and made him feel welcome and valued. The other parson, Egbert Trommel, had been in post for four years. Egbert was sixty-four at that time and considered his position as parson in the village of Easington to be his retirement. He thought himself overworked and taken for granted, and was dismissive of the ancient traditions, particularly the people's reverence and respect for a "witch". Egbert lived alone, and Hubert suspected that his irascibility was probably no more than a mechanism for keeping people at bay. Despite the considerable difference in age between them, Hubert began to believe they may have something in common.

It had taken Hubert a very long time to win Egbert's confidence, but despite all the obstacles they'd been close companions for the last sixteen years. And now his life's most precious friend had reached the end of his journey.

Egbert's hands had become shrivelled over the years, frail and twisted with arthritis. Hubert sat next to Egbert's bed, their right hands clasped. Egbert opened his eyes, clouded with cataracts, and tried to speak.

"I..."

Hubert leaned closer, trying to catch the words.

"Hubert...I..." Egbert's face was moist. Perhaps the tears were a sign of extreme old age.

"You don't have to say anything, Egbert."

"I want to tell you…"

Hubert began to tremble with emotion. He tried to hide it, determined to remain calm.

"You…" Egbert's hand tightened.

"Egbert, I know. You don't have to tell me. I feel the same for you." With his other hand, Hubert reached out and touched Egbert's cheek.

There was silence for a while. The older man did not release the younger from his gaze. Then Egbert sighed and said, "My friend."

They were his last words. A few minutes later, he closed his eyes, and his breathing ceased.

The celebrations were in full swing at Borrowby Farm. The band had worked hard to prepare music for the dancing; they didn't want to embarrass themselves in front of the two Jameses – Kirby and Nares. It was probably the best performance they'd ever given – many people commented on how good it was, and Parson Kirby himself congratulated them.

James Nares asked Hazel Priestly to dance with him.

"So, Mr Nares. I understand you're visiting us from York," said Hazel.

"Indeed so, madam."

"An organist."

"Again, the truth. You're well informed."

"I have never danced with an organist before," said Hazel.

"And, if I may be so bold, Mrs Priestly," replied James, "I have never danced with a witch before."

Hazel broke away from him, bent forward, hands on knees, and burst into laughter. James couldn't hold back a smile and allowed himself to join in her mirth. The other dancers watched in amusement while the two recovered themselves, found their place in the formation and continued.

Between bouts of suppressed guffaws, Hazel said, "You're a

bold one, sir. Are all organists as entertaining as you?"

"Alas, Mrs Priestly, I fear we're a dry bunch for the most part. I take my hilarity where I can find it." He was quiet for a moment. "You are a delight, madam. You have a happy wit, and you dance like an angel."

"Flatterer," she said.

They found themselves standing next to James's wife, Jane. Jane was partnered with Hugh Flesher, who asked, "Is she bewitching you, Mr Nares? She bewitches everyone."

Jane shook her head. "James! Always the flirt."

Not far away, Holly Robinson danced with James Kirby's brother, Andrew. At twenty-two, he was Holly's senior by seven years and was clearly entranced by her, gazing into her eyes or at her figure the whole time they were engaged. Holly smiled, encouraged him, but thought, *He's very handsome – and he worships me, but – he's not a prince...*

The number of invitations issued for the wedding had been limited by the church's small size, but the reception was open to all. Meadow Reid was one of many who appeared only for the post-ceremony celebrations. As always, she'd come alone. Her parents, Sigbert and Persephone, never attended local events, reserving their social contact only to like-minded libertines, although they allowed Meadow to come and go as she pleased. Young Henry Flesher, sitting with James Kirby's parents Philip and Margery, watched her, his idol, as she danced with his sister Louise.

"You watch that girl with rapt attention, Henry," said Philip.

"She's going to be my wife," Henry replied.

"Your wife! But isn't she older than you?"

"She's fourteen, like my sister."

"And you're..."

"Twelve, sir."

"She is a pretty girl – Louise too. They make an attractive

pair, dancing together."

Henry didn't reply straight away. Then he said, "She mocks me now, but one day she'll do as I tell her."

Philip and Margery looked at him, eyebrows raised. Margery thought, *What an extraordinary thing to say!*

Nine-year-old Buffy Miller looked around her in panic. She'd been given charge of little Kate Swithenbank for the duration of this dance and had lost sight of the child. She began to run from place to place, a cold sweat gathering, panic rising.

Kate was squatting down in the field margin by the hedge. She'd found a tiny mouse, dry and long dead, and was cradling it lovingly in her hands, singing to it, picturing it in her mind alive and happy. *Little mouse, little mouse, wake up, go home to your ma...*

"There you are!" said Buffy with relief, seeing the little girl crouched down before the hedge. "You gave me a fright." Her heart began to calm.

Kate stood, held out her arms and ran happily towards her. "Pond Girl!"

Beneath the hedge, a small mouse scurried away; energetic, inquisitive, alive.

The weather was miserable on the day of Egbert's funeral, with curtains of drizzle creeping off the moor in a listless breeze. The service was conducted by Cornelius East, although Hubert gave the eulogy – a lengthy speech telling Egbert's life story. Parson Trommel had served the parish of Easington for nearly thirty years, and the church was packed.

The people dispersed after the burial, huddled in their coats. Several of them disappeared into the Tiger Inn to warm themselves and down a few drinks in Egbert's honour. Cornelius and Hubert sheltered in the church porch, waiting for the former's carriage to Glaisdale.

"So," said Cornelius, "you're leaving us."

"Yes," replied Hubert. "The house will be cleared of our things by this time tomorrow. I'll sleep in Whitby tomorrow night and begin the coach journey from there on Thursday morning."

"We'll miss you; I'll miss you."

The carriage pulled into view. Hubert took hold of Cornelius's arm. "I've been lucky. Many people go through this life and never find themselves, never really wake up."

Cornelius waited, half expecting him to say more. "You're going home?"

"I'm going back to my mother in Exeter. She still gets about, but she's in her eighties now. Perhaps she'll need me one day soon. Anyway, it'll be nice to see the old place again."

The carriage arrived and drew to a halt by the porch.

Cornelius held out his hand, and Hubert took it. "Well, goodbye then." He cupped Hubert's hand in both of his. "And good luck to you, friend."

"God bless you, Cornelius."

The carriage was dripping with water; the rain had become more insistent. Cornelius climbed into the coach and sat down by the window, facing away from the direction of travel. Hubert closed the door, smiled one last time at the occupant, and raised his hand goodbye. Cornelius smiled in response, his eyes moistening. He'd never been good at farewells.

Hubert stood in the rain and watched the coach as it pulled away from the church and along the road, the wheels splashing brown water from the ruts and puddles. They never saw each other again.

7. IRELAND
1751-54

Alexander was in no hurry. He was walking to find a new life, wherever it might present itself. He had an idea that he might find it in Dublin, without any real reason for believing so other than the vague notion that anything and everything might be possible in such a great city.

That first day in early December was cold but bright. He easily managed the seventeen miles to Cork, arriving in the city at about six in the evening. He felt tired after his journey, although the walk had buoyed up his sense of purpose. He'd enjoyed the fields, the open sky. He chose an inn, ate a hearty meal and settled down for the night.

In the morning, he bought himself some food for lunch and set out again. In just over half an hour the city was behind him, and he was once more under the open sky. Towards evening it started to rain, and Xander began to look for somewhere to stay, soon arriving cold and wet at the little hamlet of Fermoy. It was a tiny place on the River Blackwater – just a few small cottages and a modest inn. He thought his luck was out. Why would anyone stop here at this time of year? The inn was probably closed.

But he was lucky. The door was open, and there was a room for him. The three other customers in the bar, all elderly men with facial hair it must have taken decades to grow, watched him with curiosity, although were reluctant to talk. The landlord described them as *fixtures*, a term that Xander took to denote permanent residents. The food was good, and the bed was comfortable.

The rain continued through the night and well into the next morning. It was almost noon before he was able to take up his journey again.

The ground was sodden, and the sky remained dark all afternoon. It was cold despite his vigorous walking, and by five o'clock it was raining hard. Minutes later the downpour became torrential and he was soon soaked to the skin.

It was grim, lonely, the fields empty of animals, not a soul in sight. He began to think fondly of his warm room in Francis's house, even of the barn he'd left behind in Ballinadee, but he splashed on, determined. In a while he came across a milestone telling him that Kilbehenny was three miles ahead.

The village inn was dark and appeared to be closed up. Xander knocked hard. No answer. This time, he thought, his luck really had run out. He tried again, and a moment later the door was opened by a dark-haired girl, probably in her late teens. She looked him up and down; his sodden clothes, waterlogged hat, the raging deluge behind him.

"You're wet," she said.

Alexander didn't think it warranted an answer.

The girl said, "Are you wanting a room? Here? In December?" She seemed incredulous.

Someone approached from behind her, a man in his forties. "Don't stand there with the sky pissing in. Who's that?"

The girl opened the door wider and motioned to Xander. "You better come in." He walked inside and muttered his thanks. "Sit yourself down," said the girl, indicating the blazing hearth. The warmth was a blessed relief, and he removed his soaked hat and coat. His shirt, waistcoat and breeches stuck to him, and water drained in runnels from his boots.

"Is it a room you're looking for?" asked the man.

"It is," Xander replied. "Are you closed? I'll wait a while and move on if you like. I don't want you to go to any trouble on my account."

"You will not," said the man. "You can't go anywhere in

this anyway. No, we'll put you up. Are you hungry?" Xander looked at him, but the man went on before he could answer. "Ach, of course you are. Let's get you something. Will you take a drink? I'll get you some ale."

"No ale," said Xander. "Thank you. I don't drink it. Water will be fine."

"You need something to warm you," said the man. "Do you drink tea?"

"Tea?" said Xander, eyebrows raised. "I do. I'll be very grateful if you have some. Thank you."

"I'll get some on then," replied Xander's host. The girl came running, and the man named her. "Here's Ciara."

"I've got your room ready," she said. "I'll show you up. Let me take your wet things."

Ciara led him to a room on the upper floor. It was small but welcoming, and she'd lit a fire for him. You'll be needin' a wash," she said. "Settle in. I'll get you some water." She was gone, and Alexander was alone in the room. He undid his sack and took out a change of clothes. Then he removed his wet things.

The door opened, and Ciara came in carrying a jug of warm water. Alexander had nothing on. She swept a glance at him and looked quickly away while he covered himself with his wet shirt. "Sorry," she said. "I should have knocked." She opened a cupboard and took out a basin. "There you go," she said. "Take your time."

"Thank you," he said as Ciara left, closing the door. He arranged his change of clothes on the back of a wooden chair and stood it before the fire.

The warm water felt good, and Alexander splashed it through his hair. Ciara had brought soap, a sponge and a towel. He gratefully washed himself all over and put on his almost dry clothes.

His meal of mutton stew was waiting for him before the fire in the bar, and there was a pot of tea as well. Alexander had developed a real liking for tea during his sojourn with

Francis Byrne and relished the fresh bitterness of it now. It had an invigorating effect against the damp. The food was wholesome, warmed him.

"That was wonderful," he said. "Thank you so much."

"You're very welcome, so you are," said the landlord. He held out his hand. Xander rose and shook it. "John Walsh. Pleased to make your acquaintance. I won't ask your business. Just make yourself at home."

"There's no secret," said Xander. "I'm on my way to Dublin."

"Dublin's a long way. Why aren't you in the coach?"

"I'm in no hurry," Alexander replied. "I like to walk. I can think clearly when I'm plodding on my own two feet."

"Good on you then," said John. "Will you be leaving tomorrow?"

"If the weather's good I'll move on. If it's still raining, and it's no inconvenience to you, maybe I'll stay."

"As you wish," said John. "Is the food alright?"

"It's very good. Thank you. I'm grateful for your kindness."

As John moved away, Alexander caught sight of Ciara standing at the bar, watching him. She was gone through the kitchen door as soon as he caught her eye.

His bedroom was warm. Xander laid a damp turve of peat on the fire to keep it in till morning, removed all his clothes and got into bed, relishing the softness of the clean sheets on his skin. He lay still, listened to the endless torrent of water, and was soon asleep.

The soft creak of the floorboards in the passage outside his room drew him to semi-consciousness a couple of hours later. There was a scratching at his door; quiet at first, then more insistent, clearly audible above the sound of the rain. Alexander sat up and listened hard. The room was cosy, dark, rich with the smell of peat. He climbed out of bed, quietly lifted the latch and opened the door an inch. Ciara was outside. He could just see her in the light of a dim oil lamp set on a table just along the passage. She was looking at him with eyes open wide. He looked back, unsure what she expected. Then she tipped her head slightly to the right and gave it a little shake. The gesture said, *Well? Are you going to let me in or not?*

He opened the door fully, and she quickly stepped into his room and stood in front of him in her nightgown, motionless, expectant. She watched him for a second or two, then lifted the gown over her head and threw it away. Her body glowed faintly, like ivory, in the near dark. Xander had never been so close to a naked girl before. She sounded a little irritated. "You're not going to say no to me," she hissed. Ciara pushed him to the bed and a second later was on him. She was his first.

He woke alone. It was still pouring with rain. The room was lit in dull daylight. He lay still, thinking of her, touching his own body, remembering what it had done.

Her energy, her insistence, had overwhelmed him at first, but the second time she'd been beneath him, and he found more confidence. When it was over, Ciara moved away in the bed, turned her back to him and went to sleep. Alexander lay awake. He touched her, ran his hand along the slumbering curve of her body, but she didn't respond. He lay on his front, hugged his pillow and let sleep take him. She'd left quietly sometime in the night.

Later he rose, washed, dressed, went downstairs and outside to the privy. The rain was coming down with unabated force, the clouds black with water. He sat on the wooden seat and listened to the relentless noise on the roof. As he opened the back door of the inn and went inside, he heard long, booming reverberations of thunder, miles away.

John was cleaning tankards behind the bar. "Did you sleep well?"

"I did," Xander replied. "Thank you."

"You'll not be going anywhere this morning, I think."

Ciara came through from the kitchen, carrying clean bowls and cutlery. She glanced at him as she swept past, and their eyes met. There was no smile or greeting. She began to put the things away in the dresser where they belonged.

"I'll get you some breakfast," said John, "something warming to set you up for the day."

Xander nodded his thanks, and John disappeared through the kitchen door.

Ciara had almost finished tidying the dishes. "What are your plans today?" she asked.

"I'll watch the sky," he said. "Maybe move on this afternoon." He wanted to say something about the previous night but didn't know how to start – and her manner suggested that she'd forgotten it.

Ciara said nothing more. She disappeared upstairs, and Alexander was left alone in the bar, looking out at the empty road and the thrashing rain.

His breakfast was almost more than he could eat: porridge, milk, bacon, sausages, eggs, potatoes, bread, tea. It was delicious and very hearty. He wiped his lips and thanked John.

"Oh, it was nothin' at all. Make yourself at home." John removed the breakfast things.

Xander sat by the window. It dawned on him that for the first time in his life he had no task to perform. There were no pigs, there was no cleaning to be done, nothing to be repaired, he wasn't going to set out walking. There was nothing for him to do but sit and wait. He went behind the bar and tapped on the kitchen door. John pushed it open.

"Can I do anything to help?" Alexander asked.

"Help? No. No, I don't think so. Thanks for asking." He smiled and was gone, the door swinging shut behind him.

Xander sat down again by the window.

Twenty minutes later he was still there, watching the

weather emptily.

Ciara said, "Shall I get you a pack of cards?" He'd been deep in thought, and her voice made him start. He looked around in the gloom. She was at the bar, smiling at him. He thought she looked nice.

"Yes. Thank you."

A moment later she dropped a deck before him. "There you go. You can play Patience."

"Patience?"

"Patience. You play it by yourself."

He looked vacantly at her.

"You don't know it, do you?"

"No," he said.

She sat down opposite him. "I'll show you."

It was simple enough, and he learned it in a few minutes. John, moving between the kitchen and the bar, glanced at them now and then. Xander cast his eyes up at her once or twice and wondered if there might be a subtle kind of smile hiding in Ciara's expression.

He began to play the game without her guidance, and she sat there, elbows on the table, chin supported on her fists. He looked up again. She fixed him with her stare, lips creased in amusement, and said, "What do you want to say to me?"

What to reply? He had no idea what he wanted to say, if anything. His confusion showed in his face.

"How old are you?" she asked.

"Sixteen," Xander replied but immediately felt the need to be older. "Seventeen in January."

She clasped her hands and looked away. "Fuckin' hell," she said. His heart dropped. He'd disappointed her and suddenly felt wholly inadequate.

"How old are *you*?" he asked.

"Twenty-one," she replied. She got up, walked through the back door and out into the rain.

Xander sat in the alcove of the window, feeling deeply unhappy and alone. He scanned the cards on the table and felt no interest in them, no desire to play. He'd leave. He went up to his room and gathered his things together. Then he came downstairs, intending to pay and be off, but she was at the bottom of the staircase and caught him on his way down.

"What are you doing?" she asked, surprised, almost swallowing the words.

"Leaving. Going on my way."

"In this weather? You are not!"

Xander was surprised to find that he was a little angry. He wondered if it showed in his face.

"I'm sorry," she said. "I was short with you at the table. I shouldn't have behaved like that. Please stay. Wait till the rain stops." His anger was suddenly gone. "I want you to stay," she said.

"Alright," Xander replied. He turned and made his way upstairs. A few minutes later he went down to the taproom, collected the deck of cards, took it back to his room and played Patience on his bed all morning.

Lunchtime found him in the bar again. A few other people had braved the rain and sat drinking near the fire. Ciara brought him bread and soup. She gave him a warm smile and said, "There you go. My man." It made him feel good.

The bar filled a little more. John and Ciara were kept busy serving the visitors while Xander continued to watch the downpour through the window. The sky had lightened a little.

"Are you sure you'll take no ale?" asked John. Xander turned and found him standing close by.

"Thanks, but no. I never touch it."

"Wine then? Whiskey? The potcheen is good."

"No. I never touch strong drink of any kind. If you've more tea, I won't say no to that."

"Right enough," said John. "I'll get you some tea."

The bar emptied as time went on, and by three o'clock Xander was again the only customer. He fetched the cards and played at the table.

By six o'clock the rain had stopped, and the bar began to fill again. John came and asked if he'd like supper.

"That'd be grand," Xander replied.

"You'll stay with us tonight?"

"I will, if I may. If it's still dry in the morning I'll be on my way."

He made himself comfortable in the window seat and idly played his card game. Ciara brought a tray of drinks to a party of people nearby, then sat down opposite him.

"So you're away in the morning."

"I am," he replied.

She nodded. "Can I see y'again tonight?"

He looked at her. "That'd be nice," he said. "I'd like that."

They lay together side by side in the silent darkness. The rain had stopped. It was a little after two.

"You're off to find your fortune then," she said.

"I'm off to find a life – I hope. I'm not expecting a fortune."

"Where's your ma and da?"

"My da ran away years ago. Ma – she's dead and gone."

"I'm sorry to hear that."

"What happened to *your* mother?" he asked.

"My parents? They're both dead, so they are. Dead of the pox long ago."

He leaned up on one elbow, surprised. "John's not your da then?"

"No, course not."

"He's not your husband?" The possibility shocked him.

She was incredulous. "No!" She was quiet for a moment. "He's an old friend of my mother's. He promised to look after me." Quiet again. "John's a good man, so he is."

Xander lay down again. "So, what will you do with your life?" he asked.

"I don't know."

"You could come to Dublin with me."

"And do what?"

He was quiet for a moment. "I'd marry you."

She gave a little laugh. "Would you now?"

He searched inside himself and found that he meant it. "Aye, I would."

She was smiling – he heard it in her voice. "You would... And do you love me, Xander?"

He was briefly speechless but would have answered boldly, *yes*. She stopped him before he could do so.

"Shut the fuck up! Don't you dare answer that question, yer eejit!"

They both lay in silence for a while. He stroked her skin; smooth, warm. Then she said, "Anyway, I'm not leavin' John on his own here."

He leaned up again on his elbow, reached over in the darkness and ran his hand through her hair. "I'm glad I stopped here. I might never have met you."

She reached up and took his hand in hers. "You're a nice boy – you are too." He thought she might be crying a little. "I wish you all the best on your journey."

In the morning he gathered his few things, ate his breakfast and paid his bill. It was a sunny day, though cold. They said their farewells at the door.

"Godspeed then, Xander," said John, shaking his hand. "I hope you find what you're looking for in Dublin."

Alexander took Ciara's hand and found he didn't know what to say. He opened his mouth impotently and closed it again. *Goodbye* didn't seem enough. John looked at the two of them.

"Ach, away with you!" she said, pulling her hand free, dismissing him with it. "When you make your thousands, you come and find me again."

He turned and walked away. It felt as if he were leaving a

safe haven. Perhaps he should have stayed. Could he have lived his life with her? It was possible. Maybe he was actually walking away from his destiny rather than towards it, having not even recognised that it was so. When he'd gone about two hundred yards he paused and looked back. John was no longer visible, but Ciara remained standing at the porch, watching him. He waved goodbye to her, and she returned the gesture, but the distance that separated them was too great for him to see the expression on her face. He paused, profoundly aware of the attraction that wanted him to stay. Then he turned once more and went on his way.

The road was filthy, but at least the day had brightened, and there was no sign of rain. Xander set aside his doubts and decided to press forward, arriving at Cahir in time for a late lunch. He bought some food and ate it while sitting on a rock on the bank of the Suir. The sky was blue, cloudless, and the castle, sitting on its island in the river, shone in the winter sunlight.

By dusk he'd arrived at the town of Cashel, where he got a room for the night at the Hurley Inn. He'd heard of the famous Fairy Hill, the *Carraig Phádraig*, St Patrick's Rock, or Rock of Cashel, and was impressed by its majesty as he approached the town. He stayed an extra day to explore the ruins and the old graveyard. The Rock was a strange place, the ruins open, silent; tall walls mutely pleading with the sky. He tried to imagine what it must have been like when it was alive, full of people. The weight of the past was heavy there; so many had come and gone. Xander felt very small.

The day after that was bleak and drizzly, but he left Cashel early and managed to get as far as Urlingford, taking a room at the Tobin Arms.
The weather remained poor the next day, and he stayed

at the inn playing cards by himself, wishing he could read. Sadly there was no pretty girl to keep him company on this occasion. He sat alone and thought about Ciara, recalling her in the secrecy of his bed, remembering the warmth of her body, his lips on hers.

From Cashel, his journey north took him to Portlaoise, where he again spent an extra day, this time exploring the market and sitting in the coffee house watching the people come and go. Then, next day early, on to Kildare. There were few travellers on the road, it being so late in the year. Now and then he'd stop to let flocks of sheep pass by, exchanging greetings with the shepherds.

The town of Kildare was busy, and he was surprised to see so many men in brown and white religious garb. He was told they were Carmelite Friars and had a long association with the place. They seemed friendly folk, confident, caring. Xander liked them. *Could I be one of them? Maybe...*

His next stop was at Naas, another market town. There was a troupe of girls dancing in the street, but he wasn't sure why, or what the celebration may have been. They looked nice and danced with their skirts held in their hands. People clapped for them. Xander smiled and caught the eye of one of the dancers. She smiled back at him but disappeared in the crowd, and he couldn't find her again. Rooms were scarce, but he eventually found one at the White Horse. The bustle of people had noticeably increased during the last few days, the towns busier as he neared Dublin, and he felt energised by the prospect of arriving at his goal.

The next day's journey took him to The Ploughboy Inn at Rockbrook on the outskirts of Dublin. It was busy, and Alexander only got a room because its original occupant was called away unexpectedly. There were books in the bar. He took one down and opened it, tried to pick out the words. It was frustrating. How much better his prospects would be if only he could read. The pages stared at him, mocking. He knew the individual letters and numbers, but words eluded him. It was like standing in a forest and being able to see only a single tree.

Next morning he ate a good breakfast and set out at half past nine, passing through Sandyford before lunch.
Just after two in the afternoon he arrived at the little village of Dunlary and made his way down to the cove. Dublin itself lay only a few miles to the north. He found the coffee shop and sat quietly, watching a few ships pass by on their way to Dublin harbour. Later he took lodgings at the Mariners Inn, left his things in his room and set out to explore the area. He walked a mile or so along the coast in the direction of the city, watching the sea off to his right. By half past four it was already quite dark, so he retraced his steps, spent his evening over a leisurely supper and went to bed.

The following morning he breakfasted early, paid his bill, gathered up his things and walked into Dublin. It was Sunday, December 19th, and his arrival was accompanied by the sound of church bells. By noon he was established in The Elephant on Essex Street. He sat on his bed and began to ponder. His money was almost exhausted, and he would need to find work soon, just another uneducated boy in a big city. He'd look to the inns and the markets. Later that afternoon he enquired about a job at the Elephant itself but was turned down – the innkeeper was not looking for new staff. He was similarly unsuccessful in all the nearby establishments.
Xander went to bed disheartened, pitiful, no use to anyone.

The next morning at breakfast he was approached by one of the kitchen staff, a boy little more than his own age.
"You looking for a job?"
"Yes. Do you know of any?"
"You might try the Anchor Brewery on Usher Street. I

heard a couple of days ago they were looking for strong boys. Are you strong?"

"I don't know. I think so."

"Give it a go then. It's less than a mile away, just down from the Liffey."

"I will. Thanks for that."

"Good luck to you."

It was easy. Later that morning Alexander had a job as a lifter in the Anchor Brewery. He was put to work on the drays, delivering barrels to some of Dublin's two thousand alehouses. By December 23rd he'd moved out of the Elephant and into a room in a boarding house on the south side of the river, close to his place of work. He had a job and a place to live. He was independent.

Alexander woke on Christmas Day, feeling blessed and grateful. Most of his life had been a dull round of ceaseless toil without joy or hope, but this last year had been transformative for him, and he felt that he was on his way at last. He wanted to give thanks. He put on his best clothes and made his way to Holy Trinity for the Christmas Morning service.

The building was packed with people, but he found a seat and took part in the worship. The music was inspiring, uplifting, and he was filled with awe at the old building. As the service went on, he felt ever more intensely the need to renew himself. His spirit seemed aglow, and he was almost overcome with gladness, with thankfulness.

At the end of the service he sat for a while and listened to the organ. His experience of music was limited to a few fiddle tunes and songs. He'd never heard an organ before and found the sound of it strange, like music from another world. As he sat there intently listening, he became aware that someone was standing close by. Alexander looked up and met the eyes of a tall man in a black gown and white collar. He offered Xander his hand and said, "A very happy

Christmas to you, sir." Alexander stood and returned the good wishes.

"I don't think I've seen you before," said the man.

"I only arrived in town a few days ago," Xander replied.

"Are you visiting for the season then?"

"No... No, I live here." It was true. Dublin was now his home. He felt another surge of happiness in his breast, a sense of belonging. He clasped the man's right hand in both of his and said, "I'm so glad to be here."

The man looked a little puzzled but replied, "Well, you're very welcome, to be sure. What did you say your name was?"

"Alex," replied Alexander. It was the first time that particular short form had passed his lips. Xander belonged to the old days. "Alex Regan."

"Well, I'm very pleased to meet you, Mr Regan."

A few minutes after leaving the cathedral, Alex stood on the south bank of the Liffey and watched the river as it flowed past. He felt cleansed, reborn. Anything was possible. He made his way home, joyful.

The next day he was back on the drays. Alex had never worked with a horse before but said he'd be happy to learn. To this end, he was given a few lessons in the cask yard and the brewery courtyard. It wasn't so difficult, he thought. The dray waggons were often drawn by a single horse, but the bigger loads were pulled by a pair. With a little effort, he gained some skill in managing both kinds.

Alex usually went out on the rounds with Liam Doyle, his senior by six years. Liam was lean, strong, dark-haired and very popular (judging by the smiles and greetings he received from young women they passed when out on the dray). Once in a while, on the quieter streets, Liam handed the reins to Alex to give him some experience of driving in the real world. They got along well.

Liam was on first name terms with all the innkeepers and

landlords the brewery supplied. In the first few months of 1752, Alex gradually gathered all the names into his own memory. He noticed that the girls employed in the various alehouses always seemed particularly chirpy around Liam, clearly having looked forward to his visit. One day as they were driving together, Alex commented on this.

"Me?" said Liam. "Well, maybe. But they like you too, you know."

"Do you think so?"

"Sure, they do." Liam looked across at Alex. "You know what? Open up another button on your shirt there. They like a bit o' skin." He leaned over and loosened one of Alex's buttons. "That's better. It's a bit o' rough. It's all a bit of a game. You watch now."

Alex smiled and fingered his chest for a moment. It felt a bit odd, but he'd play along.

The girls seemed to like Alex well enough, although he didn't detect any significant increase in the attention they paid him just because of his newly opened shirt button. But as the weeks went by, he did begin to feel more confident in himself. He drove the dray unaided while Liam sat next to him and saluted women in the street. His comments made Alex laugh, sometimes with uncontrolled hilarity.

"Ah," said Liam. "That's Mary Dooley. Fine pair o' tits on that one." A moment later, "Jaisus! Would you look at that? There are three arses in that dress!"

In addition to his expert assessment of women, Liam had a fine singing voice and would often run through complete songs as they drove along. Alex picked up a lot of these and remembered them for the rest of his life. *Alasdair MacColla, The Sash, On the green grassy slopes of the Boyne, The shady woods of Truagh,* and *The Love Token* were just a few of them.

"You have a lovely voice, Liam; you really do."

"I know, I do. I have my mother to thank for that. She sang

like an angel."

There was a girl who became Alex's favourite. She worked in the little Unicorn alehouse on Stable Lane close to the river on the north bank. She was pretty, auburn-haired, about his own age, and reminded him of Bridget Kelly. Her name was Colleen O'Farrell. One Friday in late September, as they were crossing Barrack Bridge in the dray, Alex confessed to Liam his fondness for her.

"Are we visiting the Unicorn today, Liam?"

"We are. I wonder why you're asking that specifically."

Alex felt a surge of embarrassment.

"Ach, it's Colleen, isn't it? You're soft on her, so you are."

"I do like her. She's nice."

Liam thought for a moment. "You're right. She's a pretty one."

"Do you think she likes me?"

"Why don't you ask her?"

"How would I do that?"

"Shall I ask her for you?"

"No! Don't you dare do that!"

Liam laughed, then said, "You know – if you don't ask... If you don't say something... she'll be someone else's. Take the chance, boy. What can she say? Piss off? Then you'll know at least."

They'd crossed the bridge and were continuing straight ahead. Alex was thinking. "But I'm no good with girls," he muttered. "I wouldn't know what to say."

"You just need confidence and a bit o' practice, Alex." Liam paused, glancing sideways at his companion. "Be bold, or be polite – one of the two. Say, *I hope you don't mind me askin', but I'd very much like you to take a drink wi' me.* That's all you need to say. Then it's up to her."

"But you know I don't drink, Liam."

"Ach, I know that. Coffee then. Or just ask her to walk a little way with you. Somethin' like that."

Alex sat still and looked doubtful.

Liam said, "You've got about ten minutes to make your mind up. It's the next stop."

He'd expected that it would be, and already felt his heart beating a little faster.

But it didn't happen. Colleen was not at the Unicorn that day. Instead, they were met by Brian Murphy. Brian managed several alehouses in the vicinity, the Unicorn being the smallest of them. Alex was disappointed. They began to unload the barrels.

Liam, seeing that Alex wasn't going to ask, said to Brian, "Colleen not here today then?"

"Colleen?" replied Brian. "She's away looking after her mother. Aoife – d'you know Aoife?" Liam shook his head. "Aoife's standing in while Colleen's away."

"She'll be gone for a while then?"

"Her mother's dyin'. It'll be a wee while before we see Colleen again, I think."

Alex listened at a distance, downcast.

"You seem very interested in the girl, Liam," said Brian. "Are you sweet on her?"

"No," Liam replied. "But he is." Nodding his head in Alex's direction.

"Liam!" Alex exclaimed.

"G'warn, boy!" Brian said. "The poor girl. Her father dead all these years, mother sick and about to cross over. She's no brothers or sisters – at least, I don't think she has. It might do her some good to have a boy. There's no shame in askin' anyway."

"Thanks, Brian," said Liam. "That's just what I told the boy."

But the following week, and the next, brought no sign of Colleen. Alex didn't mention her again.

His evenings adopted a regular pattern. After work, he'd

go to one of the nearby alehouses for a drink with some of the brewery men. His abstinence was an inexhaustible butt for jokes, although they respected him for his staunchness. While they drank ale, Alex drank saloop. He'd stay with them awhile, often taking his supper in their company before retiring to his room to study. He'd bought a Bible and was teaching himself to read as best he could, laboriously picking out a few verses each evening. He went to Holy Trinity for the service every Sunday morning and occasionally came across passages in his studies that he remembered from church. Learning to read fluently was a slow process for him, but he had a determined character.

Alex wanted to be confirmed in the church, although he hadn't yet spoken about it to anyone.

Colleen returned to the Unicorn in mid-December. Her mother had died. Alex had not expected to see her again. He was thrilled when she appeared, and his heart raced. She looked right at him. Someone had told her... Liam gave him a sideways glance and opened his eyes wide. Colleen didn't break her gaze away; her smile was constant. Alex had to do something. He walked to within a few feet of her. "Would you...?"

She broke in, "Yes. Thank you." She was as nervous as he was.

"I'll come back tonight, after work. It's alright?"

"That'll be grand," she said.

So they began to see each other almost every day, and a romance quickly blossomed. They'd talk in the bar while she served, and would walk together when both were away from their jobs.

Neil Murphy, Brian's son, often worked in the alehouse, and there was another girl – Aoife Beckett – who also helped when the little bar was busy. Aoife and Colleen shared the bedroom on the upper floor, but Neil and Aoife were sweethearts, and Colleen often had to make a bed for herself in the bar when the other two wanted privacy upstairs. In February 1753, Neil announced that he was going to marry Aoife. It was just as well, said Neil's father, because Aoife was going to have a baby in June. Aoife moved out of the Unicorn and went to live with Neil and his parents in the south side of the city. That meant there was a job going in the Unicorn. Brian offered it to Alex. If he took the work, it would mean...

Colleen listened as Brian made his offer, her eyes wide.

"So..." said Alex, "I'd move in here?"

"If it suits you," said Brian.

Alex glanced at Colleen. "I'd sleep down here in the bar."

Brian nodded. "Of course you would...there being only one room upstairs. You could stay where you're living now, of course. But I'd prefer two people on the premises, for safety's sake."

So Alex handed in his notice at the brewery and bade farewell to all his friends there. They threw a party for him, peppered with suggestive comments and lewd gestures.

He moved into the Unicorn on the second Monday morning in March. Alex's first evening in his new job was dominated by an intense feeling of anticipation. They both knew what was coming, though neither spoke directly about it. He couldn't stop looking at her.

There were few customers that night, and the door was bolted by half past ten. Alex's heart was pounding. He felt that he was on the edge of a precipice. She stood at the foot of the stairs, waiting for him.

"I'll make my bed on the settle then," he said. It sounded lame.

"You will not," she said.

Neither moved.

Then Colleen said, "*You* have to say it."

He was unsure at first exactly what she meant. Then he found the words. "Let's go to bed then."

That unlocked it. She held out her hand.

In April, Alex and Colleen were guests at the marriage of Neil Murphy and Aoife Beckett. The invitation arrived on a single card addressed to the two of them.

At home, Colleen took charge of Alex's attempts at reading, and he made good progress because of her guidance. They went to Holy Trinity together every Sunday morning. He told her that he loved her, and he meant it.

Alex had never been so happy. In June, after consultation with one of the ministers at Holy Trinity, he was baptised. He and Colleen both began studies in confirmation in July. In August, he knelt before her and asked for her hand in marriage. She accepted, could hardly speak for tears. They received the sacrament of confirmation in April 1754 and were married in Christ Church the following month.

One hot August Sunday afternoon they sat together hand-in-hand on a wall overlooking the river, not far from the Unicorn. Colleen told him she was going to have a baby. That would mean juggling things around in the alehouse, possibly asking Brian Murphy to exchange them with other tenants so they'd have more room. Not for the first time, Alex reflected on his life.

"Less than four years ago I had nothing but a field of pigs. Every day was filled with blank nothing – drizzle, pig shit and despair. Now look at me. I'm a member of a community. I have friends, a beautiful wife, a child of my own on the way. God, it amazes me when I think about it. I couldn't be happier." He looked at Colleen. "You're the brightest star in my firmament. You're my love."

She smiled, brushed his cheek with the back of her fingers, and kissed him.

8. THE LOOKOUT, PEAK
1755

The house had been unoccupied for fifty years. Many of the windows had been smashed and part of the roof had fallen in, allowing the ingress of rain and hastening the decay of the woodwork and furnishings. It had become a haven for bats, rats, spiders, and the occasional tramp – although human visitors never stayed in its wreckage for very long.

The building sat in more than a thousand acres of land, much of it left untended. The grounds and fields to the rear of the house led to a rocky beach, with cliffs to the north and heathland to the south. To the west lay a walled park, long overgrown, the site of several structures in complete dilapidation. The grounds to the front of the building consisted of unmanaged trees and undergrowth through which ran a private drive of more than half a mile. The iron gates still carried the name of the house in ornate scroll-work: *The Lookout*.

The house took its name from a ruined stone tower high up on the cliff. Possibly it had been part of a guard post, perhaps a lighthouse; local tradition dated it to the twelfth century. William Wynter, who built the big house in 1643, took an immediate liking to the name and borrowed it for the new dwelling in which he and his young wife Agnes were to live.

At the time of his marriage, William Wynter was fifty-eight years old; his wife was eighteen. William was said to be a cruel, brutal man, but despite his abuse of Agnes, he had a genuine fondness for his son, Tobias, his only child.

Agnes died in the process of giving birth to a stillborn daughter five years after Tobias was born. William did not remarry but shared the Lookout with his son for twenty more years until his own death in 1668.

Tobias Wynter was a recluse. He never saw visitors and employed few servants. He talked to himself – rambling monologues about nothing – and could sometimes be heard screaming in the night. His butler was the closest thing he had to a friend, although there was little work for him to do. The maids were mostly frightened of their master, although one of them gradually eased her way into his confidence; Rosalind, thirty-two years his junior, became his companion, and the two were married in 1696. The wedding was held in the desolate church at Scrawby, a few miles from the Lookout, the windswept location chosen by Tobias because it emphasised his unhinged melancholy. The event – grey, and entirely lacking in celebration – was attended only by the couple themselves, the parson, the household servants, and Rosalind's parents.

In April 1697 Rosalind gave birth to twin boys, Lawrence and Robin. Rosalind was filled with joy as the midwife presented them to her, but Tobias looked at the babies with an expression of horror on his face, then wandered about the house, demented, screaming. The servants found him asleep in the cellar hours later, smeared with filth. He allowed them to bathe him, then shut himself in his room, where he remained for most of the next month, eating alone and avoiding his wife and new sons.

The next few years went by with little to mark them. Tobias's household was said to be grim and silent, devoid of joy, of laughter; empty even of the sound of voices, other than the whispering of the servants.

One bright summer day in 1704, without warning, Tobias generously paid off all the staff and gave them a day's notice to depart. Nothing more was said. Tobias locked the gates after them. The house remained closed to everyone; the merchants, farmers, grocers, and all who had previously had an agreement to provide supplies, found themselves locked out.

It was more than a year before anyone entered the Lookout. They had to break in through a window. Four mummified bodies were found. Rosalind was discovered in a first-floor corridor in the east wing. She'd been strangled, the cord still around her throat. Tobias was found in his study at the opposite end of the house, slumped in his leather armchair. He'd shot himself in the face.

It took some time to find the bodies of the little boys, aged seven at the time of their deaths. They'd been imprisoned in the northeast tower, the highest point of the house. The stone staircase behind the locked door spiralled upwards for sixty-four steps, ending in the tiny turret room where their dry remains were discovered.

Very few people visited the house while it lay derelict, but those few claimed to have heard the sound of pattering feet running up and down that staircase; and the voice of a woman crying, sobbing, in the night...

Now, fifty years later, Crowan stood there, in the little turret room where the boys had died. He breathed in slowly, trying to detect any remaining scent of their rotting bodies, but there was nothing. The tiny window through which he looked faced due east. It was the only place in the house that had any view of the sea. The blue could just be glimpsed, the better part of a mile away.

His years in the trade of women's flesh had sharpened his obsessive connection between sex and death. Jacob had not yet killed anyone, but he knew that he would, one day. He'd had opportunities to murder but had restrained himself so far; it was a kind of bliss, held exquisitely in check. But one day... It would feel natural; the snuffing out of life. The Lookout was ideal for his purpose; nine miles north of Scarborough, thirteen miles south of Whitby, with the tiny village of Peak less than two miles up along the coast. The house was secluded and very large. It had been held in trust all these decades and had been inexpensive to purchase, its forbidding reputation ensuring a low price. The restoration work had been completed the previous week, and the new furniture was mostly in place. The livestock, intended to supply food for the house, was due to arrive in the next few days: hens, geese, pigs, sheep and lambs, cattle. A few of the estate staff were already at work in the grounds – the gardeners, farmers and carpenters – and the others would begin to arrive soon: the domestics, the blacksmith, laundry workers, brewery men, the headmistress and her assistant, and finally the tutors. Then all would be ready for the girls. The girls...

On the face of it, the house was to become a charitable school for the education of poor young ladies. Crowan's minions were occupied with finding likely specimens from the streets and workhouses – girls aged between about ten and sixteen; orphans and outcasts. They would be brought to the house and given a long and elaborate education in elocution, reading and literature, deportment, dress, music, movement and dance, Latin, French and other subjects. In short, they would be turned into the most delightful specimens of desirable young womanhood; beautiful, perfect, innocent creatures.

Then...

9. NARA AND ALDER
Saturday September 6, 1755

Nara's second child was conceived in a field at nineteen minutes to seven in the evening on Saturday, September 6th, 1755, just as the sun melted into the horizon. She looked up into Alder's eyes and knew. And he looked down into hers and knew the same. It was a subtle thing – a tiny, crystalline, fragile certainty that snapped awake for both of them in the same instant. They were amazed, speechless, and she began to cry.

He drew free of her, lay by her side and hugged her. He couldn't tell her how much he loved her – no words could have done that – so he held her and let her cry.

The sky had darkened by the time they arrived at the Red Lion. Holly Robinson and Nicholas Miller, sharing a table together, called them over. Nara sat while Alder ordered at the bar.

"You look so happy!" said Holly. "Rosy, sunny. What have you been up to?" Nara shot her a smile, and Holly went on, "Bet I can guess."

"My man makes me happy," Nara replied.

"You've been married seven years..." Holly began.

"...and I still love him," Nara finished. "Just as much as ever."

Holly feigned an expression of resignation. "Look at me. I expect I'll be an old maid."

Nicholas cut in with a remark addressed to Nara. "She's turned me down again."

"Oh, Holly!" Nara exclaimed.

Holly looked at Nicholas. "You're my friend, Nick. I don't want to spoil a lovely friendship." She looked away. "Anyway, your twenty-nine. Ten years older than me." She realised what she'd said, looked at Nara, and apologised.

"Age is no issue," said Nara. "Alder and me, we're the same. Except I'm twenty-two, and he's fifty-two." Holly smiled, and Nara added, "It doesn't make any difference." She looked over at the bar. Alder was leaning over the counter, his back to them, chatting with Jack Morris. "Look at him – my man, my lovely man." She swallowed, emotion welling up.

"The band's getting ready out back," said Nicholas. "You up to dancing, Nara?"

"With you? If you like."

Nicholas looked at Holly. "See? Someone wants me."

But Holly's eyes were fixed on the far end of the taproom. "Speaking of someone wanting something," she nodded her head in the direction of her gaze, "what about your sister, Nick?"

Nicholas turned around and looked. Buffy was sitting in the lap of seventeen-year-old Brendan Telford. Their faces were glued to each other at the lips, eyes closed, her arms thrown round his neck, his hand exploring her body rather more thoroughly than it should have been in public.

"Excuse me," said Nicholas to his companions. He rose and walked towards the couple.

"She's only thirteen," said Holly, following Nicholas with her eyes.

"You can't stop them," said Nara. "They'll do it if they're determined enough – and they probably are. They're probably already doing it."

Brendan and Pond Girl left through the door hand-in-hand, and Nicholas returned to the table.

"Sorry about that," he said.

"What did you say to them?" asked Holly.

"I told them to find a place on the common if they wanted to behave like that, and to stop embarrassing everyone in here. I also told him to mind my sister, and take care unless he wants trouble."

Holly smiled at him. "Mean old bachelor. And where's *your* girl?"

He replied, "Sitting opposite me in your skin – only she doesn't know it."

The door opened and Apple came in, Tozer following. Holly waved. "Ma!" Alder looked behind him, saw the newcomers and offered to buy them drinks. In a moment their table was full, all of them talking loudly to get above the surrounding din. But Nara and Alder, holding hands across the table, only had eyes for each other.

"I love you," he mouthed silently.

"I love you too," she mouthed back.

The band appeared from the back room where they'd been getting ready, and everyone followed them out into the road to dance. Torches had been fixed into the sconces outside the tavern, and the street was alive with flickering light. Nara and Nicholas danced together while Alder danced with Holly. Tozer and Apple watched from the crowd, clapping the rhythm. A minute or so later, Brendan and Buffy appeared from the darkness of the common and joined in, smiling at each other.

"Your wife loves you with all her heart," said Holly to Alder.

"I know," said Alder. "She's everything to me."

"You're so lucky, you two."

Alder watched Nara as she danced. "Look at her," he said. "She's beautiful."

Holly poked him. "Alder, you're not paying attention to your dancing partner."

He smiled. "Sorry, Holly. You're beautiful too."

"I know," she said.

10. CAPPLEMAN FARM
May 1756

Hazel Priestly was busy in her kitchen, preparing a complex medicine for Miriam Exley's young boy Amos, who'd been complaining of painful breathing. The preparation of this particular substance was a painstaking one, involving Elder tree bark and various flowers and berries.

Hazel had a lot on her mind, and it was a struggle to concentrate. Maria Buckley, one of her dearest friends, had fallen down the stairs in the big house three days before, breaking both her legs. There were fractured ribs, and Hazel suspected internal injuries as well. She'd helped as much as she was able but was frustrated that it might not have been enough. Doctor Levinson visited, checked Hazel's binding of the broken limbs, and said he probably couldn't do much more than she'd already done. Hazel hoped that Maria would be alright, although the woman was sixty-two, overweight, and hadn't been in the best of health for some time.

There was a knock at the door. She frowned, frustrated by the interruption, reluctantly left what she was doing and went to greet her visitor. Robert Forest stood there, looking embarrassed.

Robert, a young man of twenty-five, had arrived in Easington four years previously to become parson after old Egbert's death. Like his predecessor, he was opposed to anything that wasn't sanctioned in print by the Lord God. He was friendly enough with most of the local folk but remained deliberately aloof from Hazel and her family, so his arrival at her front door was a surprise.

She raised her eyebrows and tried to look welcoming.

"Robert! An unexpected pleasure. What can I do for you?"

He sighed. "Mrs Priestly, I beg your forbearance. You must know that I come to see you as a last resort. Please forgive me – I hope my honesty doesn't offend you."

"Of course not, Robert. What's the matter?"

"I've seen Doctor Levinson twice this last week, but I fear he's at a loss with me. My complaint is not an unusual one – or so I understand – but the common remedies appear to have no effect."

Her gaze was focused on him; his discomfort was obvious. "Do you want to come inside and talk about it?"

"I would prefer to stand here in the sunlight – if it's no offence to you."

"As you wish," said Hazel. She gripped the doorframe and waited. "You'd better just come straight out with it, Robert."

"I'm...unable..."

Hazel interrupted his dithering. "Well, it's either a woman or you're constipated."

"It is the latter. Thank you. Very perceptive."

"How long have you been affected?"

"Well, for years actually..."

"No – I mean, when were you last able to...?"

"Oh, I'm sorry. It's almost a week now."

"And you feel..."

"Uncomfortable, restless. It's painful."

"I suppose Neil's tried all the usual methods? Enema, fingers up the rear...?"

"He suggested I seek your help. He holds you in high esteem."

Hazel made an affirmative noise in her throat. "Just a moment." She moved away into the interior of her house. Robert looked up at the Green Man above the lintel. It looked down at him as if he were an insignificant nothing; as if he were a pitiful salesman of pointless, out of place values. It intimidated him. He began to scratch the inside of his elbow, a habit that always manifested when he felt self-conscious.

After a minute or so, Hazel returned with a small wooden pot which she handed to him. He took the lid off and looked inside, half expecting to find a frog (despite his four years in the vicinity, Robert's conception of witches and witchcraft remained infantile). The pot contained some kind of thick, sticky substance.

"What is it?" he asked.

"It's a paste. Dissolve it completely – all of it – in about half a pint of warm water. Drink it all at once, then go for a long, vigorous walk."

"Might I ask what's in it?"

"Ash leaves – various things, all mixed together. Don't worry – It won't kill you."

He looked from the pot to Hazel and back again, then replaced the lid.

"Did you come on foot all the way from Easington?" she asked. "I can't see a horse."

"I did," he replied. "I wondered if the exercise itself might achieve some result."

"And you're walking all the way back presumably."

"That is so."

She put out her hand. "Then let me prepare it for you now. The walk home should do the rest." He returned the pot to her, and she disappeared once more into the house.

Robert waited, trying to avoid the temptation to look at the smiling figure watching over him. He pushed up his sleeve and scratched vigorously at his other elbow, drawing little beads of blood. Cursing himself for weakness, he pulled the sleeve down and rubbed the injured spot through the fabric.

Hazel came back carrying a steaming mug. "There we are," she said. "Down it goes."

Robert drained the contents, then raised his eyebrows. "Not so bad!"

143

She laughed. "What were you expecting?"

"I honestly don't know," he replied.

She took back the mug.

"Thank you," he said. "I must pay you."

"Pay me when you're better, Robert. Let me know how you get on."

"I will. Thank you again, Mrs Priestly."

"Hazel," she said, nodding him good-day.

"Indeed so." He raised his hat, turned, and was gone.

Hazel stood at her open door and watched him as he began his walk home.

Tozer Robinson, on his way to help with a day of repairs at the watermill, saluted Robert as the latter approached him, striding purposefully in the opposite direction.

"Vicar."

"Good morning Tozer," said Robert, passing him. "All well, I hope?"

"As well as could ever be, sir!" smiled Tozer. "Thank you." He walked on a few more steps and noticed Hazel standing at her front door. "Mrs Priestly. How's Nara? Your second grandchild arrived yet?"

Hazel waved at him. "No, Tozer. Not today. It'll be a week or two yet."

Tozer went on his way, turning right on Watermill Lane, a field of grazing sheep away to his left beyond the Esk.

He was a happy man, although his house was less full than it used to be. His daughter Hazel had married Tudor Green, one of the farm carpenters, the previous summer, and she, like Nara, was now expecting a child. But Tozer was already a grandfather. His eldest daughter Willow had given birth twice since her marriage to parson Kirby: first "Young" Tozer a year after her wedding (that made "old" Tozer's heart swell with pride); then Margery in 1754, named after James's mother. That left only Cedar and Holly at home with Tozer and Apple. Tozer was a little puzzled that Cedar seemed to develop no real friendships with girls. The boy was twenty-five, handsome and could have taken his pick of any number of young women. Instead, he was quiet, studious, polite, seemed to like his own company. When not at work on the farm, the boy was fond of taking long walks, always alone.

Holly had only just turned twenty. She'd had a few male friends but never took any of them seriously. Tozer was aware of his daughter's fondness for children, and said to her one day, "You could get wed, you know, Holly. You're a pretty girl. You could have bairns of your own." She replied that her "prince" hadn't found her yet...

Alone again in the kitchen, Hazel continued with her work. There'd soon be another voice in the house, and she found herself smiling at the prospect of it; a brother or sister for happy, chatty, seven-year-old Kate.

Why on earth had it taken them so long to have a second child? It was a question Hazel often asked herself, and it genuinely puzzled her. It certainly wasn't for want of effort; the noises that leaked from the bedroom Alder shared with Nara sometimes kept Hazel awake at night. Even Adam and William (themselves no strangers to such activity) complained occasionally. Once or twice she'd even climbed out of bed, trundled along the landing and tapped on their door.

"Shhh. Keep the noise down, you rabbits. We're trying to sleep."

An instant, embarrassed silence; then, "Sorry, mum."

But the months and years had passed, and despite all the ploughing and planting, there'd been no crop.

"Maybe you should see the doctor," Hazel suggested. "It could be Alder..."

"Don't fret about it, ma. It'll happen, if it's going to happen."

And eventually, just when Hazel had accepted the fact that

her daughter would never have another child, it *had* happened. And the house was going to celebrate the arrival of a new life yet again. Hazel felt the excitement bubbling away inside her, and began to sing to herself, songs her own mother had sung to her as a child, rehearsing them for the new baby: *Ding Dong Bell; Jack Sprat; Rain, Rain, Go Away; Three Blind Mice; The Grand Old Duke of York...*

Beatrice Swift (ten) and Grace Buckley (nine) had been entrusted with the task of looking after Kate Swithenbank as she went about among the hedgerows, gathering plants, herbs, bark and various other growths for her grandmother. Although Kate was the youngest of the three, she was really the leader, the older girls thinking of themselves as her helpers. Catherine Swithenbank could do amazing things. She took the dried-out old bodies of dead animals and made them alive again. Beatrice and Grace had watched the miracle on several occasions, their mouths open, expressions lengthening in astonishment as the rotten flesh filled out, and the little twitching movements began. They copied her and tried to achieve the same results, never with success.

Kate knew she was different. She was like her grandmother. The two of them – they were not the same as other people.

"Ma," said Nara, "people are saying things about Kate."
"Mm..." Hazel replied quietly, lips closed.
The younger woman, heavily pregnant with her second child, sat in the kitchen sipping from a mug of small beer while her mother went about her work.
"Have you seen what she does?" she asked.
"Yes," Hazel replied. "I watched once or twice."
"It doesn't trouble you?"
"Kate's going to be a strong one. You're her mother – you know that, Nara."

But Nara was worried about Catherine. To have the ability to pull life back from wherever it had gone; to make creatures that had been dead live again? Where would that stop? For now, Kate only played with little things: birds, mice, rats. What next? Sheep? Bulls?... The course of logic suggested horrific possibilities. It had been a long time since anyone had been executed for witchcraft, but with such provocative powers... where might Kate's gift lead?

"I think I should stop her," said Nara.

Hazel responded immediately. "You won't be able to. She's too strong-willed. She'll just do it behind your back, and that'll bring tension between you." She paused, leaned on the kitchen table and looked at Nara. "Kate's going to be one of the great ones – the kind that comes only once every century or two. She's going to have abilities that you and I can't even imagine. Leave her be. Let people make of her what they will. She'll find her own boundaries as she grows up."

Nara heard, and knew that her mother was right, but her concern remained. She wanted a quiet, happy life for Kate. Power brought responsibility.

Wednesday June 2, 1756

Kate pressed herself into her grandmother's lap, legs drawn up, hands clutched tight, eyes squeezed shut, face pushing hard into her shoulder – harder, harder, burrowing – trying to find a way through, out the other side of this world, away from the shock, the horror, into some quiet place where there was calm and they were all still happy; tearing backwards through time, reversing what had happened.

Hazel held her granddaughter tightly, cradling her head in her hands, overwhelmed with grief. She hadn't expected this – she'd thought all would be well.

Florence Swift, patches of blood on her apron, stood at the window, lips parted, eyes wide, unbelieving, in shock.

Apple Robinson had run to the barn to fetch Adam and William. They'd been working with Richard Swift and had intended to hurry back as soon as there was news of the birth.

Alder sat outside the house, on the wall by the river in the pouring rain, looking up at the sky, face twisted in anguish and riven with tears, mind awash with despair and disbelief. The labour had begun well, but things had taken a turn for the worse.

In the bedroom, Nara lay dead, her lifeless baby son beside her. Neil Levinson, appalled by the rapid descent into tragedy, felt that he must be responsible in some way for what had occurred. He'd failed.

"I'm so sorry, Hazel." He was trying to hold his emotions in check. "There was nothing else I could have done." He stood close, his hand on her shoulder, needing her forgiveness, although he knew she was too distraught to supply it.

"I know," she sobbed and took his hand in hers, holding on to Kate as she did so. "I know you did everything you could."

The door burst open, and the boys came running in. "Say it's not true!" pleaded William. Hazel couldn't form any words. She looked at him, her face broken and tear-stained, lips quivering.

"Oh, no, no!" William's grief broke out of him.

"Where's Alder?" asked Adam, voice cracked.

"Gone out," said Hazel. It was all she could manage.

The boys retraced their steps and saw Alder slumped on the wall, his back to them, shoulders heaving in the pouring rain. They splashed across the muddy track, vaulted the stonework and sat next to him, one on his right, the other on his left, and shrouded him with their arms.

The sky darkened further. The rain beat into the sodden earth.

The farm was deadened with mourning. The loss of such a

beloved member of its community brought deep sadness, and Vine Cottage soon filled with flowers sent in Nara's memory. Kate became quiet, drawn in, and clung to her grandmother.

Maria Buckley died less than a month after Nara's death, adding still more weight to Hazel's sorrow.

Despite the support and consolation of his many friends, Alder began to drink heavily. The love of his life was gone. The light in his soul went out.

July 1756 – March 1757

Nara's death crushed Hazel. Her characteristic optimism, so familiar to those who knew her, disappeared, and she aged quickly and visibly. Her face creased, her hair thinned, and she developed a stoop that became increasingly marked. Fewer people called at her door to ask for remedies and advice, and those who'd regularly come to have the Wise Woman read their cards reduced in number to just two or three. She rarely went out of doors.

Adam and William stayed home as much as they could to keep her company, but Alder's drinking continued, and he was often away overnight, usually lying in a ditch or field. Hazel's daughter, her husband, her father, her mother – they were all gone. Many of the dear friends she'd known were gone too, and she knew that her own time was drawing to a close, so she set about teaching Kate everything she knew.

The girl was growing up fast and frequently expressed irritation at her father's boozing.

"Daddy, why do you do that? You drink so hard it's like you're not really there. You're asleep most of the time."

"I do it to forget," he replied.

"Ma's gone," said Kate, "but I'm still here. I need you."

But Alder was a spent force and lacked the willpower to break out of his stupor.

Kate wandered around the farm, exploring, learning, gathering things she needed for her studies with Hazel. She became familiar with the rhythm of the land, the weather, the birds, animals, insects. She liked to sit in the wood up beyond the warren and listen to the trees, the voices in the wind, in the ground. She read eagerly and widely.

"I can teach you to read, dad. It's amazing! The world is really wonderful. People write astonishing things, and we can read them. We can get into their heads, look through their eyes, feel what they feel. We can learn so much. We can grow and become wiser and better. If you'd just wake up, I could help you!"

"One day Kate. Tomorrow... or the next day..."

Kate felt in her heart that both her parents had gone, and that deepened her sadness. But she also sensed that her life had a purpose; there were things to accomplish. She felt the future rushing towards her.

Kate liked to walk along Watermill Lane. She liked to stand on slippery, moss-laden Beggar's Bridge and watch the Esk as it flowed beneath the old stonework. A little further down the lane, to the left of the road and beyond the perimeter of the farm, lay the watermill. The millwheel itself was not visible from the lane, but the building looked romantic, worn, dilapidated. She'd heard stories about the man who lived there – had been warned about him.

(Hazel: "Hugo Ash lives there alone. Don't stray from the lane if you go that way, Kate. He doesn't like strangers. The Ashes have always kept themselves to themselves; never wanted to mix. Best stay away. Anyway, the mill itself is not a good place, so they say."

Kate (curious): "What do you mean?"

Hazel: "This world, Kate – it's not always what you think it is. Things linger beyond our lives. Sometimes they're lovely things – and those things can make a place happy – they can make *people happy. But bad things, they can settle as well. You feel the bad things in buildings – in the stones, or in the rooms. Places like that – people call those places haunted."*

Kate: "So the mill's haunted?"

Hazel: "It's not a happy place, Kate. The coldness that lives there flows up over the stream and into the road – even on a bright, sunny day...")

But there was no surer way to arouse the curiosity of an inquisitive young girl. She wandered beyond the bridge on several occasions, stood at the edge of the road and looked down at the mill, and the pond...

11. THE WATERMILL
Thursday March 31 to Friday April 8, 1757

The River Esk, a modest flow gathered from three moorland streams, rose on Westerdale Moor and took its course twenty-eight miles through the Eskdale Valley and out into the North Sea at Whitby. It flowed down through the woods above Cappleman Farm, dividing the farmland from the village of Glaisdale. The Flesher family drew off some of its water for irrigation in the fields, but the main flow pressed on towards the meadow and Vine Cottage, where it veered south. Watermill Lane followed the river's course out of the farm, the road rising over Beggar's Bridge a little less than half a mile southeast of Vine Cottage. The Esk spanned almost forty feet by the time it reached the old bridge. A leat had been cut a few hundred yards south of the bridge to carry water to the mill, which lay a short distance east of the lane and the main watercourse. The tailrace from the mill, and the overspill channel from the millpond, fed the water back to the Esk downstream.

The watermill itself, a tall structure built in the last years of the sixteenth century, was used primarily to grind corn. It worked two sets of millstones driven by a single undershot vertical wheel, fixed to the rear of the building. Fragmentary ruins of large, ancient structure lay nearby, said to be all that remained of a watermill that had operated on the site since before the arrival of King William.

The mill's hermit-like occupant lived in the small, damp cottage, entirely hidden from the lane, attached to the building's north wall. Hugo Ash had taken over responsibility for the place when his father died. The family history was an ugly one, and Hugo had no wish to pass it down to future generations, so he kept himself private and never married.

The mill lay beyond the boundary of Cappleman Farm and had initially been independent of it. Generations of Hugo's ancestors had run it as their own concern, taking grain from local clients and turning it into flour, but the Ashes had a long tradition of unrest. There'd been a great deal of violence and abuse within the family, including domestic battery and incest. The Ash family was a necessary evil that the local community had to bear.

Hugo's mother, Rosa, suffered greatly at the hands of her husband. Walter Ash, twenty-seven years older than his wife, conducted affairs with local women throughout his life, all flaunted before Rosa's eyes. When Rosa fell ill and died in the summer of 1726, just short of her thirty-sixth birthday, her husband began an incestuous relationship with his twelve-year-old daughter, Cristina.

Walter died just three years after his wife. His life was over-shadowed by alcohol, and he drank himself to death one night. Hugo, then aged twenty, felt almost nothing when he discovered his father's lifeless body lying in dual pools of vomit and excrement. He rode to fetch the undertaker, arranged for the burial – and took up his father's place in Cristina's bed. She was fifteen by then and accepted the abuse as normal, having never known anything else.

Fortunately, the girl never conceived, despite more than a decade of her brother's attention. She eventually escaped, whisked away by handsome David Ward, seven years her junior, steward to one of the farmers nearer to the coast. Hugo was left alone. For the first time in his life he knew something close to peace. His relationship with Cristina had been one of habit, bound together by mutual dislike and an innate belief that fate had only suffering in store for them. Neither of them hoped to see the other again.

He ran the mill alone whenever possible – which was most of the time. When he was very young, his father had reached an agreement with Benjamin Flesher. The farm would supply the Ash family with all the victuals they required in return for limited free access to the mill and a small percentage of its overall profits. It was a good deal, and by the time Hugo lived alone, it meant that he only ever had to leave his burrow to collect booze or whores. He kept a solitary horse and cart for the purpose.

On the rare occasions when demand for the mill was high, or when it needed repairs, Hugo would send to the farm for help. Other than that, he rarely saw anyone and had no friends. From time to time his body told him it wanted a woman. On those occasions he'd drive to Whitby, pick up one of the prostitutes and bring her back to the mill. When he'd done with them, usually after two or three days, he'd drive them home. Occasionally he was impressed enough with a girl to invite her back more than once, but he never allowed himself to become overly fond of any particular one. If he felt his affections rise beyond the merely physical, he made a point of never seeing that particular female again.

It was his habit every morning to wash away the cobwebs of the previous night's solitary drinking by bathing in the millpond, whatever the temperature, unless it was frozen over. One chilly March morning in 1757 he pulled himself out of the freezing water and stretched, naked, in the low sun. Looking over to his left, he saw her, up in the lane, watching him – the pretty, young red-haired girl from Vine Cottage – the witch's granddaughter. She was dressed in a cape against the cold, with the hood hanging loose behind, holding a basket in her right hand. She didn't try to run away, didn't try to pretend she wasn't looking. Hugo turned to face her. At forty-eight, he was well built, strong, with a thick head of dark hair streaked with grey, his black, well-trimmed beard also peppered. He was handsomely endowed – the women from Whitby sometimes commented on it, fearing they might be hurt – and he made

154

no attempt to shield himself from the young girl's view. It became a kind of contest to see who would flinch first. He didn't know her name but had seen her in the lane several times, gathering things in the hedgerow. She was bold, made no movement, didn't smile (as far as he could see across the distance that separated them), but just gazed. He took a step towards her, then another. She turned to her left and walked away in the direction of her home, unhurried and without glancing at him. Hugo followed her with his eyes until she disappeared from view. He stood motionless for a moment, then wiped the moisture from his lips with the knuckle of his right index finger and walked the short distance back to his cottage.

Kate woke that night in the dark, thinking about the man in the millpond. She'd had to concentrate hard to see him clearly. The sun hadn't risen very far, and the low ground had been partly obscured in shadow. He seemed to Kate to be quite a handsome man, and she'd tried to sketch him from memory, although she was unhappy with her skills as an artist. She'd accidentally caught her father naked on a few occasions, Adam once, and had now and then seen men swimming nude in the river, so male anatomy was not entirely new to her. But Hugo's physique (if indeed it had been Hugo) struck her as being of a superior kind, and her inability to capture it in graphite was a source of frustration for her. Her work looked absurd, she felt, and the representation of those parts, in particular, was an irritation she seemed unable to overcome despite multiple attempts.

She began to wonder about Hugo's personality. What made him so bad? There were terrible stories about his parents and about an "unnatural" relationship with his own sister. It was all very curious, intriguing, and needed deeper investigation.

Hugo stood in the early sunshine, invigorated by the icy kisses of the black pond. The morning was warmer than of late, and he felt the promise of spring on his skin, although the lake water seemed reluctant to release winter's chill. He shook himself, iridescent water droplets bright with the spark of daylight firing away from his skin and hair as if he were a dog.

The girl was there again, up on the edge of the lane, picked out by the sun, watching him as she had before. Hugo had been thinking of one of his favourite whores during his morning bathe, and the memory of the woman had engendered a physical response that had not entirely subsided. He wondered if the red-haired girl could see it from where she stood – a distance of perhaps three hundred yards – and thought it likely that she could.

He took ten steps towards her, expecting her to walk away as she'd done previously, but she stood her ground, so he continued his approach, halving the distance between them. By the time he halted, his body had forgotten the prostitute's flesh.

He called to the girl. "It's not the first time you've spied on me."

"Sorry," she called back. "I didn't mean to spy. I didn't think you'd mind."

"It's difficult to hear you. Come here." He expected her to run away but was surprised to see her step forward from the lane and walk down the incline towards him. She got as far as the little wooden bridge at the overflow stream.

"That's far enough," he called, stepping to the opposite side of the bridge, just twenty feet from where she stood.

"I'm Kate," she said, "from Vine Cottage."

"I know where you're from."

"You're Hugo."

He nodded. "You've heard of me."

"You live by yourself in the mill."

"It suits me." He waited, but the girl offered no answer. "How old are you?"

"Eight," she said.

"Aren't you frightened?"

She frowned. "Why would I be frightened?"

"What am I wearing?"

"Nothing."

"I could hurt you."

"Why would you do that?"

"My family have always hurt each other. Perhaps it would amuse me to hurt you."

She watched him for a moment, then said, "But I don't think you will."

He was impressed, folded his arms. "Kate," he said, nodding his head slightly.

"Hugo," she replied.

He felt bewitched, a little amazed at her. "You're an unusual child," he said.

"How would you know?" she asked, "shut up here all by yourself... Maybe I'm completely ordinary."

He laughed out loud. "I like you!" He looked across the water at her and saw that she was smiling. "Why do you watch me bathing?"

"I watch a lot of things," she answered.

"Are you used to seeing unclothed men?"

She thought. "No. That would suggest that I see such things regularly – and that's not the case."

"You speak very clearly for a child – your thoughts seem well organised."

"I read a lot," she said. "Think a lot too."

"I also think a lot," he said. "I have time for that here."

"Men and women bathe in the river sometimes – upstream where it flows through the woods. I've noticed them now and then. It didn't occur to me that you might mind if I watched you."

"I don't mind, as it happens," he replied. "But – if you don't

157

mind my saying – it's a little naïve of you to simply *assume* that I wouldn't. Why did you run away last time I saw you?"

She was silent for a long while before replying. "I'd rather not say."

"Now I really am curious," he said. "You must tell me." Hugo heard her breathe out nervously through her nose. "Tell me," he repeated.

"I thought you might chase me."

"And you wanted to get a head start?"

"Something like that. Sorry – it was a stupid instinct. I've thought about it since. It was a silly reaction."

"Not silly at all," he said. "Very sensible."

"I was intimidated..."

He waited for more, and she went on.

"You're a strong man – like my dad – and your..." she pointed, "...it's fat – big."

"You were scared," he suggested.

Kate agreed. "Yes. I don't know why."

Hugo nodded. "Do you feel scared now?"

"No," she said. "I just feel silly. I wish I hadn't told you."

He gave a hint of a laugh through his nose. "I don't think you're silly at all. I think you're extraordinary."

"I won't watch you again."

"Do what you like, Kate. You're very welcome here. In fact, you're more welcome here than anyone."

She joined her hands together. It was a pretty gesture, oddly demure.

"What do you do here, all alone?" she asked.

"You mean apart from running the mill?" She nodded, so he told her. "I drink – a lot. Apart from that, I piss, shit, and fuck women. And bathe in the pond."

"That sounds rather empty." She said it with such honesty – and it seemed so accurate – that he felt briefly overwhelmed. "Do you read?"

"Enough to conduct the business." He unclasped his arms

158

and scratched behind his ear.

"I meant real reading. Books, plays, poems – things like that."

"I have none of those things."

"I think you should read. I'll bring you a book. You'll spend a couple of weeks reading it, and I'll read a book at the same time. When the two weeks are up, I'll collect your book and give you the one I just finished. Then you'll read that one, and I'll read another. Every two weeks we'll have a proper conversation about what we've read. What do you think?"

He laughed. "Are you serious?"

"Of course."

The absurdity of the situation struck him forcibly. Here they were, the two of them alone, almost certainly out of sight of any other living soul. He could have taken her, raped her, torn her in half in the process. But she was primly suggesting an exchange of literature, a kind of regular poetic tryst. And here he was, naked, potent and dangerous, listening to her like a baby.

"I love it!" he exclaimed, consumed with hilarity. "Only because it's you. We'll do it."

She seemed pleased. "Good. Tomorrow afternoon I'll bring you a book."

"I'll wait for you," he said. "I'll have a fire going and a spit ready. I'll have my knives freshly sharpened. I'll skin you and eat you. You'll feed me for two days."

Kate was still smiling. "No, you won't," she said. "I'm not frightened of you. See you tomorrow."

Hugo held up his hand. "Until tomorrow." She turned and walked away. When she'd reached the lane, she looked down at him and raised her hand in farewell. He returned the gesture and watched her disappear from view. He felt renewed in some way – enriched.

She was as good as her word and turned up at noon next

day. Hugo was working in the mill but caught sight of her through the window as she approached. He felt oddly excited that she'd remembered him; as if he were a child and she was his best friend. The fact that she'd returned meant that she'd been thinking about him. It was as if she cared – it was a completely new sensation. He tried to suppress his smile as he opened the door.

"Hello," she said.

"I didn't really expect you to come."

"We have an arrangement," she said, handing him the book she'd brought. "Here's a story about a man like you, who lives alone, with only his own company." She handed him her copy of *Robinson Crusoe*.

Hugo looked at the spine and opened the book to the title page. "Two weeks…"

"Can you do it?"

"Yes, I can do it."

"Good." Kate smiled.

"Would you like to come in and see the mill?"

"Next time," she said.

"I'm sorry I joked about hurting you," he said. "It was a stupid thing to say – I didn't mean it."

"I know," she said. "I'll come in next time. I don't have long this afternoon. Don't worry, Hugo. I'm not frightened of you. I think you're a nice man."

He nodded, swallowed, unexpectedly moved.

"Two weeks," said Kate and began to walk away."

"Kate!" called Hugo, holding up the book. "Thank you."

12. THE LOOKOUT
Friday April 15, 1757

When Cady Weston joined the Lookout staff in January 1757 at the age of twenty-two, she found herself the youngest of the maids, except for Sarah Alston, two years her junior.

Molly Weston, Cady's mother, had served for many years as cook in one of the big houses in York, and her daughter grew up there as a kitchen maid. Cady was rather pale and thin, though still pretty enough to be the target of several of the below-stairs male staff. But these would-be lovers always suffered disappointment, because the poles of Cady's romantic magnet were reversed, and the base passions of men had no effect upon her.

She had a spiteful sense of humour and mimicked her suitors with painful accuracy and inflated drama, to the amusement of the other staff and the humiliation of the unfortunate individuals portrayed:

" 'Let me see you in secret,' he whispered to me. 'I burn, burn for you, my beauty. My body pulses with desire.'

"Well, I did have a quick look, but I wasn't sure if it was s'posed to be a present for me, or if it was somethin' he was offerin' sixpence a pound that we could mix with the other garden vegetables. I've never seen anythin' quite that orange."

From her early years, Cady knew she was interested in girls, especially girls of a certain age, so when the post at the Lookout was advertised, an institution entirely for young ladies, she jumped at the chance.

Vivianne Stamper had been studying at the Lookout for about twenty months and had become a favourite of the headmaster, Mr Crowan, because of her unusual talent in writing: poetry, stories, essays, plays. She was unusually gifted – she fascinated him. He'd asked if she'd mind sharing a dormitory with three of the older girls, between two and four years her senior; a kind of experiment to see how she might integrate and interact. Viv, pleased with Crowan's appreciation of her, willingly agreed to move in with Kim Hurley, Holly Graham and Anne Smyth.

It was her birthday, and the other girls made a fuss of her at dinner.

"Pity you had to work today," said Anne, dressed in dark blue silk, her soft brown hair arranged in tresses.

"I didn't mind," Viv replied. "I'm going for a walk tomorrow, along the coast with Orla and Nana. That'll be my birthday treat. You can come if you like."

"Thanks," Anne replied. "But I've promised to look after Barney at the forge."

"Oh, dear," said Viv. "He'll keep you busy. Not sure I'd have the patience to look after a five-year-old."

The older girl smiled. "He's a good boy."

Anne had managed to keep her six-month affair with Alan Blake a complete secret. No-one knew that once a month she visited him at the forge while his wife shopped in Scarborough. Little Barney was shut safely in his room while Anne spent the afternoon in Alan's bed. The smith was strong, muscular, forceful, and his lovemaking was red-hot-hard as the iron he worked with. He'd told her he was going to leave his wife.

At nine o'clock, Vivianne undressed in her dormitory and put on her robe. She'd asked the maids to fill a bath for her – a nice, deep, soapy one for her birthday. It was standard practice for the maids to accompany the girls to their tubs, wash their hair, scrub their backs, tidy their nails. Cady was waiting for her.

"Hello, Viv," she said. "Happy birthday! Fourteen today."

"Thanks, Cady," Vivianne replied.

Cady shut the bathroom door. They were alone.

The room was whitewashed, lit with several lanterns, and warmed by a peat fire. The bath stood near the hearth, and was more than half full with hot water, brought up in pitchers on the kitchen lift. Cady had tested the temperature, added soap and made everything comfortable and cosy for her charge.

"Here we are then," she said. "Let's get your robe off."

Vivianne had never bathed under Cady's supervision before, but overcame her self-consciousness and allowed the maid to undress her.

"My," said Cady, half-smiling. "You're a pretty one. With your lovely big doe-eyes." She looked at the naked girl in silence for a second or two, moistened her lips, and added, "and your lovely long hair." She reached out and ran her hands through it. Her smile broadened, and she became more animated. "In you get then, dear."

Vivianne stepped into the water and sat down. "It's nice," she said. "Just right."

"Course it is," said Cady. "I made sure of it. Don't want you to get scalded; nice soft skin like yours."

Vivianne began to soap herself while Cady knelt and washed the girl's hair, humming under her breath.

"Where are you from?" she asked.

"York originally – then Oulston," said Viv.

"North of the city?"

"That's it," Viv replied. "What about you?"

"Me? I'm from York too. My ma's in service – cook."

"Ah," said Viv. "I don't have a mum any more. She went missing a long time ago."

"That's sad," Cady replied, eyebrows raised. "You don't know what happened to her?"

"I think she must be dead," Vivianne replied. "We lost our house suddenly and got separated. She said she'd come back. But she never did."

Cady felt sorry for the girl. "It's always sad to hear stories like that. What about your dad?"

"He died years ago," said Vivianne. "I was small. Don't remember much about him, except...he was nice, kind."

"I never knew my dad," said Cady.

"Is he dead?"

Cady continued to rinse Viv's hair. "Don't know," she replied. "Not sure my mum ever knew his name. Unless it was *Your Bastard Father*."

Vivianne laughed.

"You've got a nice laugh," said Cady. "Do you sing?"

"I try," Vivianne replied.

"Shall we sing a song?"

Vivianne was relaxed and smiling. She'd warmed to her maid and was enjoying her company.

Cady began:

"On yonder hill there stands a lady,
Who she is I do not know;
I will court her for her beauty,
She must answer, yes or no."

Cady pointed at Vivianne and joined her in the refrain:

"Oh, no, no, no, no, no, no, no!"

The pattern continued for each subsequent verse, Vivianne becoming ever more consumed with laughter:

"On her bosom are bunches of posies,
On her breast where flowers grow.
If I should chance to touch that posy,
She must answer, yes or no.
Oh, no, no, no, no, no, no, no!

"Madam, I am come for to court you,
If your favour I can gain.
If you will but entertain me,
Perhaps then I might come again.

Oh, no, no, no, no, no, no, no!

"My husband was a Spanish captain,
Went to sea a month ago.
The very last time we kissed and parted,
Bid me always answer, "No!"
Oh, no, no, no, no, no, no, no!

"Madam, in your face is beauty,
In your bosom flowers do grow.
In your bedroom there is pleasure,"

Cady leaned forward and kissed Vivianne's cheek. Viv stopped laughing – but she watched Cady's face closely and continued to smile as she went on singing:

"Shall I view it? Yes or no
Oh, no, no, no, no, no, no, no!

"Madam, shall I tie your garter,
Tie it a little above your knee?
If my hand should slip a little farther,
Would you think it amiss of me?
Oh, no, no, no, no, no, no, no!

Vivianne was entranced, excited, her heart racing. Cady sang the last verse, Viv subvocalizing the chorus:

"My love and I went a-bed together,
There we lay till cocks did crow;
Unclose your arms, my dearest jewel,
Unclose your arms and let me go.
Oh, no, no, no, no, no, no, no!"

The bathroom was still, except for the rumble of the burning peat and the soft lap of the bathwater. Cady was smiling at her but said nothing. Vivianne's mind was whirling. *Go on, go on, go on! Don't stop!* "More," she whispered.
Cady opened her mouth a little, and her tongue briefly ap-

peared, licking her lips. She leaned forward and ran her fingers gently around Vivianne's face.

"Alright," Cady said softly and began to sing again:

"I sowed the seeds of love
And I sowed them in the spring,
I gathered them up in the morning so soon,
While the small birds do sweetly sing,
While the small birds do sweetly sing.

"My garden was planted well
With flowers everywhere
But I had not the liberty to choose for myself
Of the flowers that I love so dear,
Of the flowers that I love so dear.

"The gardener he stood by
And I asked him to choose for me..."

She crept forward on her knees and whispered the next line into Vivianne's ear, softly and slowly:

"He chose me the violet, the lily and the pink..."

Cady kissed Vivianne's ear, pulled away, and delivered the verse's final two lines:

"But those I refused all three,
But those I refused all three."

The next verse was not sung, but whispered, slowly, with certain words emphasised. It was not completed:

"For in June there's a red rosebud,
And that is the flower for me.
I often have plucked that red rosebud..."

Cady's voice faded away.
A lot of soapy water erupted suddenly onto the floor, produced by the surprised thrashings of the bath's occupant. It

ran down the cleverly designed incline to a circular drain in a channel at the rear wall, leaving a trail of suds and bubbles. The alarmed cries that had accompanied the initial splashing faded into gasps that melted away.

The fire continued to rumble. The lanterns continued to glow their golden light.

Someone whispered, "Happy birthday..."

13. EGTON MILL
Friday April 22 to Friday May 20, 1757

"Kate, do you know what the word *wilful* means?"

"Of course I do, grandma. I also know what the words pulchritudinous, consanguineous, tergiversation, jentacular and sialoquent mean. I read – you and ma taught me to do it."

Hazel roared with laughter and took some time to recover. "Alright, Little Miss Show-off. I too know what tergiversation means – and you are a tergiversator."

Kate had been caught in the act of smuggling *The Pilgrim's Progress* out of the house. Hazel assumed the girl was going to spend the afternoon reading with Grace and asked if it was indeed so. Kate, thinking quickly, realised that she was close to being caught out. She didn't want to lie about where she was going but was also reluctant to admit that she'd ignored her grandmother's advice about avoiding the watermill. So she told Hazel that Hugo Ash had asked to borrow the book – and immediately realised that she'd dropped herself into the fire. It was a stupid thing to say and opened up a stream of inevitable questions.

"How on earth did you meet Hugo Ash?"

"I was walking over the bridge a couple of weeks ago, and he was there, and we got talking..."

Hazel broke in, disbelief on her face. "Kate..."

Kate sighed, knowing full well that deception, tergiversation, wasn't going to work. "Sorry, grandma." She bowed her head; she was found out. "I saw him from the lane one morning. He was swimming."

"Swimming?"

"Bathing. In the millpond."

"Bathing…"

Kate felt cornered but looked up and answered defensively, "He's a nice man. Not like the stories. I spoke to him. I lent him *Robinson Crusoe*. He said he'd read it, and I said we'd exchange books every two weeks and swap thoughts. I liked him."

And that was when Hazel asked if Kate knew what *wilful* meant.

She knelt down, took hold of Kate's arms and looked into her eyes. "Never try to deceive me, Kate. Always be better than that."

Kate felt ashamed. Her lips began to tremble. "Sorry."

Hazel hugged her and said, "That's it then. We'll forget it. But I'm coming to the mill with you now, so Hugo understands that I know where you are."

Kate was instantly flooded with embarrassment. "Don't do that, grandma. I'll feel like a baby!"

"Kate, you're only eight years old. Do you know what he could do to you?"

"I'll tell him you know where I am. Look, if I'm not back by half past two you can come and look for me then."

Hazel stood, troubled. "Do you know what husbands and wives do together, Kate?"

Kate flushed red. "Yes, I think so. You mean…"

"What they do together at night, secretly, in bed?"

"I know what they do."

"How do you know?"

Kate mumbled, "People talk. Amy, Walter, Grace. Children talk, grandma. It's not wrong, is it?"

"No, it's not wrong – but you need to know this: Hugo Ash did those things with his own sister – not just once (although that would have been bad enough), but for years and years. And they say it was the same with his father. His father – with his own daughter. It's depraved, Kate. If Hugo could do that with his own flesh and blood, think what he might do with you." Kate looked at Hazel from beneath lowered brows. "There'd be no-one there to protect you, Kate."

"He won't hurt me."

"How do you know?"

"I know."

Hazel pursed her lips and stared hard at her granddaughter. "*Do* you know?"

"I do. I know." The statement was emphatic, delivered with quiet assurance.

Hazel paused, then sighed and lowered her gaze. She spoke slowly, deliberately. "Alright. You and me – I think we understand what we mean when we tell each other *we know*." She shook her head. "It's not the same as what other people mean when they use that phrase. Do you understand what I'm talking about, Kate?"

Kate nodded and said softly, "Yes."

"So, when you say *you know* that you'll be safe with him, I understand that to indicate a profound certainty. Is that what you mean?"

"Yes."

Hazel swallowed, looked at the girl for a moment, and said, "Alright. You can go."

Hugo couldn't hide his pleasure at seeing her. He wore his warmest smile as he opened the door.

"I didn't really think you'd come."

"Why? I said I would."

"People only come here when they have to – for work or repairs."

"Or the women," said Kate.

He tried to think of some witticism but gave up. "Yes, them too."

She offered him the book she'd brought, and he thanked her, setting it down on a small table nearby. "Let me show you round," he said, moving aside so she could enter. Kate stepped over the threshold, and he closed the door – just the two of them, alone. Hazel's words rang in her ears. If Hugo wanted to hurt her, she wouldn't be able to stop him. She felt nervous despite her previous certainty that she'd be safe. He sensed her unease. "Don't worry. The door's not locked. I have a bad reputation, I know."

"My grandmother didn't want me to come."

He nodded. "But you came anyway."

"We talked about it. She told me about your sister."

Hugo sighed. "It's true. It isn't a secret."

"Why did you do it?"

"Honestly? I don't know. My father was bad – and his father too..."

"If it was your father standing here now, and not you – would *he* be nice to me? Like *you're* being nice to me?"

Hugo thought for a moment. "No, probably not. He'd send you packing, maybe worse."

She looked up at him, eyes big, and said quietly, "I trust you."

Her simplicity, her honesty, touched Hugo's heart, and he felt his eyes fill with tears. The reaction took him by surprise. He turned quickly so she couldn't see his face, wiped away the moisture, sniffed and pulled himself together.

"I'm glad," he said. "Do you want to see the mill?"

She said she did.

The windows were all small, and the inside of the building was gloomy, frightening. The most intimidating machinery was on the ground floor, the Meal Floor. The huge, dark cogwheels had a menacing appearance; the pitwheel looked particularly terrifying, sharing its axle with the waterwheel on the building's exterior, and half-sunken in its narrow, black abyss in the floor. *What would become of a child if she fell into that hole?* Kate wondered. She'd be crushed in the mechanism, ground to a bloody pulp, her bones split into a thousand bitter fragments... She shivered.

"Upstairs?" asked Hugo.

"Mm," she agreed, frowning, reluctant.

There were voices whispering in the building. She'd become aware of them as soon as he'd closed the door.

"There are people," she said quietly.

"People?"

"In the mill. In the walls."

Hugo looked at her in silence. "Do you want to go outside?"

"No, let's keep going."

At the top of the first flight of stairs, they arrived at what he called the Stone Floor, only a fraction better illuminated than the floor below. There were the two sets of millwheels, lying horizontally in their cases.

"You should visit when it's in operation," said Hugo. "It all looks dead now, but it's impressive when all the equipment is spinning, and the pulleys and hoists are moving – quite a sensation."

Kate nodded but said nothing. The voices were muttering. The people were watching her, knew she was there.

The second floor, he called the Bin Floor. There was a little more light than below, but she felt just as uncomfortable. The room was dominated by two huge containers, ready to feed the grain to the machinery below.

"One more level," he said and led her up the final flight of stairs into the loft, tall and almost impenetrably dark. Her eyes adjusted, and looking high up among the beams of the ceiling, she saw the big pulley wheel that hoisted the grain sacks up from outside.

"What do you think?" asked Hugo.

"It's big," Kate replied. "Scary."

"No place for girls?"

"I don't mind the dark," she said. "But the people frighten me."

"You heard them straight away, didn't you?"

She nodded. "Who are they?"

"I don't know – I've never known. I'm amazed you can hear them."

172

"They know I'm here. They can see me."

He frowned. "Most people can't hear them. I've lived with them all my life. They've always been here. We've always heard them – my father, his father. The voices have always lived in the mill."

"They're angry, frightened," said Kate. She shook her head, frowned. "Some of them are not nice." She listened intently. "There are children too…"

"I think you've had enough," said Hugo. "Let's get you outside."

They descended quickly to ground level, and Hugo opened the door. Kate picked up the book they'd left on the table and stepped outside. It was a relief to stand in the sunlight again. She looked at him. "Did you finish the book I brought last time?"

He smiled. "I did. It's in the cottage. I'll get it."

"Can I come in?"

"Do you want to?"

"We could talk about what we've been reading."

He nodded. "Alright."

She followed him across the tailrace and past the millwheel. The cottage abutted the north wall of the watermill, accessed by a small wooden bridge over the leat stream. He opened the door and said, "Welcome to my den." Kate stepped inside and glimpsed a naked woman as she ran across the narrow corridor from one side of the dwelling to the other.

"That was Roz," said Hugo. "Don't mind her." He showed her to the kitchen and said, "I don't have much to drink, I'm afraid – only booze. I don't think your grandmother would approve if I gave you gin."

"No tea?" asked Kate.

"I'm afraid not. Sorry – I should have thought. I didn't think you'd want to come in here. I'll get some tea for next time. There's water of course. I could boil that."

"Don't worry," said Kate. "I'm not thirsty. I'll bring a picnic next time."

Roz appeared at the door; late twenties, long dark hair tied behind her, eyelids painted blue, lips scarlet, wrapped in a blanket, her bare feet brushing the stone floor. "Hello," she said.

Hugo introduced them. "Kate, this is Roz. Roz, Kate."

"Pretty girl," said Roz, entering the kitchen and sitting down. She reached out and ran her hand through Kate's hair, dropping the blanket and exposing one of her breasts. "Pretty girl," she repeated. "From the village?"

"From the farm," said Kate, glancing at Roz's nipple, fascinatingly large and dark.

Hugo said, "Roz hears the whispers."

The woman covered herself and raised her eyebrows in surprise. "You can hear them?" she asked Kate.

"Yes," she replied. "Can you hear what they say?"

Roz shook her head. "No. I hate them."

"I've had about fifty girls here since Cristina left," said Hugo. "Roz is only the third to hear the voices."

"They're ghosts," said Roz. "In the mill. They're hateful. I only come here because he pays good money." She indicated Hugo with a nod of her head, then looked directly at Kate. "How old are you?" Kate told her, and the woman continued, "Eight? Aren't you frightened? Most children would run all the way to Whitby if they heard noises like that."

"I didn't say I liked them," Kate replied.

Hugo interrupted. "Roz – Kate and I have got things to talk about. Go and warm the bed. I'll be there in half an hour."

She stood. "Gin."

Hugo indicated the appropriate bottle. "Don't get drunk."

Roz collected the flask and left the room, blowing Kate a kiss as she went. "Pretty girl..."

"Sorry about that," said Hugo.

At least she's not your sister, Kate thought. "So, what did you make of the book?"

"I enjoyed it," he said. "I didn't expect to, but once I'd made myself get into it – and found a good reading speed – I ate it up. Here it is." He collected the volume from the window-sill. "What's next?"

Their meetings continued throughout May. On the 6th she brought him *Travels into several remote nations of the world*, by Lemuel Gulliver; on the 20th, *The History of Tom Jones, a Foundling*, by Henry Fielding.

"You must have quite a library at your house," he said.

"My grandmother likes to read. So did my mother."

"Your mother's dead," he said.

"Yes. Last year."

"I'd heard that. As remote as I am here, that news reached even me. I'm very sorry."

"I miss her."

"Of course you do." He paused. "I had a good mother…"

Kate waited for more, but Hugo said nothing. His eyes were unfocused, images, memories playing in his mind.

"I think you should get out of the mill," said Kate. "Come and live on the farm."

"They'd never accept me," he replied. "I'm the outsider."

"You're not an outsider to me."

Hugo was quiet for a while, looking at her. "Do you know how important you've become for me? When I think of you, my mind is filled with the notion, *Friend*. You're the only friend I've ever had."

Kate felt embarrassed. "But you have the women from Whitby."

"They're not friends in that way – not in the way that you're a friend, Kate." He looked away. "Sorry – I shouldn't speak like that. I don't want to frighten you away."

"I won't run away. I'm glad we're friends. And my grandma's used to me coming here. She knows I'm safe with you."

14. THE LOOKOUT
Monday May 30, 1757, 2.38pm

The Lookout was built in the shape of a huge square with its southernmost side missing, the west and east wings joined at right angles to the long central span. It was four stories tall, excluding the low attic spaces, mostly unused. The labyrinthine cellars were vast and gave access to a subterranean passage that led to an icehouse a short distance to the west. The Lookout was not quite true to the east-west axis but was skewed twenty degrees so that its southwest corner was the most southerly point.

A narrow turret capped each of the outermost four corners of the edifice, that on the northeast extremity sitting atop a tower uniquely rising forty feet above the roof. Inside the turret at the top of this tower was the little room where the Wynter twins had perished half a century earlier. Like the other three turrets, it was surmounted by a short, tapered spire. Atop this particular minaret, the highest point of the building, sat a weathercock, mute and worn.

If the tower had been twenty feet higher – and if the weathercock had been a conscious living thing – and had this conscious living thing rotated through a clockwise circle beginning with the view directly to the north – it would have seen...

...the elevated village of Peak, slightly west of due north, almost two miles distant beyond woods and heathland, overlooking the cliffs and the sea. And half a mile inland – to the west of the village – the main road north to Whitby.

The weathercock commencing its rotation, the land's fractured edge comes into view, the North Sea rolling in. As the wind blows the weathercock further round, it follows the line of the coast southward, the woods falling back, exposing the open clifftop. In a hollow at the edge of the cliff, facing the wind and the sea, equidistant between the house and the village, our weathercock is just able to see a naked woman, blonde and fleshy, standing motionless, arms outstretched as if welcoming some elemental sea lover. A little south of her, and perched on the precipice itself, is the ruined tower from which the house takes its name.

Blown to face due east, the weathercock traces the fringe of the land as it descends, giving way to a rocky shoreline and shingle beach a little more than half a mile distant.

Fanned further, now facing southeast, the weathercock follows the rising gradient to more heathland, carved here and there by the silver trails of streams; a few trees, sculpted by the wind.

Continuing the rotation to face due south, the mute observer spies, in the far distance, Scarborough North Cliff, the road from Whitby running towards it in the right of the frame of vision.

Finally, the view to the west reveals the day's vault reflected in a distant lake. A large enclosure encompasses overgrown grounds full of ruined buildings and forgotten gardens, untended for fifty years, now without shape or form, extending half a mile to the wall at the estate's western edge. The drive can be seen running away to the iron gates and the road. Beyond the road, open country, woodland. On a clear day, it's just possible to see the moors in the distance...

A cool breeze ran through this elevated circle of observation – a breath of wind that was not present at ground level.

The newly constructed staff house, in the same shape as the school itself but of more modest dimensions, sat within its own gardens east of the Lookout, warming in the sun. Other buildings lay beyond that: the laundry; a cottage intended for the use of guests; the brewhouse; the carpenters' shop. A large and elaborate hedge-maze, set twenty yards southeast of the main building, waited for those who would risk losing themselves, its mouth open, inviting.

Delia Tweddle and Fanny Kirkbride were at work in the kitchen garden that lay close to the west wing; and Theo Westmoreland, footman, lazed in the nearby orchard with Rye Ousby, playing cards.

A low hedge separated the kitchen garden and orchard from a track that led directly from the drive. The runs for the hens and geese were on the far side of the track; the dairy, cowshed, and milking yard further along. Then came the peat bunker, the coach house and the paddock. Fifteen-year-old Nolly Arkwright was grooming the horses in the stable block, singing to them, petting them, naming them: Athena, Demeter, Hera, Aphrodite, Artemis, Nemesis...

Further out in the grounds behind the house lay more pens and enclosures, including the pigsty and the sheep shelters. Beyond those were two fields, scattered with grazing animals. A block of terraced cottages of the same age as the main house – dwellings for the farmers and gardeners – was set at the top of the fields. Beyond that, and hidden from view, lay the forge and the smith's cottage.

It was a calm, bright day with just a few wisps of thin cloud in the azure sky. Seventy girls, aged between ten and eighteen, were at their lessons, some singly, others in groups of up to ten. Some conjugated verbs in French, others translated texts from Latin; some read aloud from Shakespeare, others sat quietly at needlepoint; some wrestled with mathematical puzzles, others sang in harmony. Lovely, golden-locked Orla Stapleton, twelve years old, played a sarabande on the harpsichord while her tutor, Rider Browning, watched her, trying to imagine how indescribably beautiful she would be at the age of fifteen, sixteen...

Miss Stella Tenley, headmistress, sat in her office taking

afternoon tea with her assistant, Miss Ruth Marlowe. There was nothing of any import to communicate, and neither was good at small talk, so the room was quiet except for the occasional offering of "another cup?" or "another biscuit?" Ruth, always ill at ease around Stella, pretended to be absorbed with documents.

The four housemistresses (all spinsters in their twenties) – Denise Trent, Lettice Shelley, Eleanor Rodman and Eve Miller – were similarly at rest in their parlour, although they were noisier and more excitable, discussing the various attributes of particular gentlemen, a perpetual source of amusement.

Major Alfred Bentley – forty-six, rotund, moustachioed, endowed with an almost regal dignity that suited his role as porter – captained a group of men as they sat drinking Alvina Rowley's delicious lemon water on the benches in the turning circle at the main entrance: the school's medic, Doctor Hollis Wayland; the drivers, Kipp Nibley and Stanley Tanner; and the three carpenters, Chad Sandon, Ferret Colborn and Tom Thorne. Tom stood from time to time, unsuccessfully adjusting his testicles, seemingly unable to find enough room for them in his breeches. Hollis found the action so distracting that he wondered if, by some oversight of the Almighty, the man had been blessed with three.

"Nice to see you today, Doctor Wayland," said Ferret, filthy brown teeth glistening in his smile.

The doctor, dapper as ever, raised his glass to the man. "Similarly, Mr Colborn."

"Any of the girls need our attention?" Chad and Tom sniggered.

"Well, they're not made of wood, if that's what you mean," said the doctor, asking himself (not for the first time) how it was possible that these three silly, flesh-obsessed carpenters had been able to land jobs in a school for girls.

"More's the pity," said Chad. "I could spend a pleasant afternoon varnishing Annie Smyth."

His two colleagues guffawed in response, and Tom echoed, "...Annie Smyth."

Alfred Bentley shook his head in disgust. "You three – you never talk about anything else."

"In a place like this?" answered Ferret. "Surrounded by fair ladies? Come on, Alf – you can't say your immune."

"...immune," said Tom.

Kipp Nibley interrupted, hoping to deflect the subject. "Chad, I need you to look at a couple of carriage wheels."

"Aye-aye, sir. We'll do that for you," said Chad, and the affirmation echoed from Tom's mouth. "Aye-aye..."

Hollis Wayland downed his drink and stood. "That's me done, gentlemen. I'm back to work."

"See you at supper?" asked Alfred.

"Indeed you will," Hollis replied. "There's a rumour that roast beef'll be on the table. My favourite!"

Behind the house, far away above the top field, six men sat smoking on a wall, idly watching the young lambs. From right to left, these were: Speck Beckwith, John Eldenshaw, Tranter Tickle (farmers), and Ned Silden, young Solly Birtwistle and gnarled old Rabbit Shipley (gardeners). Speck's dog, Bastard, lay obediently beneath the feet of his master.

Speck Beckwith and John Eldenshaw were the two quiet ones. At forty-one, John was Speck's senior by three years. They'd arrived at the Lookout at almost the same time in 1755, and this would be their third summer working together. Their mutual introspection gave them a kind of bond that was not shared by the others. John had always been solitary, and Speck still mourned the loss of his wife, dead fourteen years. Despite the inward-looking nature that was common to them both, each made an effort to fit in with the others, and they half-listened to the discussion that was taking place. The men had voted Anne Smyth the best-looking female in the school, and the conversation was now becoming more specific.

"Alright," said Ned. "If Anne wins the top prize, does she also win the prize for best chest?"

"Oh, yes," said old Rabbit. "No doubt about that."

"Seconded," said Ned.

Solly pointed out that Ned's own young wife, Pixie, might be a contender in that category. "Your missus is pretty respectable in the frontage stakes, Ned."

Ned Silden thought for a moment and nodded. "You're right. Am I allowed to vote for my own set, though?"

"Course you are," Solly replied. "I'd vote for Pixie's bubs, even above Anne's."

"She'll be pleased you said that," Ned replied. "I'll pass your opinion on."

"What about Denise?" asked Tranter Tickle.

"Denise?" said Solly, frowning.

"Denise Trent," Tranter clarified. "Housemistress."

Eyebrows shot up along the row of men.

"Denise Trent..." said John Eldenshaw, nodding.

All six growled in agreement, and the bleating of the young animals in the field suggested concordance even from the livestock.

Rabbit took a deep draw on his pipe, held the smoke for a moment, blew it out through his nose, and said, "I wish I was thirty years younger..."

There was a pause, and Ned said quietly, "Eleanor Merrick." The name was rewarded with a few appreciative murmurs and a couple of explicit gestures.

Bastard lay asleep at his master's feet, content as far as it was possible to tell. His opinion on the subject in question remained obscure.

The seven maids designated as the girls' staff, not being required while lessons were in progress, were out on the Whitby to Scarborough road, enjoying an afternoon walk with the tutors' servants, Oswald and Portia Packard. Oswald wore his best hat and carried his shiniest cane.

"A fine afternoon, ladies!"

"Oh yes, Oswald!" they chirruped. "A lovely day." There were a few stifled giggles. Portia, thirty-one, blonde and pretty, glanced back at them, her face a hilarious caricature of her husband's pomposity. The maids burst into fits of girlish laughter. Oswald didn't care. He strutted along proudly, his ruddy complexion glowing, paunch proudly pressed to the fore, like a rooster in charge of eight hens.

Ethel Coombs, following on behind, was complaining again about men to Nellie Brent. Cady Weston, sick of listening to Ethel's moaning, stuck her fingers in her ears and rolled up her eyes, making Sarah Alston cackle.

The kitchen was a bustle of activity. Edie Ashton, Kim Kelsey, Maisie Blythe, Opal Clayden and Annie Alby were all involved in cleaning the dishes from the recently consumed lunch. Alvina Rowley (head cook) and her husband Rodney sat at the table with their feet up, drinking tea and watching their minions hard at work.

The cleaning staff were freshening the girls' dormitories on the second floor, although one of their number was missing.

"Where's Mabel?" asked Birdie Wade.

"She's around somewhere," replied Tillie Haley. "Maybe she's in the east wing."

But Mabel Stanton was not in the house. She was standing high up on the cliff, almost a mile away, lips slightly parted, eyes closed, arms outstretched, blonde hair brushed back by the light breeze, enjoying the sensation of the cool moss on her bare feet firmly planted a few inches apart, the kiss of the wind on her naked skin.

Twelve-year-old Slade Stone and his friend Lucas Dent, two of the soil-boys, lay asleep in their little room by the cellar door, very close, warm, more than best friends. They would wake late at night and begin the long job of freshening all the ash buckets and taking the full privy pails to the midden on their lantern-lit trolley. Jude Farlam, the third soil-boy, was already at work, emptying the privies in the staff building.

Milton York and Janet Illif, personal servants to Jacob Crowan and Stella Tenley, sat quietly in their office, alert for the summons of the master or mistress. The two had been in service together for many years in one of the big houses in Hull; their recent move to the Lookout had been at Milton's suggestion. Both were in middle age. They were grey, quiet, efficient. Milton was portly and as dignified as a naval vessel. He liked to study the Bible, and read sermons and associated theological texts. Janet was modest and lived in Milton's shadow. She made clothes for her nephews and nieces, all far away on the other side of the country.

Jacob Crowan, headmaster, sat at the desk in his study. His secretary, Knox Quinton – squat, muscular and ferocious in appearance – occupied a chair at the side of the room, close to a window. Opposite Jacob sat his visitor, Edgar Foxley, all the way from London.

"You've put together an impressive setup Crowan. I knew you would."

"Thank you," said Jacob. "I'm glad you approve."

"Approve? This is the finest school I've seen. The establishments at Tavistock and Aberystwyth are admirable enough, but this, this…factory that you've built is a model."

Jacob nodded, acknowledging the compliment.

"How many people do you support here?"

"More than a hundred and fifty, including the girls."

"In addition to the domestic staff, you'll be paying professional fees to your tutors – and you have a lot of them."

"Of course. Everyone here is well recompensed for their labours."

"And the cost of purchasing the house and grounds, the

restoration work – which I understand was extensive – and the designing and erection of the new lodgings for the tutors and staff..."

"Yes, it was a substantial sum, but more than adequately covered by those who will eventually enjoy the fruits of their investment."

Foxley smiled. "Good man." He sat forward in his chair and asked, "Are there any pitfalls, any potential hazards? How do you deal with mail?"

"There's been no problem so far. The girls all come from the street, or from workhouses, poorhouses, prisons – as you know. None of them has any parents or siblings – at least none that we know of – so there's no-one to whom they would write, or who might write to them. Most of the girls are illiterate anyway when they arrive here – and they're often in poor condition."

"Yes," said Foxley. "The scouts we use are skilled people. Your girls are supplied by Daphne Harlan and her group, aren't they?"

"That's right," Jacob acknowledged. "Very reliable people."

"Yes," Foxley agreed. "I have a lot of respect for Daphne." He paused a moment, recalling the brief affair he'd had with her almost ten years earlier. She'd ended it, but he didn't hold it against her.

"She's professional," said Jacob. "Calm – down to earth."

"Just so," said Foxley. "It can't be easy to spot genuine potential through half an inch of filth." He furrowed his brow and continued. "But surely, the girls must make friends here among themselves. Won't they write to each other?"

The problem had not yet arisen. Crowan's first consignment of ten girls, aged between sixteen and eighteen, would be travelling to London shortly. They'd be the first who might want to write home to their friends here in the school.

"We've thought of that," said Crowan. "We'll intercept incoming mail. I don't envisage a problem with letters on the

184

way out – those should be innocent enough."

"Of course. That sounds like the same kind of solution the other schools are planning," said Foxley. He thought for a moment and asked, "How many of your people know…?"

Jacob indicated Knox Quinton with a nod of his head. "Other than Quinton, only Stella Tenley. Even Stella's assistant, Ruth, is ignorant. So there are only three of us."

"That is excellent. No danger of spillages there. And all is on track for the first delivery?"

"Yes, ten girls, all ripe and ready, will be delivered to you in early July."

"Very fine, very fine. And among those ten…"

"Anne Smyth, yes." Jacob had been aware of Foxley's interest in Anne during their tour of the school and grounds that morning.

Foxley was picturing the girl in his mind. He'd meet the coach at King's Place and personally welcome Miss Smyth; personally show her what was expected of her.

"I shall look forward to seeing her in London," he said.

There appeared to be nothing more to say; the meeting was at an end. Foxley stood up, held out his hand, and Jacob rose and took it. "You are a genuine asset to our enterprise Crowan. And you shall continue to be well-rewarded. You have my sincerest congratulations."

"Thank you, Edgar. Have a safe trip home. Kipp will run you to the terminus."

As Jacob rang for his servant, Foxley turned to Knox Quinton. "Quinton," he saluted, "Very good to see you."

"Mr Foxley." Knox returned the gesture.

The door opened, and Milton York appeared. "York," said Crowan. "Mr Foxley will be leaving now. Ask Kipp to drive him to Scarborough, please."

York acknowledged the order and escorted Foxley from the room, closing the door behind him.

Crowan looked at Knox. "I knew he'd be impressed. I think we deserve a glass of sherry. Don't you?"

"I do most heartily concur."
Jacob gave a brief snort. Success delighted him.

15. EGTON MILL
June to September 1757

Something chased Hugo in his dreams. The voices that had been there all his life increased in intensity. Filthy mutterings, fevered images of fingers – his fingers – clawing a young body. He woke up drenched in sweat, panicking.

His cries, his thrashings, terrified the girls who occasionally shared his bed. They'd wake in fright, fearful for their lives – run away and lock themselves in one of the empty bedrooms. Roz visited only once more and told him she couldn't bear the voices any longer.

There was a particular menacing presence that frightened Hugo more than the rest. It was always there, night and day, rasping above the murmurings of the other souls, whispering to him, inciting him to dreadful things. It was an old voice, ancient; it had followed him for as long as he could remember, but now it wanted something specific.

Hugo's frenzied terror-riven sleep was filled with Kate – her flesh, soft as butter, separating beneath a sharp blade; screaming – her body hung on a hook as he peeled her skin away from the raw, bloody carcass beneath.

Crush her softness. The voice was strangely distorted, as if several men spoke at once. *Rape her. Split her open. She's a gift for you. Cut her – drink her virgin blood.*

He surfaced from the red realms of nightmare, horrified to find that his body wanted the child. "Who are you?" he cried out. "Leave me alone!"

The echoing voice laughed in the dark of the night, mocking him. *We are that which gives you authority to do as you please. She's yours to enjoy – yours to tear.*

When Kate appeared on July 1st, carrying Samuel Richardson's *Pamela* with her, Hugo wouldn't allow her into the cottage, fearing what he might do. Instead, they picnicked for the afternoon on the far side of the millpond. But the voices (he thought there might be three although they spoke as one) followed him even there.

Take her now! There was an urgency in the command. *No-one can see – she's undefended. Press her down, lift her skirts, force her, open her.*

Hugo stood. "Kate, go home."

She was alarmed. "What's wrong?"

"Go home. Now. Right now – please. Do as I say."

"You're frightening me."

He clenched his fists and strode away towards the mill cottage, trembling with the determination it took, his eyes fixed ahead. There was a crash of thunder in the clear blue sky, angry; it rumbled away, echoes running out to the encircling horizon.

Kate collected her things and left, fearful and confused.

The voice again, in the night. *We know this one from before, from long ago when this land was young. You see only a child; we see one who must bleed, one who must suffer. Slit her throat; cut her into pieces and boil off her flesh. Nail her skull to the lintel of your door for good luck.*

Kate returned only once more, two weeks later, on the 15th. She knocked at the door of the cottage, but receiving no answer, tried the mill. Hugo opened the door as she approached. He'd been waiting for her. He didn't smile, didn't say anything, but stood aside so she could enter, then closed the door – and locked it.

Fear gripped her heart straight away. "Hugo?"

"Kate."

"Why have you locked me in?"

"The girls from Whitby," he said. "I don't allow them to wear clothes when they come here. I think you should follow the same rule."

"Please don't talk like that."

"It's the rules. I'm afraid I'll have to tear your clothes if you don't do as I say."

"Let me out." She began to cry. Her heart hammered.

Hugo's impassive face crumbled. He blinked, looked at the door, then at Kate as if he'd only just woken up. "Oh, God..." he muttered. "Did I hurt you?"

"Please let me go," said Kate, voice trembling, lips quivering, cheeks wet.

Hugo unlocked the door and swung it open. "Away. Don't come back. It's not safe anymore. Stay away from here."

She needed no further prompting but left immediately, shaking with fright, eyes full of tears, basket gripped in her right hand.

Kate never saw Hugo again; their fortnightly ritual was over. A number of people visited the mill with cartloads of grain during the days and weeks that followed, but the door remained shut and the millwheel silent, fixed. The work that should have come to Egton Mill went elsewhere.

It was an unusually hot summer with a few ferocious thunderstorms. Hugh Flesher went to the watermill on several occasions, banged on the door, tried to peer through the small windows. Hugo Ash was known to be eccentric – often very drunk – and extended periods of non-communication were nothing new. But as the first autumn leaves fell, Hugh began to wonder what might lay waiting to be discovered behind the locked door.

On Monday, September 19th Hugh, Elys Buckley and Richard Swift broke into the mill cottage expecting to find Hugo dead in his bed; but the house was empty, the food rotten in the larder, the kitchen full of flies. The place had been unoccupied for weeks. They looked at each other in grim silence, returned to the mill itself and broke in through the meal floor entrance. The stifling air, shut inside for months, puffed out through the door, carrying with it the unmistakable stench of decay. They found Hugo in the loft. He'd shortened the rope that hung from the pulley wheel, fashioned the end into a noose, and hanged himself, kicking a chair away from beneath his feet. He'd been there all summer.

They cut him down and arranged for his burial at Glaisdale. Cristina was invited but didn't come. Only Hugh and Cornelius were at the graveside.

Hugo's suicide added even more darkness to the mill's reputation, and Hugh decided to have it boarded up and abandoned. He took his business to the windmill at Mickleby instead.

Hugo had left a note, prominently marked for Kate, on the table just inside the mill's entrance. Hugh was concerned that it might contain something upsetting, so he opened it and read it before passing it on.

Egton Mill
July 15

Dear Kate,
I have been troubled with terrible thoughts and have become concerned for your wellbeing. I think my time is up, and have decided to go before matters become still more unbearable. I'm very glad we met each other. You brought me more happiness in the short time we spent together than I knew in my whole life. Please do not feel sad for me. God bless you.
Your Hugo

Hugh handed the note to Hazel, who read it and passed it on to her granddaughter. Kate was distraught, and her recovery from the shock took months. She insisted on knowing how Hugo had killed himself. Hazel tried to hide it from her, but Kate became angry. Hugo had been her friend – she couldn't begin to grieve unless she knew. Hazel heard the wisdom in her granddaughter's plea and gave in.

The details haunted Kate. She imagined Hugo hanging there in the dark in his last moments, struggling, unable to breathe, frightened, alone in the silence with only the voices of the dead around him.

But Hazel was glad that Hugo's final message was a positive one. "You made him happy, love. When everyone else hated him, you brought love into his life. You can bring love into the lives of everyone. Make him proud of you."

16. CAPPLEMAN FARM
1757-59

The farm community diminished in size. Hugh Flesher's mother, Emmeline, died in December 1757 at the age of seventy-nine. Several of the men went off to join the fight against France in the summer of 1758, so Hugh was obliged to search among the nearby villages to find extra labour for the harvest.

Henry Flesher's infatuation with Meadow Reid remained firm, but Meadow lost interest in teasing him. She'd grown bored with the game as the years passed, especially since her friend Louise also appeared to find the spectacle tedious and predictable. Meadow felt entirely directionless. She didn't enjoy anything and found her monotonous existence pointless. She had no friends other than Louise and hated the vacuous libertine lifestyle that beckoned.

Her parents (particularly her mother) wanted her to join in with "The New Enlightenment". That meant taking part in their round of orgies. For her eighteenth birthday, Persephone had presented her daughter with a sheep-gut condom and a box of "powders", accompanied by a big smile that was intended to invite her into the wonderful world of newly liberated feminine "pleasures". But Meadow was now twenty-one, and the gifts remained in their boxes, unused. In any case, she found her parents' friends odious. She'd become used to seeing the act of copulation close up, having walked through the drawing room, packed with thrusting sweaty bodies, during several "celebrations", the grunts and moans, both male and female, conjuring in her mind the image of a pigpen. Her father would be bouncing some hopeful young actress in his lap, while her mother

– impaled beneath a flabby politician or bishop – would hold out her hand to Meadow and implore her to embrace the joys of the modern age.

It revolted her. She didn't want any part of it. What she *did* want was to utterly reject her parents' milieu, and that meant using their promiscuity against them. She needed to copulate off-compass – to find someone entirely outside their social circle and dangle the act in front of them. She needed to rut with someone they would consider to be a pig.

The thought of sex with Alder Swithenbank had never crossed her mind, but she found him by chance one Saturday evening, passed out on the riverbank near the watermill. Meadow, depressed and bored as usual, had been on her way to see Louise in the manor house but paused at the sight of the sodden man lying in the moss. She climbed over the wall, made her way down to him and kicked him gently, trying to get his attention. He turned over, and she saw who it was. He'd clearly been there for some time, but the pool of sick in which he was lying had not completely melted into the ground.

"Alder?" she said.

Alder groaned and didn't reply, although his eyes seemed to focus on her.

The light was dimming; it would be dusk in a while. Meadow checked the road and the watermill but could see no one. She unbuttoned her dress and slid her arms out of the sleeves, then worked her hands through the shoulders of her shift and pushed both layers of clothing down to her waist, exposing her breasts. She knelt on the ground next to Alder and waited for his reaction. He didn't move, although he stared fixedly at her. She wondered if he was even conscious enough to be aware of what was happening. Leaning forward, she unbuttoned his breeches and slipped her hand inside, but there was no reaction in Alder's flesh despite a minute or so of encouragement. He was too drunk to be of any use. She removed her hand. It was greasy, and stank. He was exactly what she was looking for.

Meadow stood up and dressed herself. Alder continued to watch but gave no sign that he actually saw anything.

"Remember me," she said, then went to the river and washed her hands. As she passed him on her way back to the lane, she paused, looked down at him. "Next time," she said, and was gone.

Hazel Priestly had schooled her daughter Nara very thoroughly, and Nara had done the same with Kate. At nine years of age, Kate was a sharp-witted, well-read, intelligent child who could reason clearly and was perceptive enough to pick up and interpret the tiniest vibrations of character and disposition in the people she knew.

When Alder staggered through the door after his encounter with Meadow, he found his daughter reading *The Adventures of Roderick Random* to Hazel. Kate had a different voice for each character. She stopped what she was doing and looked at him. He was filthy; mud, and worse, caked his skin, hair and clothes. His breeches looked as if they'd been buttoned by a two-year-old.

Hazel sighed. "Alder, you have to wake up out of this. You look terrible."

"Sorry," Alder managed, sitting on one of the wooden kitchen chairs.

"I'll fill the tub for you," said Hazel, getting up.

"I'll stop drinking...from today. Not another drop."

While Hazel was busying herself with setting up the bath and heating the water, Kate was thinking, *Something's happened – there's something new.* She'd detected a tiny note of determination in his voice.

"You've seen someone," she said.

Alder looked up at her, his astonishment burning a hole through his inebriation. "Seen someone...?"

"You've seen a woman."

Hazel glanced at him from where she stood gathering towels, her eyebrows raised.

"No, no," said Alder. "I've been asleep by the millpond. No women, just booze."

He rested his forearms on the table and allowed his head to fall on them, unconsciousness overtaking him once more.

During the next week or so, Alder began to return to something resembling his old self. He cleaned himself up and avoided alcohol. In the two years since Nara's death, he'd allowed flabbiness to creep up on him, but now he actively sought to reverse the decay, walking and running vigorously every day and applying himself with determination to his work on the farm. Hazel was amazed and found herself smiling now and then. Even Alder's sense of humour was returning. Kate thought, *He's after some woman.*

Tozer was happy to see his old friend regaining his former health, and like Kate, accurately guessed the reason.

"Who is she then, Alder?"

"I can't say yet," Alder replied. "Nothing's happened – maybe nothing will. But I feel better than I've felt in a long while. If she comes to me, all well and good. If she don't, there's a lot more tail in the world."

Nearly four months passed, and Alder began to think that his encounter with the bare-breasted girl had been a drunken dream. Then, one cold day in early February 1759, he looked up from his plough and saw her watching him from the road beyond the field. He stopped and shielded his eyes from the piercing low sunlight. At this distance, he couldn't be sure if it was the same girl, but she seemed to be staring at him intently. Tozer was in the next furrow along. He looked over at Alder and brought his animals to a halt before following the line of his friend's gaze.

"Friend of yours?" asked Tozer.

"Maybe," Alder replied. "Let's keep going."

They set the ploughs in motion once more and worked forward towards the road. As they got closer, Alder began to nod. "It is she," he said.

They both turned their animals at the top of the furrow, ready to return down the field; but Alder released his plough, nodded to Tozer and walked towards the watcher. Tozer observed from a distance.

"Do you remember me?" asked Meadow. The breeze had blown her hair across her face. She brushed it away and waited for Alder's reply.

"I do," Alder replied.

She looked him up and down. "You've got fit."

"I'm fit enough," said Alder.

Meadow was breathing deeply – felt she was falling from a height. There were no handholds, and it could only end one way. The course of events was fixed, inevitable – and she wanted it to be so.

"You're Alder," she said. "You were married to Nara."

"You know me," said Alder, his own excitement heightening.

"Do you know who I am?" asked Meadow.

"I know you by sight. I don't know your name."

"I'm Meadow." She pressed her lips together, moistened them, and asked, "Ever ploughed a meadow?"

Alder stared at her, heated, like the old days. He wanted her.

"Not one like you."

"Where?" she asked, voice trembling.

"It's a cold day, but I know a warm place," said Alder.

Meadow nodded, *yes*.

He looked back at the plough, at his friend. Tozer stood motionless, fascinated, observing the brief courtship. Then Alder led Meadow to the hayloft.

That evening Alder returned home to find that Hazel had been taken ill. Neil Levinson was upstairs in her room, and

Adam and William sat in the kitchen quietly awaiting his assessment. The boys had come back to the house at about four o'clock and found her collapsed on the floor. They'd lifted her upstairs onto her bed and managed to bring her round, but she had no memory of what had happened and remained very weak. William saddled a horse and rode to Easington to fetch the doctor.

Alder took the stairs two at a time and knocked at Hazel's door. The doctor's voice gave permission, and Alder entered the room. Hazel was lying on the bed, Neil taking her pulse. She looked bad, slick with perspiration, ashen white. Kate was cuddled up next to her on the bed. The girl was still cold, having only recently returned to the house from an afternoon of foraging in the winter hedges with Beatrice Swift and Grace Buckley.

"What's wrong?" asked Alder.

Neil shook his head. "Heart, I think."

Kate cast an anxious glance at her father, then turned back to Hazel and squeezed her arm. "Don't worry, grandma. You'll be alright." Hazel weakly hugged her granddaughter in return.

"Can you do anything?" Alder asked Neil.

"I've done all I can," said Neil. "We'll just have to wait and hope."

There was a knock at the front door. Alder gestured to the doctor, *back shortly,* and hurried down to the kitchen, but Adam had already let in Hugh and Amelia Flesher.

"Elys said he'd seen William galloping here with the doctor," said Hugh. "What's wrong?"

Alder said simply, "It's Hazel. Heart, Neil says."

Adam looked at him, concerned, and asked, "It *is* her heart then?"

Alder nodded. "Looks like it."

"Can we see her?" asked Hugh. Alder stood aside and motioned aloft.

Hugh and Amelia made their way upstairs, greeted Hazel

and the doctor, and sat on the edge of the bed. Amelia smiled at Kate, wishing she could reassure her. Hazel seemed a little more alert than before, was able to speak more easily and seemed calm enough.

William ran to Glaisdale to fetch Cornelius. By the time they returned, the company had swelled to include Bernard and Florence Swift, and Elys, Sally and Alicia Buckley. Alder managed to coax Kate downstairs to help with drinks and cake for all the visitors. Word had continued to spread – Apple arrived half an hour later. Hazel's guests sat with her two or three at a time.

"You're all making such a fuss," she said from her prone position.

"You're very loved, Hazel," said Hugh. "We want you to stay with us for many years yet."

It had been a strange day for Alder. His concern for Hazel was punctuated by the necessity of looking after all the visitors; and his mind was filled with Meadow – the scent of her skin, the memory of her body.

"You alright, Alder?" asked Neil, interrupting his reverie.

"Things are looking positive. I think she might pull round."

Hazel improved over the next few days, although she remained in bed most of the time. Kate felt a growing sense of relief. She'd lost her ma – she didn't want to lose her grandma too.

One tragedy seemed to have been averted, but another took its place. Three days after Hazel had been taken ill, Holly Robinson was found dead.

It was nearly noon, and the girl hadn't surfaced from her bedroom. Apple went to investigate and found that her twenty-three-year-old daughter had died in the night. It plunged the family deeply into grief. Their home had always been a happy one, and the hole left by bubbly, sunny Holly was one that could never be filled.

Her funeral was riven with sobbing and disbelief. Even Cornelius, steeled by thirty-five years of burials, could barely hold his emotions together. He had to pause repeatedly during his introduction, the prayers and his address, and only just managed to get through without breaking down. No-one ever knew why she'd died. Poor Holly's prince had never found her.

17. CLARA

Charles Sutherland was a lucky man. He came from a wealthy family, received a good education at Oxford and secured a well-paid job in the Bank of England, to which he travelled each day from his large house in Charles Street, Westminster.

His attractive but domineering wife was a musician – a harpist – and had gathered a flourishing stable of young lady students. Juno Sutherland never wanted a family – she only wanted luxury, money and respect. She wanted to rise above her peers; to always be at least one step ahead of them; to always be better dressed and finer looking than they were. And she succeeded; she was happy with her life – until she became pregnant with her daughter Clara. Children had not been part of her grand plan; such a thing could not be permitted to happen again.

She and Charles came to an understanding. He would no longer sleep in her bed; their intimate relations would cease. He was free to take a mistress as long as he kept her to himself and didn't bring her near the house. The arrangement suited Charles, and he took up with Drusilla Glanville, visiting her at home in Vine Street, just a few minutes' walk south past the new Westminster Bridge. Drusilla was married. But her husband didn't care – he preferred the maids, and in any case, had mistresses of his own.

Charles and Juno continued happily enough, and it appeared to the outside world that nothing had changed – except they had a lovely little daughter.

Clara learned to play the harp under her mother's instruction. She grew long-legged and beautiful, with a mass of black hair, and brown eyes that had an intriguing tint of red in them. Her parents made a point of behaving well in front of her, but she knew something was missing in their marriage and once or twice caught sight of her father and Drusilla in the street.

By the time Clara reached her seventeenth birthday she could play the harp rather better than her mother and began to gather students of her own. Juno was not happy about her daughter's rivalry, and their relationship developed a frostiness that it never threw off. Juno could be mean and vindictive, so Clara developed the same kind of selfish nature in response.

Sensing her mother's prudishness, Clara became promiscuous to spite her. Her first targets were the two footmen and the driver. They were dismissed by Juno and replaced with others who were made to understand that any fraternisation with their mistress's daughter would result in immediate termination of their employment, without reference. (Juno never found out about Clara's relationships with the maids.)

Juno was the second of four children. Her elder brother, Vincent Mortimer, was a well-respected maker of violins – and Vincent's son Peter was an apprentice organ builder. Robbed of the ministrations of the footmen, Clara made her way across London to the organ builder's workshop and made herself available to her cousin, who cleared a space for her, after hours, on the floor of the pipe shop.

Clara wanted to get out from under her mother's thumb. Peter, well aware of Clara's expertise as a harpist, told her about a new school in Yorkshire.

"We're building an organ for the chapel there," he said. He indicated a few pipes, set upright nearby. "There's the trumpet stop, half-finished." He pointed elsewhere. "And there you can see the keyboards, and some of the action coming together behind. It'll go in next year."

"Organs are boring," said Clara. "I don't come here because of the pipework."

The reply was on the tip of his tongue, but he stopped himself – it was just too cheap a joke.

"I know. But I'm telling you this because they teach music. It's a school for girls. Nice place; pots of money. I've been up there. I think you'd love it. I bet they don't have a harp teacher."

He gave her the address, and she wrote for details.

Clara moved out of London, and out of her mother's life, in April 1758, just before her twentieth birthday. Peter had been right. She loved the Lookout.

Clara and Vivianne. Saturday October 21, 1758

"Who are you going to see?" asked Viv. She lay on her side in Clara's bed and watched the older woman brush her hair.

"Kipp," replied Clara. "You can stay here as long as you like. Go to sleep. I might not be more than an hour or two. You can keep the bed warm."

"What's it like?" asked Viv.

"You mean what's it like with Kipp? He's good – better than a lot of men." Her voice gained a dismissive tone. "Better than Rider."

"I like Jacob," said Viv.

Clara stopped brushing and looked at her. "Why?"

Viv lay on her back and looked at the ceiling. "He takes me seriously."

"*I* take you seriously."

"I know you do. But he reads what I write. Sometimes I sit and watch his face while he reads. He reads properly, deeply. I feel valued when he concentrates that way on my work. I mean, I feel as if I've written something that's *worth* his attention. I suppose I write for him – more than anybody. He really cares. He's constructive, complimentary. He makes me feel good. He doesn't treat me like a girl."

"Well, you write very well, Viv. It's not surprising that he appreciates your stuff."

"No-one else has ever read my stuff the way he does. It makes me like him. I appreciate him because he appreciates me. I think I love him a little."

Clara turned her attention back to her hair. "Sounds like you'd be an adoring little ramrod-polisher."

Neither spoke for a while. Then Viv said, "How old do you think Jacob is?"

"I don't know for sure. About thirty."

"Am I too young for him?"

"Yes."

Viv looked directly at her. "That was a very quick answer."

"Well, you *are* too young for him – of course you are."

"I'm fifteen."

"Too young."

"Not too young for *you,* though."

"No, not too young for me."

"So why am I too young for Jacob? I'm old enough to get married. I don't have any parents to stop me – I could do it if I wanted."

Clara put down her brush and looked at Viv. "Listen. Wait a few years. Keep writing. Jacob's an intelligent man. He appreciates maturity. He'll value you more and more. Go carefully, be subtle."

"*You're* telling *me* to be subtle?"

Clara stood, ready for her encounter behind the stables with the coachman.

"Don't do as I do – do as I say. We want different things, you and me. You want love – I just want attention."

"Thanks, Clara. I'll write your biography one day."

Clara laughed, threw a cushion at her friend, opened the door and left.

18. DUBLIN
1755-59

Colleen was happier than she'd ever been. Her only sorrow was that her mother had never met Alex, had never known that such a good man wanted her. Alex was warm, tender. They'd lie together in bed in the dawn light, she on her left side, he pressing in behind her, their bodies as one. He'd say, "Colleen, I love you." She'd softly reply, "I know you do, my sweet one." They liked to have the window open unless it was very cold, the breeze, like the sky's kiss, brushing them in the room. There'd be the cries of the gulls, the crows, the wind, the early morning sounds of Dublin.

Colleen lost her baby at seven months. She'd known since early morning that something was wrong. Alex fetched the midwife, and the three of them waited together in the bedroom at the Unicorn. Colleen bled steadily for most of the day, but at about five in the afternoon there was a tremendous surge of blood. All over the mattress. It was shocking; she hadn't realised there was so much blood in her. Alex was horrified – struck into stillness, didn't know what to do or say. A moment later the baby was there, a boy, lying in the slick red pool, completely still. The midwife wrapped him in a blanket and handed him to Colleen. Alex looked at his son. The tiny child was fully formed; dark hair, soft fingernails already long, the intricate patterns in the skin of his fingertips...
Colleen quietly said, "Our baby."
The midwife looked at Alex and asked if he would like to hold the child. Alex shook his head. He couldn't bring himself to touch the boy. It was a decision he'd regret to the end of his life.

Then Colleen vomited, her eyes turned white, and she collapsed, unconscious.

The midwife expected Colleen to die and sent Alex running for a priest. He performed the task as quickly as possible, not wanting to be away from Colleen, and was back within twenty minutes. The priest slapped a small box containing the consecrated host on the bedroom table and stood over Colleen as he uttered the words of the last rites. There followed a much-truncated version of the prayer of the Eucharist, then the midwife opened Colleen's mouth, and the priest placed a tiny fragment of the Body of Christ on her tongue before concluding the ritual with a blessing in the name of the Pope. Alex sat, confused and horrified, lips parted, unable to believe what was happening. The priest left, "Bless you, son," giving Alex a gentle pat on the shoulder as he passed by.

But against all the odds, Colleen didn't die. She lay unconscious all that night and most of the following day but eventually woke up, extremely weak and unable to walk. The midwife fetched a doctor, and Alex looked after Colleen under his guidance. The process of recovery was a lengthy one, and the Unicorn remained closed during its course, but in about six weeks Alex's wife was able to take short walks with him in the open air.

He was overwhelmed with relief that Colleen had survived, but the fact of her survival dominated his thoughts so completely that it took him months, years, to fully realise what a profound mistake he'd made in not handling his child. That physical contact might have given him the means he needed to close a wound that never healed.

In the fullness of time, the Unicorn reopened with a party at which the regular customers welcomed back their familiar landlords. Brian Murphy was glad to see the two at work again. He was fond of them; they lent the place a unique atmosphere.

Colleen fully recovered. She knew that Alex was grateful to

get her back, and their life regained most of its former contentment, although there was a hole of deep sadness, rarely articulated, that should have been filled by the missing child. Alex's early morning lovemaking was as caring as ever, and Colleen often lay facing him afterwards, descending into warm sleep as he cradled her in the crook of his arm and caressed her body, her head nestled beneath his chin while he kissed her hair. She felt so safe with him.

Despite all their efforts, Colleen was never able to conceive again. The months turned into years. Their physical relationship cooled, although they remained devoted to each other. They kept up their association with Holy Trinity, attending every Sunday and occasional feast days. They both knew they would never have a family, and Colleen irrationally felt that part of the blame was hers. It was *her* body that had let them down. More than once, she stood naked and looked at herself in the long mirror in their bedroom (a wedding gift from the Murphys). The sight made her sad. She'd cup her hand over her belly, knowing it didn't work. The tears she shed were mostly inside; she knew she was partly dead already.

Fortunately, she was still close enough to Alex that they could talk about such things, and he listened, heartbroken when she told him how she felt, his helpless love for her swelling up. Something important was broken in her spirit.

Colleen began to hurt herself. She would sit quietly and cut her forearms with a knife, needing to feel the pain, watch the slow trickle of blood. She was a failure as a wife and as a mother. She deserved the pain, although there was a kind of calmness in watching the wound heal too. It broke Alex's heart when he saw this, and Colleen could find no words that adequately explained to him why she had to do it.

And then Fintan O'Rourke came into their lives. Fintan was

in his early forties – a big, powerful labourer who worked on the docks. He sat drinking in the Unicorn and took a liking to Colleen.

"I dream about you at night, little girl." She was fascinated by his determination to get her. Alex never spoke like Fintan – he would never be so bold or forceful.

"You're a pretty wee thing, so you are…with your soft skin and your angel's hair."

Alex watched Fintan's advances from a distance, dreading the touch that would necessitate a response.

But Fintan was not so clumsy; he pressed ahead inch by inch, backing his prey into a corner. "I could show you a thing or two…you know?"

"Could you now?"

"Aye, I could. Just on the quiet. Your man – he'd never know."

She looked across the bar at him, disgusted but also in the drag of his magnetism.

"You'll be thinking about me. You will," he muttered, with practised seduction.

There was a storm of conflicting emotions in her head. Part of it was self-loathing brought about by her failure to become a mother. She needed to embrace the physical action of unfaithfulness to sufficiently inflame her self-hatred. Part of her wanted to give Alex a reason to leave her – to go away and find someone who could genuinely provide a family for him. If she took Fintan to bed, she wouldn't have to plead with Alex to leave. She'd give him the justification – take all the blame for the failure of their marriage on herself – make it easy for him. She decided to make use of the brute.

Colleen waited for Alex to spend a few hours away; then she made herself available for the big, powerful docker. She was astonished at Fintan's vigour. His copulation was aggressive to the point of violence, and he swore continuously while it was taking place, heightening his excitement by mouthing foul things to her about what he was doing. The more abusive he became, the more Colleen felt she deserved his abuse. She actually began to feel grateful to him, as if she were receiving punishment long overdue.

She timed their next coupling in the expectation that Alex would find them. He'd gone to Ormond Market to buy fish, and Colleen knew he'd be no more than half an hour. What she was doing would hurt him terribly, but she'd made up her mind it was the simplest and most direct course of action.

Alex returned to the Unicorn and heard Fintan's abusive growling as it drifted downstairs from the bedroom. He set his basket of fish on one of the tables and ascended to the upper floor, where he found his wife in bed beneath the big man. Colleen heard the stairs creak and watched as the door opened. Fintan caught the direction of her gaze and looked around over his left shoulder.

"You fuckin' peepin' little gobshite!" he cried. He was furious, leapt from Colleen and came straight at Alex, despite his priapic nakedness. Alex stood motionless, stunned, mutely watching his wife as she rose from the bed in alarm. Fintan punched Alex in the face, a blow so hard that it knocked him through the bedroom door and down the stairs.

"Fintan!" shouted Colleen, running at him.

"Shut the fuck up, woman!" he yelled, turning to face her.

Colleen screamed, "Fuck off out of here, yer fuckin' animal!" She tried to slap him, but Fintan sidestepped the blow and kicked her squarely between the legs, sending her flying back towards the bed. She landed on the floor, struck her head on the wooden frame, and howled in pain. Fintan quickly pulled his clothes on, gobbed on Colleen as she lay massaging herself in agony, and left. She heard him curse as he booted Alex before slamming the door.

There was silence. She listened hard. No sound at all downstairs. A pigeon began its gentle call nearby. After a

208

moment, Colleen got to her feet, knees pressed together, hands cupping her crotch. She'd never before suffered such a blow. She looked at her fingers, her palms, red with blood. The soreness made it difficult to dress, but she managed to get her shift on and eased down the stairs a step at a time. Alex was sitting at a table, his head in his hands. She settled opposite him, wincing in misery.

"Are you alright?" she asked.

He looked at her, didn't reply straight away. He was crushed inside – she could see it.

"Why?" he asked, his brow furrowed, head shaking.

She looked down, felt frightened. The structured reasoning with which she'd planned these events suddenly seemed false. The beating administered by Fintan, and the heartbreak she saw in Alex's eyes, joined to become a kind of absolution for the "sin" of her failure as a wife. She no longer wanted him to go.

"I'm sorry," she said. "Please forgive me."

He looked at her, nursing her wound, rocking back and forth with the discomfort.

"Are you hurt?"

She nodded.

"Can I see?"

She nodded again and allowed him to take her upstairs. The position she had to adopt for Alex to see the injury was similar to that in which she'd vented her dead baby, and she began to cry pitifully. The flesh was split, red, swollen, dripping blood; she'd soon be black with bruising. He fetched water and some towels and cleaned her up as best he could.

Colleen stayed in bed for a few days while the wound healed, and Alex joined her at night, held her in his arms as he always had. But the simple, intimate trust that had previously been at the core of their relationship was gone and never came back. They rarely smiled at each other. Both knew they were broken.

One Friday morning, about two months after the incident, Alex fetched Aoife to the Unicorn so Colleen wouldn't be alone. Aoife sat silently in the bar and waited. Alex packed his things into a sack as he'd done for his long walk from Bandon years before. Colleen watched as he did so, then followed him downstairs. Aoife sat at a distance and observed but took no part in their farewell.

Alex and Colleen stood silently a foot apart; then he reached out, looked into her eyes and gently squeezed her left arm. It was the end. The next moment he was gone. She stood quietly, looking at the closed door.

Colleen slept alone that night, and the next, and the next. She would wake early in the morning, her husband's side of the bed cold, and listen to the wind, and the cries of the gulls, the crows...

Alex took the packet-boat from Dublin Bay and left Ireland for the first time in his life. As the vessel set sail, he looked back at the city and made himself reflect on what he was leaving behind. He was deliberately abandoning the woman he loved. It had taken him weeks to come to this decision; it had seemed the best thing to do. He reasoned that he wanted the two of them to separate while there was still fondness between them. He'd convinced himself that they'd only drift further apart if he stayed; they would begin to resent each other, then perhaps to hate each other. He still loved her; he wanted to always love the memory of her. But now, as the buildings grew smaller with distance and the ship gathered speed in the wind, he wasn't so sure. If he acted immediately he might be able to swim back, to take her in his arms, to say sorry, tell her he loved her... His chest heaved, and the tears began to flow.

But within minutes it was too late. There was no going back.

The crossing to Liverpool took fifteen hours. The sea was

choppy, and it rained for most of the journey. Alex had heard of seasickness, so wasn't entirely surprised when he found himself retching over the side. He managed to find a bench below decks on which to sleep, but his rest was damp and fitful, full of remorse and indecision. Perhaps he should turn around at Liverpool and go straight home. Would Colleen have him if he did?

The boat arrived in the very early morning. Alex lay on his side, stiff and uncomfortable, as it creaked into harbour. He'd changed his mind again – decided to look to the future, to an entirely new life. So he made his way along the plank to the dock and set out north, confidently and without hesitation. He had no specific idea of where he was going but had read about the English Lakes, and there was a vision of hills and water in his mind.

The journey began well despite the continuing rain, but he soon found himself flagging, fatigued. He stopped at Maghull for lunch, then struggled on to Ormskirk for the evening, taking a room at the Castle Inn. His mind was filled with Colleen. He'd been a fool. He must return to her. He'd write her a letter and tell her he was coming home.

Having arrived at this decision, he felt calmer and was able to sleep.

The morning found him well refreshed. The determination he'd felt in the dark hours had turned about, and he now felt that having set his resolve ahead, he must continue. He would carry on deeper into England, although he would write to Colleen soon.

Alex set out after breakfast and reached Brig by dusk, securing a room at the Cherry Tree. The night found him in very low spirits. He felt immature, thoughtless, selfish, full of regret. He couldn't get to sleep but sat most of the night at the window looking at the stars and the empty road. What was she doing? Cursing him probably. Was she crying alone? The thought made him feel horrible. He should be with her, comforting her.

Alex woke very late the next day, having sat at his window till dawn. He felt ill and avoided breakfast. Picking up his bag, he wondered if he should stay another day and recover but decided against it. It was a bright day in late October; the rain had stopped. He should make the best of it.

He set out at noon but felt increasingly worse and was forced to drop his breeches in a nearby field to relieve himself.

(*Oh, that's not good...*)

Dizziness overcame him when he stood, and he had to slump on a nearby wall for twenty minutes, feeling dreadful. He was sick – it was obvious. He staggered on for a mile or two, his heart beating fast with the effort, but soon collapsed behind a hedge and slept for most of the afternoon.

Alex woke in the cool dusk. Sensing he was a little recovered, he took up his bag and walked on for about two hours, but his bowels still bit, and he paused several times at their command. The sky grew dark, and no town was in sight. His weakness returned, and he realised he couldn't go on. He dropped his sack of belongings and sat down at the side of the road.

Faint sounds approached; voices, possibly horses too. Perhaps he could ask for help. There was enough moonlight to distinguish the approach of two mounted men. Alex stood up and hailed them as they approached.

"Could you direct me to an inn please, sirs?" he said.

The horses drew to a halt, and one of the men leaned towards him. "Irish?"

"I am, sir. Arrived a few days ago."

"What's in your sack?"

He was immediately fearful. "Just a few things."

The men dismounted. "Just a few things," one of them repeated, readying his pistol. The other man approached from the left.

"I don't want any trouble," said Alex, but it was too late. They set about him with their fists; one of them clubbed him savagely with the butt of his gun for good measure. When Alexander was down, they kicked him into unconsciousness. Then they stripped him, stole his bag and rode off, leaving him for dead.

19. CAPPLEMAN FARM
February-April 1759

Meadow decided not to tell her parents about her coupling with Alder, fearing they simply wouldn't believe it, thus wasting her efforts. She needed to be sure she could rub their noses in what she'd done – make them see how deeply she despised their way of life, their empty values. If she moved in with Alder – that would do it. But how? Alder was just a piece of equipment she'd used to break herself out of her parents' world. She certainly didn't love him, although the physical process she'd been through at his hands had not been entirely unpleasant – she admitted it to herself. But to move into Alder's house would involve her acceptance by the other members of his household. She knew that Hazel Priestly was still there, although apparently bedridden. Then there were the two sons, Adam and William. How would they feel about this potential cuckoo in their nest? And Kate? Meadow didn't like children much. Kate was said to be a sensitive child with a sharp tongue. They'd probably hate each other. She couldn't decide how to progress her plans.

The days began to lengthen. Meadow wanted to keep her association with Alder simmering so she could have it ready to display should a suitable opportunity present itself.

One Wednesday in mid-March, she woke to find the spring sun blazing brilliantly through her bedroom window. The bright morning light energised her, and she went looking for Alder. As she strode purposefully over Beggar's Bridge she decided to plant in Alder's family the first awareness of her presence. She rounded the corner at the top of Watermill Lane, opened the gate to Vine Cottage and knocked at the door. Kate, a slender, strikingly beautiful girl, opened it and looked up at Meadow.

"Hello," she said.

Meadow nodded. "Is Alder at home?"

"No," said Kate. A pause. "Is it *you* then?"

Meadow was unprepared for such a direct question, albeit an oblique one. "I'm not sure what you mean."

"He doesn't drink any more. That's probably because of you."

Meadow felt she was being addressed by someone her own age, but Kate hadn't even reached her tenth birthday. There was something about the child that made Meadow feel very uneasy. Kate's hair was shockingly red, and her hazel eyes were intensely piercing, as if she were able to see all the way to the bottom of Meadow's soul. Perhaps Kate could see everything that made Meadow who she was. Could she even see her schemed pursuit of Alder? The impression cut through her, knocking her off-balance for a brief moment, defensive. But then she thought, *Mind your own business! What's it got to do with you?*

"He's just a friend," she said.

Hazel called from within, "Who is it, Kate?"

Kate turned and shouted, "It's daddy's girlfriend."

Molten embarrassment flooded through Meadow. Her eyes widened in shock, and she turned and strode back along the short path to the gate. Kate called after her, "He's working in the woods. You'll need to go all the way to the warren."

Meadow didn't acknowledge the information but walked quickly away in the direction of the barns and livestock sheds. She felt as if she'd received a slap in the face, but couldn't tell if the slap had been an insult or a bizarre kind of greeting. She was disoriented, confused. As she furiously stamped off her indignation, Meadow wondered if the girl was always like that – unpredictable, abrasive.

The labourers' dwellings and the big wooden water pump appeared in the distance, and Meadow slowed her pace.

Am I really going to walk all the way to the warren?

If she took the road to the village and then turned right along the west side of the common, the journey would take more than an hour. She stopped walking, looked down and thought, *Honestly, can I be bothered?* But then Kate's face appeared fresh in her mind, as if in mockery.

I will, damn it. I'll find him. He'll do as I tell him, whenever I tell him to do it!

Opposite the lower gate of the meadow, she turned right and took a shortcut north following the hedges. The lower field, on her left side, was planted with cereals; the upper field beyond it was prepared for the planting of potatoes the following month. The field on her right was full of heavily pregnant cows and a few calves. In her haste, Meadow had forgotten about the large area of marshland above the fields. She cursed and traced her way west along the top of the upper field, eventually arriving at the bank of the Esk, at which point she turned north again and followed its course upstream, the land rising and becoming dryer. Soon she was able to see the western edge of the wood, Glaisdale common behind her, away beyond the bend of the river. She left the bank and walked uphill towards the warren.

I'm a complete fool, she thought. *I've come all this way – for what? Indignation? Obsession? Idiot!*

She was exhausted and sat down on the trunk of an old tree to get her breath.

As she rested there, almost overcome with futility, she looked up and caught sight of a cottage at the edge of the woods, just outside the ring ditch. Perhaps whoever lived there might direct her to where the men were working.

Buffy Miller opened the door in response to her knocking. "Meadow! You're a long way from home."

"Pond Girl!" exclaimed Meadow. "So this is where you live."

Buffy, seventeen, pretty, freckled, light brown hair plaited into a single long tail, invited Meadow inside. The cottage was dark, smelled damp and was cluttered with things. "Ma's stuff," said Buffy. "She keeps everything. Sorry about the mess."

There was a surprised shout from deeper in the house. "Buffy? We got visitors?"

"It's Meadow Reid, ma."

Natty Miller came rushing into the parlour, wiping her hands on her apron. She looked as mad as ever, grey hair all over the place, eyes wide, several teeth missing from her smile, grimy. "We never 'ave visitors!" she exclaimed, then widened her eyes in demonic suggestion. " 'Ave some gin!"

The invitation surprised Meadow, but a second's reflection suggested that it was an excellent idea, particularly after her exertions in getting to this spot, so glasses were brought and the bottle opened. Buffy drank slowly, but Natty downed the spirit in one swallow. Meadow was familiar with hard drink but not in such large quantities. Nevertheless, she felt goaded by Natty's display and joined her in a second glass. Then a third.

Pond Girl's first measure sat only half consumed on the table. "Meadow," she said. "Do you think this is a good idea?"

Meadow yawned and opened her eyes wide in response to Buffy's question. It was intended to be a comical gesture: *Do I look like I care?*

" 'Nother one?" crowed Natty.

"Well...How could I refuse? Thank you." It was her fourth glass. The room was spinning clockwise. Why was she here? There had been a reason..."I'm looking for Alder," she managed.

"Alder?" replied Natty, seemingly unaffected by the alcohol. "He's working just over in the woods with Nicholas and the others. Pollarding."

Meadow finished her final drink and stood. "Well..." she

217

felt very dizzy and thought she would fall, but Buffy rose and steadied her. "I'd better go and find him, hadn't I?"

"I'll go with you," said Buffy, concerned.

"Thank you," said Meadow in a drawn-out hoot.

As the two passed through the open door, Natty called, "Come again, Meadow! I've got a lovely bit o' rum!" Meadow didn't turn but raised her hand in a rear salute.

The men were not far away. Buffy's brother Nicholas was there – also Alder, Brendan Telford and a few others. Alder saw Meadow coming, supported on Buffy's arm. "What's this...?" he said. Work ceased, and they all watched in silence. Brendan opened his mouth, about to make a joke, but immediately thought better of it.

Buffy let go of Meadow and allowed her to walk the last few steps towards Alder unaided. The two stood facing each other. It was clear to all present that there was some connection between them. But then Meadow frowned, and her hand went to her mouth. She collapsed on all fours, moaned, and threw up violently. As she knelt there, weak, helpless, it occurred to her that the roles adopted by Alder and she at their first meeting had been reversed.

Alder squatted, put his hand on her back. "Get it all up," he said.

"Oh God!" said Meadow. "I feel sick."

Nicholas and Buffy looked at each other. "Ma?" asked Nicholas.

Buffy nodded and replied, "Four gins. Big ones."

Alder addressed the workmen. "We finished here for the day?" There was a murmur of agreement, and they began to gather up their things.

He knelt by Meadow's side for a while longer, rubbing her back, comforting, then asked, "Can you stand?"

She didn't reply but cautiously got to her feet, Alder helping. Having arrived more or less at the vertical, she bent forward, hands on knees, and whispered, "Oh my God, oh my God..." while a sticky thread of drool spilt idly from her lower lip.

The men had prepared the cart to take them home and fixed the horse back into its traces. Alder made a place for Meadow behind the driver's box. "Come on," he said. "Up you come." She put her arms around his neck, and he lifted her into the waggon.

"Thank you," she managed, shuffled to her spot, lay on her side, curled up and passed out. The other men clambered in, glancing with fascination at the unconscious young woman.

Nicholas and Buffy waved them off, and Alder drove south along the edge of the common, through Glaisdale and left, into the farm. Brendan and the others jumped out one by one as they passed their dwellings, and Alder drove on to Vine Cottage, pulling up at the front gate.

Meadow was still fast asleep, snoring noisily. Adam, William and Kate, all arranged at the kitchen table, watched in bewilderment as Alder carried her into the house.

William voiced the question. "Who's this?..."

Kate's face was cracked into a little grin. "That's dad's fancy-lady."

"Watch what you say there," warned Alder as he carried the inert girl upstairs, taking care not to knock her head where the staircase turned beneath the landing.

Adam and William looked at each other, eyes wide, brows raised.

Alder set Meadow down on his own bed, fully dressed, ensured she was as comfortable as possible and returned to the kitchen, where he pulled out a chair and sat down at the table, avoiding all eye contact.

"Dish of tea?" William asked quietly, and Alder nodded.

Adam went to stable the horse and put the cart away.

That night Alder slept on the kitchen settle.

He left early in the morning to get back to the pollarding, and the brothers went to the calving shortly afterwards.

Hazel rarely left her bedroom, so Kate was alone down-stairs in the cottage. The morning grew late, and there was no sign of Meadow.

At eleven o'clock Kate boiled some water and took tea to the door of Alder's room, knocking gently in case the occupant was still asleep.

"Who is it?" Meadow's voice – subdued, weak.

"I made you some tea," said Kate and opened the door.

The windows were open; there was a breeze in the room. Meadow was fully clothed and perched unashamedly on Alder's close stool, her dress arranged to cover her, feeling too ill to care who saw her there. She looked up briefly. "Thank you."

"How do you feel?" asked Kate.

Meadow shook her head, eyes closed.

Kate stood silently for a moment. "It'll pass in a while."

Very quietly, "Mm."

"I'll get you some warm water. Have a wash. It might help." Then she was gone.

Meadow resumed the slumped posture she'd settled into before Kate's arrival and could easily have gone back to sleep right where she sat. She'd never felt so bad in all her life.

Sometime later she managed to get to her feet with sufficient confidence to wash all over. Kate was right – the action of cleansing herself did seem to help in the recovery, although her head throbbed and she felt weak. The cool of the room freshened her, and she began to think she might not die.

At half past one she dressed herself and went downstairs. There was no sign of Kate, but Hazel was sitting in the kitchen. Meadow had seen her several times from a distance, but they'd never spoken before. She was shocked at the older woman's appearance. Hazel looked old and tired, and the act of standing to greet her visitor seemed to require an effort.

"Meadow."

"Mrs Priestly. How are you?"

Hazel motioned her guest to a chair and reseated herself.

"I'm well. How are you?"

"I made a stupid mistake yesterday," said Meadow.

"Never mind," said Hazel. "You're not likely to make it again."

"No," Meadow agreed.

Hazel was looking at her, smiling.

She wants to know about me and Alder.

But the old woman said nothing. Meadow quickly assessed the state of play and made the next move. It was the right one.

"I'm… friends… with Alder."

Hazel breathed out and nodded. "That's nice." Then, "Would you like to eat something?"

"No, thank you. I'd like to get some air. I'll go for a walk."

"Of course, dear. Will you come back later?"

Meadow hadn't thought that far. "I don't know. Possibly."

"As you wish. I'll go back to bed." She rose.

"It was nice to meet you," said Meadow.

"Similarly, dear."

Hazel had some difficulty mounting the stairs unaided. Meadow watched for three steps or so, then called, "Can I help?"

"No," said Hazel, "Don't worry. I'm used to it."

Meadow listened as Hazel's bedroom door closed, then she returned to Alder's room, retrieved the bucket from his close stool and emptied the contents into the privy in the yard. She cleaned the receptacle with water from the cottage handpump, put it back in place and closed the lid. The activity made her feel a little better; she decided to visit Louise.

As she walked up the hill towards the manor house – the smithy and carpenters' shop on her left, the big field on her right – she began to feel better. A few minutes later, as the house came into view, with the dwellings of the Buckleys and the Swifts nearby, she felt the clouds in her head part. It was like the sun breaking through fog, and it happened so quickly that she was astonished. The rapid dispersal of her headache had a euphoric effect. She felt instantly happy, as if she could achieve anything she wanted.

She strode on to the house and told Louise about Alder.

Alder Swithenbank returned from his work that evening, hoping that Meadow would be at home waiting for him. But she wasn't.

Hazel was in bed. Kate was perched in the big chair in the parlour, the one they called Scarlet's chair, reading to herself. The brothers were yet to return from the fields.

"She's gone then?" he said.

"She hasn't come back," Kate replied.

Alder was disappointed. He'd been looking forward to her.

But Meadow had gone home. Louise had punctured her joy.

"Alder Swithenbank?! What's wrong with you?"

Meadow tried to explain her reasoning – tried to make Louise see that what she'd done was a reaction against her parents' stifling libertinism.

"But you don't need to grind a labourer to register your discontent. Just move out of the house. Come and live here. Daddy wouldn't mind."

The suggestion filled Meadow with confusion. She walked home to her parents' house, casting a glance at Vine Cottage as she turned left onto Watermill Lane. She no longer knew what she wanted.

Meadow stayed at home for more than two weeks, miserable and empty. Nothing seemed real. Her life consisted only of pampered pointlessness. She wasn't doing anything, wasn't achieving anything. Her existence was sterile and vacant. The one thing that seemed to cut through the vacuous emptiness was the memory of what she'd become in Alder's hands. He'd wanted her, and that was the only sliver of real meaning that she had.

Locked in her room, Meadow's frantic, gasping, lonely fantasies about Alder became her most precious moments.

So she set out once more with renewed determination. This was it. Today she would, to all intents and purposes, become Alder's wife. Her feet carried her resolutely towards her goal, past the boarded-up watermill and over the bridge.

As she approached the cottage, it became clear that something was taking place there. A crowd of people, all dressed in black, stood in the road, and a waggon with two big, dressed horses waited near the gate. Several more carriages formed a line, ready to depart. Meadow stood by the wall, transfixed, while the river purled innocently close by.

The coffin appeared at the cottage doorway, supported by Alder, Adam, William, Hugh Flesher, Richard Swift and Elys Buckley. Meadow's left hand flew to her mouth in shock. She could scarcely breathe. Kate appeared, dressed in black like everyone else, together with Grace Buckley and the two young Swift girls, Amy and Beatrice. The long wooden box was hoisted onto the cart, and the assembled people found their seats in the cortège of carriages. As the procession moved off, Kate turned and looked directly at Meadow, expressionless. Meadow's hand remained covering her mouth, and she felt the first sobs pull at her chest. Tears filled her eyes, escaped and flowed down her cheeks. She turned and hurried home.

20. POTHOS EST IN
DOMUM SUAM
Egton, Friday December 21, 1759
Winter Solstice Celebration

The day was cold. There'd been a light fall of snow over-night and the carriage journey from the Lookout that morning had been cautious, but now they were approaching the little village of Egton, just a few miles inland from Whitby. Crowan, well wrapped against the penetrating chill, sat opposite Edgar Foxley.

"Nearly there," said Foxley as they passed the first cottages. It was nearly half past one in the afternoon, and Jacob hoped they would be welcomed with a good lunch. He'd never visited this remote part of the county before and had come as Edgar's guest. Foxley had promised, "an evening of pretentious debauchery such as you've never known...". It all sounded rather tedious to Jacob, but he'd agreed to come along to keep his business partner happy.

They drove through the village and out into the country-side beyond. A cemetery and a mediaeval church appeared on the brow of the next hill, but the carriage pulled into a driveway on the left before those landmarks were achieved. A stone archway over the drive's entrance carried the inscription in bold Latin capitals: POTHOS EST IN DOMUM SUAM. Pothos, son of Eros, an acolyte of Aphro-dite. Crowan grunted a mocking laugh. Foxley smiled.

The carriage drew up in front of a substantial house. A similar vehicle, having just unloaded its occupants, pulled away as they arrived. Sigbert and Persephone Reid emerged from the portico and descended the stone steps to greet the new arrivals. Sigbert was a portly, ginger-haired man in his middle fifties, with an impressive beard and moustache. He was quite loud. Persephone was about ten years younger than her husband. She looked artistically delicate, pale-skinned, with prematurely greying hair. The effect was not unattractive.

"Mr Crowan," she held out her hand for Jacob to kiss. "Edgar has told us so much about you."

"An honour, Mrs Reid," Jacob replied. "It's a particular delight to meet such a beautiful hostess."

Persephone blushed a charming pink beneath her pale complexion. "You flatter me, Mr Crowan," she smiled.

"Jacob, please, Mrs Reid," Crowan replied.

She returned his invitation. "Call me Persephone."

He smiled at her, simultaneously aware that they were being watched from a window on the upper floor. His hostess took his arm and led him into the house, Sigbert following with Edgar.

Meadow watched the arrival of the carriages from the window of her room. A few flakes of snow began to fall as Edgar Foxley arrived. Foxley and her father were old pals who'd got to know each other in the early days of her father's London stage successes, at around the time Meadow was born. He'd been attending Sigbert's Yorkshire depravities for as long as Meadow could remember. But there was someone new with him this time, a young man of thirty or so. The men who attended these events were usually of her parents' generation or older, although the women were often younger; mostly obsequious, fawning actresses come to give themselves to Sigbert. It was unusual to see a young male. Meadow wondered if her father might feel intimidated. She certainly hoped that he would.

The servants were never present at the parties. They'd prepare the house and arrange an elaborate cold buffet; then they'd be sent away to their homes, or to a Whitby inn. They all knew what was going on, of course, but they never had the opportunity to watch.

Sigbert and Persephone tolerated their daughter's reluctance to join in the main entertainment on the understanding that she would make herself available for introduction to the guests, and to assist with a little hostessing if needed. Meadow endured the indignity, thankful that she didn't have to take part in the ensuing orgiastic carnage.

Sigbert introduced her to Crowan.

"Mr Crowan; my daughter, Meadow."

He kissed her hand. "What a beautiful name." Sigbert walked away, leaving the two alone.

"Thank you," said Meadow. "What's yours?"

"Jacob," he said.

"You must be the youngest man here," said Meadow.

Jacob looked around the room. "And you must be the youngest woman."

"I probably am," she replied. "I'm twenty-two."

"A fine age," he said. "Very ripe."

She paused. He was already trying to seduce her. She allowed a tiny smile to register on her lips. "You know what this is, don't you?"

"This?" he said, eyebrows raised.

"This place, this…temple of absurdity."

"I believe so," he said.

Meadow noticed her mother watching closely from a nearby double-ended chaise longue. The fat man on her left was already sliding his hand back and forth on her thigh. Persephone was hoping that Meadow might finally lose her virginity this evening (being unaware that she'd already lost it). Jacob followed the line of Meadow's glance.

"My mother is wondering if my… cherry… might be yours." She emphasised the word, rendering it ridiculous.

Jacob laughed. Meadow smiled and looked again at her mother, who returned her glance with an expression that

226

said, *At last!*

"And will it?" asked Jacob.

Meadow had become momentarily distracted by her mother's amusement. She looked back at Jacob as he uttered his question.

"What?..."

"Your cherry. Shall it be mine?"

She found him attractive and could easily have given herself to him for the evening, but she was enjoying the chase too much for that.

"No sir, it shall not."

Jacob looked genuinely disappointed. "Don't you like me?" he asked.

"I like you well enough, but my cherry has already been acquired by another."

"Indeed? He is a lucky man." He looked around the room. "Is he here?"

The thought of Alder Swithenbank being present at one of her parents' orgies was so ridiculous that Meadow burst into laughter. The room was instantly silent, and everyone looked at her. She blushed, regained control of herself and muttered her apologies to the assemblage. The hum of conversation resumed.

"No," she said, suppressing her mirth. "He's not here."

"That's a pity," said Jacob. "Perhaps I could have challenged him to a duel."

"I would pay good money to see such a thing," she replied.

"You are very interesting, madam. I am intrigued to know what kind of qualities tempted you."

She was playing with him. "Are you?"

"I am."

"He was an illiterate farmer. And I lay naked with him in a hayloft."

Jacob was silent. His smile remained, but his stare drilled deeply into her.

"I think you're telling the truth," he said quietly.

Meadow smiled back at him. She wasn't going to confirm or deny it.

"And me?" he said. "Am I to be the second?"

It was tempting, but the sexual pursuit was too entertaining to terminate.

"No," she said.

"Why not?" asked Jacob.

"Because I like you too much," Meadow replied.

"That is a fine compliment," he said. "May I at least kiss you?"

"That will be in order," she said. "I allow it."

Jacob placed his hand behind her head and drew her to him. They kissed deeply and at length. Again the room became silent, all eyes on the pair of them. She pulled away, watching him as she did so, licked her lips, and whispered, "Don't follow me." She turned and left the party, leaving him alone.

Meadow spent most of the afternoon in her own room but listened to the distant sounds as the festivities progressed. The entertainment's etiquette required the various couplings and intimacies to be undertaken in plain sight, but now and then individual couples opted for more privacy, flitting away to their appointed bedrooms for half an hour or so before rejoining the cast. Meadow heard occasional footsteps and subdued voices in the corridor, together with the click of softly closing doors.

She wondered what had become of Jacob and decided to brave the cattle market of the drawing room. A middle-aged couple in high spirits passed her on the huge, sweeping staircase as she made her way down. The woman was in her shift, the man bare-chested, his breeches partly unbuttoned.

"I wonder if you'll find me guilty," giggled the woman, whose name Meadow couldn't remember.

"I can't wait to view the exhibits," the man replied

(Meadow remembered his name; Charles Jackson, a justice of the peace). "And I shall pass sentence too..."

In their excitement, they took no notice of Meadow but continued their vigorous ascent, he grasping and slapping on the way.

The lamplit drawing room presented the usual shadowy scene of heaving pink-white bodies, and the smell of sweat was heavy in the air despite the brass bowls of smouldering incense. There were about thirty people in the room; a few of them glanced at Meadow as she made her way among them. None spoke to her.

It took her only seconds to find Jacob, lying on his back on the chaise longue that had earlier been occupied by Persephone. He was looking at Meadow and seemed quite calm and uninvolved despite what was happening. Her mother was on top of him, leaning forward, one hand on either side of his shoulders, in motion, her pale skin speckled red.

Meadow had seen it all before. It was no more or less nauseating this time. She returned to her bedroom, got into her nightdress and went to sleep.

There was a knock shortly before three o'clock. It shocked her into consciousness, and she felt suddenly alarmed. The oil lamp was burning very low, the fire had reduced to embers, and the room was in near darkness. She turned up the light and stepped quietly to the door.

"Who is it?"

"Jacob."

"What do you want?"

"Just to talk. Nothing more."

Meadow opened the door and let him in. He was fully dressed.

"How did you know this was my room?"

"You were watching when we arrived. I counted the windows."

Meadow was quiet for a moment. "That was damned observant of you," she said, resenting the sensation of being
under surveillance.

"I'm glad you approve," he said.

"I don't," Meadow replied. "It's late. What do you want
exactly?"

"You intrigue me. You seem... angry, discontented, keen
to offend, rebellious... but passionate, intelligent. I'm not
sure I've ever met anyone quite like you before."

"Did you enjoy my mother?"

Jacob smiled and snorted. "Not particularly."

Meadow stared at him mutely.

"Can we sit?" asked Jacob.

"On my bed?" Meadow replied in a tone that suggested, *I
know what you want.*

Jacob allowed the silence to settle in the room before he
replied quietly, "I won't eat you..."

"But I think you're a wolf," said Meadow.

Again Jacob allowed the walls of the room to watch in stillness before he answered. When he replied, it was in a whisper. "You're right. I *am* a wolf..."

The darkness of the room; she vulnerable in her nightdress; the clandestine nature of their encounter; the duel-
ling parries of their conversation... Meadow realised with
a start that she was entirely under his spell. He could
have taken her on the spot – she would have let him. If
he'd reached out and touched her, she would have been on
him like a lioness. Jacob knew it too. He remembered the
first time he'd felt sexual tension wound as tightly as this.
It was that day in his father's shop, his stepmother's gun
pointed at the two assailants, wanting so keenly to kill
them.

He stood his ground and watched her. If she were to signal,
Do it! he would have obeyed the command. But both rode
out the moment of tension in rigid immobility.

After a few seconds, Jacob's face showed a tiny smile, and

his breathing eased. Meadow was both relieved and disappointed. "Damn you," she said and sat on her bed, eyes cast down. Jacob sat next to her.

"I hate," he said. "You hate too."

She looked at him, curious as to where his monologue might go.

"We're alike in some ways," he continued. "We're both intelligent, you unusually so. But we differ in this: I *love* to hate, I thrive on it – but *your* hate is diffuse, wasted. You despise your parents, but the hate you manifest towards them is really the result of your own sense of emptiness, lack of opportunity. You have ambition but no direction and no goal. Am I right?"

"I don't know," she replied. "All I know is that I hate my life. I wish I were dead. There's no value at all in living."

Jacob looked at her intently for almost half a minute. His expression was strange. Meadow began to feel a little frightened. "What are you doing?" she asked.

Jacob said, "I could use these next few moments to the benefit of both of us. I could make you understand how much you really do treasure life, and you could give me more pleasure than anyone ever has."

"What do you mean?"

There was an odd tranquillity about him; he seemed utterly self-assured. "Do you trust me? You'll have to trust me completely."

She was uneasy but didn't want this to stop. "Alright," she said.

He told her to lie on her back, and she obeyed. Then he sat astride her pelvis, put his hands around her neck, leaned forward with the mass of his body behind his grip, and squeezed. She was instantly terrified and began to struggle. His weight ensured that her legs were no use to her, so she reached up in panic and tried to claw him with her hands, scratch his face. But he calmly increased his pressure on her throat. She couldn't cry out – his squeezing fingers made it impossible for her to breathe, to plead for mercy, to beg for her life. He wouldn't stop until she was dead. Her struggles weakened; spots began to cloud her vision, and the sound of the room gave way to the rumble of blood in her own head. She felt her eyes would burst; a few tears ran down the sides of her face. Her tongue felt very large. Her arms and hands became numb. She stopped moving. Blackness flooded in.

Jacob watched Meadow's brown eyes bulge, staring fixedly at his as he continued to crush her life away, her tongue protruding grotesquely. Poor child. She was very still. Her brow furrowed, and her breathing ceased. He maintained his pressure a moment longer. The closeness of death had brought him to the lip of ecstasy.

He relaxed his grip and slapped her. She breathed in, hard and raucous, clutching at her throat, horrified. Jacob climbed off her and stood by the bed. Meadow drew away from him in disbelief, sensation flooding painfully back into her flesh. She choked and retched.

"You're mad," she coughed. "You nearly killed me. You mad bastard."

"It was very close," he said. "Another second or two would have seen you on your way forever."

"How many times have you done that?" she asked.

"Never," he said.

"Then how did you know...?"

"I didn't," he replied. "But you're still alive, aren't you." It wasn't a question. "You see? You *didn't* want to die."

"You're a monster," she said. "I hate you."

"That's good. I could have killed you. I still could. I hold your life in my hands, and you know I could easily take it. You hate me for a reason. Now you feel alive."

She was quiet for a moment, massaging her crushed neck. Then she said, "Get out. I never want to see you again."

He rose. "I'm glad I met you," he said. Then he turned and left, closing her door quietly behind him.

Meadow didn't sleep that night. Her throat was very sore and it wasn't easy to breathe. She looked in her mirror in the dawn light and saw that her neck was black with bruising. It would be difficult to hide the injury from her parents.

She watched from her window as the carriages departed one by one. Tiny flakes of snow fell, and the sun rose higher, lighting the clouds a strange, sickly pink.

At about half past ten Crowan and Foxley emerged, giving their farewells to Sigbert and Persephone. Before he stepped into the coach, Crowan looked up at Meadow's window, smiled and raised his hat. She drew back, although she'd been expecting some parting gesture. Her spirit cringed from his gaze – the gaze of Satan, of one who knows the world belongs to him and is his to dispose of in any way he might wish.

21. MARGARET SIDDON

Christopher Siddon, an Essex fisherman, ran a slow but adequate trade in crabs, shrimps, cockles, whelks, mussels and the like on the beaches of Leigh, some forty miles east of the capital. He was married to Isobel, and earnings from her prostitution (a trade he actively encouraged) augmented his modest income. When their daughter Margaret was born in 1707, people commented that she had Christopher's eyes, and Isobel assured him that the child was indeed his, despite his doubts.

In reality, he didn't much care whether she was his or not. The important thing was that she grew into a good looking girl, and by the time she was thirteen was able to increase the family's income through the sale of her own body – which proved to be popular and sought after. There were usually two queues outside Christopher's door on payday; one for Izzy, one for Mags.

A fever ran through the towns and villages on the river estuary during the summer of 1724 and claimed the lives of Margaret's mother, father and young brother within a few days of each other. Their bodies were taken away for burial, and Margaret herself lay on the point of death for ten days while the undertaker waited like a vulture to box her up.

She recovered, against all expectations, although was unable to house herself without the income that her parents had provided. She was evicted from the cottage her family had shared since before she was born, and made her way to London in the hope of getting a better price for her charms. Margaret met with only modest success. She was a handsome girl – popular, richly bosomed and charmingly plump – but had little talent for looking after money and less still for long-term business strategy. She got into trouble and wound up in the Fleet Prison for debt.

During her incarceration she met Ivor Bentham, twelve years her senior. Ivor had been involved in running prostitutes for many years, and was able to maintain his business from within the prison. His band of eight girls (they called him *I've-a-Bent-One*) was run by two lieutenants who reported to him each day. Margaret never knew precisely how the business maintained itself but was pleased when Ivor took a shine to her, suggesting they go into partnership. (This was sometime after his earlier suggestion that Margaret should share his cell, mend his clothes, prepare his meals, keep him warm and entertained at night.)

The pairing was a success. In due course, Ivor was able to buy them both out of prison and set them up in a small third-floor apartment in Lovat Lane from where they ran their business. He was kind to the girls, and the enterprise flourished. Soon they moved into more spacious accommodation, first in Berwick Street, then Arlington Street, and finally King's Place.

Margaret conceived three times but suffered two stillbirths. The one child that survived, a boy, lived only to eight months. She was sad, all her babies taken from her. But Ivor was caring and did his best to keep her from despair.

"The girls, the nuns, are our children," he said. "Let's pull together and support them. They all love you."

Ivor had a son from a previous relationship but was estranged from both him and the boy's mother. Despite all the sadness, the convent in King's Place flourished in those days and developed into a happy little community. The nuns worked there because they felt it was their home, and everyone looked after each other.

It was in January 1745 that Edgar Foxley and his cronies came along and changed everything. He wanted to buy the business. He was charming, all smiles and reassurance, but

Ivor smelt trickery. Edgar wasn't interested in Margaret (she was thirty-seven by then, thirteen years his senior). He preferred younger girls, and particularly enjoyed the frisson of bondage. A peppering of slavery added spice, he thought – the terror of the cornered animal. It was a livelier, tastier way of approaching the sport. And it had its supporters – quite a lot of them – with money.

Ivor stood up to Foxley, didn't like his ideas, told him to get lost. Ivor liked the easy equilibrium in the convent and didn't want it upset.

But suddenly the problem was gone – Ivor was gone. Edgar told Margaret that her partner had seen sense; he'd had a change of heart, accepted a buyout of £5,000, and left the house in the night. Margaret naïvely swallowed the story. She was unconvinced of its truth but was concerned that she too might be "bought out in the night" if she didn't fit in. Ivor was no more – and Margaret had to toe the line.

So Foxley laid his plans, gathered together his band of subscribers and moved into King's Place...

22. CAPPLEMAN FARM
1759/60

The atmosphere in the house was bleak in the months following Hazel's death. Life was grey, like an abandoned ship, drifting aimlessly in fog. Alder and the brothers went to work as usual, but there was not much conversation among them either before they left or when they returned. Alicia Buckley and Emma Swift came to help out with the cooking, washing and other household tasks.

The community of farms and villages had lost its wise woman, but a few of Hazel's closest friends were aware that she'd been teaching Kate, and there had long been whispers about Kate's powers. As the summer began to fade into autumn a few tentative souls arrived at the cottage to ask if young Kate had any advice regarding some ailment or other, and Kate often had the solution, or knew how to obtain it. Two or three trusting souls even asked for their cards to be read, overcoming the odd sensation of receiving wisdom from a ten-year-old.

Alder dreamed about Meadow, wondering what had become of her. He would often lay awake at night, wondering if she were thinking of him as he was of her. He'd close his eyes and remember the weight of her body, the smoothness of her skin.

Kate had her friends, Amy, Beatrice and Grace, to keep her company, and sometimes Grace's brother Walter appeared with them, although he was happier in the company of the other boys. In the summer they took a few long walks with eighteen-year-old Alan Flathers, the smith's son. They went as far as Castleton, Littlebeck, and over the moor to Rosedale Abbey. One rainy day up on the high moor, they sheltered for a while in the mouth of a cave. It was eerie to stand there with the rain pouring, the big black hole behind them filled with echoes. Alan said they shouldn't go exploring – it wasn't safe. Kate was fascinated by the place. She could hear water falling somewhere deep within, in some unknown blackness in the earth. Alan told her it could be an underground river, or water falling in from the outside. Grace was frightened and sat close to the entrance, huddled in her coat, her face turned to the day-light, her back to the dark.

As the months passed, Adam and William spoke with in-creasing earnestness about joining the army or the navy. The war on the continent was widespread, and there were rumours that the French were planning to invade Britain. The naval battles between the two powers in November 1759 added further to their determination, and Kate be-came fearful that she might lose both her uncles.
"You'll be fine," they told her. "Don't worry – we'll be back when the job's done. We'll write home whenever we can so you'll know all is well."
In January 1760 the brothers informed Hugh Flesher of their decision. He wished them well and said he hoped they'd return when victory was won. They kissed Kate goodbye, hugged Alder, and went on their way.

One miserable, rainy day in mid-February, Kate sat in the window seat in the little parlour by the kitchen, looking out at the raindrops splashing in the puddles. The cottage was full of rich odours – the peat burning in the parlour fireplace, the smell of freshly baked bread drifting in from the kitchen where Alicia was preparing something nice for supper.
Hazel and Nara had both loved to sing as they worked, and Kate had picked up a lot of songs as a result, but the ballad that Alicia was singing was unknown to her. It related the

story of a young woman who was preyed upon by a selfish gentleman and left with two bastard children. Not knowing what to do, she killed the babies by stabbing them through the heart, and was then visited by their ghosts, who told her she'd go to Hell. The incongruity of it appealed to the black side of Kate's sense of humour, and she found herself grinning as she listened.

"What was that, Alicia?" she called when it was over.

"It's called *The Cruel Mother*," Alicia shouted back. "My gran used to sing it. Did you like it?"

"I did," Kate replied. "It was such a lovely story. Do you know any more like that?"

"I do." And Alicia began to sing *The Two Sisters*. Kate listened keenly to the tale of sibling rivalry. Two young sisters fighting over a man, murder by drowning, and the musical instrument that was made out of the bones and hair of the victim. Kate's ears were engaged, but her eyes remained staring through the window, watching the dismal day.

Someone appeared far down the lane, bundled up tight against the weather and hurrying towards the farm. She watched as the figure drew nearer, the outline gaining definition in the enveloping rain. It was a woman, one hand occupied with keeping the hood of her cape in place, while the other held the fabric tightly closed against the downpour. She must be on an important errand, thought Kate, to justify braving the elements on such a day. The nearest dwelling in that direction, other than the watermill, was more than a mile distant. Whoever she was, she must be soaked to the skin.

The figure passed by the window and disappeared round the corner of the house. Less than a minute later, Kate was surprised to see the same woman scurrying back in the direction from which she'd come, this time even quicker, almost running, as if she wanted to be gone before anyone had chance to see her. *It's Meadow*, thought Kate, jumping from her perch and running through the kitchen to the front door. There was a sealed note lying on the stone floor, slid under the door from outside.

Alicia looked up from the table where she was busy slicing pork. The song had ended. "News?" she asked, pushing her straw-coloured hair back from her brow. Kate looked at the envelope. It was addressed to *Alder Swithenbank* in an elegant hand.

"Not for me," Kate replied. "It's for dad."

Alicia continued with her work, and began to sing *The Bleeding Heart*: "Alas, what times here be…"

Kate took the letter into the parlour and dropped it on Scarlet's chair. Then she resumed her seat in the window and peered down the road. The rain had increased in force, and Meadow was too far away to be seen. There was a lightning flash in the distance, a rumble of thunder moments later.

Alder returned at seven o'clock, soaked. He greeted Kate and Alicia, changed out of his wet things, and washed before seating himself at the table.

"There's a letter for you, daddy," said Kate.

Alder was surprised. "For me? I don't get letters."

"I think it's from Meadow. She came running through the storm this afternoon to deliver it." Kate handed the paper to him, and he turned it over in his hands, looking at the front and the back, running his fingers over the wax seal.

"Meadow. I haven't seen Meadow for months. Did she say anything?"

"She just pushed the paper under the door and ran away."

Alder lifted it to his nose and smelled it.

Kate smiled and said, "I knew you were going to do that."

He handed the letter back to his daughter and waited. His reading skills were still very primitive despite Kate's efforts; she'd have to read it for him.

Alicia had been watching, but now said, "I'll pop upstairs

and do a bit of tidying..."

Kate carefully broke the seal and removed the outer wrapper, then unfolded the letter contained within. It was written in a flowing feminine hand. She glanced quickly at the signature.

"Yes, it's from Meadow." She paused and looked at her father. "It might be personal. Do you mind?"

He shook his head. "Go on."

She began to read:

Alder, this will come as a surprise to you, it having been a year since we were together...

Kate stopped for a moment and looked up at her father before continuing:

I was so very sorry to hear of the death of Nara's mother. It must have been dreadful for you and Kate to say nothing of her own sons. I felt it would be insensitive of me to attempt to renew our acquaintance in the wake of such a tragedy, but perhaps enough time has now passed.

I hope you will not find this letter too direct. The truth is I have thought of little else but you since that day. I long for you. Please consider me and have mercy on me. My body...

Kate's eyebrows raised as she read on in silence. "I can't read this," she said.

Alder watched her with intense concentration. "What does she say?"

But Kate was still reading silently to herself. "I thought *contrapunctum* was something to do with music." She read a little further. "Oh, I see..."

"Kate, tell me what she says."

Kate frowned. "She sounds ill."

Alder waited patiently.

"She wants you. She *really* wants you."

Kate looked up at her father. He looked back and said,

"What should I do?"

"How old am I?" she asked.

"Ten," he replied. "...and a half."

"Three quarters."

He nodded.

Kate said, "And how old are you, Pa?"

Alder thought for a moment. "Fifty-six."

"And you ask *me* what you should do?"

Alder said, "I'm just a simple old man. You are your mother's daughter. You know best. So I ask you."

Kate was astonished. For Alder, that was quite a speech.

"Alright. Then I think you should meet her."

Alder nodded.

Kate read: *If you will have me, meet me on Beggar's Bridge at noon this Sunday, 17th. I'll wait for you for half an hour. If you don't come, I won't trouble you again.*

Kate looked up. Alder was thinking, remembering, lost in himself.

Sunday dawned, bright and surprisingly spring-like, though the air remained crisp and wintry. Alder spent all morning preening himself. He got Kate to cut his hair, still thick despite his age, although it was completely grey. Then he had a bath in the kitchen, cleaning himself thoroughly, even beneath his fingernails and toenails. He wanted to smell nice, and asked Kate for advice. She smiled and said mockingly, "Aw, pa. You're asking me for a love potion."

"Away with you, girl! Do you have something or not?"

Of course she did. It was a common enough request, and she had a number of oils and ointments already prepared.

Alder spent a long time dressing himself, then got Kate to brush him and make sure he looked as presentable as possible. He inspected his hat, pulled all the muck off it and cleaned it thoroughly. Kate found his best shoes, shiny black with silver buckles, unworn since his wedding. They needed dusting, but were otherwise like new. Alder managed to squeeze into them without too much difficulty.

At the end of the process, he stood, arms outstretched, and awaited her assessment.

Kate laughed. "She'll think you own the farm!"

He looked at his pocket watch. "It's time."

"How do you feel?" asked Kate.

Alder stood a moment quietly, thinking hard. "Nervous. Like I'm an imposter about to be found out."

She made a tiny gesture with her head, understanding.

"What will you do this afternoon?" he asked.

Kate had planned her day. "I'm going to read with Grace."

Alder nodded. "I'll see you later then."

"Good luck, dad."

Alder left, closing the door behind him. Kate ran into the parlour and watched him walk away in the direction of the bridge. If her father brought Meadow back to the house straight away, they'd be here in just over half an hour. Kate put on her coat and walked to the Buckleys' house to find her friend.

He saw her there, waiting motionless at the brow of the bridge. The sunlight was very bright, rendering the moss on the old stonework a vivid green. He was aware of the splash and whisper of the Esk as it ran beneath the bridge, but his eyes were on her.

Alder slowed as he approached, and drank in the sight of her at the top of the gentle incline. In a few minutes she would be his again. He stopped in front of her, looked down into her eyes, pushed back the hood of her cape, and brushed her raven-black hair. He leaned forward, and her lips parted gently to meet his kiss. When he pulled back, he saw there were tears on her cheeks. A short-eared owl swooped low over the bridge as they stood there, the sulphurous lanterns of its eyes scanning them.

Alder lifted meadow's bag from where it rested on the

bridge, then gave her his arm. Neither had spoken. The soft, golden promise of the afternoon beckoned.

23. THE WHITE BULL, RIBCHESTER
Friday February 22, 1760

Alexander sat in the embrasure of the round window in his room and re-read the letter from Colleen. His hopes were dashed, his dreams proven worthless. He was rejected, unwanted, lost.

He was lucky to be alive. He'd lain exposed in the road all night until a shepherd stumbled on him at about ten o'clock in the morning. His body was blackened with contusions, blue with cold, and red with open wounds. He appeared to be dead, but a shallow breath suggested that life lingered. The shepherd removed his own smock, covered Alex with it, and sat by his side, praying for help.

After an hour or so, a small waggon came into view, a tinker's cart, drawn by a single elderly horse. The shepherd stood in the road, waved the vehicle to a halt, and begged assistance.

"He's been beaten. I thought he was dead. Must've been lying here for hours."

"Let's get him in the cart," said the tinker. "Ribchester's three miles that way." He indicated with his hand. "I'm going there anyway. There are good people at the inn. We'll get him under cover."

So they made room amongst the pots and pans, hoisted the unconscious man into the cart, and drove to the White Bull, where they sought assistance from the landlord, John Bennett.

"He's in a bad way," said Bennett. "Let's get him to bed. I'll send for the surgeon."

John and his wife, Sarah, had run the White Bull for more than twenty years. They were kind people and were content for Alex to occupy one of the upstairs rooms for as long as required. Sarah sat with him when she could, sewing, reading. Helen Shaw, who worked and lived at the inn, also watched over him.

Alex lay feverish and mostly unconscious for three days. Helen was in the room when he woke. His eyelids fluttered for a while before they opened fully; then he muttered something indecipherable. She thought it sounded like, "Again...?" Helen got up from her seat, and Alex said, "Francis?"

Helen entered his field of vision. He squinted, his eyes unfocused; then he found her. "Was it a dream?"

"You're very weak," she said. "Don't try to move."

"Where am I?"

"You're in Ribchester. At the White Bull."

"English...Colleen?"

"You've been here a few days. You were attacked on the road – beyond the river." He looked at her, confused. "Do you remember?" she asked.

There was a fog in his mind. He squeezed his eyes shut, then opened them again, attempting to drive the cobwebs from his thoughts. "Yes, I think so." He tried to get out of bed, but pain overtook him and he had to stop.

It took about ten days for Alex to begin to walk unaided, and a month before he was back to something approaching full health. In the third week of November he wrote to Colleen, telling her what had happened to him. He told her what a fool he'd been and how much he loved her and treasured her. He wanted to come home, and begged her to have him back. Alex handed the letter to the post-boy and prayed for a positive response.

John Bennett offered him work at the inn, and Alex gratefully accepted. He liked the village and the pretty countryside around it. There'd been a Roman fort on the site, they said, and two of the pillars that supported the portico of the inn had come from a Roman temple. The little town was known for cotton-weaving, and Alex learned something of the craft during his time there.

He came to know John and Sarah as friends and often shared meals at their table. Helen too became a good companion and accompanied him on many of his walks, whether for work or recreation. Although unremarkable in appearance she was strong and had a determined, direct character that Alex found reassuring. She always spoke her mind. Alex admired that honest quality and confided his whole story to her. She was a good listener, sympathetic, thoughtful and intelligent. She was twenty-four, estranged from her parents. Her father, a tanner in Blackburn, had beaten and abused her as a child.

Alex waited patiently for a reply from Colleen, knowing that the post took its time. His letter probably had to make its way down to London before travelling on to Dublin. It could take a month to get there and another for a response to reach him.

Christmas was a joyous affair, the inn full of laughter and celebration. It felt good to be part of a community, and he enjoyed the company of those around him. The New Year celebrations were similarly high-spirited. At midnight Helen reached up to kiss his cheek with her New Year wishes, but he instinctively turned his face and kissed her on the lips – and she kissed him back. It wasn't a long kiss, but their eyes were locked as they drew apart, both knowing they'd crossed a line.

"I'm sorry," he said quietly. She was gone, but when she returned to the party a few moments later, it was as if nothing had happened, and they were just as they'd always been together.

Two months passed since his letter had gone on its way, and there was still no reply. He continued to watch every day for the arrival of the post-boy. Alex knew roughly at what time mail might be expected, and he would sit in the embrasure of the circular window in his room, his eyes on the road.

And today it had come.

January 24, 1760

My Dear Alex,

I was so glad to get your letter – and horrified to hear what had befallen you. I hope you're well recovered now – and happy. I want very dearly for you to be happy – I always did – you were my precious man.

I hear your love in what you write. You blame yourself for what became of us, but the blame is not all yours – it is mine too. I should have been a better wife for you. I let you down in so many things, and you tried so hard, and for so long.

But time has moved on. You are making a new life for yourself. Things have moved on for me too. Alex – I'm with Liam. We've been together for a month. I hope it will last. He's a good man – but you already know that. Liam sends you his love, Alex. He's here as I write this, and says so now – he'd tell you himself if he could. I showed him your letter and he was sad. I think he loves you almost as much as I do.

Take care, my sweet Alex. God bless you.
Your Colleen

He was stunned, empty. He sat in his window and wept.

24. CAPPLEMAN FARM
March 1760

Meadow's parents were horrified at what she'd done. Persephone came to the cottage and confronted her while Alder was out on the farm. Kate heard it all from where she sat in the parlour window. It was a shouting match.

"You gave yourself to a labourer? A nobody?"

"Yes, yes, and yes!" spat Meadow.

"Who do you think you are? You can't do that! You have a position, a status in society."

"I don't want that! I never did! But *you* could never see it!"

"You could have had any man you liked without leaving the comfort of your own home!"

"I hated those people! And I hated living at home! In any case, I'm twenty-three and I can do as I like. I don't need your permission, or anyone's. I love it here. I'm not going home."

And the argument continued, becoming ever more hateful, sparkling with a degree of abuse, invective and profanity that made Kate's hair stand on end. Eventually, Meadow threw such a string of foul language at her mother that the latter turned on her heel and fled, slamming the door as she went. Meadow, red with fury, shouted after her, "BLOODY DOXY HAG!" Then she covered her face with both hands and sat down.

Kate left her seat in the parlour and came to the kitchen door. Meadow saw her there and quietly said, "I'm sorry – that was bad. I shouldn't have said that."

"It's alright," said Kate. "I didn't know what it meant anyway."

"Bet you did though," said Meadow. They looked at each

other, tried to contain the suppressed hysteria, and both burst into laughter.

Afterwards, Meadow sat in the kitchen and cried. Kate stood next to her, arm round her shoulders. "I'll make some tea," she said.

Meadow nodded and wiped her eyes.

Henry Flesher sat at the window of the manor house library, his dreams in confusion. Meadow Reid had been his obsession since childhood. He'd always thought of her as his wife in waiting, her persistent cruelty to him notwithstanding. One day, he'd hoped, she would wake up and realise at last that he was her master, not her toy. It was to be a day of enlightenment. He'd dreamt about it, run through the dialogue in his mind, over and over:

"Meadow, today is the day."

"And what day is that, little Henry?"

"The time for playing is over. We two are destined for one another. You have always known that it is so. The pretence is done with."

Her girlish smile would fade. Louise, standing nearby, would say, "Meadow, it's true. You belong to my brother and must obey him."

There would be a solemn moment in which they would gaze at each other. Then Meadow would bow her head and say, "You are a man now Henry, and my master. I submit myself to you."

"Thank you, Meadow. You shall become my wife, and bear my children."

But now his goal, the focus of his existence, had gone. Meadow, his Meadow, was warming Alder Swithenbank's bed. Henry's mind swam with excruciating imagery, vivid and explicit. He was lost, spinning out of orbit.

25. POTHOS EST IN DOMUM SUAM

Egton, Saturday June 21, 1760
Summer Solstice Celebration

Jacob had been a good lover – unhurried, considerate, appreciative. He'd told her how lovely she was – her body. He'd made her feel good, reassured – he thirty, she forty-four. Sigbert rarely invited young men to their bacchanals – he didn't like his young actresses to be distracted. But because Jacob had come along as a guest of his old friend Edgar, he'd felt compelled to welcome him.

Persephone generally coupled with men older than she – sixty, seventy, eighty – sometimes even creakier than that; excited, red-faced, overfed, priapic has-beens – usually finished in under a minute, then expecting her to tell them how wonderful they were, how much she'd enjoyed it.

But Jacob – handsome, young. Persephone remembered how much she'd relished undressing for him, there in the drawing room with all the thrashing bodies around them. She remembered Sigbert watching her from across the room – he'd commented on it afterwards. Jacob had been attentive – eyes on her all the time. The stillness of his manner as he watched her made her feel wanted. And his lovemaking was sustained, thoughtful, focused. Later that evening they'd gone upstairs together and had sex in private, in the bed in his guestroom. It was the best frisking she'd had in years.

She wanted him back. She'd insisted that Sigbert invite him to the Summer Solstice. Persephone began to exercise – to walk, run, swim – as soon as Jacob's acceptance arrived in the post. She wanted him to be pleased with her, wanted him to tell her how good she looked; wanted him to want her.

She watched the carriages pull up one by one, excited, ready for him. She almost burst when she saw him – would have taken him straight off to bed if she could have done. He greeted her enthusiastically enough but then asked after Meadow.

"Meadow doesn't live here anymore, Jacob," said Persephone. "You'll have to make do with me." She'd expected a smile, a light-hearted comment, a sweeping glance of carnal desire – at least an appreciative comment about the dress she'd put on for him. But no. In fact, he could barely hide his disappointment. Persephone suddenly felt old again – she realised that Jacob had come for her daughter, not for her.

Crowan was downcast. He'd been hoping to see Meadow again. She'd haunted his thoughts since that night six months previously.

And there was the other girl on his mind – Vivianne Stamper, one of the students at the Lookout – beautiful, dark-haired, big brown eyes... She was brilliant – a writer – probably the sharpest mind of all the girls. He'd watched her grow up over the last few years, her pen and her mind always busy. She'd be seventeen in October. Jacob had been aware for some time that Viv was fond of him. She often came to his office to ask for advice on her work – poems, stories, essays. She had a mature mind, a natural style. She astonished him; he couldn't hide his admiration. He believed she might be a genius – possibly the only one he'd ever met. And he found himself watching her, wanting her with a lust he'd never felt for any of the other girls. She could easily be his – they both knew it. But he could not allow his work to become entangled with his pleasures. Jacob had slept with no-one in the six months separating his two visits to the Reids' orgies, and he'd been hoping to quench his thirst with Meadow. But she'd gone. And her parents seemed unwilling to divulge exactly what had happened to her.

He took a few things from the buffet, complained of a headache and retired to his room. Persephone came knocking at his door in the night. He couldn't face another dull coupling with her, so he didn't answer. She tried the handle and found it locked.

Jacob lay quietly in his bed as she repeatedly tried to get in. *Pathetic dry old creature.*

It had been a wasted journey.

26. CORNELIUS
Glaisdale Church, Friday July 18, 1760

The church was alive with the colours and scents of fresh flowers, arranged during the day by the ladies of the parish so the place would be beautiful on Sunday. Cornelius sat quietly in the front pew as the sun went down, hands clasped, eyes closed, the day's events filtering through his mind. He'd attended a funeral in Easington, his presence having been requested by Norman Langton, a labourer on a farm west of the village, whose four-year-old daughter, Deborah, had been killed in an accident. Robert Forest, parson of Easington, had welcomed Cornelius's presence, no doubt fearing that the emotional strain of the event might overwhelm him. Cornelius was a local fixture, a figurehead, having worked in the area for thirty-six years. He'd become a kind of father to everyone, and Norman told him that his wife, Carol, had specifically requested his presence.

Unsurprisingly, it had been a difficult event; the church packed tight with people, many in tears. At one point, someone began to shout, "Why? Why?" and had to be accompanied outside. Cornelius led the prayers and gave a short address; Robert took the other parts of the service.

The sun was shining when the procession moved into the churchyard. It was a lovely day; the kind of day on which little children would play happily, running, laughing... Carol wept in Cornelius's arms while Robert read the committal and the tiny coffin was lowered into the earth.

After the service the mourners withdrew to the Tiger, and Cornelius and Robert accompanied the grieving parents home to sit with them for a while. Norman cradled his wife in one arm and his elder daughter, seven-year-old Susan, in the other. The two parsons sat opposite, leaning forward, offering some physical comfort by touch.

"She was so young," sobbed Carol. "Such a sweet girl."

Cornelius squeezed her hand. Norman continually wiped tears from his face. Susan climbed into her father's lap, and he put his right arm around her. The child looked stunned, her eyes wide open, the shock still not passed.

"She's in the arms of Christ Jesus," said Robert, "who called all little children to him."

The statement made Carol cry harder. "But I didn't want her to go. I wanted her to stay here – with me."

"Of course you did," said Cornelius. "You're her mother. Carol, there's no easy path through grief such as yours. The shock is very great now – and it will always be there, there's no denying it – you know it. You'll always carry it, as does every parent who loses a child. But it will harden over time, and with God's help, you'll find a way of going on."

"God?" interjected Norman. "What has God to do with this?"

Robert sat back, and Cornelius reached out his other hand and rested it on Norman's knee. "I know," he said. "I know how hard it must be to cling to trust in such sadness. I know how easy it is to lose sight of God."

"It was my fault," said Norman. "I shouldn't have let her ride in the waggon." He began to cry very hard. Carol pulled his face into her chest and covered his head with her arms.

"Mummy," said Susan, and Carol extended her reach to fold in her daughter as well.

Cornelius's tears threatened to spill out. One escaped, and he caught it on his right forefinger.

It's no good for them if you crumble too. Bear it, bear it...

He swallowed, sniffed (inaudibly, he hoped), and said, "You'll always blame yourself, Norman. But what's occurred can't be reversed. Carol and Susan are here to support you, as you'll support them in the coming days and weeks. And Robert and I will support you in any way we can, whenever you need it." Cornelius glanced at Robert, whose silent tears were flowing freely. Robert nodded and managed, "Of course."

"She wasn't baptised," said Carol.

Cornelius, seeing Robert look up in shock, reached out quickly and touched his colleague's knee. Robert looked at him, and Cornelius shook his head. Then he turned to Carol and said, "It doesn't matter. She's a child of Almighty God, and she'll have been saved, baptised or not – it makes no difference."

Carol stared at him through her grief and said, "Are you sure?"

"As sure as night turns to day," Cornelius replied.

The two parsons left the shattered family after another hour or so and returned to the parsonage at Easington, where Cornelius had often been a guest of Egbert Trommel and Hubert Cromwell. Cornelius accepted the tea that Robert offered, and the two sat opposite each other by the empty hearth.

On the journey home, Robert had expressed his horror that the little girl was unbaptised, and he repeated it now. "How could you tell them it didn't make any difference when you surely know it does?"

"Do I?" asked Cornelius. "Do I know?"

"You know the teachings of the Church as well as I, if not better, Cornelius."

Cornelius bowed his head. "The teachings of the Church." He sighed.

"The blessing of a witch is not the same as the sacrament of baptism," Robert pointed out. "It has no value at all – as you must know."

"Robert, you can't honestly believe that the Creator would allow the soul of an innocent child to be held in limbo."

"It is what the Church tells us. Our wicked souls must be washed clean."

Cornelius could see that Robert was becoming angry, and he felt his own irritation rising. "Wicked souls...," he echoed. "You've been here for eight years, Robert. You've got to know something of the old ways – at least, I hope you have. There's no religious division among these people other than that brought by the Church."

Robert's voice rose. "The Church is the salvation of these people!"

"I'm not so sure," Cornelius countered. "I've been unsure for a long time."

"Then you're in the wrong job!" said Robert.

Cornelius looked at him under lowered brows and said, "No. I'm in the *right* job. The Church is full of cobwebs, Robert – a tangle of contradictory threads woven together through centuries of sophistry, wrong turns and misunderstanding. The Church is only a force for good if it throws off all the nonsense it's buried itself in for centuries. The old religions of these people – they're pure, without conflict. What good does it do them to claim a child is sent unsaved into the darkness?"

"I'll pretend I didn't hear that, Cornelius. Look, with Hazel Priestly gone and Catherine still so young, we have an opportunity to stamp out these childish superstitions."

Cornelius felt his anger almost boil over. "Stamp out? Stamp out, you say? *That's* the voice of the Church – *that's* a voice I recognise – a voice of ignorance, intolerance! *That's* the voice that should be stamped out!"

Robert rose to the fury. "The Word of God is clearly written. Our Lord said *I am The way, I am The Truth, I am The Life!* He didn't say *I am one way of many!*"

Cornelius countered, "The Word of God is not clearly written *at all*, least of all in Holy Writ."

Robert was outraged. "What?"

"The Word of the Lord is first written in our hearts – not in

257

a set of dusty texts. We should be ashamed that we twist the lives of others around such a hoary old tree. Our Church is more than that – the Love of God is worth more than the paper our Bibles are printed on!"

"You're a Pagan!" shouted Robert.

"I doubt you even understand what the word means!" Cornelius shouted back. "I'll be part of no *stamping out*."

The other was quiet for a few seconds, and the tension lessened slightly. Then Robert said, "The other parsons are with me: Liverton, Hinderwell, Borrowby..."

"They may hear your zeal, Robert, but I doubt many will join you. Certainly not James Kirby at Roxby, and I doubt very much Eric Brough at Ellerby."

"I'll write to the Bishop about this," said Robert.

Cornelius replied, "As you wish." He rose, stood quietly for a moment, then said, "You and I must present a unified front to support the Langtons. It won't do if we're seen to argue. Do you agree?"

Robert sighed and stood. "Yes, of course I agree." He looked at his feet. "We think differently, you and I, Cornelius. I would not wish to lose your friendship." He extended his hand, and the older man took it.

Cornelius felt sadness flooding the space so recently occupied by rage. "We'll each think about what the other has said. We'll continue to strive together; we'll continue to search for the voice of God. We both know it's there, I think."

"Wise words, Cornelius – as only you know how."

Cornelius leaned forward and embraced the younger man. "God bless you, my friend," he said. Robert nodded, glad to feel the return of his colleague's love.

The sun had sunk; the light was gone, but Cornelius remained sitting quietly in the dark. He missed Hazel and feared for the community she'd left behind. The fact that Kate was so young meant that the ancestral line was broken, and the old beliefs were open to predation.

Cornelius both loved the Church and hated it. He saw the good of which it was capable and also the damage it could do. He saw the exclusion and damnation it could mete out, and was revolted by the invitation of re-assimilation on its own terms – the blind eye in the story of the sinner that repented. My way is right; your way is wrong. He recognised the danger in that doctrine; saw the opportunity to own, to repress. It provided endless opportunities for manipulation, for corruption. Such power could be abused – indeed, it *was* abused.

But the Church could be such a force for good if its shackles could be thrown off. The Bible was made for man, not man for the Bible. Cornelius heard the voices of those who would use the book to exclude or chastise others, emphasising that the Word of God says this, or the Word of God says that, holding up the printed text to prove it. In Cornelius's philosophy, if the Word of God could be used to make a misery of the lives of others, all the copies of the Holy Book should be gathered up and buried in peat for a thousand years. The Church was more than the Bible; and the Love of God was more than the Church.

Was Cornelius in the right job? Most certainly yes. He nodded to himself in the blackness.

Did Cornelius acknowledge himself held in the Love of God, the Creator and Sustainer of the Universe? Thrice yes – absolutely yes.

Was Cornelius a Pagan? Yes, he was.

Was Cornelius a follower of Christ Jesus, Light of the World? Resoundingly, wholeheartedly and proudly, yes, yes, yes, yes, yes!

27. CAPPLEMAN FARM
August to October 1760

Meadow lay in Alder's arms in the warm summer night. The open window framed tiny pinpricks of impossibly distant fire set against the infinite black silence; stars, the ancient wraiths of the gods. She blessed them for her existence. She felt intensely alive. Alder was asleep on his side behind her, breathing evenly, and she lay turned away from him, naked, nestled in the crook of his body. The room was as quiet as a midnight millpond.

She felt fulfilled. Someone desired her. She'd justified her own life by making someone else happy. Alder loved her, and showed her that he loved her. Every day she waited for him to come home. And he showed her the fierceness of his love. Over and over again.

Kate also lay awake. She was glad her father was happy but was also aware that something was wrong. Meadow was obsessed with Alder. She would fret and fidget all day, continually watching through the windows, running out into the garden and looking along the road to see if he was coming home, knowing he had a full day's work to do on the farm. Then, when the time for his return drew near, she would fuss over her appearance – her hair, her scent, her clothes – making herself as delicious and irresistible as she could for him. She'd see him approaching the house and would begin to pop with excitement. Then she'd be all over him, kissing him, hugging him. She'd give him a few minutes to clean off the grime of the day, then she'd pull him upstairs to the bedroom. Things had become steadily more intense as the weeks and months wore on.

Meadow knew almost nothing about cooking or other domestic tasks, so the household was still primarily reliant on Alicia Buckley for help. Alicia and Kate would work in the kitchen to the background of sounds from Alder's room. Alicia would frown and say, "A young girl like you shouldn't hear things like that."

In her heart, Kate knew that Meadow's need for Alder was not just an obsession – it was an illness.

Alder was, of course, teased by his workmates. They made suggestive noises when he approached, asked coarse questions, but he smiled and played along.

"Do anything interesting last night, Alder?..."; "*Up* early this morning, Alder?..."

Alder was well-liked, admired. He was the butt of jokes but could mete them out too. And of course, they were genuinely envious of him. Meadow was a beautiful woman, above Alder in social rank – and less than half his age.

Alder never spoke lewdly about Meadow; she was too precious to him for that. He knew how lucky he was, although he sometimes felt that he was a small boat in the whirlpool of her need.

Meadow no longer visited Louise, although she now lived within fifteen minutes' walk of the manor house. Her life revolved entirely around Alder, and she feared that Louise might try to dislodge it, to set her back on what she considered to be the right path. Meadow wanted to avoid any situation that might impede her giddily spinning cycle of love. She went outdoors occasionally, walking for exercise, but was careful to avoid other people. Meadow became fully alive only with Alder, in private.

But one day in early September, Louise came to the cottage to find her. Kate was out, Alder at work, Alicia not yet arrived. Meadow opened the door an inch and looked through the crack. Louise was alarmed to see one large, fearful, staring eye.

"Meadow?"

"What do you want?"

"I just came to see if you were alright."

"Thank you. Yes."

"Can I come in?"

Nothing happened for several seconds. The eye continued to stare.

"Alright." The door opened, and there was Meadow.

Louise smiled. "You look well." She didn't step in immediately but waited for Meadow to beckon her, which she did after a short pause. Louise took off her hat, and Meadow motioned her to sit down.

"I haven't seen you for a while," said Louise. "You're well?"

"I am. Thank you."

"Are you happy?"

"More than I've ever been."

Louise smiled again and took Meadow's hand. "Then I'm very glad for you." Louise was thin and severe in appearance, with dark hair and prominent cheeks, but she had a lovely smile that brightened her whole countenance. Meadow was so glad to see it that she burst into tears. Louise was shocked and put her arms round her friend.

"Oh, my goodness! What's wrong?"

"I don't know, I don't know. I'm so confused sometimes."

Louise hugged her, reassured her. "I'm always here for you. You're my oldest friend." She shed a few slow tears in response to Meadow's weeping.

"I know," muttered Meadow, sniffing, rubbing Louise's arm. "Thank you."

As September wore into October, Kate was frequently woken in the night by the sounds from Alder's bedroom and began to think that perhaps she should voice her concern to Meadow. The two of them had become good enough friends despite Meadow's natural dislike of children.

As far as Kate was aware, her grandmother had never been asked for advice on reducing someone's sexual desire (although the opposite had been commonplace) – at least Hazel hadn't passed on any such learning to Kate. But Kate had a few ideas of her own.

The confrontation had consequences that cascaded through the rest of Kate's life.

Meadow withdrew to her room after her brief interview with the girl. Two or three sentences were all that it took to set the course of events in motion. Kate had suggested that Meadow might be ill – and that she, Kate, might be able to help. The threat was there; it had to go.

Kate sat at the kitchen table, confused, unsure what had just happened. A minute ago, the two of them had been speaking on friendly terms. Kate was in mid-sentence when Meadow rose, smiled and went upstairs.

Less than half an hour later, Meadow was on her way to Egton, the first time in months, to visit her parents.

28. CAPPLEMAN FARM
Sunday October 26, 1760, 1.45pm

It was a bright autumn day, although the air carried a crisp suggestion of the approaching winter. Crowan's carriage passed by the watermill and made its way towards Beggar's Bridge.

He folded up the letter from Meadow, received two weeks earlier, and put it back in his pocket. The paper was becoming fragile – he'd read the note a dozen times:

Dear Jacob,

I wonder if you'll remember me – I'm the girl you didn't murder last December. I wonder if you've succeeded in killing anyone since then.

So you're a schoolmaster. I found out something about you from my parents after you'd left. I seem to remember you telling me that you found my mother merely passable as a lover. You'll be pleased to know that she had a similar assessment of you.

But enough of these fond recollections. When we last met I believe I gave you "great pleasure". Is it now your turn to render service to me? My father says that you take waifs and strays and turn them into fashionable ladies. I have a waif who might benefit from such a schooling.

Let me be blunt – I believe you might appreciate it. I have a new life. I've moved into the house of my bumpkin lover and am very content. Please don't mock me – he is all I need. My man is physically tireless and lacks the intelligence that would make him tedious. But his daughter is a nuisance. She is eleven years old and is an irritatingly intelligent child. It would be of great benefit to everyone if she were to be taken away. That is my request. Further details will follow if you indicate your willingness to assist.

I'm sending this with the courier and hope for a swift reply.
Yours (I'm sure you would wish it),
Meadow Reid

The letter made him laugh. He replied by return, offering today's date for an interview, and a further exchange of letters had elaborated the details.

And now he was pulling into view of the house, at the top of Watermill Lane on the left corner of the turning – Vine Cottage.

He'd been expected. The cottage door was already open, and the occupants were standing outside. Crowan's carriage drew to a halt. He opened the door, stepped down onto the running board and into the road. The three people who greeted him presented a striking tableau, and Jacob assessed it in a second:

The man in the centre was a substantial specimen, well over six feet in height, powerfully built and topped with a mop of wild grey hair. Meadow's "bumpkin lover" was a kind of gentle giant. Crowan could see at a glance why she'd chosen him, despite their unmistakable difference in age. The sheer brute force of the man no doubt complimented her own brilliant intellect. She had enough brains for two and wouldn't require any more from her partner.

Meadow herself stood close to the man, pressing herself against him, her arm through his as if to say, *It's he and me. We're fixed. Don't try to come between us. You'll be sorry if you do.* She was as beautiful as he remembered her. But something had changed; he sensed it instantly. The feeling of discontent, resentment, discord that had previously been so obvious was gone, replaced by a state of balance.

She's chosen well, thought Crowan, *an extraordinarily successful coupling of polar opposites.*

In the next second he looked directly at Catherine Swithenbank, and it was like looking into the well of his own future. The force of it briefly staggered him, and he instinctively knew that this moment would stand as a milestone in his memory. Her appearance was extraordinary. She was tall for her age, slender, delicate, aristocratic. Her hazel eyes met his with penetrating fierceness, and he took an unconscious step backwards, with the distinct impression that he'd been physically pushed away. Her hair was luxuriant and long, impossibly red. She did not look happy.

(Meadow had been avoiding Kate as much as possible ever since Kate had offered her help.
I shouldn't have said anything, thought Kate. She actually said so to Meadow. "I'm sorry. I didn't mean to upset you. I thought we were friends enough to discuss things openly."
"I don't know what you mean. I haven't taken offence. Look – I'm smiling – see?"
But something had changed. A week later they were talking about sending her away – to some school or something. Kate didn't need to go to school. She wanted to stay at home with her friends and grow up on the farm.
"It's a good opportunity, Kate," said Meadow. "You'll learn to dance properly, play music, speak foreign languages. Try it. If you don't like it, you can come home. It's not as if it's forever. Give it a week, a month."
But Kate knew that Meadow was up to something. Meadow tried to reassure Kate, reached out and brushed her hand through the girl's hair as if she were her mother. But Kate wasn't having it – resented the presumption. One of the more unusual skills Hazel had taught her came rushing forward in her mind, and she lashed out, the force instantly slapping Meadow's hand away and driving her several feet across the room as if pressed back by a strong wind, the heavy kitchen table scraping noisily a few inches along the floor at the same time. It was a reaction of instinctive anger and was the first time Kate had used the technique

against a person. She felt sorry for it straight away. Meadow was frightened, unable to comprehend what had just occurred. Kate turned away and went to her room.

But Alder seemed to think the school was a good idea too. Meadow had talked him into it, easing the pain of its acceptance with the promise that it was only an experiment. Kate could come home at any time if she didn't like it or if things didn't go well for any reason at all. The education wouldn't cost anything as the school was an entirely charitable institution. There was everything to gain and nothing to lose.

So it had been agreed that Mr Crowan would be invited to the farm to explain precisely what might be offered…)

And here he was, smartly dressed, the puffed white sleeves of his shirt protruding from his burgundy frock coat; his silk stockings startlingly white against the grime of the country road. His dark brown hair was tied back with a black ribbon, and he carried his cocked hat in his hand.

"You must be Mr Swithenbank," said Jacob, striding along the front path, hand outstretched.

Alder was set at ease by the grace of Crowan's greeting. He smiled and stepped forward, meeting the handshake. "It is indeed, sir. You're very welcome."

Jacob looked at Meadow. "Miss Reid," he said. "Such a pleasure to see you again." She offered her hand, which he kissed. Meadow said nothing more than, "Mr Crowan."

Jacob was well-practised in winning the confidence of others, and he put all his concentration into making a good impression on Kate. He knelt down, looked up at her and took her hand.

"And it is a particular honour to meet you, Catherine." But she saw right through him like a window. He recognised it instantly. She was far too perceptive to be misled; it was a hopeless task. If he were to succeed, he'd have to come clean – or at least, as clean as possible.

"You're worried. I can see that. There's no obligation – you don't need to join us if you don't want to."

"Shall we step inside?" asked Meadow. "It's chilly out here." Jacob stood, and they withdrew to the house. Tea had been waiting, and they settled to discuss the proposition, Kate eyeing Crowan suspiciously.

"The school is a charitable institution, one of three such in the country." Jacob began. "It's funded entirely through private patronage and requires no input from the girls' sponsors, should any exist. Many of the students are taken in from the streets, having had no previous support, and others are drawn from workhouses and similar institutions. The girls are aged mostly between ten and sixteen, although we occasionally admit exceptional students outside that age range. The object of the education is to provide the young ladies with a range of life choices. At the end of the course, they can choose to enter into the social circles of London or other centres, opt for specialisation in sales work, go on to study elsewhere – almost anything they like. In Catherine's case, being fortunate to have a home here, she could simply return to the farm and build her life according to her own wishes. There are absolutely no strings attached, and no particular path is ever enforced. The girls are always completely in control."

Alder said, "I like the sound of that. But it has to be Kate who chooses."

"Of course," said Jacob. "But I've become quite astute in my role over the years, and I can see that Catherine is a child of considerable intelligence. She would be a valued asset to the school and a great inspiration to the other girls, to say nothing of the staff. She would be an unusual jewel in our crown. But of course, as you say, it must be Catherine's decision."

Meadow said, "What kind of things might she study?"

"The curriculum is diverse, and our tutors are experts in their specialised fields." He drew a few strands together in his mind. "We have elocution and basic reading and writing..."

Meadow interjected, "Kate can read and write as well as any of us." (She squeezed Alder's arm apologetically).

"Of course," Jacob said, and went on: "Mathematics; presentation, dress and fashion; languages, including Latin and French; literature; needlepoint and similar skills; music, including lessons in harpsichord, harp, singing and other instruments; movement and dance..." He made a gesture that said, *Need I go on?* "The school is situated in substantial grounds, and there's plenty of opportunity for exercise: walking, running, whatever you like." He looked at Kate. "And you shan't be wanting for animals if you think you may miss them. We have our own, and a body of staff specifically to care for them. You'll be taken to the theatre, to exhibitions, to church, to lots of fairs..." He shrugged, *What is there to dislike?* "It really is very comfortable. The girls have their own group of maids; all kind, helpful, thoughtful – you'll make many new friends..."

Kate admitted to herself that she liked the sound of the place. But there was something wrong. With her usual directness, she said, "You're hiding something."

Crowan was astonished but covered it well. His already considerable admiration for Kate doubled on the spot. He looked at her for a few moments, calculating.

"You're right," he said. "You can feel my unease. May I call you Kate?"

"You may," she replied.

"Thank you," said Crowan. "You speak very directly, and I admire that..."

(Meadow watched him closely, fascinated by the subtlety of his predation.)

"...I will be equally direct. I hope you don't mind."

She gave no indication at all of whether she minded or not. Jacob thought, *She's astonishing!*

"Kate, you are terrifying, unique. You frighten me. I sit here trying to entice you into my school, but it seems to me that I'm *your* pupil. I'm intimidated, and I tried to hide it from you. But I couldn't. Because *you know...*" He emphasised the last two words.

Everything he said was true, but he'd weaponised his conceit and used it as a shield to hide what Kate was really trying to dig out. Her mind reflected from Jacob's skilfully deployed defence, and she missed the fact that he was hiding something else. It was Crowan's first victory against her. He knew it, and smiled inwardly.

Meadow was impressed with the display. She nodded to herself. *That was worth watching!*

Kate gave no outward sign of belief or otherwise, but in her heart she accepted what he said.

There was a moment of tense stillness, then he said quietly, "So, will you come?"

"I will," she said, equally quietly, nodding shallowly.

"Thank you," said Jacob. "There'll be no pressure or expectation. I'll send the carriage for you on...Wednesday, noon?" He questioned Meadow and Alder with his eyes. They both nodded their assent. He looked back at Kate. "If you change your mind, or need more time, send word and let me know – or just send the carriage away. I want you to feel completely at ease."

Kate felt reassured. She was actually beginning to like him. Jacob rose and addressed them all. "I should be going. Thank you for making me welcome." He shook Alder's hand and kissed Meadow's. She thought, *The devil himself couldn't be as cunning as you.* To Kate, he said, "I'll look forward to seeing you again, Kate."

"Mr Crowan," she said.

A moment later he was gone, his carriage on its way towards the bridge.

The interview had stimulated fresh excitement in Meadow, and she wanted Alder, but he made her wait. "Give me five minutes with Kate. I'll be there in a moment."

She nodded agreement and disappeared upstairs to wait for him.

Alder turned to his daughter. "Well?"

"I'm actually quite excited about it."

He ruffled her hair and smiled. "That's good!"

She smiled back at him.

"If you change your mind, or if anything goes wrong, you'll come straight back home."

"Thanks, daddy," she said. Kate wanted to tell Grace and the others, so she quickly dressed herself for outdoors and disappeared to the Buckleys' house.

Wednesday, October 29, 12 noon

The carriage arrived on the dot of noon. Kate, packed, dressed and excited, had been waiting in her favourite window and saw it approaching in the distance. "It's here!" she called, running to the front door. Alder had remained at home that day so he could see Kate off. He opened the door and watched the carriage pull up. The driver was different from the one who'd brought Jacob on Sunday. He called from his seat, "Mr Swithenbank?"

"I am," replied Alder.

"I'm Stanley, from the school; come to collect Miss Kate."

"That's me!" cried Kate excitedly.

"Nice to meet you, miss," said Stanley, hopping down and collecting her things.

Meadow came running downstairs. She was genuinely warmed to see Kate so animated but was also thrilled that she'd now have Alder's attentions entirely to herself.

Kate was keen to be on her way but allowed Alder to lift her off the ground for a hug. He was teary – it was the first time his daughter would be going away from home by herself. "Look after yourself, girl."

"I will, daddy. You take care too. I'll see you soon."

Meadow came forward, and Kate said, "Goodbye, Meadow.

I'm sorry I was mean to you."

Meadow smiled and hugged her. "You weren't mean to me, sweetheart. Have a lovely time."

Stanley helped Kate into the carriage, and a moment later she was on her way, waving vigorously from the open window.

She sat in the closed car and watched the scenery, felt the rise and fall of Beggar's Bridge, gazed at the abandoned watermill through the window on her left, the millpond, remembering Hugo. At the crossroads they turned east and passed by the old church and cemetery on the outskirts of Egton, the archway labelled POTHOS EST DOMUM SUAM on the right a half-mile further on. Next, they drove through Egton itself and carried on until they came to the main Whitby Road. The lanes were badly rutted and worn, so travel was slow, cautious.

Kate was enthralled. She'd never been alone on a journey before. This was a real adventure, and she felt properly grown-up.

Whitby came into view just over half an hour later. Kate had visited the town a few times, mostly for the fairs and markets, and thought of it as a real metropolis. She loved the sight of the sea and the harbour, and watched attentively as they passed through the streets, listening to the sounds of the place – the shriek of the gulls, the cries of the street vendors. Kate wondered if the people noticed her, travelling all alone like a noble lady.

It was busy. There were masses of people and vehicles, and it took some time to reach the harbour bridge, the abbey ruins nestled high up on the cliff to their left. Once they'd crossed the river estuary, the carriage turned south and took Kate away from everything she'd known.

The villages slipped behind one by one as they followed the road along the coast: Stainsacre, Hawsker, Raw… Sometimes the sea was in view, sometimes not. At three o'clock they passed close to the village of Peak, and a quarter of an hour later drew to a halt before a pair of elaborate old iron gates. Kate leaned out of the window and read the inscription in the scrolled metalwork: *The Lookout*. They'd arrived.

Stanley got down and pulled a rope that set a big bell ringing on top of one of the gateposts. A moment later, a squat, wizened elderly man came hurrying toward the gates from the far side, pipe clenched in his teeth.

"Afternoon, Stanley," he growled as he pulled open the entrance.

"Jack," Stanley replied. "Tessa well?"

"Same as ever," Jack replied. "She'll never go mountaineering again."

Stanley shook his head and laughed, then indicated Kate. "This is Kate; come to join the ladies."

Jack tugged his forelock and greeted her. "You're very welcome, miss."

"Thank you," Kate called, waving to him. "It's nice to be here."

Stanley mounted once more to the box and drove forward. When they'd passed far enough beyond the gatehouse, he called back, "That was Jack Archer. His wife's nearly eighty; been unwell for years. We don't see much of her."

They continued ahead for a few minutes. The grounds to the left and right of the drive consisted of dense, tangled undergrowth with occasional glimpses of underlying stonework – fragments of old walls. Kate imagined that a jungle must look something like this.

"Welcome to the Lookout, Miss Kate," called Stanley. She put her head out of the window and saw the hugest house she'd ever seen, with an impressive central section and two long wings. There were four stories – turrets too, one of them quite tall. She couldn't wait to go exploring.

Stanley drew up before the main entrance, got down, opened the door and helped Kate out. There was Jacob, smiling and offering his hand. A second man, large, important-looking and with an impressively sculpted moustache, stood behind him.

"Kate. It's good to see you. Did you have a pleasant journey?"

"Yes, thank you," Kate replied. She took his hand and smiled.

Jacob motioned the second man forward. "This is Alfred, our porter. He'll take your bags." Jacob signalled to Alfred, who nodded, picked up Kate's things and carried them inside.

"Let's get you freshened up," said Crowan, "then I'll show you the school."

29. THE LOOKOUT

There was a washroom and privy just inside the main entrance, and Jacob gave Kate a few minutes there while he rang for tea. When she emerged she found him waiting for her nearby at a small table laden with refreshments. He'd arranged a couple of leather armchairs, and they sat adjacent to each other.

"Mrs Rowley's lemon water," said Mr Crowan, pouring them each a glass. "Try it – and please, help yourself." He indicated the tray of food.

"Thank you," Kate replied. She lifted a small pie and took a bite.

The entrance hall was enormous, dominated by a huge, imposing square staircase in dark oak that extended to the top of the house. Impressive paintings, mostly portraits, followed its course all the way up. It awed Kate, the more so because the table at which she sat was positioned in its well, and she could see right up to the ceiling about seventy feet above.

Jacob could see she was impressed. "It's a wonderful old house," he said. "Built in 1643. We're fortunate to have acquired it. The Lookout was empty for fifty years and was in a very poor state of repair, but we were able to give it a new lease of life, adjusting the interior to suit our needs. It's an ideal place for what we do."

"It's the biggest house I've ever seen," said Kate. "It's even bigger than the manor house on the farm – ten times bigger probably."

Jacob laughed. "But they don't have to house seventy girls and all the staff we need."

A huge gong, bigger than Kate, hung in a wooden frame nearby, its striker suspended from a peg. She reached out, tapped it, and was rewarded with a deep, metallic growling.

Jacob chuckled. "The dinner gong," he said. "We don't use it. It has a rather austere, forbidding crash. Girls' stomachs tell them when it's time to eat anyway. They don't need the assistance of Mr Gong here."

They chatted for a while longer, then he suggested they begin their tour. "Let's start with the dining hall. As long as you remember where that is, you won't go hungry tonight."

The dining hall occupied the north corner of the west wing. It was a very large room with the capacity to seat perhaps a hundred people or more. The walls were adorned with several sizeable and impressive paintings: landscapes, seascapes, one of Whitby harbour, and a particularly lovely one of a large bay racehorse.

"I've always been fond of horses," said Jacob.

"He's lovely," said Kate. "What's his name?"

"This is the Godolphin Barb. You're right – he's beautiful. He died a few years ago. I never saw him in the flesh. I picked up this painting from a coffee house in London. The Lookout is full of fine paintings, but I like this one best of all."

"Do you keep horses here?" asked Kate.

Jacob pulled his gaze away from the picture. "Yes, we do. You'll meet them."

"And do you have a favourite one?"

He laughed gently. "I do as it happens. Demeter is my favourite. Such a kind, good-natured horse. She's a good listener – that probably sounds eccentric."

"No," said Kate. "I know what you mean."

The tour went on. Jacob pointed out the entrance to the kitchens further along the west wing, although he didn't take Kate to see them. The kitchen staff would be busy, he said, and she'd meet them later anyway.

He showed her the various offices situated on either side of

276

the entrance hall and then moved on to the large room at the north end of the east wing, which was laid out as a kind of lecture hall. Jacob called it "the debating chamber". He tapped on a set of double doors just round the corner in the east wing and said, "This is an elevator to the infirmary on the top floor. We've never had cause to use it, but it's kept in good order. It has space inside for a stretcher and one person standing."

"I've read about them," said Kate, "but I've never seen one. How does it work?"

"It's operated by winch from the infirmary. The mechanism is in the attic space."

"Have you been in it?"

"Yes, every time we test it, I take a ride."

Kate had a natural fascination for dark places and holes. "What's it like?"

"Dark," he replied, smiling. "Squeaky."

"And there's one person at the top, winding you up?"

"No," said Mr Crowan. "It takes two. It's too heavy for one. Come on – time to move on." Further down the east wing lay three large sitting rooms, all comfortably furnished and all currently vacant. The corridor ended in a wall in which was set a double door in the shape of an arch. Jacob opened it and said, "The chapel."

The room was a little smaller in area than the dining hall, although it was much higher, rising to about forty feet. It was dressed in dark panelling, austere but impressive. Kate walked to the middle of the space and looked behind her. There was a gallery at first-floor level, with a fine organ case. She'd never seen an organ before, although she had read about them.

Mr Crowan stood by her side. "The organ is new," he said. "It was installed last year. I believe it's a good one. You'll see the keyboards later."

They made their way back to the entrance hall, to a set of ornate double doors beneath the staircase, close to where they'd enjoyed their refreshments.

"Ready?" asked Jacob, poised to turn the handle. Kate nodded, and he drew open the doors to reveal an enormous hall that he called "the ballroom". It was the biggest room she'd ever seen, and extended the entire length of the central portion of the house, perhaps a hundred and fifty feet. The room was about forty feet deep and lined with tall windows on the far side, through which the gardens could be seen. Several chandeliers, large and spectacular, hung from the ceiling twenty feet above. The floor appeared to be of polished oak.

"What an amazing room!" said Kate.

"I thought you'd like it," said Jacob, enjoying her astonishment. "It has many functions: dances, parties, lectures. We also use it as a gymnasium."

Kate ran around the huge space, laughing. "It's unbelievable! I love it!"

Jacob waited for her to calm down, then said they should go on. He shut the double doors and led her upstairs to the first floor.

"This is where the work is done," he said. "All the classrooms are on this level."

Listening carefully, Kate heard the distant sound of voices drifting into the gallery where they were standing. "Let's say hello," said Mr Crowan. He strode along the corridor, looking at the doors, then selected one. "In this room we have Mademoiselle Ardoin teaching French – I think..." He tapped and listened for the soft voice within...

"Oui? Entrez, s'il-vous-plaît."

"I was right," he said quietly, turned the handle and motioned Kate to the doorway. The room was modest in size and well-lit by three large windows. A fire burned in the grate. There were ten girls aged about fifteen, all sitting at individual desks. At the front of the room was an elegant woman, dark-haired, not tall, well-dressed and aged about thirty. She smiled at Jacob, and they conversed briefly in

278

French. Kate was fascinated, understanding not a word of it.

Mr Crowan addressed the girls. "This is Catherine. She's joining us today." There were murmurs of welcome from the assembled students. Mademoiselle Ardoin, smiling, walked over to Kate, bent forward and said, "Nous sommes ravis de faire votre connaissance, mademoiselle Catherine."

Kate smiled in reply but didn't know what to say. Jacob gave a kind little laugh. "Don't worry, Kate. You'll pick it up soon enough." He thanked Mademoiselle Ardoin, raised his hand in farewell to the class and closed the door. "Let's try another," he said and led Kate round the corner and into the east wing.

The sound of singing became clearer as they proceeded. Kate recognised the song – *Early One Morning*. Jacob stopped outside a door near the end of the corridor and waited for the singing to end before tapping. A woman's voice called, "Come in." He opened the door, revealing a room similar in size and design to the previous one. A woman in her middle thirties stood there – plainly dressed and with light brown hair tied in a bun at the back. A choir of ten lovely girls stood before her, all aged about twelve or thirteen.

"Girls," saluted Jacob, then spoke to their teacher. "Miss Dryden, this is Catherine. She'll be joining us today."

"What amazing hair you have!" said Miss Dryden, her eyes wide. There was a soft murmur of agreement from the young singers.

"Thank you," said Kate. "I love that song. My mother used to sing it."

Miss Dryden smiled at her. "I look forward to hearing you. If your voice is as lovely as your hair, you'll be an opera singer."

Again Jacob bade farewell to the class and closed the door. "One more," he said. They retraced their steps along the corridor, past the staircase and into the west wing.

Another door, another brisk tap and another invitation to enter. Jacob turned the handle and looked in. "I hope I'm not interrupting at a crucial moment."

"Not at all." It was a man's voice. Jacob fully opened the door and invited Kate inside. The room was small, warm and contained just two people. A harpsichord lesson was in progress. The girl sitting at the two-manual instrument was breathtakingly beautiful, about sixteen years old, with long blonde hair hanging in ringlets. She wore a dress of white silk embroidered with gold. Her teacher was a handsome man in his thirties, smartly dressed in a grey waistcoat, frilled white shirt and pale brown breeches. His long brown hair was gathered up and tied in the back with a black bow. He held a pair of spectacles in his well-manicured, elegant fingers.

"Kate, this is our keyboard tutor, Mr Browning."

Mr Browning nodded to Kate. "Rider Browning, at your service."

Jacob introduced the young woman. "And Miss Orla Stapleton, in her final year with us. Kate is joining the school today."

Orla had a lovely face, soft and kind with prominent full lips. "Nice to meet you, Kate. I like your hair."

"Thank you," said Kate. "Everybody says that!" She paused a moment. "You're very beautiful."

Orla looked embarrassed. "You're a sweet one. I like you already."

Kate smiled, and Jacob seemed pleased. "Do continue," he said, then motioned Kate out of the room and closed the door.

"I almost forgot," said Jacob. "I said you'd see the organ gallery."

He led her back to the east wing, to the end of the corridor. Two doors were separated by a large painting of a tall and impressive-looking organ, sited in the west gallery of a large church. Kate looked up at it and said, "That looks amazing!"

"That is the organ in the church of St Bavo in Haarlem," said Mr Crowan. "The painting was a gift from our organ builder. He has a great fondness for the instrument depicted here. It's considered to be extremely fine." He opened the door on the right and said, "Let me show you ours. I'm assured it's one of the best in the country."

Kate stepped through the door and found herself at the side of the organ case, looking down into the chapel. Jacob invited her to sit at the keyboards. It was overwhelming, an extraordinarily complicated thing. Three keyboards were arranged on top of each other, raked backwards, the topmost much shorter than the other two, with keys only for the right hand. Two columns of wooden knobs were arranged on either side, and Kate looked at a few of the labels: Trumpet, Hautboy, Flute, Cremona, Vox Humana, Cornet, Fifteenth, and many more, some of which she had trouble reading. Open Diapason? Sesquialtera? It was quite dark in the space, particular with the ornate wooden screen on the gallery behind her. She put her hands on the keys and pressed a few notes. Nothing happened.

"How do you make it go?" she asked.

"You need a friend to pump the wind for you," he replied.

"It looks really complicated. Does anyone learn to play it?"

"A few," said Jacob. "Mr Browning provides lessons. He plays well."

Kate slid off the bench. There was a lot of space in the gallery on either side of the organ. Jacob explained that the choir stood there and sang under Mr Browning's direction. "Let's show you the rest of this floor and then we'll go on."

They returned to the west wing, and Jacob ushered Kate into a vacant room containing only a harpsichord and two chairs. A painting of a ruined castle hung on the wall above the unlit fireplace.

"Practice room," said Jacob. "There are several just like this along the corridor."

They withdrew and walked to the far end of the wing.

"And this is a little concert hall," he said, opening the last door. It was a large room with fixed benches for about a hundred people. The floor sloped gently downwards to a stage, on which sat a few instruments: harpsichord, harp, three large drums, a cello.

"Let's go on," he said.

They continued up to the second floor, which housed all the dormitories for the girls and those for the four house-mistresses. There were several domestic staff at work in the rooms, changing bed linen, cleaning. Jacob greeted them one by one as they passed. "Birdie, Jewel, Mabel."

They came to a room in the east wing, and Jacob pointed out Kate's bed.

"This is where you'll sleep. You'll be sharing the room with three others. I hope you don't mind."

Kate had been used to a space of her own, but the prospect of sharing didn't worry her, particularly as the room was large, with huge windows and a lovely view. Her bags were waiting for her next to her bed.

"I'm sure I won't mind," said Kate. Then she exclaimed, "All the girls seem so beautiful!"

"Yes," murmured Jacob, thinking, *Of course they are.* "Come," he said. "We're nearly done. I'll show you the rest of the house."

Just a few feet further along the corridor there was a gate that gave access to a narrow staircase.

"That's where your maids live," said Jacob. "They have a private space separated off from the rest of the house. Seven maids, just for the girls. Don't be frightened to make use of them. They'll help you bathe, dress – anything that needs doing. They like to walk in the afternoons if they can, so I doubt any of them are in at the moment." He paused, then said, "Are you getting tired?"

"It's a lot to take in," Kate replied.

He smiled. "We're nearly finished. Let me show you the library."

The library occupied the entire south end of the upper two floors of the east wing, with bookshelves on the lower level crammed fifteen feet high. The upper level, which housed bookcases to the height of a further five feet, was accessed by an iron spiral staircase and took the form of a gallery running round three sides of the room. Tables, chairs and various comfortable furnishings occupied the centre of the library floor, and the windows – towering to a height of twenty feet at the south end of the room – flooded the space with daylight. The library was set immediately over the chapel below, although there was no access between the two spaces. Jacob pointed out a small door in the southeast corner of the library upper level and told her that it led to a short stone staircase in the southeast turret, with a tiny room at the top. Kate loved hiding-places and set her heart on climbing up there as soon as possible. She imagined herself sitting secretly with a book in the cosy little space.

On the way back to the main staircase, Jacob opened a privy door. Kate saw what was inside, and Mr Crowan said, "There are several of these on each floor. You'll find them. We have a staff of three soil-boys responsible for keeping them in good order – Slade, Lucas and Jude – you'll see them sooner or later. They're nice lads." He closed the privy door and opened another immediately to its left, revealing a washroom all decorated in white. "And there are several washrooms throughout the house, including six on this floor expressly for the use of the girls. Two of them have baths. Please use them as you wish. The maids ensure that hot water is always available. There's a winch shaft in the west wing that makes it easy to bring heated water up from the kitchen, so you needn't be sparing."

They ascended to the top floor and paused for a moment at the rail guarding the stairwell. Kate looked down to ground level. The drop had a dizzying effect and she found it difficult to tear herself away.

Jacob didn't show Kate much of the top floor, although he did describe the layout for her. The end of the west wing housed his own suite as well as the living quarters for his secretary Mr Quinton, and for the headmistress and her personal assistant. The two head servants, Mr York and Mrs Illif, also had rooms at this level. A few guest suites were spread out along the corridor, and the doctor's apartment and infirmary were at the north end of the east wing. There was a large room in the rear corner of the house opposite the infirmary, which was structurally unsafe and remained locked. The rest of the east wing on the top floor was occupied by the girls' maids and the upper level of the library, which Kate had already inspected.

It was quite dark by the time the tour was over, and Jacob said they could explore the grounds and the other buildings in the morning. Lessons were about to conclude, and Kate would shortly meet her room-mates, so he returned her to her dormitory.

"Dinner commences at six-thirty," he said. I'll look forward to seeing you there. Please settle in – and make yourself at home!" He smiled, raised his hand in farewell, and left.

Kate began to unpack her bags. She'd been allotted a sizeable corner of the room, with a chair, trunk, wardrobe and dressing table as well as her bed, on which she found fresh towels. It was quiet in the corridor, classes having not yet finished, and Kate wandered a little way to a privy and a washroom. The latter was plain and whitewashed, just like the specimen Jacob had shown her earlier. There were several pedestals supporting large basins, and pitchers of warm water sat beside them. Two bathtubs were pushed up against the wall. The floor sloped gently towards a drain in one corner, with shallow channels cut to aid the escape of water. She inspected the drain itself, which appeared to be a vertical pipe of about three inches diameter. After washing, Kate took her basin of water and poured it onto the floor, watching as it ran gurgling away down the hole.

A moment later she heard young voices approaching, so returned to her room to await the arrival of her new companions. A few girls passed by in the corridor, briefly peeking in at Kate as they passed. One or two of them gave her a friendly wave, and Kate smiled in response.

Her three room-mates arrived simultaneously and greeted her straight away.

"You must be the new girl. Wow! Look at your hair!" The girl came over and started to fiddle with it.

"I'm Kate," said Kate.

"I'm Bip," said Bip.

"That's a nice name," said Kate. "Is it short for something?"

"Yes," said Bip, "Anne."

"Bip is short for Anne?"

"Yes." Bip was still engrossed with Kate's hair. "How do you get hair like this?" The other two girls had come to join in the admiration, all running their fingers over Kate's head.

"Apparently my great great great grandmother had it too."

"It's amazing!" The word's second syllable was drawn out.

The other girls introduced themselves.

"I'm Pammy."

"And I'm Shelagh."

"Nice to meet you," said Kate. "You're all really pretty." It was true – they were. All of them were attractive and slender, with pleasantly sculpted, distinctive faces. Bip and Shelagh had dark brown hair, while Pammy was lighter, with lovely blue eyes. They were roughly the same age as Kate.

"Where do you come from?" asked Pammy.

Kate told them a little about herself and learned something about them in return. Bip and Pammy had been brought to the Lookout from the Halifax workhouse. Pammy had vague recollections of her mother, but Bip didn't recall her parents at all. Shelagh had run away from home when she was eight, having been abused by her mother's partner. She'd been living in the gutters of Cromer for nearly two years by the time she was spotted by Mr Crowan's scouts. It had been a hard life, but she'd learned to fend for herself. Kate instinctively liked her very much – she had the hardest shell of the three.

Kate learned their full names. Bip was really Anne Pringle, although no-one called her Anne; Pammy was Pamela Heron; Shelagh's surname was Jamieson. Bip and Pammy were eleven; Shelagh had just turned twelve.

A smiley young woman, thin, blonde, pale-skinned and dressed in black, appeared in the doorway. "Let's get you ready then," she said.

Pammy introduced Kate to Cady Weston, one of the maids, explaining that she'd come to help them dress for dinner. "We have to dress specially," said Pammy. "Do you have dining clothes?"

"I have my best dress," said Kate, not entirely sure what they meant.

"I'm sure that'll do," said Pammy. "Dressing for specific events is something we learn. Watch us."

The three girls got out of their school clothes, and Cady helped them into their dinner dresses. First they put on pretty bodices, stockings and petticoats, then very fine gowns. Kate was dismayed. She had nothing to compare. Finally, they added ruffles and gleaming shoes with low heels. By the time the ritual came to an end, Kate had been sitting in her best dress for twenty minutes.

"I don't have any clothes like that," she said downcast.

Shelagh laughed. "Don't worry. Neither did we. I expect you'll be fitted out tomorrow. You look fine as you are. This isn't a formal meal anyway – there are different rules for those."

Kate shook her head, worried.

"It's confusing at first," said Shelagh, "but you'll pick it up."

"I'm so hungry I could eat one of the farmers," said Bip.

"Well, let's go and see if roast farmer's on the table," replied Pammy.

"You'll get used to the banter," said Shelagh to Kate. "Coming for dinner?"

"I am," Kate replied and followed them down the staircase to the ground floor.

Dinner was divided into three sittings. The youngest girls were served at half past six, the thirteen and fourteen-year-olds joining them at seven o'clock. At half past seven the older girls would arrive.

Mr Crowan had been watching out for Kate. He put his hand on her shoulder and asked, "How's it going? Are you settling in?"

"Yes, thank you, it's lovely."

He smiled. "I'm glad to hear it. Bip showing you the ropes?"

"Yes."

"Have a good meal then. Away you go."

The girls selected their places as the kitchen staff arrived with the soup, which was served at the table by the footmen and maids. There was small-beer to drink. Kate thought the soup was a kind of mixed vegetable broth but couldn't precisely identify all the ingredients. The second course, consisting of about twenty individual dishes, was laid in the centre of the table. There were various meats, fish and vegetables.

Kate became conscious of the ritual, the etiquette, of the table. She watched and learned. Sometimes the girls would reach for a particular dish themselves or ask their neighbour for it. If anything was out of reach, a footman would be called to fetch it. The girls never rose from where they sat.

After the main courses were finished, the maids and footmen completely changed the tablecloth before bringing in the sweet courses. Fresh cutlery was provided for the jellies, custards and creams, but there was also a selection of dry food that was eaten with the fingers: nuts, dried fruit, small cakes, various dainty confections, and cheese. A glass of wine accompanied the sweet course. Kate had tasted wine only a couple of times before and didn't care for it much. She made a face.

"You'll have to get used to it," said Shelagh. "It's all part of the instruction. You'll learn how to tell a good one from a bad one – but you don't have to drink much of it. Just take a bit and leave the rest if you like."

Kate felt very full by the time the meal was over. It had been the biggest she'd ever eaten – and she'd polished off everything on her plate.

"You don't need to eat every morsel," said Shelagh. "Just eat as much as you feel comfortable with. They don't like us to swell out much."

The older girls arrived in the hall at about half past seven. They looked splendid, stunning – like royalty.

"They're gorgeous!" said Kate breathlessly.

Shelagh smiled at her. "We'll all look like that in time."

The tutors arrived one by one as the evening wore on. Kate scanned the hall. Mr Crowan sat in a group of four at the top table. A squat, ugly man sat on his right side and two women on his left – one in her early forties, stern in appearance; the other younger, pretty and blonde. The tutors' bench was just below the top table and a little to the side. About twenty people sat there. Kate recognised the harpsichord teacher Rider Browning as well as Miss Dryden and Mademoiselle Ardoin. She cast her eyes around the rest of the hall.

"It's extraordinary!" she said.

"What's extraordinary?" Bip replied.

"They're all beautiful – all the girls – each and every one of them."

"Well, the object is to go into fashionable society at the end of the course, so I suppose they deliberately pick out the pretty girls."

"It seems a pity, though," said Kate. "You don't have to be beautiful to play music, or sing, or speak French."

"Don't complain, Kate," said Pammy. "We're all very lucky to be here."

Kate reflected. "I suppose so."

After dinner the four girls changed into casual clothes, went to the library and sat talking together. It was cosy in the room, with the comforting scent of the peat fire and the warm glow of lanterns and lamps. There were no other occupants when they arrived, but two older girls appeared shortly afterwards and introduced themselves to Kate as Harriet Dixon and Iris Little, both in Class 6, which had an average age of fifteen (Class 7 being the topmost). The two sat by themselves beneath the window and had an animated conversation – punctuated by a lot of giggling – about the contrasting qualities of the footmen. Kate picked up only fragments of what they said.

Suddenly she remembered the little door on the upper level and said, animatedly, "Can we look in the turret?"

"If you want," said Bip. "There's not much up there."

"I want to see," said Kate.

Shelagh took one of the oil lamps, and they all clattered up the iron spiral staircase and along the gallery beside the bookshelves until they reached the little door set in the corner. The topmost part of the huge window was immediately to their right, filled with night's blackness. Kate was excited and stood looking at the door handle.

"It's not locked," said Pammy.

The hinges creaked as Kate pulled the door open. It was very dark inside. Shelagh passed the lamp forward to Kate. She held it up and stepped to the doorframe. A narrow set of stone steps was revealed in the lamplight, spiralling up clockwise inside the turret. Kate clicked her fingers and listened to the brief, sharp echo.

"Wow!" she whispered. "It's like being in an old castle."

It was cold inside the turret, and the chill flowed down the stairs like liquid. Kate began to ascend, followed by the others. It wasn't a long climb – there were only sixteen steps. At the top there was a tiny six-sided room with a bench dressed into the stonework on five sides, leaving the sixth open for the ingress of the stairs. There was room for only three of the girls; Shelagh hung back on the staircase. A small window was set in each of the six faces. It was very dark outside, so Kate turned the lamp down as low as it would go and looked out.

"It's amazing up here!" she whispered. "I love it!"

Looking down from her lofty position, she was able to see the roof of the house, just a few feet below, dark in the starlight. To the west, a long way off, stood the turret on the southwest corner, identical to the one in which she now stood. Kate remembered the interior layout of the house and worked out that the southwest turret must be accessed from Mr Crowan's apartment. Her eyes were still adjusting to the darkness, but she was able to pick out the remote northwest turret at the rear corner of the house. Again she tried to deduce the position of the entrance but wasn't so sure this time, being uncertain as to whose rooms occupied that particular corner of the building. She recalled that the last turret, that on the northeast corner, was much higher than the other three, sitting on top of a narrow tower. A second later she was looking up at it. Being at the far end of the east wing, it was the closest to where she was standing, although it was still a long way off – about a hundred and thirty feet. She had to peer into the darkness of the night to pick out its details. There was an odd patch of paleness behind the distant window. With a start, Kate realised it was a face, looking right at her across the gulf of frigid night air. She shivered, gasped in shock and stepped back, bumping into Bip, who'd been standing behind her. The two of them nearly tumbled down the stairs.

"What was it? What happened?" asked Bip, alarmed.

Kate gathered her wits, shivering again. "There's someone at the window," she said. "It made me jump, that's all. I wasn't expecting to see a face."

"Which window?" asked Pammy.

"The tall turret – the one at the back of the house."

"Oh. That's odd," said Shelagh.

"Odd?" Kate replied.

"Yes, odd. The entrance to the tower is in the locked room. No-one goes in there. It isn't safe."

Kate stepped to the window and looked at the tower again, peering very hard, concentrating. The pale patch had gone; the turret stood dark and unoccupied.

"Let me see?" said Bip, stepping forward. She peered out into the night. "It's pretty stygian out there. And the tower..." She began to whisper. "Remote; unreachable; inscrutable..."

"Stop fooling around, Bip," said Shelagh.

"Maybe it was a reflection or something," said Kate doubtfully.

"I can't see anyone," said Bip. "It does look creepy, though." Pammy wanted to leave. "It's cold up here," she said. "Let's go down to the fireside."

The girls carefully descended the stairs, the light from the library dimly illuminating the lowest few steps. A moment later they were seated on the rug before the fireplace, watching the flames and swapping stories.

Kate woke in the night. The room was almost black, curtains closed against the faint light. Something had woken her. She listened for sounds in the darkness but heard only the breathing of the sleeping girls, the gentle ticking of the clock, the faint brushing of the wind.

Then she heard it, distant and intermittent. Someone was crying – a woman. It was such a forlorn, lost sound, the hopelessness in it rendered still more pitiful because of the enfolding blackness. The last time Kate had heard such sadness was from grandma when ma died. She lay listening to it for several minutes, shedding a few tears of her own in spontaneous sympathy. The crying faded after a while, leaving only the girls' breathing, the tick of the clock and the wind.

Soon Kate was deeply asleep, wrapped safe in the warmth of her new bed.

30. THE LOOKOUT
Thursday October 30

Kate awoke to the sound of a man's voice. "Breakfast, ladies!"

She was lying on her left side, facing the wall. There was movement behind her – Bip was out of bed and opening the curtains to the dull morning light.

"What time is it?" asked Kate.

"Eight o'clock," said Bip. "Wakey-wakey."

Shelagh and Pammy were through the door and on their way to the washrooms. Kate stretched and yawned. Then she remembered.

"Someone was crying in the night."

"Aha! You heard that."

"Yes, did you?"

"No, I've never heard it, but some people can."

"You don't know who it is?" asked Kate.

"No. It's just a voice. Did it wake you?"

"Yes, I think so. It was very sad."

"Well, crying usually *is* sad."

"Yes, but this was...really, really...sad." It was too early for her to find the words she wanted.

"Come on, sleepyhead!" said Bip. "Up you get."

Kate rose, yawned again, went to the jakes, then found Bip in the washroom. They stood together at their ablutions, and Kate said, "Is breakfast as formal as dinner?"

"No," said Bip. "Breakfast is a free-for-all. Everybody turns up at once. I'm hungry! Let's get dressed and go!"

The dining hall was packed. Breakfast included sausages, eggs, bacon, kidneys, kippers, cold meats, bread and butter and cheese. There was tea to drink – and coffee, which was new to Kate.

"Try a cup?" Shelagh suggested.

"Yes, alright. Thank you."

Shelagh signalled to one of the footmen.

"Mr Ousby, may we take two cups of coffee, please?"

"Of course, Miss Shelagh." He nodded.

"And a cup of chocolate, please!" called Bip.

Ousby nodded again and went to fetch what they'd asked for.

"I must try to remember their names," said Kate.

Shelagh replied, "It takes a while, but everybody knows everybody else. It's all very friendly. We've just sent Rye Ousby (Zachariah is his real name) to fetch our drinks. He's married to Flossie (Florence), one of the dairymaids (she's lovely – you'll like her). They're both obsessed with keeping fit – like to run. The other footmen are..." Shelagh looked around to see how many were present, then named them one by one, pointing them out. "That's Theo Westmorland. He's gorgeous, but married to Sukey, also a dairymaid. Erm..., let me see... There's Newt Fallowfield, over there with the straw-coloured hair... and that one is Gene (Eugene) Fenton. He's a bit shy. And I bet you haven't met many of our maids yet – or the house-mistresses."

"No, I haven't," said Kate. "Only Cady last night."

"They're all lovely," said Shelagh, "although the house-mistresses can be pretty hot in pursuit of the men. They're a bit wild – *I* think anyway. Lots of fun, though." She presented Kate with a big smile. "You'll love it here – you really will! It's full of adventures."

Shelagh's enthusiasm infected Kate; made her feel excited. Their drinks arrived. Bip took her chocolate and started on it straight away. "Lovely and creamy," she said.

Shelagh presented Kate with her coffee. The cup was of moderate size, and the liquid was very black. Kate put her nose to it and sniffed. "Smells nice."

"Try it black first," said Shelagh.

Kate took a small sip, wrinkled her face and shivered. "Ugh! It's *very* bitter!"

"But you don't have to drink it like that," said Shelagh. "Look." She lifted the lid from a small jug of cream. "Let's see what you think of this." Shelagh poured the cream into the coffee until it assumed a much friendlier brown colour, then stirred with a little silver spoon. "Now try."

The bitter taste was transformed into something very much milder, and the cream gave the drink a lovely, velvety texture.

"That's much better," said Kate.

"I thought you'd like it. You can add some sugar if you like." Shelagh opened another little pot, revealing the sweet substance within.

"Alright, let's try a bit," said Kate. Shelagh poured in one small spoonful and stirred. Kate sipped. "Oh. That's nice – I'm a coffee drinker!"

"Well done, you!" said Shelagh.

"I like you!" Kate laughed. Shelagh gave her a little peck on the cheek.

Mr Crowan suddenly appeared on Kate's right.

"All going well, Kate?"

"Yes, it's lovely, thank you, Mr Crowan."

"I'm glad to hear it. There'll be no classes for you until tomorrow. At ten o'clock this morning you'll be visited in your room by Mercy and Ada, the seamstresses. They'll take your measurements and talk to you about your preferences for clothes. It should take only half an hour or forty minutes. After that, I've arranged for Nellie Brent to take you on a tour of the grounds. Nellie is one of your maids. She'll collect you at your room and have you back in time for close of lessons and dinner. Would that be acceptable?"

"Yes. Thank you. I'll go to my room after breakfast and wait there."

"Just the thing! Have a good day!" Jacob looked past Kate

and spoke to Shelagh. "How are you today, Shelagh?"

"Very well, thank you, Mr Crowan."

"And you, Bip?"

"Very well, thank you, Mr Crowan. Looking forward to Latin today – it's my favourite."

Crowan laughed. Bip had a prized sense of humour. "I bet it is!" he replied.

Kate was sitting on her bed when the two women arrived on the dot of ten o'clock, armed with tape measures and other bits of equipment. Both appeared prim and severe, unsmiling, dressed in plain black and white. They greeted her, confirmed that she was indeed Kate, but didn't offer their own names. All Kate's measurements were acquired, including those of her feet and the circumference of her head. One of the women made the usual comment about her hair. There followed a very brief discussion about Kate's tastes in colour, fabric and design, but she assured them that she had no particular requests, preferring to leave all the details in their hands. The two women were gone in under half an hour.

Kate waited quietly for about ten minutes, then heard footsteps hurrying down the maids' staircase just next to her room. A moment later her guide appeared – a thin, mousy woman aged about thirty, with coarse fair hair and brown eyes. She wore a brown dress with a white apron and bonnet, all slung about with a cape, also brown.

"Hello. Are you Kate?" she asked.

"I am," Kate replied.

"I'm Nellie Brent. Mr Crowan asked me to take you outside. It's quite chilly. You'll need to dress warmly, and put on your boots for the mud."

Kate had anticipated the necessity of boots and was already wearing them. She quickly pulled her coat from the wardrobe and put it on.

"Good. Let's go," said Nellie.

Nellie was energetic and liked to move briskly. She led Kate downstairs to the ground floor and into the west wing, greeting several members of the domestic staff as she passed them. At the dining hall she waited a moment for Kate to catch up, then led her along the corridor and through a door on the right just before the entrance to the kitchens. Kate found herself in a plain passage, painted yellow. The fine furnishings, beautiful paintings and ornate wood panelling of the house clearly did not extend into the more functional areas. The door at the far end of the passageway was open, framing a patch of dull daylight. They made their way towards it, passing several small rooms, some cluttered, others quite bare. A boy, ragged in appearance and two or three years Kate's senior, emerged from a room on the left.

"Morning, Slade. All well with you today?" asked Nellie as they passed in the corridor.

"Yes thanks, Miss Brent." He tugged his forelock at Kate and said, "Morning, miss."

"Good morning," Kate replied as he disappeared behind them.

As they reached the exit, Nellie said, "That was Slade Stone, one of the soil-boys."

They emerged into the light, and Kate found herself on a path bordering a large kitchen garden in which three women were at work. She looked from right to left and breathed in the crisp scents of the autumn morning. A middle-aged woman rose from her task and raised a hand.

"Morning, Nellie," she called.

"Morning, Maisie. How's your back?"

"It's always worse in this cold weather," the woman replied.

The other two women were younger. They called their greetings, and Nellie replied to each in turn. "Opal. Annie." Kate looked around her while the women exchanged pleasantries. The further edge of the garden was bordered by fruit trees and a hedge. There was a road beyond, coming into view on the left, around the side of the school, then passing by the garden and running on to the peat bunker and stables and beyond.

"This is Kate," Nellie called to the women. "She's new." Then she turned to Kate and introduced the women one by one. "Kate, that's Maisie – Maisie Blythe," (indicating the middle-aged woman), "and that's Opal Clayden, and over there near the apple tree is Annie Alby." Opal and Annie appeared to be about thirty.

Greetings were exchanged, and the women went back to their work. Nellie turned and indicated the door through which they'd just emerged. "If you ever need to get in and out at night, this door's never locked."

"Isn't that dangerous?" Kate asked.

"Well, the park is secure – supposedly, anyway – and Mr Crowan reckons its safer to keep an exit open. In any case, Slade, Jude and Lucas need to come and go at night, shifting all the soil buckets. And lots of people are up early, specially in the kitchen: there's the milking to be done, butter to be made, bread and rolls to bake, breakfast to prepare, all the water drawn up for bathing, the spill jars and peat boxes to be filled... It's a lot, running a place like this. It's not often that everyone's in bed at the same time." She paused for a second, then looked at Kate and said, "Feeling up to some exercise?"

"I am," replied Kate.

"Let's go then!"

Nellie led her along by the wall of the house and turned right at the northwest corner. The exterior of the ballroom stood before them. It appeared to be an addition to the original building, standing only a single story in height while the bulk of the house towered above. Kate looked in through one of the windows. Nothing moved inside – the room was unoccupied.

Nellie waited for a moment, then drew Kate's attention to

298

the large area of benches and statuary set immediately to the rear of the ballroom.

"This area is used for parties, and for outdoor theatre productions. It's very nice in the warm weather. Looks a bit bleak now though."

Kate looked to her left and saw the flower garden, set away from the house and beyond the theatre area, running all the way from one side of the building to the other.

"The garden looks brilliant in the summer," said Nellie.

"I bet it does," Kate answered.

As they walked along beside the rear of the house, a substantial building came into view away to the left, beyond a line of trees. It was similar in design to the main house, although smaller – only two stories in height. As they walked towards it, Nellie said, "This building is new. It's where the staff live – except us maids, of course – we stay close to you girls. But the tutors live here, as well as their servants, all the cleaning staff and domestics, the footmen, the kitchen staff and dairymaids... Alfred the porter, and... a few others."

The building reproduced the shape of the older house, with a long central span and two wings projecting at right-angles. It had its own flower garden, statuary, and several outdoor sitting areas.

They walked through the staff-house garden, and Nellie pointed out the laundry just east of the new building. Sheets had been spread out to dry on lines and bushes, but the sky was darkening, and Kate thought the washing might need to be rescued in a while.

"The Staffords live in the laundry," said Nellie. "Nice, decent people – dedicated. Michael and Mary and their family: Beryl, Crispin (lovely boy, he is. He'll marry Winnie one day), Babs and Sylvia."

"Who's Winnie?" asked Kate.

"Ah, course, I forgot. You haven't met all the maids yet. Winnie Warwick is another one of your maids, like me.

Then there's Cady Weston, Sarah Alston, Mary Acker, Molly Colby and Ethel Coombs. It's a lot of names for you to remember all at once, but you'll soon get used to everyone."

They doubled back, keeping the gardens of the main house on their left. The large brick-built stable and coach house was an old building, constructed at the same time as the Lookout. The big doors were open, revealing several vehicles on the right-hand side, and the horses' stalls opposite. They walked inside and found a young man at work, grooming a horse. Nellie greeted him.

"Morning Nolly."

"Morning Nellie," the boy laughed.

Nellie looked at Kate. "Nellie and Nolly. We have a bit of a giggle about that, don't we Nolly?"

"Quite right, Nellie," replied Nolly.

"Nolly, this is Kate."

Nolly said hello.

Nellie looked at the horse, a big, coppery bay with a white diamond between its eyes. "How's Demeter today?" she patted the horse and stroked its shoulder and neck.

"She's very well. She's a good girl," replied Nolly. Then, addressing the horse, "Aren't you, my beautiful?"

"She's lovely," said Nellie.

Kate joined in the petting. "Lovely and smooth," she said. "So, you're Demeter."

"Mr Crowan likes her," said Nolly. "Takes her out for a run sometimes, all by himself."

"I love horses," said Kate.

"Do you ride?" asked Nolly.

"Not really," Kate replied. "I'd need lessons, I think."

"At your service," said Nolly and bowed.

Kate laughed and said, "Alright! I'll look forward to it!"

"Me too!" said Nolly.

Nellie led Kate outside, and they moved back towards the kitchen garden. "Nolly Arkwright," she said. "He's a good lad – been here since the place started."

Just beyond the stable there was a yard full of hens and geese. The hens clucked away in fear, but the geese came running towards the gate, flapping their wings and making a tremendous fuss, honking and hissing. Kate hurried past, startled.

"Don't worry about them," said Nellie. "Silly old things." She moved a few yards beyond the poultry enclosure, beckoned Kate to join her, and pointed out the cowshed and milking yard to the rear of the stables. Two cows stood there, pails beneath their udders, the milkmaids hard at work.

"That's..." She peered, "...Delia and Neva doing the milking."

They retraced their steps again and walked back past the stables, following the road for about a hundred yards as it curved to the north. Nellie came to a halt and pointed into the middle distance. As she did so, Kate distinctly heard someone far away shout, "BASTARD!" She looked at Nellie in puzzlement.

Nellie laughed. "That's Speck Beckwith calling his dog."

The cry came again. "BAAASTARD!"

Nellie pointed out the animal, in a field some distance away with a flock of sheep. "And there you can see Speck calling him. The dog plays him up sometimes."

A herd of cattle stood almost motionless in a nearby field, watching Kate and Nellie intently, their lower jaws munching from side to side, big blue tongues like fat lizards, licking their lips, their nostrils. Nellie pointed out the cattle shed nearby and also the paddock behind the stables. Kate counted four horses there. Various pens and enclosures, one of them containing several pigs, lay between the paddock and the two fields.

They walked a little further north. After a couple of minutes, another building came into view, up by the second field, where Bastard was still making a nuisance of himself.

"Who lives there?" asked Kate.

"The farmers and gardeners... It's a block of terraced cottages – bigger than it looks from here – quite a lot of it is out of sight behind. And the forge is a little further along that road. Alan Blake is the smithy. He's a strong man, good-looking. The maids all like him, and the housemistresses make dirty jokes about him – they're wicked, that lot. He's married though, and lives there with his wife and boy. Wife's name is Chastity. The housemistresses laugh themselves to death, makin' merry with that. The boy's nice, polite. Bartholomew – Barney. He's eight now. Growing up."

"So where does Nolly live?"

"Nolly lives in the stables with the drivers. He's got a cosy room over the horses."

They continued to walk east, the house and associated buildings falling behind. After a while, two more buildings came into view, away on the right, and Nellie identified one of these as the brewhouse. "Six men work and live in there," she said. "They have three big tanks for rainwater and use their own well too. They make all our ales and beers and some of our fruit wine as well. Mrs Rowley, the cook, is very proud of her own wine though, and only uses the brewery boys to make sure the supplies are kept topped up." She indicated the other building and went on, "and that's the carpenters' shop. Chad Sandon, Tom Thorne and Ferret Colborn live there. They don't always have much to do, so they go about peering at the girls like filthy old men. Dirty-minded old buggers. Don't take any notice o' them."

"The school is a huge place!" said Kate. "It's like a town."

"It is," Nellie agreed, eyebrows raised. "It's a nice place to live. Where have you come from?"

Kate told Nellie about herself as they went along; about life on the farm, her grandmother, her mother and father, her friends.

They were walking uphill; a gentle incline at first, then steeper. A shallow brook ran down from the high ground on their right, channelled into a little valley some distance away, and turned towards the coast. The sound of the gulls increased, and Kate smelled the ocean. A moment later they arrived at the brow of the hill, and there it was – the North Sea. Nellie came to a halt, and Kate looked about her. The rise where they stood gradually descended to rocks and a wide shingle beach straight ahead. The little brook ran into the sea away to her right. Beyond the brook, heath-land rose steadily; grasses and delicate purple heather. Kate turned and looked behind her. The school was visible but far away.

It must be impossible to see the sea from the house, she thought. *What a pity. This little hill must completely hide the view.*

To the north, the land rose gently at first but then very sharply. There were high cliffs in the middle distance, topped by a ruined stone tower. It was an impressive look-ing structure, battered by the sea wind and the ravages of time. Kate judged it to be about forty feet in height, maybe more.

"What's that?" she asked.

"It's an old lookout tower. It's where the house gets its name. That is *the* lookout."

Kate imagined herself at its top, watching the approach of a storm. Actually, it *was* becoming quite windy.

"It's fantastic," she said.

"The woods beyond the tower mark the boundary of the estate. The cliffs continue after that, and you come to Peak a little further up the coast. It's a nice walk." Nellie waited, wondering where Kate might like to go next – if she might pick her own direction. But Kate was staring at the tower and didn't seem ready to move on. After a moment, Nellie asked if she'd like to go down to the beach.

"That would be nice. Thank you."

It took them another ten minutes or so to reach the sea-shore. The ebb tide was just beginning to pull, and Kate stood on the shingle and breathed in the crisp salt air. The wind was getting cold, but the exercise had kept her warm. She loved the smell of the seaweed and the skirl of the gulls. Nellie watched her as she walked to the water's edge, knelt down and put her hands in the sea. The wind played with her hair like a rough, loving parent. She was struck by how natural a part of the landscape Kate seemed to be. For a moment Nellie had the impression that the child and the sea were the same – that the wind knew her – that she was an embodiment of the forces of nature that played around her; that she was much more than a mere girl. It was an odd sensation, eerie, disturbing. She'd never before felt such a peculiar thing and found herself frowning in puzzlement. She was silent for a while, then called, "I should get back. Work to do."

"Alright," said Kate. "Thank you for showing me round. I've had a lovely time."

"You're very welcome," Nellie replied.

They retraced their steps to the brow of the hill, the wind strengthening as they climbed, chilling the air further. The school came into sight, and Kate picked out a figure walking towards them.

"Who's this...?" mumbled Nellie. She strained to see. "It's Mabel, I think. Mabel Stanton." Nellie raised her arm in greeting, and the approaching figure returned the gesture. A few moments walking closed the gap between them, and they came to a halt. Mabel was a big woman in her middle thirties, plump, with rosy cheeks and blonde hair. Nellie asked, "Have you met Kate?"

"No, but I saw you yesterday. I was cleaning the rooms, and you came by with Mr Crowan. Nice to meet you."

"Nice to meet you too, Mabel," said Kate.

"We've just been for a walk to the beach," said Nellie.

"That's nice," Mabel replied. The wind blew her hair across

her face. She swept it away and said, "The rooms are done, and I'm away up to the scar."

"To the tower?" asked Kate with some excitement.

"I'll pass by the tower," said Mabel.

"Can I come?" asked Kate. "Do you mind?" The first question was addressed to Mabel, the second to both women.

Nellie and Mabel glanced at each other. Mabel shrugged. Nellie said, "Sure you don't mind? You'll get her back in good time, won't you?"

"Yes, alright," said Mabel.

Kate thanked Nellie again, and the two parted with a wave. Mabel began to walk in the direction of the sea. "So, your first day in the school?" she said.

"Yes," said Kate. "I love it."

They conversed as they walked along – mostly small talk about where Kate had come from, what her interests were, her impressions of her new environment. In a few moments, Mabel turned north onto a faint path towards the high ground, and they followed the track as it sloped gently upwards. The lie of the land hid the tower from view as they approached, the terrain rising ever more steeply, but it came into sight again later. The last part of the climb was very steep and needed some care, but it eased off near the top, and they emerged onto a platform of grass, heather and gorse.

The old broken building stood about ten yards from the cliff edge, looking out over the darkening North Sea. Kate drew an awed breath and stared. Its shattered countenance made a deep impression on her; she felt she was in the presence of some silent oracle from the ancient world. The rear of the tower had collapsed, the stones lying strewn about, but the ruination only added to the formidable impression, particularly with the angry storm clouds surging in. There was something elemental about it, and Kate felt an overwhelming need to be enclosed in its womb-like embrace. She walked forward and began to pick her way over the broken stonework.

Mabel remained where she was and watched as the girl disappeared from view. "Be careful," she called. "I don't know how safe it is."

Kate stood in the centre of the enclosed space. There was a great sense of stillness despite the broken wall, and the soft sounds she made with her voice were amplified as if they were being mimicked by whatever lonely god or goddess lived here. The tower was about twenty feet in diameter and about fifty in height, wider at the base than at the summit, narrowing as it rose. There were holes opposite each other in the walls on at least two upper levels, having once held joists for wooden floors. An embrasure, high above, suggested a fireplace, or perhaps the upper part of a staircase. She counted a total of six small windows, the ledges still visible, and imagined how it must have looked hundreds of years ago when it was in use. Perhaps it had been a lighthouse, a flame burning on its roof, a beacon for ships at sea. Or maybe it really had been a lookout tower, high enough to give plenty of warning against the approach of enemy ships. The crumbling, ancient stone was plastered with moss and lichen. A few plants had found cracks in the upper part of the structure and taken root, their living fingers stretching, imploring the light. Kate looked straight up at the broken circle of stone, the roof of the sky rolling storm clouds overhead like angry demons, and felt as if she were at the bottom of a well. The feeling of vertigo almost toppled her, and she staggered.

"Kate," called Mabel. "The storm's coming in fast. We'd better go home."

Kate appeared a moment later and clambered back over the stones to the older woman. "Sorry," she said. "I didn't mean to hold you up."

"Don't worry," said Mabel. "I wouldn't have got there anyway – not in weather like this."

"Were you going to Peak?" asked Kate.

"No," Mabel replied. "There's a special place I like to go – away from the estate, beyond the wood. It's quiet, private. No-one else ever goes there." Mabel expected Kate to ask about it, to ask if she could come too, but no such enquiry came. *She's a sensitive girl*, thought Mabel.

They began to make their way down the steep slope, the school coming immediately into view. It was a scramble. Mabel turned and used all fours, but Kate managed it by jumping from spot to spot. The gradient soon became more shallow, and the first drops of rain began to fall as they hurried along the path, moving gently downhill towards the main track between the house and the beach.

The downpour began in earnest as they drew closer to the school buildings. Kate, remembering the face at the window from the night before, looked up at the tower – and stopped. Two faces were looking at her; she could see them clearly despite the pouring rain. Mabel halted and turned, then followed the line of Kate's gaze. She nodded in recognition, drips falling from her nose and the hood of her cape. "You can see them," she said. The downpour became a deluge, smashing forcefully into the earth around them.

The faces were still there, looking directly at her.

"Who are they?" Kate shouted through the tumult.

"They're the Wynter twins. They starved to death up there more than fifty years ago."

"Can you see them too?"

Mabel looked hard. "No. Not this time. But I have seen them. They just stare."

"What do they want?"

Mabel shook her head, frowning. "Who knows? Their spirits are fixed in the house, like old cobwebs."

Kate shivered. The water had penetrated her clothes; she could feel the chill on her skin.

"Come on," said Mabel. "You'll catch *your* death out here."

There was a flash and a cacophonous roll of thunder. The two ran to the house, puddles exploding beneath their feet.

Bip, Pammy and Shelagh skipped noisily along the corridor and into the dormitory when lessons were over, having spent most of the afternoon in Miss Trollope's needlepoint class. Kate had been weighing up whether she should talk to them about the ghosts but decided against it. No-one had mentioned the Wynter twins the previous night when Kate glimpsed them at the tower window. Perhaps they were unaware of them. In any case, Kate didn't want to draw attention to herself – her new friends might think she was mad or silly.

Kate had never before seen a ghost, but she'd read stories involving them and once asked her grandmother if such things were real. Hazel said, "They're real enough. You *may* see a ghost one day – it's more common to *hear* them though." She'd wagged her finger. "You must be careful who you talk to about ghosts, dear. We're in an age of what's called 'Enlightenment'." Her tone of voice suggested mild scorn. "It means that people have stopped believing in a lot of things, especially more 'educated' folk. They need to have something they call 'proof'. Plain old belief – that's kept us all going for centuries – isn't good enough these days. You have to be able to see something with your own eyes for it to be considered real. If you can't measure it, it isn't there. That's what they think, more and more. And things'll get worse before they get better, I suppose. Most people will just think you're daft if you tell them you've seen a ghost, so best keep it to yourself unless you're sure that you're speaking to someone with a bit more sense."

Pammy was eager for Kate to meet the girls in the dormitory next door, so they went to say hello to Tully Gray, Aggie Carnaby, Fuzzy Craw and Gail Curwen, all Class 3 girls, aged twelve or thirteen. They'd noticed Kate's hair in the dining hall the previous evening and now had the opportunity to make a fuss of it. Kate particularly liked

Fuzzy, who had long frizzy brown hair and freckles. She was a quiet girl of thirteen who'd been found in the workhouse at York, and Kate liked her kind, modest smile. Fuzzy had been abandoned at the age of two and had no memory of her parents. She didn't know if Fuzzy was her real name or if it was a pet form of anything. In any case, people mostly called her "Fuzz".

Kate again wore her best dress to dinner, there being as yet no word of her new garments. She sat with Bip, Pammy and Shelagh but found Fuzz looking over at her from time to time as if she were curious or concerned about something. Kate smiled at her, but Fuzzy just looked away as if she'd been caught staring.

I wonder what's bothering her, thought Kate.

As dinner drew to a close, she saw Mr Crowan making his way towards her.

"Kate, the other members of staff are keen to meet you. Do you have a moment?"

"Of course," said Kate, rising from her seat immediately and accompanying Jacob to the top table. Three people sat there, two of them looking rather unfriendly: the stern-looking woman Kate had noticed the previous evening and the ugly, squat man who made Kate think of a bear or a fierce dog.

The stern-looking woman stood to greet her. She was dressed in a fine blue gown with silver brocade and gave Kate only the ghost of a smile.

"Kate, this is Mrs Tenley, headmistress."

"Welcome, Catherine. Mr Crowan has told me all about you. We're happy to have you join us at the school."

"Thank you, Mrs Tenley," said Kate, thinking, *I have to remember the names, I have to remember the names...*

Mrs Tenley sat down, and Mr Crowan introduced Kate to Mrs Tenley's personal assistant, Miss Marlowe, the blonde woman Kate had noticed the previous evening. She gave Kate a nice smile and said hello.

Next, Crowan introduced Kate to his own assistant, the bear-dog, Mr Knox Quinton. Kate instinctively disliked him. He was about forty and had a scowl for a face, with little beady eyes. He was probably very strong despite his small size. Kate thought he looked cruel and dangerous, although he stood as she was introduced to him and did his best to smile kindly.

As Jacob led Kate to the tutors' table, four young women stood up at once, all in their early to middle twenties, very animated, excited, and dressed in the height of fashion with plunging décolletages. Kate thought, *It's going to be the hair again...* and indeed it was. When the clamour died down, Jacob introduced the Misses Trent, Shelley, Rodman and Miller, housemistresses.

"But you must call us by our first names – because we're *all girls*, just like you!" said Miss Miller, "...aren't we, girls?" They all whooped their agreement. Miss Miller pointed them out one by one: "Denise Trent and Lettice Shelley are *your* housemistresses – they're both in charge of you younger ones, aged ten to twelve." (Denise and Lettice both beamed broadly); "Eleanor Rodman..." (Eleanor waved excitedly), "...she's in charge of Classes 4 and 5, that's the thirteens and fourteens; and me, Eve Miller, I do the older girls."

Jacob thanked them and steered Kate away. "They're very lively, as you can see," he said quietly to Kate. "You'll get used to them. Now let's introduce you to the teaching staff."

Kate recognised Rider Browning straight away. He elevated himself about a foot from his seat and saluted her, acknowledging Jacob's re-introduction. "Mr Browning you've already met. Next, we have Miss Dryden, who was taking the singing lesson you heard yesterday."

Golda Dryden nodded, "Nice to see you again, Kate." She wore a claret-coloured velvet dress with gold brocade around the low, square neckline, and large, loose sleeves.

Her light brown hair was modest in length and fastened closely around her head. She was not a great beauty but looked intelligent and efficient.

"And our harp tutor, Miss Clara Sutherland."

Miss Sutherland was young; Kate judged her to be about twenty-two. She was very striking – unusually tall, with extremely long coal-black hair that she wore completely loose, at odds with the prevailing fashion. She wore a black silk dress, smooth and plain, and when she stood, Kate saw what a fine figure she had, the dress hanging loose about her hips. The effect was mystic and sepulchral, alluring. She could have been Morgan le Fay, or a succubus.

But they were already moving on. "And here we have Mr and Mrs Breedon, our deportment tutors – movement and dance." They were both in late middle-age and looked oddly similar to each other, modestly dressed and unremarkable in appearance. Mrs Breedon wore her grey hair gathered up and tied behind.

"Next, we have Mr Rayden, who teaches elocution." Again, middle-aged and a little dull-looking, rather heavy. He gave her a modest salute and greeted her by name.

Jacob and Kate remained in motion throughout the introductions, rarely pausing for more than a second. He would indicate the next tutor, name them and pass on, giving only just enough time for the person to make a very short retort. Kate had already forgotten most of their names.

"This is Miss Huxley, who teaches basic reading and writing." Jacob paused for a brief moment and addressed Pearl Huxley directly. "Miss Huxley, I'm afraid Kate's skills are already advanced to the point of finality. I'm afraid you're more likely to meet in the debating chamber than in the classroom."

"Very nice to meet you nevertheless, Kate," said Miss Huxley. "Let's have a chat sometime – I'm sure we'll be good friends." Kate liked her. She was quite small, fair-haired and in her middle thirties.

"I believe you intend to teach geography too. Is that so?" asked Jacob.

"It is," she replied. "I don't feel quite ready yet, but the day is coming."

"We all look forward to it," Jacob replied, moving away. Kate looked ahead. The next man appeared to twitch his whiskers as she approached.

"This is Mr Badger, who you'll see for literature lessons."

Kate almost laughed. Mr Badger looked remarkably like his four-legged namesake. He was about forty years old, thin, had a few ragged whiskers, a pointed nose and prominent teeth – and a streak of white running through his thick black hair. When he spoke, he appeared to be sniffing out some tasty morsel he was about to dig out of the ground.

"Delighted," he said and followed his greeting with an odd, grunting sound which he repeated several times as Kate moved on.

Next was Anabelle Trollope, a pretty, fair-haired woman in her late thirties who taught needlepoint and similar skills. Bip had already spoken to Kate about Miss Trollope, who preferred to be called by her first name. She was very kind, they said.

Jacob then re-introduced Sylvie Ardoin, whom Kate had already met as she taught her class. Mademoiselle Ardoin rose and greeted Kate in French, to which she responded with a polite smile, too self-conscious to reply to the elegant French greeting in clunky English.

They were getting close to the end of the table.

"And here is Mr Hornsby, who teaches Latin, a subject beloved of young Bip Pringle."

"Is it?" said Hornsby in a surprised tone. He was rotund and in his middle fifties, hair dishevelled. "I'm touched. I had no idea." His hand was on his heart, demonstrating the sincerity of his delight. "And I'm very pleased to meet you, young madam." He bowed.

"Likewise, sir," said Kate, thinking, *I'm glad he didn't say*

312

hello in Latin…

"Here's Mr Nisbet, our mathematician." Terrel Nisbet was dressed in red and black, very dashing, his black hair brushed back and tied at the rear. He was about thirty and looked the model of efficiency. He rose from his seat and bowed. Kate thought Mr Nisbet looked like a military officer, and briefly wondered where her uncles Adam and William were at that moment and what they might be doing.

"Miss Kate, a delight." He had a lovely deep voice. Kate thought it might be described as seductive – a word that rarely came to her mind. *Oh my*, she thought. *I shan't forget you.*

"One more," said Jacob. "Here we have Miss Lynn, who teaches fashion, dressing and presentation." Etta Lynn was dressed in pink silk with cream brocade and wore an elaborate black wig with an exotic plume of cream and red feathers. She was in her early forties, and Kate found her intimidating until she smiled. The clothes she wore lent her a powerful presence, and she would certainly have been a prominent figure in a ballroom. Kate couldn't tell if the black spot on her cheek was real or not. She thought it probably wasn't.

Miss Lynn made the usual comment about Kate's hair and said she looked forward to finding clothes that might set it off.

"There's one more person you should meet," said Jacob, and introduced Kate to the last individual at the table. "This is Dr Wayland. He operates the infirmary on the top floor of the house (I believe I told you yesterday) and is available at all times. Any aches, pains, worries, illnesses or agues, Dr Wayland is your man."

Hollis Wayland stood up and bowed to Kate. "Welcome to our happy house, Miss Kate."

The younger girls had all finished their meal and left the room, so Jacob led Kate to the door. "That concludes the introductions for today. How many names do you think you'll remember?"

"I don't know. Probably not many at first."

"You'll meet everyone again, one by one. It'll be less of a struggle that way." He gestured her through the door. "The rest of the evening is yours – away you go. Have a good sleep. Classes begin in the morning. Good night."

Kate returned Jacob's wishes and bounded up the staircase to find her friends.

31. STELLA TENLEY

Stella Tenley poisoned her husband to death. He was mild-mannered, kind, dull and inconspicuous. So she killed him. Peter Tenley inherited his wealth from his father, who'd made his small fortune in the Lowestoft herring industry. Stella Seagrove (she always resented giving up her maiden name) was attractive in her youth, her hardened mean streak appearing only as her marriage matured. She initially took Peter for a man of substance but became increasingly frustrated with him.

Stella inherited his estate as his widow and expected to be well enough off. Sadly he turned out to have been a gambler, and most of what he left behind went into paying his debts. She had to sell the house and move into a modest apartment. That was when the bitterness became fixed, and the desire to see others suffer became attractive.

One day she saw Jacob Crowan's advertisement in the Suffolk Gazette. A new charitable foundation was opening north of Scarborough, a girls' school, and there was a lengthy list of positions to be filled, including that of headmistress. Stella thought that such a situation might allow her to administer the kind of prolonged, subtle cruelty she craved. She wrote for details and within days received a letter apprising her of the qualities required. The position would be decided by interview. No specific previous experience was needed – the job would be awarded to "the right person".

She was summoned in early December 1754 and took the stagecoach from Lowestoft. The journey was a lengthy one, with four overnight stays at inns along the route. It was a cold time of year to travel, but the blankets in the coach kept her reasonably comfortable, and the inn rooms she was given were all very good, the expenses having been paid in advance by her potential employers.

The school itself, the Lookout, was a building site, full of carpenters, stonemasons and glaziers, but a few rooms on the ground level of the east wing had been made ready and comfortably furnished for the interviews. She was met by an ugly individual who introduced himself as Mr Knox Quinton.

Stella soon found herself sitting in the company of four other women, all younger than herself. They chatted together but mostly excluded her, perhaps sensing an unsympathetic character. She began to feel she'd wasted her time and was about to make a fool of herself. She was wrong.

Jacob Crowan was much younger than Stella had expected, probably in his middle twenties. He wore the tiniest hint of a smile that seemed to be a permanent fixture in his countenance. He was intense and observant, conducting the interview himself while Mr Quinton sat silently on his right like a bulldog. He picked little bits of information from her as if he were a surgeon, carefully removing fragments of unrelated tissue to expose the diseased flesh.

Stella's interview was the last of the five. At its conclusion, Mr Quinton accompanied all the applicants through the throngs of workmen to the kitchens where a light meal awaited them. They were to make themselves as comfortable as possible and wait to be called. He introduced them to the head cook, Mrs Alvina Rowley and her husband Rodney, who would look after them.

The excited babble – the swapping of impressions – began as soon as Mr Quinton left. Stella was again largely excluded, although another of the applicants, Miss Ruth Marlowe, blonde and about ten years Stella's junior, sat quiet and withdrawn. Stella tried to engage her in conversation. "What do you think?" she asked.

Miss Marlowe gave a small sigh. "I think this is all too grand for me. I didn't make a good impression at all."

"Well, that makes two of us then."

Ruth appreciated the remark and felt a little less isolated because of it. "Thank you for that." She managed a slight smile.

They were served bread and soup and continued talking while they ate. Ruth had travelled from Durham, having previously worked as governess in a big house there. She told Stella that her charges had grown up and no longer required her services, hiding from her the fact that the mistress of the house had chased her out after discovering Ruth in bed with her husband.

More bread, cheese and cold meats were brought to the table, and a jug of lemon water. Requests for tea, coffee and chocolate were fulfilled. The incessant ticking of the kitchen clock heightened the general sense of anxiety.

Nearly an hour later Quinton returned and informed them that a carriage was now waiting to escort three of their number to Scarborough, where they would overnight before setting out on the stagecoach in the morning. There were dismayed glances and a few mutterings but no real fuss. Ruth and Stella were asked to accompany Mr Quinton back to the east wing.

Stella was called first and sat opposite Mr Crowan, his large desk separating them. He locked his hands together under his chin and looked at her for a long time. She held his stare in silence. Quinton watched her coldly, immobile, his cruel expression fixed like a gargoyle.

"There is no love in your soul, Mrs Tenley," said Jacob.

Stella was stunned by the remark, delivered entirely without warning. She didn't reply but allowed the shock of its impact to settle.

Jacob went on. "There is an establishment near here that is set up to appear as if it were a school for female foundlings... but in reality..." His delivery had become very slow, drawing her fascination word by word. His gaze had clawed its way deep within her being and had its talons in the cruel desires of her spirit. He'd found her. He knew what she was. "...in reality...it is a spawning pen for the production and supply of courtesans. Prostitutes. Flesh slaves."

He became silent. Stella absorbed his utterance. It thrilled her. But she said nothing. Jacob, who'd been sitting forward intently, now relaxed in his chair. He went on.

"The headmistress of such an establishment – if the right person were to be found – would be very handsomely rewarded... I imagine."

She paused a moment. "I would gladly take on such a task." Her expression gave vent to a snarl. "I would relish it!"

Jacob smiled. "I thought you would."

She waited. "Then its mine?"

"Welcome to the team, Mrs Tenley."

Her nostrils flared and she sniffed in victory. "Thank you. You won't be disappointed."

They stood. He shook her hand. "We'll send for you when the building nears completion in a few months. In the meantime you'll be paid a retaining salary."

That was it. Stella left, and Crowan sent Quinton for Ruth.

"Miss Marlowe. I'm afraid we don't feel able to offer you the post of headmistress."

Ruth was expecting it but was downcast anyway. "I know," she said. "But thank you for your time."

Jacob went on. "But we would like you to consider the position of personal assistant to Mrs Tenley, who has just accepted the responsibilities of headmistress."

Ruth thought for a moment. It wasn't what she'd hoped for, but it might be a way back to teaching. She was grateful. "Yes. Yes, thank you. I'd like that very much." She smiled and became a little tearful. Jacob handed her his handkerchief, for which she thanked him.

"We're delighted to have you with us, Miss Marlowe. And I know the girls, when they finally arrive, will appreciate

the warmth and kindness that you so naturally display."
Even Quinton was smiling.

Ruth was happy.

Jacob Crowan's apartment at the Lookout
Thursday October 30, 1760, 10.15pm

"What were you thinking, Jacob?" Stella was angry.

"It was part of a game I was playing with someone. It was my turn to render service. But now the child intrigues me. She is remarkable."

"That may be so, but this is a *business*. The girls are assets on which our sponsors expect returns. How does this girl fulfil that function?"

"Stella, I sense your annoyance, but just leave it to me."

"She has a home, Jacob. There are people waiting for her. If we send her away with the other girls at the end of her time here, her family will want to know what's happened to her. And if we send her home, we shall have to explain the wastage of funding to our benefactors. She's a liability."

Jacob had anticipated this confrontation. "I know. She is my responsibility. I will…carry out the solution when the time comes."

"You can't send her home at the end of all this."

Jacob's irritation began to show. "I've said I'm aware of that."

"And you can't send her to London."

Jacob was silent.

"You know what you'll have to do – don't you." It wasn't a question.

"Yes," said Jacob. "Say no more about it. I'll see to it – when the time comes."

32. THE LOOKOUT
Friday & Saturday, October 31
& November 1, 1760

Classes began for Kate the next day. She was well ahead in basic skills and needlepoint but had a lot of work to do elsewhere, particularly in French and Latin, which were both new to her. Mademoiselle Ardoin and Mr Hornsby arranged personal lessons so she could catch up with the other girls.

She'd been a keen reader for years, a love inherited from her grandmother, but was intrigued by all the works she heard mentioned by Mr Badger. She made a note of the titles and authors and tracked down the books in the library.

Her new clothes appeared that evening. She found some of the fastenings difficult and was glad of Cady's help. "My word Miss Kate! You'll look like the queen of France!" Cady had a high-pitched voice that she used to great effect in telling endless unlikely stories about various members of the Lookout staff. She was hilarious, outrageous, and had the girls in stitches. If there was gossip to be spread, Cady would spread it.

Bip was envious of Kate's new red gown. "Kate, you look amazing! It's not fair! I want a dress like that!"

The clothes seemed heavy and awkward, but she no longer felt out of place amongst the other girls.

Again Fuzzy watched her across the table, serious and troubled.

That night Kate lay awake again.

Far away, heartbroken and lost, the unknown woman sobbed her endless grief. The sound cut softly through the black night like a chill wind. As it faded, a tear curled down Kate's cheek.

No classes took place on Saturday and Sunday, so the maids and housemistresses proposed a walk up the coast with the younger girls. There was some initial excitement about the expedition, but the weather worsened by noon, and the rain began to fall. Someone suggested they should all set up camp in the debating chamber and play games instead, which proved a good idea. By half past twelve, everyone was playing a raucously adapted English version of the new French game of Charades.

The thirty-one youngest girls were all there, as were their housemistresses, Denise and Lettice. Nellie Brent, Cady Weston and a couple of the other maids also joined in. A few of the more confident girls ran to fetch their favourite people, which was interesting for Kate as it gave her a clue as to which staff members were popular. She could have guessed at some of the most likely faces, but a few of the others surprised her. Eighteen-year-old Nolly Arkwright was a Romeo for many of the girls, his association with the horses stoking their fondness for him. She might have guessed at Theo and Sukey Westmorland too. Theo was considered the most handsome of the footmen, and his pretty wife Sukey was a clear favourite as well, the girls treating her like a big sister, cuddly and affectionate. Wiry, athletic Flossie Ousby, another dairymaid, appeared a few minutes after Sukey, and a surge of girls ran to meet her, crying her name.

Ruth Marlowe was a surprise for Kate. The girls clearly liked her a great deal, but Kate thought she would have been too remote from them, assistant to Mrs Tenley as she was. But no, they were all over her as if she were their mother – and she had a lovely smile. Two of the tutors were there. Kate already knew that Annabelle Trollope was popular, but she was surprised to see the maths teacher, Terrel Nisbet. He appeared in casual clothes and had lost his soldierly air. He sat next to Denise Trent.

Bip leaned over to Kate and whispered in her ear. "We think Denise and Mr Nisbet are...you know..." She gave a mock-disapproving downward glance, with raised brows and pinched lips.

"You mean...?"

"Yes...you know..." (the same glance).

Kate nodded. "I know."

Aggie Carnaby had been sent on a mission to find Rider Browning, but she now returned with the news (that was imparted to only a select handful in the room) that Mr Browning was "engaged" with Class 7 and their housemistress, Eve Miller, in re-enacting fragments from Homer, while Mr Badger read the texts aloud and provided the sound effects. Orla Stapleton was playing Helen of Troy, and Mr Browning was Paris. Aggie giggled. "They're not wearing very much – just a few blankets. Even Miss Miller!"

"Shhh," issued from several quarters. Kate got the impression that something a bit scandalous was going on, and that a concerted attempt at concealment was being made by those who knew about it.

"Tell me? Please?" Kate asked Bip.

"You can guess."

"I want to hear it from you."

"I'll give you three guesses."

Kate said, "It's Orla and Mr Browning."

"See?" Bip replied. "I told you you could guess! You have to keep it quiet."

Kate nodded her understanding. She looked round the room but saw none of the domestic staff apart from the four maids. If she'd been a little more self-assured she would have gone to find Mabel Stanton, but she didn't feel quite established enough to invite her own personal favourites just yet.

As the party wore on, Kate noticed that Mr Nisbet was resting his hand on Denise's thigh. Denise was blushing, wore a little smile and was breathing quite fast. Kate thought Denise had a very pretty bosom and wondered what her own would look like in a few years. Would she be able to wear a dress like that?

Kate nudged Bip and indicated the intimate contact between the two.

Bip looked back at her with an expression that said, *I know – they're all at it*, and made a lewd gesture with her hands. Kate choked back a laugh.

Fuzzy, unsmiling and tense, cast concentrated glances at Kate throughout the afternoon.

Dinner that evening was largely uneventful, although Kate noticed the subtle play of physical signals between Mr Browning and Orla. They arrived together and briefly touched hands as they parted to their separate tables, the play of their fingers suggesting practised intimacy. Kate wondered how the situation would end. Was it common for marriages to occur between students and staff? She asked Shelagh.

"No, not at all. And I don't know what will happen if this gets out. You have to keep it secret. I think *most* of the girls know, but I'm not completely sure. Eve must know, but I've no idea about anybody else. I think they're taking a risk."

"Eve?" asked Kate.

"Eve Miller – housemistress," Shelagh replied.

"Oh yes," said Kate. "I'd forgotten."

"Names, names, names," Shelagh smiled. "Keep asking, and I'll keep reminding you."

Kate, Pammy and Bip climbed the stairs to their room after dinner, while Shelagh went to find a privy. As they walked along the line of dormitory doors, some open, others closed, Kate noticed that Fuzzy was in her room. Bip and Pammy walked on, but Kate put her head in and said,

"Fuzz, can we talk?" Fuzzy appeared to be deep in thought but looked up when she heard the voice. Kate went on, "I mean somewhere quiet, just you and me."

"Yes, alright," Fuzz replied, though with a hint of reluctance.

Kate's puzzlement grew. "I'll get out of my dinner things," she said. "Back in a moment."

A few minutes later, dressed in more casual clothes, Kate returned to Fuzzy's dormitory to find her looking still more deeply worried.

"You look so serious!" said Kate, smiling. "I'm just curious to know why you look at me with such concern. Or am I imagining it?"

Fuzz glanced down. "No...you're right. But you'll think I'm mad."

"I doubt it," said Kate. "Let's go somewhere quiet."

They tried the library but found it already occupied by several of the older girls.

"Shall we sit in the turret?" asked Kate, and Fuzzy nodded agreement. Kate took up a lamp and they ascended the iron staircase, made their way along the gallery and into the turret through the little door. Kate arrived first in the tiny room and looked briefly out through the window, trying to see the top of the northeast tower. But her eyes had not adjusted, and the lamplight was in any case too bright to allow anything outside to be seen. Nevertheless, Fuzzy had registered Kate's attempt to find the two boys. She breathed a sigh of relief and gave a rare smile. The two sat opposite each other on the stone bench. It was cold, and the dark began to consume the chamber despite the lamplight.

Fuzzy said, "You can see the boys."

Kate was not entirely surprised. "You can too."

"Yes. Have you seen the woman?"

Kate paused, wondering what she meant, then shook her head. "No."

"But you hear her crying at night?"

"Yes," said Kate, "I hear crying. It's very sad."

"It's their mother," said Fuzzy.

"Who knows about this?" Kate asked.

"Not many. A few. Probably only the ones who see them. At the moment I think that's only you and me. And Mabel. There was another girl, Penny Dyson, but she left last year."

"They're ghosts," said Kate.

"I know."

There was silence between them for a few moments. Then Kate said, "But why were you staring at me in that way?"

Fuzzy didn't answer immediately. She licked her lips, looking hard at Kate. "You have a guardian. Did you know?"

Kate was stunned. She hadn't been expecting that. Her mind whirled, and she tried to grapple with the implications. She knew she was descended from a line of powerful women, and was aware of the lineage of the Craft handed down through the first-born females and now entrusted to her. But a "guardian"? Surely, she would have sensed such a thing. She was appalled that she hadn't known. The bottom suddenly fell out of her sense of self, and her accustomed confidence hit the floor. It was an utterly new sensation. She experienced a surge of panic, as if she'd been swept overboard at sea and might drown.

Their exchange was rapid: Kate asked, "What do you mean?"

"You know what I mean."

"What do you see?"

"She's always behind your left shoulder."

"Can you see her now?"

"No, I can't see her in the dark."

"What does she look like?"

"I can't see her clearly. She's very faint. I can't see her face at all unless I look away, or look directly at you. Then the face fills in with features – nose, mouth, eyes. But when I look directly at her, there's nothing but a halo of hair."

"Just the head then?"

"Yes, I think so."

"The hair?"

"It's red, like yours."

Kate's hands flew to her mouth and she took a big, spasmodic lungful of air. Her eyes filled with tears, and she began to cry with huge, wracking sobs. It went on for some time while she sniffed and wiped the tears from her face. Fuzzy sat silently for a while, then reached out and touched her. "Sorry," she said. "I didn't want to upset you."

Kate tried to gather herself. Sniffing and swallowing, she managed, "It's alright. I just never knew. It's a shock."

"Is it your mother?" asked Fuzz.

"No, I don't think so," said Kate. "I think it must be Anne White."

"Was she in your family?"

"She was hanged for witchcraft more than a hundred years ago. My grandma told me she was the last person to have my hair."

There were a few more moments of silence. Fuzzy looked solemn, and Kate tried to claw back some control of her emotions.

"Are you alright?" asked Fuzzy. She chewed her lip, concerned.

Kate replied, "Yes, yes. I'll be fine." But she remained seated, sniffing and catching her breath for several more minutes. Fuzz waited patiently, her hands on her friend's knees in comfort.

Soon Kate's breathing steadied, and she sighed. Fuzzy said, "Fancy a drink? I think you need one."

Kate said, "Good idea."

Fuzz replied, "Come on then. I've got some gin hidden under the floorboards. Let's celebrate."

The younger girls were mostly in bed by the time Kate and Fuzzy returned to the dormitories. They got into their nightclothes, selected a nearby privy, locked themselves in and turned up the lamp.

It was smelly in the smallest room. Kate lifted the privy seat and shovelled lots of ash into the bucket while Fuzz uncorked her little earthenware flask. A moment later they were sitting side by side in the gloom, and Fuzz wordlessly offered the bottle to Kate. She put it to her lips and drew a small mouthful. It was the most overwhelming taste she'd ever experienced. Her face screwed up in revulsion and she nearly choked.

"Yeeeuch! That's...*horrible!*"

"It *is* good, isn't it?" replied Fuzzy enthusiastically, taking the flask back from her companion and drawing a long swig herself.

Kate shivered in disgust. "Where do you get that?" she asked.

"Mary Acker keeps a stash in the maids' quarters upstairs. There's a still down at the brewhouse. It's meant for the staff really – I mean the tutors and Mr Crowan and that lot – but the maids get an order in too. And Mary knows I like it. There was a lot of drink about in the workhouse, and I got used to it. Have another go – it's worth persevering."

Kate shook her head. "No, I don't think so. Does Mr Crowan know you drink that?"

Fuzz gave a little snort that said, *Not likely!* and took another draught.

They sat looking at each other for a second, Kate waiting for Fuzzy to say something. The question, when it came, was very direct.

"So, are you a witch?"

Kate had asked herself that question on many occasions and didn't really know the answer. It was a word that her grandmother had used now and then. The country people used the word freely, and Kate thought that the farm folk, particularly the older ones, had probably thought of Hazel as a witch – as *their* witch. It was a position of respect.

"I don't know," she answered. "I suppose so, in a way."

"In what way?"

"Well, I can make medicines and ointments and things…"

"That's hedgecraft, not witchcraft."

"But aren't they the same?"

"Witchcraft is more. Can you make charms?"

"Yes, I have done."

"And do they work?"

"I think so. Mostly."

"What about spell casting, magic?"

"Incantations, yes. They focus the mind."

Fuzz was silent for a moment, then said, "Can you turn a man into a frog?"

Kate laughed. "No."

"What *can* you do then?"

Kate had believed that her ability to push people away by focusing her anger at them had been a manifestation of witchcraft, but she now wondered if those actions were in fact carried out by her guardian acting on her behalf. Her self-confidence had suffered a substantial blow because of Fuzzy's revelation, and Kate wasn't sure it would ever return.

"I make dead animals alive again."

Fuzzy offered no reaction, but sat motionless, watching Kate intently. She took another swig of gin.

"You mean freshly dead? Like, a few minutes?"

"No. Very dead. Like, a few…months."

"You're joking!" exclaimed her friend, quietly.

"I'm not," said Kate. "I take their bodies, and I…concentrate very hard. I sing to them…and blow love into them. All the dryness goes out of them, they get soft and warm – then they wake up."

Fuzzy was looking at her, staring, in complete silence.

"It starts in my head," said Kate.

"Are you telling the truth?"

"Yes," said Kate.

"I want you to show me."

"Alright."

"Can you bring people back to life?"

"I don't know. I don't think so."

"Have you ever tried?"

"No. I've only done it with small animals. Birds, mice, rats, that kind of thing."

"But maybe you can, and you just haven't tried it out."

Kate shrugged. "Maybe."

"We should suffocate Mrs Tenley (she's not very nice) and then see if you can make her alive again. It would be amazing if you could do it, and it wouldn't matter much if it didn't work."

Kate laughed. Fuzzy offered her the flask again. She took it, drew on it, swilled the aggressive fluid around her teeth and swallowed, shivering with revulsion, although she admitted to herself that she might be able to get used to it.

It was getting very late, and Fuzzy was beginning to show the effects of the alcohol. Kate's own cheeks were oddly warm.

"Tell me about the crying woman," said Kate.

"Don't look at her face," said Fuzzy.

"Why not?"

"It's horrible."

"You mean ugly?"

"No. You can see she's been strangled." Kate waited for more. "Her face is all red and her eyes are bulging – staring – at nothing. Her mouth is open and her tongue is all fat and very long, black. There's a cord round her neck, pulled tight. It's horrible."

Kate imagined the sight. "That sounds horrid."

"She's on the first floor, in the corridor in the east wing. She wears a huge dress, and it's like she's sitting on a chair, except there isn't a chair. She has her face in her hands, crying. If you go closer, she suddenly appears on her back, near the floor but not quite on it, very still and dead with her tongue sticking out like I told you."

Kate sat silently, picturing it. "Why is she there?"

"I don't know. I think she's the boys' mother, but that's just a guess."

Kate was quiet for a while. Then she said, "I'd really like to get into the tall turret, the tower."

"You can't do that," said Fuzzy. "I've tried. But if you stand near the turret door you can hear the boys running up and down the stairs."

"You've been in the room? The locked room?" asked Kate with some surprise.

"Yes," Fuzzy replied. "It's difficult to get there, but I've done it a few times."

"How?" Kate asked.

"You have to crawl a long way. It's mucky and spidery." Kate waited again. "The house is full of hidden passageways, crawlspaces, hidey-holes, things like that. Maybe Mr Crowan decided to keep them when the house was rebuilt, or maybe the workmen just left them. Or maybe they just didn't find them. Have you been upstairs to the maids' rooms yet?" Kate shook her head, no. "Well, you go through the gate and up the stairs as far as the left turn. There's a loose panel in the wall just after the turn. You can lift it out, and there's a space behind. If you get into that space, you can crawl on your hands and knees inside the wall. There's a narrow crawlspace that goes all the way along the wing of the house. It runs under the windows and round the chimneys. The far end comes out in the corner room."

"That's amazing!" Kate exclaimed. "Will you take me there?"

"If you want. There's nothing in the room. Only the tower door, and you can't get in there."

"Tomorrow?" asked Kate.

"Alright. You'd better wear old clothes."

Kate took one more drink of gin, and Fuzzy finished the bottle.

They heard the sound of approaching footfalls; someone was coming. Both girls held their breath. The steps got louder, closer, and came to a halt right outside the privy door. Kate and Fuzz looked at each other in alarm. The handle turned.

The two girls said, "Just a moment," in unison, then both clapped their hands to their foreheads. Fuzzy unlocked the door and swung it open, a sheepish expression on her face, in readiness for the expected telling-off.

Slade Stone, the soil-boy, stood there, looking at the two young girls in their nightdresses, one clutching a bottle. He smiled and tugged his forelock. "A very good evening to you, ladies."

"Hello Slade," Kate slurred drunkenly.

"Hic!" said Fuzzy.

"See you in the morning," said Kate, and wobbled unsteadily across the spinning corridor to her room.

Fuzzy gave the bottle to Slade and went to bed. He looked at it, put it to his lips, found it empty, and cursed.

33. THE LOOKOUT
Sunday November 2, 1760

"Breakfast, Kate," said Shelagh, shaking her awake.

Kate opened her eyes to bright sunlight and found her head full of gravel. She sat up. "Oh dear..." she muttered, hands at her temples.

"We didn't see you at all last night. What did you get up to?"

"I was talking to Fuzz," Kate replied.

"Hm," said Shelagh. "Fuzzy isn't feeling too good either." She paused, watching, while Kate sighed and lay down again. "Coming for breakfast? Fuzzy's gone already."

"Alright," said Kate, with some reluctance.

Sheila waited while her friend washed and dressed, then accompanied her downstairs. Kate felt ill but was relieved to find that food gradually chased away the headache. She began to think she might recover.

Fuzzy's eyes were a little bloodshot, but she seemed lively enough.

"Did you have a bad head?"

"Yes, I did," Kate replied.

"It gets better with practise."

"I don't think I'll be doing that too often."

Fuzzy sniggered, smiling.

"Will we have time to visit the tower room today?" asked Kate.

"They're all walking up the coast to Peak and the Bay if the weather stays nice – lots of the girls, Denise, Eve, Eleanor – Cady, Portia and the rest. But we don't have to go. We'll pretend we're writing, or practising the harp, or snuggling the footmen or something."

"Good," said Kate.

"Don't forget – old clothes."

"I'll find something."

William Wynter had incorporated many secret passage-ways and hiding places into the original design of the Lookout, having had a fascination with such things. Many of the walls contained interior spaces, hidden compartments and concealed staircases. Most of these had been found and removed in the restoration of the building, but a few survived intact, while others became truncated or joined together. A small number remained undiscovered.

Denise, Lettice and the maids led the expedition away at eleven o'clock, and Fuzzy met Kate a quarter of an hour later. Kate had been rummaging in her belongings and found something she thought might be suitable – a worn shirt and patched-up trousers she used to wear outdoors on the farm. Fuzzy wore old rags that she always put on for just such burrowing as this.

"Are you set?" she asked. "It really is filthy – and very tight. A grown-up couldn't do this."

"Ready to try," Kate replied.

Fuzzy led the way to the gate at the bottom of the maids' staircase. She lifted the latch and opened it, beckoned Kate in behind her and ascended as far as the left turn at the eighth step, where she stood quietly, listening. After a moment she turned to Kate, whispered "It's clear," and disappeared around the corner. Kate followed her, leaping up the stairs two at a time. The staircase was L-shaped and continued its ascent after the right-angle – another twelve steps or so, Kate thought – but Fuzzy remained at the bottom, just beyond the turn. The shaft in which the stairs ascended was lined on both sides with wood panelling. Kate watched while Fuzzy tapped on the corner of a particular panel on the lower left. It tipped inwards, and she lifted it out to reveal a dark space within, big enough for them to enter with care.

"I'll go first," she said. "You'll need to reach down and pull the panel back into place. Can you do that?" Kate thought she probably could. "Good. After the hole is closed, just follow me. It'll take about fifteen minutes to get there. Keep very quiet." Kate nodded.

Fuzzy put both hands into the space and leapt up from the stairs, using her feet on the narrow wooden bannister to ease herself into the hole. Once inside, she turned immediately right and disappeared from view. Kate followed her example; then turned around, reached down for the corner of the displaced wooden panel, lifted it up into the opening and pushed it into place. Coffin-like blackness completely enclosed her. It smelt dry. She felt dust in her throat.

"Are you alright?" whispered Fuzzy, an unknown distance along the tunnel.

"I can't see anything," she whispered back.

"Don't worry. It's not all black. You'll see enough. Are you ready?"

"Yes, I think so. How will I know where you are?"

"I'll go slow. Feel carefully ahead of you. Sometimes you have to climb down – and sometimes up – to get round things. It's a bit scary first time, but safe enough. There are no big holes to fall down. You won't get lost. I'm starting now."

Kate crawled slowly on hands and knees. She knew the wall to her right was wood, at least to begin with, but wasn't sure about the wall to the left. It felt like stone, maybe brick. There were lots of cobwebs, and something ran over her fingers. Kate didn't mind spiders as long as she didn't accidentally crush them under her hands or get one in her mouth. After a few feet, the space narrowed, and she had to ease herself round a column of stonework. This must be the chimney in my room, she thought. It was a tight squeeze, but she managed to do it. A few feet later there was a very narrow beam of light, thin as a pin, cutting in from above – the result of a tiny hole in the building's fabric, between the stone blocks. She briefly caught sight of Fuzzy's bottom, illuminated in the dimness ahead of her.

They crawled carefully for about fifteen minutes. Kate's hands and knees were getting very sore, but she was soon aware of daylight ahead. A moment later she looked up and found that she was no longer looking at Fuzzy's bottom, but her calves and feet instead, framed in a square of light. The girl appeared to be standing upright. Then the legs were gone, hoisted away as if they'd flown straight up, leaving only the empty area of sunlight, filled with swirling, disturbed dust. Fuzzy had pulled herself free of the passage.

"We've arrived."

Kate looked up and saw her friend three feet above her, kneeling, looking down into the hole. She realised she was looking up through the floor of the top story of the house.

"This is it," said Fuzzy. "Wasn't so bad, was it?"

Kate stood up, her head emerging from the tunnel, and looked about her, the broken floor at the level of her chest.

"I can't believe we're actually in here," she said.

It was a large, bare, corner room with a high ceiling, and tall windows on two sides, flooding the space with brilliant noon light. There was no furniture at all, and much of the panelling had been stripped out, leaving the brick walls exposed. Part of the ceiling had collapsed, revealing the timbers of the shallow attic. The tower door, brown paint peeling, stood in the far corner, closed.

Kate scrambled up into the room, using arms and feet for leverage. She stood and rubbed her hands together, getting rid of some of the dust, then brushed her clothes down.

"They didn't do any work on this room," said Fuzzy. "Maybe they were frightened by the noises."

"The boys," Kate replied.

Fuzzy nodded. "Hear them?" she said quietly; then whispered, "They're always there – always."

Kate listened hard and couldn't hear anything at first. She walked slowly towards the door, straining to pick up the slightest sound... and then she heard them – light footsteps running up the staircase behind the door, so delicate they could have been fairies. She stood very close, her head almost touching the wood.

Someone was scratching the door on the inside.

Time seemed to be moving very slowly. Kate concentrated hard, her lips parted. She could hear Fuzzy's soft breathing in the room behind her. Particles of dust drifted slowly in the shafts of sunlight.

Kate said, quietly, "Can you hear me?" The scratching went on. "I'm Kate. Is there something I can do to help you?"

Still the scratching.

She knocked once and listened, ear against the door.

The scratching stopped.

She waited...and waited...

Suddenly the room was filled with the sound of a screaming child, impossibly loud.

"MAMAAAA!!!!"

The force of it knocked Kate away from the little door, and she stood, eyes wide, hands covering her mouth and cheeks in shock. Fuzzy screamed and ran to the door that would have provided an exit, struggled with the handle and remembered it was locked. She collapsed in the corner and covered her head. "No!"

"Sh!" said Kate loudly.

There was silence in the room, except for the panting of the two girls.

And then came the soft patter of light feet running up the staircase and out of earshot.

Kate waited a second, listening further, then let out her breath in a gasp, clasped her hands to her chest and collapsed on her knees. "God! I didn't expect that."

Fuzzy released her head from her protecting arms and turned, open-mouthed, breathing shallowly. "Fuck!" She gasped. "That was amazing!"

Kate, not yet recovered from the shock, was unable to answer. After a moment she looked at Fuzzy and give a tiny shake of the head as if to say, *Did that happen?*

"Kate, *they knew you were here!* They answered you – they answered your knock! *Your* knock!" Fuzzy's voice was ablaze with astonishment.

Kate recovered sufficiently to stand, walked stealthily to the tower door, put her ear to it and listened. There was no sound on the other side. For the first time since they'd entered the room, she tried the handle and found that the door was indeed locked. Finally, she knocked, lightly at first, then with some force, producing a long, hollow echo from the inaccessible staircase.

"They're gone," said Fuzzy

"For good?" Kate responded quietly.

"No. I don't know. I don't think so."

Kate felt helpless, as if there was something she should be doing. But she had no idea what it might be. "They want something," she said. "They need help. They're trapped."

"You can feel that? For sure?"

"Yes," said Kate. "They can't get out."

"They're ghosts," said Fuzzy. "It's not the locked door that holds them."

"No," Kate agreed. She paused; then said, "I don't know what to do."

Fuzzy said nothing for a while. Then, "Worrying about it won't bring the solution any closer. Maybe something will turn up, give us some ideas. Mabel might help?"

"Maybe," Kate replied. The tension was easing. "Have you always seen ghosts?"

Fuzzy stood, brushing the dust of the room from her clothes. "A few. In the workhouse; on the street."

"These are my first," Kate said. She stepped over to the big window facing east.

"Bet they won't be your last," said Fuzzy, joining her in the shaft of sunlight.

The staff house and the laundry lay a short distance away, the brewhouse a little further east. The girls had a clear view of the roofs from their elevated position. Seventy or eighty yards to the southeast, Kate saw what appeared to be a large hedge-maze. She pointed it out. "Is that what I think it is?"

"Yes," Fuzzy replied. "It's a maze, a big one. Nicer in the summer."

Kate looked east again and found she could just pick out the top of the old lookout tower away in the distance. It was possible to see as far as the hilltop that overlooked the final descent to the beach, but as she'd suspected, the sea itself was not visible. She suddenly realised why this one turret was much higher than the other three; it was precisely to give a view of the water.

"Are you any good at picking locks?" she asked her companion.

"I've never tried," said Fuzzy. "I'm not sure I'd know where to start."

"I wonder where the key is."

Fuzzy shook her head, *Don't know*.

Kate tried the handle again and kicked at the turret door, which remained firm.

"Why were they locked in there?" she asked.

"I'm not sure," said Fuzzy. "I think their father went mad. He strangled his wife."

"What happened to him?"

"Mabel says he shot himself."

"So – is his ghost here too?"

"I don't think so," Fuzzy replied. "I've never seen him. I don't think anyone has."

Kate looked around the room, wondering if the key might be hidden nearby, but there were not many possibilities.

She ran her fingers along the little sill over the tower door itself but found only dead flies there. A search of the cold, empty fireplace, mantel and chimney revealed nothing but dirt, and the locked door that led to the east wing offered no nooks or crannies that might conceal such a thing.

"Frustrating," she muttered.

"Hm," Fuzzy agreed, shaking her head. "We're not going to get in there."

Kate stood for a moment, impotent, then became aware of her discomfort.

"We'll have to go," she said. "I need a wee."

It took them just over ten minutes to crawl to the end of the tunnel, knock out the loose board and clamber down into the maids' staircase. Fuzzy secured the panel in place while Kate ran to a privy (*God! I'm going to wet myself!*), locked the door, dropped her trousers, sat down and let out her breath in relief.

They changed out of their filthy clothes and reconvened on Kate's bed over glasses of Mrs Rowley's lemon water, a large covered jug of the beverage being standard in all the dormitories.

"That was the most amazing thing I've ever seen," Fuzzy began.

"How did you discover the passageway?"

"I like to be by myself. I've always done a lot of exploring. In the workhouse, I found all the holes and hiding places. It's like being a mole, tunnelling. I tap and listen for empty spaces. The loose panel in the staircase was one of the first I found."

"How many times have you been in the room?"

"Can't remember. Maybe ten or so."

"Are there any other long passages like that one – that come out in completely different parts of the house?"

"There are all sorts of things. Some are just holes in the

wall, a few of them big enough to stand in. There's one really scary one. It's a shaft. You can see into it if you lift out some of the panelling in one of the music practice rooms."

Kate was excited. "Can we see now?"

"Alright – if there's no-one in the room. Let's go."

The two girls made their way down to the first floor, and Fuzzy led Kate to a practice room in the west wing. She tapped on the door, put her head inside, and finding it empty, motioned Kate to join her.

It wasn't easy to remove the wooden panels. One slid upwards nearly an inch and had to be levered out from below. A vertical slot of dark space was revealed behind it, about two inches in width. The panel to the right of the first had to be removed to create a hole big enough to look into. A rope hung vertically inside the hole, in the centre of the space. As Fuzzy propped the panel against the wall, Kate put her head in and looked down, immediately withdrawing it.

"Ugh! That's scary." She looked again, fascinated. It was a shaft about two and a half feet square, completely vertical and smooth on all sides. The rope hung all the way down the centre of it. Kate pulled it and found that it was taut, under tension. She could see about five feet down the shaft before it was engulfed in darkness.

"How deep is it?"

"I don't know."

"You've never tried to crawl down it?"

"No!"

"Is there a light?"

Fuzzy looked around. The lamp wasn't lit. The spill vase was full, but the fire was out.

"No. Drop something."

Kate looked around and found a candle stub on the mantel. She held it in the shaft and let go. About three seconds passed before they heard a faint click as it hit the bottom.

"I think it goes all the way down to the cellar," said Fuzzy.

"The cellar?" said Kate excitedly. "I hadn't even thought of a cellar!"

"There is one – big, I think. I've never been down there – the door's always locked – but I think you can get to the ice-house through the cellar. There must be a tunnel under the drive."

Kate put her head in the hole again and said, "That's amazing." Her voice echoed back. She twisted and looked up to see that the shaft ascended in equal darkness. "It's a lift shaft for wine from the cellar to the staff floor."

"Yes," said Fuzzy. "I think so too. They probably still use it. I've never seen the rope before. The lift must be at the bottom of the shaft."

Kate was impressed. "Is there anything else really exciting like this?"

"There's another lift, but that's not hidden. It has a door on each floor. They use it for water, coal and stuff."

"Yes. But I mean exciting things, scary things, like this."

"I bet you haven't been in the overgrown garden yet."

Kate made a motion with her head that said, *Where's that?*

"You can see bits of the old buildings from the windows in the concert hall. I'll show you in a minute. Let's put the panels back first."

The panels had to be replaced in reverse order, first the right, then the left. A moment later the two girls were on their way to the end of the west wing corridor. As they approached the concert hall, the door opened and Mr Browning appeared, accompanied by Orla. They seemed surprised to see Kate and Fuzzy.

"You didn't go with the other girls?" asked Orla, wiping her lips with her left forefinger.

"No," said Fuzzy. "We had things to do."

"So you're going to do some music practice," smiled Mr Browning.

Fuzzy laughed. "Maybe. I wanted to show Kate the view

from the concert hall windows. Have you finished?"

"We have," said Mr Browning. "It's all yours."

They walked away together, Mr Browning's hand on the small of Orla's back, and the two girls went into the concert hall. Fuzzy shut the door and said, "I wonder what we'd have interrupted if we'd turned up two or three minutes earlier..."

They crossed the hall and stood at the large windows on the far side of the seating area. It was still light outside, and the air was clear. Fuzzy indicated the vast expanse of uncultivated growth on the north side of the drive.

"There it is," she said. "Long ago there was a garden in there. There are buildings. If you look carefully you can see them. There's a wall behind all the undergrowth on this side," (she pointed), "and just beyond the wall there's a big house, covered in creeper." She indicated with a sweeping gesture of her hand. "You can see the roof and the back of the house. The roof's mostly fallen in. There are trees and things growing out of it. See?"

Kate squinted into the tangle and found she could see it quite easily. "Oh, yes. Of course. It's big."

"There are other buildings too – a few big old plant houses, sheds, statues, even a little castle thing. Way over in the distance (you can't see it from here) there's a little house, all overgrown and abandoned, completely ruined and fallen down."

"How do you know all this? Have you been inside?"

"Yes. Everybody goes in there. It isn't difficult. There are lots of holes in the wall further down to the right there, up near the fields – and along the drive too. It must have been lovely once, but it's all spoilt now. There's a big pond and a nice summerhouse. In the winter they cut the ice off the pond and put it in the icehouse. That's the icehouse, just there by the wall – nestled against it. See?" She pointed. "I don't know why they didn't clear out the old gardens when they restored the Lookout. It's a pity in a way, but it's

342

really exciting as it is. You can play great hiding games in there. There are orchards and big spaces, completely overgrown, that might have been lawns or something. The deer have eaten away paths for themselves, so it's not difficult to get around even though it looks like a jungle from up here."

"Deer?" asked Kate.

"Yes, they come out into the estate now and then and get shot. I like venison. Do you?"

"Yes," said Kate. "I do. Can we go in there and explore right now?" It had been an extraordinary day, and she was overwhelmed with all the excitement.

"I think we'll have to go another day," said Fuzzy, pointing at the drive. Kate saw that the girls were returning. "They'll all be eating cake in a minute, and I want some too."

34. KNOX QUINTON
Scarborough, Tuesday November 4, 1760, 6pm

Knox Quinton drove alone to Scarborough. The sky was already dark, and the carriage lanterns cut poorly into the gloom. Owls hooted; a family of deer hurried across the road. A light wind played in the trees, setting the leaves a-rustle, hissing like gossips.

He'd borrowed the little two-wheeled chaise and had Nolly prepare Athena for the journey as he did once or twice every month. This evening he'd dine in one of the town's many taverns. He wasn't in a hurry.

Knox was born on Christmas Day 1718 in the squalid room he shared with his parents and both older sisters on the top floor of a dingy house in a nameless alley off Whitechapel High Street. The room was drenched with the sounds and smells of the nearby breweries, tanneries and slaughterhouses. The bell foundry, where his Uncle Silas worked, was little more than a stone's throw away. He was an ugly child, and he wasn't wanted.

Knox was the uncomplaining butt of his sisters' jokes as he grew up, and was also the daily target of his mother's back-handers and his father's belt. He played alone in the filth of the street, the other children avoiding him because of his repul-sive appearance. Passers-by kicked him and called him worm or runt or worse. He grew up expecting ill-treatment, having re-ceived no love...

After an hour or so, the lights of Scarborough came into view, and Knox decided which of the town's alehouses would be his lair for the evening. He varied his des-tinations, trying to avoid becoming too prominent, too memorable, in any particular place. Sometimes he'd go to Whitby or Filey, sometimes inland to Pickering, Goathland or elsewhere, particularly in the summer when the evenings were longer.

He mulled over the inns he knew and selected *The Three Fishes* just off the harbour. Knox pulled the horse onto the appropriate road as he neared his goal.

In 1727 his mother and teenage sisters took him to Tyburn to watch his father and uncle hanged for robbery. Knox stood at the front of the enthusiastic crowd and held his father's gaze as his neck was placed in the noose. His mother and sisters were frantic, desperate, pleading for his life. But Knox felt nothing at all, not even hatred – not even when his father gobbed at him right before the trap was released.

He lay calmly awake that night as the three women sobbed themselves to exhaustion. What would it feel like to die that way, dangling, hands tied? He imagined the neck snapping, felt it crack, tissues pulling apart. Then he pictured himself breaking someone's neck, strangling someone. He imagined his hands around a throat. How would it feel? The soft flesh, the bone. The image took possession of him…

Knox tipped the coach house boy to look after Athena and the chaise for a couple of hours and made his way into the bar. Food was one of Knox's two great passions. Not necessarily fine food – just food. He liked to eat, particularly meat. He liked to chew, to masticate. He sat down, choosing a position from which he had a good view of the bar itself, and ordered a large meal.

He scanned the customers as they came and went, particularly those who stayed, and drank, and drank.

He killed for the first time when he was twelve years old, the unfortunate victim another ugly boy, about two years his junior. They found each other as a result of their mutual rejection and played together in the street once or twice. Knox took him into an alleyway and strangled him. The boy (he didn't even know his name) put up a feeble fight, choking, struggling for breath; but Knox had powerful fingers and was determined to get the job done. The boy's resistance ceased after a while, and Knox let the body slip to the ground. It was not what he'd imagined at all; it had been dull, unsatisfying. Something was missing.

He thought about it for two weeks and then tried again; a girl this time, about his own age, her clubfoot having excluded her from the games of her friends. Another alleyway and a different technique. This time he got behind her, steadied her body with one arm and wrenched her head with the other.

The soft sensation of cracking bone and grinding cartilage lit up his soul, and he was inflamed with joy, allowing the dead girl to slip to the ground. This was what he wanted – here was the relief, the instant of gratification that would light his life...

The bar continued to fill as the evening wore on, Knox chewing the time away and watching the patrons. He'd settled on his target – a lone man of about fifty, a determined drinker. As soon as his table was cleared, Knox made his way to the bar and befriended the man, who was already well on the way to inebriation. He bought him another drink and asked senseless questions: Did he always drink here? How did he make his living? Receiving the answers, Knox forgot them instantly. Even the man's exclamation of "God, you're an ugly one, aren't you!" went right by him without registering any impact.

Breaking necks was one of Knox's two great passions.

Knox perfected his skill as he grew older. He sharpened the efficiency of his technique and maximised the pleasure he got from rending necks. Some people relish the crush of soft peach flesh in the mouth; others crave the soft, warm yield of a plump buttock. Knox needed only the crunch and grind of the death he brought. He never developed an interest in women, or in men. Any sexual desire he might have felt was entirely channelled into that one brief, bright moment of popping, snapping, cracking tissue.

His mother died. His sisters both disappeared into prostitution. He was turned out of the house where he'd been born.

Knox lived on the streets, slept in the gutters or in doorways. He never tried to get a job. Living in the open, he was vulnerable to the predation of thugs and learned to defend himself forcefully with his fists. He gained a reputation, and found that people would pay money to see him in action. Very soon he became a good bet as a street fighter, then as a prizefighter.

In March 1746 the twenty-five-year-old Edgar Foxley saw Knox in action at a set of matches in Hyde Park. Foxley and his acquaintances were already involved in big-money prostitution and were looking for strong men to work for them. He offered Knox more money than he'd ever dreamt of and a decent place to sleep.

Knox felt no interest whatsoever in the convent girls, all of whom were afraid of him anyway, but he was happy to bodyguard them when the occasion called for it. And his employers occasionally needed him to snap necks, which gave him job satisfaction. Foxley soon got the measure of him, ensured he was well-fed, and provided a safe haven to which he could return after he'd slaked his other needs...

Knox kept his new friend well supplied with ale until nearly nine o'clock, when the latter voiced his desire to go home. His wife would be wondering where he'd got to. Knox's offer to help him to his dwelling was gladly accepted, as the poor man would – as he laughingly said – have to crawl on his hands and knees otherwise.

Knox took the man's weight on his shoulder, left the tavern, and staggered step by step for about ten minutes; then took advantage of a narrow, unlit passage...

Jacob Crowan met Knox Quinton early in 1748 when the former began his collaboration with the King's Place convents.

Jacob was nearly nineteen at that time, Knox a little more
than ten years his senior, but Jacob sensed an affinity straight
away. They never became friends as such, but Jacob under-
stood Knox's need to kill; and Knox, in the strange, animal-like
darkness of his being, recognised Jacob's longing for drawn-out,
aching cruelty, born years earlier along the barrel of a pistol in
a Ludgate Hill cobbler's shop. In a way, they were the same, but
whereas Jacob's fascination with death included a strong erotic
response, any sexual urge in Knox's obsession was subsumed in
his particular style of extinguishing life.
In 1753, when plans were drawn up for the Lookout, it seemed
logical to all involved that Crowan and Knox Quinton should
work together...

The chaise was on its way home, Athena pulling the little
carriage north, away from the lights of Scarborough. Knox
sat alone in the driver's seat, eyes front, peering at the road
in the lantern-light. He felt calm, satisfied, well-fed. He
wasn't in a hurry.

35. THE WHITE BULL, RIBCHESTER
Saturday November 15, 1760

Helen kissed him awake. Alex responded to her touch and blinked as he came to consciousness. A circle of dawn light lit the white bedcovers.

"Good morning, my lover," she said. "Wakey. There's work to be done."

Alex sighed and watched her as she climbed out of bed, walked over to the window, stretched, yawned, lowered herself into the embrasure and looked out at the street.

"It's going to be a cold, wet day."

Alex had grown particularly fond of Helen's fleshy bottom. He propped himself up in bed and watched it as she leant forward in the window. Perhaps things had turned out well after all. He'd written to Colleen again in the summer. She was happy and still had Liam. He told her about Helen, and Colleen said she was glad for him.

"I love your bum," he said.

She turned to him, smiling, swaying it for him. "Do you now?"

"I do," he said.

She sat on the edge of the bed and slid her hand under the covers. "Oh, yes. I see you do."

The inn was busy that day, a fair few guests wanting breakfast. The kitchen offered a good menu: mutton, kidneys, sausages, cold meats, several different cheeses, eggs, bacon, salmon or trout cooked specially to order. Rice pudding was also on the list, and the gooseberry pie was a speciality of the house. Ale, beer, wine, cordials and tea were available to drink.

The bar buzzed with conversation as Alex and Helen waited at tables, carefully avoiding three small children who'd been allowed to run around unguarded. A pair of men occupied a table near the rear of the room, close to the door leading outside to the privies. One of them ate enthusiastically while the other admired Helen. He beckoned her to him, and Alex saw words exchanged, although he couldn't hear what was said above the general noise of the room. The man laughed, and watched her as she walked away.

"What was that?" asked Alex.

"Cheeky swine. Don't worry about it," she said.

Alex was in the bar at noon. Breakfast was over, and the room was almost empty. Helen cleared away the last of the dirty dishes from the tables.

The two men appeared and asked for their bill. John or Sarah always dealt with the money for lodgings, so Alex called to them, and John appeared a few moments later. He totalled up their spending and presented the men with a sheet of paper.

"Very reasonable," said the man who'd earlier spoken to Helen. Then he said, "Your maid's a pretty one. I've always been fond of chubby vixens. I'll pay a guinea for half an hour. What do you say?"

There was a short pause, then John said, "This is an inn, sir. There are brothels in Blackburn, Bolton and Manchester. You'll receive a more favourable response there. No disrespect intended."

Alex tried to keep his outrage under control, but Helen sensed something amiss and walked over to him.

The traveller addressed Helen. "Ah, here she is. Well, what do *you* say then? I ask you once more; a guinea…for thirty minutes in your company. You're a pretty girl. It's a fair offer."

Alex said, "This is my wife, sir."

"Irish?"

Alex recognised the voice, and his anger ignited.

"I know you."

"I don't think so..."

"Yes. A year ago. Late at night. On the road. It was you."

"Let's go," said the other man. He sounded worried. "The horses are ready."

The first man continued to address Alex. "You're mistaken."

"I don't think so," said Alex, walking around the bar.

The two men moved quickly outside, between the Roman pillars and into the street. Alex followed them, closing in on the first man.

"Alex!" called Helen, following them into the open air.

The man was drawing his sword, but Alex was on him and punched him in the face. He went down, dropped his weapon, and Alex kicked him between the legs.

"Just like you did to me, you bastard!" A second kick, then he bent down, pulled the man up by the scruff of the neck and hit him again, flattening his nose and bursting his lip, spraying blood.

Suddenly there was a blade at his throat. The second man had got behind him and was pulling back his head.

A shot rang out, frightening the horses, and all three of them looked towards the inn. John stood there, a pistol in each hand.

"The next shot kills one of you," he said. "Alex, come here."

Alex got up and moved over to John, Helen waiting in the rear, her hands covering her cheeks in fright.

John said, "Alex, what should I do with these men?"

Alex was thinking clearly despite the excitement that surged through him. These men had almost killed him. They'd robbed him – but he hadn't had much for them to take. He'd found himself at the White Bull because of what they'd done to him. He'd met Helen – because of what they'd done to him.

"Put the guns down," he said to John.

John lowered the weapons and Alex walked over to the two men. He offered his hand to the prone one and helped him to his feet.

"Apologise to my wife," he said. The man looked at Helen, then at Alex. "Now," said Alex. "I won't ask again."

The man raised both his hands and called to Helen, "I meant no harm."

"Thank you," said Alex. "Now go. And Godspeed to you."

The two mounted their horses, the injured one with some difficulty, and rode away.

Helen's heart swelled with love for Alex. She was so proud of him – and she hadn't yet told him she was three months pregnant.

36. WHITBY
Wednesday December 3, 1760

Meadow, tense and anxious, sat opposite her mother in a tea shop near the bottom of Flowergate. Persephone had drained her cup ten minutes earlier, but Meadow's remained untouched and cooling. The older woman looked steadily at the younger. Meadow's eyes were unfocused, staring emptily at the tabletop.

The powders that Persephone had presented to her daughter on her eighteenth birthday had run out months ago, but Meadow's overwhelming need for Alder's attention had continued regardless, and she'd become pregnant.
She disliked children. She did not want to be a mother. And she did not want *any thing* to interfere with what she had with her man.
She had to lose the baby. And she had to make sure this situation could never occur again. Meadow had little idea how to terminate the pregnancy herself, so after more than three months without bleeding, went to find her mother. Persephone was not entirely displeased to see her daughter, although she was horrified at the news. Meadow stood quietly and absorbed all the abuse and ridicule before asking directly for help.
Her mother knew what to do – and where to go.

It was a bright day for the time of year, though cold. The appointment was for two o'clock in the afternoon; Persephone had instructed the driver to return for them at three.
"How do you feel?" she asked.
"Stupid," muttered Meadow.

She felt sympathy for her daughter but also a little self-righteousness. However, she was sensible enough not to utter any kind of *"You only have yourself to blame"* comment.

They sat in silence a moment longer.

"Are you ready?"

Meadow paused; then, lips closed, "Mm..." in the affirmative.

"Let's go then."

They stood, left the shop and made their way along Cliff Street as far as Pier Lane. Meadow was fearful and felt crushed, almost overwhelmed with dread. She could die; she could lose all her love – *all her love...* It was difficult to walk.

They stopped at a small terraced house, and knocked. Meadow swallowed, wrung her hands, gasped for breath, felt the tears start.

The door was opened, and they stepped inside.

It was quiet on the farm that day, and Alder was home by four o'clock, as the last of the light faded from the sky. The empty house felt strange. He'd grown accustomed to Meadow's immediate demands and felt refreshed by the opportunity to light the peat himself and sit peacefully in front of it. He made himself a pot of tea and brought the dish and cup to the fire, kicking off his boots.

Meadow had told him she was going to see her parents that day. Nothing more. He knew nothing about the pregnancy.

They arrived at Vine Cottage just after five o'clock. Alder, hearing the coach pull up, opened the front door, the lamplight from the kitchen spilling along the path. The driver, a tall, handsome African man, was helping Meadow down from the carriage. She saw Alder and held out her arms to him. He hurried forward and took her. "Thank God," she muttered close to his ear. The girl was pale, weak, and found it difficult to stand upright. Alder looked questioningly into the carriage's gloomy interior.

"Alder," Persephone greeted him.

"Mrs Reid," he said. "What's happened?"

"Meadow fell on the stairs. The doctor has looked at her and assures us that she isn't badly hurt. Make sure she gets some rest."

A carriage passed on the road as they were speaking, travelling towards the manor house.

Alder's consternation deepened in response to Persephone's words. "Of course," he said. "Thank you – for bringing her back."

"I'll come and see her in a few days," said Persephone. "Send for me if she worsens. Don't hesitate." The driver was already in his seat. Persephone tapped on the roof with her umbrella, and the carriage pulled away.

Meadow put her full weight on Alder. She was panting, in pain. "I need to go to bed."

"Of course, my love," Alder replied, concerned. The last time he'd seen her so helpless was when he'd brought her home in the cart, drunk.

"I'm sorry," she said. She was crying – not in torrents, but steadily, the moisture hanging on her cheeks.

"There's nothing to be sorry about. Let's just get you better."

He carried her upstairs to the bedroom, sat her on the edge of the bed and removed her shoes.

"Shall I help you undress?"

"No. I can manage, I think. Thank you."

"I'll light a fire."

"No, don't worry. I'll be warm enough under the covers." She began to unbutton her clothes.

"Alright." He paused, worried, feeling helpless. "Would you like some more light?"

"No. Honestly. I just want to lie down."

"Can I make you some tea, then?"

"Yes. Thank you. That would be nice." Her voice was feeble.

"Are you in pain?"

"Yes. Don't worry about it. It'll pass." Meadow slid her shoulders out of her dress and pushed it down, the material rustling.

"I could send for Doctor Levinson."

"No. Really. I just need time."

Alder nodded impotently, went downstairs and began to boil the water. He remembered Nara, how he'd lost her, and was almost breathless with anxiety.

A few minutes later he returned to the bedroom with the tea he'd prepared, and found her in bed, wrapped under the sheets, fast asleep.

Alder busied himself in the kitchen, carrying out pointless tasks, trying to keep his concern at bay. He sharpened the knives, then made a poor job of mending a pair of breeches. His repeated struggles with the latter task were interrupted by quick footsteps on the path and a brisk knock at the front door. It was Louise Flesher.

"Hello, Miss Flesher. I'm afraid Meadow's asleep."

"Is she not well?" asked Louise. "Cornelius passed by earlier and saw you carrying her into the house. Can I see her?"

"Please," said Alder, stepping aside so she could enter. Louise swept by him, removed her cloak and was already running up the stairs as he called after her, "She's fast asleep. She fell at her mother's house..."

The bedroom was almost completely dark, lit only by a single lamp, burning low. Louise called her friend's name softly, took up the lamp and approached the bed. Meadow was indeed asleep, just as Alder had said. Louise set the lamp on the bedside table, pulled up a chair, sat down, and touched Meadow's shoulder. She opened her eyes, found Louise in the dimness, and tried to sit up, the bedclothes partly falling from her.

"Oh my goodness!" said Louise. "You're not wearing anything." She covered her up and gently returned her to a prone position. "You'll catch your death. It really isn't warm in here. It's December – don't you know?"

Meadow smiled weakly. "It's alright. I always sleep like this."

Louise stopped fussing and asked, "What happened?"

"You mustn't tell anyone."

"Tell anyone what?"

"Promise."

"Alright. Of course. I promise not to tell anyone."

"I was pregnant. I went to Whitby today – to stop it."

Louise's hand flew to her mouth. "Oh, my God!" she said.

"Don't tell," Meadow whispered urgently.

Louise was crushed with sadness; moisture flooded into her eyes. "You were going to be a mother," she said, her voice breaking as the tears fell.

Meadow's mouth puckered. "I'm sorry."

Louise sat silently until she was sure she'd be able to speak. "What happened?"

"It was horrible. I bled a lot. It hurt – it still hurts."

"You must let Neil see you."

"No."

"For God's sake, Meadow! Are you still bleeding?"

"No. I don't think so. Not much anyway. Maybe a little."

"Show me."

"No. Please. It's not necessary."

Louise stood. "I'm going to look. If you won't see the doctor, at least let *me* help – as far as I can."

Meadow sighed and wiped tears from her cheeks and eyes. She sniffed, looked up at her friend but said nothing.

"I'll get some warm water." Louise dabbed away the residue of her own emotion and went downstairs. Meadow heard her talking with Alder. He was clearly concerned and wanted to help, but Louise kept him at bay. A few moments later she reappeared in the bedroom with a basin and some towels. She lit some more lamps and brought them close, standing them on two wooden chairs; then she washed her hands, dried them and set the towel down on the bed.

"Here we are then," she said, sighing. "Alright, let's see." She lifted the bedclothes aside, and Meadow lay back and drew up her knees. "Oh, dear," Louise muttered, peering. "Poor love." She sucked a breath through her teeth, leaned forward and began.

"Is it bad?" asked Meadow after a few seconds, flinching at her friend's fingers. She was sore, uncomfortable.

"Honestly?" said Louise. "I don't know. I don't even know what I'm looking for. There's a bit of blood. You've been cut, nicked – that must sting. But I can only really see the outside. It's very dark – inflamed, maybe." She tutted, concerned. "This could get infected; perhaps it already is." She went on quietly for two or three seconds more, then asked, "What did they do to you?"

Meadow winced, trying to stay relaxed. "It was an old woman – and her daughter, I think, standing by. I kept my eyes closed as much as I could and tried to imagine I was far away." She gasped. "Louise, that hurts. Please…"

Louise frowned. "Sorry. Meadow, you need a proper examination. Please let me get Neil."

"No," said Meadow. "Please don't ask me to do that. I'd have to start explaining things to Alder. I don't want him to know what I've done."

Louise withdrew her hands. Meadow lowered her legs and pulled the covers around herself once more.

Louise shook her head, looking very worried. "Meadow, listen to me. I'm not a surgeon, so I don't know for sure how bad this is. But I do know that infections can kill you." She emphasised the last words, staring at her friend. "You must get this into perspective – it might be very serious."

Meadow was becoming agitated. "No. No. Please. Look, I really don't want anyone to know. I'd rather be dead than have them know."

"That's stupid!" said Louise. "How do you think Alder would feel if you died? He loves you. It's as plain as the nose on your face. You're not being fair to him."

Meadow was quiet. She felt ashamed. "Alright. If it gets worse, I'll see Neil."

"Promise?"

"Yes. Yes, absolutely."

"I think Alder should know," said Louise, washing her hands in the basin.

"No," Meadow insisted. "Please, no. I might lose every-thing. I might lose *him*. I don't want that."

Louise rubbed her hands in a towel and stared at the bed-ridden girl.

"Please," said Meadow, shaking her head. "Promise me you won't tell him."

Louise sighed, thought hard, ran her tongue around her teeth, staring intently at her friend. "If you die, I'll blame myself."

"Please just give me till the morning. I might be better by then. *Please*."

"Meadow..." (shaking her head – disapproving – *you're being in idiot...*)

"Please, Louise."

Louise looked down, breaking eye contact *(this is silly – dangerous)*. "Alright. Till the morning."

"Thank you."

She looked up again and caught Meadow's eyes once more. "But only until the morning. If things get worse, I'm taking charge."

Meadow nodded. "Alright. Fair enough."

"Good. Thank you." Louise breathed out through her nose, a gesture that said, *That's it then; standoff for a few hours.* "You need to wash yourself thoroughly. Do you want me to do it for you?"

"No," Meadow answered. "I can do it."

"I'll check on you tomorrow. I'll look again in the daylight, so I know."

"I'll be better tomorrow," said Meadow.

There was a distant knocking at the front door – another visitor.

"See you in the morning," said Louise. "Take care of yourself – and if things get worse in the night, send Alder up to the house."

"Alright. Thanks, Louise."

"I mean it. Straight away. Don't wait for daylight."

"Yes," said Meadow. "I will. Thank you."

Louise kissed her friend, hugged her, then replaced the lights from where she'd taken them, turned them low and made her way downstairs. Cornelius was sitting at the kitchen table with Alder. Their conversation ceased when Louise appeared.

"I hear Meadow's had an accident," said Cornelius.

"Yes," Louise replied. "She'll be alright, I think – she just needs to rest."

"Should I go up?"

"I don't think so. She's very tired."

The parson nodded.

Louise addressed Alder as she got into her cape. "I'll come back tomorrow and check on her. She's convinced she's fine, and won't see Neil. If things get worse, Alder, come to the house and get me – whatever the time is."

"Thank you, Miss Flesher."

"Louise."

"Thank you…"

She opened the door, admitting a blast of winter wind, and was gone.

Cornelius resumed his conversation with Alder. "As I was saying, I have to be in Scarborough this Friday, but I could stay the night there and visit Kate on Saturday morning on the way back. Would that be alright with you?"

"Yes, thank you. It'll be nice to hear how she's doing."

"Good. I'll come and see you on Sunday afternoon – tell you all about it." He smiled.

"I'll look forward to it," said Alder. "It's kind of you to think of Kate."

"We all miss her, Alder. So many people have gone in the years I've visited this house – John, Hazel, Oswin, Nara. And now Kate's growing up... It's a strange thing, the passing of time – sweeps everything away."

Alder nodded but offered no reply; his thoughts were upstairs with Meadow. Cornelius rose, donned his black coat and shook Alder's hand.

"Alder. Until Sunday."

"See you then," Alder replied.

Alder took off his clothes quietly in the darkness and joined Meadow in bed at half past nine. He'd thought she was asleep, but she turned, put her hand on his hip, and he saw the glimmer of her eyes. He lifted her gently and slid an arm beneath her, drawing her to him. She rested her head on his chest.

Alder listened to her breathing in the stillness that followed. Then she whispered, "I'm sorry."

"Why?" he asked.

"I'm not strong."

"You'll be fine. You just need to rest."

"No. I mean, I'm not a strong person."

Meadow didn't often say such things, and Alder felt a rush of love for her. He hugged her and caressed her head.

"You don't have to be anything for me, love. I just want you to be happy."

She was silent for a while, then whispered, "You're a lovely man."

Alder said, "I'm a *lucky* man." He paused. "I was a rogue when I was young. Drunk a lot of the time, always chasing women, getting into fights. Then one day Nara came, and everything was different. That was love; that was the first real love. Then she died, and everything was mud – for a long time." The wind howled around the house, filling in his silence, and he added softly, "Then there was you... It was a miracle."

They kissed, warm in their bed, in the dark.

"I love you, Meadow," he said.

She tried to find his eyes in the blackness. He'd drawn her very close, his hand on her thigh.

"I can't..." she whispered.

"Doesn't matter," he said. "Just lie quiet and sleep, my love."

37. CAPPLEMAN FARM
Thursday December 4, 1760

"G' mornin', Miss Louise," called Stephen Flathers.

Louise had been so deep in thought that she hadn't seen him working there in the forge. She looked to her right and elevated a hand in greeting. "Good afternoon, Stephen."

The smith laughed and said, "So it is. I lose track o' time – it's the 'eat."

Stephen's son, Alan, added his greeting to his father's. Louise paused in her ascent to the manor house and called, "Busy then?"

"New 'inges for t' barn doors," called Stephen. "You can tell t' Squire they'll be ready tomorrow."

"I'll do that," said Louise. "Thank you."

"Is Meadow alreet?" asked Alan. Louise looked at him but didn't answer immediately. Alan went on, "We 'eard there'd bin an accident or somethin'."

"She's recovering," Louise answered, nodding. "She'll be fine."

"That's good to 'ear," said Alan.

The three stood for a second, looking at each other, none finding anything else to say.

"I'd be better be getting back," said Louise.

"G' day to you then, ma'am," said Stephen, raising his hand. Louise nodded and walked on.

In truth, she was still concerned for her friend. Meadow remained sore and weak. Her tissues appeared less inflamed this morning than the previous evening, but Louise could have put that down to the fact that she'd undertaken her examination in the bloom of a sunny day rather than in last night's shadowy lamplight.

"I don't think it's any worse," Louise had said, reluctantly. Her better judgement told her to send for the surgeon straight away, but Meadow delayed common sense still further by getting her friend to agree to a further postponement.

"How did you cope with Alder last night?"

"We didn't."

"Have you been up?"

"Yes, of course – to pee. I can move about. I feel no worse than yesterday. That must be a good sign..."

So this was the way it was going to go; day by day, step by step. Perhaps it would turn out well; perhaps she'd got away with it.

Louise stopped a few yards short of the Buckley's house to listen to a robin, just visible high up in a bare beech tree, perform its long, complicated song. She smiled, watching the jerking movements of the bird's head as it paused to listen to the distant reply of a mate. It was very early for the robin's spring song – the first time she'd heard it this season. The worst of the winter was yet to come, but here was the herald of the new year's life. Soon there'd be snowdrops, crocuses, then the world would come alive again.

"Grace Buckley's sweet on thee," said Stephen to his son, hammering away at the red hot metal. "It's in 'er eyes."

"Dad," said Alan, shaking his head, "she's only thirteen."

"She won't always be *only thirteen*," his father replied. "She's already a good lookin' lass."

Alan knew Grace liked him, but was embarrassed by his father's observation. "She'll grow out of it," he said.

"Maybe she will, and maybe she won't." Stephen looked up and caught Alan's eye. "She'll be fourteen in t' summer. Lasses get married younger."

"It's too young, dad. Come on – she's just a girl. Let her grow up."

Stephen sighed. "Good lad, you are. Made your ma and me

proud. Now listen to you – thoughtful, always thinkin' of others. You're a good boy – a fine catch for a girl like Grace. Your ma (God rest 'er soul), I wish she could've seen you grow up."

"Dad…" said Alan, cringing.

Stephen hammered, once, twice… again. "All I'm sayin' is – keep alert. You two – you're meant one for t' other."

38. THE LOOKOUT
Friday & Saturday, December 5 & 6, 1760

Cornelius spent all of Friday in a Scarborough hotel, taking part in a conference that drew together many Yorkshire parsons. He dined well with friends on Friday night, had a good sleep and rose early the next morning.

Saturday dawned dull and grey. Cornelius washed and took a quick, chilly walk along the strand before breakfast. The sea was choppy but the fishing boats were already out. As a boy, he'd dreamt about being a fisherman, but things had turned out differently. He'd been alone most of his life; had never married. There'd been opportunities but he hadn't taken them. Now it was too late. He stood and watched the sea – the waves crashing on the beach. In his blood, he was a fisherman.

He met a few friends at breakfast, ate heartily and was on his way north to the Lookout by half past eight.

The road was badly rutted and slow, but ten o'clock found him in front of the closed iron gates. He dismounted, found the bell chain on the left gatepost and pulled it. The bell itself was set in a frame at the top of the stone pillar and rang out boldly, summoning the gatekeeper, who emerged from his little cottage a few yards along the drive.

Cornelius raised his hand in greeting as the man approached, squat, bow-legged, in his middle sixties, wizened of face and smoking his pipe.

"Morning, sir," saluted the man, talking around the pipe clenched between his teeth.

"Good morning," Cornelius replied. "I've come to see a friend of mine, one of the girls."

"I've got no note of any visitors today."

"I know. I was engaged in meetings yesterday in Scarborough, and I'm on my way home to Glaisdale this morning. I realised I'd be passing the school and thought I'd ring the bell on the chance that an unannounced visit might be acceptable."

"I see you're a parson."

"I am."

The man swung open the left gate for Cornelius. It hadn't been locked.

"In you come, sir. Alfred'll meet you, I reckon. Just follow the drive."

"Thank you. May I ask your name?"

"Jack, sir. Jack Archer." He saluted again.

"Thank you, Mr Archer. I'm much obliged."

Cornelius rode along the drive for about six minutes before the house came into view. It was indeed an impressive edifice, one of the largest houses he'd ever seen. He located a tethering post and water trough in the area near the main entrance, secured his horse, mounted the steps and rang the bell. A moment later the door was opened by a uniformed porter, impressive of stature and sporting a notable moustache.

"Yes, sir?"

Cornelius gave his name, repeated his explanation, and was invited into the entrance hall, dominated by its immense staircase. He removed his hat.

"Take a seat, sir. I'll call for someone."

Cornelius sat down and looked about him, awestruck. There were huge landscapes on either side of the waiting area. The one over the porter's desk depicted a naval battle, while that above and behind him was a mountain scene, featuring a village dominated by a dark castle, with people fishing in a lake in the foreground.

He cast his eyes over to the staircase and looked at the portraits hanging there, wondering who they depicted. He'd heard that the Lookout had been closed for a very long time and had fallen partly into ruin. The reconstruction work was most impressive, and he wondered if the portraits might show members of the old Wynter family. If so, the likenesses must have either been returned from storage or have undergone similarly painstaking restoration.

Quick footsteps heralded the arrival of a slender, pale-haired footman. Cornelius overheard the dialogue.

"You rang, Mr Bentley?"

"I did, Newt. This gentleman, Parson East..." (he indicated Cornelius) "...has come to visit one of the girls. Would you kindly inform Mr Crowan or Mr Quinton, please?"

Newt turned and ran up the staircase. Cornelius watched him disappear from view. Mr Bentley looked across at the parson.

"Sorry to keep you waiting, sir."

Cornelius waved, *No matter,* and continued to fidget with his hat.

A few moments later Newt came running down the stairs and disappeared into the west wing from whence he'd come. A minute after that, Cornelius heard more footsteps descending – regular, leisurely – then a well-dressed squat man came into view. As he approached, Cornelius thought how unfortunate was his appearance. There was something animal-like about him that the parson attempted to set to one side, preferring to dismiss first impressions as far as possible. He found it difficult to judge the man's age – forties or fifties, tight grey hair tied back.

The man extended his hand. "Parson East? I'm Knox Quinton, Mr Crowan's secretary."

Cornelius stood and took Quinton's hand. It was stubby and powerful, with a firm grip that made Cornelius wince with pain.

"A pleasure to meet you, Mr Quinton. I'm here to visit Kate Swithenbank – if she's available. I apologise that I haven't made arrangements."

"I think we can manage that, sir. I'm not sure where she is, but perhaps you'd like to accompany me while we search for her? You'll see something of the school that way."

Cornelius was indeed eager to see more of the place. "How kind," he said. "I'd like that very much. Thank you."

"Follow me, please." Quinton led the way to the debating chamber. "There are no classes today, but we usually find some of the girls in here." He opened the door and looked briefly inside. "But Kate is not among them. Those are Class 5 girls." He paused. "Would you like to see the chapel?"

"You have a chapel? That would be most interesting."

Quinton led Cornelius to the double doors and ushered him inside.

"This is most impressive!" exclaimed the parson. "My word! You even have an organ! Do you hold services regularly?"

"Once a month, and on occasional feast-days."

"Do you employ a chaplain?"

"No," said Quinton. "We call on the goodwill of retired clergy."

"Aha!" said Cornelius. "Perhaps I know some of them?"

"More than likely," Quinton replied. "Will Surbiton, Douglas Norris, Arthur Mulgrave, Peter Exmouth..."

"Yes," said Cornelius. "Peter Exmouth. I haven't seen him for years. He used to be parson at Littlebeck. Will Surbiton – I'm sure I met him once or twice. Wasn't he at Harwood Dale?"

"I'm afraid I wouldn't know, sir." Knox paused. "Shall we continue?"

"Yes, of course," replied Cornelius. "I beg your pardon – I'm taking up your time."

"It's no trouble, sir. Let's try upstairs in the classrooms. Perhaps someone might know where she is."

As they ascended, Cornelius voiced his curiosity about the portraits, all of men – certainly as far as the first floor – although he looked up and noticed others, on the loftier ascents, that appeared to depict women.

"Are these likenesses of the Wynter family?" he asked. "Did you have them restored?"

"A few of them are Wynters," Quinton replied. "Most of them are portraits of our benefactors."

"I see," Cornelius nodded. He recognised a few faces; politicians, clergymen, gentry, royalty.

Quinton opened a few doors but to no avail. "I'm sorry," he said, "this may take some time. We'll try the library."

They ascended to the second floor and made their way along to the end of the east wing. Cornelius was astonished by the library, a room occupying two stories, filled with light and packed with books, probably twenty thousand of them, or more. While Cornelius looked around him in stunned amazement, Quinton picked out one of the girls and spoke to her.

"Bip, do you know where we can find Kate?"

"Kate's practising the harp."

"Ah, thank you," said Quinton. He turned and motioned to Cornelius. "We're closing in."

They left the library and retraced their steps to the first floor.

"She'll be in one of the practice rooms," he said, hurrying to the west side of the house. Quinton tried three rooms before they found her sitting alone with a harp, struggling through her preliminary exercises. She looked up in surprise.

"Cornelius!"

"Kate!" he exclaimed. She set the instrument down and ran the few steps that separated them. The parson embraced her warmly. "How good to see you!"

"I'll leave you. Please excuse me," said Quinton.

Cornelius straightened himself and shook Quinton's hand. "Thank you, Mr Quinton. I'm most grateful for your time and efforts."

"A pleasure, sir." He turned and was gone, leaving the two alone.

Cornelius sat on the harpsichord seat. "So, how are you? How's it been here?"

"It's amazing," said Kate. "I've made lots of friends and had loads of adventures. The house is full of surprises. And I'm learning such a lot. Look..." she showed him the book containing her harp exercises, "I can read music. I'm learning the harp – and the harpsichord."

"Good for you! What lessons are your favourites?"

Kate thought. "Well, harp..., dancing, literature of course..."

"Of course," echoed Cornelius.

"...and French. I love French!"

"Tu sembles très heureux," he said, smiling.

"Je suis!" she replied, delighted.

"That's amazing!" he said. "You're picking it all up so fast!"

Kate gave a happy laugh. "Let me show you round."

Kate began the tour with the concert hall. Some of the older girls were practising a choral piece, accompanied by Orla at the harpsichord. Mr Browning, overseeing the rehearsal, was seated at the far side of the room, but everyone stopped to greet Cornelius. The four singers introduced themselves as Nana Hall, Vivianne Stamper, Betty Elliot and Dearbhla Blackwood. They were all staggeringly beautiful, almost robbing Cornelius of breath. "My word..." he muttered to himself.

As Kate towed Cornelius towards her own dormitory, she said, "Aren't the girls lovely?"

Cornelius replied, "Lovely? I'm...speechless."

Kate laughed.

Fuzzy was reading alone on her bed.

"Fuzz, this is my friend, Cornelius. Cornelius, this is my friend, Fuzzy."

They shook hands, and Cornelius gave a little bow. "I'm very pleased to meet you, Fuzzy. I've never met a Fuzzy before!" The girl laughed, and curtsied for him.

"And this is my room," said Kate, taking him next door.

Cornelius was pleased to see it – the dormitory was comfortable, large and bright. He looked at the other three beds, and Kate pointed to each in turn. "Bip, Pammy, Shelagh. We have a great time."

"I'm glad you're so happy, Kate. I can't wait to tell your father tomorrow."

"How are things on the farm?" she asked.

"All well, I believe," he replied. "Much the same as when you left a few weeks ago. Your father is well. Meadow had an accident in her parents' house a few days ago and is recovering at home."

"Oh dear," said Kate. "Is she hurt badly?"

"I don't think so," he replied. "Louise is watching out for her. Will you be coming home for Christmas?"

"I've been thinking about it," said Kate. "I probably will. None of the other girls has a home to go to. I seem to be the odd one out."

"It would be nice to have you back for a few days," said Cornelius. "I think your father misses you."

Kate suddenly felt a little guilty about having such a good time. She frowned. "I *will* come home," she said.

"Good," said Cornelius, smiling. "Just for a few days, then we'll get you back."

"Let me show you outside," said Kate.

They made their way down to the entrance hall, and Cornelius asked Mr Bentley if someone might take care of his horse for half an hour or so.

"Of course, Mr East. I'll get the stable boy to look after it."

Kate took Cornelius around the grounds behind the house: the outdoor theatre, the gardens, the stables and the animal pens. She saw Speck Beckwith approaching as they took the path towards the fields. His dog, running ahead of him, came bounding up to Kate, panting, tongue lolling. Kate knelt down and petted him.

"Hello, Bastard! Lovely boy!"

"Bastard?" laughed Cornelius. "What a name for a dog!"

Kate laughed back.

Speck drew near, lifting his hat. "Good day, sir," he said to Cornelius. Cornelius returned the greeting. "Young Kate," said Speck, giving her a wink.

"Hello, Speck," Kate replied.

Speck passed on his way, Bastard following behind.

Kate and Cornelius took the path to the east and walked as far as the rise from which they could view the North Sea. She pointed out the old lookout tower.

"That's one of my favourite places. I feel very safe in there. I don't know why. If I could make a roof and close the hole in the wall, I'd live there."

Cornelius smiled. "You have an old soul, Kate."

The phrase struck her. Perhaps it was true.

She asked him if he'd like to climb up to the tower but he said he'd better be getting on his way. They walked back to the house, and he collected his horse.

"Well, Kate. It was *so* good to see you." He hugged her tight. "I'll tell them at home how well you are, and how happy. And we'll all look forward to seeing you later in the month." "Goodbye!" He mounted, waved and rode away.

Kate watched him as he went. She hadn't told him about the locked room. Or the boys in the tower. And she hadn't told him that the ghost of Rosalind Wynter stood at the end of her bed every night.

39. ST WILFRID'S CHURCH, RIBCHESTER
Tuesday December 16, 1760

The churchyard contained a few scattered gravestones. Those that were more recent shone in the daylight; the older ones leaned as if they were tired, their surfaces decorated with lichen, moss filling in the engraved letters. She cast a glance at the old sundial as she passed it. Two elderly women, wrapped up against the chill, hurried by in the road beyond the churchyard wall, gossiping animatedly. Helen stepped into the porch, lifted the latch and creaked open the wooden door. It was very cold in the empty church, but Helen Shaw's heart was full of warmth. Events had brought about a situation in which she'd never dreamt to find herself.

She'd grown up in a tiny terraced cottage in Blackburn. There'd been very little money in the family because Isaac, her father, squandered it. Every night he'd go straight from the tannery to the alehouse to get drunk. Then he would come home and beat her mother and herself. Helen was an average-looking child with a natural tendency to flabbiness, though her face was pretty – at least Maureen, her mother, told her it was. "You're very fair of face, Helen," she would say, cuddling her. It was the only warmth she received, and she was grateful for it. "My fair-faced child."
But she received no love from her father, whose violence increased as the years wore on. One appalling night in 1750, when she was fourteen, he came home full of drunken rage, uncontrollable and ferocious. He took his fists to Maureen until she collapsed unconscious on the

parlour floor, then proceeded to boot her mercilessly as she lay defenceless. Helen tried to stop him, smashed a kitchen pot over his head. She'd never dared strike her father before; it changed the dynamic of the situation entirely. He turned towards her, inspecting the blood from the wound she'd inflicted on the back of his skull. His gin-fuelled fury became incandescent. He took his fists to Helen as he'd done to her mother. Then he tore open her dress and raped her.

The act siphoned his violence away, and when it was done he sat down and took his head in his hands. Torn and bloody, Helen watched from where she lay, expecting a resumption of the onslaught at any moment. Instead, he rose, gave her one red glance from beneath lowered brows, buttoned his breeches and strode out of the house.

Helen pulled the remains of her dress about her and tended to her mother. Isaac didn't return that night – or the next.

Four days after his brutal attack, the man came home sober. Neither Maureen nor Helen said anything as he sat in his chair. He told them he was changed and was ashamed of what he'd done. He asked their forgiveness. Maureen, always loving, took his hand and said she would take him back, of course she would – she loved him. She kissed his forehead, told him all was forgiven, forgotten. Isaac crumpled where he sat, wracked with sobs, his head cradled in her arms.

Helen packed a few things in a sack and left home for good. She uttered not a single word to him.

In the years since that time she'd communicated with her mother by letter but had never returned home. She found employment for herself in a laundry, where she worked hard for four years; then heard that an inn at Langho was seeking kitchen staff. She took the job, and it was there that John and Sarah Bennett found her in 1757, when she was twenty-one. Sarah, in particular, took a strong liking to her and offered her work at the White Bull in Ribchester five miles distant.

And there she was when Alex was carried in, close to death, two years later. Now she had a man who loved her, who didn't mind her plainness. In her mind she heard his voice, *"I love your bum,"* and smiled with affection for him. She was going to have a child, born out of real love. Helen felt blessed and had come to church to give thanks for her life.

She knelt at the altar rail in the chancel and silently offered up her prayer. It was dark there, but the clouds pulled apart briefly, and the low morning sun cast its brilliant rays through the three tall east windows, illuminating the supplicant in a shaft of golden light. It was as if the creator of the cosmos had seen Helen, heard her thanks and reached out to bless her, His daughter. She gasped with the unexpected surprise of it, and her gratefulness overflowed within her.

Helen was well-known to most of the village folk, and she greeted a number of them as she made her way back to the White Bull, her mind filled again with Alex. He was the love of her life, the *only* love; she'd never before been in such a relationship. He was the opposite of her father. Alex was kind, affectionate, thoughtful, and never touched alcohol. She couldn't have been happier. As she approached the inn, he opened the door and appeared in the street. He'd been watching for her.

"You look lovely in the sunshine," he said.

He was the only man who'd ever told her she looked lovely. She couldn't suppress her delighted cry as he took her in his arms and kissed her. Sarah Bennett, in hat and coat, passed through the door on her way to the market and eased her way around the couple as they stood there, firm in each other's embrace, lips joined.

"Oh my goodness," she said, "look at you two!"

40. CAPPLEMAN FARM
Saturday December 20, 1760

Fair-haired Grace Buckley had been without her friend Kate for nearly two months. Today Kate was coming home, at least for a while. The carriage was due to arrive at Alder's cottage at two o'clock, and there was going to be a surprise welcoming party. Grace's brother Walter was coming – also Beatrice and Amy Swift. Pond Girl had decorated the cottage, helped by Alan Flathers from the forge. Alan was strong, with dark wiry hair. At nineteen, he was six years older than Grace – and her secret idol.

At half past one, Grace and Walter collected Amy and Beatrice from next door and made their way down the long, shallow incline to Vine Cottage. It was a cold day, though very still, and they found the front door open, a blazing fire roaring in the kitchen. The decorations were complete, with a big banner that read, WELCOME HOME KATE! in big red letters. Buffy Miller and Alicia Buckley had been in the cottage for some time, preparing the welcome meal, and Apple Robinson had come to assist. Buffy hurried from place to place, putting the final touches on a few details. Alan Flathers and Alder were in the little parlour, out of the women's way, the older man drinking tea, the younger a glass of ale.

Grace, Walter, Amy and Beatrice hung up their capes and pushed the door closed. Greetings were exchanged, and Grace asked after Meadow.

"She'll come down later," said Alicia. "She's getting better."

Meadow remained weak. She moved about the house with care but had been outside only rarely in the preceding two weeks. Louise, who came to see her almost every day, was frustrated that her friend maintained her refusal to see Neil, although she was encouraged by the fact that recovery seemed to be taking place, albeit slowly.

There would be a lot of eating this happy afternoon. The celebrations were to begin in Vine Cottage, then transfer up to the big house where there was more room – and where a second welcoming reception had been arranged. But for now, all being in place, they sat and awaited the carriage from the Lookout.

Grace took a seat at the parlour window and kept an eye on Watermill Lane. As expected, the coach appeared in the distance at two o'clock, clattered by the window and pulled up in the road by the front gate. Alder stood in the doorframe, everyone else hidden inside, while Kipp Nibley climbed down from the box and opened the carriage door, releasing the single occupant. Kate jumped down into the road, beaming with delight.

"Daddy!" she cried, running to her father.

"Kate! My Kate!" His arms were round her and he lifted her up, swinging her about in joy.

"Have a good time, Miss Kate," called Kipp, clambering up into his seat.

"Thanks, Kipp," said Kate, waving. "See you in two weeks."

There was laughter and shouting, hugs and tears when Kate walked through the front door.

Meadow sat upstairs in the bedroom. She'd managed to wash and dress and was almost ready to go down and join in, hearing the sounds of the throng below.

The weakness and pain she'd experienced following the procedure had settled into a persistent feebleness and lack of will. Every night she lay in Alder's arms, thankful for his constancy, strength and comfort, although their physical relationship had not resumed. She despised herself for what she'd done, the more so because she hadn't found the courage to admit it to her man.

Persephone, fearing a second visit to the abortionist, sent her daughter a fresh supply of powders, specially ordered from her supplier in London. The mixture had kept Persephone herself from conceiving for more than two decades. On one of her more determined days, Meadow struggled to the outhouse and emptied the entire contents of the packet into the bucket, from whence it was removed with the night-soil.

Meadow was caught in a trap she'd built herself, the bars made of her own selfishness and deceit. Her release would come about only in the wake of her confession – her confession to Alder that she'd misled him and killed his child. Alder's forgiveness was the key that would let her out. But could she expect such a thing of him after what she'd done? She would probably lose his love – the most precious thing she'd ever had. What then…?

Kate was telling everyone all about the school and her new friends there; about the secret passageways, the hiding places, the beach, the old lookout tower, the maze and the forgotten garden. She didn't tell them about the ghosts or her secret midnight gin parties with Fuzzy (of which there had been three).

Amy Swift asked excitedly, "Teach us something we can say in French!"

Kate was prepared for this question and had something ready. "Alright. Listen." She concentrated and delivered the sentence. "Tu ne penses pas que je suis la plus jolie fille de la ferme?"

Their jaws dropped in amazement. There was awed silence for a moment, then Beatrice said, "What does it mean?"

"I'll tell you in a minute," said Kate. "First you have to learn it."

"Say it again," said Walter.

Kate repeated the sentence, then broke it down to two or

three words at a time until all the parts were assembled and they could recite the phrase after her.

"Tu ne penses – pas que – je suis – la plus jolie – fille de la ferme?"

They all did it.

"Now without me," she said. There were a few stumbles and corrections at first, but they soon had it perfectly.

"Now tell us what it means," said Amy.

Kate said, "It means, *Don't you think I'm the prettiest girl on the farm?*"

They all collapsed with laughter. Before the giggles had subsided, Walter Buckley (aged fifteen) looked at Amy Swift (aged sixteen) and said quietly, "But I think you *are* the prettiest girl on the farm..."

Auburn-haired Amy blushed red, smiled and looked sheepish, while all the other girls cringed in vicarious embarrassment. But Walter meant it. He'd fallen for the girl next door, and they'd already exchanged a few secret kisses.

There was a cautious step on the stairs, and Kate glanced across the kitchen to see Meadow descending. She rose from her circle of friends, ran over and hugged her while she was still two steps from the bottom of the staircase. Kate looked so happy – Meadow felt her heart pull with affection.

"You're not well," Kate said. "Cornelius told me. Are you getting better?"

Meadow sat down on the stairs and put her arms round Kate. "I am, my love. I've been silly – a silly accident, but I'm nearly better."

Kate kissed her cheek warmly, and Meadow was suddenly so overwhelmed with remorse that she burst into tears. Everyone else fell silent, unsure what had happened. Alder, alarmed, rose from where he sat at the kitchen table and hurried to her.

"What is it, my love?" He put his arms round Meadow, and Kate backed away in confusion.

Meadow couldn't speak. She tried to form a few words, but it was useless and she gave up, waving her hand and allowing the tears to flow, sniffing. Alder hugged her and motioned to Kate that everything was fine; it wasn't her fault. Alicia drew Kate away, reassuring her. Meadow was ill, she said, and very fragile. She'd be better in a minute – just give her a moment.

Kate was herself close to tears. "Alright," she said, and watched her father and Meadow from a distance.

The cottage remained silent while Meadow calmed, and the stillness exposed the sound of Cornelius's carriage pulling up outside. A moment later he was knocking at the door. Alder wanted to continue comforting his partner, so Apple let Cornelius into the house. His arrival drew attention away from Meadow, and the buzz of conversation resumed. Kate ran to meet him, and he stooped to throw his arms round her.

"Cornelius," she said. "Thank you for coming."

"I wouldn't have missed you, lovely one," he replied. He looked beyond her and caught sight of Meadow, sitting on the stairs in Alder's embrace. Kate kissed his cheek, drew away, and returned to her friends. Apple remained standing at the door, and Cornelius raised his eyebrows, questioning.

"It's alright," she said. "Let it sort itself out."

Cornelius knew Apple to be a caring, sensitive soul, and he was very fond of her. Holly's death had aged her mother. Apple's face, which had been so youthful and rosy, was now lined; her hair, once full and filled with sun, had become thin and grey. She looked older than her fifty-two years. The funeral service had been one of the most difficult of Cornelius's life, and although it had taken place almost two years ago, the memory was still painfully vivid. He looked into her eyes and put his hand on her arm.

"How are you, Apple?"

"We're coping. Still got Cedar at home."

"And Tozer?"

"Tozer busies himself and smokes his pipe. Life goes on."

"And what about Young Tozer and Margery. See much of them?"

"Yes. James and Willow bring them over. They're both growing up now."

"And Oak? He'll be four years old by now."

"Yes, he's well. Happy wee boy." The thought of little Oak, son of her daughter Hazel and Tudor Green, brought a smile to her face.

"Time's a great healer."

"I know, Cornelius. Thank you."

"God bless you, Apple." He rubbed her arm, a gesture of solidarity and friendship.

Cornelius made his way through the crowded kitchen to where Alder sat cradling Meadow, and put his hand on Alder's shoulder. "All well?" Alder looked at him and nodded. Meadow had quietened, though her face was red with crying. "Will you come with us, Meadow?" Cornelius asked. "I'll drive you in the coach." He could tell she was about to decline, but he knelt before her and cut in quietly before she could form the words. "Please come."

She paused, then said, "Alright. Let me wash my face."

"Of course."

Meadow returned upstairs, and Alder looked to the parson. "Thank you, Cornelius."

"It's nothing. I'll wait for her if you like, and you can escort the others up to the house."

Alder nodded his agreement, stood and encouraged everyone to don their outdoor clothes. A few moments later they were gone.

Cornelius sat in the kitchen of the almost silent house, waiting for Meadow. He clasped his hands and thought. Something was wrong – Meadow was deeply troubled. He'd seen guilt before and knew what it looked like. A few moments later she appeared on the stairs. He rose and offered his hand to help her down, and she gratefully accepted. When she'd descended the bottom step and stood before him in the kitchen he kept hold of her hand and looked into her eyes. She returned his gaze, her eyes widening, lips quivering, the corners turning down in sadness.

"Meadow. Tell me. It might help."

She stood for a moment, defences failing, trying to hold the tears in, but it was no good. Cornelius took her in his arms and let her sob freely. In the next ten minutes she told him everything.

There was a crowd waiting at the manor house: Hugh, Amelia and Louise Flesher; all the Swifts and Buckleys who weren't already present at Vine Cottage; Dr Levinson; Tozer and Cedar Robinson; James and Willow Kirby and their two children, Young Tozer and Margery. There were lots more shouts, hugs, pies, cakes, jellies and ice creams.

Buffy Miller, always eager for the company of children, volunteered to look after Margery and Young Tozer, who were both full of excitement at the approach of Christmas. The house was busy, everyone wanting to know about Kate's adventures.

Alder, standing proudly to one side and watching the throng gathered round his daughter, suddenly became aware that Louise was by his side.

"Isn't Meadow coming?" she asked.

"Yes," he replied, "Cornelius is bringing her in the carriage."

"How is she today?"

"The same, more or less."

She nodded and went to stand by the door, watching for the coach.

Alder's next visitor was plump Florence Swift, her grey hair tied back beneath a white bonnet. Florence was two years younger than Alder, rosy-faced and always wore a smile. Her husband Bernard (temporarily released from his role as butler so that he could enjoy the day with everyone else) was seated nearby, listening with rapt attention to Kate, while his granddaughter Beatrice and her friend Grace occupied his knees, one girl on each.

"You must be very proud of young Catherine," said Florence.

"I am – of course I am," said Alder.

"And now, you and Meadow – you could have more children."

"At my age? I'm even older than you!"

"You cheeky devil!" She mock-swiped his head, then was quiet for a while. "You ought to marry her, you know."

"Meadow? You're right, I know. But I still don't know what she sees in me. I'm just an old man. I can't read nor write, not more than a few words anyway. And her – she's young." Alder noticed Henry Flesher standing nearby, surely within earshot. He looked morose, unsmiling.

But Florence didn't seem aware of him. She answered Alder. "She's that right enough. Lovely-looking she is too. You say you wonder what she sees in you, but you didn't kick her out of your bed, did you, you rogue!" She poked him, laughing, then pressed herself close against him and said quietly, slowly, "I bet she warms you at night hot as an oven."

Alder gave a sly smile. "I've no cause for complaint, Florence."

Henry's countenance darkened further, and he walked away, filling his pipe.

The front door was pushed open, and Meadow appeared, supported on one side by Louise, on the other by Cornelius. Her eyes searched anxiously for Alder and found him. He waved at her across the room, and she smiled, relieved. Louise spoke to Cornelius. "I can take her – it's alright, I can manage."

"Very well," said Cornelius. "If you're sure." She nodded. Cornelius removed his cape and made his way across the hallway to Hugh.

Louise steered Meadow through the crowded drawing room and into the empty study beyond. She closed the door behind her and sat her friend down.

"Feeling any better today?"

"I think so," said Meadow.

"How are things with Alder?"

"He's lovely – he's always lovely. We haven't...you know, since that day, but he's patient – he doesn't seem to mind."

"No more sign of your mother?"

"No, not since she dropped off the package of stuff..."

"...which you threw away."

"...which I threw away."

They were quiet for a moment; then Meadow said, "I told Cornelius."

"...and..."

"He listened – understood, I think." She was silent, cast her gaze to the floor, and said, "God, Louise – I wish I hadn't done it."

Louise rested her hand on her friend's knee, sympathy surging through her. "You can't change it now. Does Alder know?"

"I have to tell Alder. Cornelius says so too. I can't go on with this big lie in the house – I can't live with it."

"Anything you want me to do, I'm always here," said Louise.

"I know you are," said Meadow. "You're a love, a real friend to me."

Again they were quiet for a moment. Then Louise said, "You know, you've changed an awful lot since you found Alder."

"I know," said Meadow. "I feel like a girl who used to be a rat. I did horrible things. I sent Kate away."

Louise was surprised. "What do you mean?"

"It was me. I wanted Kate out of the way so I could have Alder to myself, all the time. I called in a favour and got rid of her."

"But...it's worked out well, hasn't it? Look at what she's doing, what she's learning. See how happy she is. Are you blaming yourself for making her happy?"

"There's something wrong, Louise. She's in danger, I know it. The man who runs the school – he came to my parents' house – that's where I met him. He's sly, evil."

Louise was quiet, brows furrowed. "You can't know that. Perhaps it was just an impression."

"No," said Meadow. "I'm sure of it."

There was another pause. Louise rubbed her lips with the side of her left forefinger. "So what are you going to do about it?"

"I'm going to tell her," said Meadow. "She mustn't go back there."

"Kate's a very bright child," Louise replied. "She's probably more than capable of looking after herself, and the education she's getting is a rare and precious thing."

"I have to tell her. To save my own soul, there can be no more secrets."

Louise sat back in her chair, nodding shallowly. "And Alder?"

"Alder has to know too. He has to know everything."

Louise sat forward, clasped her hands and looked down at the table. "Give her a few days," she said, "if you can. Perhaps till after Christmas. Then tell her – and Alder too. I think you're doing the right thing, for what it's worth." She looked up at Meadow. "You've become a noble creature – I admire you."

The remark startled Meadow. She'd never imagined that she herself might be so described – even by Louise, her closest friend. She opened her eyes wide and said, "Thank you...thank you. That means a lot."

Louise stood and held out her hand. "Come on. Let's go and join in."

Henry, bitter and hurt, watched as Louise led Meadow

back into the drawing room. She was clearly weak and unable to support herself easily. His mind was filled with images of she and Alder – together. She'd been the obsession of his childhood, and now fate had decided that she was not for him. He wondered if she could feel his resentment from across the room and wasn't surprised when she lifted her head and found him with her eyes. He didn't acknowledge her gaze, but pinned her with his dark stare until she looked away. He drew heavily on his pipe. Old Tozer, another pipe smoker, walked over and stood by his side.

"Henry," Tozer greeted him.

Henry glanced briefly at Tozer.

"We smokers should stick together," Tozer went on.

It was an empty comment and Henry did not acknowledge it.

"Coming to say hello to Kate?"

Henry had no wish to fraternise with Alder's family. "No," he said.

Tozer raised his eyebrows in indifference. "Suit yourself then," he said and walked away.

He didn't know it then, but the day was coming when Henry Flesher would crave Kate's company more than anything.

41. THE LOOKOUT
Friday December 26, 1760, 1am

Jacob lay in his bed, waiting for sleep to take him. He always rested well, there being little in life to trouble him. He knew who he was, understood himself, his requirements. He knew how the world functioned for him, having engineered his own course year by year since his early days. Now, at the age of thirty-one, he felt accomplished, at peace.

It had been another well planned and successful Christmas Day. Breakfast had been followed by a service in the chapel led by old Will Surbiton. Jacob liked to keep the ancient traditions alive, and the service always began with the procession of the boar's head, held aloft on a platter, its tusks smeared dark, flesh roasted and glazed, orange thrust into its mouth, eyes reduced to mush by the heat of the oven. The display of such an ugly thing in surroundings so beautiful appealed to Jacob's sense of humour. He liked the procession to be led by one of the prettiest girls from class 4 or class 5. This year he'd selected thirteen-year-old Flora Ogilvie. She was going to be one of his jewels by the time she'd reached fifteen or sixteen – another Orla. The girl's soft, wavy auburn hair, worn long and loose, made a stark contrast with the painted flesh of the dead animal. She had to practise her procession, not having expected the combined weight of the head and the platter to be quite so great, but it had all gone excellently, and the assembled girls had been awestruck at the beauty and barbarity of it. The music had been excellent, with a choir of eight of the best singers positioned in the organ gallery, led by Mr Browning – Pammy Heron and Hilda Dodds (surprisingly strong at the age of ten) pumping the wind for him. The closing music, an arrangement of the *Hallelujah Chorus* from Mr Handel's oratorio *Messiah*, had been most rousing. The girls sang brilliantly, and Mr Browning brought out the basses and trumpets on the organ to great effect. Everybody sat listening and gave it a tumultuous reception (which was not appreciated by old Will, who believed that such an ostentatious secular reaction had no place in a church or chapel).

After the service there was a reception in the ballroom, with sherry and Christmas cake, the girls fawning around old Will in his black cassock, starched white collar and old-style Canterbury cap. He'd confided to Jacob that this particular service had become the highlight of his year; the opportunity to preach to seventy of the most beautiful young ladies he'd ever seen made his heart sing. He had a particular softness for the older girls and had little objection to the fashionably low-cut dresses they wore to chapel, and none at all when they were in conversation with him afterwards. Looking down at them from the height of the pulpit, he frequently lost his place in his sermon.

It was a cold, bright day. The sun, low in the south on its trajectory from east to west, did little to illuminate the ballroom, so all the chandeliers, lamps and lanterns were lit, and the big space came alive with a warm, festive glow. The maids and footmen had decorated the room with garlands of ivy, holly and mistletoe. Floral displays hung from the ceiling; others were set in the windows. The scent of lavender, rose, and rosemary was heavy in the air. The Yule log, wrapped in hazel twigs, was ablaze in the massive fireplace, a discreet iron screen set before it to guard against accidents.

There was a timetable of games in the afternoon: charades, bob apple, blind man's buff and Fox-in-thy-hole. As the afternoon wore on, Mr Browning played the harpsichord so the girls could dance. Jacob accepted an invitation from sixteen-year-old Nana Hall to join her in the almand, courante and jig, which delighted him. Nana was one of his favourites; delicate and elegant, with hair that was almost white, built up into an exotic fantasy.

Later, he allowed himself to dance with Vivianne Stamper, despite the danger. She'd been watching him all afternoon, waiting for an opportunity. She danced expertly, pressed her body close to his and gazed into his eyes, wanting him to know he could have her. He admired her. Her writing – her poetry in particular – had become extraordinary in the last year or so, and he found her not only intriguing but intoxicating. Flirtation was too trite a word for what passed between them. From her earliest days in the school, she'd valued his opinion of her work; and they met regularly, alone in his study. The sexual charge between them developed over a period of years, and had now achieved an exquisite tension that could easily have spilt over. Her brown eyes were like wells. There was a ruthless streak in her – a determination – that fascinated him. He'd never felt so attracted to one of the girls, and had to keep telling himself that she was an item to be sold – part of the business. If he'd been just a little weaker, he would have taken her to bed.

The tutors and house mistresses, together with Ruth Marlow, Dr Wayland and Alfred the porter, played snap-dragon in the later afternoon, while Jacob made his way to the brewhouse to join the various husbandmen and domestic staff in their own celebrations. The labourers, gardeners, groundsmen, farmers, drivers and cleaning staff were all there; and Alan Blake, the blacksmith, had come down from the forge together with his wife Chastity and his son Barney. Jacob had arranged for food to be sent over to the brewery for the occasion, and the party was in full swing when he arrived. The brewers had created a special Christmas ale, and Jacob enjoyed a glass of that followed by a dance with Teresa Tickle, wife of Tranter, one of the farmers. Teresa was rosy-faced, full-bosomed and nearly twenty years older than Jacob. She'd already drunk quite a lot, told Jacob what a fine figure of a man he was, and let him know that she was alone at home most afternoons. Jacob smiled, thanked her for the pleasure of the dance and kissed her hand. Lastly, he wished them all a Happy Christmas and returned to the big house.

The evening was dominated by dinner, for which old Will gave the blessing. Here too, Jacob liked to preserve something of the old ways, so there was peacock and swan in addition to goose, roast beef, roast pork and turkey. The sweets included fruit pies and plum pudding. Drinks included the new Christmas ale and sweet wine. There was punch with and without alcohol, spiced wine, fruit wines and cordials. Everyone was merry; even Stella and Knox displayed some festive spirit.

After the meal they returned to the ballroom for the presents, of which there were a great many. Everyone – girls, staff and tutors – received something on behalf of the school from funds provided for the purpose by the benefactors. Gifts were presented to the girls by the tutors, five or six students allocated to each of them. In addition, there were a few special, personal gifts. Rider Browning had chosen a particular kind of nightdress for Orla, having imagined the moonlight shining through it, picking out her gentle curves. He had intended to present it to her privately, but alcohol had worn away the edge of caution, and he'd passed it to her where she sat near the blazing fire via a series of hands. *"Pass this to Orla, please..."*, and off it had gone. He watched its course until it reached her. She looked over to him, knowing he'd sent it. There was a general rustle of excited *"Open it!"* requests, so she'd torn away the wrapping paper and revealed it, holding it up in front of the fire to make clear how easily the light penetrated it. The gasps were clearly audible, but Rider wasn't sure if they meant *That's lovely!* or *He wants you to wear that for him!?*

Jacob watched from a distance, aware that Stella's eyes were gauging his reaction. He turned to her and said, "I know. Don't worry about it." She disapproved, he knew. She'd said it before and he could hear her saying it now. *"These girls are market animals for which we have responsibility. We are required to deliver them perfect and whole, their virginity intact. We must not allow sexual relationships to develop between them and the staff. It's an insult to those who support us."* But Jacob had carved out this life for his own gratification, his own fulfilment. In his way, he loved the girls. He wanted them to develop individuality based on their own interests and pleasures – to have distinct personalities of their own. Fraternisation between the tutors and the girls was a rarity, and Jacob found this particular manifestation of it between Rider and Orla fascinating. He'd been aware for some time of the increasing intimacy of their touches, and had spied on her now and then from the supposedly locked corner room when she'd scurried away at night to sleep with her lover in the staff house. He hoped they were being careful, although he had a plan mapped out if Orla became pregnant.

The girls eventually retired to bed, and Jacob went to the west wing to thank the kitchen staff, see that they had their gifts, and wish them Happy Christmas. He stayed for a few minutes and took a drink with them. Speck Beckwith was there, having paid a visit with his curiously named dog.

Only one task remained for the evening, and all was organised for that. He retired to one of the smaller rooms in the east wing and celebrated Knox's forty-second birthday with him. Stella, Ruth, Alfred Bentley, Dr Wayland, Milton York and Janet Illif were all there. Knox's choice of celebratory food for his birthday was always the same: a thick, juicy piece of beef held between two slices of bread. The others partook of smaller versions of the same in honour of his special day. Knox favoured no particular drink, so the opportunity was taken to further deplete anything that remained from earlier in the day.

By half past midnight, the final good wishes having been exchanged, they all retired to sleep.

Lying awake in the dark of his room, Jacob felt very pleased with his lot. The only minor irritation at the school was Stella, who would have preferred a more rigid set of ground rules. Despite the friction between them, she was effective in her role, and Jacob believed he'd made the right decision in appointing her. He always listened to her concerns, of course, but she was not the captain of this ship. Stella was anxious about Catherine Swithenbank and often reminded him of the dangers of taking her in at the school.

"She has a home, a father, people who know her," Stella pleaded. "Catherine isn't like the other girls – she can't just disappear in the way that all the others can. What's the next step? What will you say if she asks to take Bip home with her for a holiday? Or Pamela, or any of the friends she's made here? Will you forbid it? What reason will you give? This is a disaster in waiting. There's a possibility that friendships could form away from the school. If that happens, it opens up the likelihood of communication between the London convents and an unmonitored address in Yorkshire. We cannot intercept mail sent to a neutral address. This situation could be fatal to our business. And we would be held responsible by our patrons for negligence with their investment."

He knew Kate was a danger, but she fascinated him. The easiest solution would be to find some reason to eject her from the school right now and send her home for good. But he didn't want to do that. Jacob wanted to watch her as she grew, to see at first-hand what she would become. His overwhelming curiosity got the better of his common sense – he knew it was so. He'd mapped out a number of plans to deal with Kate and could bring them into operation straight away if a problem arose. He assured Stella of it, but he knew she was not convinced.

Kate had gone home to her father for Christmas, and Jacob was sorry that she'd missed all the celebrations at the Lookout.

He lay quietly, sleep eluding him as his mind wandered.

Orla would almost certainly be in the staff building, and Rider Browning would surely have had the delight of his generous Christmas gift by now.

He thought of Vivianne and felt his body responding. Would he miss her when she was gone? Yes, indeed he would. Could he risk…? No, most certainly he could not.

Jacob saw each of the girls for what they were – unique, each and every one. It made the final execution more exquisite. He sometimes thought of himself as a farmer raising livestock. He got to know each animal personally, by temperament, by name, by identity. He came to understand their ways, their individuality, their loves and their hates. Then, smiling at them all the while, he led them to the market, the stockyard, the shambles, and said goodbye.

42. CAPPLEMAN FARM
Sunday December 28, 1760, 8.25am

Alder watched through parted lids as she climbed out of bed and stood in the glow of the sunrise, stretching and yawning, her long black hair reaching almost to the small of her back, pale skin lit by the soft kiss of the early light. Meadow had become stronger in the last few days, her recovery encouraged by some inner conviction. Today they had to talk, she said. He'd wanted her in the night, but she'd said they must wait one more day; there were things to discuss.

Alder was born on April 2nd 1703, on a farm near Burford, Oxfordshire, where his father was a labourer. William and Heather Swithenbank had been good parents and had intended to bring up their boy to be thoughtful and caring, but young Alder soon found that he was stronger than any of the other lads and could always get his own way in whatever he wanted. He was a bully who gathered similar characters around him. As he grew into his teenage years he became feared and respected by boys, and sought after by girls, despite their parents' pleas to stay away from him. A few days before his thirteenth birthday, he and buxom Ada Broadbent, two years his senior, presented each other with their respective virginities in a secluded spot on the bank of the Windrush. After that, the pursuit of women became his primary distraction. He was a father by the time he was fourteen. Sixteen-year-old Effie Crosthwaite's parents were furious and demanded that he marry their daughter. Alder stayed out of sight as far as possible, although not before he'd got two other girls with child. Three sets of furious parents came hammering at his door.

Heather Swithenbank was disgusted with her son. Her husband William supported her, although he dropped the boy the occasional wink and encouraging gesture in sly admiration.

Alder was determined not to get hooked. His physical strength meant that he could easily get a job elsewhere, so he fled from his fatherly obligations and found work on Albion farm, a mile east of Chipping Norton, where he quickly became popular with the other young hardmen.

In his four years at Albion he learned to love drink. Work on the farm was hard, but in the evenings he'd jump in the back of a waggon with his mates and visit the local alehouses, where he frequently drank himself to oblivion. Their favourite haunts were *The Blue Boar*, close by in Chipping Norton, *The Fox* in Middle Barton, *The Falkland Arms* in Great Tew, *The Quiet Woman* in Enstone, *The Black Horse* in Woodstock. In the summer months, when there was more light in the evening, they'd drive as far as *The Reindeer* in Banbury or, if Alder dared take the risk of being so close to his roots, *The Shaven Crown* in Shipton under Wychwood. The Albion men were well-known as a gang of toughs, and Alder, as he continued to grow into manhood, became their tallest, most muscular mascot. Women flocked to him, and by the time he was eighteen he'd fathered two more children from different girls, although he never offered any kind of support or showed much interest in his offspring.

Things came to a head in June 1722 when the daughter of the new rector of St Mary's, Chipping Norton became pregnant. Reverend William Slate locked Alison in her room, took his pistol and strode furiously to Albion farm, the terrified townsfolk parting like the Red Sea before his blind rage. Twenty minutes later Alder was on his knees looking up the barrel of Bill Slate's gun.

"Marry her, or you're a dead man!"

Alder's friends didn't seem so hard right at that moment,

cowering behind a hay waggon. He promised straight away to wed the girl.

"Good," said Bill, turning up the muzzle. "You'll come with me now and tell her yourself, then I'll make the arrangements."

The rector walked behind Alder on the way back to town, ensuring that he didn't run away. There were a few bursts of applause from onlookers as the two passed among them. But Alder was not to be caught. Without warning, he muscled into a dense crowd of customers at a market stall, ducked down, crawled to the road and disappeared out of sight under a passing cart. Bill tried to follow him, ducking and weaving with his gun, doing his best to keep up, but Alder sprinted through the door of *The Joker* alehouse, leapt over the bar, up the stairs and through an open bedroom window. He picked his way carefully along the roofs of the terraced buildings and jumped down into the lane at the rear. Next he sprinted two streets south, found an open coal shed and hid until nightfall. Then he took the road north.

Alder walked for a week, watching the horizon for pursuers, sleeping in ditches, knowing he had to get some distance between murderous Bill and himself.

By the middle of July he was working in a coal mine near Barnsley. The occupation was new to him, but the hard work kept his muscles toned. There were several bell-shaped pits on the coalfield, effectively wells all about two hundred feet deep, cut to reach the seam. Alder, two other miners and two boys, went down each morning on the winch to hack out the coal, with just a couple of lanterns for illumination. The boys' job was to fill the baskets and signal the women above to winch up the load. The winching itself was done by a pair of elderly horses, ironically named Hercules and Goliath. The heat in the chamber could be overwhelming, and the work was hard, dirty and sweaty.

Alder took a room in nearby Darton and played as hard in the evening as he worked during the day. Heavy drinking was the norm every night, and women were always on his mind. In March 1723 he was confronted late in the evening by a large group of his fellow miners. Two of their daughters were pregnant and had identified Alder as the father. There was no choice of bride or bullet this time. Alder got a hard kicking and was left bloodied and on his back in the street.

That was it – he was on the road again. As he walked, Alder began for the first time to ponder his own nature. He was a hard worker but also a troublemaker. He had scant regard for others, the sole purpose of his existence being to seek gratification for himself. Was he ready to grow up? He wasn't sure, but at least the seed of self-realisation had germinated.

He began calling at the great houses he passed, seeking any employment they might offer. For days there was no luck, and he kept walking, sleeping in fields and living off anything he could find. He passed through York, briefly looking in at the Minster, and eventually came to Helmsley where he was at last successful in finding work as the gardener's assistant in a modest country house. He slept in a hut in the garden and tried to keep booze and naked women out of his head.

Alder was successful for nearly a year. The only strong drink that passed his lips was distilled secretly from potatoes and barley by Tom Berridge, the gardener. It was good strong stuff, but Alder missed his ale.

There were other temptations too. Charlotte, his employer's daughter, was nineteen, attractive, rebellious, and interested. She often came to tease him in the garden, and the harder Alder tried to shake her off, the more persistent she was. Tom Berridge thought it was hilarious and bit hard on his pipe, trying not to laugh.

"I admire your patience, Alder," he said.

Alder replied, "Well, what can I do? I've had trouble with women all me life."

"All your life!" said Tom. "What are you, twenty? If I were twenty again I'd've 'ad her on 'er back before now." Tom was laughing. Alder looked at him, frowning. Maybe he was right. He was indeed twenty and ought to be having a good time.

The next time Charlotte came into the garden to tease him, he took her into the shed and gave her exactly what he thought she wanted. All seemed to go well, and Charlotte seemed pleased enough as the operation proceeded, but afterwards things took an immediate turn for the worse. She shouted at him as she pulled her clothes together. Who did he think he was to treat her like that? She'd been assaulted, raped. Her father would hear about it straight away. She marched off back to the house.

"Oh Christ!" said Alder. "Here we go again." He muttered his goodbye to Tom, shook his hand and was gone.

Alder walked for two days with no idea of where he was going or what he would do next. He passed through Lastingham, Stape, Goathland, Beck Hole and Egton Bridge before arriving at Glaisdale, where he sat at a table outside the Red Lion alehouse, exhausted. It was a Saturday in late April 1724, and he was twenty-one years old. He had a string of nameless children behind him and felt lost, without purpose.

Nineteen-year-old Tozer Robinson saw him sitting there and sensed his emptiness. He ordered two jars of ale, sat down beside him, handed the drink to Alder and said, "Get your lips round that."

Alder was surprised, thanked him and took the ale. It was delicious, the first he'd had for more than a year. Tozer watched as he downed it in one.

"Ho-ho! You were thirsty!" He put out his hand. "Tozer Robinson. Pleased to make your acquaintance."

"Alder," said Alder. "Alder Swithenbank."

"Alder! That's a tree. A tree... That's a good name!"

That night Alder slept at Tozer's cottage. On Monday, Tozer took him to the big house, introduced him to Ben Flesher, and asked if work might be found for the new man. On Tuesday Alder began life as a labourer on Cappleman Farm. It felt like coming home, and he was very grateful.

The drinking went on, but Alder decided there'd be no more womanising in the workplace. Whenever the need took him (which it frequently did), he walked or took a ride the nine miles to the brothels in Whitby, always alone. Over the next twenty years he watched the young prostitutes turn into middle-aged women. Some died, others came along, new ones began their trade.

As the years went on, he grew steadily more disillusioned with his life. It had no direction. Even the boozing began to appear senseless. He was fortunate that he never picked up a serious disease from his regular visits to the dockside pleasure-gardens. There was the odd bout of this or that, but Dr Clover always sorted it out for him, while administering the usual textbook admonition.

Early in 1744 he made a decision. There'd be no more women. He was almost forty-one and had got bored with it all.

Alder began to feel calmer, at peace. He drank with Tozer and his other friends in the Red Lion but rejoiced in his newfound celibacy. He saw the women looking at him as they always had, and smiled at them kindly. He could breathe easy. He was done with it.

But then, early in 1748, Alder became bewitched by a young girl. And there was nothing he could do to escape...

Meadow disappeared behind the screen, and a moment later Alder heard her peeing into the close-stool. He tried unsuccessfully to catch the faint scent of her water, and rubbed the sleep out of his eyes as the soft gold light strengthened in the window.

Alder breathed in this woman every day, and the familiarity of her had become part of him. The subtle odour of her body, the warm smoothness of her skin, the exquisite sleekness of her hair, her big brown eyes in her delicately sculpted face, her soft lips...

She reappeared, and Alder lifted the bedclothes. "Come back to bed, little girl."

Meadow smiled and joined him, Alder enfolding the two of them with the sheets, crushing her body to his. She was deliciously cold, skin chilled in the winter morning.

"You're so warm," she said, snuggling into him.

He brushed her hair with his right hand and kissed her forehead. She quietly told him she loved him, and he knew it was true.

"Whatever it is, just tell me now," he whispered.

"I can't," she replied, "not like this. I will though. Today."

She was asleep almost immediately, breathing evenly in his arms.

Kate had been up since seven o'clock, wandering around the hedgerows in the pre-dawn, gathering things. The farm was quiet and still – not another living soul in sight. There'd been a light snowfall in the night, and the ground was dusted white. She returned to the house at nine, made tea for herself and waited for her father and Meadow to appear. She sat in Scarlet's chair in the parlour and read, listening for sounds from above, but at a quarter to ten, when there was still no sign of activity, she prepared fresh tea and took it up to their room. Alder responded to Kate's tap with a mumbled "Come in," and Kate pushed open the door. Alder was in bed, Meadow cuddled close, her head on his chest, asleep.

"I made you some tea," she whispered.

"Thank you, lovely," said her father.

Kate set down the tray and said, "I'll get breakfast ready. Half an hour?"

"Forty minutes," whispered Alder. He put out his arm, and Kate leaned forward to join in his embrace. As Alder reached up to kiss his daughter, Meadow woke and turned her head towards Kate.

"Morning, love," she said sleepily.

"Morning, Meadow," said Kate and kissed her cheek.

After Kate had gone, Meadow again settled onto Alder's chest. "She's so lovely," she said.

"I know," said Alder. "This is a happy house."

Meadow lay quietly. The revelations she had to make today could easily change all this. There may never be another warm, loving morning.

At Meadow's request, Alder asked his daughter to go out and spend an hour with Grace. Kate sensed that something important was about to happen. She didn't ask any questions but donned her hat and coat, put on her boots, and left the house.

The cottage was quiet, except for the cracking of the fires. It was time.

Alder sat down in the little parlour and looked up at Meadow, standing before him in a plain, pale yellow cotton dress, wringing her hands. Her apprehension was obvious; she was deeply, deeply troubled about something and was about to throw herself on his mercy. His instinct told him that much. She knelt before him, took his hands in hers and looked directly up into his eyes.

"Meadow," said Alder, taken aback, "don't do that." He tried to raise her from her kneeling position.

"No," she said. "I need you to see how I feel. When you've heard me, you'll understand that I don't deserve forgiveness; but I need you to know how sorry, sad and full of... self-loathing I am."

Alder was almost overcome with emotion. "What is it then? Set it loose."

She glanced down, trying to keep control of herself, then

looked up at him again.

"I didn't fall when I went to see my mother. I…"

"Ah," said Alder, "that's it. I wondered."

"What?"

"Meadow, I know."

She stared at him, her lips quivering, breathing shallowly, heart beating fast. "What do you know?"

"You were pregnant."

She pressed her lips hard together, and the tears began to fall. She couldn't speak. He was squeezing her hands tightly, tightly.

"It's alright," said Alder.

"I'm so sorry," she managed, then lost control, buried her head in his lap and cried bitterly, with long deep sobs.

Alder stroked her head gently, his own tears coursing down his cheeks. "Shhh…" he whispered, quiet and calm.

It took Meadow a long time to cry it all away, but eventually her flow of grief calmed to a few sighs and catches of breath, the tears mostly turned to sniffs. She lifted her head from his lap but was not able to look at his face. With downcast eyes, she said, "It was your baby – I killed it."

"Meadow," he replied, "I don't know how many children I have. I ran away from them all – except Kate. Never even saw them. I was a bad man. This life – we all make mistakes, all have regrets…"

"I'll never do it again," she interjected quickly and quietly.

He stopped in mid-sentence and looked at her. "I want you to be happy," he said.

"I want you to love me," she said. "I *need* your love." She began to cry again.

He took her face in his hands and leaned towards her. "You will always have it, Meadow. Always."

She still looked frightened, concerned. Her eyes were wide, watery, her lips pressed tensely together.

"There's more."

"Go on," said Alder, curious.

"Kate's school. I organised it."

"I know," said Alder. "You told me – you'd met Mr Crowan at your parents' house."

"I did it all for the wrong reasons, Alder. I wanted Kate gone so I could have you to myself. There was no other reason."

He sat back and looked at her in puzzlement.

"It wasn't because I didn't like her – I've always liked Kate. But I was ill – I think – I may have been ill. I'm..." She'd lost her train of thought and seemed unsure how to go on.

Alder said, "But where's the harm?" He felt some confusion. "Kate's very happy – you've seen how happy she is."

She looked directly into his eyes. "Kate is in danger, Alder."

"What do you mean?"

"Crowan, the man who came here, he's not the person he pretends to be."

Alder shook his head, *I don't understand.*

"I don't know for sure what he's up to at that school, but whatever it is, it's only to please himself."

"You really think she's not safe there?"

"I'm sure of it."

Again, he shook his head shallowly. "Then the answer is simple. We won't send her back."

But Kate was not having that. "What about my friends? What about my French lessons? And all the rest? I'll never see Fuzz or Mabel again – or the tower, or anything." She was upset and angry.

"Kate," said Alder, "we think it may be dangerous. Meadow's met Mr Crowan before and doesn't trust him..."

"But he's perfectly nice to me."

"Yes," said Meadow, "He would be. He's like that. Listen, Kate. When I arranged for him to come here, I was ill, selfish. I wanted to get you away so I could have your dad to myself. But things are different now. I'm better – at least I hope I am – and I'm worried about you."

"But I can look after myself." She paused. "In any case, there are things I have to do there."

"What do you mean?" asked Alder.

"I can't tell you."

"Secrets?" Alder again.

"Not secrets – just things you might not... understand."

"Why not?"

Kate thought. "Dad, did you ever see Grandma Hazel do anything special?"

He wondered what she meant for a moment but then remembered Hazel sitting opposite him in the Red Lion, her finger boiling his ale away. He nodded his head slowly. "Yes."

"Then trust me. I'm like grandma. I'm a first-born girl just like she was."

Meadow knew about the witchcraft stories and remembered the bizarre sensation that day when she'd been on the receiving end of Kate's displeasure. But it was strange to hear Kate speaking directly about it.

There was silence in the room. Alder waited for his daughter to continue. She said, "In any case, nothing can harm me – not Mr Crowan – not anything."

Meadow was very apprehensive about resuming full relations with Alder. She was worried that the termination procedure might have permanently changed her body. Perhaps the internal wounds had healed in such a way as to render sex painful or unpleasant. Perhaps it would be altogether impossible. How would he react if she were no longer able to properly sleep with him? She'd shared her concerns with Louise, who'd again said she should allow Dr Levinson to examine her. But she hadn't done it – whether out of shame or embarrassment, probably a combination of both – and she'd gone on worrying.

But now she lay here in bed, in the enclosing dark of the night with Alder, and the time had come. He was holding her very close, kissing her, breathing hard, kneading her body, crushing her breasts, climbing onto her, pressing himself between her legs. It was going to happen.

Her heart hammered fast in panic. "Alder." He stopped moving and waited for her to continue. "It might hurt. I'm frightened."

He paused, cooling his excitement. "That's alright," he replied. "You're in control. Whatever you want."

"Thank you," she muttered.

They lay in each other's arms for a few minutes, he on his back, she drawn in against him, head on his chest, arm thrown over his body. The damp peat fire glowed dully in the winter chill of the room.

"I do want to," she said. She felt him reaching to kiss her forehead, but turned up her face and met his lips with hers. She was quiet and still for a few moments, gathering courage. "Alder..." she said quietly, touching him. She climbed on top, straddled his body, and nervously threaded herself onto him. There was no pain, and the action was as easy as it had always been. Alder sighed and whispered something she couldn't catch. He caressed her thighs, her hips. His breathing deepened. She sat motionless, his fulness inside her. The sense of relief was overwhelming. She opened her mouth and let out her breath in a long sigh that terminated in a brief, quiet chuckle.

Alder felt the vibration run through her. "How is it?"

"It's alright I think. It feels fine. Hmm." There was a smile in her voice. She ran her hands over his chest.

Alder reached up and lightly brushed her left breast with the back of his hand. "I think you and me should be married. Will you marry me, Meadow Reid?"

She gave a tiny, delighted laugh, "Yes. Yes, I will, my lovely man!" and began to move with a steady, easy rhythm. All was well.

The New Year celebration at the big house turned into a farewell for Kate. Everyone wore party clothes, and there was lots of food, drink and dancing. A few of the younger children found quiet corners in which to fall asleep after midnight.

Henry appeared briefly but returned upstairs to his room when he saw Alder and Meadow sitting lovingly together, hands clasped.

At half past one in the morning, Richard Swift and Elys Buckley drove the carriages down through the farm's snow-covered roads, dropping off the revellers at their respective dwellings, Cornelius following behind in his chaise.

Alder opened the door of Vine Cottage and lit the lamps while Meadow and Kate removed their coats. The kitchen fire had gone out, but Alder relit it and the place soon began to warm up. Kate was tired but content. "I'm glad you're both happy again."

Meadow embraced her. "We love you, Kate! Happy New Year."

Kate woke late and spent the day out in the snow with Grace, Walter, Beatrice and Amy. The crisp sparkling white crunched beneath their boots, and the bright sun made the farm stark and vivid. A few warmly dressed people greeted them as they passed, on their way to the Red Lion for a New Year meal. "Kate! I hope we'll see you again soon!" Kate waved, smiled and wished them a Happy New Year.

Alicia came to the cottage in the afternoon and prepared a special meal for the evening, warming and delicious; a kind of suet pudding with beef and kidney pieces, all juicy in Alicia's own spicy meat sauce. None of them had ever tasted anything like it before. She made a lovely moist fruit cake for the sweet.

The next morning Kate woke at eight o'clock and packed her things. At a quarter past nine she delivered tea to Alder's room. There was no answer to her knock, so she lifted the latch and opened the door an inch. Alder lay on his back in bed, looking at the door and nodding gently at Kate, giving her permission to enter. She carried the tea quietly to the bedside, and Alder mouthed his thanks silently so as not to wake Meadow. They looked cosy. She was lying face down on top of him, fast asleep, arms flung up about his neck, face turned to the wall. The bedclothes were in disarray, and Meadow's back was partly exposed. Kate thought she looked lovely – vulnerable and white in her sleep. She wished she could have painted the scene and wondered, not for the first time, why painting was not taught at the Lookout.

"She's beautiful," whispered Kate.

"So are you," Alder whispered back.

Kipp arrived with the carriage at noon, having rested overnight at the Red Lion. Kate was ready to go. She handed up her bags and gave Alder and Meadow one last hug.

"Take care," said Meadow.

"And you take care too," Kate replied, kissing her cheek.

Kipp helped Kate up into the coach and closed the door. Then he bade farewell to "Mr Swithenbank, Mrs Swithenbank" and drove away.

The two stood hand in hand in the snow and watched the carriage pull into the distance down Watermill Lane and out of sight.

43. THE LOOKOUT
Saturday & Sunday, January 3 & 4, 1761

The temperature tumbled on Friday night, and there was a heavy snowfall. Kate occupied herself with music practice on Saturday, taking a few of her simple keyboard exercises into the freezing chapel in the afternoon and trying them out on the organ while Bip pumped the wind. It was so cold that she had to play in her coat, her breath visible in the chill air. Some of the sounds were very strange and made her laugh, particularly when the knobs were only partly pulled out and nothing sounded in tune. The stop marked *Trumpet* was her favourite. If she held down a key and drew out the register knob slowly, it made a noise like a frail old man about to die. Bip thought it was hilarious. Both girls doubled up in laughter trying to imitate the sound with their voices.

After dinner, Fuzzy celebrated Kate's return by hosting a midnight gin session in her dormitory. Shelagh, Pammy and Bip came along for a while; Fuzzy's room-mates, Gail Curwen (always serious), short-haired and boyish Tully Gray, and white-skinned Aggie Carnaby joined in too, although their enthusiasm for the spirit didn't match that of the two more seasoned drinkers. They soon retired to bed, leaving Fuzz to search for a second bottle under the floorboards before retiring to the usual privy with Kate. At a quarter to two Slade Stone found them locked in and still talking. He'd become accustomed to this and tapped on the door politely.

"Pardon me, ladies."

The door opened and the girls passed on either side of him, Fuzz dropping the bottle into his hands. "Saved you a drop," she slurred.

Kate woke briefly at twenty minutes past three, as she often did, and saw the ghost of Rosalind Wynter standing motionless at the foot of her bed, face to the wall. She wore a mantua of red and gold silk, her hair in tight brown curls at both sides of her head and tied up at the rear. She never made any sound or movement, and Kate had never seen her face, the apparition always having its back to her. She manifested for no more than about a quarter of an hour, always between twenty past three and twenty to four. Kate never noticed her arrive or saw her leave.

There was no more snow overnight, although the temperature remained well below freezing. The peat fire in the bedroom hearth had reduced to embers by morning, but both the big dining hall fireplaces were roaring at breakfast. Kate wanted to explore the forgotten garden despite the cold and the snow. She'd been into the enclosure only once before, late one afternoon with Fuzzy. They hadn't penetrated very far on that occasion because it had got dark and Fuzz said it wasn't safe, but today was crisp, bright and dry despite the settled snow.

She looked across her breakfast plate at Fuzzy and said, "Let's go into the old garden today. The weather's good, and we'll have hours."

"Let's *all* go," said Shelagh, "It'll be fun! I haven't been in there for ages."

Mabel Stanton was tidying Kate's dormitory when the girls returned from breakfast. She hadn't seen Kate since before Christmas, and gave her a warm welcome.

"We're going to explore in the old garden," said Kate. "You could come too."

Mabel thought for a moment. She hadn't finished cleaning the rooms, but the prospect of joining the girls on an adventure was tempting. In any case, it wasn't entirely safe in the grounds beyond the wall; it might be just as well if they had an adult to look after them.

"Alright, I will," she said. "Give me a few minutes. I'll need to get my warm things from the other building."

The dower house grounds occupied all the space between the west side of the school and the main Scarborough to Whitby road – an area measuring half a mile east to west, and about six hundred yards north to south, broadening to eight hundred yards by the time it reached the main road. The grounds were surrounded by a high brick wall that had collapsed in several places because of neglect, weathering or the undermining effect of tree roots. The brickwork was almost completely obscured by climbing plants: ivy, honeysuckle, dog roses, gorse, brambles and more. Many trees – oak, elm, ash, birch, and others – had been planted some distance beyond the north wall when the house was under construction in 1643, but like the house itself, they'd been left untended for over fifty years, and their descendants had marched outwards, colonising ever greater circles. The east wall – that closest to the school – remained intact and contained the original wooden gate, now dilapidated, that opened on the path directly to the rear of the dower house. But the gate was locked and the key long since lost, ensuring that no access was possible from the east without the means of a ladder. The south wall followed the drive as it snaked from the school to the entrance gates.

Mabel and the girls crunched through the snow beyond the north wall. They passed the animal pens on their right, the fields and the groundsmen's cottages coming into view in the distance. After about a hundred and fifty yards an opening appeared in the wall to their left where the brickwork had collapsed, taking a substantial amount of the undergrowth with it, although brambles had sprung up and partially straddled the breach. Mabel stepped gingerly over the rubble and helped the girls through one by one.

They stood in the snow facing a thick tangle of spindly winter growth. It wasn't possible to make out any particular shape or design, everything having run amok. Some distance away and a little to the left, there was a very long building, and Mabel led the way carefully towards it, picking her way around gorse and brambles to do so. The rear of the structure consisted of an unbroken wall about three hundred feet long, mostly intact, running east to west. But when they rounded its western end and saw the front of the building, its utter ruination was obvious. It must once have been spectacular, about thirty-five feet high, with large windows cut into the south wall at regular intervals. "This was the orangery," said Mabel. "All kinds of exotic fruit was grown in here. I was brave enough to get inside once. Maybe it's still possible."

Kate was awestruck. She began to walk forward along the front of the building, the others following behind. It wasn't easy. There'd once been paths – that much was clear – but they were completely broken up now, overtaken with foliage. In the summer, she thought, this passage would be even more difficult; all the undergrowth would be alive and active, thickened into a dense green prickly jungle.

Soon they came to an entrance, the door hanging open, fixed on a single rusty hinge. Kate squeezed a yard or two inside and looked about. She could see the hulking remains of ancient orange trees, picked open by time and insects. There was growth everywhere – ivy, honeysuckle and dog roses, their bright red hips peppering the chaos. Ferns – brown and dank – were abundant, and the snow lay as evenly inside the building as it did outside. Kate looked up and saw that the ceiling had collapsed along almost the entire length of the building. She heard someone say "Wow!" behind her, was briefly distracted by the exclamation and stepped forward without looking.

There was no floor – she was falling…

Mabel caught her and pulled her back. "Watch where you're going," she said.

Kate shuddered at the scene below her. The stone floor of the building's central area had crumbled apart, revealing a wide space about three feet deep in the building's foundations. A few stone columns that had once supported the floor punched dimly through the layer of settled snow.

"It's the heating system," Mabel explained. "They had to keep the fruit trees warm."

A small rat scurried through the dull white in the subterranean hypocaust. "Rats, mice – all the buildings are full of them." Two or three of the girls squealed in horror and rushed to get out. "Let's move on," said Mabel. "I doubt there's much more to see. It's a real struggle to climb about in there anyway."

They retraced their steps and stood by the door. Mabel pointed over to the right. "There are two more plant houses over there, similar to this but much smaller. The nearest one is covered with climbing plants, but you can see the corner of the roof, just there." Kate followed Mabel's pointed finger and saw the structure, just visible in the morass of vegetation. "Let's go this way," Mabel went on, indicating the opposite direction. "It might be easier to get round."

She led the way southeast, and they soon came across a clear path. "Deer," she said. "They eat their way along, munching the tree bark and pretty much everything up to shoulder height. Makes it easier for us to move from place to place." She looked behind her. "Everybody alright?" There were a few murmurs of assent.

Two minutes later they came to an area of low growth. Kate recognised bushes of yew and box, and several herbs that had run wild – rosemary, sage, lavender, marjoram and a few others, not all looking happy in the extreme chill. "This was a knot garden," she said. "There's one at the big house on the farm." The original box hedges had colonised much of the surrounding area, spreading out well beyond their designated spaces and reverting to their natural shapes.

"Very good," Mabel replied. "I think you're right, although you'd hardly know it now, it's all so wild."

They pressed forward a few more steps, and the dower house itself came into view on their left, tragic and breathtaking in its ruination. The other girls had been there before, but Kate was seeing it for the first time. She gasped in amazement. It was a wide two-storey building with a central entrance and three sets of large mullioned windows either side of the door at ground level, seven more on the upper storey. The roof had partly collapsed, and daylight showed through the higher windows, a few of which retained their glass. Ivy, honeysuckle and other creeping plants ran over the whole structure, and growth had climbed out beyond the roof, branches and stems reaching to the sky.

A balustraded staircase of eight stone steps laid out in the shape of a fan led up to a large terrace that fronted the house and overlooked the knot garden.

"This is so sad!" said Kate. "Why didn't they restore this with the big house?"

"I don't really know," said Mabel. "It would have been too small to use as the staff house. Maybe they didn't have enough money. I just don't know – there could be any number of reasons." She was quiet for a moment. "It is a pity, though – you're right. It must have been a lovely house."

"Can we get in?"

"The front door is locked – and still strong," she replied, "but the side door's broken open. Look – the girls are waiting over there for us." Fuzz and the others had run up the steps, crossed the terrace, and were standing at the building's northwest corner.

"Come on, Kate," called Pammy. "It's amazing in here!"

Kate and Mabel stepped through the snow and joined them. The wooden side door, white paint mostly stripped away by time, hung open, precariously leaning on its lower hinge, the upper rusted through and torn free. The space beyond was dark, although some details could be picked out as their eyes adjusted to the gloom of the interior.

"This leads into the kitchen," said Mabel. "Don't put any weight on the floor just here but step right across to the kitchen door itself – just to be safe. There's a hole on the left, just here..." (she indicated with her hand) "...where the cellar stairs used to be..." Kate peered around the corner into a void. The cellar door was gone, and there was no sign of the stairs. Presumably they'd collapsed, leaving only a long, pitch-black hole in the floor, like the entrance to Hell. It looked frightful, and Kate stepped backed in horror.

"That's horrible," she muttered. "Is it really safe to go in?"

Mabel replied, "Just watch how you go. Follow me." She stepped forwards over the rotten floorboards of the little entrance vestibule and into the kitchen beyond, then turned and held out her hand. Kate took it, hopped across the treacherous area and into the house, the other girls following.

The kitchen was dark and cobwebby, although a small amount of light penetrated the creepers that covered the window. The room was still recognisable as a kitchen. A wooden table and two benches occupied the centre of the space, probably undisturbed in all this time. A black kettle hung on a chain in the fireplace, its tilter still in place, ready for use at any moment. Piles of mouldering firewood were stacked at either side of the fireplace, covered with thick layers of cobweb. Most of the shelving had collapsed, but many objects could still be identified where they'd fallen: an urn, pots, dishes, spoons, ladles, skimmers, a roasting spit and a cradle spit, sugar cutters, lemon squeezer, rushlight holders, a biscuit pricker, a salt box and other items, all now homes for spiders and mice. The ceiling seemed solid, although it was festooned with spiderwebs and birds' nests.

Kate shivered. "It's almost like they're still living here – might come back and tidy everything up."

"That's time, Kate," said Mabel. "In the silence of time, in the wake of life, these things, and us, are left behind."

The phrase struck Kate to her heart. She looked at Mabel in wonder and could think of nothing to say. She felt the brush of eternity pass over her.

Fuzz and the others were waiting for the expedition to proceed. Mabel walked carefully across the kitchen and through the next door. "Just follow my footsteps as closely as you can. There are a few rotten floorboards, but it's pretty safe – I hope."

The kitchen door opened into the corner of a narrow L-shaped passage, one branch of which ran to the front of the house, where it gave access to the servants' staircase. Fuzz, Shelagh, Bip and Pammy all ran on ahead to the foot of the narrow stairs, then walked carefully up them, one girl at a time. The treads seemed solid enough, and Mabel encouraged Kate to ascend. The staircase led to a narrow landing that gave access to two doors, one of which Kate found open. It was a servant's bedroom, rotten bedframe still in place, rusty fire irons ready in the grate. The floor and ceiling seemed surprisingly intact, and daylight illuminated the room despite all the foliage in the window frames. A few panes were cracked but the windows themselves were mostly sound, though slung with multiple layers of hammock-like cobwebs.

"What do you think, Kate?" said Bip. "We could run away and live here. In the spring and summer I bet it's full of fairies."

Kate smiled. Yes, it would be an adventure to hide away here.

There was a similar room to the rear of the first – darker,

but intact apart from a few broken floorboards. On the far side of this rear room there was another door. Mabel clutched the handle, preparing to pull it open. "Are you ready?" she asked.

"Go on..." said Bip quietly. Mabel turned the handle and pulled hard. The door ground against the floor, and she had to apply the weight of her body to drag it open. Kate gasped in amazement – the space beyond was full of daylight. The door opened onto a gallery that ran round the main stair-case. The gallery itself was intact, but the roof of the house had entirely fallen in and exposed the centre of the building to the sky. Plants, bushes and trees had taken root and grown up beyond the top of the house. A few startled birds – crows and jackdaws – flew up into the daylight and out of sight. Two bushy-tailed chestnut-red squirrels clung motionless to the opposite bannister, curiously observing the newcomers.

Kate looked down over the gallery rail. Large pieces of the shattered roof poked out of the foliage and snow like broken teeth. The scene was simultaneously terrifying and beautiful.

"Don't lean on the bannister, Kate," warned Mabel.

Kate said, "It's heartbreaking."

Shelagh, standing a few feet further along the gallery, said, "It is, but the house is still lived in by so many creatures. You can see the squirrels there, and all the birds' nests..." She pointed some out, clinging to the few remaining pieces of overhanging ceiling. "There are bats in the cellar too. You see them flying around the school at night. They'll be hibernating now."

Kate nodded. "It's amazing, frightening – like all the people left the world but everything else carried on." She paused. "Can we get deeper into the house?"

"It's possible," said Mabel, "but the rest of the upstairs is like this. A few of the downstairs rooms on the other side are not too bad, but you have to climb through all that mess to get there. We *could* do that, or we could go on and see the rest of the grounds."

Most of the girls signalled their desire to move on. Kate thought she'd come back alone one day and explore right round the house. "Alright," she said. "Let's go on."

They retraced their steps, emerged into the open and made their way along the rear of the house. It wasn't too tricky, deer having forced a path between the brambles, gorse and the thick climbing plants on the house wall. Kate peered through the windows as they went – many of them broken – and was able to make out a few details of the rooms within. Some of the furnishings were still there – chairs, sofas, settles, tables – but it was too dark inside for her to judge their condition.

They came to a narrow door on the far side of the house, closed, impassable, with a step down and a path running into the undergrowth.

"That leads to the locked gate in the garden wall," said Mabel. "It would have been the quickest route home from the Lookout."

Beyond the south wall of the house, they ran into a dense jungle of impenetrable growth. Mabel said, "This is all wild now, but I think it must have been a bowling lawn. Just inside the back door of the house there's a cupboard that contains all the equipment."

They went on, squeezing between the suspected bowling lawn and the south wall of the house. Soon they emerged into open space, the terrace and ruined knot garden to their right. From that point there was a clear path that led southwest, bordered by an extensive area of undergrowth on their right, which Mabel said had probably been a lawn. The expanse had been colonised by damson trees, most likely seeded by birds.

Pammy, Bip and Shelagh ran on ahead. "Worry not, My Lord!" shouted Bip. "Help is at hand." They all laughed, and Kate suddenly saw the folly. It was built in the form of

418

a little two-storey castle with a crenellated parapet. The arched door was closed but not locked, and by the time Kate, Fuzzy and Mabel got there the other girls had already entered the building, climbed the stone stairs to the roof and stood laughing and waving at them.

"We shall repel any siege!" shouted Bip. Pammy and Shelagh giggled excitedly.

Kate peered into the dark, windowless room to the right of the stairs at ground level.

"There's nothing in there but old cricket equipment," said Mabel.

The narrow spiral staircase gave access to a little first-floor room with small windows in its north, west and south walls. An old wooden chair stood upright in the middle of the otherwise empty space. Kate and Mabel continued upwards and emerged into bright sunlight on the snow-covered roof.

"Welcome to my castle," said Bip graciously. "I am Anne, Queen of Bipland..." (Pammy and Shelagh sniggered) "... and these are my subjects." The two girls so indicated wittered like sycophantic royal hangers-on.

Kate curtseyed and said, "And I am Catherine, Princess of the Swithen Bank."

Bip reached out and put her hand on Kate's shoulder. "Then I dub thee Lady Kate of Bipland. Thou shalt be my chief bath-filler." They all laughed hard at that, including Mabel. "What would we do without your sense of humour, Bip?" said Mabel, smiling.

Kate looked out from the roof. Much of the surrounding undergrowth rose to a similar height as the top of the folly. To the north she was able to see the topmost parts of the orangery and the two other plant houses. The top of the dower house was visible to the northeast, and beyond that, the upper storeys of the Lookout, with the northeast turret away in the distance, too small to make out any details. She wondered if the boys were at the window looking at her. The jungle-like growth of the lost lawn, all dusted white with snow, stretched unbroken for a long way to the northwest, and the neglect was repeated in the area immediately to the west of the folly itself. The scattered trees seemed sugar-coated in the frosty air.

"That was a cricket ground," said Mabel, pointing directly west of the folly. "I imagine they used to sit up here and watch the game."

In the distance, beyond the overgrown cricket ground, a huge area of silver glowed brilliantly, reflecting the sunlight.

"The lake," said Mabel.

"Wow!" said Kate. "Is it frozen?"

"It looks like it. Let's go and see."

A narrow deer track allowed access between the undergrowth that had taken control of the cricket pitch and the vegetation that had overrun the lawn. Ten minutes later they emerged from the tunnel of dark winter foliage and stood on the lakeshore. Kate was overwhelmed by the silent, icy beauty of the scene.

The surface seemed entirely frozen, with alders, willows and birches leaning over the ice. It was beautiful – silver-white and shimmering, stretching away for about two hundred yards, a few ducks slipping about drunkenly.

"Is it safe to walk on?" asked Fuzzy.

"I don't think you should try," Mabel replied. "They usually cut the ice and cart it to the icehouse. Looks as if they don't need this."

"How deep is the lake?" asked Kate.

Mabel said, "It's deep, but I don't know exactly how deep. At least thirty feet in the centre, I think – maybe more. It's full of life when it's warmer – fish – quite big ones, newts, tadpoles, frogs. Lots of greenery in the water – spawning places." She looked at Kate. "Do you swim?"

"Not very well," said Kate. "Do you think I could practice here?"

"I don't see why not. But somebody would need to watch out for you while you did it."

Kate smiled. "That could be you."

Mabel looked at Kate. *There's something special about you*, she thought. "Alright. When it gets warmer we'll swim together."

"Good," said Kate quietly. "We'll be good friends, you and me."

Pammy put her hand on Kate's shoulder and pointed into the distance beyond the lake. "Can you see the summerhouse?"

Kate peered and saw it – a red-brick domed tower beyond the lake. The glare of the reflected sun on the ice had hidden it from view, but with a little effort it became visible.

Fuzzy said, "It's the only building in the dower house grounds that's in reasonably good condition."

"Yes," said Bip. "And that's nice for certain people we know, isn't it?"

Kate glanced at Mabel for clarification, but she only pursed her lips and shook her head as if to say, *Trust you, Bip!*

Bip was already on her way. "Come on," she called, and they all followed around the southern edge of the lake. There were several ornamental statues, a few still upright, all covered in lichen and creeper. Twice they passed over terraced platforms with short flights of steps leading down to the water's edge. Eventually, they came to the summerhouse, the east side of which, though covered in thin, bleak creeper, seemed intact and sound. It was a circular building with four protruding arms in the manner of a Greek cross, entirely of red brick – even the domed roof, which was topped with an ornamental lantern that appeared to be copper under a patina of verdigris. The building was about thirty feet in height and twenty-five from side to side. The door, about eight feet tall and made of dark oak, faced the lake at ground level; and a large, arched window with many lights stood above it in the upper storey, its wooden frame showing clear signs of decay even through the accumulated foliage.

Kate tried the door. "It's locked."

Bip responded, "A-ha-ha-ha-ha-ha-haa…" She skipped into the undergrowth to the south side of the building and returned a moment later with a large key. "Well, well. Look what I've found."

Pammy said, "Everybody knows where the key is hidden."

"Yes," said Bip, "but *they* think only *they* know the secret."

"Who?" asked Kate.

Mabel interjected, "Bip, you're such a gossip."

Bip ignored her. "Who do you think?" and made a lewd up-and-down gesture that involved the key in her right hand slipping in and out of a ring formed by the thumb and forefinger of her left. "*She* keeps the lock oiled, and *he* has the nice big key that fits it." As Bip spoke, she inserted the key in the lock and turned it. "See how easy that was? That's because it goes in and out *a lot*." The other girls were giggling. Mabel had become genuinely irritated at Bip's remarks. "Bip, that's enough. Practise a little subtlety, please."

"Ah," said Kate, "you mean Orla and…"

Bip cut back in, "…and Rider, yes. *Rider…*". She drew out the word, filling it with suggestive innuendo. "This is one of their f***ing places."

Mabel raised her voice, obliterating the sound of the word. "Bip. That's enough. Any more, and I'll take you home."

Bip looked mock-sheepish. "Sorry, Miss Stanton." She hid her grin from Mabel but displayed it to Kate, who suppressed a smile.

Bip turned the handle. The door opened easily, admitting them to a circular chamber about ten feet in height with windows on three sides, although the enclosing creeper admitted very little daylight. The room was clean and contained nothing but a few wooden chairs. A flight of stone steps to the left of the door gave access to the upper level. Shelagh, aware of Mabel's increasing frustration, sought to calm the tension by asking permission to ascend. "Shall we...?"

Mabel nodded. "Alright. But don't touch anything!"

Shelagh led the ascent. The upper floor was very much brighter, the window overlooking the lake having been partly cleared of growth. The three other windows remained overgrown although they were not entirely obscured – and a small amount of light was admitted through the lantern twenty feet above their heads in the domed ceiling. The room was painted completely white and had a strange acoustic that produced a long fluttery echo. There was a small fireplace and a large bucket of wood. The only piece of furniture (apart from a couple of rugs rolled up against the wall) was a small wooden bed, dressed ready for its occupants. Bip looked at Kate, winked and licked her lips thoroughly from side to side, exposing half an inch of pink tongue whilst fluttering her eyelids in mock ecstasy. Kate found it almost impossible to keep a straight face.

"How did he get the bed in here?" asked Pammy.

"It's so cold!" said Fuzz, banging her hands on opposing elbows to generate a little warmth. "Even colder than outside!"

Bip risked one more comment. "You just need love to keep you warm, Fuzz." Mabel ignored it.

"Have we seen all we need to see?" asked Mabel. The girls all mumbled in the affirmative and made their way back down the stairs and outside. Bip locked the door and replaced the key where she'd found it.

There was another huge area of dense foliage to the north of the lake. "That looks like it was a garden," said Kate. "I'm not sure the trees are meant to be there." She pointed out a few – damson, silver birch and sycamore.

"You seem to know a lot about this, Kate," said Mabel.

"My grandma taught me. It was what she did."

"All this growth," said Mabel, "it looks solid, but actually it's easy enough to get inside if you're determined. Like I told you, the deer graze up to their own height, and the plant cover is preserved above that, so when you look down on it – from the upper floor windows of the school, say – you see a canopy that appears solid. But it's not. You can spend all day exploring – trying not to get lost. There's nothing in there except a few little sheds for tools and things. There's probably a potting shed somewhere, but I've never found it. The same with all the other overgrown areas; you can get into all of them if you don't mind making a bit of an effort – the lawn, the bowling green and the cricket pitch – and the orchard, which is where we'll go next." She looked around. "Where's Fuzz and Pammy?"

"Gone for a wizz," said Bip, clearing her dark brown hair of cobwebs that she'd only just noticed. Mabel waited for the girls to reappear, then led the way northwest from the summerhouse, pushing through snow-laden undergrowth. After just a few minutes it became clear, despite the infilling of vegetation, that they were standing in an orchard. There was an ordered pattern of veteran apple trees – and even a few younger ones – that had withstood the foraging of the deer. As they made their way through the orchard, Kate noticed a few surviving pear trees. There was even evidence of old peach trees, although they were all dead, and no new ones had risen to replace them. Damsons had self-seeded abundantly, and there were a few invaders – hawthorn, yew, a lot of ash. Bracken had climbed over almost everything and occupied much of the ground space as well, protecting seedlings that would otherwise have been exposed to foraging animals. The area to the west of the orchard seemed to be woodland, and the whole area – wood and orchard – was full of rabbit holes, fox dens, badger sets and molehills.

The sky darkened as they made their way, and snow began to fall lightly, accumulating on top of that which had already settled.

Soon another building came into view in the shade of the trees. It was of moderate size, two stories high and made of wood. The growth that covered it seemed to be drawing it to the ground – as if it were pulling the structure beneath the earth.

"That's the old gamekeeper's cottage," said Mabel, pointing it out.

As they got closer to the house, the full extent of the dilapidation became apparent. The building was in a state of complete collapse, the upper floor and roof having given way and entirely fallen in at the rear. The front door stood open as if inviting access. It might have been possible to get into one or two of the downstairs rooms, but Mabel wouldn't allow them to try, fearing an accident or further structural collapse. They peered in at the front door and surveyed the wreckage in the hallway. The bottom of the staircase was intact, but the higher part tumbled precariously backwards and then broke away completely from the upper floor, which had slid into the back garden carrying part of the roof with it. The place looked like a secret grave for wraiths or vampyres.

"It'll be full of rats," said Mabel. Then she turned to face them all. "But the outhouse is still good. Anyone?"

"I'll go," said Bip, and quickly disappeared round the north side of the house. The others followed her slowly through the snow at a more leisurely pace.

The outhouse was indeed strangely undamaged by the ravages of time, standing proudly to the rear of the plot, ready for the sprays and strains of the next passer-by. Bip stood at the open door, looked in, and waited for Mabel and the girls to catch her up.

"I can't go in there," she said. The interior was draped so heavily from side to side with thick spiderwebs that it would have taken a desperate individual indeed to tear down the multi-layered fleeces of dusty, corpse-filled silk and expose the seat to view.

"Find a spot, Bip," said Mabel, but Bip was already hopping away through the snow to search for a friendlier location. Another small wooden building, probably a tool shed, occupied the opposite side of the yard. She dipped out of view behind that.

Kate inspected the rear of the cottage while they waited for Bip. It was a complete wreck and hardly resembled a house at all when viewed from this angle. Given the devastation, Kate thought it was astonishing that the front of the building still retained something of the aspect of a dwelling.

The snow fell harder, and the sky grew darker even though it was not yet three o'clock. Bip came running back towards them.

"Better?" asked Mabel.

"Yes," said Bip. "Those nettles needed my attention!"

"Let's go home then," said Mabel and steered them towards the north.

Kate said, "So what *haven't* we seen today?"

Mabel answered, "You've seen almost everything, I think. You didn't get to see the two plant houses, but you haven't missed much there – they're very ruined – worse even than the orangery. Apart from that...No, I think that's all."

"So, where are we now?"

"We're walking north, in the direction of Peak. Once we're through the enclosure wall, you'll see the fields behind the Lookout away to the northeast. Over there..." (she pointed to the left) "...is the wall that separates the estate from the main road. And behind us..." (Mabel turned and walked backwards as she pointed to the south) "...is the end of the main drive and the gatekeeper's cottage, where Jack and Tessa Archer live. Directly over there..." (she indicated due east) "...is the dower house and the school. You can't see any of it from here."

The undergrowth thinned, and the wall separating the dower house grounds from the Lookout park came into view. This part of the barrier had clearly fallen a long time ago. Its tumbled stones were covered in moss, lichen and other growth and were barely visible at all.

"This is the exit the deer mostly use when they come out into the park," Mabel said.

"We haven't seen any deer today," Kate answered.

"There are lots, but they mostly stay hidden. I think we have them all though – roe and fallow, even some big red deer. It's the roe deer that appear most often – and it's them that wind up at dinner."

The snow continued to fall as they crossed over the shattered barrier and into the Lookout estate.

"Thanks for taking us, Mabel," said Shelagh.

"You're very welcome, my dear. Now let's get home before we all freeze."

44. THE LOOKOUT
January to April, 1761

The year wore on towards spring. Kate's mind was like a sponge. She read widely, practised her music almost every day, continually ran over French and Latin phrases in her head (dance steps too), and focused her attention in every subject so she remembered what she was taught. She was any teacher's ideal student. The timetable was demanding, but there was still time for her friends.

She wanted art classes – wanted to sketch, to paint – and cornered Mr Crowan about it. He raised no objection, and recalled from her interview that Golda Dryden, currently employed as singing tutor, was a keen painter. She was easily persuaded to offer an optional weekly class in the ballroom, and by the middle of February the "Art Club" had become a fixture, open to anyone, staff or students. Jacob ordered the supplies from London and looked in at one of the early sessions to find nearly twenty girls – and several members of the teaching and domestic staff – occupied in a still life study. He was genuinely impressed.

Kate hadn't forgotten Nolly's offer of riding lessons. Horses were not new to her – she'd grown up on a farm – but she'd never become a really competent rider. Some of the other girls (many of them secretly in love with Nolly) thought lessons were a great idea, and the boy was soon in charge of a flock of young ladies. The Lookout possessed only six horses, so the girls had to take turns. Kipp and Stanley watched with amusement and teased the boy endlessly about his "wives".

Whenever she could, Kate also spent time in the kitchen, watching the head cook, plump fifty-year-old Alvina Rowley, at work. Alvina introduced her to her husband Rodney and to the five kitchen maids: Edie Ashton, Kim Kelsey, Maisie Blythe, Opal Clayden and Annie Alby. She became particularly fond of middle-aged Maisie, who was a good friend of Mabel. Kate liked to watch the preparation of the food, and Mrs Rowley let her help in its production now and then.

She made friends with the Staffords in the laundry, although she found the laundry itself too hot and stifling for a lengthy visit. It was a large building, full of copper boilers, vats and mangles. The laundry used water from the little river that ran off the heathland close to the building's rear. It had its own store of coal and firewood, regularly replenished, and the building was perpetually full of steam, the big fires always lit. Michael Stafford and his wife were both plump, middle-aged, grey-haired people who always seemed happy despite the laborious nature of their occupation. Twenty-three-year-old Beryl was the eldest of their children and looked like a younger version of Mary, her mother. Crispin (who, in Nellie Brent's words, would "one day wed Winnie Warwick") was a handsome dark-haired young man of twenty-two. The two younger girls, Barbara and Sylvia, looked like twins, although they were separated by two years. Sylvia, aged eighteen, reminded Kate of Beatrice Swift back at the farm.

Fuzzy liked to visit the brewhouse on Saturday mornings, and Kate sometimes accompanied her. Alcoholic drink was a great passion with Fuzzy, who was not only a keen consumer but thought of herself as a brewer in waiting. The head man was Dennis McCallum, and three of the other five brewers also had names beginning with the letter D: Douglas Trivet, David Fielding and Donald Fitzroy. Of the other two, Richard Brent was universally known as Dick, while Franklyn Egan changed his name to Daniel in order to fit in. Fuzzy had dreams of joining them in business one day. She'd already designed the company banner: *Den, Dan,*

Don, Doug, Dave, Dick and Fuzz; there never were Truer Brewers. The six men loved her – she was their favourite girl, and Fuzz felt more naturally at ease in their company than she did with most of the other girls, Kate excepted.

In the early days of her explorations, Kate made a single visit to the carpenters' shop – against Fuzzy's advice.

"I wouldn't bother if I were you, Kate. They're just three dirty old men. Doesn't matter how young or how old you are – class 1 to class 7 – they just look at you and leer as if you're not wearing anything."

But Kate wanted to see for herself, so one Saturday morning while Fuzz was carousing with the brewers, she continued on the track past the brewhouse, knocked on the door of the carpenters' building and went inside. The place consisted of a large single room with doors off at the rear, presumably leading to their living quarters. It smelt of sawdust, sweat and (for some reason) urine.

Chad Sandon, Ferret Colborn and Tom Thorne stopped what they were doing and focused their three sets of beady eyes on the tasty morsel that had blown in. Kate felt uncomfortable straight away. Chad and Ferret were in their early forties, both with sweaty, untidy grey hair; Tom was a bit younger – perhaps thirty-five, although he was almost completely bald. None wore a beard as such, although it looked as if they hadn't shaved for four or five days. They were dressed in ragged old clothes, and all appeared to be salivating as if they were going to fire up the oven and bundle the pretty red-haired girl inside.

" 'Ello, sweetie," said Chad, face screwed into a nasty grin. "What you lookin' for then?"

"I just came to say hello," she replied. "I'm Kate."

"I bet you are," said Ferret, and laughed like a rat might – if a rat could laugh. Kate didn't understand his remark.

Tom played with his trousers, and Kate squirmed inwardly.

"Soft, ain't you..." said Chad, moving towards her round

the work table. "Soft..." He licked his lips. "We don't get many little girls in 'ere."

"...little girls in 'ere," echoed Tom, pulling his trousers about.

"Come to look at the tools, have you?" asked Ferret.

"...tools?" Tom, half a beat behind.

Ferret went on without stopping. "The nails, the drills? The bangin'?"

"Bangin'!"

"We 'ave vices in 'ere," said Chad.

"Vices..."

"Screws are nice too," Chad went on. "Would Pretty like a screw?"

Tom laughed. "...like a screw?"

"Well," said Kate, lifting her hand. "Have a lovely day." She retraced her steps and left the building. After a few seconds she turned and saw them watching her as she hurried towards the Lookout. Chad still wore his filthy grin. For some reason, Ferret stood with his tongue poked out – a disturbing sight that entered Kate's nightmares once or twice. Tom Thorne was fiddling with himself.

"What did you expect?" asked Fuzzy. "I told you not to bother."

Kate never visited the carpenters' shop again, although her voyages of friendship continued elsewhere. She wanted to know everyone.

(*Here she comes*, thought Speck Beckwith. *She'll want to play with the dog. Why does she make me feel like this – as if the world stands still?*)

Speck's dog, Bastard, loved Kate. Their first meeting had been memorable. The dog was always daft in the company of a new face, bounding about, showing off. But with Kate it had been different. Bastard behaved as if he knew the girl but had been separated from her for a long, long time. The animal had been overjoyed, barking, jumping up, running round her, pressing its rear end low in that way that happy dogs do. Speck had never seen an animal so overcome with elation.

And then Speck had met the child's eyes...

(*There's something special about you,* Speck frowned, watching her approach. *I felt it the moment I first saw you. It was as if I recognised you – as if I'd always known you – all my life, even before you were born.*

Someone was calling to him from deep within his soul, but the voice was unfamiliar, and he couldn't make out the words. He always felt a kind of shock, a pinprick of amazement in her presence, and didn't understand why.)

One Saturday noon in March, the three farmers – Speck, Tranter Tickle and John Eldenshaw – sat smoking together in their accustomed place on the wall by the top field. Kate, Shelagh and Bip were playing with the dog a few yards away, and the three men watched the young girls with affection, having just concluded a reflective discussion about their own childhoods. It was a bright day, and there was a little heat in the sunshine despite the prevailing chill.

A sudden, dramatic shaft of brilliant sunshine illuminated the three clay tobacco pipes in heavenly gold as they were simultaneously lifted clear of the men's lips as if in ordained synchronisation. Only Tranter noticed this, but it made such an impact on him that he was moved to ask, "I wonder if they've ever smoked..."

"Now there's a thought..." Speck replied. "Wait a while..." He hopped off the wall and walked away in the direction of the groundsmen's houses, returning a few minutes later with three short clay pipes, which he held up and described as *spares*. He pointed the pipes in the direction of the girls and was about to say something.

"You're leading them girls astray, Speck," said John Eldenshaw.

"They'll all be led astray soon enough, John, like all females of the species, said Tranter. "No reason they shouldn't try out a few of life's little pleasures first."

Speck called his dog, "Bastard!" The animal came running to his master, panting, happy tongue lolling to one side, and the three girls followed him.

"Speck!" said Bip. "Did you see what happened?"

"What was that?" asked Speck.

"Well," Bip replied, "we threw a stick for Bastard and he chased after it very fast. He caught it in his mouth just as it hit the ground – and tried to skid to a halt. Well, the *front* legs stopped running, but the *back* legs went on – with disastrous consequences…"

The three men laughed, Shelagh and Kate joining in. Bastard barked and ran round in a tight circle.

Speck held up one of the new pipes. "You ladies ever…?" They all answered in the negative. "Would you like to?"

"Isn't it smelly?" asked Shelagh.

"Well," said Speck, "it smells like tobacco."

"I'll do it!" said Bip.

"Good on you!" Speck replied and began tapping tobacco into the bowl. "Kate?"

She said, "Do you have to breathe it in?"

"No, you don't have to. You can if you want – I do, but you don't have to."

"Is it hot?"

"Well, you feel the heat in the bowl, around the fingers – a bit, but no, it's not hot. Go on – have a go."

She paused. "Alright."

"I'll light them for you."

Speck pressed down the tobacco in Bip's pipe, took the stem in his mouth and lit it with his flint and steel striker. Years of practice produced instant success, and he drew on the pipe until the tobacco glowed and smoke rose easily. Then he handed it to Bip. "There you go. Draw on that. Take the smoke into your mouth, hold it, then blow it out. If you like it and want to try inhaling – breathing it into the chest – take a second draw."

Bip took the pipe nervously and put it to her lips while Speck began to fill the second one. She drew, and Kate watched the bowl light up.

"What's it like?" she asked.

Bip took the stem out of her mouth and stood still, holding the smoke for a few seconds before blowing it out. She opened her lips and waggled her tongue from side to side, then said, "It's actually...quite nice." But the second draw, this time inhaled into the lungs, produced an instant fit of coughing.

"Gently does it!" said Speck. "Just a little at first. You'll soon get used to it." John and Tranter laughed but also congratulated her and offered encouragement.

Bip tried again, just a shallow breath. The coughing reflex was still there, though reduced. "Uck, uck, uck!" she said. "It needs practice."

"That's the spirit!" Speck replied. "Keep the pipe – it's yours. And here's a knob of tobacco for your pocket." He turned to Kate. "Yes?"

She looked a little uncertain, brows furrowed, lips set – but nodded. "Alright."

Speck lit the second pipe, and Kate's experiment produced roughly the same result as Bip's, but she agreed to try again at a later date and accepted Speck's gift.

Shelagh declined. "No, I don't think so. Not for me."

The girls bade the three farmers good day and made their way northeast to the forge where coffee and cake awaited them along with the company of Chastity Blake, the blacksmith's wife. Nine-year-old Barney had been looking forward to the girls' visit as it provided him with an excuse to feast on his mother's celebrated fruit cake, sweet and juicy. Chastity was about forty years old, buxom and voluptuous, with light brown hair that was beginning to turn grey. They lived just beyond the smithy, at the end of the farm track, close to the wood and entirely out of sight of the Lookout and the other buildings. It was a peaceful setting, the only sounds apart from the wind and the wildlife being those that Alan Blake made in the forge. He was busy when the girls arrived but joined them later to say hello. Alan was a muscular, handsome man in his middle forties who was often the subject of the torrid, improvised fantasy games that were a feature of parties thrown by the house-mistresses. Kate had overheard one or two as the women passed round the narrative, fragment by fragment, building up an unlikely chain of fiction:

"I was walking past the forge the other day..." (guffaws and encouraging comments).

"...when I saw Alan Blake dressed only in..."

"...Chastity's hat!" (Hysterics).

"I said, 'I'm looking for a poker'..." Shrieks of uncontrolled laughter.

"...and he said, 'I've only got this big one, I'm afraid, but at least the end is hot and glows red...'"

And so it went on.

Kate got to know the three gardeners. Gnarled, weathered Rabbit Shipley made her welcome, as did his enthusiastic young assistant, Solly Birtwistle. Both were impressed with her encyclopaedic knowledge of herbs, shrubs, trees, flowers and everything found in the hedgerows.

Shy, quiet Ned Silden and his younger, noisier wife, Pixie, became very fond of the girl and told her she was always welcome at their table in the groundsmen's house.

Slade Stone, Lucas Dent and Jude Farlam, the Lookout's little squad of teenage privy-men, were allowed to organise their own rota of freshening the jakes-pails, and they carried out their slippery task with efficiency and regularity. It was an indication of the boys' reliability that those who used the privies rarely gave a thought as to how and when they were emptied, yet the task was a substantial one. The Lookout itself was equipped with no fewer than forty jakes, including the close-stools in the private apartments. There was also an outdoor privy block with four pails. The staff house contained eight privies and a further four buckets in its own outdoor block. There was another outdoor block of two pails behind the laundry and yet another, of four pails, behind the brewhouse. There was also a single one, always filthy, near the carpenters' shop. Chad, Ferret and Tom were not accurate in their aim. The boys' duties did not extend to the stables, the groundsmen's dwellings or the forge.

The allocation of localities in the nocturnal cleaning rota often involved disputes between Jude and Slade over whose turn it was to clean the jakes on the dormitory floor, Jude hoping for a glimpse of bare female skin, Slade looking forward to a few drops of gin left over from Kate and Fuzzy's boozy lock-ins. Kate became friends with both boys. She never knew it, but she was the subject of many of Jude's sticky fantasies.

Lucas Dent was shy, quieter than the other two, and carried out his duties inconspicuously in the less exciting parts of the house and grounds. He was gentle and rarely heard to speak. It was a secret known only to the three boys that fourteen-year-old Lucas was Slade's special friend. Kate saw him once and commented on the silver whistle he kept on a string round his neck. He smiled, pleased to have her interest, took it off and blew it for her. Kate loved his smile and warmed to him straight away.

"I wish I had a whistle that made such a nice sound!" she said.

"Slade gave it to me," he replied. "It's my most precious thing."

Kate gradually gathered everyone at the Lookout into her circle of acquaintances – a considerable undertaking, seeing that the school and park housed more than a hundred and sixty people. By the time spring arrived, Jack and frail old Tessa Archer were the only people to whom she'd not properly introduced herself, so she made her way along the drive in the direction of the iron gates and the gatekeeper's cottage. Sadly, Jack was not pleased to see her, and waved her back to the school with his pipe, saying she shouldn't venture this far alone. Kate apologised and decided she wouldn't try again.

There was a big service in the chapel on Easter Sunday, March 22nd, with lots of music, and celebrations afterwards.

While the girls were fussing over Old Will at the reception, Jacob asked Kate if she'd be going home for her birthday. She'd already given it some thought and had decided to remain at the Lookout, and go home for a while in the summer instead. She asked to send a letter home, and Jacob promised to have Kipp deliver it. The reply came straight back. Meadow and Alder were glad Kate was happy, wished her a joyful birthday with her friends, and said they looked forward to seeing her later in the year.

Kate's birthday was held in the debating chamber the following Sunday, March 29th. Mrs Rowley made her a special cake, very large so that as many people as possible could share it. There were lots of games, and almost everyone looked in during the afternoon. The housemistresses and Ruth Marlowe stayed all day and helped organise things, simultaneously ensuring that the festivities were as noisy as possible. Denise Trent, soon to be Mrs Nisbet, looked beautiful and sunny. The higher staff – Jacob, Quinton and Mrs Tenley – appeared together at one point to wish Kate "Many Happy Returns of the Day", and most of the maids, footmen and others visited to hug her as well. Nolly Arkwright gave her a kiss on the cheek and held her hand for a moment, drawing envious gasps from many of the girls.

Kate, bold as brass, but also in reaction to the girls' excitement, took Nolly's face in her hands and kissed him on the lips. He'd expected that his little kiss might elicit a modest thrill in the watchers but was not prepared for Kate's response, which made him blush bright pink in embarrassment. He put his hand to his lips and muttered, "Oh, Kate..."

She smiled broadly. "Thank you for my riding lessons." The girls erupted in laughter, and Nolly grinned happily, pleased to be made the centre of attention by such a pretty girl.

Nearly all the tutors appeared at some point or other, except Sylvie Ardoin and mysterious, seductive Clara Sutherland. As the afternoon drew on, Kate asked Bip if they'd gone away for the day, or were ill.

"Oh no," said Bip, "they're just canoodling somewhere, I should think."

Kate, expressionless, waited for more.

"Oh, come on Kate! Don't feign innocence!"

Kate dropped her gaze. "Alright, I had wondered. It's not always easy to read Clara, though. I wasn't completely sure..."

Bip cut in. "Don't assume *too* much. Clara may be unpredictable, but she gets around – one at a time. She likes men too. Before Orla was grown up enough to..." (she made brief bouncing movements with both hands at breast level) "...interest Mr Browning, Clara and he used to...compare fingerings. A bit before my time, of course, but I've heard the stories. I think she's run Kipp a few times round the paddock too. But Sylvie's more a girl's girl, I'm pretty sure. No men allowed in *her* chamber."

But wherever they'd been, both of the absent women looked in for a few minutes towards five o'clock, Sylvie looking elegant and aristocratic in a petite, bejewelled kind of way, while white-skinned Clara, tall and dressed in her characteristic plain dark silk with provocative décolletage, looked as ready as ever for a night of crimson debauchery.

Kate loved life at the Lookout. She had nearly everything she ever wanted.

The events of the following Saturday, April 4th, had been long anticipated. The wedding of Denise and Terrel took place in the chapel at ten o'clock in the morning and was followed by a lavish wedding breakfast. Arthur Mulgrave took the service, Old Will being unavailable. Arthur was astonished at the number of people in attendance, having been used to the more usual handful of close family and a few guests. But the chapel was full, and the event felt like a major religious feast.

Arthur was sixty, and no longer had a parish of his own. There'd been a number of complaints about him in his last job, and the bishop had asked him to retire. He'd never married, and lived quietly alone. But he was pleased to be asked to officiate at occasional ceremonies such as this even though the girls didn't have the same appeal for him as they did for Old Will.

Denise looked breath-taking in a dress that emphasised her various attributes. It had been determined by the gardeners and farmers, after extended debate, that she possessed the finest bosom at the Lookout, and most of them attended the ceremony to watch it as it processed in and out. Tranter, John, Rabbit, Solly and Ned sat at the back of the chapel in order to avail themselves of the most extended view of the exit procession. No words were exchanged among them as the magnificent, twin-globed figurehead passed by, although the air was peppered with appreciative mumbles and a couple of sighs.

Terrel was dressed in red, his sword shining like polished silver. He liked to give the impression that he was a member of the armed forces, although he'd never served, the teaching of mathematics having been his lifelong calling.

He was aware that his profession made him appear rather dry, so tried to make up for it with visible dash and an energetic manner. Denise certainly appreciated it, and Terrel was in turn captivated by her gentle softness...among other things.

Speck saw Denise and Terrel separately the day before their wedding, and offered his best wishes and apologies. April 4th was the twentieth anniversary of his wife's death, and he wanted to be alone with her memory. He took his dog and spent the day walking on the moor.

45. THE LOOKOUT
KITCHEN PARLOUR
Friday April 24, 1761
Sukey & Theo's 5th Wedding Anniversary

Thirty-two was a tight squeeze in the servants' parlour but they just managed it, seated round two parallel tables, fifteen at each, with Sukey and Theo at the top so they could see everybody. The kitchen staff, the dairymaids, the footmen, the girls' maids, the cleaners and the soil boys were all present. Supper was over, and the conversation was quietening. Sukey pressed his hand; it was time for him to speak. Theo rose, and the room fell silent, all eyes turned towards him.

"I'd better start by saying what a lovely feast that was." He raised his glass, picked out those who'd been responsible for producing the meal, and acknowledged each in turn. "Thank you, Alvina, Rodney, Edie, Kim, Maisie, Opal, Annie."

His gratitude was met with a resounding cheer and much applause.

He continued, "I must say – I never thought Mrs Tenley would taste so good."

The room erupted with laughter, stamping and table slapping.

Theo grinned, waited for the din to settle, and went on. "Seriously though, I'd like to say..." He looked down at Sukey by his side. "We'd *both* like to say how lucky we feel to live and work here, and to have such friends and colleagues as all of you. It's our fifth wedding anniversary – as you know, of course. We were both young when we got married. I was nearly eighteen; Sukey was a few months short of sixteen. People said we were still children." He shook his head and admitted, "Maybe we were. The first two years were hard, living in Scarborough in a tiny room. I was working on the docks; she was in the Fisherman's Arms." There was a flurry of suggestive noises and lewd comments. Theo continued, "I mean, she was *behind the bar* in the Fisherman's Arms." He cast his eyes over the crowd and wagged his finger. "But you're right. She was as pretty then as she is now." Sukey began to blush – she'd always been shy. "And it wasn't always easy to keep the men off – especially when they'd drunk a bit. She wasn't happy." He paused again, then went on, head nodding. "But then we got the chance to work here, and our lives changed. And it's not just this place – it's all of you – lovely people. Our friends." He took Sukey's hand and drew her to her feet.

Alvina sniffed, wiped a tear from her eye, rose and raised her glass. "Ladies and gentlemen," she said. "A toast – Theodore and Susannah Westmoreland. May your first five years be only the start." Everyone stood and drank the couple's health. Three cheers ensued. Theo waved in acknowledgement and the couple sat down.

"That was a lovely speech," said Sukey to her husband as the general hubbub of conversation resumed.

"Did I sound nervous?" he asked, holding her hand.

"No," she said. "You sounded really confident. I was proud of you."

He was pleased. "That's good. Can I have a kiss then?"

"You can," she said and kissed him lightly on the lips.

The end of the evening was informal, and people began to peel away to bed fairly quickly, but enough activity remained in the kitchen for Rodney Rowley to uncork a few more bottles.

Neva Hutton, Flossie Ousby and Delia Tweddle, three of Sukey's dairy colleagues, sat giggling together at the far end of one of the tables. Mabel Stanton and Maisie Blythe came to sit with them.

442

Mabel scanned the three dairymaids and said, "Kate Swithenbank told me she was coming to you so she could learn how to milk, make butter and everything. How's she doing?"

"She's amazing," said Delia, pushing back her thick dark hair. "She picks up everything so quickly."

"Kate's lovely," said Flossie. "Thoughtful girl. You only need to tell her something once, and she remembers it straight away."

"She's Mabel's favourite," said Maisie.

"She is nice," said Mabel. "It's true. I'm fond of Kate. She's a special girl."

Maisie went on, "She reminds me of my daughter when she was that age. Jess was like that – polite, listened to what you said."

"Have you seen Jess recently, Maisie?" asked Neva.

"Last November," said Maisie. "I spent a week with them in Northallerton."

"How many grandchildren have you got?" asked Delia.

"Three now," said Maisie. "Two boys and a girl."

Flossie said, "You don't look old enough to have grandchildren, Maisie."

"Go on with you!" Maisie replied. "My grandkids are twelve, ten and five. My daughter's thirty-three."

"Never!" Delia exclaimed.

"It's true," said Maisie. "I'm fifty-five."

Mabel smiled and rested her hand on Maisie's arm. "She's not lying – she's old enough to be my mother!" The comment earned her an elbow in the ribs from her friend.

A knot of women occupied the far end of the other table, questioning Winnie Warwick.

"You ought to get wed, Winnie," said Molly Colby. "You should pin Crispin down and make him promise you. You've been with him for more than a year."

It was true. Crispin Stafford, Michael and Mary's son, had been Winnie's sweetheart since Christmas 1759. His wooing had been persistent, and she'd eventually accepted his advances (and allowed him what he wanted – although no-one else knew that for sure). But he was five years younger than she, and Winnie had decided not to hurry him.

"Crispin'll get round to it before too long," she said. "He's true to me."

"It's not fair to keep you waiting though," said Ethel Coombs. Ethel, greying prematurely in her late thirties, had grown disillusioned with men, having been let down three times in earlier life. She'd accepted that she was likely to remain unmarried, and was already thinking of running away to Ireland or to the continent to become a nun.

"He's still only a boy," Winnie insisted. "Give him time."

Sarah Alston turned away from the conversation and said to Cady Weston, "Men. Who'd have the patience with them?"

Cady rubbed her hand along Sarah's thigh and replied, "We don't need them anyway. We're the superior race."

Cady and Sarah had been together for just over a year. They were committed to each other, but Sarah disliked Cady's fondling of the younger girls, and insisted it had to stop if their relationship was to continue. Cady was sad about that, but realised she was genuinely in love for the first time in her life and agreed to comply with Sarah's demand. Even so, she missed the pretty young bodies, and often looked with longing at what she couldn't have.

Rye Ousby, Gene Fenton, Jude Farlam and Slade Stone sat together, joking and drinking, while Lucas Dent lay asleep on the bench, his head in Slade's lap. Rye was telling a story – long, lewd and physically impossible – which the others punctuated with raucous guffaws. Delicate, yellow-haired Newt Fallowfield sat apart, looking bored. The joke was a crude story about an owl living in a large woman's pubic hair, and he didn't think it was funny. He rose, offered a quiet goodnight, and left.

444

Birdie Wade tapped Mabel on the shoulder and said, "We're going out to get some air. Just for a quick smoke and a wander. Come along?"

"Alright," Mabel agreed, drawing herself out from the bench, first one leg, then the other. "Maisie? Coming?"

"Aye," said Maisie. "I'll join you."

The night was calm and bright, the moon a few days past full. The kitchen door opened, and a clutch of ten women strolled around the side of the house and away down the drive, seven of them smoking their pipes. Birdie's signature cough pricked the night every few seconds, and Mabel wondered (not for the first time) just how ill she was. The woman was nearly sixty, and her eyes sagged with the heaviest bags that Mabel had ever seen in a face. She smoked continuously.

"Your cough's not getting any better, Birdie," said Mabel. "You should see the doctor about it."

"I'm fine," Birdie replied. "The pipe does me good. It's worse when I can't light up."

"Maybe you should stop for a while and see. It might do you good. You're coughing more – and for longer."

"Well, I'm gettin' old," said Birdie. "What d'you expect? Me husband died ten years ago and left me all alone; baccy's all I've got." She paused, and added, "Smokin' never did *'im* no 'arm neither."

Suddenly four pink objects ran past them from behind. Birdie ceased her coughing, stared, and doubled up with laughter. Mabel peered and realised she was looking at the unclothed rears of Jewel Springfield, Tillie Haley, Margaret York and Leafy Crosthwaite. "What…?" she muttered.

Nellie Brent stepped up beside her. "They've 'ad a bit too much to drink. They stripped off back at the 'ouse and laid bets who could run quickest to the gatehouse and back bare-arsed."

"Old Jack Archer'll have a heart attack!" said Mabel.

A voice from behind called, "Kim and me are going swimming in the lake. Anybody else?" Mabel turned and saw Edie Ashton and Kim Kelsey, two of the kitchen staff, hanging back expectantly. "We're going now," said Edie. "It's calm. It'll be nice."

Opal Clayden and Annie Alby, two more kitchen girls, looked at each other. Opal called, "Wait for us," then turned and bade goodnight to Mabel and the others.

"Me too," said little Fanny Kirkbride.

"You pulling your clothes off and going in the water?" asked Maisie, with some surprise. Fanny was the shyest of the young dairymaids. This was out of character. "It'll be freezing!"

"I've 'ad a good night," said Fanny. "I feel frisky!" She shook herself, smiled, and ran to join her adventurous friends.

Mabel looked back at the house in the moonlight. They'd walked a little over three hundred yards. Birdie's mirthful response to the nude runners had become a violent, hacking cough. She was bent forward, hands on knees, convulsed. Maisie patted her back and said, "Dear, oh dear, oh dear!"

Mary Acker, in her middle forties the eldest of the girls' maids, stepped up beside Mabel and said, "I'm off to bed. I'm too old to lark about like this. See you tomorrow."

Mabel nodded. "Goodnight then, Mary. Sleep well."

Mary walked back towards the school while Mabel and Maisie stood waiting for Birdie to recover – or die...

Jack Archer was fast asleep and dreaming of his mother when the urgent knocking shocked him awake. He opened his eyes and listened. TAP-TAP-TAP-TAP-TAP-TAP! Rattling knocks, overlapping as if delivered by several hands. Some disaster must be in progress. He jumped out of bed and looked at Tessa. Incredibly, she was undisturbed, snoring as if in competition with all the other snorers of Yorkshire. TAP-TAP-TAP-TAP-TAP-TAP! Jack pulled his dressing-gown about him and quickly checked the clock. It was a few minutes to midnight. What on earth...? TAP-TAP-TAP-TAP-TAP-TAP- TAP-TAP-TAP! He took up his lamp, hurried to the front door, drew back the bolts and opened it to the night.

Cool, still air greeted him; owls hooted. No-one was there. He looked along the drive at the iron gates. There was no-one; the gates were closed and lonely.

Then he heard the distant giggling, turned his head in the other direction, and saw four naked bottoms, shining in the moonlight, hurrying away as fast as they could go.

"Did you have a good night?" asked Theo, cradling his wife in their warm bed.

"It was lovely," said Sukey. "You spoke *so* well. It was a happy party."

"It was," said Theo. "Aren't we lucky?"

"We are," she replied. "You and me, together forever."

"Forever," he said, and kissed her forehead.

46. HORSFORTH CASTLE ESTATE
Saturday May 2, 1761

Sir Valentine Parker-Sinden, 3rd Earl of Horsforth – middle-aged, dark-dyed hair tied back – sat in his little shelter on the hilltop, his telescope pressed to his eye, and watched the proceedings in the meadow a little less than half a mile away. He paid his mercenaries good money to entertain him, and to keep their mouths shut about what took place on the estate.

It was a sunny day. The roof of the shelter had been lifted away so that he could enjoy the wind's cool breath. He chewed on a chicken leg while his manservant poured him a third glass of wine.

The girl had been given a twelve-minute head start – two minutes more than was usually permitted. He'd been fond of her and was keen to prolong his amusement.

Louise was nineteen and had been Valentine's favourite mistress for more than a year. He'd found her in the village of Baildon. She was a lovely creature – blonde, happy, with a pleasing figure – just an ounce or two of extra softness low on the tummy. He liked that. Her parents scratched a living as basket makers and were pleased when His Lordship offered their daughter a position at the castle.

"She'll want for nothing," he said. "My wife will soon be needing a new maid, and I'm sure that Louise will give satisfaction."

Valentine set the girl up in her own little cottage, a dwelling in which he'd housed his sweets on many occasions, some considerable distance from the castle. She was upset when she discovered what was really in store for her, but

Valentine assured her of his devotion, his love. She really didn't have any choice but to do as he ordered – especially with the perpetual double guard outside her door.

She surrendered her body to him on the first night, and he won her heart steadily as the months went by. He told her she would soon come and live in the castle – he'd grown tired of his wife (he said) and had prepared a fine wardrobe for Louise. She'd have servants, pets, anything she wanted. Louise began to smile, began to believe him, began to dream.

Valentine's toys usually kept him distracted for just a few months, so Louise's year-and-a-day (it was actually a little more than that, but he liked to think in fanciful terms) was unusual. He always tired of them after a while, became bored, wanted to move on to the next one. He became particularly irritated if the silly things became pregnant too early. He didn't want any more screeching brats than he had already, and he found the sight of naked women bloated in pregnancy entirely unappealing. To her credit, Louise had taken well over eight months to become infected with child and was only just beginning to develop outward signs.

He threw away the chicken bone and called for further nourishment. "Pay attention!" he snapped at his man.

"Apologies, sir," said servant Drew, handing his master a large piece of succulent chicken breast.

Valentine had sent men to Baildon the previous night in order to execute Louise's parents so as to avoid any sticky questions or awkward situations. The two elderly folk hadn't put up a fight. His assassins reported that Louise's mother had become a gibbering wreck as soon as her husband's throat was slit in front of her. And a quick sword thrust through the heart had seen her off, poor thing.

His men knew what their master expected. The girl went running off, usually in a blind panic, over the fields. They'd count the agreed advantage of time, then set off noisily after her. The pursuers always numbered thirteen (Valentine thought of this as a *Horsforth Dozen*). When they caught up with her, they were to use their imaginations. Anything was permitted as long as it was done within sight of Valentine's spyglass. Nothing was to be quick – the entertainment was to be vivid, unexpected and drawn out. Of course, the first half-hour or so of the show was predictable, and the victim's screams carried clearly to Valentine's hill. Sometimes the girl would call his name, begging for mercy. That always made him smile. There were occasions when the spectacle resembled the behaviour of a pack of dogs with a rabbit, but it was usually a little more subtle than that. Once they'd all sated themselves with the girl, anything was permitted – torture, fire, animals, mutilation, dismemberment – always remembering that the observer on the hill got his money's worth. There was but one stipulation: the victim must be dead before it became too dark for the master to pick out the details.

The men were all on horseback, the girl in her bare feet. Valentine stood and watched with excitement as she was cornered and surrounded. The laughter of the men, the despair of the quarry – he relished it. He saw, but could not hear, the tearing of her clothes.

He hurriedly finished his food, unbuttoned his breeches, and transferred his spyglass to his left hand...

47. THE WHITE BULL, RIBCHESTER
Monday May 18, 1761

Alexander Regan was a father. He found it hard to believe, cradling his tiny child in his arms. Helen was tired but happy, and Janet, the midwife, was clearing up the room. She'd been sent for at half past seven that morning, and the baby was delivered just after noon. It had been a good birth, she said; uncomplicated, straightforward. Alex had remained in the room, although he spent some of the tenser moments peering out of the window, pessimistically expecting complications. It was easier to leave the work to Janet and Sarah, who clearly knew what they were doing.

But Janet didn't allow him to escape entirely. "Alex! Get over here. Your wife needs you."

He'd obeyed, sat on the edge of the bed and held his sweating wife in his arms as she went through the birth, kissing her and whispering encouragement, reassuring her of his love. And soon it was done. Helen felt blessed, grateful and cherished, hearing the tiny cries of the child. She looked at Alex, tears in her eyes, and told him she loved him. Then the baby was in her arms.

They'd spent some considerable time discussing names and had eventually agreed that the choice would be Alex's if the child were a boy, Helen's if it were a girl. She chose Abigail, after her grandmother. But they now cradled their son, Francis, named after Francis Byrne, the first person who showed Alex kindness all those years ago in Bandon.

"Francis..." whispered Helen, peering at the boy's tiny face, slipping her finger into his hand.

"Our son," said Alex, eyes moist with tears. "It's impossible."

"Congratulations, both of you," said Sarah. "I'll go and let them know downstairs."

She left, and seconds later a thunderous cheer and shouts of congratulations carried up from below. It seemed most of the village had turned out to await the news.

There was a knock at the door, and John appeared with coffee. "Bet you could both do with this," he said, putting the tray down on a nearby table. "Janet, come on down and eat something. Everybody's waiting – they think you're a hero."

"Well, thank you! Actually, I don't mind if I do. I haven't eaten anything since yesterday." She looked again at Helen. "I'll be back shortly to see how you're doing. Well done again! And Alex, you did very well too – good man!"

"Thank you, Janet," he replied. "You were amazing. I'm glad it was you."

"Me too," Helen agreed.

Janet returned to the bedside and kissed Helen's cheek. "Och, you're so sweet, you two – and your little man as well. It was lovely to be here with you."

John held the door open for Janet and followed her down the stairs. There was the sound of footsteps descending, then a roar of welcome and congratulation.

Helen stroked Francis's head. "We're so lucky, Alex. Can there be anybody as blessed as we are?"

48. CLIFFS NEAR THE LOOKOUT
Sunday May 24, 1761

French had become a fascination for Kate. Not just the language but the landscape and history as well. One warm Sunday in May, after breakfast, she loaded up a basket with books on the subject, together with her vocabulary and grammar exercises, and made her way to the old lookout tower. It was too dim to read in the structure itself, so she walked round to the front of it, found a large stone that had tumbled from its height some unknown time in the past, and settled down to study.

She was about twenty feet from the edge of the cliff, the old tower at her back like a watchful parent. The gulls whirled in circles on the light breeze, and the North Sea, stretching to the horizon, whispered to her like the subdued voices of her ancestors.

She was at peace. Her eyes became unfocused, and she allowed her mind to float, felt the edges of her body dissolve and the fabric of time stretch so she could penetrate beyond the present, her spirit like a fish in the sea of eternity. She wasn't alone. Fingers of past love tugged in her chest *("Ma...grandma...").* The wind gusted briefly as if in response, tousling her hair. She was inseparable from the natural world in which she sat, her soul in the wind, in the sea, the sun. She was rising...

"Kate?"

The utterance startled her, and she looked around. It was Mabel.

"Are you alright?"

"Yes, thank you," Kate smiled. "I've just come up here to work for a while."

"You're quite close to the edge."

"I'll be fine."

Mabel continued to look at her, not sure quite what was happening. When she'd caught sight of Kate from behind, it had seemed there were three women with her, one with flaming red hair, just like Kate's. But she no longer saw them. It was the strangest sensation – as if she'd been encased in amber, time stopped, awoken only by the sound of her own voice. She squeezed her eyes shut and shook her head as if to wake herself from sleep, then looked at the child again.

"Are you alone?"

"Yes," Kate replied.

Mabel nodded, then paused, still trying to chase the strangeness away. "Alright. I'm going to my special place."

"Have a lovely day."

"You too, Kate. Watch your step up here."

"Don't worry."

Mabel held up her hand in farewell and was gone.

Kate took three books from her basket and read for just over an hour under the blue sky, aware that her bladder was calling to her with increasing urgency. When the need to pee began to cancel out her concentration, she rose from her perch, stretched, and went to find a suitable place.

A short distance to the northeast of the tower, the gorse gave way to a dense wood, the trees all blown back by the sea wind, and she chose a secluded spot in the shelter of a stunted oak tree, its trunk twisted to the rear, branches flailing like a drunken man. She squatted there and looked to the north, wondering where Mabel might have gone. It was dark in the wood, the tree canopy filtering the daylight, and the underwood was thick with growth, but there seemed to be a faint path leading away. She finished, and stood; allowed her clothing to drop into place, and began to follow the trail.

It was pleasantly cool in the leafy shade, and she walked

454

rhythmically, making patterns of French verbs in her head as if she were rehearsing a song. At the same time, she glanced about her, noting the various flora that she would be back to forage another day.

After about fifteen minutes the trees began to thin, and the light increased. A stone wall appeared, covered in lichen and herb-robert, with a crossing point and steps on either side. Kate climbed over the wall, carefully avoiding the masses of nettles that grew at its base, into an area dominated by brambles and bracken, and peppered with the purple flowers of ground ivy. The wood was much thinner beyond the wall, and there were two paths leading away; one tracking directly ahead, following the direction she'd been travelling, the other following the wall east towards the sea in a gentle upward gradient. She guessed that the path ahead would lead to the village of Peak a mile or so distant, so she followed the line of the wall instead.

The trees dropped away entirely after two or three minutes, the rising land levelled out, and the stonework ended in a heap of collapsed, moss-covered rubble, the sea visible beyond. Kate began to doubt this was the path Mabel had taken. She slowed and looked about, preparing to retrace her steps. Then she saw her, away to the left and a little lower down, standing in a natural hollow in the cliff edge. She wasn't wearing anything, her pink flesh exposed to the sun, blonde hair blowing in the wind, the palms of her hands turned to face the sea breeze. Kate took a few steps forward, keeping as silent as possible, not wanting to disturb her. But then Mabel spoke.

"Kate."

Kate paused before answering. "Yes."

"I knew you were there."

"I'm sorry. I didn't mean to disturb you. I'll go."

"It's alright," said Mabel. "Come down."

Mabel hadn't moved during their discourse but remained squarely planted on the cliff edge, eyes closed, lips gently parted, palms facing the wind as if they were drawing some power from the elements. Kate carefully climbed down the incline into the hollow and stood at her side, looking up at her face. Mabel was in communion with the world that enfolded her, in just the same way that Kate often was in such circumstances – as she had been just a little earlier that day. She was part of the wind, the sunlight, the sea, as Kate had been.

"You feel this too," said Mabel.

Kate looked out at the horizon. "I do."

"I like to feel the kiss of the breeze. Clothes get in the way. You're not embarrassed." This last was not a question, but a statement. Mabel knew that Kate understood.

"No," said Kate.

They stood quietly together, then Mabel said, "My mother taught me to do this. We lived on the eastern edge of Flamborough, just my mother and me – my father died when I was very small. We'd go up to the cliffs at the head, among the kittiwakes and gannets..."

Kate looked at Mabel's face. There were a few tears, perhaps brought about by the wind – but she thought not.

"Old Joe at the lighthouse, he got used to us. Thought we were mad, I expect."

You're like my mother, thought Kate. *You're like Nara.* It was such an intense feeling that she instinctively took the woman's hand, startling Mabel out of her trance. She knelt and took Kate into her arms, hugged her tightly.

"You're special, Kate. I feel it. There's something in you that's very precious." Mabel sniffed. Now there were a few real tears, which she wiped away.

"You're lovely, Mabel," said Kate. "You make me think of my mum."

Mabel stroked the girl's face in silence for a moment and looked deep into her eyes. "Are you busy?" she asked.

"I don't have to be," Kate replied.

"Then let's go for a swim in the lake."

49. CAPPLEMAN FARM
Friday May 29, 1761

Persephone arrived at Alder's house just after noon and instructed John, her driver, to return at two. She opened the front gate as the carriage pulled away, and walked up to the door. The image of the Green Man smiled down at her as she knocked. It always struck her as vaguely erotic in an earthy kind of way, and she reflected that it could be seen as a symbol for what Meadow's life had become. Alder was a "Green Man" – potent, powerful, ploughing life into the fields. And her girl – she *was* the field, that which is ploughed. It all slipped into place – click! – and the rightness of it struck home fully for the first time.

She'd expected her daughter to come to her senses – to wake up, realise what an idiot she'd been and come home. But it hadn't happened. Weeks had passed – months. Sigbert did not register his opinion; it didn't seem to matter to him whether Meadow was in the house or not. He simply got on with his writing, smoked his pipe, whistled his irritating happy tunes and looked forward to the next carriage-load of ripe young flesh to stretch on his bowsprit.
Meadow wasn't coming home. And the more time that passed, the more Persephone wanted reconciliation. Despite everything, she did genuinely love Meadow, and finally understood that her daughter was as free a spirit as she herself – and if she wanted to spend her days as the mate of an illiterate labourer then she must be allowed to do so.
So peace had broken out between them, although Persephone avoided Alder as far as she was able. Today (she'd been led to believe), he would be working at the other end of the

farm.

Meadow opened the door to her knock. "Mother," she said. Persephone stepped back to look at her from top to toe and congratulated herself on having created such an exquisite creature. The girl was dressed as a farmer's wife, in a simple straw-coloured cotton dress and white apron. Her soft, coal-black hair was pinned up, and she wore no cosmetics or adornments at all. *Well*, Persephone thought, *quite honestly, she doesn't need to.*

"You...look...ravishing," she said, shaking her head subtly in appreciation.

"Thank you, mother," said Meadow, stepping back and inviting her into the house. Persephone removed her cape and handed it to her daughter.

"He treats you well, that's obvious," she said. Meadow smiled in response, knowing that she didn't need to say very much.

"Would you like a dish of tea?" she offered.

"A glass of wine would be more welcome."

Meadow pursed her lips in regret and shook her head. "No wine – sorry. There is a little ale, though. Alder doesn't drink, but we keep some in the house for guests."

"Oh, dear," her mother replied. "It had better be tea then. How dreary."

Meadow invited her visitor to be seated and produced a plate of little cakes. "I do have these though..."

The older woman looked at them suspiciously. "What are they?"

"Ratafia-cakes – with a difference. Try one."

Persephone lifted one of the smaller examples in her delicate fingers and sniffed it. "Wine. Sherry?"

Meadow smiled. "*I* made them."

"*You* made them? You never took an interest in such things at home." She took a bite and savoured it for a moment, rolling it around on her tongue. "My God! You're a proper little chef, aren't you? That's bloody good!"

"Alicia Buckley teaches me. I'm almost passable now."

Meadow prepared the tea while Persephone consumed most of the contents of the plate. A second array of ratafia-cakes was brought forth, and her mother continued to graze.

"So…dear girl. What's this about?"

"I'm not getting pregnant." Meadow drew out a chair, sat opposite her mother and rested her hands on the tabletop.

"I know you're not. You told me you didn't want children."

"Yes, I know. But now I *do* – and I can't."

"You're scheming to make me a grandmother."

Meadow watched her, waiting for a considered response rather than a flippant one.

"Well, how often do you…?"

"Every day," Meadow cut in. "Several times every day."

"My God. You're nothing if not enthusiastic."

"I think the termination sterilised me."

"Are you still having your moons?"

"Regularly, on cue every month, despite everything."

"Have you seen a doctor?"

"I have. He can't see anything wrong."

Persephone thought for a moment. "How old is Alder? (I dread to ask…)"

"Fifty-eight," Meadow replied.

"My God, he's the same age as your father," she whispered.

"He's everything I want."

"Clearly, since you're actually going to marry him. This quaint procedure that we're invited to attend – it *is* a marriage, I suppose?"

"It is. It's what Alder wants – and if he wants it, I want it too."

Persephone nodded shallowly and said nothing more, although she continued to look into her daughter's eyes. She lifted another cake and popped it into her mouth.

"Are you coming?" asked Meadow.

"I'll be there," said Persephone.

"And father?"

"I don't know. Does it make any difference if he doesn't come?"

"It would be nice if you were both there, but it won't change anything if you're not."

Another nod of the head. "Try resting Alder for a few days. No sex."

"None at all?"

"None at all. Give it five days and try again. He's not young. Perhaps he just needs time to... enrich the nectar."

Steps approached on the front path, and a knock announced the arrival of Apple Robinson.

"Hello, Meadow. Tozer's working with Alder and the others today, so I thought you might be by yourself here. I've brought a carrot cake so we can binge together if you like." She held up the basket she was carrying.

Meadow invited her in and introduced the two women.

"Apple," said Persephone. "What a pretty name!"

"Thank you, Mrs Reid." She turned to Meadow. "Shall I come back another time?"

"No, no," said Meadow. "I'm sure my mother is about to become your biggest admirer. Let's get some plates out."

50. JANET ILLIF

Janet Cross was born in Whitehaven in 1704, the fourth of seven children. Her father, Simeon, was a tailor, always unwell, always had trouble with his chest. Her mother, Ava, was unhappy with her lot, often irritated with her husband and short with her children. She'd hoped for better things – more money, a bigger house, time to spend by herself or with her friends. She wanted a more comfortable life – she didn't want to be trapped in a daily cycle of toil with a houseful of screaming children and a husband who was always sick – who didn't pull his weight.

Ava and Simeon were married in 1697. Their courtship had been pleasant enough, and early married life was successful, but things had taken a turn for the worse with the arrival of the first child. Ava no longer had time for herself – and Simeon's health was worsening. A second child followed two years later, and a third two years after that. The fourth was really not wanted – and to make matters worse, the child (it was Janet) wasn't pretty like the others had been. It was wrinkled, squat-faced, with a ghastly screech of a cry. Ava, already unhappy, began to vent her discontent in anger.

But that didn't stop twins arriving in 1706, and yet another child, a boy, in 1709. Mercifully Simeon died two years after that, leaving the family relatively well off.

The years passed, the sound of crying babies faded from the house, and the children grew. But Ava still wasn't happy. She wanted her brood gone so she could begin a life of her own, whatever that might be. It would surely be easy enough to get most of them married off and away from her responsibility. Janet was the only plain one, the one that might linger.

The plan began well. John, her firstborn, went into service in St Bees and wed one of the maids there in 1719, and Anne, her eldest daughter, got married the following year. Five to go.

Martha was next on the list, eighteen years old, good-looking and surely wanted by somebody. Old Thomas Illif, undertaker, lived across the street. He was well-respected in the Cumbrian death industry, had run his business successfully for well over four decades, and was known to be worth a pretty penny. His wife had been dead for more than ten years – and Ava often caught him looking at her daughters. He'd do.

But Martha didn't want him – he was too old – and too ugly. Alright, thought Ava – what about Janet? The girl's figure was reasonable enough, although she was a bit stocky, and her face had the character of a frying pan. Ava proposed the match to old Thomas. Janet was his if he wanted her. She ought to be serviceable as long as there was no light in the bedroom. The girl was a few weeks short of seventeen, plump and juicy, just the thing for a lustful old man. Ava thought it sounded like a workable proposition, and Thomas (then aged sixty-four) knew it was the best deal he was likely to get. Janet wasn't pleased about it but did as she was told. They were married in April 1721.

Thomas was proud of his new young wife, and found the unclothed version of the girl more than satisfactory, but it was apparent from the first night of their marriage that he would be unable to perform all the functions of a husband. Janet, who'd been filled with dread at the prospect of sexual relations with Whitehaven's grand old man of the eternity box, now found herself oddly disappointed. She'd steeled herself to walk through the flames only to find that the fire had gone out. Their marriage remained unconsummated, and Thomas died next to her in bed six years later.

At least she'd inherit Thomas's estate. Wouldn't she? The truth was revealed shortly after his burial. He'd never altered his will. All his worldly goods were left to the children of his first marriage. Janet had nothing – and there was no alternative but to walk back across the street and move in with her mother.

Ava had got rid of almost all her offspring by that time – eighteen-year-old David was the last one left in the house. She didn't want Janet back, and suggested her daughter should seek work and a place of her own. She was twenty-three after all and ought to be able to make herself useful somewhere.

Janet was fed up and decided to look further afield, to escape the stifling single street that had been her life's only stage so far. She took what little money she had and travelled across the country to Grimsby, where she found work as a maid in a hotel.

It was there, one night in 1728, that she finally parted with her virginity. The said item was removed by her employer, landlord Peter Tilson, twelve years her senior, who visited her in the small hours and carried out the procedure "whether she liked it or not". Actually, she didn't totally dislike it, and went on to accommodate him until his wife found out in 1731.

His wife also found out about Peter's servicing of the other maid's: Lilly, Elizabeth, Margaret, Elsa, Sarah, Tessa and Prim. Elizabeth and Sarah both had children they'd claimed to be by a certain member of the taproom staff, "Long Ron", who Peter had dismissed as a result. But once the truth began to unravel, it didn't stop until every thread was exposed. The children were, of course, all Peter's. To make matters still more complicated, Elsa was pregnant, and Elizabeth was expecting her second child. Janet, though regularly watered, had brought forth no fruit.

All the maids had to go; so said Cecilia, Peter's wife. And Peter had to submit himself entirely to Cecilia's will. It was his last chance, she told him. He bowed his head, accepted responsibility and took his chastisement.

But Cecilia recognised that the major culprit was her husband, not the girls, and she allowed him to give them all acceptable references. As a result, Janet moved across the Humber to Kingston upon Hull, where she went into service as lady's maid in one of the great houses. There she met Milton York, valet to the master.

Janet missed the masculine attention she'd received in Grimsby. It wasn't a loss she felt every day, but now and then she was overcome with a deep physical need that she couldn't assuage by herself.

After about four months in her new employment (and feeling that she'd become good enough friends with Milton), she gathered her courage together and asked him for his services – just once, and with no further expectations. It had taken weeks of mental preparation – and nerves of steel – to ask that question. And it completely backfired. Milton was horrified, disgusted, threatened to have her thrown out. Janet was immediately apologetic, on her knees begging his forgiveness, imploring his mercy.

He'd forget her vulgar proposition, he said – on the condition that it was never repeated. She agreed and scurried away, crushed, sweaty with fright.

But the need, the ache, was still there. It was more than a year before she was able to gather courage again. She watched the two footmen, the hall boy, the boot boy, the gardeners, the groundsmen, and got to know them all, sized them up, trying to decide who might be the safest.

One afternoon in September 1733, while her mistress was away, Janet sat by the paddock, talking with eighteen-year-old Frank Smart, the stable boy. She was twenty-nine by then. It wasn't the first time they'd spoken together. In fact, they'd become quite good friends. It was a warm day – they were both alone – they found themselves chatting easily. Frank didn't find her so bad-looking. He had a girl of his own, so he knew how it went. And his girl wasn't around that day...

It must have been difficult, he said, to have been widowed so young.

She'd been unfortunate with men, she told him.

They both watched the horses for a few moments.

He asked her if she had a man now.

She told him no.

He asked her if she missed...you know...

She looked at him and said she did – sometimes very much indeed.

He looked at her, his breath quickening, and put his hand on her knee.

An hour later, when she was getting back into her clothes in the stable loft, she told him he must keep quiet about what had happened. She was honest with him – she didn't want any commitment, only his friendship – and his body once in a while. Frank was happy with that, not wanting to replace his pretty teenage lover with sad, lonely Janet – although he was delighted to have the occasional use of the latter's flesh.

The arrangement worked well for twelve years, despite Frank's marriage in 1737. Janet was content, and Frank was always pleased to see her, delighted that things could be so simple. She never conceived. Something must be wrong with her internal arrangements, she thought. But it never worried her. Her childhood hadn't been a happy one, and she didn't want to risk any offspring of her own repeating the experience.

In 1745 Frank and his young family (he had three children by then) moved away to Bridlington, where he was to have chief responsibility for a stud farm. It was a good job, with very much more money than he was earning in Hull. He was saddened to say goodbye to Janet, and she was equally sorrowful to watch him go, fearing loneliness again. But there was a new stable boy – nineteen-year-old Ryan Slater. Frank told young Ryan a little about Janet. "She may look dull," he said, "and she may be twice your age, but she's hot as an oven. And she's more than presentable once her skins are off."

Frank engineered their meeting. He told Janet that Ryan was lonely, had just lost his girl, and needed comfort. It worked like magic. Ryan stepped right into Frank's shoes. He and Janet met regularly in the stable loft, except on the rare winter occasions when he felt brave enough to infiltrate the house and find his way to her room so they could spend a long, warm night in each other's company.

But time marched on, and Janet's hair was greying, her face wrinkling. She was increasingly friendly with Milton, who'd come to believe he'd been unduly mean to her that day in 1732. He'd suffered for two decades with the guilt of mistreating her, and although he could never bring himself to apologise, he did want to see the best for her. Of course, he knew nothing about her twenty-year fraternisation with the stable boys.

Towards the end of 1754, he chanced on an advertisement in the Hull Journal, drawing attention to senior service positions in a new school fifty miles further up the coast, in Yorkshire. He admitted it was a little late in life to start thinking afresh – he was fifty-two, Janet was fifty – but he felt the need to redeem himself by suggesting to her that they might embark on a new adventure together – as friends, of course, nothing more. She agreed that he could write away for the details, although the prospect of leaving Ryan saddened her. He'd moved up in the house's hierarchy and was the master's driver by that time. Ryan was twenty-eight, had not yet married, and had become very fond of Janet. One insane night he'd actually asked her to marry him – had got down on one knee and begged her. It made her cry. She was twenty-two years his senior. For his own sake, she refused him. She was concerned that she may have held him up in life, may have prevented him from finding someone suitable, closer to his own age – and now there was an opportunity to set him loose. She took it, and went for interview at the Lookout with Milton. They moved into the school in 1755, in separate apartments on either side of the top floor.

But the old ache came back, and the same solution suggested itself. She liked Speck Beckwith. He was handsome, strong, masculine, romantic in appearance, with his weathered, windswept skin and long grey hair. She spoke to him once or twice, but he never divulged much about himself. He lived alone and kept silent about his past. She didn't know if he'd ever been married or if he had a family somewhere. She guessed him to be about forty but never found out for sure. He was quiet, sensitive, instinctive, his eyes communicative, his gaze intense, penetrating. One grey day in January 1756, she decided to ask him directly. But he saw it coming.

"Speck. I'm a middle-aged woman, unattractive and lonely. I wouldn't ask much…" (He was already shaking his head, watching her) "…Just a little affection once in a while…"

"I'm sorry, Janet. I have my own ghosts. I live my life alone. Let's be friends, but not more. I'll always listen if you want to talk."

He covered her hand with his. She looked at it, felt her eyes moisten, swallowed. "Thank you," she said, brokenly; sniffed, waited a moment, then rose and thanked him again before walking away.

As the months went on, Janet got to know all the staff – in a superficial kind of way. Milton was kind, but that was the end of it. She also appreciated the smiles and thoughtfulness of her employers, particularly Jacob. Stella was harder. Stella's smile always appeared thin and forced. She was brusque, brittle, short-tempered at times, and rarely offered any conversation. But Janet settled in and enjoyed the job for which she was employed. Her duties were light and included the role of librarian, which she loved.

A year passed, two. Her monthly bleeding ceased in 1758,

but her intermittent craving went on. Old age approached, and she had no-one. In the evenings she'd sometimes play cards with Milton. Now and then Ruth visited and they spent a few quiet hours together. Janet read a little but filled most of her time watching the fire in her room and making clothes for her nephews and nieces. Her siblings all had families; she was an aunt twenty times over and a great aunt more times than she could count, although she never saw any of the children. Her mother was still alive, now aged eighty-two, and living with David and his family. Janet was the forgotten one, the unwanted one, left out in the cold, alone, childless, failed, with superficial acquaintances but no real friends. Every day her sadness grew a little deeper.

Then, one cold night in November 1759, with hardly any conscious thought, she walked out of the Lookout, made her way to the groundsmen's dwellings and tapped lightly on John Eldenshaw's door. She'd spoken to him a few times, never at length, knew almost nothing about him.

"Janet. Are you alright? You've been crying."

Her lips quivered, and she sniffed, looked down.

He asked her in and closed the door. Then she looked at him.

Sunday, May 31, 1761. About 2am

Now, eighteen months later, she lay in his arms, content. He was asleep. She pressed her body close against him, rested her hand on his chest. He was twelve years younger than she. Only a few words ever passed between them, but he was kind to her, caring, gentle; and she believed that, in his quiet way, he loved her just a little... and "just a little" was enough.

Everyone, more or less, knew about Orla and Rider, but no-one knew for sure about John and Janet. Slade Stone once saw her leave the Lookout in the small hours of the morning; and Pixie Silden thought she saw a figure hurrying away from John's cottage, long before one winter sunrise.

But theirs was not the only spark of secret warmth in the velvet dark. Other lovers slept in each other's arms that night, unknown to anyone – or almost so:

Kipp Nibley and Lettice Shelley, illuminated in the soft flickering light of the fire, made slow, intense love in his room behind the stables, her long auburn hair spread out on his pillow the way he liked, each whispering the other's name as their moment drew closer.

In the dark of the soil boys' room, Lucas Dent and Slade Stone slept, tangled close, warm, intimate. Jude Farlam dozed on the opposite cot, facing away. He preferred girls – he'd never understand why two boys should be attracted to each other in *that* way.

In the summerhouse by the lake, Orla and Rider lay joined, heated bodies only just beginning to calm from their passion, hearts slowing from the apogee of transformation.

"I love you, Orla," he whispered.

"I know you do. You make me happy. I love you too."

The clouds parted, and the moonlight washed into the room like a silver sea.

"Orla."

"My love."

"I have something to ask you..."

51. THE LOOKOUT
Sunday May 31, 1761, 8.20am

Nana Hall was dressing for breakfast when Orla came running into the dormitory, breathless and excited. Their eyes met, and Orla dropped onto her bed, hands pressed together before her. Nana's eyes widened in expectation of some great revelation.

"He asked me to marry him!"

Nana was not surprised. "Well, I should think so!"

"We spent all night together in the summerhouse. It was so romantic!"

"How did he ask? Was he on his knees?"

Orla's blush deepened. "No...I can't tell you that. He was *very* passionate."

Nana brushed her hair. "Well, I'm very pleased for you. Does Jacob know?"

"No. Rider's going to tell him today."

"So what does this mean for our coming out in London in July?"

"Well, I just won't," said Orla. "My life is with him now. No need to be a grand lady."

"But aren't you a bit disappointed, not having the prospect of wild parties with the rest of us?"

"Not really – I have my..." (her right hand moved to her chest and she gasped quietly, vocalising the word in its new implication for the first time) "...my husband." She paused, allowing it to settle into her awareness. "And that's all I want."

"Will you make a big announcement?"

"I don't know. I don't think so. I won't tell anyone else until Rider's told Jacob."

"It'll leak. You won't be able to keep it to yourself."
"I'll try."

But by ten o'clock all the other class 7 girls knew, as did the housemistresses. Denise Nisbet could keep a secret, but the other three...

Rider Browning, as good as his word, called on Jacob at one o'clock. But Jacob already knew; he'd picked up the buzz at breakfast.
"So, Rider," smiled Jacob, his hands joined to each other at the fingertips. "I believe you have some news."
"Jacob, I've asked Orla to be my wife."
"And she's accepted?"
"She has."
"Then, seeing things have progressed so far, I'm very pleased for you. What are your plans?"
"I hope we can continue to live here," said Rider. "Perhaps Orla can busy herself with some kind of work on the estate? Or not. I'm more than happy to support her."
Jacob nodded. "Do you have a date in mind?"
"She won't be going to London now with the rest of them. I thought perhaps we'd be married in July so that Nana and the others might attend the ceremony."
"You'll have to work fast to meet that date. If you were to wait until September the arrangements would be easier – and I'd be pleased to help with those. The other girls could return from London for a few days. It would be easy to arrange. In fact, I could make *all* the arrangements for you if you wish."
"That's very kind of you," he said. "September..."
"Yes. Of course, if the short delay would upset your future wife..."
"No, no. We haven't spoken yet about a specific day. If you're sure that we could have the other girls back..."
"It would present no problem at all, I assure you."

"Then, I'm happy." Rider stood and held out his hand, which Jacob shook.

"Again, many congratulations."

The cat was out of the bag. Within an hour everybody knew.

"And what do you intend to do about *that*?" asked Stella, in suppressed fury.

Jacob replied, "I believe there is only one thing that can be done. Leave it to me. I'll set things in motion."

"In future we must forbid these relationships between the staff and the girls."

"If we were to begin enforcing such things, it would turn this foundation, this fascinating zoo of human interaction, into a mere factory. And that is not how I wish to see it run. I prefer to observe, and surgically remove problems individually as they arise. Don't worry. This will be clean and efficient."

"I do not share your scientific curiosity. If I were in charge here, things would be done differently." She was angrier than he'd ever seen her.

"But you're *not* in charge, Stella. And you will see that my orders are carried out precisely as I instruct." There was a subtle, threatening crescendo in his declaration.

She was quiet, expecting his fury to intensify; but it didn't, and he was instantly calm.

"And we will very soon need another keyboard tutor."

52. THE LOOKOUT
June 1761

Golda Dryden's Art Club gained in popularity, with numbers swelling towards the maximum that could be accommodated at a single sitting. The girls in classes 5 and 6 joined forces to request what they called a "life room", at which they might have the opportunity to study unclothed models. Golda was dumbstruck at first and thought it was too dangerous an idea, but the girls pointed out that the ancient Greeks had clearly thought it essential, and that it had been standard practice in civilised lands in the modern world since the fifteenth century. But she still refused, so the girls allowed word to leak to Mr Crowan.

"I understand your objection," he told Golda, "but for the sake of enlightenment, I would say try it."

"But surely, it's a scandalous idea!" She looked at him doubtfully. "Isn't it?"

"Hardly, since it's centuries old. In fact, I would encourage it."

"Yes, it *is* an old practice, you're right, but the students – the artists *and* the models – have almost universally been men, not impressionable young girls."

He shrugged. "I pride myself that we think ahead of our time. Is there a model?"

"No. At least, I don't think so – unless they've already got together and schemed amongst themselves."

"Well, the idea has my support, so feel free to proceed – if you wish. I'll leave it to you."

Of course, Stella was outraged, but Jacob followed the progress with interest.

Golda confronted her class. "Alright. After much thought and consultation, we've agreed to give it a go."

There was a resounding cheer.

"So who is going to be the model?"

There was a resounding silence.

Golda smiled. "Well, that settles that then..."

But it was not to be dismissed so easily.

Kate operated a busy post-dinner timetable, and in addition to her gin-drinking with fuzzy, tobacco smoking with Speck, horse riding with Nolly, and any number of other social activities, she'd added chess with Ned Silden. Ned had been teaching her to play the game since April, and she was already passably good, having lain awake at night imagining strategies. Of the three gardeners, Ned was the only one to be married, and his wife Pixie kept both he and Kate supplied with ale and biscuits during their tournaments. Ned had attended a couple of Golda's initial classes but had given up, believing he had no talent for it. One night, as the endgame approached and the rushlight neared extinction, he asked Kate how things were going.

"Very well, I think," she replied. "Zoe Scott, Midge Fenwick and a few of the others asked for nude models, but no one wanted to pose."

There was a brief pause. Then Pixie said, "I'll do it."

"You won't," Ned replied.

"It's only for the girls," Pixie insisted.

Ned said, "There are a few fellows in there as well. No."

"Well," continued Pixie, "I'm disappointed to hear you so insistent, Ned. I thought you were more free-thinking than that."

"I *am* free-thinking," he replied. "But there are limits."

Pixie was silent for a few seconds while an image formed in her imagination. "Well, what about *you*, then?"

"Me?" Ned looked up from the chessboard and almost dropped his pipe.

"Yes, you. Doesn't have to be a woman, does it, Kate?"

"No," said Kate, apprehensively, "I suppose not."

"You must be joking," said Ned, horrified.

"Good looking fellow like you," said Pixie. "You'd make a fine model, I reckon."

Ned continued to stare at his wife, eyes wide, mouth open in disbelief.

Pixie looked at Kate. "My husband would be good enough, Kate, wouldn't he?"

Kate was unsure which side to take, and wished she'd never mentioned it at all. "I suppose so..."

"I'm not doing it," said Ned. "You must be out of your mind."

So, on Saturday morning, June 13th, Ned Silden, heart beating fit to burst and much goaded by his wife, stepped up onto a low platform in front of twenty-five young ladies. The four footmen came along too, having decided to "show support" for their colleague. They sat at the rear, easels, brushes and colours ready, although not one of them intended to do any painting.

Golda had done her best to reassure Ned that this would be easy, and she now stood, arm outstretched, waiting to receive his gown. He was mortified with fright and couldn't move.

Kate stood within four feet of him, wearing a patient expression that said, *Get it over with. It's just skin*. Ned focused on that, slid out of his robe and handed it to Golda. There was an instant flutter of applause, and he gave a little bow, feeling immediately more at ease.

"Ned," said Bip, "You're a bloody hero. That deserves ten out of ten."

Golda said, "Language, Bip," and nodded her thanks to Ned. After a few minutes, he found himself wondering why he'd been so concerned about it. Being naked in front of them was not the most difficult thing about the class – the most difficult thing was to hold a pose for any length of time. His muscles tired quickly, and it was always a relief when Golda snapped, "next," leaving him to adopt a posture that relieved the tension produced by the previous one.

Kate had seen naked men before, in the river and in the millpond – Hugo of course; her father and uncles by accident on a few occasions – but she'd never had the opportunity to scrutinise one in such detail, staring, close up. She was fascinated by both the similarities and the contrasts between the male body and her own. There were the obvious differences, of course, but she was intrigued by the subtler things too. Men's hips seemed less exaggerated than women's – their waists didn't seem to narrow as much as women's waists. Ned was much hairier than she'd imagined he would be. She was particularly pleased when Golda turned him round – even his back was hairy, and his buttocks were flatter, less padded than she'd expected. There were short hairs on his legs and feet that proved very difficult to adequately represent. The parts of him that were uniquely male (*cock*, she thought. *Call a thing by its name*) were the most problematic of all. It was easy to render a crude picture of his genitalia, but she was utterly unable to capture all the detail and complexity. Kate frowned, inspected her work from the distance of a few feet and found it wholly inadequate, clumsy and ridiculous.

"This is not easy," she said, unhappy.

There was one tricky moment for Ned towards the end of the session. Two of the loveliest Class 7 girls sat close by – Nana Hall and Viv Stamper. Ned's eyes briefly met Nana's, and she blew him a kiss. Golda noticed the gesture and quietly reprimanded her, but a reaction had already set in. Viv smiled and tutted at her companion. "Bad, bad girl," she whispered.

"Death in the family, Ned?" said Bip.

Ned looked at her, puzzled. "Death? No…"

She pointed with her brush. "Flag's at half-mast."

Golda noticed and immediately handed him his robe. "I think that concludes proceedings for today, girls," she said, "and I believe Mr Silden deserves your noisy appreciation." Before she'd finished her sentence, the room was in uproar, with applause and foot-stamping. Ned felt exhilarated, and Pixie, who'd come into the room for the final ten minutes, received her husband with pride.

"Well done, love! Wasn't so bad, was it?"

"No," he said, "it wasn't." He was very pleased with himself and grinned broadly.

Nana brushed past him, caught his eye and said, "You look good."

Pixie overheard the comment. "And he's mine!"

Nana replied, "I bet you look good too, Pixie. You next time."

And indeed it was so. On Saturday morning, June 20th, Pixie posed for the class. Ned sat at the back, prepared to do his best to produce a likeness of his loved one. Tranter Tickle sat next to him, brushes ready, and Ned tried to give the impression that he didn't mind his colleague's presence. When Pixie handed her robe to Golda, Tranter leaned forward, peered closely, and said, "She's not bad, your missus."

"Well, get working then," Ned replied, irritated.

"Me, paint?" said Tranter. "I ain't paintin' – I just come for the view!"

Kate wasn't there for Pixie's debut. She had an important event to attend. She'd returned to the farm to be present at her father's marriage.

53. CAPPLEMAN FARM
Sunday June 21, 1761

Against all expectations, Sigbert Reid agreed to present his daughter in heathen marriage to the labourer Alder Swithenbank. Something about the sheer barbarity of it appealed to the Pagan in him, and the promise of a torch-lit procession, together with the sheer phallic rawness of the old traditions, fired up inspiration for his next play – which would be a tremendous success, he was sure. He could even see it as an opera. There'd be a knighthood somewhere along that road.

Sigbert and Persephone had accepted an invitation from Hugh and Amelia Flesher for drinks prior to the celebrations, so they dressed fit for the King's birthday party and set out for the farm.

The two couples had never met before despite living so close to each other. Sigbert found the Fleshers dull. Hugh was kind, effusive, seemingly without a single granule of darkness in him; Amelia was attractive enough though somewhat blank in character. They were briefly introduced to the two children, who proved rather more interesting. Louise was already known to Persephone by name; Meadow described her as her best friend. She was severe, thin, with an unfortunately mean-looking countenance, although she broke her troubled mask with a genuine enough smile. The other, Henry, was darker still; morose, uncommunicative, offered only the most insignificant of greetings. Sigbert filed away his impression of them both for dramatic use in the future.

Kate and Grace sat in the meadow in the early evening, watching the shining dragonflies hovering above the Esk.

The riverbank bloomed with the purples, blues, pinks, yellows and whites of bluebells, daisies, clover, dog rose, yarrow, hawthorn, foxglove and campion. Even at six o'clock, the air was warm, and the sun remained high, encouraging the lofty acrobatics of swallows. Half the meadow had been cut for hay, allowing space for the midsummer ceremony to take place within its confines.

Grace was sad she saw Kate so rarely, but looked forward with keen anticipation to her visits home, and remembered with fondness the limited time they spent together. "It's nice to have you back," she said.

Kate hugged her friend. "It's nice to see you. I have three weeks, so we'll have lots of time."

"We can go for walks, swim, all those things."

"Yes," said Kate. "I've got so much to tell you."

The bonfires were being lit. Richard Swift fired the big one at the top of the meadow, and they could see another in the distance, way up beyond the farm near the warren, probably enkindled by Nicholas Miller.

A waggon approached from the east – from the manor house.

"Here comes the feast," said Grace.

The cart pulled across the bridge and into the meadow, where a few tables had been set up in readiness, the ale, cordials and many other drinks already prepared. The horses drew to a halt, and most of the Swifts and Buckleys jumped out of the waggon to begin setting up the food. Soon after that, a second carriage drew into the field, carrying Hugh Flesher, Amelia and Louise, and Meadow's parents.

"It's nearly time," said Kate. "We'll see the procession in a few minutes." They stood and looked west.

Alder and Meadow watched from an upstairs window in Vine Cottage as the preparations took place in the nearby field. Shortly after half-past six, as the sky turned from pale blue to a subtly darker hue, Meadow pointed out the distant lights on the road, and a moment later the music became audible.

The carnival began with a good deal of initial carousing at the Red Lion. Torches were lit, and the revellers – many bedecked with flowers and fruit – made their way onto the farm and towards the meadow, musicians in front, dancers behind. The waggon carrying the celebrant came next; the long, flaming procession following after. A few of the bolder girls were bare-breasted, bodies painted blue and white.

There'd been much debate about who should lead the midsummer proceedings, the farm being without a wise woman. The overwhelming feeling was that the chosen person should be a *character*, an eccentric, drawn from within the community. For better or worse, the ballot had shown Natty Miller, Pond Girl's mother, as the clear favourite, and it was she who now stood upright in the approaching waggon, crying out incantations to the sun god.

"We should get ready," said Alder.

For Meadow it was easy. She wore nothing but a long, pure white cotton dress, simple and without ornament, and a pair of flat shoes. Alder put on the same clothes he'd worn for his marriage to Nara – crisp white tunic, open at the neck, dark breeches and best shoes.

Meadow sat and waited for him as the music became louder, closer. The earth beckoned her; the spirits of the fields smiled on her. Tonight she and her man would become one, never to part.

Henry Flesher, having decided to remain at home and have nothing to do with the proceedings, now felt an acute need to watch. He had to see with his own eyes the final act that would seal Meadow from him forever. He took his pipe and tobacco pouch and made his way down the shallow hill towards Vine Cottage and the meadow.

The dancing, torch-waving procession turned into the field just as Henry reached the junction with Watermill Lane. If he could have stopped the world, he would have done so.

The crowd was quiet for Natty's opening declaration, which was simple but delivered with her usual dramatic insanity, concluding with a scream that brought the field to uproar.

The feasting commenced straight away, with music for the dance striking up a few minutes later. The Fleshers and the Reids exchanged partners, as was customary, Hugh pairing with Persephone, Sigbert with Amelia. At close range, Sigbert found Amelia not so dull and wondered if her patina of plainness might just be a mask she adopted to hide from predators such as himself.

"You dance very well, Mrs Flesher."

"As do you, Mr Reid."

"How long have you been married?"

"Twenty-five years."

"You surprise me. You can't be more than thirty-seven, thirty-eight."

"You flatter me deliberately. My children are twenty-two and twenty-four. I'm forty-eight years old."

He decided that honesty might elicit a better response.

"I suppose you're happy?"

"You suppose correctly."

"Hm. I find you quite attractive."

She smiled at him and gave a laugh. "You have a lovely wife already."

"Yes, Seph is a good wife, a good companion. But we have an understanding..."

"I don't think so," Amelia cut in.

He was disappointed, but gracious enough to concede, at least for now. "Forgive me if I've offended you. I meant no harm."

"You're forgiven," she said. "And call me Amelia, please."

So, there was a small advance. "Amelia," he muttered.

Cornelius was there, lending the merriment his support as he always did. James and Willow Kirby were there too, together with Margery and Young Tozer. The two clergymen saluted each other across the throng of dancers.

Robert Forest was not present, wanting nothing to do with such ungodly proceedings. The man's continuing unwillingness to accept the local traditions was a source of great sadness for Cornelius and James, who felt themselves bound to apologise on his behalf.

But there were deeper tensions to come in the years ahead, the ongoing absence of a wise-woman creating an ever-wider rift. It was as if a garden had lost its gardener. Strong, alien vegetation would take the opportunity to invade more aggressively, while the native flora would evolve in a hostile way in order to resist the unwanted growth. Ever more damaging divisions were coming between the church and the old ways. Cornelius smelt it like the ash of an approaching moorland fire, and James was beginning to think of taking his family away.

Alder and Meadow had been hiding, taking part in the feast but not yet joining in the festivities. At eight o'clock, Apple and Buffy came to them, carrying the adornments the bridal couple would wear at their marriage. For Meadow, a garland of summer fruits: strawberries, raspberries, cherries, blackcurrants, gooseberries and elderflower, and a crown of red roses. Alder, in honour of the Green Man, was to wear a head-dress of mistletoe.

"You look lovely, Meadow," said Apple.

"And you do too, Alder," added Buffy. He reached down and kissed Buffy's cheek. Then, for good measure, he put his hands on Apple's shoulders and kissed her too.

Natty called the crowd to attention. Her extraordinary

voice had the screeching quality of a barn owl, though even louder. It shocked the throng into instant silence.

"AND NOW!" (that did it – all eyes turned to face her), "IT'S COME THE TIME FOR TWO TO WED. LET'S WELCOME THE OAK KING AND HIS CHOSEN QUEEN."

That was their cue. Alder took Meadow's hand. They walked to the top of the field, close to the blazing bonfire, and came to a halt in front of Natty. Tozer stepped up behind Alder as his witness; Sigbert, his jacket removed, stood near Meadow.

The couple faced each other, the bonfire picking out Meadow's body through her thin white dress. She looked intoxicating, elemental, the bride of the fields. The sight of her brought the crowd to complete stillness, although everyone knew why she was so dressed – and what was shortly to occur.

Natty's voice became a little quieter. "We come to fasten Alder and Meadow in union..."

Henry stood at some distance, the words of the ceremony just audible. He guessed that Meadow had written the vows. They made him feel sick. She promised to be Alder's forever, body and mind, *his* wife and *his* alone. Alder stumbled over his words but found them with a bit of prompting.

As they exchanged their tokens, Henry became aware that someone was standing behind him, to his left. It was a man, dressed warmly for the time of year and wearing a tricorn hat. Henry had never seen him before.

"Isn't she something?" said the man.

"Yes," said Henry, "she is. Are you a friend?"

"In a way."

Henry turned back and followed the proceedings for a moment or two.

"I wanted her once," said the voice behind him.

Henry suppressed a laugh. "You too."

Natty produced the cords for the knot-tying. Alder and Meadow joined hands, wrists crossed, and waited as the woman wrapped the cords over and around. She'd practised hard at home in her cottage, with Nicholas and Buffy acting as the couple while her cat Brownie tried to catch the dangling ends of the cables. It was difficult at first, but she'd persevered and mastered it.

But it didn't work now. The couple pulled apart and the knot collapsed, strands separating. There was a sigh of disappointment from the crowd.

(Henry said to his dark companion, "Ha! Let's hope that's an omen.")

Natty, clumsiness set in and confidence gone, tried again, with similar lack of success.

"Oh no..." she said. "Oh dear, I can't do it..."

She was about to try for a third time when Kate appeared at her side. "I'll tie the knot," she said. "You just say the words. Don't worry – you're doing very well."

Natty breathed out in relief and patted Kate's shoulder in thanks as the ribbons were correctly arranged and loosely tied.

Kate stood away. "Say it again, dad."

Alder looked at Meadow and said, "These hands will be your protection, always."

Meadow echoed the phrase. "These hands will be your protection forever."

The two stepped apart, holding onto the ribbons as they did so. The knot tightened and held firm as the field erupted in joyous shouts and cheers.

While the noise subsided, Natty took the cords and handed them to Kate, who melted back into the crowd.

Buffy came forward, lifted off Meadow's crown and garland, and helped to tie up her hair.

("My God," said Henry. "Here it is." There was no reply from behind him, and Henry turned to find the unknown man standing motionless, watching the ritual in tight concentration as if to burn the images into his memory.)

The sun was setting, its vast red orb melting into the hill directly behind the bonfire, painting the sky pink, a few bloody patches thrown onto the soft low clouds, like flecks from the brush of an excited artist. The lick of the breeze had increased as the darkening air cooled.

"And now," said Natty, "there's one last rite to perform..." She stepped aside. All sound ceased, except for the crackling flames.

Persephone, standing close by with Hugh and Amelia, felt the tension and said, "What's happening?"

Hugh answered, "It's for fertility. The fire – life, renewal."

"What...?" Persephone was suddenly fearful, frowning. She realised what was about to happen. "Meadow," she called out, her voice rising, "be careful..."

Alder walked to the far side of the bonfire and stood waiting for his wife. Meadow lifted her white cotton dress over her head and stood naked in the field, except for her shoes.

"Oh, my God..." Sigbert muttered.

She handed her dress to Buffy, and with no hesitation, ran forward and leapt through the bonfire. Alder caught her on the far side and held her tightly to him, lifted her off the ground, pressed his lips to hers. Meadow embraced him with all her limbs and kissed him back. The crowd's response was explosive.

Sigbert stood open-mouthed, astonished. Hugh was quietly amused. "It's just not safe to do that with your clothes on," he said.

Sigbert looked at him and said, "No...I suppose not."

Buffy stepped around the fire and waited for Meadow and Alder to separate. It took a while – they were locked together in a tight embrace, lips joined. A few encouraging laughs and shouts arose from the crowd as the seconds ticked by and the kiss went on, but eventually the two drew apart. Buffy handed Meadow her dress, and she put it on straight away.

Hugh, watching the embrace, was moved by the honesty of it, the fullness of love it expressed. He thought of Amelia, then remembered that his guest was still by his side. "You'll see lots of others do the same thing now. Wives, lovers, I expect twenty or more will leap through that fire tonight. And the other bonfires around: there..." (he pointed up to the warren, and to two others, still more remote, that had become visible in the fading light), "...there, and there... There'll be people doing more or less what we're seeing here now."

"It's astonishing!" said Sigbert. "I never imagined such things still took place. It's exultant! Transformative!" He laughed, and Hugh joined in his laughter.

Henry stood expressionless, his soul filled with ice. "Tell me how you knew her," he said. "I've never seen you before." There was no reply. He turned and found himself alone. Jacob had left.

The celebrations continued well into the night. Sigbert watched for a while and found that Hugh's prediction was accurate. There was indeed a queue of nude girls waiting to risk their lives leaping through the roaring fire into the arms of their partners. Meadow had been only the first of them.

Looking over to the north side of the meadow, he noticed that several large bundles of burning gorse were being carried across the bridge towards the farm buildings.

"What's going on there?" he asked.

"They're going to carry the gorse torches around the livestock pens. It's to protect the animals from disease and accidents."

"Extraordinary! Does it work?"

"Of course it works!" said Hugh.

Looking back at the bonfire, Sigbert saw that the column

of leaping girls had been replaced by a line of unclothed men, jumping through the flames, delicate parts exposed to the blaze.

"I have to say, Hugh," said Sigbert, indicating the young farmers, "I don't think I'll be doing that."

"Don't worry – I shan't set you an example myself. It's for regeneration. Fertility, potency, as I explained before; but also for the fertility of the crops. It ensures a good harvest."

"You're going to tell me it wards off evil spirits, aren't you?"

Hugh laughed again. "You're right! It *does* ward off evil spirits!"

Without warning, a hawk suddenly flew low across the meadow, its brown wings spread for gliding, piercing black eyes searching, the bright orange flash on its beak catching the glow of the bonfire. A few startled folk ducked to avoid it, then it was gone. Voices were raised in surprise.

Sigbert was impressed. "Was that planned?"

"No," said Hugh.

"Was it a portent?"

"I don't know," said Hugh, frowning. "It was looking for someone."

Natty searched for Kate when the ceremony was over and found her eating bread and pork with Grace.

"Hello Kate," she said, scuttling up to the two girls. "Thank you for steppin' in. I *can* do it..." she was nodding vigorously, "...but not under pressure, it seems."

"It's alright," Kate replied. "Grandma taught me how."

"Course she did," said Natty. She paused to think, then put her hand deep into one of her voluminous pockets, fished about and pulled out a handful of random objects, most of which she threw away.

"I wonder if *you'll* be wed, Kate," she said, smiling.

Kate said nothing, waiting for more.

Natty held out her hand and said, "Did your grandma tell

yer 'bout this?"

Kate inspected the object. It was a small chunk of brittle black rock. "It's a piece of coal," she said. Grace peered over and looked at it, muttering her agreement.

Natty said deliberately, "It'll tell you who your 'usband'll be."

"Ah," said Kate. "You found it under a rat-tail plantain, a broadleaf."

"I did," said Natty, surprised. "A long, long time ago. My word, your grandma taught you everythin'!"

Kate smiled and nodded.

"Put it under piller tonight," said Natty. "It'll work…"

Tozer and Apple, both drinking ale, sat opposite Alder as he cradled a flagon of fruit punch. A goblet of elderflower wine stood waiting for Meadow, who'd returned to Vine Cottage to put on a few more layers of clothing.

"You're a married man again, Alder," said Apple. "And to such a beauty. You must be dead proud of yourself."

"I'm a lucky man," said Alder. "I never, never expected to find myself here."

Tozer covered Apple's hand with his own. He looked at Alder and said, "We've all known bright blessings, and we've all known terrible loss. It makes us who we are – and offer thanks for those we've known."

Persephone appeared, carrying a glass of wine. "May I join you?"

Alder rose and greeted her. "Of course, Mrs Reid."

She sat down next to Alder and looked across the table. "Hello, Apple."

"Mrs Reid. This is my husband, Tozer."

Persephone reached over and shook Tozer's hand. "Very nice to meet you, Mr Robinson."

Tozer replied, "Please call me Tozer, Mrs Reid."

"Well, you'd better call me Persephone. No, call me Seph, like my husband – especially you, Apple. I'd better be on pet-name terms with you because I want much more of your cake."

Apple laughed. "You're very welcome."

There was silence for a moment, none of them entirely at ease with the attractive, well-dressed, bejewelled newcomer. Persephone, sensing the awkwardness, turned to Alder and said, "So, Alder. You're my son-in-law."

"It would seem so, Mrs Reid," he smiled.

Persephone nodded and glanced round the group. *Will I ever be one of you? She thought. Am I too remote? How can I fit in? How can I become who you are?*

Apple said, "You have a lovely daughter, Seph."

At least she's trying, thought Persephone. She was grateful for that.

"Thank you," said Persephone. "I know."

"She takes after you," said Apple.

Persephone was unexpectedly, deeply touched. "Does she? Do you really think so? That's such a kind thing to say. Thank you, Apple. I really appreciate that."

"And here she comes," said Tozer, rising from his seat and looking away to his left.

Alder stood and held out his arms to Meadow as she strode towards the table. "Mrs Swithenbank!" he said. She returned his embrace, her eyes meeting her mother's as she did so.

The sky had become dark, the table illuminated in the lantern-light. Meadow sat on Alder's right, Persephone on his left. Louise, who'd been waiting for Meadow's return, now came forward from where she'd been standing and sat by Apple.

Persephone said, "Meadow, that was some performance. You must have been terrified."

Meadow shook her head. "No, not really. Alder was there. Nothing could have gone wrong."

Alder put his arm round his wife's shoulders and cuddled her, rubbing his head against hers.

"But you must have practised it."

"No."

There was a further moment of silence, then Meadow asked, "Where's Buffy?"

Tozer stood and scanned the field, muttering, "Pond Girl, Pond Girl..."

Louise said, "She's down by the river, looking after the children. Your grandchildren are there." She motioned towards Apple and Tozer.

"Of course she is," said Meadow. "She's lovely with children. Wherever there are little ones to look after, there's Buffy."

Apple gazed at Meadow and said, "You'll have children of your own soon, Meadow. And you too, Alder. At your great age, when you'd expect to be settling down in the garden every day with your pipe, quiet under the sun – you'll be surrounded with a squall of young'uns."

They all laughed – even Persephone smiled. Meadow thought, *I hope you're right. I pray that I haven't finished it for good.* She directed a prayer upwards: *Please help me...*

It was one of the happiest nights Kate ever spent on the farm. The partying, dancing, and general carousing went on well into the small hours, and by the time she settled down to sleep, the glow of dawn was already seeping into the eastern sky. She put Natty's coal under her pillow and drifted towards oblivion...

...she was high up in a dim room, her back pressed to the ceiling as if she were fixed there, looking down. It was her father's bedroom. He was in bed below Kate's vantage point, Meadow beneath him, loving. Meadow whispered to him, encouraging him as his body wove with hers. Nara was there too, standing silently at the bedside, watching. There was a crowd of tiny faces at the other side of the bed, stretching out beyond the walls of the room. Kate realised they were the souls of children, waiting,

hoping. One by one they wept, breaking into silent tears, their faces dissolving to darkness.

There was something else – another voice, far away. She raised her head and found herself outside the house, beyond the roof. Someone was calling her from a great distance – a man. Kate couldn't see him, but she knew he was advancing towards her – had already come a long way, from a land across the sea. There was something wrong. He was lost, deeply unhappy. His voice called her, though they'd never met. She couldn't go to him, couldn't see him. There was a shape on a distant hilltop. It was a cross, an X. She saw an eye nearby – it was Henry Flesher's eye. Suddenly a voice, very close by, whispered, "You're mine!" She turned her head sharply to see the X close by, Henry's eye immediately closer, more threatening, on the other side. She looked down between the two visions and saw her clumsy drawing of Ned Silden's genitalia.

She was becoming frightened, trying to cry out, to wake up, but she couldn't produce more than a whimper; her throat seemed full of earth.

Someone was behind her, had taken her neck in an arm-hold. She was at the Lookout, falling down the huge stairwell. A woman's voice screamed "Xander!" and she felt her neck break.

Kate woke in a panic, sweaty, heart racing. She sat up, breathless, trying to scream.

A moment later the door opened and Alder came running in, a towel draped round him. "What is it?"

She looked at him in confusion.

"You were shouting," he said, "crying out."

Meadow appeared behind him, naked, carrying a light. "Is she alright?"

Kate was confused, panting, but gradually woke to her surroundings. She was speechless for a moment, trying to shake off the horror of the nightmare.

"You were dreaming," said Alder.

"I'll get her something to drink," said Meadow and disappeared from view.

"I'm sorry," said Kate, breathlessly, "I've never had…"

"That's alright," said Alder, "it was just a dream." He sat on her bed and rubbed her arm. "Nothing to worry about."

Kate's head was still spinning with the intensity of the experience. "I'm sorry," she repeated, blinking hard. "I'll be fine. Don't worry."

Meadow reappeared carrying a beaker of fruit cordial. "There you go, love," she said, handing it to Kate, who took it and drank straight away. She sat next to Kate at the top of her bed, by the pillow, and put her arm round her. Kate kissed her shoulder and whispered, "Thank you."

The three sat quietly for a while, Meadow hugging Kate and Alder stroking her hair and face as she finished her drink.

"That was the scariest dream I've ever had," she said.

"What happened?" asked Alder.

Kate thought she understood the early part of the dream but didn't want to tell them. It would be too upsetting. The second part she didn't understand anyway.

"I don't know. There were people far away, someone calling out. Near the end, I knew I was going to die. That's when I woke up."

Meadow pulled her close. "It was just a dream, love."

"I know," she replied. "I'll be fine now. Don't worry about me.

"Are you sure?" said Alder, standing.

"Yes. Thank you."

Kate lay down and drew the covers round her. She smiled and looked at her stepmother. "You were amazing tonight, Meadow."

Meadow kissed her. "And you were a treasure, coming straight up to help out like that."

Alder smiled, moved to see such affection between the two. "Sleep tight, Kate," he said.

"Goodnight, dad. Thank you."

When the bedroom door was closed, Kate removed the

coal from beneath her pillow, opened the window and threw it out of the house.

At eleven o'clock the next morning, Hugh and Amelia stood at the door of the manor house, waving goodbye to Sigbert and Persephone as their carriage pulled away.

"Well, that was interesting," said Hugh. "The famous Sigbert Reid."

"He invited me to his bed," Amelia replied.

Hugh laughed. "Did you give him a piece of your mind?"

Amelia raised her eyebrows. "In a way, it was quite flattering."

Hugh glanced at her over the top of his spectacles. "Seph was more subtle. Quite intelligent, I thought."

"Seph, eh? She obviously made an impression on you."

"I think they came here expecting to be the luminaries in a farmyard of country bumpkins." He removed his glasses and started to polish the lenses with his handkerchief.

"You enjoyed entertaining them, didn't you?"

"In a way." He raised his eyebrows. "I didn't dislike them."

"How shall we reply if we get an invitation to one of their... indulgences?"

He looked at her. "How would you *like* me to reply?"

Amelia was silent for a moment. "She's on your mind. I think you quite liked her."

Hugh looked along the road to the point where the carriage had disappeared from view, returned his handkerchief to his pocket and put on his glasses. "I think life is already as complicated as it needs to be." He looked back at his wife. "Anyway, you're enough for me."

The carriage stopped briefly at the corner of Watermill Lane so that Meadow's parents could offer their goodbyes.

"Alder," said Sigbert. "It was good to meet you at last."

"And you too, Mr Reid. Safe journey home."

Kate ran to the door, and Alder introduced her. "My daughter, Catherine."

"Yes," said Persephone, smiling. "We saw you last night." She ran a hand lightly over Kate's hair, and Kate prepared herself to receive the usual comment. "Look at your hair! It's on fire! I've never seen the like."

"Nice to see you, Mrs Reid," said Kate.

Meadow came forward from inside the house and addressed Kate. "You have to call her Grandma Seph." She looked at Persephone. "Isn't that right, mother?"

Persephone didn't answer, but instead fixed her daughter with a rigid smile that said, *I'll get you for that, see if I don't.*

As they mounted Beggars Bridge on the brief journey home, Persephone asked, "Well, what did you make of that?"

"I thought it was extraordinary, I have to say. It was an inspiration, in fact. To feel the intensity of it all. There were moments last night when I thought I was going to burst. And to see Meadow filled with such raw, animal energy. I've never seen her so alive... My God, Seph, but isn't she beautiful? She looked like the goddess of the sky, and when she stood like that in front of the pyre, it was as if she were tempting the sun himself..."

Persephone cut in. "Yes, well, I can see you're moved."

"Sorry," he said. "I'm being a bore."

There was silence for a few moments as the carriage approached the entrance to their drive.

"You liked her, didn't you?" said Persephone.

"I did," her husband replied. He glanced at his wife. "And him? You liked him?"

"He was kind," she said. "I wouldn't have turned him down." The carriage pulled to a halt, and they dismounted. "And Alder?" she asked.

"He's like his name. A tree. Solid, dependable, fixed...constant, reassuring."

Persephone stood still and thought, head cast down. Then

she looked up and straight into his eyes. "You know, you are a bloody good judge of character. That's it in a nutshell. You've just described *exactly* what he is. That's what she wanted, and that's exactly what she's got. No wonder she's so happy. She found her own way, no help from us."

He stood silently for a moment, smiling, then reached out and took her hand. "Come on. Let's go inside. I want to make some notes."

54. THE LOOKOUT
Wednesday June 24, 1761

Jack Archer had been expecting the carriage since noon, so when the gate bell clanged just after two o'clock, it came as no surprise to him. *"The coach will be carrying five men and a chest of funds for the school,"* Jacob had told him. Jack took a pull on his pipe, stepped through his front door, and made his way along the drive. The black coach that stood waiting was drawn by four fine-looking horses.

Jack raised his cap and spoke to the driver. "Afternoon, sir."

"We're for the school," said the driver, lifting his hand in greeting. "I believe we're expected. You must be Mr Archer."

"That I am, sir," Jack replied. He opened the gate and let them through.

The driver thanked him, and Jack briefly greeted the four men in the vehicle's interior as it passed by.

They knew where they were going, and drove straight to the coach house. Nolly heard them arrive and untethered their horses while they unloaded a large trunk from the roof of their transport and made their way to the school's main entrance.

Alfred answered the door to their ring and took an instant dislike to them. They were all in their thirties, well-dressed in similar uniform, with frock coats and uncocked hats despite the warmth of the day. All fixed Alfred with an unsmiling similarity of expression. The foremost addressed him by name.

"Major Bentley?"

"It is. I believe you're expected."

"Thank you. We are." He stepped forward into the building, Alfred retreating and simultaneously opening the door. The other four entered, carrying the trunk between them, one corner handle to each man. They headed directly for the stairs with no further word. Alfred thought they were a surly bunch, chilly and aloof. The group soon passed out of sight, although he could hear them labouring away with their load all the way to the top of the house.

Stella patrolled the west wing corridor on the first floor, waiting for Harriet Dixon's harpsichord lesson to end. It would be her last for a while, so it seemed right to allow it to run its course. Stella's heart beat fast with a strange mixture of emotions. She wasn't sure which was the uppermost sensation: fear, guilt, horror, or the pleasure of being able to inflict such cruelty – on both Rider and Orla. She was to be instrumental in bringing about the suffering of others, and that went some way towards filling the empty space where her soul might once have been.

At a quarter past three, the door clicked open and pretty, auburn-haired Harriet appeared. Stella took the door handle and smiled at her as she departed, music clutched under her arm. She looked into the room and found Rider slipping into his jacket.

"Rider. Mr Crowan wants a word, if it's no trouble."

He was surprised to see her but answered straight away. "Of course. In his room?"

"In his room," she confirmed.

"I'll go straight up."

He passed two of the class 4 girls on the stairs – pale, delicate Ali Bromfield and Flora Ogilvie, already startlingly beautiful at the age of just thirteen.

"Hello girls," he said as he passed.

They returned his greeting in unison: "Good afternoon, Mr Browning."

Within two minutes he was knocking at the door of Jacob's suite. It was opened by Quinton, who greeted him and ushered him inside, closing the door. "Please go straight in," he said. Rider walked through the sitting room to Crowan's study door and opened it. Jacob was sitting behind his desk, his hands joined at the fingertips at the level of his chin. He looked directly at Rider and offered a warm smile. "Rider. Thank you for coming."

Rider walked forward into the room and only then noticed the five hatted men standing to his rear. They looked piercingly at him, and he was instantly afraid.

"Take a seat." Jacob motioned. "This won't take much of your time."

Rider remained standing, wide-eyed, looking at the men. He wanted to run. Two of them came forward, each taking one of his arms, and pinned him into the seat opposite Jacob, who continued to present his calm, friendly smile. Then Knox came up behind Rider's chair, took his head into the well-rehearsed arm-lock, pressed it down and wrenched it violently to one side, expertly breaking his neck. There was the usual sensation of popping, crunching cartilage, and Quinton's mouth dropped open in pleasure. He remained in position for a few seconds, Rider's head held loosely in his arms; then he sighed, as one might in the moment following the climax of a satisfying sexual union, released his victim and stepped aside. The two men who'd secured the unfortunate man's arms now let go, and he fell forward, head banging hard on Jacob's desk before his body slid to the floor.

Jacob stood. "Efficiently done, gentlemen. And thank you, Quinton – expert as always. Now let's get him boxed up and out of the house." He looked at one of the men and said, "Thomas, we'll move to phase two. You should be in position in twenty minutes." Thomas nodded and checked his pocket watch. He would expect to intercept the target at twenty minutes to four. Crowan went on. "Quinton, you'll accompany Thomas and see that he's undisturbed and has privacy to make his preparations."

Thomas and Quinton left the room while the remaining four men folded Rider's body into the trunk. Jacob held open the door as they carried their burden out of his suite, then followed them downstairs as far as the first floor, where he met briefly with Stella while the men continued down.

"All is going according to plan. You can send Orla to meet me in ten minutes."

"He's dead?"

"That was the plan. The plan is proceeding according to our arrangements."

Orla would be finishing her harp lesson at half past three. Stella made her way to the room Clara used for teaching, and stood watching in the corridor like a cat waiting for the mouse to appear.

"Hello, Mrs Tenley," said Orla, closing the door. "How are you?"

"Very well, thank you, dear," she said, and offered her grimacing teeth in substitution for a smile. "Jacob is hoping for a quick word with you downstairs. He's just seeing a guest out of the building. It won't take more than a minute or two."

Orla was a little puzzled, then thought it might have something to do with her wedding arrangements. She smiled and went on her way.

Jacob, meanwhile, had sent Alfred off on a pointless errand to the brewhouse to order a firkin of special ale for Doctor Wayland's birthday. Alfred thought the task beneath him but was pleased to get the opportunity for a walk in the sun, smoking his pipe.

The hall was clear – there was not a soul in sight.

At just after twenty-five minutes to four Orla came tripping happily down the stairs. Jacob waited for her, smiling as she approached. He mounted the staircase to the fifth step and met her there, holding out his hand which, innocently, she took.

"Thank you for coming, Orla," he said. "This will be brief."
The fifth step provided a good view of the first portrait on
the staircase. It showed a slightly rotund, bearded gentleman in his early fifties, standing in what was perhaps the
drawing room of a great house. He was finely dressed in a
red justacorps with gold braiding, dark stockings, extravagantly frilled cuffs and ruff, and a long brown wig filled
with curls. He supported himself on a thin cane held in his
right hand.
"Do you know who this gentleman is?" asked Jacob.
"I think so," Orla replied. "Isn't he the Earl of Horsforth?"
"Very good," said Jacob. "He is Sir Valentine Parker-Sinden,
3rd Earl of Horsforth."
"One of the school's patrons," said Orla.
"One of the school's patrons," repeated Jacob, "…as you say.
And many of these men…" (he indicated the portraits with
a sweep of his arm) "…in fact all that you can see from here,
support the school with their fortunes. Their contribution
pays for your education, the maintenance of the buildings,
the wages of all the staff. It is a huge commitment."
Orla was growing uneasy.
"A huge commitment…" Jacob paused and looked at her,
smiling. "…for which they expect the pleasure…the pleasure…" (he emphasised the phrase with a nod of his head,
then paused) "…of a return."
She was frightened, her brows knit, staring at him. Her
heart was beating fast. Something was wrong – she felt
panic rising.
Jacob smiled. "There's someone I'd like you to meet. Come
with me." He stepped down the stairs and she followed
him, breathing quickly, afraid. He led her into the west
wing towards the kitchens. Quinton was there in the passage, waiting.
"What's happening?" she said. She couldn't control her lips
and found it difficult to form the words. Then she saw another man, waiting in the doorframe of the dining hall. He

was holding an object in his right hand – a cloth, a thick piece of material. Something was dripping from it. He stepped out and looked at her, holding the fabric at waist height. Jacob came forward and stood very close, gazing into her eyes, enjoying her terror. Her mouth was open – she was panting in fright. Then he was touching her, stroking her with tenderness – her face, her arm, her lips. She wanted to scream but couldn't find the breath.

"We'll miss you," said Jacob. "I'll miss you."

The unknown man was suddenly behind her, left arm around her body, right hand pressing the cloth to her face. There was an overwhelming smell. She found her strength, struggled hard, tried to break his grip, drew in her breath to scream – but the cloth was there, covering her nose and mouth, and she was breathing the wet substance in. She became dizzy, and her strength dissolved, her legs liquified. She was falling...

Quinton took Orla's lower body, hooking his arms behind her knees, while Thomas supported the bulk of her weight, her head resting against his chest. Jacob opened the door that led into the yellow passageway, enabling them to carry the drugged girl inside, then ran ahead to unlock the entrance to the cellar.

Without warning, Lucas Dent emerged from the soil-boys' room and saw Thomas and Quinton manoeuvring the unconscious Orla onto the stairs that led beneath the house. Jacob assessed the situation quickly as the three passed out of sight. He put his hand in his pocket and drew out five guineas, more money than the boy had ever seen in his life. "Listen to me," he said. "There's someone after Orla. We have to hide her. Will you help us? This is yours if you do." Lucas was too surprised to answer. "It'll only take a moment."

The boy nodded, and preceded Jacob down into the cellar. Thomas and Quinton stood at the bottom of the steps, Orla suspended between them. Quinton had prepared a few lamps earlier, so their passage was adequately lit.

"This is Lucas," said Jacob. "He's agreed to help."

The other men nodded their understanding and proceeded on their way, following the maze of rooms and passage-ways.

Lucas had never been in the cellar before. He was over-whelmed by the size and complexity of it and found the darkness frightening. After a minute or so of low ceilings, tight corners and stunted corridors, they came to a long straight passageway that sloped downwards and led to a single door. Mr Crowan opened the door, and the bottom of a flight of stone steps was revealed. The passage in which they stood was suddenly filled with a deep, shocking cold-ness as if a crawling, living thing had escaped from the staircase and invaded the cellar. Lucas clutched his arms about him.

The conical ice-well was thirty feet deep, entirely sunken into the earth and capped with a domed brick ceiling ris-ing twenty feet above the well's rim. Only ten feet of the building's exterior was visible above ground – and that was hidden beneath undergrowth and huddled against the south wall of the dower house grounds, maximising insu-lation. The well itself was packed with ice cut from the lake in winter and insulated with layers of wood and straw. The building could be accessed from the outside or from the passage that ran beneath the drive from the cellar of the Lookout. A circular flight of stairs followed the well shaft from the ice chamber above to the level of the subter-ranean passage in which they stood.

Quinton and Thomas carried Orla up the stairs past boxes of foodstuffs set in niches in the walls, their footsteps echoing in a strange, tight flutter.

Jacob looked at Lucas. "Up you go," he said.

The boy did as he was told and followed Thomas and Quin-ton up the stairs, banging his arms against his sides in re-action to the fierce chill. There was very little light on the

502

stairs, the only illumination being from a lamp at the bottom and another at the top. He was scared. Something was wrong. He wished Slade was here.

Forty-eight steps brought them to the ice chamber, where the mouth of the well, covered with insulating frames made of wood and packed with straw, gaped to a width of sixteen feet. Their subdued voices, and the tapping of their feet, produced a sustained echo in the high, domed space. Lucas looked around himself in amazement. It was like being underwater.

Jacob emerged last from the staircase and told Quinton and Thomas to move on. A second flight of steps, much shorter than the first, led up to the little corridor that gave access to the outside world. Quinton unlocked the door and swung it outwards.

"Luke," said Jacob. "Run and tell us if the carriage is there." Lucas nodded and did as he was told, relieved to find he had a function, and glad to be out of the dark. Seconds later he returned and said that yes, there was a carriage present. Jacob motioned Thomas and Knox to go ahead and carry Orla out into the daylight. They emerged from the gloom and stood in the open air, concealed from view by the body of the carriage. The other men came forward, took the girl, and lifted her into the coach.

"Thank you, Luke," said Jacob, at the same time signalling to Thomas that he would like the use of his sword. Thomas handed the weapon over, and Jacob again turned to the boy. "Now, let me pay you." He motioned to the dense undergrowth beyond the icehouse and gently pressed Lucas ahead of him and out of sight of the others. The men waited in silence for a moment; then Jacob re-emerged from the foliage, wiping the blood from Thomas's blade before handing back the weapon.

"That was unfortunate," he said. "Quinton, please remove the body after nightfall if you'd be so kind, and find a suitable place to bury it."

Knox indicated his understanding with a brief inclination of the head.

Jacob glanced up at the coach, the trunk containing Rider's body fixed in place, the driver already in his seat. "Thank you, gentlemen. We're done here. Have a good journey."

Thomas and the others joined the comatose girl in the carriage, and the vehicle pulled away.

Crowan followed it with his eyes until it vanished round the bend in the drive, then said to Quinton, "It could have been smoother, but overall not too bad. I'll need to expand the cover story to account for the disappearance of Luke." He gave a half sigh. "That was a pity – he was a good lad."

Quinton looked at him but said nothing.

Alfred Bentley appeared from beyond the far side of the house on his return journey from the brewery. Knox and Jacob walked towards him, rounding the corner of the west wing, raising their hands in greeting as they converged at the main entrance.

It was a sunny afternoon, warm, with lots of birdsong; a bright, calm summer day.

55. IN THE COACH
Wednesday to Friday, June 24 to 26, 1761

The girl lay unconscious as they made their way south. They'd been instructed to travel as fast as possible without drawing attention to themselves, the journey to London expected to take no more than two and a half days. They were to see that the woman was adequately looked after, reassured as far as possible, and delivered safely. They were not to divulge anything to her about her destination, her future, or her lover. They were to dispose of the man's body at some convenient secluded spot. The horses would need to be changed fifteen times along the route, and locations had been identified and paid for in advance. Fresh food and drink would be provided at the same points. They were not to use coaching inns. They were not to pause in their journey more than necessary. Everything had been worked out and taken care of.

The carriage itself was of the most modern design with steel spring suspension, able to travel comfortably at eight miles an hour. The driver's footboard seat had been modified to accommodate armed guards on either side whenever it was deemed necessary, and there was a raised seat at the rear, enabling another guard to see over the carriage roof.

The girl occupied the entire forward-facing seat inside the carriage. Thomas, Harry and William sat opposite her, while Marcus took the guard's place in the external rear seat. Saul drove. They carried ten pistols between them, all loaded, and there were other weapons ready in the case on the roof. The merchandise they were carrying was of the highest value, and they were being paid well to guard it with their lives.

Harry and Will managed to get to sleep shortly after the coach pulled away from the Lookout, leaving Thomas to watch over the woman. He could hear Saul, up on the box, entertaining himself with a few songs. It was a sunny afternoon and the road, though rutted, could have been worse. Progress was easy. As they approached Scarborough, Thomas drew the window blinds to avoid the possibility of anyone spying in from outside. He began to get hungry.

They were soon on the road out of town, and the air began to chill. He stood, reached up to the rack above the opposite seat, pulled out one of the blankets and draped it over the girl. She lay quite still, breathing easily as far as he could tell. Thomas had no idea what was in the mixture he'd held over her face, although he'd used it before. It smelled foul, overwhelming. The girl would experience a strong physical reaction when she woke up – as if she'd drunk two bottles of gin on an empty stomach. He'd seen it before on many occasions. It was not pretty, but he knew what to expect, knew what to do.

Shortly after half past six they pulled into a farm on an estate near Yedingham and drew to a halt in front of the farmhouse. Thomas opened the door, stepped down and waited. Two middle-aged men and a younger woman emerged from the building and walked towards the carriage. One of the men was well dressed – probably had money invested in the girl; the other man, rougher, was clearly a servant. The woman carried a basket of food and drink which she handed to Thomas while the lackey began to unharness the horses. Thomas leaned into the interior and deposited the basket on the seat.

Marcus and Saul jumped down from their respective positions, and Saul asked directions to the jakes. The well-dressed man strode passed Thomas, climbed up onto the step of the coach and waved Harry and Will out of the carriage so he could get in and inspect the sleeping girl. From where he stood, Thomas could see him lifting her skirts, looking at her legs, running his hands over them. He emerged from the interior and said, "She's a pretty one. Worth the effort." Thomas said nothing in reply. Silence was the way they worked, as few words as possible.

It took just two or three minutes to tether the fresh horses, and the men exchanged positions while the process took place, Will climbing up to drive and Harry taking the rear-guard seat. Marcus and Saul returned from the jakes, Saul scratching and adjusting his crotch as he approached the vehicle. They both climbed inside while Thomas thanked the three nameless people. A moment later they were on the road again.

The next section of the journey passed without incident, although the sky darkened and the temperature dropped. The girl lay motionless. The five men ate and drank as they travelled, drawing to a halt briefly at one point for the usual reason.

At twenty minutes past nine they arrived at a great house on an estate near Stamford Bridge. Fresh horses were ready for them, and they were on their way with barely a pause. Marcus took the reins, Harry on guard at his side, Saul in the rear seat, pistols ready. The possibility of attack from highwaymen increased after dark.

Thomas continued to watch over the girl, counting the hours, expecting her to wake at any moment, ready to hammer for the coach to stop so he could get her outside in the few seconds he'd have. But for the time being she continued her peaceful slumber. Will dozed in the opposite corner, snoring lightly.

Saul, watching in the rear-guard, continued his irritating singing. Thomas tolerated it for a few minutes, then stuck his head out of the window and told him to shut up.

"Sorry, Tom. No offence, mate. Di'n't know I was doin' it."

It was peaceful at last, except for the clatter and rumble of the wheels and the rippling purr of Will's oblivion.

The woman began to stir shortly after eleven. Thomas stopped the coach, opened the door and stepped down into the road. It was a clear night, the moon in its last quarter, the fields lit in the soft silver light. He looked around searching for water – a stream, a brook, a lake; an animal trough would be better than nothing. The sound of a river pricked the stillness close by, up ahead in the crook of the road's right turn. *It's the Ouse,* he thought. *That's a bit of luck.* He made his way back and looked through the open door. Will had the girl's change of clothes ready, folded on the seat next to him.

She was moving, groaning. He removed the blanket that covered her, and waited. A few seconds later she opened her eyes, lifted her head slightly and looked about in confusion. Thomas had the door open ready, but there was still not enough time. She sat up, clutched at her mouth and vomited violently, spraying Thomas, the floor of the carriage and the seat opposite.

"Ach, God!" said Thomas in disgust, flinging the acrid mess from his hands. "Let's get you out quick." He took hold of her and pulled her forward, through the door and down to the ground. She tried to find her feet, swayed in the moonlight, then dropped to all fours and vomited again – and the rest. She tried to catch her breath, supporting herself as best she could in the stinking pool of fluids and sludge, retching drily, her clothes soiled, ruined. After a few moments she collapsed and lay in the dirt, wretched and filthy.

Thomas always felt sorry for them – it must be dreadful, waking up so sick in an unknown place surrounded by strange faces. He knelt down and put his hand on her back. She felt warm, hot, the clamminess sweating through her clothes.

"It'll pass in a moment," he said. He stood up and addressed Saul. "You got some water up there? I need to clean this off." Saul searched in the basket and found a flask. He stepped down from his perch, uncorked it and motioned for Thomas to present his hands for washing. Once that was accomplished, Thomas took the flask and cleaned his clothes as best he could. Then he looked down at the girl. "Can you stand?" There was no reply, so he prodded her with his foot. She lifted herself to a kneeling position, then reached over to the carriage step and pulled herself upright. "Well done," said Thomas. "Hold out your hands." She did so, and he poured water over them. "We're going for a very short walk. Can you manage?" She nodded weakly. He looked into the carriage and spoke to Will. "I'll need my change of clothes too." He looked down at himself. "These things are done for." Will had anticipated this and passed a sack of fresh clothes through the door to Thomas.

Thomas held out his hand to the girl and she took it. She was very weak and slow. He had to lift her over the wall so they could get down to the water's edge, getting more of her filth onto his clothes in the process.

"Your things are ruined," he said. "Take them off and clean yourself in the river. I have fresh clothes for you here."

She looked at him, unsure, lips trembling in fear.

"Don't worry," he said. "No-one's going to hurt you. You're completely safe. We're here to look after you."

She paused a moment longer, then quickly removed all her clothes and stepped into the river, supporting herself on undergrowth and rocks so she wouldn't slip. While she busied herself, Thomas took off his own soiled garments, washed himself, and donned the fresh ones. When he was done, he stood on the bank, arms folded, waiting for her. She was splashing water onto her face and rinsing her hair, taking more time than he was comfortable with.

"We need to go. We can't spend long here."

She became still, and was silent for a moment. Then she

rose, stepped out of the water and stood before him, covering herself with her hands and arms, shivering with chill and exhaustion.

She looked vulnerable, defenceless.

He could...if he wanted... She was probably expecting it after everything else that had happened to her. He felt his body respond to her nakedness, ran his tongue around his teeth. He could almost taste her.

"Hands," he said quietly, motioning that she should drop them, which she did. He looked at her for a few moments, her wet skin glowing in the moonlight, then said, "Turn round." She obeyed. He understood why she was so precious to them and wondered what she was worth, what she'd make. Hundreds of pounds probably – thousands before too long. One night with her would cost more than he earned in a year. He was suddenly aware that he was grinding his teeth, breathing hard.

"Put these on," he said.

She turned back to face him, took the clothes he offered and dressed herself in them immediately, relieved to be covered. Thomas collected all the soiled garments – his and hers – and put them in the sack. They'd need to be disposed of, buried somewhere.

"Your shoes are ruined, I'm afraid. You'll have to do without until we get you home safe and dry."

"Where are you taking me?"

"I can't tell you that."

"Where's Rider?"

He paused. "I don't know anyone of that name."

"My husband."

He shook his head. "Sorry, I can't help you."

"Where am I?"

"You're on a journey."

She looked around desperately.

He shook his head, discouraging her. "Don't run. If you run, I'll have to shoot you." She looked at him, lips quivering in despair. Thomas held out his hand. "Come on. The coach should be cleaned up by now."

She paused a moment longer, then took his hand and allowed herself to be led back to the carriage.

Will and Saul were still scrubbing out the mess but took only a few more minutes to complete the task. Thomas and the girl stood close by and waited.

"You're frightened," he said.

She didn't reply, eyes cast down, lips trembling.

"You'll be fine," he went on. "No harm will come to you."

"I want my husband," she said, very quietly.

He said nothing for a while – then, "What's your name?" She didn't reply. "I'm Thomas." Still she was silent. He said, "You don't have to tell me."

"Orla," she said.

He nodded. "Orla. That's a nice name. I don't think I know anyone else with that name."

"We're ready," said Will from within the carriage.

Thomas helped Orla up into the coach, then clambered in behind her and shut the door.

The coach arrived at Brayton at twenty minutes to one in the morning, forty minutes late. The man who met them – bald, hatless, in his middle forties – raised his hand in greeting but expressed irritation at their delay as he changed the horses. His younger female companion stood silently, her face impassive, lantern raised, trying to see through the open carriage window. Orla leaned close to the opening and met her gaze. "Help me," she said. The woman didn't answer but stepped back, shaking her head, fear visible on her face.

"Don't do that," said Thomas quietly. He leaned over and pulled Orla away, then drew up the glass and fixed the blind in place. He opened the door, stepped out of the coach and collected the basket of food that lay on the ground near the woman's feet. She moved further away, frightened.

It was Harry's turn to drive, and Will's turn to take rear-guard. There was some disagreement about who should be upfront next to the driver. The rotation on which they'd agreed suggested that it was Thomas's turn, but he didn't want to give up guarding the girl – not yet.

"Marcus, you sit up front for now. Saul, you're inside with me. I'll ride on top at the next change." They arranged themselves as instructed, and the carriage pulled away.

The unknown woman, her heart full of sorrow for the poor captive child, followed the coach with her eyes as it left.

They needed to get the body buried before dawn, so the three men on top began to search for a suitable place to pull in. There was a track leading into woodland on the road south of Eggborough. Marcus saw it first, and Harry stopped the coach at the side of the road. Saul opened the door, stepped out, and joined the others as they hauled the trunk off the rack.

Orla looked at Thomas. "What are they doing?"

"Nothing for you to worry about," he replied.

It was very dark in the carriage, the lantern turned down low, and she was acutely aware of the scraping sounds above.

"They're taking something off the roof," she said.

"Try to get some sleep," said Thomas. "We'll be here for a while."

The four men gathered shovels and lights, took up their burden and carried it away into the wood. Orla glimpsed them through the shaded window as they passed out of sight. They were carrying something between them – a large box. She began to sob.

"Did you kill him?"

Thomas sat quietly for a moment. "I can't tell you any-thing."

Orla was instantly out of control. She rose to her feet and

attacked him, screaming, "TELL ME, YOU BASTARD! TELL ME!"

He rose to meet her assault, slapped her hard with the back of his hand – and again. "Sit down!" She collapsed, her hands pressed to her stinging face, gasping, sobbing.

Thomas took his seat once more, hating himself for having struck her. "I have a job to do," he said. "It's not a job I enjoy, but I have to get it done. I'm under orders. I'm not at liberty to tell you anything. I'm sorry. I wish it were otherwise."

She leaned away from him in her seat, quietening.

"I'm sorry I hit you. Please don't make me do it again. I'll have to gag you and tie your hands if you make trouble. I don't want to do that. I know you're worried. I can hardly imagine how frightened you must be, but no-one wants to hurt you."

"Tell me where you're taking me."

"I'm sorry. I can't."

"Did you kill him?"

"None of us killed anyone."

She paused a moment. "Is he dead?"

Thomas said nothing. He couldn't bring himself to lie to her, but was equally unable to offer reassurance.

Orla began to cry bitterly – long, drawn-out keening, and her tears almost broke Thomas's heart. "He's dead," she sobbed.

There was nothing to be done. He couldn't touch her, couldn't offer her comfort. He searched for something to say, but everything felt hollow, empty. She cried for nearly half an hour. Sometimes she'd almost stop, catching her breath, but the next moment would start afresh – deep, despairing, drawn-out wails fragmenting into sniffs and sobs, a repeating pattern. He was glad for the darkness in the vehicle, aware that she might have seen the emotion in his face if there'd been more light. He wanted this to be over.

Dawn was breaking by the time the others returned to the

coach, their task complete. They fixed the empty trunk back into position on the roof and added Rider's clothes to the sack containing those previously discarded by Thomas and Orla. Thomas raised the window shades and looked at the young woman in the early light. She was motionless, head resting on her chest, eyes closed, sleeping, exhausted by her grief.

Poor, sad, sad girl.

The sky brightened as they proceeded south, the carriage rocking and bumping in the rutted track. They'd expected to run into trouble at some point, and it arrived soon after four o'clock.

Orla was still sleeping, Thomas watching her, when Marcus rapped twice in quick succession on the roof – the signal for danger. The alert was delivered loudly enough to wake the girl, and she jerked up her head, catching Thomas's gaze. A couple of seconds later, Marcus knocked again – once, twice – indicating the likely number of targets. Thomas felt a surge of excitement, exchanged a glance with Saul, and drew one of his pistols. He raised a finger and stared at Orla, indicating that she must stay quiet.

The carriage slowed, and they heard the command, "Stop, or we'll fire."

Without further warning, there was a rapid exchange of six shots. The vehicle lurched, the horses alarmed at the snap of gunfire, but Harry regained control almost immediately. In the silence that followed, a horse and rider passed by the right side of the coach, and a moment later, Will appeared at the window, gesturing for the use of a weapon. Thomas handed over his own gun, and Will disappeared, walking back along the road, the crunch of his footsteps mingling with the calm of the dawn, the singing of the birds. A single shot rang out. Thomas got to his feet, opened the door and stepped out of the carriage, instructing Saul to watch Orla. Will was walking back towards the coach, Thomas's pistol in his hand. A dead man lay in the road behind him, another just ahead of the vehicle. The robbers' horses stood idly by, evidently used to the sound of shots.

"Hit them both first time," said Will, "but that one tried to run." He pointed along the road to the man he'd just killed. "Couldn't stay on his horse though. Bastard. Right between the eyes." He brandished Thomas's pistol and handed it back to him.

Harry called from the box. "Marcus is hit."

Thomas and Will hurried to the front of the carriage. "Badly?" asked Thomas. "Marcus?"

Marcus opened his cape, and they saw that his waistcoat was covered with blood.

"Shit!" said Thomas. "Is it as bad as it looks?"

"I don't know," Marcus replied. "Probably."

"Alright. We have to move as fast as we can. Can you get down and into the coach?"

Marcus managed it with difficulty, the wound causing him to cry out with pain. Orla watched as Saul helped the injured man into the interior, settling him in the corner diagonally opposite her. He was dripping blood, gasping with agony, clutching at his abdomen.

"What happened?" she asked, eyes wide.

"Highwaymen," Thomas replied from where he stood in the road. "They're dead."

Harry and Will waited for instructions while Saul tried to make Marcus as comfortable as possible.

"We can't stop here," said Thomas. "We have to keep going."

"What about the bodies?" asked Will.

"Leave them," Thomas replied. "We have to get moving. Will – you're fore-guard; Harry – you're at the rear." The two men assumed their positions, and Thomas leaned into the coach. "Saul – you're driving. Away – up you go." He

515

stepped aside, giving his man room to exit, then looked again into the interior. "Marcus – can you hear me?" The man turned his ashen, sweaty countenance towards his captain, and Thomas went on. "Adwick is an hour ahead. Can you hold on till then?" Marcus closed his eyes and nodded weakly. Thomas called up to Saul, "Let's go," then got into the vehicle as it pulled away, resuming his seat opposite Orla.

"Is it bad?" she asked.

Thomas was glaring out of the window, furious at the situation, and angry with himself for having allowed it to happen. If they'd followed the planned rotation, it would have been him sitting in the corner with a chestful of lead. He ignored Orla's question and muttered instead, "We can't stay here. We have to keep going – get off the road." He looked at her. "How are you?"

She stared back and didn't answer him.

"Sorry," he mumbled. "That was stupid."

The day was already bright when they drew to a halt in front of a large and impressive country house close to the village of Adwick le Street. Thomas rang the bell, and the front door was opened by a servant, his master, dressed in a green linen morning gown, following behind.

"We expected you some time ago," said Sir Arthur Holywell.

"I'm sorry," Thomas replied. "We had a small task to perform – and we ran into trouble. I have a wounded companion. Can we get him inside?"

"Of course," said Sir Arthur, hurrying down the steps and into the drive. "Was it an accident, or was it blackguards?"

"Two highwaymen..."

"Bastards!" interjected Sir Arthur as they arrived at the side of the coach.

"We took care of them, but one of my men is hit," concluded Thomas.

516

Sir Arthur put his head inside the carriage, his attention immediately arrested by Orla, who sat quietly in a cocoon of anxiety. "Hello," he said, then awoke to the task and looked at Marcus, waxen and bloody. He withdrew from the vehicle and spoke to Thomas, shaking his head. "Looks bad. Let's get him inside." He called to his servant, "Fox, prepare a place in the hall."

Saul and Will helped Marcus out of the carriage and walked him to the house, Harry following behind. It was a struggle, Marcus unable to support himself. Thomas followed with Orla. She had no shoes, and the drive was scattered with sharp stones. "Sorry," he said. "You must be uncomfortable walking on this. I'll carry you if you like."

"No," she replied, shaking her head, revolted at the thought of having him touch her.

The hall carpet felt good after the discomfort of the drive. Orla looked around. The grandeur of the room reminded her of the Lookout, although this was smaller. There were fine paintings, expensive wood panelling. The space was lined with lots of small, upholstered armchairs as if for a meeting.

Thomas spoke to her. "Please sit down and wait over there." He indicated a place where she'd be in his line of sight while he helped with Marcus. "I'm sorry you have to see this."

They'd laid the injured man on a couch near the entrance, weak, confused, panting, slick with sweat. His eyes appeared unfocused, and he was deathly pale. Will opened his shirt.

"Damn it!" he said. "There are two wounds, not one. God knows how much blood he's lost."

Sir Arthur addressed his servant. "Fox, take a horse and ride to the village for the doctor. Quick as you can." The man left, and Sir Arthur looked at Thomas. "You'd better think of a story fast."

Just then a woman came briskly down the stairs. She was

about sixty years old, grey-haired and wore a banyan of similar hue to her husband's morning gown. She saw them all kneeling around the bloodied man and cried, "What on earth…?"

"He's been shot," said her husband. "Fox has gone for the doctor. There's nothing you can do, Dora. Go back to bed."

Dora's eyes alit on Orla, sitting quietly by herself. The scene was confusing, and Dora was not able to piece together quite what was going on. She descended the remaining steps, walked to the young woman and settled in the chair next to hers. Their eyes met, Orla's lost and alone, Dora's full of incomprehension, her mouth open.

"My husband's dead," said Orla blankly.

"Oh, my dear!" Dora replied, putting one hand on Orla's arm and motioning towards Marcus with the other. "Is he your husband?"

"No, not him," said Orla.

Thomas looked at the two of them and called, "That's enough."

"Who are you?" Dora asked the girl.

"Orla."

Thomas stood. "Madam, I must beg you to leave the woman alone."

Dora stared at him. "What's going on here?"

Sir Arthur rose from where he squatted by the injured man, and looked at his wife. "Dora, go to bed. Now."

Dora pushed herself up from her seat, frowning at her husband. Orla said, "Help me, please."

Things began to cohere in Dora's mind. "Where are you taking her?"

Thomas quietly addressed Sir Arthur. "We can't have this."

Arthur looked coolly at his wife. "Dora – you *know*. There's no secret here. And this is not something that you need to see. Go to bed."

Her face reddened with rage. "Men!" she spat, igniting. "Vile, disgusting creatures!" She pointed at Orla and shouted, "She's not a slave! And she's not going with you!" She turned to the girl. "Come with me. They won't take you." Dora grasped Orla's hand, pulled her up from where she sat, and hurried with her towards a door at the rear of the staircase. Thomas came running after them and tore them forcibly apart.

"That will not be possible," he said. "I have my orders to carry out, and the girl will be coming with us."

Dora flew at Thomas with her fingernails, astonishing him with the ferocity of her attack. He briefly let go of Orla so he could defend himself, and she took the opportunity to sprint for the open front door. Arthur hastened to the fray, secured his wife in an arm-hold from behind, manhandled her into the cellar and locked the door. She began to bang loudly from within, outraged for both herself and the girl. Thomas looked around, expecting to have to charge after Orla, but Will had brought her down and was sitting astride her on the floor.

"For God's sake, don't hurt her," Thomas cried, fearing for the young woman's ribs.

"Don't worry," said Will. "She's undamaged."

On the outside, thought Thomas. He looked at Arthur. "I'm sorry about that. We'll need to tie the girl up. Do you have something?"

"I think I can supply what you need," said Arthur. He disappeared for a few moments and returned with rope and some rags. Saul bound Orla's hands and feet, testing the knots as he went, while Will restrained her struggles. Then Saul bundled up a ball of rags, forced it into her mouth and gagged her. She was helpless. Will, no longer required to pinion the girl, settled at Marcus's side.

Thomas inspected the gag and bindings. "That'll do. Good. You two..." (he indicated Harry and Saul), "...carry her to the coach. Saul, you stay out there and watch her; Harry, you come back here." The two lifted Orla between them and disappeared through the front door.

Thomas knelt once more by the couch. Marcus was still, breathing only shallowly, and looked close to death. Arthur shook his head and said, "I'm sorry to say…"

Thomas nodded in reluctant agreement. "I think we may have lost him." He clenched his jaw and fought away his tears, unable to speak for a while. Then he said, "This man has a young wife – married for three years – and a two-year-old son who loves him."

"Linda's her name," said Will. "Jack's his son – little Jack. Please God, don't let this man die." Thomas heard the tremor in his colleague's voice.

"I'm very sorry indeed," said Arthur.

Again, Thomas was quiet. Then he sighed and said, "It could have been any of us." He reached across the dying man and rested his hand on Will's back, a gesture of comfort. After a few seconds he stood, looked down at Marcus and moved away, wandering slowly and aimlessly around the hallway, arms folded, thinking. Arthur followed him with his eyes, saddened at the course of events. Dora's noise had stopped, the tranquillity of the house pierced only by the warbling of pigeons and the distant thrustings of a bull.

A few minutes passed, and Thomas began to wonder why Harry was taking so long to return from the coach. "I'm going to check outside," he said, unfolded his arms and stepped towards the open door. But at that moment Harry appeared. "All well?" asked Thomas.

"All good," said Harry. "She's trussed up tight."

Thomas looked at him and thought, *What did you do with her?* but said nothing.

" 'Ow's Marcus?"

Thomas shook his head.

"Poor bastard. 'E di'n't deserve that."

Just then, Fox arrived with the doctor. Harry sat to one side and waited.

As soon as she heard fresh voices, Dora began to pound on

the cellar door, shouting, "They've got a girl! They're kidnapping her!"

The doctor's brow furrowed, and he looked at Sir Arthur. "What's this?"

Arthur replied, "This man's been shot."

The doctor knelt, examined the patient, and shook his head. "He's dead."

"Damn it all!" muttered Thomas under his breath, and turned away. Will rose from Marcus's side and hurried outside, unwilling to allow the others to see his emotion.

The doctor got to his feet. "And what's this about kidnapping?" he asked. "Why is Dora locked up?"

Arthur had anticipated this. He put his hand in his pocket and drew out a banknote for £100. "You were never here, doctor. I hope that clarifies everything."

The doctor frowned over his spectacles at Sir Arthur, paused for a moment, then took the money and left.

"Thank you," said Thomas. "We didn't need him after all, but none of us was to know that." Arthur nodded. Thomas sighed. "We can't take the body with us. I'm afraid I'll have to ask you to take care of him."

"Leave it to me," said Arthur. "I'll have a coffin made up and send him on to London in a day or two. I'm sorry you've had all this to cope with. And I'm very sorry about my wife's behaviour."

"What will you do?" asked Thomas.

"She'll calm down – she has to. That's a problem for me, not for you – you have enough worries, I think." He motioned to his servant. "Fox, please exchange their horses." The man left the house, Harry following.

Thomas removed Marcus's pistols and personal items and made his way out into the daylight. Fox was leading the tired horses away, and Saul was harnessing the new ones. Will was some distance down the drive, leaning on a fence, gazing out over a field. Harry stood away to the right, pissing into a hedge.

Thomas checked on Orla. She was lying on the rear seat in the carriage, bound, gagged and helpless. She met his eyes, and he saw that she'd been crying. He suspected that Harry and Saul had entertained themselves with her in some way, although he wasn't sure exactly what form it had taken. He said nothing to her but busied himself with cleaning away as much of Marcus's blood as he could from the corner of the opposite seat. He was filled with grief for his companion and was angry with the girl for trying to run. He wondered what Harry and Saul might do with her if they were left alone for a good length of time.

Harry was standing close to the vehicle when Thomas emerged, and the two exchanged a glance. Sir Arthur waited silently at his front door, ready to see the coach off. The distant bull was still exerting himself.

The horses were in place, and Saul was on the box, ready to drive. Thomas looked up at him. "No. You ride inside with Harry. I'll drive."

Saul raised his eyebrows, guessing his superior's intentions. "Alright," he said, handing over the reins as Thomas clambered up.

"No marks," muttered Thomas. Saul sniffed and climbed down. The coach door closed. Orla was shut in with the two men.

Thomas called back to Will, who'd arranged himself once more in the rear-guard. "Will, are you alright for another session at that?"

"No problem," he answered.

Thomas nodded, raised his hand in salute to Sir Arthur, and pulled away.

The road from Adwick le Street was a poor one, rutted and bumpy. A few farm buildings could be seen across the fields, but there was little activity at this time of the morning. The grazing sheep and cattle they passed paid them no attention.

Will peered down through the rear roof light into the carriage below. At thirty years of age, he was the youngest member of the group and had been associated with them for only six months. He was sickened by what he glimpsed in the dimness of the compartment, thinking of his own love, Anna, soft and pure, waiting for him in London. No matter how hard he tried to concentrate on the road, his eyes were frequently drawn to the scene beneath him. After twenty minutes he could stand it no longer.

"Tom," he called. Thomas half turned to catch his words. "Stop for a moment." The carriage was duly drawn to a halt, and Will dismounted and joined his companion in the fore-guard position. Thomas restarted the horses and they continued on their way, glancing briefly at each other.

Will said, "Are you aware of what's happening in the coach?"

Thomas replied, "Marcus was their friend. They've worked together for years. They're angry, shocked, grieving."

"But it's not the girl's fault," said Will.

Thomas's eyes remained on the road, and he took some time to answer. "I know that."

"Then why…?"

"She tried to run," he cut in rapidly. "After all my assurances that she'd come to no harm, she took the first chance to bolt."

"But isn't that exactly what you'd expect? Isn't that what you'd do? She's having her freedom, her life, taken away."

Thomas said nothing.

"We're taking her into slavery," said Will forcefully. "Against her will."

"A lot of people are slaves. It's the natural order of things," Thomas replied. He looked piercingly at Will. "There's the strong, and there's the weak. The strong take what they can and possess it; the weak are taken." He looked back at the road and added quietly, "It's the way things are."

Will watched him for a moment. "You can't tell me you

think that's right. I've only known you for a few weeks, but I know you don't believe that."

"I do believe it."

"This is wrong," said Will.

"I think you'd better keep your mouth shut," said Thomas. A tense silence fell between them. Will began to think that he might turn his gun on Thomas. What would happen if he did? The others would emerge from the coach, shoot him and continue on their way.

Thomas guessed what Will was thinking. "When we next stop, you'll rape the girl."

Will's voice was bitter, hard. "I will not."

Thomas looked at him. "You have to learn. You'll do it – at gunpoint if necessary."

Will drew his pistol and pointed it at Thomas. "I'm not doing this. Stop the coach."

Thomas looked at the muzzle of Will's pistol. "You're making a mistake," He said. "You'll die here."

"Stop the coach. I won't tell you again."

"Think," said Thomas. "Exactly what will happen if I stop the coach? The others will see what you're doing up here, and they'll pick you off. Even if you shoot me, you won't have time to do anything else."

Will continued to stare at him, pistol pointed in his face.

"You've got a sweetheart, haven't you? What good will you be to her if you're dead? This girl in the coach – she's one girl among thousands of others. There's nothing new here. Her life will go on, and she'll adapt to it. Marcus is gone forever. His wife, his boy, they'll never see him again. That's the greatest sadness here today – not what's happening to that girl down there. Put the gun down, Will, and see sense."

Will's resolve was crumbling. Thomas went on. "I know it's hard. To see this and accept it, it's hard. You're right – I hate it too. But it's the order of things. One day this world may change – people may stop using each other. I hope so. But that time is not today, and we have our own worries, the burdens of our own lives to carry." He paused. "Put your pistol down, Will."

Will was silent for a moment. "I won't abuse her."

"Alright," said Thomas. "I'm sorry I said that. I respect your feelings."

"You mean it?"

"I do."

Will lowered his pistol and put the safety back on, half expecting Thomas to jump him. But he didn't.

"Well done," said Thomas. "It's hard, this life."

Will said nothing more, but gazed grimly ahead.

They passed near Doncaster and continued south. The road was quiet except for a few farm waggons and occasional flocks of sheep driven by shepherds and their dogs. A team of drovers crossed their path at one point, some on horseback, with a great many cattle. Thomas saluted the men as they came near. He was fond of the smell of animal dung, and flared his nostrils, breathing in the fresh stink.

About ninety minutes further on, he noticed a lake in the distance, away to the left, the sun transforming its surface into a fiery dish. He pointed and said to Will, "We'll stop there. She'll want to wash, and we can eat something."

There was a good track leading off the road, and twenty minutes later Thomas pulled the horses to a halt at the waterside, turned and tapped on the roof. "Five minutes and you're ready to come out," he called.

Tom and Will sat quietly together on the box and looked at the water. It was a calm scene, brightened by birdsong. Butterflies danced among the flowers, and honey bees busied themselves gathering pollen. The sound of distant sheep and cattle drifted to them, although no buildings were visible. The land rose gently toward the east beyond the lake.

After a few minutes the doors opened. Saul and Harry

climbed down from the interior. Will looked at them but said nothing. Thomas gave two pats on Will's thigh and addressed the other two men. "All well?"

Saul nodded. "All well."

Thomas took a deep breath and dismounted. "We'll breakfast here," he said. "We'll give ourselves an hour or so." He looked up at Will and asked, "You alright?" Will nodded, though unease showed in his face. "Good man," said Thomas.

Orla was sitting upright in the carriage, still gagged, her face filthy with sweat and sticky with tears. Her hands, which had been tied behind her, were now tied in front, and her ankles were unbound. She looked at Thomas, the whites of her eyes shot with red.

"If I remove the gag, will you be quiet?" he asked.

She paused, then nodded yes.

"If you shout out, or make any trouble at all, you'll be gagged again for the rest of the journey. Do you understand?"

She nodded again. He cut the tight band of material from around her head, and she spat out the plug of cloth from her mouth, retching as she did so, her tongue protruding so far it looked as if it might detach itself. Thick strands of saliva dangled from her lips. She tried to wipe her mouth as best she could with her bound hands.

"I'd like to untie you, but I'm not sure I can trust you." She looked hard at him, then held out her wrists. He lifted her chin with his knife, running its blade gently from side to side, leaving no mark, looking into her eyes. The threat was clear; her life was in his hands. She didn't flinch. He cut the cords that shackled her, and she rubbed her wrists, gasping with relief. He stood watching.

"You know what they did to me," she mumbled.

He said nothing.

"You could have stopped it."

"You ran," he said. "You took advantage of a dying man, and

526

you tried to escape."

"I'm not your *thing*," she spat.

"You've been punished," he said. "Don't make me punish you again."

"I hate you," she said. "All of you. You're all hateful."

He offered her his hand. "Come. There's water. And we have some time."

She hesitated, then dropped her gaze from his eyes, took his hand and stepped down from the carriage. The other men looked at her as she came into view. They were eating, drinking as if nothing unusual was taking place. She felt ashamed, crushed, unable to meet their eyes. "Save some breakfast for us," said Thomas.

There was a large willow tree about fifty yards away on the lakeshore. He released her hand and pointed to it. "We'll go there," he said.

As soon as she was in the shade of the tree and out of sight of the coach, she took off her clothes and stepped into the lake, finding a place where she could squat, the water at shoulder height. First, she cleaned the men away, repeatedly and at length; then she washed her face and hair, then the rest of her body, very thoroughly. After that, she sat motionless, eyes vacant, submerged except for her head.

Thomas watched quietly, intently. He tried to imagine how she must feel but was not a shallow enough fool to believe he could actually do so. He wished he could comfort her but knew that such a thing would be both impossible and hypocritical. Anything he could say, even if spoken from the heart, would sound vacant and empty. Yet silence seemed callous.

"What's going to happen to me?" she asked.

"You'll be delivered safely to your destination. You'll be looked after, fed well. You'll be comfortable; you'll have friends."

"Am I going to be sold?"

Thomas raised his eyebrows. He found the wording curious, unexpected. "Sold? What happens to you is not my business. My task is only to deliver you."

She waited a moment, then said, "I expect you're in a hurry to go."

"No," he replied. "Take your time. I'll wait as long as you wish."

The water was cold, but Orla had got used to it. The stillness was calming. She looked across the surface and saw a family of swans, free, untroubled.

"What time is it?" she asked.

He looked at his watch. "Nearly half past eight."

"Half past eight," she muttered. "Yesterday I was free. I had my own life – a man who loved me."

Again, he wished there were something he could say that might make things easier for her, but there wasn't – so he said blankly, "There's nothing I can say to help you. I wish there were."

She looked at him. "Why? Why do you do this?"

The answer was simple, but he couldn't bring himself to say it out loud, couldn't tell her that she was just money to him. "That's enough," he said. "No more talking."

Orla crouched in the water for a few more minutes, then said, "Alright. We may as well go." She stood up and walked to where she'd left her clothes.

"I don't have another change of clothes," said Thomas. "I'm sorry. Will those do?"

"I'll rinse them," she replied, picked them up and took them to the water's edge. Thomas looked at her as she crouched there, cleaning her dress and shift in the lake. She was beautiful, her arched back, glowing flesh, soft hair... The cruelty of what he was doing almost overcame him.

"Did they hurt you?"

"Of course they hurt me," she replied scornfully.

He clarified. "I mean, did they mark you?"

She paused. "No. I don't think so."

"Can I see? You can say no."

But she stood up, spread out her arms and allowed him to walk round her. "Is the item in good order?" she asked.

"Get dressed," he said. "We should go."

As they neared the coach, Thomas noticed a farm waggon coming towards them from further up the track. There was a man driving, a boy behind him standing in the cart. Thomas said, "If you shout out or call for help, I'll have to kill them – both, including the boy."

Orla stood in her sopping wet clothes, smiling and waving as they passed. The boy, dark-haired and sun-browned, no more than about eight, gave her a huge, happy, toothy smile and a delighted laugh. Thomas raised his hand in salute to the driver. When the waggon had passed out of earshot he turned to Orla and said, "Thank you. That was well done."

They drew close to the carriage. "I'd prefer not to bind you again. No more harm will come to you if I can trust you. What do you think?" She looked down and nodded her head. "Good," he said. "I'm grateful to you."

Will, Harry and Saul stood by the coach, ready to climb on board. Thomas said, "Orla will be unbound from now on. There'll be no more trouble, no more punishment." He looked at her.

She remained mute, head cast down. "Saul, you're driving. Harry, you're rear-guard. Will, you're inside with me."

They took up their positions and a moment later were on their way once more.

The basket containing the remains of breakfast lay on the seat next to Thomas. He looked across at Orla.

"Would you care to eat something?"

"No."

"You should at least drink," he said, lifting a flask. "It's ale. Strong and good." He removed the bung and offered it to her. She took it from him and pressed it to her lips – just a small sip at first, but then much more deeply. When she was done, she handed it back to him, and he put it to his own lips. He smiled, glad to see her take the ale. It was the first smile she'd seen on his face. In other circumstances it would have made him look human.

He sat back. "It's good to see you drink."

Five minutes later Orla was fast asleep.

Clouds drew in, and a light rain began to fall at about eleven o'clock. It cleared by the time they reached the next change of horses but came on again soon afterwards and developed into a torrential downpour a few minutes after noon. The sky darkened further, thunder growled, and flashes of furious white ruptured the heavens. Orla continued to sleep until a nearby lightning strike tore the world apart at about half past twelve, its cacophonous explosion startling her awake and lighting the carriage interior a vivid yellow. She leapt forward and looked around her.

"It's just the weather," said Thomas.

She closed her eyes, sat back, and tried to withdraw into slumber once more. Her clothes were still damp, and she was cold. Thomas covered her with two extra blankets and said, "You must eat. It must be almost twenty-four hours since you ate anything at all."

She shook her head. He handed her a piece of cheese from the basket and tore off some bread to go with it. "Try," he said. "What's the point of not eating?" She reached out a hand, palm open, and he dropped the food into it. It looked strange to her. Why would she want to eat? Why would she want to stay alive? She took a bite and held it in her mouth. Thomas nodded. "We'll stop for lunch in a few miles anyway."

Orla waited for the substance on her tongue to turn to mush. She looked out of the carriage window at the dark, waterlogged landscape, and felt numb, cancelled out of existence. Her mind was filled with grey images of Rider, of

Jacob – no longer the kind, constant figure she'd thought him to be – and of what had occurred in the coach just a few hours since. Her past life was that of another person, a dream. She'd died and was on her way to hell.

At some point in the early evening, Orla woke and found Saul and Harry sitting opposite her – watching her. She looked around. The carriage was in motion. The other two must be outside, one driving, the other on guard. They'd left her undefended with these two again – her rapists. She felt panic rising; her heart began to race. The two men stared at her, enjoying her terror, deliberately frightening her.

Harry rose, stood just inches away and began to unbutton his breeches. She closed her eyes – it was going to happen again.

There was a sudden furious rapping on the top of the coach. She looked up and saw Thomas staring angrily down through the roof-light. "NO!" he shouted. The carriage came to a stop, and Harry quickly buttoned himself up. Three seconds later Thomas was in the cabin, his pistol jammed point-blank in Harry's face, his voice intense, enraged. "If I see the contents of your trousers again I'll shoot it off. Understand?"

Harry held his hands defensively and nodded in comprehension. "Sorry. I wasn't gonna do anythin'."

Thomas continued to stare at him. "Alright. You're up on the roof. Get out."

A moment later Harry had gone, the carriage was moving again, and Thomas was once more sitting opposite Orla.

"Are you alright?"

"He didn't hurt me," she said, "not this time."

The rain had stopped, the sky was darkening, evening setting in, and Thomas began to worry once more about robbers.

They were south of Leicester, close to the village of Dunton Bassett, when they ran into trouble again. Thomas was driving, Harry next to him and Saul in rear-guard. They were approached by a single masked man on horseback. Harry saw the glint of the carriage lantern reflect off the robber's gun as it was raised for use.

"Stop, or you're…" said the thief.

But Harry had already fired, simultaneously uttering the word, "Sorry." The man tumbled to the ground, his startled mount running a short distance. The coach horses reared at the shot, but Thomas calmed them with the reins and his voice. Harry jumped down to check on the highwayman, then dragged the body to the side of the road.

"Easy kill," he said, returning to the coach. "Just a kid."

"Good shot," said Thomas. "Keep your eyes open. There may be more."

But the night passed calm and untroubled, and by sunrise they were south of Daventry.

Margaret Siddon, plump, fifty-four years old, sat at luncheon with Edgar Foxley, their table in the convent office arranged so they could look out at the people and carriages passing by in the sunshine on King's Place. The hour was approaching two o'clock in the afternoon, and Edgar expected the arrival of the coach from the Lookout sometime later in the day.

"These little spiced sausages are excellent," said Margaret, picking one up with her fingers and biting off half of it.

"Yes, I like them too," said Foxley, helping himself to another. "Indian spices – fascinating."

"You've always had a taste for the new," she said.

"It's true," Foxley replied. "New tastes, new smells. Keeps me fresh."

"Indeed so," she replied. "Fresh food, fresh drink, fresh ladies. Good for business."

"Yes. It'll be interesting to see what Jacob sends us. I haven't been up to the Lookout for a while, so I don't think I'll recognise any of the new ones. I should have paid him a visit I suppose, but things have been busy, as you know, and it's such a long way to Scarborough."

"We won't be disappointed, I'm sure," said Margaret. "He's always reliable – the stable he sends is always top class. Everyone says so. I expect our gentlemen are looking forward to the new stock even more than we are."

"You can be sure of that. This one arriving today though…"

"Hmm. I know. It must be very upsetting for her. But you don't feel badly about it, do you?" She raised her eyebrows questioningly. "Or perhaps you do…"

"I expect she'll fit in, one way or another."

"Yes," Margaret went on. "Life carries on. We'll make her welcome."

"Of course you will," said Foxley. "You always do. You're very kind to them."

Margaret ate another sausage. "So, one today and the other nine…"

Foxley completed the sentence, "…in about three weeks."

"Exciting," said Margaret. "The best ones – they're always the girls from the Lookout. He has a gift, does Jacob."

"He does," said Foxley. "We always thought so. He's a talented sausage."

Foxley laughed out loud and Margaret joined in, reaching for the next little tube of spiced meat. "I can't resist these," she said, popping it into her mouth. She chewed for a while, enjoying the subtle heat of the spices, then said, "How will you manage the difficult girl?"

"Her name is Orla – Orla Stapleton – nice name." He sighed and leaned back, cradling the rear of his head in his linked fingers. "She may remember Holly Graham. Holly came from the Lookout too. She's here in the convent today…"

"Holly, yes, of course…"

"Holly remembers the girl. Orla would have been about

thirteen when Holly came to join us. Younger girls often have their idols in the older ranks, and she'll likely remember Holly. On the assumption that a familiar face is a comforting one, I've asked Holly to take charge of Orla when she arrives."

Margaret nodded. "Yes, that sounds like a good idea. When do you think that might be?"

"Not sure. Anytime between about three or four today and early tomorrow morning."

"I'm looking forward to it," said Margaret.

Foxley replied, "So am I."

The carriage pulled into the yard at King's Place at a quarter to nine that evening. Orla peered out of the window anxiously as Thomas opened the door and stepped down. He extended his hand for her and said, "Welcome to London." She took the offered assistance and climbed out of the coach, nervously looking around her. She was in the courtyard of a huge house. The street beyond the entrance archway was noisy, but the sounds were subdued here in the quadrangle, surrounded by the building's walls. She gazed upwards. It was a cool evening – the sun had set. The stars were the same as those she saw at the Lookout. Nothing had changed for them. They didn't care where she was. The carriage was already moving away, William driving, Saul and Harry inside. Thomas rang the house bell and turned to Orla. "I may never see you again," he said. "Good luck. I hope you have a long and happy life."

She couldn't think of anything to say in reply. Thomas nodded, and as the door began to open, he quietly left, dissolving into the shadows. A young woman of about twenty stood in the frame, illuminated in lanternlight. "Orla?" she said.

Orla was surprised. For some reason, she hadn't been expecting to see another female. She frowned in concentration and stepped forward. The woman was familiar from somewhere. But where? "Helen...?" she said, but it wasn't right – she knew it wasn't right.

The woman smiled and said, "Holly. Holly Graham. I remember you. You were just a little thing back then."

Relief flooded through Orla. She ran forward, collapsed before Holly, flung her arms around her legs and burst into tears.

Twenty minutes later they were sitting together in a warm room on the ground floor of the house, sharing a pot of tea, while Orla told her everything that had occurred. Holly listened, empathised and held Orla when she cried, which was often.

"You've had a horrible ordeal," said Holly. "It's been much worse for you than for most of us."

"Most of us?" said Orla, but she'd had two days to arrange the pieces in her mind and already had a good idea of what was really going on.

"The Lookout," said Holly, "and other schools, are institutions for training courtesans – prostitutes."

Orla nodded. "I thought so," she said quietly. "It's horrible. We're all deceived for seven years..."

"I've been here for three years," said Holly.

Orla looked up. "You're a...?"

Holly nodded. "Mm," affirmative, lips closed.

"Where are the others? All the others I knew?"

"They're here. Or working nearby. Most of them."

"It doesn't feel real," said Orla, shaking her head. "It's monstrous."

Holly sighed. "Yes. But it hardens you if you can stand it. Orla, I won't pretend – I've been given the job of acclimatising you."

Orla looked up in horror. "Acclimatising? They murdered the man who asked me to marry him! They raped me!"

Holly covered Orla's hand with hers. "I know, Orla. But you're here, and they won't let you get away. You have to fit in, or..." she widened her eyes and shook her head.

"They'll kill me?" Orla gasped.

Holly looked at her intently for a few moments. "You wouldn't be the first."

Holly's subdued tone conveyed such blackness that Orla's hand flew to her mouth in fright.

"It's not all darkness," Holly went on. "Now and then, a man takes a real liking for some particular girl and buys her from the convent. There've been several, and some of those girls are happy. Do you remember Annie Smyth?"

Orla searched her memory, brows knit. "I'm not sure. Can't think clearly."

"You'd have been about twelve when she left the Lookout. She was always the prettiest girl – you'd probably remember her if you saw her. Anyway, she's married. She worked here for two years, then got bought out by some politician who wanted her just for himself. She was his mistress for a year, then he divorced his wife and married her."

Orla listened open-mouthed but said nothing.

"You have to make a go of it, Orla. There's no other choice." Holly stood and held out her hand. "I have to take you to your room and give you a bath."

Orla's room was comfortable and large. It was warmly lit, though not bright, and contained a wardrobe, a trunk, a commode chair, several armchairs, an ornate longcase clock and a large double bed. The walls were pink, the rug was red, the ceiling was a soft cream colour. There were three large vases of flowers that lent their fragrances to the already pleasant scent of the room itself, and also a table, on which sat a bowl of soap and several jars that Orla guessed contained oils, perfumes and creams. Food and drink had been arranged on a table opposite the window overlooking the courtyard into which she'd arrived. A small fire burned in the grate against the cool of the evening. A bath stood ready for her, steaming, inviting.

Holly indicated the soap and the towels and said, "I'll leave you for half an hour. Eat something, have a nice bath and make yourself comfortable."

A moment later she was alone, sick with horror and fear, in the room that was to be her new home. She used the commode, undressed, and climbed into the bath, wondering if she would be able to drown herself. But she couldn't do it and sat still in the water instead, eyes unfocused. The heat was calming, and she felt her body relax despite everything. She thought of Rider and began to weep again.

When Holly returned after half an hour, she found Orla fast asleep in the cooling water.

"Wake up, sleepyhead," she said, shaking her. Orla opened her eyes. "Come on," said Holly. "We have to get you ready."

"Ready?" said Orla. She stepped out of the bath and allowed Holly to start rubbing her dry with the towel.

"Yes," said Holly. "Ready. Tomorrow I'll come back, and we'll talk about how you managed, then we'll have breakfast, coffee, and go for a nice walk in the park. They'll probably let us take the dogs. How does that sound?"

"Sounds good," said Orla, her mind drawing itself in, hiding.

"Think about that," said Holly. "Think about tomorrow."

Orla looked at her. "I've got no clothes."

"We'll worry about that in the morning," replied Holly. She'd mostly finished drying the girl, although her hair was still damp. She looked at the clock. It was twenty minutes past ten.

"We should make you smell nice," said Holly, opening a few of the perfume jars and applying scents to various parts of Orla's body, ending with two dabs behind the knees.

"Behind the knees?" said Orla.

Holly explained, "It rises nicely from there."

"What's happening?" asked Orla.

"I've brought you a nightdress," said Holly. "Here, put it

on." Orla obeyed. It was a nice, floor-length cotton gown. Holly opened the bedclothes. "We're ready," she said.

"Ready," echoed Orla dully.

Holly heard the staircase creak. She looked at Orla standing helplessly in the centre of the room and brushed the girl's face with her hand. "Be good," she whispered. "For your own sake. And think of tomorrow."

There was a soft tap at the door. It opened, and Foxley entered the room. He was wrapped in an expensive silk dressing gown, cream in colour, with red and blue flowers.

"Hello, Orla," he said.

Holly said, "Orla, this is Mr Foxley." Orla, eyes questioning, mind tumbling deeper, looked at Holly. Holly nodded. "Yes," she said.

"Thank you, Holly," said Foxley, "I'll take it from here."

Holly left the room, closing the door behind her. She didn't look back.

56. STELLA – KNOX – RUTH

Stella's duties at the Lookout were very light. In the early days, she'd wondered at times why she was there at all.

"You're a figurehead," Jacob had told her. "This is a school full of girls. There has to be a woman in a position of authority – even if she does almost nothing. Having said that, you're free to mix with the girls as you wish. Enjoy yourself – get to know them as I do. They are fascinating, delightful people. I love them all."

"You love them," she mocked. "Yet look what you have planned for them."

"If you love the one you kill," he replied, "it makes the execution more exquisite."

Stella liked that. Of course, Jacob was right, and he could see by her reaction that she enjoyed his comment. "You're a free agent here," he said. "Live as you want. Mix or not, as you wish. Be fulfilled."

Stella had never trained as a teacher, never taught before in any capacity. Nevertheless, she would step in to take a class if one of the tutors was ill. Her skills were limited – she could only do a little reading and needlework, being untrained in everything else. If she was asked to look after a class of girls who expected a French lesson, she simply got them to read a play aloud or recite poetry. It filled the time.

There were the timetables to draw up – that task fell mainly to her, and she relied on Ruth's assistance to adequately complete the job. Ruth was well organised and efficient. They drank tea together now and then but didn't develop any genuine friendship.

And there was the girls' mail of course. There was never very much, but it all had to be opened, assessed and censored. That task fell entirely on Stella's shoulders, Ruth being ignorant of the real situation. A few letters from girls already working in King's Place got through to the Lookout even though measures were in force in London to see that they didn't. They were probably smuggled out or dropped from windows. The small number of letters that successfully made the journey all the way to the school were read by Stella and committed to the flames.

The outgoing mail, written by the younger girls to their heroes who had made the transition to London, was usually safe. Now and then, if she was sure she could do it convincingly, Stella would fake a letter from London, telling the Lookout girls how exciting the new life was. They could look forward to their thrilling futures with confidence and joy, she wrote, smiling at the gross deception.

Stella liked to write – it was one of her chief pleasures. She liked to sit quietly in her suite and write stories about a murderess – a middle-aged woman who travelled the country, killing people at random. She imagined all kinds of scenarios. One of her tales was set on a ship at sea. Her heroine (she named her Miss Shadow) knifed the crew one by one at night. Soon only Miss Shadow and the captain remained alive, facing each other in a storm. He knew the killer was she, but she was too beautiful to extinguish. She offered him her body – and slit his throat during the act of love.

Stella loved that one and read it to herself over and over again. But there were many more – she'd been writing for years and had a substantial collection of manuscripts. There were several stories in which she killed all the Lookout girls. There was one in which she tied them up and knifed them one by one. She transcribed their terrified pleading, their pitiful last words before the blade slid into their soft bodies. In another story, she poisoned them all at dinner and watched them die in agony, dressed in their ridiculous finery. Another tale had them all starve slowly, locked in and beyond help as she walked amongst them like the angel of destiny. In yet another, she hanged them from the top of the staircase – all in their nightdresses – and watched their little dancing feet as they choked to death.

She had a technique for regenerating her ideas. Whenever she felt her inspiration was drying up, she put on her boots and went out for a long walk, marching vigorously in no particular direction. She was almost blind to the external scenery and would keep striding along until she caught the corner of an idea. And when that happened, she returned to her room and worked out the story, pulling on the exposed corner until the details formed and the characters came alive.

Murdering, killing – it wasn't always fiction. Miss Shadow. Sometimes she crept out into the real world...

Ruth had even less to do than Stella, although she befriended many of the girls and made more effort than her superior when asked to fill in at lessons. Other than the girls, Ruth got on well with the housemistresses. She was less raucous than they but enjoyed their company nevertheless – when they'd have her.

Sometimes she'd spend an evening with Janet Illif. Ruth would read, Janet would make clothes, they'd both watch the fire. Ruth told Janet a little about her past (but not the bit about losing her job in Durham), and Janet listened, always attentive. Janet never said much about herself except that she'd come from Whitehaven and had met Milton in Hull.

Ruth was really rather meek and mild. She looked at Kipp sometimes (and knew he looked at her once in a while), but she was too timid to get close. In any case, he had a reputation for getting round the maids. He was risky – probably thought her dull anyway. Those were Ruth's thoughts – and her own self-assessment.

The years were passing and it was beginning to look as if she would be forgotten. She'd be an old maid – like Janet.

When not occupied in his work at the school, when he was not chewing or breaking necks, Knox liked to hit things. He had a suspended punch bag in his room. He'd strip down to his waist – or strip altogether – and pummel the thing into oblivion for hours on end. It kept him fit and concentrated. He often imagined the bag was his father, but only because of the way his father had died – suspended on the end of a rope like Knox's punchbag. It seemed logical to pummel the old man's body until it burst. Finally, the worthless gobbing nobody was good for something.

And the boy – the boy he'd had to bury. Knox rarely felt much, but the dead boy had been difficult, even for him. Lucas Dent had been an outsider, alone; Knox was an outsider, alone. Lucas was quiet, kept himself to himself; Knox was the same.

He'd slung the body over the wall, then gone into the grounds of the dower house and buried it in a shallow grave on the old bowling lawn. It was likely that the rotting meat would stink, even though it was buried, and he'd gone searching for some decoy to mask the decay. The body of a fox would do, he thought – or a hare perhaps. As luck would have it, he came across a large, freshly dead badger in the undergrowth near one of the old plant houses. He carried it back to the bowling lawn and dropped it close to the boy's grave. That should do it.

But the task had disturbed him, and he had to punch it out, punch it out, punch it out. There was the bag – and there was his father's face (*BANG!*). And there was Jacob's face (*BANG!*) – for making him do that.

542

57. THE LOOKOUT
Sunday July 12, 1761

Bip and Fuzzy had been busy during Kate's absence. They'd forced their way through the undergrowth in the dower house hall and infiltrated the rooms on the far side.

The largest and most impressive chamber they called "the drawing room", and that's probably exactly what it had been in better days. It occupied the front of the house and looked out onto the terrace. A door at the far end of the drawing room opened into a smaller room that had perhaps been a study. It still contained a moderately sized wooden desk, riddled with woodworm.

There was a long, narrow gallery-like room at the back of the house, accessed through a door at the rear of the drawing room. At the north end of this long room there was a locked door that would have allowed the girls to get directly into the servants' corridor, enabling easy passage all the way from the kitchen to the south end of the house, avoiding the jungle in the hall. Sadly, the door was immovable. They tried forcing it, tried to break the lock, but it held firm.

A small vestibule with hooks for coats and capes lay at the other end of this long rear room, separated from it by a doorframe, although the door itself was missing.

The house's rear exit (which was not locked but only bolted) opened into the little cloakroom, and faced a narrow staircase that led to the upper floor. A cupboard under the stairs contained the bowling equipment that Mabel had told them of.

Many of the soft furnishings were still in place, but they were mouldy and eaten out by rodents. The windows and ceilings were full of spiders, many of which the girls managed to brush out, although it took determination and a lot of screaming.

The tables were still usable (when they'd been properly cleaned), and they brought in some of the small wooden chairs from the folly and the summerhouse. After much struggling, they managed to get a few of the windows open, and the all-pervasive damp they'd initially encountered began to diminish as the rooms were aired.

Sadly, the upper level resisted the girls' colonisation, although they braved the staircase's visible rot to find out. There were three large bedrooms, the frail wooden floors of which supported their weight (just about, despite some worryingly spongy places), but the roof was full of large holes, and the plaster ceiling had entirely collapsed. Plant-life had taken over where human beings had once slept, and the three chambers had become host to a mass of tendrils and greenery. Moss covered most of the hard surfaces, and the beds and chairs had become cities for insects. In the warmth of the summer the place was alive with wasps, bees and birds. Huge multi-storeyed, myriad-gilled canopies of fungus smiled from all the corners. Despite its romantic, lost, forgotten, faraway, desert-island-like atmosphere of abandonment, it was no place for a pair of girls.

But they'd made a cosy, secret parlour of the downstairs rooms, despite the near-constant dripping of water from above; and it was here, on the afternoon of Sunday, July 12th, that they sat with Kate, relating the story blow by blow, of all that had come to pass during her three weeks holiday.

"That sounds mad," said Kate, shaking her head.

"Yes," said Fuzzy. "No-one ever expected anything like that."

"But Mr Browning *did have* an impulsive kind of character," said Bip. "I mean, if he'd just stopped to think, he'd have realised what a daft idea it was to flip-flap with one of his own pupils. I mean, if Stella had been in charge he'd have been out – no job, no reference. And goodness knows what might have become of Orla."

"So," said Kate, trying to get the sequence of events clear in her mind, "he knew the strong-box was arriving that day..."

"...or caught sight of it as it came in..." interjected Fuzz.

"...took a chance, somehow got into Jacob's office..."

"...and filled his pockets with money," Bip finished. "Yes, that's about it."

"Five thousand pounds," said Kate. Bip nodded. "That's an incredible amount."

"Must have weighed a bit too. Apparently, a lot of it was in banknotes – you know, the pieces of paper that nobs use for bets. A hundred pounds, five hundred pounds – there were even a couple of dockets for a thousand pounds apiece, so they say. But a lot of what he took was in gold, sovereigns. It must have weighed a ton! I wonder how easy it'll be to get rid of the notes..."

"So do you think Orla knew about it?" asked Kate.

"How do we know?" Bip replied, shrugging. "She's gone. We don't know where they went."

"But what's the connection with Lucas?" asked Kate. It all felt like some kind of joke. Any minute now, someone would drop the punch-line, and the world would tip back into focus.

"Who knows?" said Bip. "Maybe Luke was Orla's secret brother."

"That's ridiculous," said Kate.

"Is it?" said Bip. "What's ridiculous? It's *all* ridiculous. Life's ridiculous. Everything's ridiculous."

"What about Slade?" asked Kate.

"Slade doesn't know anything," Bip replied. "He's upset – says Lucas wouldn't run off. No-one really knew Luke except Slade, and Slade says he couldn't have had anything to do with it."

"Has Jacob questioned Slade?"

"No," Bip replied. "But Betty Elliot has."

"Betty?"

"Ah," said Bip. "There are things even you don't know. Betty and Jude had a thing last year, and she got to know Slade a little better than most of *us* ever have. Slade is very upset. His best friend is suddenly gone, and he doesn't know why."

"That's horrible," said Kate. "Jacob has to do something."

"Do you think Jacob knows about Slade and Luke?" asked Fuzzy.

"I don't know," said Kate. "He's not always easy to read. Sometimes I think he's very broadminded; sometimes, I think he holds things back. It wouldn't surprise me if he knew."

Kate had dismissed Meadow's warning about Jacob, having decided that her stepmother had misjudged him – the result of an encounter that had gone wrong in some way. But now it rose again to the top of her mind, and she felt a stab of unease.

"Maybe *you* should talk to Slade first, Kate," said Bip. "Before anyone goes to Jacob."

Kate thought. She shook away her ponderings and tried to imagine how Slade must be suffering. What could she say to him? How could she help? "Alright. I'll do that. He must be distraught – abandoned. It's horrible – just think of it..."

"Jude's there," said Fuzzy. "Jude's kind. He'll be helping."

Kate frowned. "I can't comprehend any of this," she said. "It's not real. One way or another, by design or by accident, Mr Browning robbed the school, then calmly walked off accompanied by Orla and Luke. They didn't even take a horse – they just walked away, pockets full of money."

"That's about it," said Fuzzy. "They probably walked to Scarborough or Whitby – it would have taken them three, four, five hours – maybe stayed overnight. Jacob didn't notice the money was gone until very late. The first sign that something was amiss was when the privies didn't get emptied on the Wednesday evening. No-one put two and two together and realised the three of them had vanished until Thursday morning."

Bip seconded the assessment. "That's right. And by that time, they could have hired or bought horses, booked themselves onto a stagecoach – even *bought* their own coach if they'd wanted."

"But even with the theft of all that money, Jacob..." began Kate.

Bip finished for her. "...just wanted them back. *'It's only money,'* he said. *'Our friends were tempted and fell.'* It was like he was giving us a lesson in forgiveness or something. He posted notices in all the newspapers, basically saying 'Come back, all is forgiven'."

Kate screwed up her face in disbelief. "It's absurd. And all that money was just replaced without question?"

"Apparently so," said Fuzzy. "Even if Jacob wanted to go after Rider (which he didn't), the school benefactors told him to forget it. They just replaced the money, patted him on the back and told him 'what rotten luck'."

"But can't something be done to trace them? I mean..." Kate began.

"Why?" asked Bip. "What's lost? The money's back; Rider, Orla and presumably Lucas are living a great life, happy-dappy somewhere. Who would trace them anyway? The Scarborough constables? They're just a pair of fishermen – they're not going to go running about after people."

Kate thought, then said, "Supposing it's all a lie?"

"Alright," said Bip. "We've thought of a few possibilities. What's yours?"

"Jacob didn't want Rider and Orla to get married."

"Why not?" asked Bip.

"I don't know, just suppose for a moment. Maybe he's got them both locked up somewhere, and stole the money himself..."

"...Or murdered them..." said Bip.

"No," said Kate. She paused again. "That doesn't make sense either."

They sat quietly for a moment, shafts of shattered sunlight breaking through the creepers on the windows.

"I hope Orla's happy," said Fuzzy.

"So do I," said Kate. "We won't be going to their wedding now. I was looking forward to that."

"We all were," said Bip.

There was another pause. Then Kate changed the subject, "So we won't be seeing Nana again, or Viv, Betty, Dearbhla..."

"That's right," Bip replied. "They've all gone to London to become great ladies, to meet adoring gentlemen. Jacob makes a big thing of it. Kipp and Stanley take them down to Scarborough. They all stay there overnight – Jacob, Stella and the ten girls (nine, of course, this time). Then they travel all the way down in a pair of specially hired stagecoaches. He treats them like royalty. He makes up a pamphlet for them, so they'll know where they going to stay – pretty houses, inns with romantic names, menus and wines all laid on for them. I think he uses the same places every year. Looks like a real adventure. This journey, it's like Jacob's last present to them. They left three days ago – probably got as far as Cambridge by now."

"I'm not thinking clearly," said Kate. "This all feels false – like a dream. I'm not awake." She stood. "I'm going for a walk round the house."

"Let's all go," said Fuzzy. "Come on, Bip. We'll be Kate's guard in case she gets kidnapped."

They left by the back exit and strolled anti-clockwise around the house. The door into the kitchen was open, as it always was. Kate put her head round the corner and peered into the darkness of the cellar, trying to hear the bats, but there was no sound at all in the sepulchral blackness, and they went on, pausing briefly on the terrace overlooking the knot garden. Now that summer was here, the growth had filled out, and the plants, herbs, bushes and trees had burgeoned into life. The ivy covering the house had become rich and green, and the dog roses and honeysuckle had flourished along with convolvulus. Brambles and nettles were everywhere; geraniums and blackthorn. The exploded knot garden itself was rich with rosemary, sage, myrtle, thyme. Further away, beyond the sprawling box bushes, Kate picked out hyssop, gooseberries, currant bushes and more, all flourishing in the sun. The garden was awash with life. The sound of insects enlivened the warm air, and the flowers welcomed the fleeting visits of bees and butterflies.

"I wonder if Eden was anything like this," said Fuzzy.

"...Walking in the cool of the morning..." Kate muttered, her eyes unfocused, staring into the sky of her mind.

"It's three o'clock in the afternoon," said Bip.

"I know," said Kate. "I was lost for a moment – reflective. Sorry – it won't happen again." She looked at Fuzzy. "Got any gin?"

"Got any? I keep a bottle in the house. Shall we go back and fuddle our caps?"

"Let's do that," said Kate. "I've got my pipe too. I didn't dare smoke at home for fear of horrifying my dad."

The three girls continued their anti-clockwise course. As they made their way along the south side of the house towards the back door, Kate noticed the smell – the sickly stench of an animal's rotting flesh. She wrinkled her nose. "That's not nice."

"It's been there for a while," Bip replied. "It's a badger, dead on the bowling lawn. Not the first time something's died in there. It'll pass."

Kate stopped and looked at Bip. "You sure it's a badger?"

Bip pursed her lips. "You think it's Orla – or Luke. Rotting, murdered..."

"I think that sounds more likely than the story we've been

told," Kate replied.

"Well, it isn't," said Bip. She looked at Fuzzy, then back at Kate. "The same thing crossed our minds, and we went to see. It's a badger – a big one."

Kate sighed and continued towards the back door. "Alright," she said. "Gin then. Gin's definitely required today. I haven't been glorious for nearly a month."

58. THE ROAD HOME
Friday to Monday, July 17 to 20, 1761

At twenty minutes past four on Friday morning, Jacob set out from King's Place in the drizzling rain to walk the mile and a half to the Black Swan Inn, Holborn, where he would board the stagecoach to York. Edgar had offered the use of the convent's carriage, but Jacob enjoyed the early morning exercise. In any case, he wanted to be fully awake – sharply, exquisitely awake. He wasn't quite the same man as he'd been the day before. He turned his face up to the damp and allowed the tiny drops of moisture to spike his skin.

These annual visits always left him with an overwhelming sense of *ennui,* but things had proceeded differently this year. He relished the freshness of it but equally felt disturbed at how events had developed. Throughout his life, he'd avoided emotional involvement as far as possible, though not always with complete success. Once in a while he'd felt the pull of a kindred spirit, was briefly attracted by its gravity, then escaped without having become ensnared in its orbit. After each such occasion he was filled with a sense of loss, of having passed over the chance to obtain something precious. His brief flirtation with Meadow Reid had been one such, and now there was another. He felt an overwhelming sense of frustration, inadequacy, and he was fiercely walking it off on the dawn streets of London.

The journey south had been more subdued this year than it usually was, the nine girls saddened by the loss of the tenth; disheartened that she'd been led astray by a man who'd turned out to be an opportunist. Nevertheless, something of the usual excitement remained. Their years of study had all been leading to this; the moment they would emerge from their chrysalises and become beautiful butterflies. Stella always enjoyed the journey, and it made Jacob smile to see her partying with the girls, so very different in character from the headmistress they'd known all these years. They bonded with her in a way that hadn't been possible at the school. Of course, Stella was doubly joyous, anticipating what was to come.

Jacob joined in with their celebrations, their games. Once or twice, in earlier years, he'd become the unwitting object of the passion of one or more of their number, and had developed a considerate method of deflecting their attention: an affectionate smile, a harmless peck on the cheek, the suggestion that perhaps they'd drunk enough. But this year it had been more difficult; he'd known it would be. For the first time, there was a girl to whom he felt genuinely attracted. Beautiful, brilliant Vivianne Stamper sat next to him at dinner and put her hand on his thigh beneath the table. In all the time he'd known her she'd never been so bold. He allowed her touch to continue for a moment and looked directly at her.

"You know," she whispered. "It's the last chance."

She wasn't stupid – she knew he liked her. He rested his hand on hers, allowed it to linger briefly, felt the charge of their mutual desire race between them through the contact, skin to skin, then lifted her touch away. "Vivianne," he whispered. "It's difficult to say no, but it has to be *no*."

She looked downcast. The conversation around the table had dwindled, and Jacob thought a few of the others might have noticed what had passed between them. He put his hand on Vivianne's arm, attempting some kind of comfort. She glanced at him, then away, eyes unfocused. He said, "I'm genuinely sorry."

The Carriage

By the time Jacob arrived at the Black Swan the drizzle had turned into a steady downpour, and the streets had begun to resemble shallow rivers. The carriage was already in position, awaiting departure. He handed up his bag for securing to the roof.

"Poor weather for travelling," he commented to the driver.

"Aye, sir. It'll be a wet start right enough."

Jacob opened the coach door and climbed inside, the coachman closing it firmly behind him. He bade good morning to the two other occupants, took off his wet cape, sat down and pushed the garment under his seat, fearing that it might drip on him if he deposited it on the overhead rack.

It felt oddly still in the cab, the rain pounding on the roof, splashing in the puddles, distant cries of people braving the early morning. He sat in the offside corner of the forward-facing seat. A thin young man occupied the corner diagonally opposite. He faced away from Jacob, motionless, gazing intently out of the window. Jacob looked at the woman sitting directly across from him and noted her dense grey-white cataracts. She seemed to be staring straight at him, but it was obvious that she was blind. She was dressed entirely in black, her grey hair pinned severely above her head and tied in the back. Jacob guessed she was in her middle sixties, possibly as old as seventy. Her black bag and black hat occupied the rack above her head.

"A miserable morning," he offered.

She said nothing. Jacob wondered if she might be deaf. He sat back and made himself comfortable. The driver clicked the horses into motion and the carriage pulled away. Jacob watched the miserable streets through the rain-spattered window, the unsmiling bedraggled people on the way to their labour.

A few minutes later they drew to a halt at Smithfield market, already busy, the cattle pens almost full. A few butchers' stalls were open, even though the day was so young, and early sales were in progress, servants out to purchase fresh supplies for their masters' breakfasts. But there was no-one else for the coach, and within a few minutes they were once more on their way.

The carriage followed the road north, and a further fifteen minutes found them at the Angel, where several passengers waited. A large middle-aged man and his equally large, slightly younger wife joined the party within the coach, together with their teenage son, who looked as if he'd rather be somewhere else. At least three other people climbed into the carriage's external rear seats, and a guard joined the driver in front. The vehicle was on its way by twenty minutes to six.

The married couple argued with each other and scolded their son, who sat scowling at them. In the far corner, the uncommunicative young man looked out of the window as the city passed behind them, and continued his mute observation as they rode through succeeding villages. The elderly blind woman opposite continued to stare fixedly at Jacob, and believing her sightless, he stared back. After a minute or two, her face adopted a subtle smile, as if she'd found him out, discovered him, uncovered his secrets. The effect was unnerving, and he felt compelled to look away.

In his mind he heard Viv's voice. "For God's sake, Jacob! If it has to be someone, it may as well be you."

King's Place

His short sojourn in King's Place had largely followed the pattern of previous years. He and Stella handed over their cargo to Foxley, Margaret and the guards, and then absented themselves, leaving the girls to discover their fate. For the next two or three nights, Jacob would spy on them from an adjacent room as they individually underwent deflowering by customers who paid enormous sums for their virginity. It was Jacob's reward – the climax of years of nurturing the girls. Stella watched the spectacle too, although from a room on the opposite side, Jacob preferring to observe in isolation. The bolder, stronger girls resisted, cried for help, shrieked in protest; but often the procedure would pass quietly, submissively, the girls numb, in shock, paralysed with fright. There were almost always tears, to a greater or lesser degree. Despair was common, but it usually faded with time.

Jacob knew them all – knew how each one would be feeling. Each was achingly unique for him; each like a fine wine saved for this day.

But this year...

The Carriage

The coach lurched and bumped along the rutted road, the two parents and their irritating child squabbling almost all the time. Jacob was glad when they stopped at Edgware for the first change of horses. The rain had ceased, so he dismounted from the coach and stretched, yawning. The three passengers in the rear – two men and a blonde woman in their late twenties or early thirties – also hopped down and stamped about, trying to drive the cramps and aches out of their bodies.

"At least the rain's stopped," one of the men called to Jacob.

"Going far?" Jacob asked, making conversation.

"To Stilton. We're being collected there and taken home to Yaxley."

"Yaxley," said Jacob, eyebrows raised in friendly enquiry. "I've never been there."

"Well," said the blonde woman, "no reason why you would. Yaxley is really somewhere you start from in order to go somewhere interesting."

"Oh, not fair!" said the second man. "Yaxley's a pretty enough place. And the church is very fine."

"Sorry, Jed," said the girl. "I was being flippant – flippant, you see? It's a damp morning, and flippancy – *flippancy* – keeps me warm."

"I think you're quite warm enough, Mary," said Jed, chasing her, arms outstretched.

Jacob turned away, allowing them to banter among themselves. Two women were bringing refreshments out to the coach from the nearby inn. Jacob was hungry, and breakfast was most welcome.

They ate in the cabin while the horses were changed. Jacob leant forward and addressed the blind woman. "We have some breakfast. Can I help you to something?"

"No, thank you," said the woman. "I have my own breakfast here." She produced a box that had been tucked into the seat by her left thigh. It appeared to be made of brass, perhaps a tobacco box. She removed the lid and revealed what looked like a fruit cake cut into small squares.

"Would you care for a piece?" she asked Jacob.

"How very kind," he replied, took a piece and balanced it on his thigh, intending to consume it in the wake of the meat pie with which he was currently engaged.

The woman ate a piece of her own cake, then immediately inserted her hand through the neck of her dress and brought forth a large flask that had been slung beneath her left armpit. Jacob couldn't withhold a chuckle. The revealing of the object had been so deft and skilful that it had something of the appearance of a conjuring trick. "Ha!" he said, "that was well done, if you don't mind me saying so."

"Not at all," said the woman, uncorking the vessel. "Would you care for a drop?"

"What is it?" he asked.

"Rum," she replied. "I never go anywhere without it."

"Rum!" he replied. "No. But thank you. It's a little early for me."

She took a swig and followed it immediately with another of her little cakelets.

The carriage was beginning to move again, lurching, rocking on its springs.

"Are you going far?" asked Jacob.

"To York," she replied.

"Then we shall be fellow travellers all the way."

The woman said nothing but resumed her stare, smiling. Jacob found it unsettling.

"I've been to London on business," he volunteered.

Again, silence.

"And you, if I dare ask," he went on. "Visiting friends in the capital?"

"No," she replied. "I've been to my husband's burial in Corfe."

Jacob leaned back in his seat, hands on knees, regretting his faux-pas. "Oh," he said. "Please forgive me. I'm most terribly sorry."

"*I'm* not sorry," she said. "Not sorry at all."

King's Place

"Jacob, the new nuns are all so graceful, so beautiful," said Margaret. "We're very glad that you're one of us. What you do is beyond any reward we can give."

"I gather my own reward," he replied. "Believe me, if I found the work unsatisfying I'd be doing something else. The pleasure I gain from my involvement remains undiminished."

"That is delightful to hear," she replied (Foxley nodded his agreement). "But Edgar and I have been talking, and we feel you should be offered something more."

"I have all the money I require..." he began, hands raised in a gesture of contentment.

"Yes," said Margaret. She paused. "We both feel that you should take one of the new nuns. We know you watch, but we both think that you should... you know. Wouldn't you like that?"

Jacob paused, wondering if he'd heard correctly. "You mean..."

"Yes," said Margaret. "I know it's not much... a gesture to show how much we appreciate you."

He sat for a while in silence, thinking. His own particular pleasure lay in anticipation, not in fulfilment; if it had been otherwise, he would have consummated his erotic frisson with Vivianne long ago. There had been rare occasions when he felt the raw animal urge that was common with many men, and at those times he rode to Whitby, Scarborough or elsewhere and paid for its assuagement, as he had in the old days in London. But his own girls, these girls, were special, and he felt no desire to sully them by allowing himself to become the instrument of their ravishment.

"No," he said slowly. "I don't think so. Thank you, but I don't believe that would be a good idea."

"Come on, Crowan," said Foxley. "Take one of them. You've earned it."

This is going to get tedious, thought Jacob. *They believe they're doing me a great big favour.* He thought for a moment and decided that the simplest thing would be to select a girl, sit quietly in her room for a while, and then emerge a satisfied customer.

"Alright. Nana, then; Nana Hall."

The Carriage

The coach continued on its way north while breakfast reached a conclusion within its confines, the married couple arguing over who should eat the remaining morsel of cheese. Jacob thought it really was the pettiest of arguments, the two prattling at each other like apes. The elderly blind woman clearly shared his opinion. She sighed, thrust out her tin blindly to the centre of the carriage and said, "Please help yourselves. This is a fruit cake made to my own recipe. Everybody commends it."

Jacob reinforced the recommendation. "I can vouch for that. It's some of the finest cake I've ever eaten."

The elderly woman smiled in his direction. "Thank you for your endorsement. How kind you are, sir."

"Jacob," he replied. "Please call me Jacob."

She did not offer her name but instead held her cake box firmly while the family helped themselves to its contents. The silent young man in the opposite corner did not turn or acknowledge the invitation to partake, but instead continued to stare out of the window. The blind woman replaced the lid of her receptacle, casting Jacob a smile as she did so.

The coach rumbled onwards, conversation inside having ceased except for the odd snipe between the two parents. Jacob began to doze despite the bumpy road.

King's Place

Foxley and Margaret cast each other a glance.

"Er, possibly not Nana," said Foxley.

Jacob raised his eyebrows in enquiry.

Margaret explained, "Nana is an extraordinary beauty, really quite unique. And the surgeon has confirmed that she is still a virgin."

"I see," said Jacob, realising his error. "Although I'm sure they're all virgins. I keep a close eye on them and would know otherwise."

"No offence, Crowan," said Foxley. "It's simply to do with turnover. We're sure we can auction Nana's first night for well over four figures. She's worth a huge sum of money – probably more than any girl in London."

"Of course," Jacob replied. "Stupid of me."

"Not at all!" Foxley returned. "Your own value to us far exceeds such a sum; of course it does. But for the sake of practicality – if you don't mind..."

Jacob was already nodding in reassurance as Margaret said, "Of course, if you have your heart set on Nana..."

"Not a bit," said Jacob, waving the suggestion away with both hands.

"What about Orla?" Foxley suggested. "She hasn't smiled yet, but she's obedient – making an effort to fit in..."

Jacob gave a half laugh and interjected, "No, I don't think that would be a good idea."

"Dearbhla then," Foxley tried. "She's a pretty thing, lovely wavy hair. And I'm told it's her birthday today! Eighteen. There we are. You can give her a birthday kiss. She hasn't been unlocked yet. Neither has Vivianne or Carol. You'd be doing the honours."

Jacob thought for a moment. "If it's all the same with you, I'll take Vivianne. Viv Stamper."

Margaret nodded her approval, and Foxley said, "Certainly. Viv it is, then. She's yours for the night. I'll have her made ready." He looked at his watch. "Thirty minutes?"

The Carriage

Jacob woke to the sound of choking. He looked to his left to see the large man doubled up, hands at his throat, face bright red, clearly in extreme discomfort. His wife, no longer arguing and chastising, was in a panic, shouting, gesticulating. The boy leaned away from his parents, his face a mixture of concern and disgust. The woman thrust her head out of the far window and shouted up to the coachman. "Stop, my husband's ill."

The carriage drew to a halt and the driver came down to inspect the sufferer, who appeared to be worsening, his face developing an alarming purple hue.

"There's an inn at Hatfield a mile ahead," said the driver. "We'll summon help there."

"Can I do something?" asked Jacob.

"Are you are a physician?" called the driver, raising his

voice over the unfortunate man's spluttering.

"No," Jacob replied.

"Then sit tight, sir. I'll go as quick as I can."

In seconds the coach was moving again, the poor wretch continuing to choke and struggle for breath. It was a frightful spectacle.

Jacob scanned the carriage for the reactions of the other passengers. The silent man in the corner continued to stare out of the window, motionless. The blind woman opposite sat rigidly upright, sightless eyes fixed on Jacob, the corners of her lips turned up in her strange, fixed smile.

Jacob changed places with the teenage boy and inspected the agonised man, but he was at a loss. Beyond a few simple remedies and the treatment of superficial wounds he had almost no medical knowledge and could think of nothing useful. The poor man's face continued to darken, and his hands became crimson and swollen.

"I'm sorry," he said to the large woman. "I don't know what to do." She was frantic, beside herself, shouted and cried to her husband, exhorting him to stand up, move, breathe. But her pleas brought no response.

Mercifully, the coach pulled into the stage at Hatfield just a few minutes later. The driver dismounted, called to the innkeeper and then ran back to the vehicle. The people on the rear jumped down and looked through the open door, the young woman turning away in horror at the sight, while one of the men leapt into the cabin and opened the sick man's collar, although it appeared to do no good.

Fortunately, there was a surgeon who'd been waiting at the inn for the arrival of the coach. He had the distressed man removed from the carriage and taken into the hostelry, the large woman and her son following behind. The three rear passengers, the driver, and the guard formed a group of concerned spectators and followed the unhappy family into the building.

The coach was suddenly quiet. Jacob returned to his corner, shaken by the experience. The silent thin man seemed unmoved and remained staring out of his window. The blind woman was calm, still, and appeared utterly unconcerned about what was taking place.

"He'll probably survive," she said, then offered him her newly opened cake tin. "Another?"

Jacob said nothing, but looked from her face to the cakelets, his soul chilled. *But we all ate them*, he thought, *except that odd creature over there in the corner.*

The blind woman leaned forward, her smile hardening. She whispered, "You think I'm a dark one – but you are a darker creature than I. *I smell you.*" The words were delivered in a steadily quieter tone, the last three syllables long, drawn-out, emphasised, as if she were carefully exposing a fragile black bud to the eyes of something that wished to eat it.

Jacob pressed himself back into his seat. "Who are you?" he said quietly.

The woman resumed her calm, upright posture and replaced the lid on her cake box. "Just the wife of a poor, deceased parson."

He looked again at the third occupant of the coach. There was no change. As far as Jacob was aware, the small man had not altered his position an inch during the entire journey. The thought occurred to Crowan that the carriage was not going to York at all, but was spiralling steadily down into the earth on its way to some flame-red nightmare. Perhaps his travelling companions were not even human...

The vehicle lurched, and Jacob came to himself with a start. The rear passengers had re-boarded, and the guard had mounted the box. The driver looked in at the open door and said, "They'll be staying here with the doctor. We're moving on."

"How is he?" asked Jacob.

"Not sure," said the driver. "The doctor reckons he ate something that disagreed with him."

Jacob looked again at the elderly blind woman. She seemed

calm, even serene, smiling her little smile.

In a moment the coach was moving again.

The woman whispered, "Blessed peace."

King's Place

"I hope I'll have the chance to visit you up there in the north sometime before next summer," said Edgar. "I could do with a bit of sea air. I'm afraid I've rather lost contact with the Reids. I really must make more of an effort."

"The Lookout is always at your disposal, Edgar," said Crowan, "as you know."

"You're very kind, as always." They shook hands. "So, you're on the five o'clock coach," Edgar went on. "I shan't be up at that hour, so I'll say goodbye now."

"Till next time, Edgar."

"Indeed so." Foxley paused, then said, "Up you go then. I hope your lovely dark-haired young nun appreciates the blessing you're about to bestow upon her."

Jacob smiled, turned and climbed the staircase, aware that Foxley was watching him. When he'd reached the first-floor landing, he stopped and listened to the creaking floorboards that traced Edgar's withdrawal to another part of the house. Jacob swallowed. He'd really rather not see Vivianne, but for simplicity's sake, he knew he had to press on and somehow get this situation over. So he walked to the end of the landing, took hold of the banister, and ascended further.

Vivianne's room, he'd been told, was on the third floor, at the end of the corridor, immediately before the next flight of stairs. He was surprised to find his heart racing, and stood outside the door for a few moments without knocking. He swallowed, cognizant of the choice that faced him, unsure if his resolve would hold once he was alone with her. He held up his hand, looked at his knuckles, paused once more, then knocked.

"Yes." A voice from within. Jacob pushed open the door. Vivianne stood in the centre of the bedroom, the firelight shining behind her. She was a creature prepared for sacrifice, Holly at her side holding a hairbrush, having just administered the final touches for her surrender. "Jacob," Holly greeted him quietly.

"Holly," said Jacob. "It's good to see you again." He stepped forward.

Viv looked at him with incredulity. "You?!" Holly left the room hurriedly, shutting the door behind her.

"Vivianne," he said and looked at her from top to toe, her body clearly visible beneath the fragile fabric, his own body helplessly responding at the sight of her.

She was angry. "They send *you* in here? *You?! Of all people!*"

He said nothing.

"You evil bastard!"

Jacob didn't know what to say. He shrugged, and shook his head impotently.

"Not you," she said. "I won't submit to you – not now."

He held up his hands, palms forward as if to silence her. "Shh. Be still. Calm yourself. I won't hurt you."

She'd expected him to force her. Instead, he walked to the window, sat down, and cast his gaze to the floor. "Do you have something to put on? It's very...disturbing to look at you."

Viv briefly surveyed herself and said, "No. They took my clothes away."

"Perhaps if you just got into bed then," he said.

She turned around, stepped to the bed and sat on its edge. "What are you going to do?"

"Nothing," he replied. "I'll just sit here if I may."

She got into bed, leaned up on the pillows and looked at him. "Tell me why," she said. "All those years, all that nurturing, *all for this?*"

"It's what I've always done," said Jacob.

"We were promised a rich, fulfilled life," Viv replied, cutting in before he'd finished his sentence.

Jacob spoke across her statement. "Where did we find you, Viv?"

"Where did you find me?" She felt a little of her outrage crumble. "Oulston. I was living in a loft next to a hen coop, above a pigsty."

"In a pigsty." He nodded. "I remember the story. You were among the first. You were rescued in the summer of 1755 and arrived at the Lookout that autumn. You were twelve years old, abandoned by your mother..."

"Don't you mention my mother!" Vivianne shouted at him. "She was good! I loved her!"

But Jacob had gone on, ignoring her outrage and continuing unabated, his voice rising. "... grew up with the pigs. You lived with their filth. Another year and you'd have been sharing your master's bed. You'd have been a mother by the time you were fourteen, fifteen, probably dead before you were twenty. Look at you now. You're an educated woman: eloquent, intelligent, beautiful. You would never have become the person you are now if it were not for the Lookout – if it were not for me." He'd quietened by the time he reached the end.

"Orla's here," she said.

"I know," he replied.

"Tell me what you did."

He was puzzled. "What do you mean?"

"You know what I mean. How low did you sink? Where's Rider? Orla thinks you murdered him."

Jacob said nothing for a while but just looked at her. Eventually, he said, "Go to sleep, Viv. I'll be gone before you wake." He rose and extinguished the lamp, leaving the dwindling fire as the only source of illumination in the room, then walked back to his chair, sat down and closed his eyes, aware that she was still watching him in the dimness.

The Carriage – Biggleswade

Shortly after noon, the carriage pulled into the coach house at the Crown Inn, Biggleswade. Jacob had been dozing again but was awakened by the bustle of voices in the inn yard. The rear passengers, driver and guard had already dismounted, and the carriage was empty except for Jacob, the elderly woman and the motionless man.

"It appears we've stopped for lunch," said Jacob. "May I help you down?"

"How kind," she replied and presented her hand. Jacob opened the door, assisted her to the ground and walked her the few steps to the inn. The taproom was busy, but a few tables remained unoccupied. Jacob selected one and saw that his companion was comfortably seated.

"I'd like to buy you luncheon, if you'd allow me the honour," he said.

"How thoughtful you are," she said. "I accept. Thank you. I'll just take a little cheese, bread and cold meat if I may."

"Of course," said Jacob. "I'll see to it. What would you like to drink?"

"If there's a strong ale, I'll have some of that. How kind."

"It's my pleasure." He looked about for the serving girl, but seeing that she was occupied at another table, rose and ordered their meal at the bar, returning a few moments later with two flagons of ale. Their simple meal arrived almost immediately.

Jacob cast his eyes around him as they ate. The three people from the rear seats were having a great time, the young woman in fits of laughter. The driver and guard occupied a table by themselves near the door. There was no sign of the odd young man. Perhaps he was sitting outside, or maybe this was his destination and he'd gone on his way. The inn was busy, popular, abuzz with conversation and full of colour and character.

Jacob, enjoying a piece of pungent yellow cheese, looked across at his companion and said, "You still haven't told me your name."

"No," she said, "but *your* name is Jacob. You told me."

"You're a mysterious woman, if I may be so bold," said Jacob. "You tell me that I'm a dark creature, that you can *smell me out*, yet you withhold your name. You intrigue me."

She looked sightlessly at him, a piece of bread held in her fingers. "Names are powerful things, Jacob. They should not be easily given away."

He nodded. "Of course not."

"But you can call me...Maria. I've always liked the name."

"But it's not your real name."

"What do *you* think?" she said. "Perhaps it is."

"It seems to me that you are rather dark yourself," said Jacob.

"You flatter me," she said. "I'm just an old woman in mourning for her husband."

"That wasn't the impression you gave earlier," Jacob ventured.

She took a draught of her ale – then set down the flagon, brought forth the flask of rum from her armpit, poured half the contents into the ale, swilled the mixture about and sampled the result.

"Much improved," she said.

Jacob took a swallow of his own ale, identical to hers. He'd asked for the strongest in the house, and it was indeed quite potent enough – without the addition of rum. He laughed. "You're a fascinating creature."

"What do you do, Jacob?"

"I'm the headmaster of a charitable school for young ladies."

She raised her eyebrows. "Indeed so? How interesting."

"And you," said Jacob. "Were you always married to a parson?"

"Not at all," she said. "I was married in 1716, when I was twenty-two years old."

"A good age for a woman to marry," said Jacob. "Do you have any children?"

"No," she replied. "That, at least, was a blessing."

"You were not happy in your marriage?"

"As a very young woman, I was ambitious," she said. "I was a student of the chymical arts..."

"Fascinating," Jacob interjected, eyebrows raised.

"It is a most diverting subject," she said. "I studied with Viktor Distler."

"I'm afraid I don't recognise the name," said Jacob.

"No," said she. "But perhaps you know the name, Robert Boyle."

"Of course," Jacob replied. "The famous philosopher, himself a noted chymist."

She nodded. "Very good, Jacob. You have an enquiring mind. In his later years, Robert Boyle confined himself to his sister's house in London – he withdrew almost entirely from public life. Viktor Distler visited the house on many occasions in Robert's last ten years and became well acquainted with both Robert and his sister Katherine, Lady Ranelagh. Robert immersed himself in many pursuits and procedures that remained incomplete at the time of his death. They would have been lost, but Viktor, my Viktor – they lived on in him. And in me. They'll die with me."

Jacob was enthralled. "This is fascinating," he said. "Tell me more."

Maria sighed. "Do you know, I'm rather tired. I think I would like to return to the coach."

He was disappointed, but pleased that they'd have further opportunity for discussion as the journey went on. "Of course," he said. "Let's get you back."

"Jacob, I would like to visit the house of office. Would you be so good as to guide me?"

"Of course, here's my hand."

568

Maria took nearly a quarter of an hour in the jakes while Jacob wandered about the yard. He watched the queue build up at the privy door, some of its members becoming visibly irritated at the delay. Maria ignored their grumbles when she emerged, and Jacob escorted her to the carriage, which stood ready with fresh horses. In less than a minute she was fast asleep.

Rum, he thought. *Good idea.* He returned to the bar and purchased a large bottle of the spirit and a second flagon of strong ale, checking his watch to ensure there was adequate time to drink the latter. He had a quarter of an hour in hand, so he wandered into the field at the rear of the inn and sat on the wall there, drinking his ale in the sun.

It had turned out to be a warm day, the rain of the morning long forgotten. There were a few cows in the field, some of them watching him, their long tongues licking into their nostrils, tails swiping idly at flies. Beyond the field lay the splendid old church of St Andrew. The tower was new, the mediaeval one having collapsed at the turn of the century. The bells were being rung, but whether in rehearsal or for a specific event, Jacob had no way of knowing. He counted five tones, five bells. As he sat, ale in hand, eyes unfocused, counting the pitches, he became aware of a figure standing in the field, between the cows and the church. He concentrated his vision and realised it was the strange young man from the coach. He was facing the church, his back to Jacob, perfectly still.

Jacob frowned, his flagon half raised. There was something strange about the sight, the young man standing in the grasses while the cows walked untroubled around him. He was tempted to call out, to get the boy's attention, but was reluctant to puncture the scene with his voice.

He checked his watch. Five minutes. Jacob downed the rest of his ale, took the flagon to the bar, thanked the innkeeper and made his way out to the coach, finding himself the last to board. The strange young man was back in his place, staring out of the window. Maria was fast asleep, snoring. The driver signalled the horses to move off, and they were once more on the road.

King's Place

Jacob sat quietly in his chair and hoped that Vivianne would go to sleep. The minutes passed and the fire continued to die down, the room darkening further. He detected no change in her breathing, although she seemed to become less restless, the stir of the bedclothes diminishing. He closed his eyes and allowed his mind to drift. Soon he was sleeping, head slumped forward, dreamless.

He woke in the near black. The fire had gone out, leaving only glowing embers. He was unsure how long he'd been unconscious but realised that he needed to find a privy. He sat forward and listened. Viv's breathing, even and deep, suggested she was asleep. He rose from his seat and let himself out of the room.

A single oil lamp burned low on a table at the other end of the landing. The only sound was that of a ticking clock on the floor below. He crept along, trying all the doors, not wanting to disturb anyone, wincing at the squeaking floorboards, and eventually found what he wanted.

A few minutes later he stole back to Viv's bedroom, opened the door silently, passed inside and closed it behind him.

"I thought you'd left," she whispered as he tiptoed back to his chair.

"No," Jacob replied softly. "I just had to find..." He could see her dimly, sitting up in bed.

"You must have a room of your own here. If you're not going to...," she left the phrase unfinished, "...what are you doing?"

"Watching over you – for the night," he said.

"Why?"

He sighed. "Suicide is a danger on the first night."

"My God," she replied. "You're sitting there to see I don't kill myself..."

"This place, and the realisation of what you have to do, is a shock to new nuns, as you've found out..."

"Nuns?" Her incredulity was apparent in the tone of her voice.

"It's a term we use," he replied. "And you're living in a convent."

"And is there a mother superior?"

"There's an abbess."

"This is unbelievable."

"The ecclesiastical terms have a long association with the profession."

"This'll make a fine, long story!"

"And I'm sure you'll write it well. There's your new calling. Think of this as gathering material."

She was quiet, and Jacob sensed her concentration. "You're inspired," he said, "aren't you? I can hear your mind working."

She answered him obliquely. "Supposing I were to write this book. Would you see that I was deprived of pen and ink? Would you seek to make its creation impossible for me?"

"No Viv, I wouldn't do that. I'll say nothing to anybody. I'll look forward to reading your work. I've always taken pleasure in your writing – you're well aware of that. You have a talent – I would not wish to see it extinguished."

She paused a moment. "You're a difficult one to understand, Jacob. You're a destroyer – and a nurturer."

"It'll be something to do with power," he said. "The closer one is to death, the more one appreciates the fragility of life."

"We should have had this conversation a year ago, two years ago," she replied. "I'd have had a better understanding of you. We could have had an altogether different relationship, and I might not now be here."

"It's too late now," he quickly interjected. "You *are* here. You've been delivered."

She absorbed the finality of his statement. "So what happens now?"

"I'll sit here until the dawn comes up..."

"No," she said. "I mean, what happens to me?"

"In the long run? You'll absorb this experience and grow – you're intelligent and strong. That is my assessment of you personally."

"And the others?"

"Most of them have already been...initiated into the order, last night or the night before. I think there's only you, Nana, Dearbhla and Carol remaining. The first night is the most traumatic – the baptism into the life – but almost all survive it. The second encounter is usually easier. After that, it becomes routine. The initial despair fades – the sense of hopelessness. From that point you make a go of it, or you don't. You won't be here forever. The working life is a short one – you'll retire long before you're thirty, with enough money to keep you and your family in comfort for generations." He'd expected her to reply to that, but nothing was forthcoming, so he went on. "There's no violence here – it isn't permitted..."

"No violence?" she scoffed.

"I mean, you'll be protected – you won't be beaten. This is not a cheap establishment – this is among the most elite convents in London. Only the rich and powerful find themselves in this house."

"Go on," she said.

"Disease is rare here. The house surgeons check regularly. It is safe, relatively speaking."

"Relatively speaking?"

"A few nuns have died; I won't hide it from you."

"Anybody I know?"

"Yes."

She was quiet for a moment, the horror of this single word sinking in. "Alright. Don't tell me any more, please."

Only the faintest glow remained in the embers. The silence in the room seemed to thicken, to become denser.

"I thought I knew you," she said. "I even liked you – in that naïve way that girls do. But I didn't know you at all. Now I see who you are."

No adequate reply occurred to Jacob, so he said nothing.

"Supposing I write a book that exposes you? Suppose I write a book about a London brothel serviced by a fake school in Yorkshire? Suppose I name the headmaster Jacob Crowan?"

"I'm sure you'll do just that," said Jacob, "but it won't do any good. We'd just deny it as a work of fiction, a fantasy."

She thought, then said. "Suppose I send copies to the Lookout? Then the girls would all know. They'd rise up against you."

"Mail to the Lookout is strictly monitored. It would never get through."

"I'd send the book to the newspapers then. They'd expose you."

"Viv, the newspapers are run by the people who fund these schools and convents. Do you think they'd publish your story?"

"Alright, then I'd send the book to parliament..."

"Your visitors here will include many lords and politicians..."

"To the King then, the royal family..."

"I think you're going to be very surprised..." he said.

"I'll find a way," she finished.

"I admire your determination," he said, "and wish you the best of luck."

The sustained creaking of the bed frame and the extended angry rustling of the linen suggested that Viv had either got out of bed or had lain down and indignantly pulled the sheets around her. Jacob waited, eyes unfocused in the gloom. There was complete silence for a long time. Then she said, "Why don't you just do it?"

"You mean...?"

"Yes," she said. "It's you and me alone in a room. I can't stop you. Why don't you just do it?"

"I...prefer to watch."

"You must hate me," she said.

He was puzzled, frowned. "I don't hate you at all."

"You told me the first night is the worst; that the second is easier."

He saw where this was going. "Yes..."

"So, if that's true, you could make things easier for me rather than sit there and string out my suffering for another day."

"Viv..."

"Why aren't you in this bed, you coward?"

"I..."

"For God's sake, Jacob!" she cried. "If it has to be someone, it may as well be you."

The Carriage

Crowan woke with a jolt, driven from his dream by Viv's shout. He thought he may actually have cried out. The cabin came into focus as sleep dropped away – the young man fixed to the window, Maria opposite, smiling, cataracts shining. "I beg your pardon," he said.

"You were talking in your sleep, muttering," said Maria.

Jacob looked out of the window. The sky was much darker, filled with threatening clouds.

"Where are we?" he asked.

"A few miles north of Alconbury," she said. "We've just changed horses for the last time today. You've been asleep all afternoon."

Jacob checked his watch and found that it was half past five. "I'm terribly sorry," he said. "The ale must have been

574

stronger than I thought."

"No matter," she replied. "I've been asleep too."

"We'll soon be at Stilton," said Jacob.

"Yes," she confirmed. "About seven o'clock. On schedule, more or less. I'm looking forward to some fine cheese."

The first drops of rain appeared on the carriage windows. Jacob decided to try conversation with the coach's other occupant. He leaned towards the young man. "Excuse me, sir. Good day to you. Are you travelling far?"

"Good Lord!" said Maria, pressing herself forward, alert. "Is there someone else in the coach? I thought we were alone."

Jacob glanced at her, surprised that she hadn't sensed the young man's presence. "No, I assure you, we have a companion." He returned his attention to the other, who remained fixedly staring out of the far window, his back to them. Jacob was about to repeat his question, but was startled by the forceful impact of an unnaturally large splash of bird dung across the windows on the far side of the coach, almost completely obscuring the young man's view of the passing world beyond. Jacob leapt back in his seat, shocked, as if the carriage were under attack. The young man exhibited no surprise, no movement, no reaction at all to the sudden explosion, but remained immobile as if carved from a particularly dark alabaster.

Jacob gave up and resumed his seat, frowning. Maria's smile had disappeared. She sat rigidly upright, staring emptily, her countenance greyer than it had previously been.

The gloom in the cabin deepened suddenly as if a cloak had been laid over the world, and the sky unleashed a torrent of water that beat down on the vehicle with deafening force, flushing away the mess on the window in two or three seconds. The coach halted, and the three travellers riding in the open seat at the rear jumped down, opened the carriage door and bundled themselves inside. Once settled and the door closed, the carriage pulled away.

"It's teeming down out there!" said the young woman.

Maria produced her cake tin, removed the lid and offered the contents to the newcomers. "Have a cake," she said. "I made them myself."

Jacob looked at Maria in alarm, then at their new companions, all of whom were already consuming the offered refreshment. There was nothing to be done. He watched curiously as they chatted amongst themselves. Five minutes, ten minutes, fifteen. There were no ill effects. He glanced up at Maria and found her smiling broadly, almost to the point of bursting into laughter. Was she mocking him?

"My baking is celebrated far and wide," she said, took a piece herself, bit off half and crushed it in her mouth. "Take some, Jacob." She pushed the box in his direction.

He pressed himself into the upholstery and said, "That's very kind of you, but I won't at this stage if you don't mind. It'll soon be dinnertime, and I want to preserve my appetite."

"Of course you do," she said, withdrew the tin and replaced the lid.

At seven o'clock the carriage pulled through the archway of the Bell Inn at the village of Stilton, where everyone dismounted. The three young people bade goodbye to Jacob and Maria, their transport to Yaxley already waiting to carry them away. Crowan helped his companion down from the carriage, then glanced across at the far side of the coach, but the fixed young man was already gone, his door hanging open. Jacob stood in the coachyard as the driver handed down their respective bags, then escorted Maria into the inn, where they checked in and were given adjacent rooms.

"Shall we eat together?" he asked.

"I shall look forward to that," she replied. Shall we say half an hour?"

"I'll give you a knock," said Jacob.

His room was well lit, and he was relieved to find a basin

and warm water already provided. After a quick visit to the privy in the coachyard, he freshened himself up and sat down, reflecting on the events of the last twenty-four hours, pleased to be settled in a chair that wasn't constantly in motion.

At a quarter to eight, the two sat opposite each other at a table in the bar. Jacob ordered food for them both and carried two flagons of strong ale to their table. Maria tasted it and reached for her flask of rum, but Jacob stayed her hand and said, "Allow me." From his pocket he produced the bottle he'd purchased at Biggleswade, opened it and poured a quantity into Maria's ale. She took a draught, smiled and laughed. "You learn quickly, young Jacob."

"The pleasure is mine," he said.

"It's good to have company," said Maria, setting down her flagon. "I had expected the journey to be without incident, but I find you very diverting."

"And I you, madam," he replied. "Earlier you were telling me about your studies with Viktor Distler, and the secrets of Robert Boyle."

"Are you a man of science, Jacob?"

"If you mean the natural philosophies, no, I fear not. But I have a hungry mind, and you have an arresting manner, so I am curious to listen."

She was quiet for a moment, then said, "I acquired an understanding of – hidden knowledge, shall we say? – that proved useful to me in later life. Of course, in my younger days I had my sight; and learning – experimentation – was easier. I never met Boyle; he died three years before I was born. But my Viktor assisted him for nearly a decade..."

"Were you married?"

"To Viktor? No. No, but I should have been. I studied with him from 1710 until his death five years later. I was sixteen when we met. He was sixty-two."

"That is a huge age difference," said Jacob. Maria was silent. "You were lovers then?"

"That is the modern expression, I believe. Yes, we were, from my nineteenth year."

Their dinner arrived, and the conversation paused while the dishes were laid on the table.

"Pardon my ignorance if I prove too forward," said Jacob. "Can I offer you any assistance with your meal?"

"No, no," she replied. "I'm quite used to fending for myself. Please, go on and enjoy your food."

Jacob began to eat, simultaneously observing the techniques Maria used for mapping and navigating her way around the table. After a while, he asked, "So, what did you study with Viktor?"

"Many things," she said. "The behaviour of gasses. We experimented with vacuums and speculated about the nature of corpuscular matter, amongst other things. All fascinating, but there were other studies too, involving all kinds of substances from vegetable extracts to liquid metals. Some of the results proved very useful – to me."

Jacob wanted to ask her about the cake but couldn't find an acceptable form of words. As it turned out, he didn't have to.

"You're wondering about my cake, aren't you?" she said.

"Well…" he began.

"But you ate a piece, didn't you?"

"Yes, I did."

"And you saw me eat some?"

"Yes."

"And you saw other passengers take some too, yes?"

"I did."

"Well, there we are then," she finished. That particular part of the conversation appeared to have come to an end.

She suddenly turned her face towards him, impaled him with her blazing cataracts. "Where's your wife?"

He was briefly knocked off balance. "My wife? I'm not married."

"But you've been with a woman. I mean, you've slept with

a woman – very recently."

He frowned, his brows knit. "How did you know?"

"I can smell them," she said.

Jacob set down his knife and fork and waited for more.

Maria went on. "I was distraught when Viktor died. He was sixty-seven – not young, but hardly a great age. I was deeply in love with him and found myself suddenly alone – vulnerable, I suppose – a target for predators, particularly those in the clothing of shepherds. I married my husband in 1716. I was twenty-two (I believe I told you before). He was ten years older than me, the rector of one of the fine new London churches. Shall I tell you which? No, I don't think so. But his name – let's call him…Solomon. It is apt."

"I'm not sure I understand," said Jacob.

"Not know your bible? Tut-tut, Jacob. No matter. But perhaps you're not interested in the complaints of an old woman."

"I assure you that I'm listening with rapt attention," Jacob replied. "I beg you to continue."

"My husband, Solomon, was a proud and bold conveyer of the spirit of the Lord. He wasted no time in filling me with the spirit – quite forcibly so – one September afternoon. He was so overcome with his passionate desire to preach to me that I could not close my ears to him. He stretched out his spear like Joshua and subdued me. We were married a few weeks later."

"I understand," said Jacob.

"Of course you do," Maria went on. "But like many persuasive missionaries, he went on to convert others. My friends were the easiest targets. They'd come to the house to visit me, but in a few days he'd have them under the thrall of Aaron's rod, converting them. Often he'd convert them in our marriage bed, sometimes while I was in the house. One after another they fell to him, all pierced with the lance of Longinus. His preaching was most persuasive. Sometimes I'd listen outside the bedroom door and hear the women –

my friends – speaking in tongues, begging him not to stop, to go on stuffing them with the good news. He was vigorous, relentless, determined to plant the seed of his faith wherever he could. His not the sinew that shrank. He drove his doctrine into them with the mitre of his righteousness, the great rod of Moses.

"We went on, year after year, the decades passing by, he bringing his gospel to the women, always thirsty for his holy wine. Oh yes, he was an expert. But me – me, he treated like a leper. He'd grown bored with me. I was as nothing to him. He though – the great man; the great Solomon; king of seven hundred wives – he spent his years distributing the water of life from the blessed fountain of his virtue." She paused. "That's why I'm so practised at smelling women."

Jacob let her words settle, then said, "I'm very sorry for you."

"Don't be," she replied. "You see, I had my own little gospel to share with him. I taught it to him very gradually. In a little while the staff of Moses became a snake, then a worm. The women lost interest in him. They stopped calling, and he couldn't pursue them – the uprightness had faded from his faith. Drop by drop, day by day, I fed him my own spirit of the Lord. He became bedridden, lost the use of his hands, his legs, his eyes, his ears. Slowly, steadily. My spirit of the Lord became very heavy within him. One day it became so heavy – that it pushed him six feet under the ground."

Her monologue had become steadily quieter, slower, more emphatic. When she finished, Jacob found himself leaning forward, utterly enthralled. He'd been absorbing every syllable, her words like rain in the desert. Now he sat back in his seat and looked at her in silence. She bent forward across the half-eaten meal and quietly said, "You think my soul is damned." She pointed at him. "But you carry death in yours also." He was unable to respond; it was as if he'd been cornered by a huge, inescapable predator...

There was a clatter at the side of the table, and Jacob, startled, looked to his right. A large-breasted serving woman stood there with a platter of fine blue-veined cheese and fresh bread.

"Our local cheese," she said, "made nearby and much admired." She curtseyed and retired.

"Stilton cheese!" said Maria. "Wonderful. Nothing like it. Let's get down to business!"

Jacob pulled himself together and took up his knife with relief. "Here. I'll cut you a piece."

"Thank you, young Jacob," she said. "Tomorrow you must tell me *your* story. Mine must have bored you senseless."

Jacob felt cast adrift by the strangeness of events, separated from the person he'd thought himself to be. He was troubled by Maria's instinctive assessment of him, expressed with such precision. And he was overwhelmed by the memory of Vivianne, both emotional and tactile. Lying in the darkness of his room, he imagined her in bed next to him, recreated her softness in his mind, his hand running gently along the curve of her flank, her thigh, and was disturbed at the fierceness with which his body wanted hers.

She'd said nothing as he removed his clothes in the near dark, although he could hear that she was breathing nervously through her mouth. When he pulled aside the bedclothes to get in with her, she lifted her nightgown over her head and threw it away. She was in his hands in the same second, and in the next they were coupled, he in motion, she beneath.

"Don't let me stay here," she whispered. "You can take me away with you."

He said nothing, but continued on to his peak. She felt its approach and voiced his name, a plea. "Jacob? Please? Don't leave me here."

Afterwards, they lay together in the stillness, neither

speaking. But he was wide awake in the dark, touching her, exploring the landscape of her body, and within a few minutes he wanted her again.

The second time was slower, more sustained. He'd never enjoyed the act of love so much. He felt her heart thundering as they neared the end, and her breathing came in short gasps. He muttered her name, and she whispered something rapid and incoherent in reply. Then they were at the summit, and it was over.

The faint light reflected in her eyes in the silence that followed. She was looking up at him. He kissed her, and she returned his kiss. That was the moment when things changed for him. It was the first such kiss of his life. "Jacob..." she whispered. He traced her lips with his fingers, brushed her cheek. He knew what the words were, but he couldn't bring them forward, couldn't give them voice.

In a few moments she was asleep, and he settled on his back in the gloom, trying to find the scattered pieces of himself. Jacob lay next to Vivianne for almost an hour, then rose and dressed as best he could in the darkness. She was still sleeping when he left. He made his way to his room and packed his things in readiness for the early coach, reeling from what had happened. Was it genuine, or had she acted it? But in his heart he knew it had been real – and he walked away from it...

Now, alone in his hotel room, far away, he ached for her, cursed himself for not having taken his chance with her much sooner. They could have had a life together at the Lookout. He could have loved her. At this very minute she'd almost certainly be with someone else, and he was maddened at the thought.

Creak...

The sound startled him to full consciousness like the splash of cold water on his skin. He was instantly alert, ears tightly focused in the silent darkness, breath stilled, immobile... nothing... nothing... nothing...

Creak...

There it was again. Someone was standing outside his door – he knew it with absolute certainty. Not just passing by on the landing but standing an inch or two from the door itself, facing it, as if they were about to enter.

Creak...

It was unmistakable. Had he locked the door? He held his breath and continued to listen, fascinated. There was no shuffling, no rustle of clothes – only the creaking. He listened for a minute, two, then got out of bed as quietly as he could and stood in the almost complete blackness. The floorboards creaked again. He crept to the door, turned the handle and pulled it open.

There was no-one. The lamp on the far side of the landing burned very low, but his eyes had become used to the darkness of his bedroom, so the spark of illumination seemed bright. He looked up the stairs to his left, walked out to the banister rail and peered into the blackness below. Nothing moved, yet he was certain that someone had been there.

Jacob shivered, chilled inside and out. He went back to his room, located the spill jar and relit one of his lamps from that on the landing. Then he climbed back into bed and lay staring at the ceiling, mind in turmoil, lost.

As the fingers of dawn began to creep into the room, he realised he hadn't felt so bereft of confidence since he was a boy. He'd known where he was going ever since that day he'd held the two men at gunpoint in his father's shop. He'd been completely sure of his destiny, had never looked back, never stumbled, never questioned himself – until now.

At five o'clock he rose, packed his things and made his way out to the coachyard. He was the last to board and was surprised to find the carriage full. Four passengers were settled in the rear seat, huddled up against the chill of the morning, and there were eight packed inside, Jacob being the last. Maria was in her spot in the corner, smiling at him as he greeted her. She'd saved his seat for him. A thin, fragile-looking woman in her forties sat next to Maria, eyes cast down, basket in her lap. Next to her was one of the most rotund men Jacob had ever seen, hatted, frowning and leaning forward on his stick. Jacob found himself wondering unkindly if the driver had tethered a second team of horses to cope with the extra weight. The thin young man was squashed into the corner beyond the fat man, facing the window in the usual way, the back of his head presented to the occupants of the carriage. Two well-dressed middle-aged men sat to Jacob's left, a young woman in a bonnet occupying the seat next to the window, opposite the strange young man. Jacob couldn't see her clearly in the gloom but formed the impression that she was quite attractive, in her late twenties or early thirties.

After a few moments, the driver and guard mounted, and the coach pulled out onto the road.

"Did you sleep well, Jacob?" asked Maria.

"No, actually," he replied. "I wasn't able to sleep at all."

"I'm sorry to hear that," she said. "Perhaps you were afraid you might have nightmares."

He looked at her. The smile was still there, confident, all-knowing. Jacob wondered if she were laughing at him. He said, "I have a lot on my mind."

"I'm sure you do," she said. "I should try to get a few winks now if I were you."

The sky was already bright with day, but Jacob, soothed by the motion of the carriage and the reassuring smells of other folks' lives, was soon unconscious.

Maria shook him awake. He'd been deeply asleep and now looked around himself, not immediately sure where he was. The carriage was motionless, empty except for the two of them.

"We're at Grantham," she said. "You haven't uttered a

sound the whole journey."

"What time is it?" he asked, rubbing his eyes.

"It's half past one. We've stopped for lunch. You missed breakfast long ago."

He sat up, astonished. "Half past one? It can't be." He checked his watch and found that it was indeed so.

"We'd better hurry if you want to eat something," she said.

"Of course," he muttered. "I'm terribly sorry. I've been no company at all."

"No matter," she said. "You slept as if you had nothing on your conscience. Well done."

It was an odd thing to say, and he glanced at her, puzzled.

The inn was bustling, and there was nowhere to sit, so they purchased some cold food and ale and brought their luncheon back to the coach.

"Jacob, you listened patiently to my ramblings last night, but you've told me virtually nothing about yourself."

"There's not much to tell," he replied. "My father was a London cobbler, and I grew up in the trade. It was a tedious profession, and I'm afraid I gave it up in my teenage years."

"Interesting," she said. "Do you think you could make a decent pair of shoes now?"

He thought. "Yes, I think so. I believe I could pick it up again easily enough."

"I imagine it might be a craft that could be adapted. Supposing you worked on a ship, for example. You could probably turn your hand to any of the material repairs – sails, rigging, that kind of thing."

He nodded. "Yes, I suppose that's true. Curious that you should single out maritime work."

"I can smell the ocean in your hair," she replied. "I have a feeling you might travel widely."

His brows furrowed. He briefly stopped chewing on his pie, then swallowed and said, "You say such curious things. It's as if your mind flows in a different direction from that of most people – or runs at a different rate. You seem able to pick out details of the landscape of fate of which others, including myself, are completely unaware."

"Jacob, I think you flatter me."

"It was just an observation. But you speak like an oracle; puzzling, yet with directness and clarity." He gave a little laugh and said, "I wonder what else you can see," then immediately regretted it, wondering what he'd invited.

He looked up, and found her staring at him with such force that he began to believe her cataracts were false, and asked her directly, "Maria, can you see me?"

She paused, and when she replied, her voice was intense, her delivery focused tight. "You're full of secrets and darkness, Jacob. Yes, I can see you..." she pointed to her eyes, "... but not with these."

Her manner alarmed him, but he rose to the challenge. "What can you see?"

"You tell me you have charge of a charitable school for girls. I sense this is true, but you're hiding something there – a dark, wicked secret. You're used to deception on a gargantuan scale – you enjoy living with risk; your way of life is precarious. You stand atop a grand tower that is likely to crumble." She was silent for a second, then went on, her expression unchanged. "There are others like you, whose hair is full of salt. I see their blackened, burned skin, their roasted flesh. I hear their cries for mercy – they're terrified. And you, like me – you have blood on your hands." Her voice softened, and the delivery became fractionally less intense. "But I also see that you love. You run from rare, precious things that could save you – even now. You're thinking of a woman. All the time we've been travelling together, I see her in your mind. She's beautiful, young. You doubt yourself. *It can't be true*, you think. But you love her. It's a fresh, bright love, full of joy, delight, exhilaration. But you're running away from it, back to death, back to hate." Maria paused, and her brows knit. "But there's another coming. Also young, with flaming red hair." She stopped abruptly, dropped her food, opened her sightless eyes wide and flung herself back in her seat as if struck. "Oh, no! I can't look at her!" She covered her mouth with both hands and spoke through her fingers. "I've said too much!"

Jacob was shocked by her sudden terror but was also astonished at the preceding revelations, prophecies, whatever they were. His scalp tingled as if his hair were standing on end, and he was trembling with...he didn't know what – fright, awe, foreboding? He fished out his bottle of rum, picked out the cork and handed it to her.

"Calm yourself, Maria. Here's the rum – take it."

She grasped the bottle with both hands and downed half the remaining contents.

"Are you alright?" asked Jacob.

"Enough," she replied. "Here's your rum. Thank you."

The door on the opposite side of the carriage opened, and the other passengers began to arrive. The young woman at the far side of Jacob's seat looked at the two of them, sensed the dissipating tension and said, "Is everything alright. Do you need help?"

Jacob held up his hand and said, "Everything is fine, thank you. There's no need to worry." He sat back in his seat and looked across at Maria. Her hand was at her chest, and her mouth was open. She appeared to be recovering from some huge, unexpected shock. As the carriage filled, he said, "Are you sure you're alright? We could step down from the coach if you wish. I'm in no hurry."

She shook her head. "Leave me be," she said. "I'll say nothing more."

He sat back in his seat. The carriage began to move.

Blood. At the time, he hadn't even thought of it.

Lucas had been his first kill. Seeing the boy there in the corridor – puzzled rather than afraid, innocently watching them as they carried Orla into the cellar – Jacob had known what had to be done; hadn't questioned the necessity of it. He'd simply taken the boy aside and run him through the heart. There'd been no sound, no struggle. It had been clean. One second, Luke's body held the spark of life within it; the next, it had flown away through a hole in his chest. Although Jacob regretted the boy's death, he hadn't felt personally responsible for it.

But now, in the coach, rejected by Maria, he began to wonder about him. Who had his mother been? Might his father, whoever he was, have cared about his son's extinguishment? Had anyone ever doted on him, loved him?

From there, his mind jumped immediately to Vivianne, and he realised how empty his own life was. He was selfish, thoughtless – he existed only to bring suffering, to torture, to make money for himself and others. His was a shallow, black existence. He would die hated, alone, loveless.

Jacob looked around the carriage and wondered who these people were. Was there one more wretched than he? Maria was motionless, head cast down. The shy, mousy woman next to her seemed determined not to meet anyone's gaze. The huge man on her right sat upright as if he were a statue to the honour of gluttony and pomposity; he'd never contemplated himself in his life – Jacob could see the self-important blinkers in his eyes. The odd creature beyond the fat man, squashed into an absurdly small space at the end of the seat, stared fixedly out of the window as he always did. With his face constantly hidden, it was impossible to know anything about him. The woman sitting opposite the strange boy seemed the most sympathetic person in the coach. Her profile suggested a thoughtful nature, kind. The two men immediately to Jacob's left appeared to be sleeping, their faces impassive, remote, disinterested. Who were they?

No-one spoke. The carriage rolled on. Jacob thought, *I wonder what she's doing right now...*

They arrived at the White Hart, Retford, at a quarter to

eight that evening. Maria allowed Jacob to help her down from the coach and into the inn but declined further contact.

"I apologise if I've said or done something to offend you," he offered.

"For now we've shared enough," she replied. "Perhaps tomorrow we may find something to say. Have a good supper, Jacob." She was led away to her room by one of the staff.

Jacob ate alone that night. There were only about twenty people in the bar, and more than half of those were from the carriage. The hum of conversation was subdued. Maria, evidently quite capable of looking after herself, and needing no assistance, was seated at a table some distance away. She appeared unemotional, impassive, although she sat bolt upright in her chair at times, food ignored in front of her, staring blindly at nothing.

She's deep in thought. Is she thinking about me? What did she see?

He sat up until midnight, reading Samuel Richardson's *Clarissa*, resolved to the likelihood that he'd be again unable to sleep. But he was wrong and fell into a deep slumber within minutes of putting down the book, his mind filled with the novel's heroine and the underhanded exploits of her ravisher, Lovelace, with whom he felt some affinity.

But Clarissa didn't appear in his dreams – he dreamt about Vivianne. She was beneath him, her soft, warm body enfolding him, her breast moulded in his hand. She loved him – wanted him to stay. *Don't go, Jacob. Stay with me. We need each other*. She was kissing him, her arms and thighs around him. He reached down and took one of her feet in his hand, her ankle, the soft skin of her sole, his fingers slipping into the secret spaces between her toes...

Jacob woke suddenly in the near dark, heated by his dream. The room was deathly cold, unnaturally so. He didn't rise or make a sound, but opened his eyes wide in anticipation, knowing that something was about to happen. He felt clammy in the freezing air, his flesh squeezed in the fingers of dread.

Someone sat down on the bed, the mattress sinking to accommodate the weight of their body. Jacob's soul turned to ice, his hackles on end. For a moment he couldn't speak, then managed, "Who are you?" The room was silent except for the creaking of the bed as his visitor altered position. Was this person watching him? Jacob had left the lamp burning low at his bedside. He reached out, turned up the wick, then sat and looked along the bed. There was no-one. The room was still. It was a warm summer night.

The coach left at six o'clock. He was relieved to hear Maria greet him as he boarded.

"I'm so glad to hear you address me," he said. "I'd come to believe the rift between us must be irreparable."

"There's no rift, Jacob. Sometimes one needs a little space, that's all. Did you sleep well?"

"I was awoken in the night," he replied.

"Noisy neighbours?"

"No," he said, thinking. "No, it wasn't that."

She paused. "Were you alone?"

Why did she ask that? He thought. "Yes," he said. "Quite alone."

Maria nodded.

Nine o'clock found them at the Red Lion in Doncaster, where they paused for breakfast and the first change of horses. The morning was already warm, and some of the passengers settled on a wall outside the inn to consume their food in the sun. Jacob, sitting close to the huge man, decided to strike up a conversation.

"It's going to be a fine day."

The man looked up and said, "I think so. A clear blue sky, birds are singing. We're in for a stuffy journey."

"I'm Jacob Crowan." He held out his hand and the man

shook it.

"Abel Dashford. Pleased to make your acquaintance."

"Are you travelling far?"

"To York," said Abel. "On from there to Edinburgh."

"A long journey," said Jacob.

"Indeed. But worth the effort, I hope."

"Business?"

"Of sorts. I shall be meeting a young woman. Her father wishes to enter into business with me."

"Interesting," said Jacob. "What's the role of the young woman?"

"We've agreed that our business partnership shall be sealed by my marriage to his daughter. She's a pretty thing. Ripe." He emphasised the last word with a rolled *Rrr*.

Jacob nodded. "You're in love with her?"

"Love?" said Abel, arching his eyebrows, a sausage raised aloft on its way to his mouth. "There's flesh, sir – and heirs. But love? Is there such a thing? Except in the imaginations of women?"

Jacob nodded again. "Yes," he said. "There is such a thing. A thing not easily found, perhaps – and not always appreciated until it's too late."

Abel looked at him. "I'm an older man than you, Mr Crowan. Trust me – you'll grow out of it."

Jacob had been watching the privy door for the emergence of Maria. Seeing her appear in the open, he said to his companion. "Please excuse me, Mr Dashford. Perhaps we'll have the opportunity to talk again later."

Dashford raised his hand. "Indeed so." He looked past Jacob and said, "Gawd, sir! *She's* not your love, I hope!"

They were both mistaken about the weather. By the time the coach reached The Golden Lion at Ferrybridge, the air had cooled, the sky was grey, and the dismal rain was falling in repetitive curtains. The passengers, driver and guard sheltered inside the inn with a light meal and ale while the coach was cleaned and the horses changed. The fire roared as if it were Christmas.

Maria sat opposite Jacob. Dashford and the others were spread out around the otherwise empty bar. Jacob called out, "We were quite wrong about the weather Mr Dashford."

"Just as well I didn't put any money on it," Dashford called back.

"The voice of an oaf," muttered Maria.

Jacob looked across at her and smiled. "How's your fish?"

"It's delicious, I must say," she returned. "I smell your food," she went on, "but I'm completely unfamiliar with the aroma. What is it?"

"I've never eaten it before," he replied, "but I was curious to taste it. It is quite delicious. Apparently the technique comes from India. It's called Rabbit Curry. It contains a great deal of onion, turmeric and ginger, thrown together with the diced meat in a large quantity of cream and lemon juice, served with rice. I wonder if I can get the cook at my school to serve this to the girls."

"It sounds intriguing. Might I try it?"

"Of course," said Jacob. "I'll put some on your plate."

Maria paused very briefly before replying. "Feed me."

Jacob found the request, and its delivery, unnerving – and also oddly erotic, seductive. He smiled and rose to the challenge.

"Very well, my lady," he said, "It will be my pleasure." He filled his fork, and in a tone designed to match the suggestive nature of her request, said, "Open wide."

Maria licked her lips, opened her mouth and received the implement, drawing off its load and savouring it with her teeth and tongue. She swallowed, then moistened her lips again, daintily. "Delicious," she muttered. "And the food was good too…"

Jacob laughed out loud. "Madam, you are a delight!"

"A delight," she said, smiling. "Well, perhaps I was once. I wish I were fifty years younger and had my vision. I think then you might have been delighted with me."

Jacob felt his heart swell with affection for her. He reached out, took her hand and kissed it. "You are a delight now. What an astonishing, refreshing woman you are."

"Be careful, Jacob," she replied. I'm still aflame inside. You might get singed."

They made their way out to the coach together, trotting through the rain. Jacob shut the door behind them and noticed the strange young man already keeping sentinel at his window.

"Have you had lunch?" called Jacob, but got no reply, of course.

They sat and waited, Maria smiling strangely at him.

The coach doors remained closed. No-one else emerged from the inn except the driver and guard. Jacob, hearing the coachman click the horses into motion, looked up in surprise.

"But where are the others?" he asked in alarm. "There's only the three of us here."

"They're not coming any further," said Maria.

"But Dashford," said Jacob. "I know he's going to York – and travelling on to Scotland from there. He told me."

"He's not coming," she said. "None of them are coming. It's just you and me."

Jacob stared at her, his brows knit. "The three of us, you mean."

"No, Jacob," she said. "There's just you and me in the coach."

Jacob gazed at the strange, motionless young man and felt his blood freeze.

"But..." he said, pointing.

"You don't travel alone, Jacob," she said. "No-one who has taken the life of another ever travels alone."

Jacob looked across at the other side of the carriage, eyes

wide in fear. The countryside beyond the windows was a blur, as if they were moving at an extraordinary speed, yet there was absolutely no sensation of motion in the coach. The strange young man slowly rose from his seat and turned. Jacob cowered back into the corner. The young man had no face, only a grey, featureless blankness.

"No!" Jacob called out, terrified. "Stay away!" He shielded his face behind his raised hands. The young man moved towards him, and Jacob saw the pinprick of blood on his shirt, over his heart. "Luke?" Jacob gasped. Then the greyness vanished, and Lucas's features appeared, expressionless, dead. He sat next to Jacob and pressed into his side like a loving son, his thumb in his mouth. Jacob's face was a mask of horror. He felt the warm physical weight of the boy, reached out, embraced him, and suddenly found himself in tears. "My God!" he said out loud, "What have I come to?" He squeezed his eyes shut and held the boy close, wishing it were possible to reverse what he'd done.

The coach flew on, without sound or motion.

After a while, Jacob sensed that he was rising, floating upwards from some dark space deep within the earth, ascending towards the light. Silence surrounded him, peace. He looked up. Maria was gone. He looked for the boy, but there was no sign of him.

Then he realised there was no coach. He was standing outside The Black Swan in York, his bag in his hand. It was half past seven. The sky was almost dark.

Jacob's head tingled that evening, and he felt himself moving in a world that was only half real. He ate, but didn't taste the food; drank, but drew no pleasure from the liquor. In the bar, he was approached by a pretty prostitute but found himself unable to form any words to return her conversation. She left him with a shake of her head and a muttered invitation that he immediately forgot.

594

Lying in bed, he had the vague impression that his room was slowly rotating. He couldn't see Lucas but knew that he was there. *I'm mad*, he thought, *insane – glued to the underside of the world, looking at the ravings of the dead in Hades. I'm lost, and I can't get back.*

The next morning, he remembered that he was to take the stagecoach to Scarborough, but wasn't able to see the vehicle even though it stood right in front of him outside the inn. He looked to one side, his hands clawing vaguely at his face, eyes unfocused.

"Scarborough, sir?" asked the driver.

"Yes," Jacob muttered, not seeing him.

"Let me take your bag."

Jacob held it up and sensed the removal of its weight when the driver lifted it away.

"Thank you..."

"Can I help you inside, sir?"

"Yes... Thank you."

He held out his hand and a moment later found himself in a moving coach with two other passengers. One of them greeted him, but Jacob didn't respond; only turned to the window and stared out. They stopped at Malton for lunch while the horses were changed. Jacob managed to step down from the carriage unaided and purchased a meat pie, of which he was able to eat a small amount. He stood in the open and looked across the fields, feeling the wind on his face. The world began to solidify, bit by bit.

One of the passengers approached him, a man. "Are you alright, sir? You seem withdrawn, troubled."

Jacob turned to him. "Thank you. I... I've had a shock." He nodded to himself. "A shock – yes. I think I'm alright."

"You must say if you need help, my friend." The man laid his hand on Jacob's arm, and Jacob felt moved by the gesture, almost beyond words. He looked at the man and wondered if he might start weeping again.

"Thank you," he said. "Thank you for your concern." He

wanted to say something more but couldn't find the appropriate words. The man nodded and walked away.

How much was real? thought Jacob. *Was Maria real? Lucas? Vivianne?*

He became gradually more alert as the coach moved on. Towards the end of the journey he began to smell the sea, and closed his eyes in relief.

Almost home. He frowned. *But she won't be there. She'll never be there again.*

His heart was filled with sadness.

The carriage arrived at The Ship Inn, Scarborough, just after five o'clock. Kipp was waiting for him with the coach from the Lookout.

"Mr Crowan," he said. "Nice to have you home."

"Thank you, Kipp. It's a relief to see you."

"Good trip?"

Jacob was about to answer with the expected banality, but caught himself, shook his head and said, "I honestly couldn't say."

59. MISS SHADOW

Stella remained in London for almost a week after Jacob's departure so she could see every last one of the girls launched into their new life. It was the highlight of her year.

The *Sale of the Top Girl* was always a particular pleasure. Twenty-five wealthy men attended the auction for Nana's virginity, each charged twenty pounds admission just to be in the room. Stella sat among them and watched the girl brought in, powdered, dressed in frills. Nana was silent during the proceedings, face fixed, lips set hard, eyes staring into space. Her appearance in the pen caused quite a frisson among the assembled priapic males. She'd probably have seen Stella sitting next to Foxley among the spectators, smiling happily at her as Margaret began the bidding, although no sign of recognition crossed her face.

The event was a resounding success and took the highest figure ever. Nana's first night was sold for £1,750 – a colossal sum – and she was led away to be prepared for her violation while her purchaser stood and acknowledged the applause, congratulations and lewd gestures of his comrades. Stella was beside herself with glee, while Foxley slapped his thigh and cried, "Jolly good bargain for such a filly if you ask me!" The men were an absurd bunch, thought Stella; ridiculous, braying oafs, in competition with each other not just for the purchased item, but to brag about how much money they could expend on such a thing. Children, they were – like stupid little boys. She had nothing but scorn for them.

But the defilement of the girls was not the only pleasure Stella took in city life. She had another love. Another love, in the form of an eight-inch, needle-sharp blade that she'd purchased from a pedlar in Whitby a few years previously. It was dark in hue, elegantly thin, and kept lovingly polished. The handle was crowned with a small finger-guard that enabled the instrument to be employed with force and precision. And she'd sown a shallow steel sheath into the sleeve of her dress where the weapon's point rested when not in play. The blade could be concealed there and brought swiftly into action from its resting position. It was attached by a leather strap to a harness buckled around her upper arm, so there was no danger of dropping the weapon or losing it.

On the night that Nana was sold, after the bidding had been completed and the prize won, Stella celebrated with a visit to one of the Drury Lane theatres. She had a soft spot for Shakespeare and was delighted to find a performance of Henry VI, Part 3. With luck, there would be some particularly bloody and gruesome stage murders.

The elderly gentleman who sat by himself in the third bay along on the upper right, two rows back, had been a devotee of Shakespeare for almost sixty years. He was a familiar figure at the theatre, a well-dressed kindly widower who was on first name terms with many of the staff and actors. He had eleven doting grandchildren and was hoping for a romance with his neighbour, herself recently widowed. He'd led a happy, blameless life.

The area of the theatre in which he sat was rather dark, and there were few people nearby. Indeed, he'd deliberately selected a spot in one of the less populated areas specifically because he liked a little privacy.

The woman who sat immediately to his rear selected her seat for very different reasons.

The performance ended. The applause faded away, and the patrons left the building. All except the elderly gentleman in the third bay along on the upper right, two rows back, who wouldn't be coming to the theatre again. His shirtfront and his lap were soaked in blood, his neck having been perforated clean through from behind by a long, sharp, needle-like implement.

Miss Shadow wove swiftly through the crowd in the street on her way back to King's Place. She looked neither right nor left but produced her barb several times, jabbing it swiftly out and up at waist height, without pausing in her course, enjoying the gentle pull of resistance as it penetrated flesh, and the cries of agony and confusion that accumulated in her wake. The sleeve of her dress was slimy and red by the time she arrived home, but her heart was full of joy.

60. KATE – DREAMS
– AWAKENING
Summer 1761 to May 9, 1762

She was locked in.

It was very dark, damp. Water dripped somewhere. There was a well close by – she was certain of it. She felt brickwork to her right and thought the well shaft might be behind it. If only she could be sure of where to dig with her fingers. Things scurried in the darkness – rats. Her clothes were torn, her lip was swollen, split. She was frightened, alone, needed to get out...

It was suddenly hot, she was sweaty, someone was pressing her down. She cried out but couldn't get her voice to work. She writhed on her back, turned over...

Calm... Lying on her side in bed. The darkness remained, but it was a different dark. There was a man sleeping next to her, warm. He was a nice man. She'd been a gift to him – her mother wanted her to be safe, so she'd given her to the man. She almost remembered his name – almost... "Anhaga". There it was – she had it. His name brought other details: eating at his table, watching him lead Mass in the dark church, the feel of his lips. She remembered how frightened she'd been when he first took her to his bed, remembered him lifting away her clothes, his hands on her skin.

"Don't hurt me..."

"I won't hurt you. Pretty girl – Willa."

With the utterance of her own name came an image of her mother's face. "Eldrida"...

It was dawn, but she didn't want to wake up – she knew how sad she'd be if she let in the day. Pale light filtered through her closed eyelids. She was alone, her skin wrinkled, breasts shrivelled, vision fading, hair silver-white.

Her husband was dead, his funeral over, all the people gone home. And now she would grow old alone and die unloved. The tears came. She searched for his name, couldn't remember it. Clouds filled her mind; she couldn't breathe...

"Kate!"

Kate's eyes snapped open.

Nothing was familiar. Soft light penetrated tall curtains. She lay on her side, sticky with sweat. There were three other beds, three young girls looking at her, their eyes anxious, frightened.

Her old age dispersed. The memory of her husband dissolved. She was in her bed at the Lookout. She burst into tears, and Bip ran to her.

"I was dreaming," she sobbed.

"I thought you were. You were calling out." Kate sat up in bed and Bip hugged her. "Look - it's still early. I'll sleep in your bed." She lifted the covers, climbed in with Kate and held her as they lay down together. "There we are, Lovely." Bip stroked her head and kissed her brow.

"Sorry," Kate whispered.

"Ssh," said Bip. "You're safe. I'm here."

Slade and Kate sat side by side on the bench in the kitchen garden.

"Luke was kind. He'd never have run away without telling me." Slade paused and looked down. "He was my friend, you know? My friend."

"I know," Kate replied. "You knew him better than anyone. What do you think happened?"

Slade shook his head. "I don't know. He wouldn't have just run away with two people he hardly knew." He paused again. "I think something else happened to him. I don't think it has anything to do with Mr Browning and Orla. I think someone came and took Luke – maybe someone who knew he was my friend. I think he's dead. And I think it was because we were friends."

Kate was shocked. "Slade, you mustn't think that! Who would do such a thing? There's no-one here like that."

"Isn't there? Are you sure?"

Kate thought quickly, but she was certain that if such paltry prejudice existed at the Lookout, she would have sensed it. "Yes, I am."

"It says in the Bible though…"

"Slade, the Bible's just a book."

"But there are people who hate because of it. I reckon there are people who'd kill because of it."

"Trust me, Slade. I know everyone here, and I'm sure there's no-one who's that small-minded."

He looked at her. "It must have been someone from outside then."

"Someone from outside wouldn't have known about you and Luke." Slade was quiet. Kate went on. "Maybe it was an accident. Maybe he wandered away and got into trouble somewhere."

"That's possible," Slade replied. "I've thought of that. I've looked for him everywhere."

"Of course you have," said Kate and covered his hand with hers. "It must be dreadful to lose someone in the way you have. I lost my ma – and my grandma. But at least I knew where they went. For someone to just disappear – and for you not to know – that's bad."

He began to cry. Kate put her arm round him and hugged him. "Don't give up hope," she said. "He may turn up some-where. In the meantime, *I'm* your friend. You know where I am. You're not alone."

The heat of the summer deepened. The smell of the rotting badger on the old bowling green became steadily worse for a couple of weeks, then faded. By the time August came to an end, only the faintest scent remained. For her own peace of mind, Kate penetrated the undergrowth and found the animal's body, open and alive with maggots. She couldn't bring herself to drag it away – it had to stay there until nature was done with it.

France had become an obsession with Kate. As summer rolled on into autumn, she began to imagine herself a French girl and made herself think in the language to the point at which it became second nature. She was fluent and read as widely in French as she did in English.

A new keyboard teacher arrived at the school in September. Felix Hadleigh was prematurely grey in his middle thirties and appeared rather shy and academic. Kate was intrigued by his interest in unusual repertoire and enjoyed the rarities he gave her to learn – particularly the French music: d'Anglebert, Lebègue, Marchand, Dumage, Clérambault, the two Couperins, and more. They became good friends.

"Kate, you're staggering. I've never known anyone able to assimilate so much music so quickly – and play it so well. You make the harpsichord sing. I feel you should be teaching me; not me you."

"No," she replied. "Keep listening. I'm learning a tremendous amount. I'd never have discovered half this stuff without you."

She watched Etta Lynn and Clara Sutherland and thought she'd try designing her own clothes. It was a struggle initially, but her determination brought increasing success and had Etta nodding her head in approval.

"You're going to be good at this," she said. "I ran a fashion house in Vienna years ago – it's where I made my name. If someone your age had brought me some of the things you've designed, I would have signed them into the business right away. You have a knack. You could go far. Just keep on doing what you do. You have a fine eye and a unique flare."

Etta's comments delighted Kate. She'd always thought of

her teacher as somewhat aloof, but now saw the warmth of her personality. The endorsement of her ideas from such a lofty quarter gave Kate a considerable boost of confidence. Word got round, and she began to receive commissions from the other girls – too many to complete alone, so she drew up the designs herself, then had the seamstresses, Mercy and Ada, do most of the manufacture. *Kate's fashions* were increasingly on display at dinner, modelled by their proud owners.

The day I made up my mind to come here to the school, she thought. *That was the luckiest day of my life. It opened entire new worlds.*

She remained unsatisfied with her work in Golda's art classes, particularly her inability to accurately depict the male form. It just never looked right. Shelagh, Bip and the others told her she was taking things much too seriously. They were able to skate over it themselves, and when Kate compared their work with her own, she realised that she was aspiring to a degree of detail not attempted by the other girls. More than that: she was trying to express a profundity, a kind of symbolism, of which the others seemed entirely unaware. There was something in Kate's head trying to get out, something that wanted itself known.

"It's just a cock and balls for God's sake, Kate," said Bip. "Don't take it so seriously. It's not as if you're going to cut it off and stuff it, after all. It's just a spicket and a pair of tarriwags. Every cove's got a set, and they're all the same – so I hear…"

Deep down, Kate knew what the root of the problem was, and could remember exactly when the seed of fascination had been planted, but she wasn't yet ready to bring it into her full awareness; didn't yet feel ready to examine it. The associated memories were still too disturbing for her. But she didn't want the obsession, compulsion, fetish – however it might best and most honestly be described – to wane, so she caught Ned Silden at the end of one of Golda's Art Clubs and boldly asked him to model privately for her. "Certainly not!" he said.

"Why not? You do it here, in the ballroom in front of loads of people. It wouldn't be anything new."

"But why?"

"Because I want to get it right – just exactly right."

His eyes widened. He paused. "Are you ill?"

"No more than anyone else – I think," she replied.

Pixie, overhearing something of the conversation, came to stand at her husband's side, and Ned, boldened by the presence of his wife, asked, "Kate, if it were the other way round, and I asked you to strip off down to the buff so I could paint you, would you do it?"

"Yes," she said, without hesitation. "If it were to help you. Of course." She shrugged. Pixie grinned.

Ned was rendered silent, and stood looking hard at Kate, his jaw set. He spoke after a few seconds. "I didn't say that – and you didn't answer. The last half-minute..." He shook his head. "It didn't happen."

"Go on, Ned," said Pixie. "For goodness sake. Pretend you're a man."

"I am a man," he rounded. "That's just it."

Kate withdrew her request. "Sorry I asked. I didn't think you'd be so upset."

Ned sensed her disappointment and felt his resolve begin to melt. He looked at Pixie. She smiled back at him.

"Alright," he said quietly, common sense beaten back. "Alright then. But I want to know you really take it seriously." He cast his eyes upwards and muttered, "God, what am I doing? I should learn to say no..."

Pixie squeezed his hand. "Ned. Course she's serious about it. I'll be there. Don't worry – you'll come to no harm."

"Saturday morning, your place?" asked Kate.

"Saturday morning," said Ned. "Bloody hell..."

605

Kate probably took Art Club more seriously than anyone else. Some of the aspiring artists were genuinely dedicated, but others used it as a platform for dares and hilarity.

The maids, full of gin one night, thought it would make a good game if they drew lots to determine which of their number would pose nude. The "winner" was Mary Acker. Mary was in her middle forties and no longer the slender beauty she'd been twenty years earlier, but having agreed to take part in the lottery, she felt obliged to keep the bargain.

When she ascended the plinth, she got a rousing cheer from the girls, and cries of "Good for you, Mary" from the gentlemen present. It won her a lot of respect, gave her a sense of achievement, and increased her confidence. Her quiet, withdrawn manner instantly became more outgoing. She began to sing to herself, quietly at first, then more boldly, as she went about her work.

"Mary! You're a singer!" said Kate one evening when the woman was dressing her hair for dinner.

"No, Kate. Not really. I'm just happy – so I sing. I used to sing all the time when I was younger. I was happy then."

"Ever been married?"

"Used to be. He left. That's when I stopped singing."

Her words moved Kate, and she reached up, took Mary's hand and kissed it. "But you're happier now?"

"I must be, I suppose."

"We all love you," said Kate. "All the girls."

The footmen were not to be outdone and decided to hold a similar ballot. It was risky; there were only four of them, so the stakes were high, and there was no going back. One of their number would have to be the willing sacrifice.

At the appointed hour, Newt Fallowfield nervously took the stand amidst appreciative mumbles from the girls. For a few moments, Kate was distracted by his delicate straw-coloured hair, which threw certain details of his body into unanticipated relief. He was very different from Ned; more delicate, his physical presence more refined.

Golda had studied medicine and anatomy in her younger years, and liked to use anatomical labels at the life classes in the belief that it would lend them a formal air. Everyone got used to hearing the Latin terms for the muscles: *pectoralis major, trapezius, rectus abdominis, triceps brachii, sartorius, biceps femoris* and the like. Some of the terms she used felt uncomfortable in the room. *Gluteus maximus* was one (the girls liked to draw pictures of this large-buttocked Roman centurion); *mons pubis* was another. The most excruciating was *penis*. This last always drew embarrassed giggles from the girls, and made the model raise his eyes to heaven. Kate understood the comedic aspect of it as much as the other girls but became irritated at the predictability of the reaction. It seemed to be generally accepted that penes were funny, but she couldn't really see why, beyond the fact that people simply *thought they were.* It seemed stupid.

Kate loved to dance. Her studies of harpsichord dance suites extended into Isabella and Edgar Breedon's dancing classes, and she became a real master. She got to like Bella and Ed very much. They were simple, straightforward people – always gentle, happy and smiling.

Some of the other subjects were more of a problem. Latin was challenging and dull, although she did her best. The lessons might have been easier if Mr Hornsby had managed to stay awake more often.

Mathematics bored her senseless, even with such a handsome tutor as Terrel Nisbet. Bip hated it too. "God!" she said, banging her head repeatedly on the desktop. "Bloody numbers! Numbers, numbers, numbers!"

The less formal studies – those outside the building – were

sometimes the most enjoyable. Kate had learned as much about riding from Nolly as she was likely to, and got to know the characters of all the horses. She often went to the stables in the company of three or four other girls, and they'd all ride together.

Pammy Heron seemed to be Nolly's favourite. The two had a way of looking at each other that Kate found intriguing. The boy always seemed to be touching Pammy's arms and hands. Sometimes it appeared to Kate as if Nolly thought the girl might be a kind of sweet food; as if he wanted to lick her or put her in his mouth. She asked him about it on one occasion.

"You like her."

"Like Pammy? Of course I like Pammy. I like all of you."

"No," said Kate. "I don't mean that. You know what I mean."

Nolly reddened, and said simply, "You're *all* nice."

Now and then, Kate went off to the brewhouse with Fuzzy, who introduced her to the brewers. It was like a little family there, the six men all hearty friends with each other. And Fuzzy was a kind of pet to them. Kate noticed how Fuzzy flirted with Doug Trivet. The display made her feel uncomfortable; it was deeper and more daring than Nolly and Pammy.

"Are you and Doug...?"

Fuzzy denied it. "No. It's just playing."

"It looks very serious to me," said Kate.

"It's only a game."

Kate thought for a second. "You'd tell me, wouldn't you? You must tell me if anything really happens."

Fuzzy said, "You'll be the first to know."

Kate tried hard to match Fuzzy's expertise in drinking but was never quite able to do it. She watched Fuzzy keeping level with Doug, flagon for flagon, and thought to herself, *One day I'll be able to top you. I'll keep practising till I do.*

Her other "vice" (that's what Bip called it) was smoking. There were times when Speck Beckwith wished he hadn't introduced Kate to tobacco, but she applied herself to its study as thoroughly as she did everything else. Speck brought out his entire collection of pipes for her experimentation – a variety of materials, bowls and stem lengths. She tried different tobaccos and mixtures but decided that the one she enjoyed most was Speck's own – a mixture he'd developed himself many years earlier. He was glad of that – it made him feel as if he'd done something right.

Whatever time she had left in the day was spent in the company of the other girls, or with Mabel in the lake or at the cliff edge where they stood together in the wind and the sun, as if they were mother and daughter.

Kate often saw the ghosts of the twins standing at the window of the tower. She smiled and waved but never received a response. The two boys looked blankly at her, their faces pale and grey. Rosalind Wynter continued to appear, silent and motionless, at Kate's bedside for about twenty minutes in the deadest point of every night.

Mr Crowan seemed quieter since his return from London, spent more time out of sight in his study, and sometimes failed to join the company at meals. Bip joked that he'd probably been unhappy in love.

Hastings Rayden, tutor in Elocution, cheered himself up, lost quite a lot of weight and adopted a snappier style of dress, having received advice from Terrel Nisbet and Oswald Packard. According to Bip, he was "sniffing round" Ruth Marlowe, who'd apparently given him some encouragement even though he was twenty years her senior ("Nothing wrong with that," said Bip. "Older men are more interesting, more lived in. I bet they give you a stiffer buttering too." "Bip!" said Kate, mock-horrified).

Twelve-year-old Edwin Elvet, rescued from the Middlesbrough workhouse, joined Slade and Jude as the third soil boy. There was no news of what had become of Lucas, Mr Browning or Orla.

Slade and Kate met and spoke several times together. She was always there when he needed to talk to someone. Lucas never faded from Slade's mind, but he was glad to have young Edwin around. A corner of his depression lifted, and a ray of light penetrated into the dark of his loss. In early December, Denise announced that she and Terrel were expecting a baby, due in May. Everyone was thrilled – especially the other housemistresses – and there was a big party in the ballroom. Kate danced with Mr Crowan.

(*Actually*, she thought, *he's very handsome, and he has firm, strong hands. He seems sad though. I wonder why. He looks at me strangely. I think he's starting to like me.*)

Kate returned to the farm for Christmas, as she had the previous year, and was delighted to find both her uncles safely home from the wars. Meadow and Alder were as happy together as they'd always been, doting on each other with undiminished love, although there was still no sign of a child. It was nice to have the house full.

She spent lots of time with Grace and Beatrice, reading together or wandering on the farm, talking about things. Pond Girl joined them for a walk three days after Christmas – a crisp, chilly Monday. The four girls visited the graves of Kate's mother and grandmother in the yard behind Glaisdale church and then spent an hour in the parsonage, chatting with Cornelius and drinking tea. Later in the afternoon they found themselves trudging through the snow at the north end of Glaisdale Common, the warren and the woods in the distance on their right, beyond the river.

"Buffy," said Kate. Buffy turned her face towards the younger girl. "Do you still see Brendan?"

"Brendan Telford?" Pond Girl asked.

"Yes," Kate replied, wracking her brains, attempting to recall if there was another so named.

"No," said Pond Girl. "Well – yes, I *see* him out and about, but not like *that*. That was years ago."

"I always thought you two would get married," said Beatrice. "You were together a long time."

"We were," Buffy replied. "But we grew apart. I think we just got to the bottom of each other, and there wasn't any more to find out."

"You got bored?" asked Kate.

"Yes," sighed Buffy. "We got bored – saw each other less and less. Then it just stopped." They crunched on for a few more yards, and she added, "Better that way than going on, pretending there was something worthwhile."

"Pity," said Grace.

"Is it?" asked Buffy, then answered the question herself. "Probably not. We were close for a long while though. I think you always feel close to your first one."

"So, is there someone now?" asked Beatrice.

"No," said Buffy. "I'm not really looking. I sit at home, help ma. And I spend a lot of time in the Red Lion with Nick. I'm happy enough."

"What about Cedar?" asked Kate.

Buffy seemed puzzled. "Why?"

"He's nice," Kate replied. "Quiet, unattached."

"Cedar's over thirty," Buffy replied. "More than ten years older than me."

"Does it matter?" Kate asked.

"Not really... I suppose," said Buffy. She frowned and said, "Why are you keen to get me married off?"

"You'll be twenty in March," said Kate. "Time's running away."

"Twenty's not old," Buffy replied, brows knit. Kate's expression said, *It is though*, and Buffy insisted, "No it's not. It just seems old to you."

"I'll be thirteen at the end of March," said Kate. "Just two years younger than my mother when she got married."

"Fifteen is very young to get married," said Buffy. "Just because it worked for your mum doesn't mean it might have worked for me. I remember your mum very well. She was older and wiser at my age than I'll *ever* be. Some fifteen-year-olds are fifteen; others are much older. Sometimes wise old people live in young bodies. I'm not ready to get married."

"I'll be fifteen in May," said Grace.

"And do *you* feel ready to get married?" asked Buffy.

"No," Grace laughed.

"But you're fond of Alan," said Beatrice.

"That's true," Grace replied. "And we've got close. I've liked him for a long time, and I know he's fond of me – he's told me so..."

"What?!" Buffy exclaimed, eyebrows flying. This was news to her.

"Yes, he has," said Grace. "And I think, one day..." She looked to the side and found Kate smiling at her. "Nothing's happened," Grace added firmly.

"Nothing?" asked Kate.

"Nothing," Grace insisted. "Not so much as a little kiss."

Kate nodded to herself, thinking, *Bet it won't be long though...*

"But I can't say the same for my brother..." said Grace.

The other three looked at her, and Pond Girl asked, "You mean him and Amy?"

"They've been canoodling for a long time," Kate observed.

"I know," said Grace, "but they're hands-on now..."

"Grace! You little gossip!" exclaimed Buffy.

"What do you mean, hands-on?" asked Kate.

"Smooching," said Grace. "Kissy, kissy, kissy."

Beatrice interrupted firmly, "But not anything else."

"You sure?" asked Grace.

"Absolutely," Beatrice replied. "I've caught Amy kissing Walter too, but she says that's as far as it's gone, and I believe her."

"But they're older than all of you anyway," said Buffy. "Walter will be seventeen next summer, and Amy's a year older than him. That's alright."

612

Grace changed the subject. "I need a wee. Cornelius's tea's gone right through me. Look the other way for a minute."

The three girls stood where they were, and Grace hurried off to find a tree or bush away from their sight. She'd been gone only a few seconds when Beatrice, gazing over towards the wood, cried, "Look at that!"

It was a swirling black cloud of starlings, tens of thousands of them, oscillating, expanding, rippling in the air like smoke, up above the warren. The sight took Kate's breath away.

"That's amazing!" she exclaimed. "The biggest I've ever seen!"

"It's breathtaking, isn't it?" said Buffy. "We see them a lot from the cottage. It amazes me every time. It's like they're dancing for joy. Can you imagine such happiness?"

Grace came running back through the snow. "My goodness!" she said. "Aren't they just beautiful?"

"Makes you glad to be alive, doesn't it, when you see such a thing?" said Beatrice. "Makes you see all over again how beautiful the world is. It's like a poem in the sky."

Yes, thought Kate. *How lucky I am – to have this life, my friends, my home, the school, music, everything; to be able to see such things as this.*

The four girls continued to stand in awed silence, and Kate thought, *I wonder if the Wynter twins can see the starlings. I wonder if they feel joy like I do...*

At the end of February 1762, Adam and William visited Kate at the Lookout. It made her happy to see them there, and she took a lot of pleasure in showing them round the house and park, but they brought bad news. Bernard Swift, Beatrice's grandfather, butler at the manor house, had died suddenly at the age of sixty-five. Kate returned for his funeral and sat next to Beatrice in the church. It was another sad day for the community, and the loss of yet another old friend for Cornelius.

Grace's father, Elys, became the new butler.

"Going home for your birthday, then?" asked Alfred. Kate sat near the porter's desk, waiting for Kipp to bring the carriage round.

"Yes," she replied. It's the day after tomorrow. "I'll be thirteen."

"I thought so," he replied. "You're growing up fast. You don't look thirteen at all."

"Don't I? How old do I look?"

"Well, if I didn't know, I'd say you were..." He scrutinised her closely before replying. "Fifteen. Yes, fifteen."

Kate liked that. "Am I pretty?"

Alfred laughed. "Yes, Kate, you're a pretty girl. I think you know that very well."

She heard the carriage draw up and said goodbye to Alfred. Kipp opened the coach door and helped her up onto the step. She was surprised to find Lettice Shelley inside.

"Hello, Lettice," she said. "Are you going somewhere too?" The door closed behind her. Kate sat down and rested her bag on the seat by her side.

Lettice made a *shh* gesture with her finger at her lips and said, "Kipp and I are going to the Red Lion in Glaisdale for a few days. Jacob said we could have some time off. It's a long distance for the horses to travel in a single day – to your farm and back, so they're getting a rest while Kipp and me have a little time together."

"It's true then," said Kate, smiling. "You're together." The carriage began to move.

"Doesn't necessarily mean anything – yet," said Lettice. "We just like each other, that's all. Don't go spreading it about."

Kate said nothing but continued to look at Lettice, face in a fixed grin.

"Look at you – Miss Smileygirl," said Lettice. "What do you know? You're still not quite thirteen."

"I know you look happy," said Kate. She leaned forward. "You love him."

"Enough, Miss Swithenbank!" exclaimed Lettice, blushing. "Talk about something else."

Kate didn't sleep well the night before her birthday. She was uncomfortable, sweaty. Her head ached dully, and she had vague stomach cramps. But breakfast was nice. William and Adam were there, and Meadow made kippers for her. Kate loved kippers at breakfast. There were kidneys too, and bacon, eggs and sausages. Her headache disappeared while she drank her tea, although the discomfort in her tummy remained.

"You're a teenage girl now," said Adam. "You'll soon be wed."

"I don't think so," Kate replied. "I'm busy with finer things."

"Ha!" Meadow exclaimed. "Well said, Kate!" Adam laughed, Alder smiled, and William tousled her hair.

At half past ten, Kate put on her cape and shoes and walked down Watermill Lane and over the bridge. She'd gone that way only rarely since Hugo's death, not wanting to open the old memories. But it was different today. She had to go – something was calling her there.

She stopped at the low wall and looked down at the mill, boarded up and empty. It looked strange – like a corpse; a shell enclosing a dark, forgotten space. She imagined the interior, reconstructing it from her memory.

Is the mechanism still inside, silent in the gloom? Probably. And the pitwheel, dormant in its deep slot in the floor – like a surgeon's knife arrested in the action of making an incision. All still, all enclosed in sticky spidery blackness.

Up in the loft, is the big pulley-wheel still there, up in the rafters where he'd hanged himself? And the rope...is the rope still there...? Was he frightened, hanging helpless above the floor, dying, alone in the stillness, watching the dust-motes lazily drifting in the sunbeams while he choked, reddened, blackened, tongue swelling, thickening, veins bulging, the light of life going out?

Is Hugo in the walls now, with the others? If I were inside the mill, would I hear his voice...?

She looked at the millpond and saw him again in the eye of her mind as he was that day they first spoke – close by, just beyond the overflow stream. The world around her faded – her eyes disengaged. She saw only Hugo, naked, strong, his penis thick, heavy (*penis, penis* – the word pulsed in her mind). Despite her display of boldness, of confidence that day, she'd been frightened. The fear remained as she held the image in her mind, but now it was joined by something else, a sensation that was new to her. She moistened her lips, felt her heart hasten, her breath quicken...

You like that, don't you...

It was a strange voice (in her head?), oddly amplified and resonant, as if more than one person spoke. It had a mocking quality that she didn't like. She'd heard it before somewhere, long ago...

The vision was gone. She felt dizzy, looked left and right, lifted up her clothes and found a strange sticky sweatiness between her legs. She frowned, wiped her hand on her cape and walked home.

There was a big party for her that evening, with lots of cakes, creams, pastries and games. But she didn't feel well, and the sore head returned. Her skin was clammy, her breasts ached, seemed swollen, and her thoughts were filled with Hugo.

On the morning of March 30th, Kate woke to find her bedclothes soiled with blood. Most of her friends were already menstruating, so she wasn't really surprised. Meadow was motherly, sympathetic, but decided together with Alder that Kate shouldn't return to the Lookout that day. *My little girl,* Alder thought, *all grown up.*

Kipp and Lettice arrived at noon with the carriage. Alder smiled at the attractive auburn-haired woman and looked her up and down more than once. *In the old days...* Meadow elbowed him and said, "Hey! *I'm* your wife."

Meadow served the two visitors with cake and ale and told Lettice what had come to pass with Kate. Kipp said he'd return at the same time the following week, and the carriage went back to the school without its youngest passenger.

The delay meant that Kate was at home on April 2nd for her father's fifty-ninth birthday. It was another memorable event, with visits from Cornelius, Hugh and Amelia Flesher; Tozer, Apple and Cedar; Elys, Sally and Alicia Buckley, and Stephen and Alan Flathers from the forge. Florence Swift was still in mourning for Bernard, but Richard and Emma visited for a while, bringing her apologies.

Alicia prepared the food with assistance from Adam and William. The house was overflowing, but fortunately the weather was good enough for the partying to spill outside. In the afternoon many of them walked to Glaisdale and met more friends at the Red Lion. Alder drank only lemon water. Meadow squeezed close and hugged him, cradling a glass of elderflower wine. Cornelius sat next to Kate and drank a flagon of ale. Kate drank lemon water like her father, thinking, *Shall I ask for some gin?* She was on the point of daring it when Meadow looked at her and said, "Kate, would you like to share my wine?"

"Are you sure?" she asked.

"Go on," said Meadow, pushing the glass towards her. "I bet you're used to stronger stuff anyway."

Kate lifted the wine to her lips, gazed at her stepmother across the lip of the glass, and thought, *If only you knew...*

Her bleeding lasted for only three days. The symptoms she'd had – the aches, cramps, sweats – disappeared. The images of Hugo dispersed, and she spent the rest of her unexpected free week with Grace and the others.

And she forgot about the strange voice she'd heard on the road by the watermill.

Kate's dreams became clearer, more vivid, in the days and weeks following her return to the Lookout. She no longer emerged from them in tears but often felt sad on waking. She lay in her bed, thinking quietly, pondering what she'd seen: the tall rectangular church; the worshippers from the marsh villages; the visitors from the monastery; the hanging; the dark; so many people, friends, growing old, dying. She felt the immense depth of time that lay behind her, and gradually admitted to herself what she'd always known. They were not dreams – they were memories. Once she'd accepted that, she found that she could shut them out, turn her back on them. *I just want to be me*, she thought. *I just want it to be now. I want to be Kate.*

Sunday, May 9th dawned bright, and the air was already warm by breakfast time. Someone brought news that Denise was in labour, and word spread like fire. By ten o'clock the entire school was in a state of tense excitement. The Nisbet's child would be the first born at the Lookout since the Wynter twins in 1697.

Kate made her way to the staff house and knocked at Terrel's door to offer help. Denise had already asked Ruth Marlowe to be on hand, and it was Ruth who opened the door to Kate and gained Denise's permission for the girl to enter. Doctor Wayland was there, and the expectant mother looked as comfortable as it was possible to look in such a situation. Terrel, about to enter into fatherhood, was perched nervously at Denise's side.

"My grandma did some midwifery," said Kate. "Do you mind if I stay? I mean, I might be useful, and I'd like to watch how it goes."

No-one voiced any objection – in fact, Denise seemed to appreciate Kate's inquisitiveness.

The birth was easy and proceeded without complication. Kate was fascinated but wasn't actually required to do anything other than a couple of simple tasks suggested by Ruth to make her feel involved.

Elizabeth Ruth Nisbet was born just before three o'clock in the afternoon. Ruth Marlowe, after whom the new girl had received one of her names, was overcome with emotion, and Kate sacrificed her handkerchief to the woman's tears. Hollis Wayland, wiping his hands, said, "Well, that's a piece of history. Well done, everyone – and particularly well done you, Denise. Top marks; ten out of ten."

The other three housemistresses – Lettice, Eleanor and Eve – had been popping with excitement in the Nisbets' parlour, and appeared in the bedroom minutes later to inspect the new addition. There'd be extravagant partying later in the day.

At half past three, Kate sat quietly holding the new life in her arms, enthralled. "Little girl," she whispered, brushing the child's head and looking into her eyes. "Little girl..."

That night Kate had a vivid dream in which she was present at a birth:

The window was open, and there was a refreshing breeze in the room. The woman on the bed was in some discomfort, and seemed rather old to be having a baby, perhaps in her early forties. Two midwives encouraged her to push. Kate saw the child's head appear as the mother cried out.

"Nearly there," said one of the midwives. "One more push and we'll be done."

A moment later the child was born. There was quite a lot of blood. Kate looked out of the window and saw that the sky was red too. There was a storm coming on. A bell began to ring nearby, probably from a church tower. Kate thought it was chiming the hour, but she counted twenty-one strokes. The air in the room was becoming pink, and the light was fading. She felt herself falling up, out of the dream but just caught a snippet

of conversation as the scene faded to black.
"What's he to be called Mrs Ottershaw?"
"Giles. His name is Giles, after his grandfather."

61. COVENT GARDEN
July 1762

Jacob and Stella took the ten eldest girls to London in the summer as usual, Jacob with a hardened resolve not to allow a repetition of the preceding year's events.

He watched through his familiar spyhole as the initiations of Iris Little, Lilith Robson, Jane Young, and Midge Fenwick took place in the next room. The star of 1762 was pretty Harriet Dixon, heading for auction in the same way as Nana the year before.

"Take a girl," said Foxley, but Jacob was prepared this time, and claimed an "intimate illness".

"Jacob! How careless of you!" chastised Foxley.

"A moment of idiocy," Jacob replied. "It won't happen again. But how are the girls from last year? How's Orla?"

Foxley raised his eyebrows and said, "Orla was a problem for quite some time. We thought it likely she might kill herself and had to make sure there was nothing sharp in her room; no curtain cords; nothing she could... you know. I don't think she ever actually tried to do it, but she was *very* unhappy. It was a nasty business, that liaison with the music teacher – set her up for a bad start. I felt sorry for the poor creature, I must say. I have a sympathetic nature, as you know." He drew in his breath and changed his tone. "But now things have rather moved on, and it's starting to look as if we might lose her. She has a regular – one of our more recent patrons – young fellow, baronet; not exactly a noble, though he's popular, well-connected. He comes to see the girl at least twice a week. Good chap, knows the rules. He's even taken her out once or twice. Obviously, we keep the jewels in the house if the girls venture outside, so they're not as magnificently bedecked as they are at home. Can't risk theft, you know." Jacob laughed. Foxley smiled and went on. "The fellow will need a tidy sum if he's really going to buy her. We wait and see."

"Well, that sounds promising," Jacob commented. "And Nana?"

"Nana is popular with everyone. She's a good girl. The younger nuns go running to her with all the worries that girls have, you know. She's worth her weight in gold, that one. And what a pretty thing! My word, she's one of the gems. We earned a colossal amount of money for her breaking-in, as you know. Things have settled down now, but she's still a hundred and fifty guineas an hour."

Jacob couldn't resist pressing on. "How's Viv?"

"Viv," Foxley replied. "Viv is most impressive. I would rate her the most intellectual nun in the order. She's a particular favourite of the more learned gentlemen. I believe they visit her just as much for a literature lesson as for a fuck." Foxley looked thoughtful. "Of course, you were with her a year ago."

Jacob smarted at the throwaway use of vulgar profanity in relation to Vivianne, but he tried not to show it.

"I was," he said. "I wonder if she recalls it."

"I should imagine she recalls it very well," said Foxley, "although she doesn't speak about it – not to me anyway. She keeps herself occupied – when she's not being *kept* occupied. Writes a lot."

"Yes," said Jacob. "She was always a writer."

"If it wasn't for your blasted pox, Crowan, you could have spent the night with her. I'm sure she'd be a good girl for you. What a pity!" Foxley thought for a moment, drawing on his pipe, then said, "She has the nicest bum in the convent, in my opinion."

Jacob could bear no more. "I'm away to bed, Edgar. Not feeling too well. Goodnight."

They shook hands. "Sorry about your health Crowan. Take

care of yourself. We can't afford to lose you."

Jacob was on his way north early the following morning, but Stella remained and watched Harriet's sale. £1,275. Not quite up to Nana, but still pretty impressive. Things might have gone a little better if the poor girl hadn't cried the whole time.

After the auction, Stella and her sharp little friend were once again out on the streets of London. She began her annual jamboree by perforating two elderly women as they sat in their places in the upper level of the Theatre Royal, Covent Garden. Both died quietly. The first received the blade through the neck from behind, the second in an upward jab under the chin as she turned to confront her attacker. It was cleanly done, and Miss Shadow was away into the night, swimming through the crowds like a shark, feeding on the living bodies she passed, administering blind, random death.

She lost count of the number of times her needle was deployed, but left the busy streets after a minute or two and turned into a quiet alleyway, a short cut home to King's Place. Almost immediately there came the sound of footsteps, hurrying after her in urgent pursuit.

"Stop there!" The order was barked loudly, a command. Stella obeyed and turned. The man was smartly dressed and armed with a club of some kind, long and heavy.

"I saw what you did! Hand over your weapon and come with me."

"Are you a Runner?" she asked, never having seen one of the little band before.

"Give me your blade," the man demanded. But Miss Shadow was quick, well-practised, and a second later the needle bored a hole through his heart. She withdrew the weapon instantly, enjoying the soft spatter of thick, bloody droplets as it pulled free. The unfortunate man stared at her for a moment in disbelief, then fell to his knees and collapsed to the ground, dead. Stella turned and hurried home.

The story was in the newspapers two days later:

BOW STREET RUNNER SLAIN

It has become apparent that a MURDERER walks the streets of Covent Garden annually in the summer. The killings occur within theatre buildings or in the open street, the victims – seemingly selected at random – receiving a single deep stab wound to the neck, chest or abdomen. Constables have noted that these BRUTAL SLAYINGS occur annually in July, and those poor souls fallen this year have included a mere child and a constable. The public is asked to remain vigilant at all times so that the **COVENT GARDEN VAMPYRE** *may be cornered and exposed...*

That was worthwhile. Stella was happy.

62. COVENT GARDEN
Sunday August 8, 1762

My God, look at them, he thought. *Five in a row, more shining than the angels.*

He was going to pass right by them. How long would he able to look? Half a minute? Then they'd be behind him. Five young women, as radiant and colourful as a rainbow, impossibly beautiful, with two fashionable, well-behaved little spaniels on leashes, their long brown and white coats groomed till they shimmered.

They're Foxley's girls, he thought. *Only Foxley has such goddesses. Where are their guards?* He looked right and left and saw the two men, walking at a distance, one on either side. *Oh my, my, my, my – what wouldn't I give for the white-haired girl? They're like exquisite dolls – that one, blonde hair in ringlets. My God! Look at her figure! She's magnificent.*

His being turned to water at the sight of them, his body like a sigh. The young women were very close now; he'd have to look away at any moment. But then the black-haired one caught his eye – and he realised he knew her. He'd actually spoken to her in the theatre. She was smiling at him – smiling! At *him*! His mouth dropped open in astonishment.

"Hello, Luke." She raised her hand in greeting. His heart melted, and he felt helpless – that such a creature should speak to him. A ridiculous, inane grin spread out like butter on his face. His mother would have called the expression "gaumless".

"Hello, Vivianne." He returned her salute. "You look lovely. Well, you all do, of course. So beautiful – like the day..." He continued garbling for a moment, stumbling over his words, felt a complete fool. They'd gone anyway – they were continuing on their way, and he was left spinning in their wake.

"Who was that?" asked Nana.

"Luke Black," said Vivianne. "He's an actor. I've seen him a couple of times."

"Is he a customer?" asked Orla.

"No!" said Vivianne. "He's not famous enough to have money. We're out of his price range. He's nice, though – intelligent, well-read. We had a conversation about Coriolanus during the interval."

Harriet Dixon craned her head forward, peered at Vivianne and asked, "You're allowed to go to the theatre?"

"Not by yourself," Vivianne replied. "They'll let you go with a client if they're sure they can trust him – or they'll let you go with one of the guards. I've been a couple of times with Will."

"Him?" Harriet nodded to the right, to one of their minders. "Will Jones?"

"Yes," said Viv. "He's alright. He's kind. Not like some of them." She nodded in the other direction, indicating Harry Clarke, shadowing them on the path by the hedge about thirty yards distant.

"Harry's a bastard," said Orla. "A total, hateful bastard."

Both dogs began to make a fuss, barking at a Pomeranian as its owner, a middle-aged man out for a walk in the sunshine, dragged it past. "Merry! Fiddler!" called Nana, holding both their leashes. "Stop it!" She apologised to the owner of the other dog. The gentleman smiled and lifted his hat, then stood and watched the girls from behind as they moved away from him.

"Harry was one of yours, wasn't he?" Kim Hurley asked Orla. "One of the men who got you."

"Got me?" said Orla. "They raped me in the carriage – him and Saul Butcher."

626

Kim looked ahead and made a disapproving noise. "Hm. They weren't supposed to do that."

Orla went on. "Saul's an evil shit. Always humming his stupid little tunes; whistling to himself. He even did it while he was... while he was..." She couldn't say it, fury rising at the memory. "Sick bastard. If I ever get the chance..."

Kim raised her voice and cut in, irritated at Orla's persistent complaining. "But you won't, will you. You won't. Because you're going. Aren't you? You're getting out."

Orla quietened. "I don't know yet. It's possible."

"He's nice – your man, James," said Nana, hoping to defuse the tension. "Talks about you all the time."

"He's been with you then?" said Orla in an accusative tone, anger rising again.

Nana realised she'd made a stupid mistake. She swallowed, fussed with the dogs for a moment. "Come on, Orla. You know we can't refuse them."

Harriet was curious, looked at Orla and asked, "But do you actually like him? James?"

"He's alright," Orla replied with some reluctance. "Between staying in this place or going with him – I'll go with him."

"Jumping ship," said Kim.

The remark was meant to be harmless, a meaningless fragment of banter, but it ignited Orla's fury, and she rounded on the older woman. "Fuck you!" she spat. "And *all* you people who think this is any kind of life. They *killed* the man I loved. Don't forget that. And don't try to justify *any* of this. These people are parasites – and you're just a happy little fish in someone else's pond. *Don't you dare criticise me!*"

Vivianne put her arm round Orla. "Shh. Calm down. We know what happened. Kim knows too. You're one of us. We care about you."

"I'm sorry, Orla," said Kim. "I didn't mean to upset you. I know it was very bad for you, coming here."

Orla brushed her eyes and sniffed. Vivianne produced a handkerchief and gave it to her. "Thank you," she muttered, wiping her cheeks.

They were approaching a long bench on which sat two slender young men, about twenty years old, one dressed in red, the other in pale green, both hatless.

"Let's have a breather," said Kim.

The two men gawped open-mouthed as the ladies bore down on them. Kim made a brushing motion with her hand and said, "Hello there. Would you like to piss off, please? Go on, off you piss." The two stood, fidgeting, intimidated. "Go on," insisted Kim, continuing her dismissive brushing action. "Piss, piss, piss, pisssssssssss...." The two ran away, and the girls sat down. Nana passed the leashes to Harriet, and the dogs settled at her feet.

Harriet looked at Kim. "How can you stand this?"

Kim shrugged. "Money," she said. "I came down from the Lookout four years ago. It was horrible at first – I was just as upset as anyone. But it's not such a bad life once you're used to it. And we're lucky – we're the cream of the bunch. We're protected. We're precious to them – to Mags and Mr Punch."

"Foxley, you mean?" asked Harriet.

"Yes," said Kim. "Mr Punch." She waved her fingers vigorously at the sides of her face. "Because of his red cheeks and his big chin. Haven't you heard him called that?" Harriet shook her head. "Don't let him hear you say it though – he doesn't like it."

"Alright," said Harriet. "But you said money. What do you mean, *money*?"

"What do I mean?" Kim gazed incredulously at the younger girl, her brows furrowed. "You really don't know how this works do you?" Harriet shook her head, and Kim went on. "We're not cheap, you know – any of us. The men who come here – they pay more for a few hours with one of us than they pay all their servants together in a year."

"I know that," said Harriet, looking away.

"We're the best," said Kim. "The most educated, the most cultivated, the most prized. We cost a lot. Do you know how much money was given for your first time?"

"Course I do," Harriet replied.

Kim continued, "One man paid all that for you – a fortune. He thought you were worth that much. What was it? Twelve hundred and fifty pounds?" She paused, allowing the vastness of the figure to sink in. "That's more money than most people earn in their whole lives – just for a pop at you."

Harriet stared at the ground and swallowed. The other girls surveyed the park while Kim filled in the rest of the details. They'd heard it all before, but none of them really believed it.

"They save us a percentage of what we earn. We work for them till we're twenty-six, twenty-seven, twenty-eight; then they pay us our percentage and cut us loose. We have free lives after that; we can do as we please. And the amount of money we get is about twenty-five times what was paid for your first night. That's more money than you can dream of. All you need to do is lie down and tell whichever idiot's on top of you what a big boy he is, how much you admire him, how much you look forward to his visits. You just have to make the right noises – any old rubbish you think he wants to hear. Pant a bit, gasp at all the right moments, tell him he's better than anyone. You put up with it for a few years, then you go and buy a castle, drink wine and eat sweets for the rest of your life. It's not a bad deal."

Nana laughed. "You make it sound pretty dreamy, Kim. How many nuns have been right through and come out at the far end of the process? How many ex-nuns are there, living in castles and eating sweets?"

Kim scowled. "None – yet. But that's because the business is still young. The rewards come after ten years of service, and the business is only seven years old. Foxley and Mags have been running this show for ages, but this exclusive setup, involving schools and high-class girls, only began seven years ago. The first of the new girls arrived in 1755 – before the Lookout was in the picture. Those nuns will retire around 1765 or 1766. Then we'll see the whole procedure in operation: school – convent – rewards. The first girls from the Lookout arrived in 1757. They'll come out the far end five years from now. It's a constant stream, refreshed every season – everybody comes out happy."

Nana laughed. "Happy! How do you know Foxley'll keep his word? How do you know he won't just have us killed when he's done with us and pocket the money? They're willing to commit murder when it suits them – you know that."

Kim reddened. "Because we – the ones who are left – will always keep in touch with those who've gone."

"You mean like the censored mail from here to the Lookout?" laughed Viv. "They'll just lie to you."

"No – we'll keep in touch personally – we'll go and see them – we'll know they're safe. In any case, what's Mr Punch got to lose? He's already rich – he wants to keep good relations – there's no reason for him to renege."

Harriet cut in immediately. "What's to stop the freed girls going back to the Lookout in person and telling everyone there what's going on?"

"Why would they do that?" asked Kim, irritated. "What would they say? *Look at me – see how rich I am. Pity you can't have it too – we've come to save you from this evil life and take all your prospects away.*" She was silent for a moment, then went on with reduced energy. "Anyway, I dread to think what would happen to anyone who tried that. And I dread to think what would happen to the people at the school."

Harriet asked quietly, "What do you mean? You mean they'd kill them all? Everyone?"

"They would if they felt threatened," Kim replied. "Think

how much money's involved. Better murder a hundred and fifty people than risk exposure. It'd be safer to wipe everything out and start again."

All five sat in silence for a minute, faces expressionless, as if they were waiting for sentence to be passed.

An ancient couple shuffled by, bent, shrivelled, both supported on walking sticks. "Good morning, ladies," saluted the white-haired gentleman, but received no answer except a glance and smile from Nana.

"What is wrong with young people these days?" asked the wrinkled woman as the pair moved on, their voices fading into the distance. "Why people can't be civil and receive a greeting gracefully, I have no idea. I remember when I was a girl…"

Harriet, entirely ignoring the couple's passage, proposed a new idea. "Then, supposing the retired girls told powerful people about all this. Supposing they told the King?"

Kim replied, "Have you been visited by royalty yet, Harriet?"

"Yes," the other admitted, eyes cast into her lap.

The dogs were restless, standing on their hind legs, pawing at the girls, begging for attention. Harriet looked right and left. The two guards watched them from a distance, waiting patiently, Harry smoking his pipe.

Harriet said, "Supposing we just all run then? Now. There are five of us – four if you want to stay, Kim. And there are only two of them."

"Where would you run to?" asked Kim. "Even if they didn't catch you, could you be sure that we who are left behind wouldn't suffer the consequences?"

Harriet snorted her contempt and spat, acidly, "I hate it here!"

Kim's voice was quiet. "Just play the game."

Orla and Nana glanced at Vivianne. Viv knew what to do. It was a secret shared between only the three of them. Viv was going to sink it all.

63. THE LOOKOUT
Early August to Early September, 1762

The month of August was considered to be a holiday at the Lookout. Lessons ceased, and the girls were free to do more or less as they pleased. Some chose to study alone, others applied themselves to their own particular favourite subject: a musical instrument, singing, reading, dancing or whatever. Or they could simply relax and unwind, spend time with friends, swim, or organise a play for their own enjoyment. The outdoor theatre was regularly used for just such things.

Walks and picnics were popular, often led by the girls' maids, the housemistresses noisily tagging along and frightening the men they passed. Sometimes they were joined by a few of the footmen and dairymaids.

Occasionally there was something more formal, involving a coach trip to Whitby or Scarborough to visit the theatre or go to a fair. Up to ten girls at a time were allowed, with two staff members – tutors or maids – looking after them. The older girls – classes 5, 6 and 7 – were usually released from authority and allowed to roam free, even in town. Fraternising with the town boys was discouraged, although brief adventures were not unknown, mostly harmless. Occasionally there was a bit of gossip in the homeward bound carriages, but the excursions were too infrequent to allow genuine romances to develop.

Jacob smiled, overhearing their stories, thrilling with their little excitements. He sometimes wished it were possible to cut the Lookout off from King's Place and run it as the benign establishment it pretended to be.

Some loves remained as they had been a year previously;

others changed. Kipp and Lettice were still together. It was rare for Kipp to sustain a relationship for so long. He was beginning to feel that Lettice was almost his wife. He became restless once in a while and found himself looking at the older girls – Elizabeth Redesdale, Zoe Scott or Yvette Maxwell – although he knew he couldn't touch them. *Is it her, then? Lettice, is she the one?* He thought. *Is that it? Is it time to make things official?*

Clara and Sylvie were long-term partners. Sylvie was completely monogamous, wholly faithful, but Clara always needed change. She'd had a one-nighter with Theo Westmoreland *(bet he hasn't told his wife)* and a somewhat longer fling with Solly Birtwistle. There was something raw and earthy about Solly that excited Clara. Their meetings (now at an end) had mostly taken place on the floor of the potting shed. Solly always threw down a few blankets, but she still got splinters in her back.

One of Clara's early conquests at the Lookout had been Hollis Wayland, the doctor. He was in his thirties, straightforward, handsome, kind, and actually quite a good lover. Clara liked him a lot but found him a little dull at times. Sex in the infirmary was safe and predictable, and although their relationship was not continuous, she liked to return there once in a while. Hollis would open the door, and there she'd be.

"Hello, Clara…"

"Hello, Hollis. Got time?"

He rarely turned her away.

Eleanor Rodman had been at Golda's life class on the occasion that Newt Fallowfield fulfilled his modelling lottery. Eleanor had felt alone that day, depressed, and something in Newt's face touched her – a loneliness that was similar to her own. She was attractive: slender, small-breasted, intriguing, intellectual, kept her blonde hair cut extremely short. She'd never really thought of herself as a woman. She joked with Denise, Eve and Lettice, played her part in their bawdy games, but there was something missing or misplaced in her – she'd always known it. Eleanor was an outsider, like Newt. She looked across the ballroom that Saturday morning and saw the otherness in him too, never having noticed it there before. His spirit seemed as exposed to her as his body.

She waited for him after the class and caught him as he was leaving.

"Newt."

"Eleanor."

"You looked good up there. I mean..." She fixed him with her gaze – tried to get her eyes to say what her lips hadn't.

Newt didn't know how to reply. In all the years he'd worked at the Lookout, he'd exchanged probably less than a hundred words with Eleanor. He looked down and tried to think of a throwaway witticism.

She watched him for a few seconds as he fumbled for words, then quietly said, "You like boys, don't you?"

He looked at her but said nothing.

She put her hand on his chest. "I can be a boy..."

Janet Illif's nocturnal visits to John Eldenshaw continued, though they were rare – only once every two or three months. She was concerned that he might become irritated or bored with her, so visited him only when her loneliness bit too deep for her to bear. They'd make love and then lie quietly for a while, talking in the dark. He knew most of her life story, and she knew most of his, but she never told him how much she really needed him – never told him that if it wasn't for him, she might have already walked into the sea.

This warm August night, she lay sleeping soundly in his arms, snoring quietly. John smiled to himself, stroked her grey hair, her right shoulder. She was warm, loving, vulnerable. How could it be, he wondered, that she'd passed right through her life and no-one had noticed what a wonderful, thoughtful, special, tender woman she was?

Kate had changed since that day on Watermill Lane when she'd had her vision of Hugo. His image was often in her mind, particularly that part of him. Her innocence in the life classes was gone, and she admitted to herself that she felt a new excitement looking at the unclothed male models. Her failure to adequately portray men remained an irritation to her, but there was also a new fascination. It disturbed her, and she tried to set it to one side, to overcome the unwelcome frisson.

One Tuesday morning, she took up her sketching equipment and set out to find Ned, determined to crack the problem. Today was the day, she told herself; she was going to get it right at last.

Things were quiet in the park. In the distance, down by the fields, she saw John Eldenshaw and Speck Beckwith standing together. Speck seemed downcast, and John's hand rested on his friend's shoulder as if in sympathy. John was speaking; Speck was quiet. Unusually, Bastard was nowhere to be seen. *Something's happened,* thought Kate.

"Morning, Miss Kate." It was Solly Birtwistle, on his hands and knees in one of the flowerbeds.

"Morning, Solly," Kate replied. "Have you seen Ned?"

"Not yet," Solly called. "He's probably still at home."

Kate continued on towards the groundsmen's dwellings. Speck and John were no longer in sight, and there was little activity in the pens and fields as far as she could see, the animals left to themselves.

Pixie Silden was in the little garden at the front of her house, hanging out her washing. She saw Kate coming, waved in greeting and stood, hands on hips, waiting for her.

"Morning, Pixie," said Kate.

"Morning, Kate. Now let me guess what you want."

"Is it alright? Is he in?"

"He is," said Pixie. "You know Kate, some people might

think that what you do is a bit odd."

"Really?" Kate replied. She thought, then said, "I suppose I know what you mean. But I really want to get it right."

"I know," said Pixie, in a tone of voice that said, *The rest of us will just have to do as we're told until you're satisfied.* "Follow me. I admire your determination."

Pixie pushed open her front door and called, "Ned. Kate's here. Get your breeches off."

Ned had become used to Kate's perfectionism and was agreeable enough to do what was necessary on the understanding that she kept his compliance to herself. He didn't want to invite such detailed scrutiny from any other lone "perfectionists".

It was no use, though. Whatever Kate did, it looked silly, and she became increasingly frustrated – the more so because she knew that frustration wouldn't help. She was trying to frame something beyond what she saw; some symbol, some emblem that she couldn't quite reach.

It must be possible to capture it on paper, she thought. *Why can I never do it? I'm missing the essence of it.*

She knew that if she drew an eye, she could capture the *eyeness* of it – the idea of eye from which all eyes might proceed. A leg, the same – the essence was there; she could do it. An arm, a foot, a hand, even a knee. But this? This thing, she couldn't do. It just looked absurd – always.

Kate held her work at arm's length, frowned and said, "That's useless. What am I not understanding? I've tried this a hundred times, and I never get any closer."

"Let's have a look, my love," said Pixie, taking Kate's work in her hand and scanning the various attempts. She frowned, eyebrows knit. "What's wrong with them? Looks good to me. They're *really* good, in fact. What a talent you've got." She paused, then added, "Mind you, I'm not sure I'd like to show them to my mother."

Pixie seemed genuinely impressed, but Kate remained unsatisfied. "But they don't look *natural*, do they? I mean, women I have no problem with – mostly. Men too, I can generally do – except for *that*. *That* always looks wrong – always dead, unconvincing, childish."

Pixie shook her head. "I can't see anything wrong with it," she said. "I reckon if you sketched the bits of ten idiots and hung 'em up on a wall, I could tell easily enough which was Ned's."

"Maybe that's it," said Kate. "Ten of them, all different. I had trouble with faces at first – because every face is different. I got better, though. Perhaps I just need more of them."

Ned, silent until this point, said, "Ask old Rabbit Shipley. That'd be a challenge, I bet."

Pixie replied, "Yes. And I can just hear his answer now…"

"Anyway," said Kate, "I'm done for today. Thank you, Ned, as always."

"That's alright, Kate," said Ned, pulling his clothes on. "I'm off to see how poor old Speck is. He might be pleased to see you too if you've got time."

"What's happened?" asked Kate.

"Bastard died," Pixie explained. "Just this morning. He had an accident yesterday."

"Oh, no!" said Kate. "Oh no, that's dreadful."

Speck lived right next door to Ned and Pixie. Kate hugged him as soon as she saw him. "Speck, I'm so sorry."

He ruffled her hair, and she heard the sadness in his voice. "Ah well, he was good'un, and a friend, so far as a dog can be. I'll miss him."

Speck ushered Kate and Ned inside. It was the first time Kate had been in Speck's dwelling. It was clearly the home of a solitary man: untidy, dusty, a bit mucky, filled with the smells of sweat, earth, tobacco, booze – and dog.

"What happened?" she asked.

"He hurt himself yesterday afternoon, running about, jumping over fences, having a mad hour. It was something sharp, maybe a nail or a broken fence post or something. I looked around but couldn't find anything that might have done it. I saw straight away he was in pain – felt around him. He was all opened up underneath, trying to lick himself. I knew he was gone. I carried him back here, settled him where he liked to be, under the kitchen table and sat with him till he died."

Ned sighed. "We'll all miss him, Speck."

"Yep," Speck replied. "We'll need another dog, that's for sure. I'll have to train one up quick for the sheep. Should always have had two, really. We learn by our mistakes."

Kate had been thinking. "Where is he? Have you buried him yet?"

"He's in the kitchen, Kate. He'll go in the ground this afternoon. I've got a few things to do before I can attend to him, poor fellow."

"Can I stay with him?" she asked.

Speck looked at her and said, "You were as fond of old Bastard as I was, weren't you?"

"I was," Kate replied. "I loved him."

"You can keep him company if you like."

Speck led her into his kitchen. Bastard was lying on a blood-soaked blanket under the table, his sightless eyes half-open, lips drawn back in death, teeth exposed.

"He's not a pretty sight," said Speck. "And he doesn't know you're here, so just leave when you want."

"Thank you," she said. "I'll stay awhile."

"You're a good girl, Kate. Bless you."

Then he was gone, and Kate was left alone with the body of the dog.

It had been quite some time since Kate had tried to resurrect anything, and she'd never attempted the procedure with anything like as large as a dog.

She made sure that Ned and Speck had left, then knelt down next to Bastard and laid her hand on him. His skin felt strangely loose. The dog looked very dead indeed, and the cool stillness of his body – no heartbeat, no muscular response – intimidated her. She wasn't sure if she could really manage this. And if she did, how was she going to explain it to Speck and everyone else? How much time did she have before Speck returned? Birds and mice took only minutes to bring back, but a big creature such as this? Who could tell? It might require hours. If she was really going to try, she had to start right away.

I need something in the air, she thought, not knowing quite why. Scent wasn't something that Speck was likely to have, so Kate returned to Pixie's house, explained that she was watching over Bastard ("...you're a strange one, Kate, stranger and stranger...") and asked if she had something that would help concentration, like incense or scent – something with a pleasant odour. Pixie was puzzled but lent her a perfume burner with a few pastilles of rosewater, myrtle and orange, together with a little charcoal. She offered the girl a flint striker, but Kate proudly produced her pipe and smoking equipment. "Got my own, thanks!"

She set the perfume burner going on the floor of Speck's kitchen, dragged out the blanket on which lay Bastard's body, made herself as comfortable as she could, closed her eyes, and lost herself in deep concentration. She hummed quietly, improvising little snatches of melody, caressing the dog, calling his name, willing him back...

Speck returned at half past three. He'd been thinking of his companion all day and was steeled to the task of burying him.

But it wasn't going to happen. Bastard was there to greet him even before the door was properly open – jumping up, barking, tongue lolling, happy, as daft as ever.

What?? What is this? How?

Speck knelt and hugged the dog, his mind in confusion. He must have been dreaming. It was the strangest sensation –

as if two universes had collided. In one, the dog was dead; in the other, he was alive, and Speck had slipped between the two. He laughed, although his joy was shot through with disbelief. He petted Bastard, tickled him, made a fuss of him. Then the dog ran off into the cottage. Speck stood up from where he knelt and noticed for the first time how sweet the house smelt. He looked up and saw Kate leaning in the kitchen doorframe, exhausted, Bastard sitting obediently at her feet.

"...How...?" he asked, unable to form the question.

"I just hugged him," said Kate. "It took a long time. I've always been able to do it with small animals, but I had to really concentrate this time."

"But it's impossible!" said Speck as Bastard ran back to him.

"Well – you can see it isn't," she replied, pointing at the happy dog, very alive.

"He was dead, Kate!"

"But he couldn't have been," said Kate. "It just takes determination to wake them."

Speck felt around his dog's underside. "Where's the wound?"

"Gone," said Kate.

Speck was lost for words. He stepped into the kitchen, found a chair and sat down. Bastard settled obediently at his feet, looking up at him, watching for his master's next move. Speck opened his mouth in mute incomprehension. He cocked his head to one side and looked askance at Kate, questioning.

"I just wanted him back, like you did," she said.

"I don't understand," he said quietly. Bastard had jumped up, his front paws on Speck's lap, panting, tongue dangling idly to the right, hung on his teeth as if it were out to dry. Speck took the dog's head in his hands and played with his ears. He smiled at Bastard and said, "So you're back, boy! Are you really back?"

Kate stood silently for a moment, then said, "All's well.

Sometimes nice things happen, unexpected things."

"How did you do it, Kate? Really. I need to know."

Her face fell. "Are you cross with me?"

His eyes widened in alarm. "Cross? No! I just want to understand."

"I'm not sure I can tell you. I'm not sure I really know. It's just something I've always been able to do. Only little things before, just tiny animals. I didn't think it would work with Bastard, but it did. Aren't you happy? I wanted you to be happy."

He held out his hand, and Kate came forward and took it. "Of course I'm happy. I'm amazed."

"It might be best if you didn't tell too many people," said Kate. "I don't want them to think differently of me or be frightened. Is it alright?"

"How can I repay you for this?" he asked.

Kate thought for a moment, then let go of his hand and said, "Actually, there is something. But it's going to sound very odd."

He frowned and waited. Kate's request required a little explanation and back story. She told him what she'd been doing that morning in Ned's house next door, and then asked him point-blank.

Speck's expression steadily gathered incredulity as he saw her question approach. "What?" He laughed. "You want me to do what?"

Kate laughed too. "Say no if you like. I shan't be offended."

But Speck could say neither yes nor no. This new universe he found himself in had just shifted again.

Kate, realising that her actions would have consequences, braced herself for the inevitable questions. Those few people who'd seen the dog dead, and knew how serious his injuries had been, were the most unsettled. Kate tried to explain Bastard's resurrection by basically telling the truth, the same as she'd done with Speck. What calmed the sceptics most was her insistence that the technique must have a basis in natural science for which there was not yet an adequate explanation. In the meantime, Bastard was safe and well. Wasn't that a good thing?

The story that got around was that Bastard had been very ill, believed dead, and that Kate had made him better. A few people said there was some kind of magic involved, but Kate dismissed the idea, and any real excitement there might otherwise have been was minimised.

Nevertheless, Kate's status in the community had changed. To some, she was a hero; to others, a mystery.

The other girls sought her out more and more, asked her advice, wanted to be close to her. One of the more imaginative maids, Molly Colby, having convinced herself that Kate must have a connection with the spirit world, asked if she could see the future. Kate replied in the negative but told Molly she could read her cards if that was any use. Soon there was a deluge of people – girls, maids and others – wanting the same service.

"They say the girl raised Speck's dog from the dead," said Stella.

"That can hardly be," Jacob replied. "Nothing ever comes back from the everlasting blackness."

"Kate herself says the reports are exaggerated, but others are very sure in what they believe. Her grandmother was a witch; is that not true?"

"That word hardly has a place in the modern world, Stella. I really think people are blowing up a tempest where none exists. Forget about it. Let it die down. The excitement will pass."

"You're not going to investigate the matter?"

He took off his spectacles, dropped them on his desk and sat back in his chair. "I know Kate is different; I've always known it – ever since the first moment I saw her. She's been here for two years now, and I've watched her carefully, from a distance. She learns at an extraordinary rate. Have you heard her play the harpsichord?"

"No," Stella replied.

"You should," said Jacob. "She plays like a professional. You'd think she'd been studying for ten years. I'd like her development to continue without obstruction."

"I wasn't suggesting any kind of restriction as such," Stella replied. "I simply thought it would be a good idea to nip superstition in the bud."

"I understand your concern. I'll have a word with her. In the meantime, let her be popular. She'll manage her celebrity in her own way."

Jacob caught Kate immediately after dinner on the first Friday of September.

"Kate. Do you have a moment to speak?"

"Yes, of course. I've been wanting a word anyway," she replied.

They made their way to a table in the entrance hall, close to the gong, while the girls milled about on their way to various evening activities. Once seated, Jacob asked her if all was well.

"Yes, I think so," she replied. "I'm always very busy; there are so many things to do…"

"And people to see," he interjected. "I hear you're sought after."

"Ever since Speck's dog," she replied. "I don't mind. I still get all my work done."

"Tell me about the dog," he prompted.

"It was nothing," she said. "I just sat with him, and he woke up."

"No magic involved then?"

"Magic?" said Kate, fixing him with an enquiring stare.

He felt a little ridiculous. "I mean…in earlier times, to put it bluntly, such a thing might have had you arrested – for witchcraft. You might have been hanged."

Kate looked at him for a long time in silence, her expression fixed. Jacob began to feel unnerved, and after a few moments it appeared to him that he was looking into the face of someone else, a woman perhaps twice Kate's age, unsmiling, piercing him with her eyes. It was eerie, chilling. He frowned and shrank away, leaning back a few inches in his chair.

Suddenly it was Kate again. "I know," she said.

He swallowed, unsure what he'd just seen.

Without warning, Kate said, "I'd like to go into the turret on the tower."

He shook his head, lips downturned. "Why? There's nothing there."

"I've been in the corner room," she said, "but the tower door is locked."

"So is the room," he said. "How did you get inside?"

"There's a tunnel in the wall. It's a tight squeeze. When I first arrived here, I could get through it, but now I can't. I've got bigger, and I can't manage it anymore."

He looked briefly away from her. "Ah, I see. I knew there was a cavity in the wall on the second floor, but I thought it was too small to be used for anything. It must be very dark. It could have been quite dangerous. That was pretty foolhardy of you. The wall is built in two layers, and the chimneys rise between them. If there'd been a roaring fire, you might have been roasted trying to get round the brickwork."

"I didn't think about the hazards," she said. "I just wanted to get into the room."

"But there's nothing in that room, as you know. Apart from you, I don't suppose anyone's been in there for the last eight years. It was never finished – the floor is unsafe."

"Why wasn't it finished?" she asked.

Jacob raised his eyebrows, pursed his lips and said, "The workmen wouldn't go in there. They complained of noises."

"Noises?" she said.

"I imagine you know what happened in the house decades ago. There are old stories of ghosts – all nonsense of course..." He seemed to lose track of his thoughts for a moment, his mind elsewhere.

"Ghosts?" she prompted.

"Two young boys died in that tower. They were locked in and starved to death. The workmen claimed to hear the sound of their feet on the staircase. I don't think it's a place for you – or *any* of the girls."

"Please, Mr Crowan," she said. "I'd very much like to go into the room again. And into the tower."

He looked at her for a long time. "Kate, if access to that room were to be sought by any other girl, I would flatly refuse. I only consider your request because it comes from you."

"Why?" she asked. "I mean, why – only from me?"

He thought before replying. "People come to you because you tell their future in cards. That's what I hear. Is it correct?"

"My grandmother showed me how to do it, but the cards are just tools – there's no magic involved. They offer clues as to what *could* be. They don't specifically predict the future, but they do supply symbols from which you can draw your own conclusions. The symbols can be specific, or not, depending on what the drawer thinks they represent."

"And what do you mean by that exactly?"

"That sometimes you recognise what's to come. Sometimes the future shapes itself according to what you believe it ought to be."

He looked at her in silence, his left hand loosely clenched, his thumb gently rubbing the side of his forefinger. It was an unconscious gesture she'd seen him make several times when he was deep in thought.

She went on. "Have you ever had your cards read, Mr Crowan?"

"No," he said.

"Would you like me to read them for you?"

He thought, then replied, "No."

The atmosphere between them had become strangely charged. "I can go into the room? Into the tower?"

"I'll find the keys for you. This is on the condition that you tell no-one else, no-one. That room is unsound. I wouldn't want to see anyone hurt. I must have your promise."

"You have it," she said. "I promise."

64. THE LOOKOUT –
CLARA – THE TURRET
Tuesday September 7, 1762

Kate often felt a little uneasy in the presence of Clara Sutherland. The woman was so tactile, her movements sinuous and feline, and she always wore gowns that clung about her figure, accentuating the lines and curves of her body, throwing her breasts and hips into relief. Clara liked to touch Kate's hands and arms during her harp lessons, and Kate found her subtle approaches both fascinating and disturbing. Clara had big eyes, full moist lips and a resonant alto voice. Fangs would have looked quite natural in her smile. Kate, who hadn't yet had any amorous encounters at all, was uncertain whether she'd jump inwards or outwards if Clara's touches became more insistent. Shelagh had long ago warned her to be careful – Clara was known to indulge in affairs with her students.

For several days Kate's head had been filled with a piece of music she'd been learning on the harp. *Captain O'Kane,* it was called, written by Turlough O'Carolan. The room would vanish during her less absorbing classes; she'd close her eyes and allow the piece to play in her mind, transporting her far away to a land where mathematical calculations and Latin verbs had little significance. She brought it to her lesson on Tuesday afternoon at three o'clock and performed it for Clara. When she'd finished, her teacher's hand was on her knee.

"Kate," she said, "That was beautiful. I love old Turlough's music, and you made it sing as if you were improvising it. You're born for this." Her hand caressed Kate's thigh through her clothing. "You are a *very* fine musician. You could do anything with this instrument." Kate's heart beat faster, and her breathing deepened. She was warmed by her teacher's opinion of her musicianship but apprehensive about what might happen next.

There was a knock at the door, and Clara quickly withdrew her touch. "Enter," she called.

The door opened, and Jacob looked in. Kate seemed strangely pink, flushed. "Am I interrupting?" he asked.

"Not at all," Clara replied.

"Good," he said. "Thank you." He stepped into the room and handed Kate a ring on which hung two keys – one large, one small, both rusty. Clara watched, eyebrows raised.

"Here are the keys, Kate," he said. "Remember our agreement."

She took them and said, "I won't forget. Thank you, Mr Crowan."

Jacob apologised to Clara for the intrusion, then turned and left, pulling the door closed behind him.

"So," said Clara. "What will you play next?"

There was no more touching during the lesson. Kate was simultaneously relieved, disappointed and surprised. *My God! She can't think that Jacob and I...*

As soon as the lesson was over at half past three, Kate ran to her dormitory and was pleased to find it empty. She locked herself inside for a few minutes.

She woke suddenly. The room was dark, but she could see the outline of Rosalind Wynter standing by the door beyond the bed where Bip was sleeping.

She wants me to go – now.

Kate had intended to rise early and visit the tower before breakfast, but now she knew it wouldn't wait – she had to leave her nice warm nest and go immediately.

Alright. I'm coming.

She swung her legs out of bed, felt under her pillow for the tower keys, and crept out into the corridor, past the sleeping girls. A glance right and left confirmed that no-one was in sight. Rosalind had vanished. The house was totally silent.

There was a lamp, burning low in the corner, left there so people could find their way to the privy at night. She took it, made her way to the staircase as quietly as she could, and ascended.

The top floor of the house was still relatively unknown to her. Jacob had his apartment here, as did Quinton, Stella, Ruth, and their two servants, Milton and Janet. The infirmary was up here of course, and Dr Wayland's rooms. Kate knew that Jacob's suite occupied the end of the west wing, and she knew where the infirmary was, but was uncertain as to how the other rooms were distributed. She imagined there'd be no mistaking the door to the room on the northeast corner, although she'd previously seen it only from within the room itself.

She walked stealthily, keeping the banister rail and the black maw of the stairwell to her right. The clock in the entrance hall seventy feet below chimed two. *Shhh*, she thought, listening for any activity. There were a couple of creaky floorboards that she thought someone must surely hear – felt them give a little beneath her feet – but a moment later she was standing outside the door, hoping it was the correct one.

Kate held the lamp in her left hand, the keys in her right. Careful to avoid clatter, she inserted the larger of the two into the lock, turned it, but met resistance. *It's been eight years,* she thought, and exerted a little pressure. The lock clicked; the key rotated. She withdrew it, turned the handle and pushed open the door.

The moon, high in the west, was four days past full, and the room was bathed in silver light. Kate closed the door behind her and turned the key. The entrance to the tower lay in the opposite corner of the room. She approached it carefully, remembering Jacob's warning that the floor was unsafe. The hole in the ceiling overhead gaped like a frightful black mouth, the darkness inside too complete to pick out any detail.

At the tower door, she held her breath and listened. There was no sound, not even the wraith of the wind moving on the staircase. She inserted the small key into the lock and turned. It yielded immediately. Kate was suddenly aware of the chill in the room, and her nervousness increased. She looked behind her, half expecting to find Rosalind standing there, but the room remained empty. She turned the handle and pulled open the door.

The staircase was invisible at first, but Kate's lamp, held aloft, revealed the lowest few steps, curling upwards clockwise. She began to ascend, counting the stairs, the chill deepening as she rose higher. Twenty steps, thirty. It was freezing. She wore nothing other than her nightdress; in the need to get here, she hadn't thought to reach for warmer clothing, and now regretted it. Forty steps, fifty. There was light above – it would be the moon shining through the turret windows.

At the fifty-sixth step, Kate saw the two boys. They were standing motionless in the tiny room, looking down the stairs at her. She paused and greeted them.

"Hello. I'm Kate. I knew you'd be here."

They said nothing and made no move, but gazed intently at her. Kate ascended to the top of the stairs and stood between the twins in the lonely little room where they'd died. She put down the lamp and the keys on the narrow stone seat that encircled the space, and knelt in front of the boys. They shifted to accommodate her movements, though remained silent and expressionless. The two looked almost identical, both with delicate shoulder-length hair, very light in colour – ash white. They were dressed the same, in brown silk suits, white ruffs at the neck, white stockings and brown shoes.

"You must be Lawrence and Robin," she said, "But which

is which? Can you tell me?" They didn't respond but continued to look directly into her eyes. Kate raised her hands and touched their faces, stroked their hair. They felt real, but she was shocked at the iciness of their skin.

"You're frozen!"

She sat on the little stone bench and drew the boys to her, hugging them both as tightly as she could.

"The door is open," she said. "Can you come with me?" But there was no response.

Kate didn't know what to do. It was unnaturally cold, and she began to shiver. After a few minutes she heard a sound at the bottom of the staircase that could only be the door swinging shut. Was it the draught from the turret, or had someone closed it? Was she shut in?

"I'll be back in a moment."

She rose, took up the lamp and descended the stairs as quickly as her chilled feet allowed. The door was closed but not locked.

Does it shut by itself?

She set the door ajar, stood quietly, and watched the gentle warm breath blown from her mouth cloud in the room's arctic night. The door didn't move but remained gaping open. Kate set it closer to the frame and waited for it to close unaided. But it didn't. Farther away – the same result. After about ten minutes, she retraced her steps to the turret room and set down the lamp. The boys' eyes remained fixed on her.

"I need to think what to do next," she said. "I'll be back for you." She hugged first one, then the other, and kissed them both. They felt frigid, and their faces remained impassive.

She took up the lamp and the keys, made her way down the staircase and locked the door. Finally, she let herself out of the room, turned the key in the lock and carefully crept downstairs, returning the lamp to its accustomed spot before quietly tiptoeing to her bed.

Kate wrapped the covers around her and pulled them tight

up to her neck, relieved to be warm once more.
But she didn't sleep.

65. MARGATE
Saturday October 9, 1762

Orla sat at her window, looking out at the sands and the sea. The day was warm for the time of year, and the strand was busy with people. She'd slept late, her lover having kept her occupied for much of the night. He'd dressed himself at ten, kissed her and said he'd return before noon. The maid arrived half an hour later with breakfast, and now she sat quietly, thinking.

James had paid extravagantly to take her away for a whole week. He'd first visited her at King's Place a few weeks before the previous Christmas, apparently on a recommendation by a friend of his, and she thought he'd be just like the others – casual, kindly enough, but with no interest beyond the obvious immediate physical one. A week or so after their initial encounter he'd taken her to the theatre, and they'd spent the evening together watching a play, eating a meal, before going back to her room. There was nothing particularly unusual in that; Orla, like many of the Covent Garden nuns, looked impressive on the arm of a man, and being educated, she was able to engage in genuine conversation. But he'd come back the following week – and then again. By the end of January it was clear that he was infatuated with her. He thought of nothing but her, he said. He dreamt about her every night. Orla listened, responded thoughtfully, caressed his face when he told her how much he wanted her. After a while, she began to look forward to his visits, and now here they were in Margate, living together for a week like husband and wife.

They broke the journey at Canterbury and took a room at an inn close to the centre of town. On the morning following their arrival, they walked through the narrow streets towards the cathedral and paused for refreshment at a little coffee shop near the archway to the precinct. He held her hand across the table, pressed it to his lips and told her he loved her, needed her, didn't want to be without her. She listened, eyes moist.

They entered the ancient building hand-in-hand through the southwest porch. It was cool in the vast, lofty space, and the two strolled together, admiring the architecture and the stained glass. There were several visitors, some in groups, some solitary; a few couples, perhaps lovers like themselves. They sat for a while in the choir, Orla looking across at the organ and thinking sadly about Rider. After a few moments, someone arrived to play, a boy in tow to pump the bellows. The organist sat down, made himself comfortable and drew the stops he required.

"Are you ready, Tom?" he said, Orla just catching the words. "Yes, Mr Porter," the boy replied and began to operate the wooden pump handle.

The first notes of the opening slow movement sang into the colossal space, serene, sublime, free, and Orla's heart broke. She knew the music, played the piece herself, Rider having taught her. It was the Voluntary in C major, Op. 5, No. 1 by John Stanley, the famous blind organist of the Temple Church, London. "From a new set of ten", Rider had told her, "published in 1748". She felt his lips on hers; her soul filled with love for him.

Orla couldn't bear to hear it; the loss was intolerable. She stood up in anguish and begged to leave. James was instantly on his feet, arms around her, and escorting her from the cathedral. They hurried, and arrived at the porch just as the lively trumpet tune began to play. He knew what was wrong; she'd hidden nothing from him.

Once in the open air, Orla found a seat and collapsed. "I'm sorry," she said. "I can't listen to that music."

He sat next to her and took her in his arms. "Don't worry,

my love. All the pain, it's still very recent for you."

And it was true – it was still fresh. Orla liked James a lot, but she didn't love him as she'd loved Rider. She'd had a lot of time to think during the fifteen months she'd spent in her enforced profession. The most acute ache, the most pressing concern, was that Rider had been murdered – and there must surely be some justice for that.

Having acknowledged that priority, she then attempted to come to an understanding of herself. Orla had grown up with her mother in a hovel in Sheffield, never having known her father. She wasn't sure how Martha Stapleton paid for their living, although she suspected the money came from work at the low end of the profession in which Orla now found herself. In any case, Martha had become too ill to work by 1754, and they'd been evicted from the slum in which they lived, and forced into the workhouse, where Martha died a few months later.

The scouts from the Lookout found Orla there when she was ten years old. She was nothing, she had nothing, she would have become nothing. Of that, she was certain. Then she'd spent all those happy years at the school, become educated, made friends and memories to last her lifetime. The Orla she recognised grew there.

But it was all for this courtesans' life. If she'd known at the start that it would all lead here, would she have turned it down? Seven happy years at the Lookout, then die? Or seven happy years, then this? Choose. If she'd known in advance, would it have made any difference, given the circumstances from which she'd begun?

But the difference was that the *choice* had been taken away. The girls were promised that at the end of their education, they would have the opportunity to decide about the rest of their lives. They looked forward to that time; that time when they'd launch like ships into waters of their own choosing.

But it was all a lie.

Orla told James everything, and he listened with sympathy. Prostitution itself was not generally considered illegal, he said. Orla knew that, of course, but the level of deception involved was surely scandalous, at least. He agreed that it was but also pointed out the value of the education she'd received. Weighing the benefits of the school against the deception, would its abolishment do more harm than good? In any case, it was unlikely that the powerful men who provided its funding, and benefited from its fruit, would ever permit its undoing.

Orla understood all that, but she also understood something else. The Lookout had shaped her soul. But what was the point of having such a finely fashioned soul if it were destined to be sucked out?

She and others at King's Place were quietly determined to bring about change. Vivianne was writing a book, and one day, somehow, the whole sick edifice would come crashing down.

Sir Charles Clarke was a successful architect, inherited wealth from his father, made money of his own and married into it too. He sent his son James to Oxford to study theology, although the boy showed little interest in it, or aptitude for it.

James was twenty-three years old and married to Anna, with whom he had nothing in common. He was a good enough lad but hadn't found much direction in life – until now. He'd done some research, and he had a plan. And he was in love.

Just after noon, James returned to the Margate love-nest in which he was spending a few days with Orla and presented her with a huge bouquet of flowers.

"Oh, James, look at them!" she said, rising from her seat. "They're lovely!"

"Not as lovely as you," he replied. "Nothing in the world is as lovely as you, Orla."

"You're so kind to me," she said.

In addition to the flowers, he'd been carrying a large flat black case, which he now held out to her. She put down the bouquet and took this second offering. "What's this?" she asked. "James, what have you done?"

"Open it," he prompted.

She did so, and immediately collapsed onto the chaise-longue in astonishment. "My God!" she whispered. "James..." Orla was speechless. He was delighted at her reaction. She held the case in her right hand while her left covered her mouth. A few tears rolled down both cheeks.

"It's yours, my love," he said. "I knew it was yours the moment I saw it."

She was stunned, shaking her head. It was a necklace consisting of twenty-six silver links, each set with seven diamonds. A large diamond-encrusted pendant hung at the bottom of the chain, fashioned into two parts: a butterfly at the top and a teardrop below. She didn't know what to say. It must surely be worth more than her life.

"There are more than three hundred diamonds in it," he said, "but you outshine all of them." He stepped forward. "Can I put it on you?" She stood up, nodding, wiping away tears. He fastened the clasp and walked her over to the tall glass. The effect was dazzling. She mouthed words, but no sound came.

"You look like a goddess," he said softly. "I want you to be mine. I'll take you away from London, and you'll live here in Margate. This town is growing, and I'm going into business here. You can be part of it too. We'll see each other a lot. We'll be so happy." He stood behind her, kissing her neck, reaching beneath her arms and crushing her breasts with his hands. "You'll have everything you need, everything you want. You'll have your own house, your own life. You'll be mine. Please say you'll do it, Orla. I want you; I love you."

She looked at her eyes in the mirror, at the necklace, at James, his chin resting on her shoulder, eyes on hers, pleading. His arms enfolded her from behind, pulling her body against his.

She heard herself say, "Yes, I will. I'm yours."

66. THE TURRET
Sunday to Friday, October 24 to 29, 1762

A tremendous storm came crashing around the school that Sunday morning. Kate knelt on the hard stone bench in the tower turret, the boys behind her, and looked out at the elements. It crossed her mind that she was in the most elevated part of the building. If the lightning struck the house, it would very likely connect right here, the roof that capped this little room, just above her head.

The rain was so thick, the atmosphere so grey, that she could see little further than the roof of the house itself, about twenty-five feet below. She could make out the library turret easily enough, but the other two, over on the corners of the west wing, were much harder to see through the torrent. The sound of the rain falling around her was deafening, but when the thunder crashed the effect was cacophonous, the sky torn apart by jagged streaks of shocking white fury. It was exhilarating, terrifying.

"Isn't it thrilling!" Kate said, burning with excitement.

The boys stood silent, impassive, looking only at her. The lead strips in the windows were not as tightly fixed as they once had been, and the cold rainwater found its way in, running down the panes of glass in thin rivulets. Kate dipped her finger into a small puddle that had collected on the narrow sill, watched the drip as it hung on her fingertip, then deposited it on her tongue. The water, so recently escaped from the tumbling clouds overhead, mingled with her saliva, and she imagined it energising her, renewing her life, charging her with the power of the sky. She closed her eyes and silently gave thanks for the privilege of life. Somewhere, everywhere, she knew that the sentient forces of existence, the energies that enfolded her and everything, every particle, were smiling at her, loved her.

"Anne," she whispered against the raging of the firmament, eyes closed, "are you here?"

There was no reply, of course, but Kate knew she was close. It had been seven weeks since Jacob had granted her sole access to the tower, and during that period she'd visited the twins more than ten times, mostly at night but occasionally, as now, during the hours of daylight. The boys remained always the same. They never spoke, they never looked at anything but Kate, their appearance never altered, their expressions remained fixed. They never left the turret room, although they changed position to allow Kate to move about, and also to maximise the directness of their observation of her. They never ventured down the staircase.

Rosalind still visited Kate every night, but something had changed since Kate's first entry to the tower. She no longer manifested at a distance, her face turned away; instead, she appeared directly at Kate's bedside, facing her. As Fuzzy had warned, it was a horrific sight – the strangled expression, bulging eyes, black tongue protruding in the agony of death. Kate felt compelled to look the first time and found the spectre's appearance so dreadful that she cried out and threw the blankets over her head. Bip, Shelagh and Pammy all woke and brightened the lamps, believing Kate to be dreaming again. Rosalind had vanished – the other girls probably wouldn't have been able to see her anyway. Kate pretended she'd had a nightmare. The subsequent manifestations were easier, although Kate tried to keep her eyes turned away from the ghost's face.

Rosalind had a voice. Not the voice that cried in the night, but another. Her second voice was the door at the foot of the tower. Each time Kate visited the twins, the voice became louder. On the first occasion, the door had been closed calmly, just loud enough for Kate to hear from the turret above. The second time she visited, the door was closed with more emphasis than before, and the third time was a distinct slam as if to say *Listen!* By Kate's fifth visit, the banging of the door had become a violent, angry statement; and the sixth, seventh, eighth... Kate gradually came to understand what the message was.

"I'll do it," she said. The thunder rolled, though less angrily than before. The clouds parted, and in the distance Kate saw the sea. "I'll do it." She turned, hugged the boys, kissed their cheeks and ran down the stairs.

"What exactly are you asking me to do, Kate?" asked Jacob.
"I know it sounds mad, but trust me – I'll come to no harm."
His eyes drilled into her. "Why do you want to do this?"
She thought about telling him but rejected the idea. "It would take too long to explain, and I'm not sure I could do a good job of telling the story."
He thought long, looking at her, his left thumb brushing the side of his left forefinger in his usual mannerism. "It must be to do with the boys who died."
"And their mother," Kate volunteered.
He thought carefully. "Have you seen them?"
"I have."
Jacob turned his gaze away, and his expression softened. He looked sad. "I also have ghosts."
She was surprised but said nothing in reply.
"Alright," he said. "I hope you know what you're doing."

Kate told her friends that she'd be going away for a few days. After supper on Friday, October 29th, she climbed the stairs with Jacob to the top of the house. The sun had long set, so she took a lamp from the corridor and unlocked the door to the corner room. They went inside together, and Kate held the lamp aloft, illuminating the stark, broken interior. Then she walked over to the turret door, opened it and handed Jacob the keys.

"You're really sure about this?" he asked.

"I am," she said. "It's the only way."

He nodded. "Good luck to you."

"Thank you," she replied, and stepped through onto the staircase. Jacob closed the door behind her, and Kate heard the key turn in the lock. She stood quietly, listening to his footsteps as he walked away. Then she heard the door to the corridor open and close. Finally, the sound of the lock turning.

It was cold and dark. She set down the lamp and reached for her things, having already prepared the tower for her arrival. There was a basket containing the few items she'd need, a privy bucket, and a bucket of ashes. She got out of her clothes and put on her nightdress. The thin garment gave no protection from the icy air. It was the quickest and simplest way of doing what had to be done. She wore nothing else. Her feet were bare. She turned down the oil lamp and blew it out, then mounted the stairs to the boys. They were waiting for her, as they always were. She greeted them, sat down and hugged them both close, one on either side. Their bodies gave no warmth.

Jacob walked away, both troubled and relieved. He had a great affection for Kate and was reluctant to see her come to harm. On the other hand, this was an ideal opportunity to get rid of her. As Stella said, she was the odd one out and could not be sent to work with the other girls. He would have had to dispose of her at some stage anyway, and this present turn of events was timely. Kate would perish in the tower; no-one knew she was there; her disappearance would be a mystery. It would probably be years before any-one else entered that turret room.

67. THE TURRET
Saturday October 30, 1762

It was an unusually cold night for late October. Kate knelt on the stone bench, shivering while the boys watched her. After an hour or so, she lay down on the floor and allowed herself to doze in the freezing air, fully accepting the fact that she might not wake.

She came back to consciousness with the dawn, and looking up, noticed the curious shadows floating in the red daybreak. Despite the profound chill in her body, she managed to pull herself to her feet and peer out of the window. It was snowing – huge soft white flakes, slowly drifting from the sky like fairies from heaven; dancing, brushing against the glass. The sun sat low over the sea, painting the underside of the clouds a vivid crimson. It had evidently been snowing for a while. The roof of the house was buried under a thick sheet of white, and the estate had become a silvery wilderness. The staff house, the laundry, the brewery, the carpenters' shop – all white. She could see the top of the old lookout tower away in the distance. It gazed out over the ocean as it had for centuries, facing away from her, its womb-like comfort beyond reach.

She sat down on the bench, white, shivering, hardly able to catch her breath, hands and feet numb. She was so frozen she could barely move.

The sun rose higher and the little room filled with the light of day – red, then golden.

Oblivion beckoned, and she could no longer sit upright, so she returned to the stone floor and settled on her side.

The dead boys sat motionless, and waited.

That night Dennis McCallum, head brewer, came trudging

through the snow on his way home from the forge where he'd spent the evening playing chess with Alan Blake. It was a monthly ritual. Dennis would arrive pulling a cart loaded with one of the new brews, Chastity would make dinner, then Dennis and Alan would sit down together in front of the fire and engage in an evening's strategy with the old game. Barney would often sit quietly and watch. Tonight's contest had been a long one, ending in Dennis's defeat; not an unusual outcome. Alan was a good player, and the struggle was always rewarding.

But it wasn't only the monthly game of chess that Dennis looked forward to. He had a fondness for Chastity and liked to watch her as she went about her tasks. She had a roundness that Dennis found warm, appealing. She was modest, too, seemingly unaware of her soft, gentle charm. Despite his friendship with Alan, Dennis often dreamt of taking Chastity to bed. But he was forty-seven, and she was now over forty, and the possibility receded with each passing year. As he stepped carefully through the crisp white, he reflected on how sad it was, to be fond of someone year after year but never to have the courage to tell them, always passing over the opportunity to love.

Deep in his ponderings, he looked up at the dark, star-filled sky, the changeless, silent Milky Way, a cataract of ice adrift in the eternal vault. The night was deathly still except for the crunch of his own boots in the snow. There was no sound at all, not even the hoot of an owl or the distant wash of the sea. He stopped moving, stood completely still and listened. His ears told him the universe had vanished. Only his eyes bore witness to the fact that it still existed in the dead of night. The black hulk of the Lookout lay four hundred yards ahead, all in darkness except for a faint red glow in the high turret on the northeast corner. He frowned. Curious. He'd never noticed a light there before. Someone was up late.

68. THE WORLD BEYOND THE MAUSOLEUM
Sunday October 31 to Saturday November 6, 1762

The sudden unexpected fall of snow that hit the east coast from Kent to Edinburgh at the end of October was gone by November 1st, having lain on the ground for only a couple of days. The air remained cold, but the snow did not return.

Things moved swiftly for Orla. James meant what he'd said and paid a fortune to have her released from King's Place. Her career as a courtesan was over. She belonged to James alone, and he treated her with adoration. She was aware he was married and had another life elsewhere, but she never asked about it, and he rarely volunteered any information. On the morning of Tuesday, November 2nd she and James moved into their new home, a large apartment spread over three floors, close to where they'd stayed the previous month. It had a sweeping view overlooking the bay and was close to the guesthouse that James had bought just along the street. Margate was going to become a popular seaside resort for Londoners, he said. He'd engaged staff for the business and planned to open in the spring.

He suggested that Orla hire a maid who might double as a cook, and invited her to conduct the interviews herself. There were six applicants for the position, aged between twenty-three and fifty, all from nearby. Orla appointed plain, dark-haired Kitty Smith, aged twenty-five, largely because of her easy manner and happy smile.

"You'll be my first maid," said Orla. "I've never had one

before."

"I'm sure it'll be a pleasure, milady," she said.

Orla laughed. "Don't call me that! I shan't know who you mean!"

"Thank you, milady," she replied, joining in the laugh. "What should I say then?"

"Call me Orla," said Orla. "It's my name."

"Miss Orla," said Kitty.

"Alright," Orla replied.

"And how should I address the master?"

"Better just call him sir until he says otherwise." Orla wrinkled her nose and smiled, nodded her head.

"Very well, milady,"

"Orla."

"Thank you, Miss Orla."

(Three seconds pause...)

"I hope we'll be friends, Kitty."

"Oh, so do I milady!"

Late on Tuesday night, Dennis McCallum stepped outside the brewhouse for a smoke in the cool air. He lit his pipe and stood listening. The snow was mostly gone, and the wildlife seemed a little more active. The hooting of owls came to him on the still air, and he glimpsed a pair of roe deer in the distance beyond the fields, trotting towards the dower house wall. He breathed in the tobacco smoke and held it in his lungs for a moment before allowing it to peel out through his nostrils. Not for the first time, he gave thanks for the opportunity to live and work in such a beautiful place. He looked to his left. The strange orange glow in the turret was still there, and he wondered for whom the light burned, so high above the ground.

In the still, small hours of Wednesday morning, miles away on Cappleman Farm, Meadow lay snug in Alder's arms. He was fast asleep, but she lay awake, listening to the sounds of the night. She liked to sleep with the window open even when it was quite cold. Her husband was always toasty, and Meadow enjoyed the contrast between the chill of the breeze and the heat of his body. She snuggled into his glow, and he instinctively held her closer.

There would be no child – she'd accepted it. Her stupid selfishness had ruined their chances of having a family together, and she sometimes wept in Alder's embrace, cursing herself and apologising to him. But he was Alder – steadfast and true. His love for her was undiminished, and she felt blessed.

And warm.

Mabel grew concerned. *"I'll be away for a few days,"* Kate had said. The girl was up to something. Mabel thought that "a few days" meant the weekend, but it was now midweek and there was no sign of her, no word. As far as she could tell, no-one at all knew where she was.

"Bip, did Kate tell you where she was going?"

"No, I'm sure she's fine, though. She didn't tell Fuzz or Shelagh either."

"I've got a bad feeling about this..."

"Ned might know," Bip suggested. "Kate's friendly with Ned and Pixie. Or Speck, maybe? They smoke together."

"I'll go and ask," said Mabel.

"You could try Nolly too. Kate goes riding with him sometimes."

Mabel was suddenly as curious as a girl. She knit her eyebrows. "Are they...?"

"No..." said Bip. "At least... I don't think so. I think she'd have told me."

So Mabel put on her cape, walked out into the drizzling Wednesday afternoon and visited the stable and the groundsmen's houses. Nolly, Ned and Pixie had been told the same story as everyone else – that she'd be away for a "few days". Speck wasn't even aware that she was gone.

"Kate? No. She came to see me a few times after that business with the dog, but I haven't seen her for a while. You think something's happened to her?"

"No. I don't know. It's a feeling I've got. Something's wrong..."

On Wednesday night, November 3rd, at half past eight, the brewers were joined by their favourite girl, mascot, and brewer-in-waiting, Fuzzy Craw. She sat in Doug Trivet's lap while Dennis McCallum and Donald Fitzroy prepared dinner for them all.

"Don't you go leading that girl astray now, Douglas," warned Dennis.

"I wouldn't do any such thing," said Doug. He looked at the girl in his lap and squeezed her thigh. "Would I?" he asked her.

She nuzzled into his shoulder and teased huskily, "Go on, Doug – lead me astray."

There was a buzz of suggestive laughter from the others. Dick Brent said, "Be careful with him, Fuzz. He's more fragile than he looks. You could easily do him an injury." Doug gave a snort in response.

"Any news up at the school then?" asked Dennis, bringing some dishes to the table.

"Not really," Fuzzy replied. "Kate's gone missing. She said she'd be away for a while but didn't tell anybody where. Not really like her, but I expect she'll turn up some time. Everything else is the same as ever."

"Kate, the witch girl?" said Dan (Franklyn).

"Yes, that's her," Fuzzy replied. "She's lovely – special."

"Special?" said David Fielding.

Doug squeezed Fuzzy to him in a close embrace, his hand groping around the rear of her right thigh, fingers exploring their way to her buttock. "You're not – you know – a girls' girl, are you?"

She broke free of his grasp and stood up. "No!" she said. "I'm a brewers' girl – you know that." She pursed her lips and blew him a kiss.

"Grubs up," said Dennis. "Come on, Fuzz. Tuck in."

Just after ten o'clock, Dennis stood outside with his pipe once more, watching Fuzzy as she walked back to the Lookout. He glanced up at the building, illuminated in the clear light of the full moon. The orange glow was gone. The turret was dark.

At eleven o'clock on Thursday morning, Vivianne sat at the table in her room, writing her novel. Despite the constant demands of her occupation at King's Place, she still managed to get about two hours every day for writing. Mr Punch and the abbess raised no objection to her having all the paper and ink she needed. They probably never imagined that anything she wrote would find its way beyond the door of her room.

Like all the nuns, she was fed well, regularly checked by the doctor, and allowed a limited amount of time outside with the others. Their walks in the park were intended primarily as a shop front – five, six, seven nuns at a time, accompanied by their minders. They were never permitted to dress casually out of doors but were expected to look magnificent and expensive at all times.

"You are the top of the range," Foxley told them. "The elite. The way you dress, the way you walk; everything about you must be superb. Nothing less will do."

Occasionally they'd visit a restaurant or coffee shop, where they'd invariably attract the attention of any males present. It was an act, a bit of theatre.

Their patrons were considerate in the privacy of the nuns' cells, kind – within the parameters that were possible given the nature of the transaction. She even liked a few of them. Things could have been worse.

But Vivianne still recognised it for what it was. It was slavery; a way of life she'd been forced into without consultation. She'd had her freedom amputated; any life choices she might have wanted, taken away. She was like a farm animal, fattened up for the sole purpose of gratifying the raw physical desires of rich men. Her flesh had been purchased to make others wealthy. She was owned.

But it wouldn't always be so. One day, with the force of her written word, she would break this business open, and those who were responsible for it would pay for what they'd done.

She rarely thought of Jacob.

Sylvie Ardoin and Clara Sutherland sat next to each at dinner on Thursday evening, both finely dressed: Clara in her usual clinging, seductive fantasy with only the thinnest shift beneath, deep décolletage, nipples visibly lifting the silky fabric; Sylvie more modest, in a gold and white linen gown, bejewelled, wearing a tiara. (Etta Lynn had encouraged the tiara, telling Sylvie it would soon be the fashion.)

"Où est Kate?" asked Clara.

"Je ne sais pas. Loin pour quelques jours je pense."

"C'est une fille douce. Je l'aime beaucoup."

"Pas trop j'espère. A moins que nous puissions partager..."

"Je pense que Jacob la baise."

"Non! Je n'y crois pas! Elle est trop jeune pour lui." She thought, then added, "Bref, Jacob ne baise pas."

"Non?"

"Non."

"Ce n'est pas parce qu'il ne t'a pas baisé qu'il ne baise pas."

"Jacob ne t'a pas baisé..."

Clara looked directly at her and said, "Non pas encore. Bref, Kate n'est pas trop jeune pour moi..."

Jacob sat at the top table with Stella, Knox and Ruth.

"This is delicious!" said Stella.

"Yes," Jacob replied. "It's a big success, by the look of it." He surveyed the assembled girls, unusually quiet, enjoying the new dish. "I knew they'd like it. Mrs Rowley took some persuading, but I think she's convinced now. Rabbit Curry. I discovered it at an inn on the way from London. What about you, Quinton? Not enough to chew, probably?"

"It's tasty enough," Knox replied, "but the pieces of meat are small. Bigger pieces – more fun for the teeth..."

"Ruth," said Jacob, peering at her around Stella. "Your opinion?"

"It's delicious!" she replied. "I like it a lot."

"Good," said Jacob. "We must experiment with other meats and different mixtures of spices. Pork, beef, mutton, pigeon, venison...Fish."

They ate in silence for a while.

"What's happened to Kate?" asked Stella. "I haven't seen her for a few days."

"Don't worry about Kate," Jacob replied quietly. Stella looked at him. "I don't think we'll be seeing her again."

Stella cast her eyes down to her plate, pondering for a moment, wondering what he meant. "She's gone back to her family?"

"No."

Again, silence as she gathered her next question. She turned towards him as if to speak, but he raised his hand and calmly said, "Don't ask..."

The bonfire was impressively tall and broad. It had taken days to build and now popped, cracked and blazed brilliantly in celebration of the night. People were already enjoying the potatoes that had been buried hours earlier in the base of the fire – they hooked them out of the flames with irons, split them open, mashed herbs and butter into the soft flesh and scooped the delicious mixture into their mouths. Other folk used the irons to roast sausages, livers, and chops of meat.

Alex loved the smell of bonfires. He held little Francis in his lap and smiled at Helen. He was happy – happier than he'd ever been. John and Sarah Bennet sat beyond Helen, and the bar staff, kitchen staff, domestics, locals and visitors wandered around the fire or nearby in the field. The rear of the White Bull was lit up in the glow of the flames.

It was November 5th. The moon was bright, just two days past full, and the clear sky was peppered with stars.

"Don't you love it?" said John. "The smells and the sounds of this night?"

"Yes," said Alex, "1605. What's that – a hundred and fifty-seven years ago?"

"Gunpowder Treason Day," said John. "Cheers, Mr Fawkes!" He raised his flagon of ale.

"We live in more enlightened times now," said Sarah. "How blessed we are."

Helen looked at Alex, squeezed his hand and whispered, "How blest are *we*?"

"Look at you two," said Sarah. "You're as much in love now as when you first knew each other."

Alex raised his glass to her.

John said, "Is Francis going to have a sister? Or a brother?"

"Maybe, John, maybe," Helen replied. "It won't be for lack of effort from Alex, I'll say that."

"Alex, you devil!" exclaimed Sarah.

"Sarah," he called, leaning forward and calling across Helen, "I fell in love with my wife from the bottom up."

His remark drew exclamations of mock horror from both the women, and noisy cheers and guffaws from all who were within earshot. Helen looked at Alex and shook her head, lips pressed together in an expression that said, *Only you would say a thing like that.* He put his hand behind her head, drew her to him and kissed her on the lips.

There was a cacophony of hoots, *wha-heys,* applause and demands for an encore.

Orla found herself alone on Saturday morning, James having returned to London. She guessed he was spending time with his wife but didn't ask, not wanting to introduce any friction between them. In the early days, when she sensed that their relationship had gained some solidity, Orla decided that she'd allow James to deal with his domestic arrangements as he saw fit. She believed that her quiet acceptance of the situation was one reason he treasured her as much as he did. The time he spent away from her meant he was filled with passion when he returned; his lust would remain inflamed as long as his marriage endured.

She'd been living in her apartment for only a few days and hadn't yet had the opportunity to venture out and seek new friends, so she'd taken Kitty for a walk along the bay and found a coffee shop where they now sat looking out at the boats and watching the passers-by.

They'd received a few curious glances from the gentlemen seated in the establishment as they entered – a few frowns and shaken heads, the older men recalling the civilised days when women were not seen in such places. But coffee shops were no longer the sacred haunts of males. It remained unusual to see unaccompanied women there, but gone were the days when they could be sent packing to where they belonged. In any case, Orla had decided that if she was going to live in Margate, she was going to make it her own, and wasn't going to be intimidated by tradition.

"It's very kind of you to treat me, Miss Orla. Thank you."

"It's my pleasure, Kitty. I hope you like coffee."

"Ooh, I do."

"Let's get something to nibble," said Orla and signalled to the serving woman.

They were soon sitting cosily in their own feminine cocoon of coffee, cream, sugar and biscuits.

"How's your family, Kitty?" asked Orla.

"Thank you, Miss Orla, they're very well."

"So your mother works in the laundry, and your brother…"

"Works on the boats with my father, milady. They're fishermen." She nodded at the window. "If we sit here for long enough we might see them."

"And your brother's name...?"

"John, milady. He's two years younger than me – twenty-three."

"John Smith," said Orla quietly.

"That's right, Miss Orla. And my mam and dad are Mary and Peter."

Orla nodded and looked idly out of the window. "I never knew my father. My mother's name was Martha. She died a long time ago."

"I'm sorry to hear that, milady. Did you have brothers and sisters?"

"No," Orla replied. "I was quite alone."

Kitty was about to enquire who'd been responsible for her mistress's upbringing, but sensed it was not her place to ask such a question. She cast her gaze down into her lap instead.

"I've had a very... complicated life," said Orla quietly, "... with lots of..." She paused for a long time, remembering him – felt her eyes moisten but managed to blink away the tears before they were shed. "It hasn't all been good. Sometimes it's been horrible." She emphasised the last word. After a moment, she shook her head and said, "I'm sorry. I shouldn't be burdening you with my concerns." She sniffed.

"That's alright, Miss Orla," Kitty replied. "I'm a good listener – if it makes any difference."

Orla looked at her. "Thank you. I think things are better now. I'm very glad to have you here." She reached out and covered Kitty's hand with hers. Kitty smiled and held her mistress's fingers.

69. THE CLIFF – THE TOWER – THE TURRET
Sunday November 7, 1762

Sunday afternoon found Mabel alone on the cliff edge, naked, facing the sea. It was warm for early November, but the wind blowing in off the water still bit her skin hard. This would probably be the last opportunity of the year. She stood with her eyes closed, palms open, catching the breeze, feet planted a little apart so that the sky's fingers could touch her all over. She opened her mouth and let the chill inside, filling her lungs with cool salt air.

Where's Kate? she thought, begging the sea, the sky, for an answer. *Something isn't right. Something's happened to her. Show me.* She concentrated hard, waiting for a response, but the elements wouldn't help.

After half an hour she put her clothes on and made her way back – along the wall and through the wood to the lookout tower. She slowed as she approached the old structure, looked up, squinted at its jagged peak. Something drew her awareness. There was something up there – something just beyond seeing.

"Kate?" she said. Then shouted. "Kate!" No answer. She ran forward and scrambled over the broken stones that had fallen from the rear of the tower in ages past, opening it to the elements and weakening its structure. In a moment she stood inside, peering up at the top, fifty feet above, searching. "Kate!" she shouted, her voice resonating in the stonework. A pair of startled crows took off from a hidden cranny high up in the wall and flapped noisily into the sky. "Kate!" she cried again, as loud as she could, the echo skating around the walls, up and away. The empty wind re-

675

turned; there was nothing but the sky's white indifference. Mabel scrambled back out of the tower, walked round to the front and looked over the cliff edge; a drop of perhaps eighty or ninety feet to the surf. *What am I looking for?* she thought. *A body?* She stood in the space between the tower and the land's splintered lip and shouted once more, stretching the syllable out. "Kaaaate!"

There was no reply. Mabel shook her head, puzzled. For some reason she'd been convinced that Kate was nearby, had been sure she was about to spot her. "Where are you?" she said out loud, hopelessly. She stood for a moment, impotent, facing the sea, hands hanging idly – then returned to the rear of the tower, picked her way down the hillside to the level ground below and began to walk toward the Lookout.

The wind was picking up, the clouds moving overhead with increasing rapidity. She saw a few figures in the distance walking away from the house and toward the fields – Speck, Rabbit, Solly, Ned. As she walked, Mabel felt her eyes drawn to the high turret. She peered harder as she approached the house, unable to look away, her pace slowing. The two boys, gazing through their little window. She'd seen them before, several times, high up. The twins. Mabel's steps became heavy. She stopped moving.

The two boys...

But three figures stood there, forlornly looking out.

And the middle one was Kate.

Mabel's face became a mask of horror, and her soul filled with ice. "No..." she mumbled, and began to run toward the school. She hurried around the house and crashed through the side door by the kitchen garden. By the time she arrived in the entrance hall, she was screaming, beside herself, mounting the stairs three at a time. Those in her path pressed themselves against the wall or the banister, wide-eyed, fearing she'd plough right through them.

"Kate!" she shouted. "Kate's in the tower!"

676

A few people gathered in her wake, and by the time she reached the top floor there was a train of about twelve. She ran to the door of the corner room, turned the handle, found it locked and began to hammer on it with all her might, like a madwoman.

"KATE!"

Hollis Wayland, busy in the infirmary, opened his door and looked out.

"What on earth is going on?" he shouted.

Mabel stopped her assault and turned. "Kate's locked in the tower! She's probably been there for days!"

"How can that be?" answered Hollis, "That door is..."

"KATE IS LOCKED IN THE TOWER!!" Mabel shrieked, eyebrows knit in fury. "BREAK IN! BREAK THE DOOR OPEN! NOW!!"

Hollis was shocked by Mabel's ferocity. She looked as if she could tear someone apart with her bare hands. "Right," he said. "Let's do it. Stand away." Mabel retreated into the gathering crowd. Stella, Ruth, Milton and Janet had been drawn out of their apartments by the noise and now joined the rear of the assemblage, watching.

Hollis kicked the door. It buckled briefly but held firm. And again – the same result. Then he attacked it with his shoulder, running from a distance. No good. He withdrew, wincing and rubbing his arm.

Knox elbowed through the crowd and motioned Hollis to stand aside. A single powerful and efficient kick close to the lock did it. The door slammed inwards against the wall; screws flew free of the hinges.

Jacob appeared right at that moment. "Careful in there!" he said. "The floor is unsafe."

Mabel looked at him. "Kate's locked in the tower." Her face was red, sticky.

"How can she be locked in the tower?" said Jacob, irritated. "This room's inaccessible."

"I saw her. She's in the tower."

Jacob stared at the woman for a moment, his face tense, eyes small; then said, "Alright. Hollis, you come with me."

Jacob and the doctor hurried across the room to the tower door while the others watched from the corridor.

"It's locked," said Jacob, trying the handle. "And there's no key to this door."

Hollis said, "Then we must break it open. Knox, can you open this?"

Quinton came forward, but Jacob held up his hand, fixing Hollis with his glare. "There cannot be anyone in that tower."

Hollis felt his anger rising. He faced Crowan and said deliberately, "Open the door, Jacob."

Jacob met his gaze squarely for a moment, then looked at Knox and said, his voice pinched, "Alright. Do it."

The tower door proved more resistant to force than the other. It was smaller, and constructed to open outwards. Knox had to kick his way through the wood, then tear the door off at the hinges. It was an impressive demonstration of brute force that took almost two minutes.

Hollis was the first through onto the stone staircase. "There are slop buckets in here," he said, lifting them by the handles and depositing them in the room. "My God! She *is* up there!"

Mabel came running into the room as Hollis sprinted up the staircase. Jacob put up his hands and tried to stop her. "Mabel..." But she shot him a look that would have killed had her eyes been poisoned darts, and he stepped away, allowing her to follow the doctor into the tower.

Hollis was kneeling at the top of the staircase, leaning into the tiny space. Mabel, coming up behind him, could not see into the little room, although the daylight entering through the windows illuminated the doctor's crouched back. He was bent close over something on the floor.

"It's Kate isn't it?" she asked.

"Yes," he said. "I'm afraid she's dead."

70. THE GULL

Kate was in the clouds high over the ocean, falling freely, swooping almost into the waves, then breasting the wind and soaring aloft once more. To the south she could easily pick out Scarborough and the coast beyond; to the north, Whitby, Staithes, Boulby village and communities still more distant. With a little more concentration she probably could have made out Glaisdale, Easington, Roxby, perhaps even her father's house.

She was free; there was no anxiety, no hurry, no guilt, no cold. She knew the twins were nearby, and their mother. They were happy. Nara was here, Hazel. Kate felt their hands on her shoulders, turned upwards into the sky and found them smiling at her, greeting her. There were others too, older ones she hadn't known before. Willa. Where was Anne?

Kate was on the top of the old tower. Everything was still. The wind had calmed, although the clouds continued to roll slowly in. She felt the cool of the old stonework beneath her and looked to her right. There was a big gull perched on the broken rim of the tower just a few feet away. It looked directly at her, its bright red beak opening and closing, bright red eyes staring. It was looking after her; Kate was sure of it.

The crisp air felt good, refreshing.

Her body had no weight. She could just fall forward from the tower, kiss the sea at the foot of the cliff and soar aloft again, her spirit mingled with the soul of the gull. She could go anywhere...

"Kate!"

She looked around and down to the west of the tower.

Mabel was there, looking up at her. She ran forward out of Kate's line of sight but reappeared a moment later down below, within the tower, looking up directly at her.

"Kate!"

She wanted to reply but found she had no voice. A pair of crows flapped angrily past her from below, startled from their perch in the tower wall.

"Kate!"

Kate wanted to answer her, to reassure her, but was powerless to do so. She looked down, meeting Mabel's gaze, apparently unseen. Mabel turned and climbed out of the tower. A few seconds later she was at the cliff edge, looking down into the sea. Kate wanted to call, *Mabel, I'm up here!* But no sound came.

"Kaaaate!"

What can I do? I can't reply. But it doesn't matter. She'll know one day. Everything's alright.

She heard her friend say, "Where are you?" and smiled. Mabel knew Kate was here.

She looked at the red-eyed gull; the gull stared back and squealed – a question. The sea called. Kate and the wind could be one forever. She could whirl with the gulls to the end of time and beyond. There was no need to go back.

Mabel was gone. Kate saw her far away, walking toward the school. She watched her halt, then break into a run. The gull was aloft, crying out, and Kate was riding in the grey clouds as they flowed over the Lookout.

She was outside the turret, looking in through the window. There was a dead girl curled up on the stone floor, skin as white as the thin nightdress she wore. The gull perched on the weathercock; Hazel and Nara were in the wind on either side of Kate, ready to comfort her. Someone appeared, running up the stairs – Doctor Wayland. He knelt over the girl, turned her onto her back and put his ear to her chest, checked for breathing, felt her skin, searched for some sign of life. Mabel appeared on the stairs behind him. Doctor

680

Wayland said something; his frantic movements slowed. He lifted the dead girl – not an easy thing to do in such a confined space – stood as straight as he could in the little room, turned and walked carefully downstairs. Kate heard shrieks and cries below.

She was inside the house, on the ceiling of the corridor, looking down. Doctor Wayland was carrying the body through a crowd of shocked people. There was a lot of noise, crying, exclamations of horror, despair. Mabel was beside herself with grief, surrounded by people trying to comfort her. Kate looked at the dead girl in the doctor's arms. The girl's right arm hung loosely as he walked. Her head was thrown back, mouth open, eyes rolled up, exposed in death.

Hollis carried her into the infirmary and laid her down on one of the beds. Mabel forced her way through the crowd of people and knelt by the bedside, holding the girl's hand.

"My God! She's so cold," she exclaimed through her tears.

"She's been dead for a while," said Hollis. "A few days at least. I'm so sorry, Mabel. I know how fond of her you were."

Mabel sniffed, stroking Kate's forehead. "Oh, my love. What happened to you? What were you doing?"

Jacob appeared, Stella by his side. "There's no hope then?" he said.

Stella came forward and looked down at the lifeless body. She reached out and touched Kate's skin.

"She's dead, Jacob. Very dead," Hollis replied.

"She's cold," whispered Stella.

"Of course she's cold," Hollis replied. He turned to Jacob. "She was locked in. How is that possible?"

"How can I tell?" Jacob replied. "No-one has visited that room since the restoration of the house. I have no key for it."

"I didn't see a key on the inside of the door." Hollis

looked around and searched for a suitable person among the crowd gathered at the infirmary entrance. "Annabelle, would you mind going back to the tower and searching for a key? There's a basket at the foot of the stairs. Check all the steps and the room at the top." He searched for a second person and said, "And you, Nellie, if you wouldn't mind, bring the two slop buckets directly in here to me."

"What are you suggesting?" said Jacob.

"I'm preserving the evidence," Hollis replied. "I can't help recalling that you tried to prevent me from opening the door."

Jacob was angry. "I won't hear that," he said coldly. "Are you accusing me of murdering the girl?"

"I'm not accusing anyone of anything. I just want to get to the bottom of why she died. There's something amiss here."

Nellie appeared with the two buckets and set them down out of harm's way. Fuzzy, Bip and Shelagh wove through the crowd and ran into the infirmary.

"No...!" cried Bip, catching sight of the body.

Hollis looked beyond them to the assembled people. "Please keep the girls away. This is no place for them." Hands were extended, and the girls were drawn back, but Fuzzy broke free and ran to Kate's bedside.

"Oh no..." she said, and burst into tears.

Mabel hugged her and spoke through her own sobbing. "There's nothing we can do. It's too late."

Kate, watching from the ceiling of the room, felt the pull of the sky, the lift of the breeze that wanted to take her away. Hazel and Nara watched her, waiting to see what she would do. She felt the wings of the red-eyed gull fold around her head, and followed the thread of light as it descended to the body below.

Kate muttered, "Mabel..."

All sound in the room ceased. Hollis felt his hair stand on end. Mabel and Fuzzy stopped crying. Stella retreated from the bedside. Jacob's eyes widened...

"Kate...?" whispered Mabel.

Hollis, quietly, "It isn't possible."

Kate whispered, "...cold..."

"My God! This can't be happening," said Hollis, but Mabel was already gathering more blankets.

Fuzzy kicked off her shoes, climbed into the bed under the covers with Kate and hugged her, sharing the warmth of her own body.

Hollis motioned to Bip and Shelagh. "Come over and rub her hands and feet. It'll help to get the circulation moving."

Kate blinked, once, twice, focused her eyes on the ceiling. Mabel cried out incoherently and took a step back. Hollis felt the girl's forehead. "She's as cold as the grave. How can this be happening?"

"Ask the questions later," said Mabel. "She's alive."

Hollis took one of Kate's wrists and felt for a pulse. He nodded, eyes wide in astonishment. "She's alive. I've never seen anything..." He was too dumbfounded to complete the sentence.

"Can I do anything?" asked Jacob.

"A warm drink, perhaps. A cup of tea?" Hollis replied. He motioned to his private apartment. "There's a pot in my room, just a few minutes old."

Jacob hurried into Hollis's flat at the far end of the infirmary.

"Fuzzy," said Kate, turning her head to look at her friend.

Fuzzy rubbed Kate's cheek and said, "What happened? Where were you?"

"In the tower," whispered Kate. "It's all over. It worked."

"What did you do?" asked Fuzzy.

"Save the questions till later, Fuzzy," said Hollis. "I don't know how fragile she is."

Fuzzy kissed Kate's nose and said, "Get well. Talk later."

Jacob returned with a china cup. "Here's some tea. Are you able to drink it?" Fuzzy helped Kate up, plumping up the pillows to support her. She took the cup from Jacob and held it to Kate's lips.

"That's warm," said Kate after taking a sip. She sighed and looked directly at Jacob. "Thank you, Jacob. Thank you for everything."

He found himself almost overwhelmed with emotion and couldn't understand why. It had something to do with Kate's use of his first name under these circumstances. Not wanting anyone to notice his weakness, he mumbled an incoherent excuse to Hollis and left the room.

Kate closed her eyes. She felt comfortable, her body warming. Hazel and Nara were nearby, their strength feeding her. The gull was in her chest. She slept.

Annabelle searched the tower thoroughly: the area round the door, all the steps, the room at the top, the windows, ledges, the roof. She descended the turret stairs as the crowd was dispersing and caught sight of Ruth Marlowe in the corridor.

"Belle!" she said excitedly. "Kate's alive. She's recovering."

Annabelle's eyes widened in amazement. "But she was dead. I saw her."

Ruth shook her head. "She's alive. Go and see."

"Kate?" said Annabelle, stepping into the infirmary. Hollis moved towards her and motioned with his hand. "Shh. She's sleeping. God knows how..."

"A miracle," said Annabelle.

"A miracle," Hollis agreed. "In all my days..."

"There's no key as far as I can see," said Annabelle. "I checked everywhere. Unless the key is on Kate herself."

"There are no broken panes of glass?" said Hollis. "She couldn't have slipped it outside?"

"I checked the windows. They're all tight, the glass firm."

"You checked the roof of the room?"

"Yes. There's nowhere she could have hidden a key. It could be in the slop buckets."

"I'll check later," he said.

Hollis looked worried. Annabelle rested her hand on his arm. "Are you alright?"

"I'm fine," he said, covering her hand with his. "Just a bit shaken up. I'm afraid I got rather ragged with Jacob."

"Do you want me to stay?"

"No," he smiled. "Thanks, Belle."

"You know where I am," she said.

Hollis kissed her on the cheek, and she left, closing the door behind her.

Mabel, Bip and Shelagh were huddled around Kate's bed. Fuzzy remained snuggled up to her friend inside it. Hollis joined them.

"Well," he said quietly. "This is indeed a miracle."

"A miracle, yes," Mabel agreed. "Thank you, Hollis."

"For what? I don't think I did very much."

"You were quick," she replied. "And insistent when Jacob tried to resist."

"How did you know she was there?" he asked.

She had to tell him, even though she knew it would make her sound ridiculous. "I saw her standing at the window."

He knit his brows and returned, "That's not possible. There's no way she could have stood up to make herself visible."

"I saw her ghost..."

He raised his hands and closed his eyes in rejection.

"It doesn't matter if you don't believe me," said Mabel. "We found her. That's what counts."

Bip interjected, "You saw her ghost?"

"Yes," Mabel shrugged. "I saw her ghost."

"She'll need to eat something," said Hollis. "And we must have plenty of liquids ready as well. She'll be dehydrated."

"I'll go to the maids' rooms and sort something out," said

Shelagh, rising from where she'd been kneeling at Kate's side.

"Kate must stay here in the infirmary until she's stronger," said Hollis. "You could stay with her, Mabel, if you like. I'll be in my room. Please call straight away if you need anything."

Kate woke in the evening. The fire crackled vigorously, but the infirmary was otherwise quiet and dimly lit. Only Mabel remained at her bedside, the girls having been sent away by the doctor.

"Mabel?" Kate's voice sounded dry, husky.

"My love, I'm here," she said, hurrying forward. "How do you feel?"

"Tired. Worn out."

Hollis was writing his journal at the desk in his apartment, but hearing voices through the open door, he emerged to check on the patient. Kate was thirsty, and the doctor had her drink slowly, carefully.

"Easy does it, old girl. You've been through a rough time." Mabel helped her sit up, and she ate some bread and butter and a few small pieces of cold meat while Hollis watched.

"She's doing well," he said. "But she probably won't be able to eat a lot."

"I'm getting better," said Kate.

"You are," said Hollis. "But go carefully. Take as long as you need." To Mabel, he said, "I must get back to my writing. I need to note down everything that happened today. Call me if..."

There was a knock at the door. Hollis apologised, hurried to open it, but had already identified Clara's distinctive tapping. He opened the door, and there she was. Hollis stood in the doorframe. "Hello, Clara."

"I heard..." she began.

Hollis nodded and replied, "She's here. Resting."

"Can I see her?"

"Give her a day or two. She's very weak."

"Will she be alright?"

"I think so."

"Everyone's talking about it: Felix, Alfred, the Breedons, Golda..."

Hollis was nodding as she spoke. "It's all a puzzle, but mercifully she's still here. We haven't lost her."

Clara paused, staring at him. She opened her lips as if to speak, closed them again; then said, "And you? Are you alright?"

He reached out, smiled, and rested his hand on her arm. "I'm fine. Just... upside-down. I feel like I've seen the Raising of Lazarus."

Clara's eyes moistened. She stepped forward, slipped her arm round Hollis and kissed him on the lips. "Can I do anything? Do you want me?"

"Always, Clara. You know that." He kissed her forehead. "But I must be vigilant tonight."

She nodded. "Of course you must."

Hollis loved her; had asked her several times to marry him but was always turned down. He stroked her cheek, helpless.

"Give her my love," said Clara.

"I will. Thank you."

"Give her everyone's love."

"Of course."

She was silent for a few seconds; could think of nothing more to say. She looked away from him, turned, and was gone. Hollis shut the door and returned to Kate's bedside.

"She's sleeping," Mabel whispered.

"Good," Hollis replied. "Mabel, you're more than welcome to stay here overnight."

"Thank you. I might do that."

Kate woke a couple of hours later, needing to pee. She wasn't able to walk by herself, so Mabel carried her the short distance to the infirmary privy. The girl was asleep again as soon as she returned to bed. Mabel watched over her for a while, then chose a bed nearby and lay down.

At twenty past three in the morning, Kate woke again, sure even before her eyes were open that Rosalind Wynter was in the room. The fire had almost burned out, but there was still enough light to see. Rosalind stood at the side of Kate's bed, her two boys holding her hands.

"Hello," Kate whispered. The twins looked at her, faces impassive. "I still don't know which is which," she said. "Lawrence?" Rosalind stroked the head of the boy on her right. "And Robin," said Kate. Rosalind stroked the head of the boy on her left. Kate looked up at their mother. The hideous vision was gone – she was smiling, eyes glistening. She knelt down at Kate's bedside, reached out and stroked her head. Her hand felt warm, soft. She leaned forward and kissed Kate's forehead, then took her hand and kissed that too. "I'm glad," said Kate.

Prompted by his mother, Lawrence stepped forward and kissed Kate's cheek, then Robin did the same. After that, the three moved away past the fire and disappeared into the darkness at the far end of the infirmary.

The room was quiet for a few moments, the dying fire popping, its light dancing on the wall.

"You freed them." It was Mabel's voice. Kate hadn't realised she was awake.

"Hm," Kate replied quietly. "They don't have to stay here anymore."

"How did you know what to do?"

"Their ma showed me."

Mabel was quiet for a moment. "It could only have been you, Kate. No-one else could have done it."

"Can I come and sleep in your bed?" said Kate.

"Of course you can, my love. Can you manage?"

"I think so."

A moment later Kate was asleep in Mabel's arms. "Kate," she whispered, "you're an angel."

71. THE INFIRMARY – THE SEA – THE MUSINGS OF GENTLEMEN
Monday November 8, 1762

Hollis examined Kate the following day and found her, as far as he could tell, fully recovered. He sat on a chair close to her bed and watched the girl as she put on her dress.

"How long were you there, Kate?"

"A little more than a week, I think."

"And how much of it do you remember?"

"I remember the first two or three days in the tower – after that, things changed."

"Changed?"

"Yes. You'd probably say I was hallucinating."

He smiled. "Ghosts."

"If you like."

"How did you come to be shut in without a key?"

"I needed help to do that. I asked someone to lock me in."

"Why?"

"So that I'd die and have no way to stop it happening."

"You wanted to die?"

"I needed to die."

"Why?"

"I'm not saying any more. Sorry." She looked right at him and added, "I don't mean any disrespect."

"Will you tell me who locked you in?"

"No. Sorry."

He sat thinking, then sighed and said, "Very well, Kate. You can go."

She walked over to him, crouched, and kissed his cheek. "Thank you, Hollis."

Doctor Wayland looked up in surprise, touching his face

where she'd kissed him. "Kate…"

"You did everything right," she said.

Something had changed in her. She seemed very self-assured, no longer the girl he'd previously known.

"Thank you," he said as she left. "You know I'm always here…"

Kate decided not to attend lessons that day. Few people would have expected her to do so anyway. She went down to her dormitory, changed into one of the colourful dresses she'd designed herself, put on her cape, left the house and walked to the sea alone.

The day was bright but windy, and the tide was out. She took off her shoes and walked as far as she could on the mud till she was a long way from the stony shore. Then she pushed back her hood and looked up at the sky.

They were all there, she knew, but she was no longer able to see them, dressed in her body as she was. She lifted an arm and waved, her heart full of love. The wind hammered on the waves, stirring the water to white froth, driving the low tide inward. She watched the gulls gliding in huge, ecstatic circles and longed to join them.

"I love you!" she cried out, and the wind battered her in response, blowing her flaming hair into streamers, skimming her face and neck. Kate opened her mouth to the cool air and allowed a few tears to drain from her eyes. "Mum…" she whispered, emotion catching in her throat.

Speck Beckwith, Tranter Tickle, Rabbit Shipley, Ned Silden and Solly Birtwistle were sitting in their accustomed place on the wall by the top field, smoking, Bastard at their feet, when one of their number picked out the distant figure of Catherine Swithenbank as she made her way back to the school.

"Look who's coming…" said Solly.

"It's the witch," Tranter replied.

Speck watched the girl but said nothing.

"She were dead yesterday," said Tranter.

Old Rabbit replied, "She ain't dead no more."

"She's a special one," said Speck. "She's different from us; doesn't follow the same rules as everyone else. I'm not surprised to see her up and walking about."

They were quiet for a moment.

"Wonder where she's been," said Solly.

Rabbit took his pipe from his mouth and said, slowly and thoughtfully, "Casting spells with the sea..."

"Bare-arsed, I shouldn't wonder," said Tranter.

"Why so?" asked young Solly, his interest aroused.

Tranter brought his imagination into full flow. " 'S what witches do, i'n't it? They dance on' 'illtops; copulate wi' Beelzebub."

"Beelzebub?" asked Solly.

"Beelzebub," Tranter replied. "Old Nick, Lucifer, Satan – wi' 'is 'orns, 'is tail, 'is cloven feet – an' 'is 'uge stiff red staff."

"What's copulate?" asked Ned.

They all shot him a look of derision.

"Copulate!" exclaimed Tranter. "Like you do at night wi' Pixie when you get 'er nightdress up."

Ned's expression registered his understanding.

There was silence for a moment, the men's eyes following Kate as she approached the point where she'd need to turn left to return to the Lookout.

"Any road..." said Tranter, and paused. They all removed their pipes and looked at him, expecting more. "...I've seen 'er up on t' cliffs wi' Mabel, norra stitch on – neither of 'em. I've seen everythin' – tits, arse, tinder box."

"You haven't..." scowled Solly.

"I 'ave!" returned Tranter. "Two or three times. They strip off and stand there like they're waitin' to be stuffed by pirates."

"Don't sound like they're doin' it for you, you dirty

bugger," said Solly, enraged. "You shouldn't go spyin' on women like that. Should be ashamed of yourself." He stuck his pipe back between his lips and angrily chewed on the mouthpiece.

Kate arrived at the crossroads and turned left towards the school.

"Kate!" Speck shouted. She halted, turned and waved.

"Look at 'er," muttered Solly. "Ain't she lovely...?"

"Join us for a pipe?" Speck called loudly.

"Another time," she cried back. "I'll see you soon." She turned and walked on her way.

"*See you soon*, eh, Speck?" Tranter repeated suggestively, his eyes small, accusative.

"Piss off," said Speck.

Ned looked at Speck and said, "But she *is* seeing you, isn't she? Saturday morning, I reckon – after me."

Speck looked at Ned in irritation. His expression said, *You dunce. We agreed to keep that quiet.*

There was an embarrassed silence, then Tranter said, "... what? What's this...?"

Solly looked curiously at Ned and Speck, and said, "Does she...do you too, then?"

Ned and Speck mumbled in unison, vaguely in the affirmative. Speck leaned forward, peered at Solly, and asked, "So you're on the parade as well, are you?"

Ancient, weather-beaten Rabbit clutched his pipe and laughed, eyes squeezed shut, slapping his knee. The other four men looked at him, tobacco smoke rising from the bowls of their pipes. Rabbit squinted at them, stabbed a finger at himself and continued to guffaw noisily.

"Rabbit, you old devil!" said Speck. "Even you?"

The venerable gentleman was so convulsed with laughter, he could barely draw breath.

Solly's incredulity showed in his expression and in his voice. "Really? Bugger! Why? Twisted, dry old spindle yours must be. Probably hollow and full of spiders."

Speck and Ned were both hooting with laughter.

"What?" said Tranter. "What...?"

72. THE ORGAN
Thursday November 11, 1762

Jacob was anxious to speak with Kate, but time eluded him. He studied her at dinner on Thursday evening as she sat surrounded by a crowd of adoring younger girls and noticed, not for the first time, what an attractive young woman she'd become. She was going to be beautiful. The thought set him reflecting first on Vivianne, then on Maria's shocked reaction to her own visions in the York coach: *"...there's another coming...young, with flaming red hair...Oh no! I can't look at her!"* In his heart, Jacob knew that the *young woman with flaming red hair* was Kate. He watched as she rose from the table, a pair of class 2 girls in tow. Perhaps there'd be an opportunity to talk if he followed. He excused himself to Stella, Knox and Ruth, left his place and moved towards the door.

There was no sign of Kate when he arrived in the entrance hall. Jacob looked about him, but the direction she'd taken was anybody's guess. He took a couple of steps towards the porter's desk.

"Alfred, did you see Kate Swithenbank come this way just now?"

Alfred was busy with something in one of the desk drawers. "Sorry, Mr Crowan. I've been sorting keys. I missed her if she came this way."

Jacob retraced his steps to the dining hall and found many of the girls who'd made up Kate's recent audience still eating. He approached them and enquired where she might have gone. Eleven-year-old Gwendolyn Spooner, all auburn hair and freckles, smiled at him and said, "She's in the chapel. Babs and May are blowing the organ for her."

Jacob thanked them and set out once more.

He heard the distant voice of the organ as he passed through the entrance hall, and decided to listen for a while. Having heard Kate play the harpsichord on several occasions, he was curious to hear how she'd be on the larger instrument. He walked on to the chapel and pulled open the door, allowing the impressive tone to briefly flood the east wing as he entered.

The lanterns were lit, but the pews were empty. Jacob selected a seat just below the gallery and sat down.

Barbara Lea and May Roberts took turns at the pump handle while Kate played. It had been more than two weeks since she'd last practised the instrument, and she found herself enjoying the grandeur of the sound as it rolled around the chapel walls and roof. Riding the melodies was like whirling with the gulls, and the tension in the discords and suspensions brought back the sensation of hovering in the air before diving to the sea. It was like being free, bodiless – exhilarating. Felix Hadleigh had suggested that Kate dip into the new set of six voluntaries by the Oxford organist William Walond, and she'd diligently learnt every one of them.

The chapel instrument was resourceful and contained all the sounds required for the performance of the pieces: the pair of noble diapasons for the slow movements; the powerful cornet stop with its thrilling ring, like the energetic cry of a kestrel; the graceful solo flute that skipped through the figuration like a butterfly dancing among flowers; and the grand, tragic, full organ.

She was well into the third piece when Clara suddenly appeared on her left. The breadth of the organ sound masked the opening of the gallery door, and she was startled at the sudden appearance of her visitor. Clara signalled an apology, and Kate played on without pause, the chapel ringing with the music's drama. It took just over two minutes to get to the end. She lifted her hands from the final chord, and the echo of the sound faded into the walls.

Clara allowed the silence to return before she spoke. "What a strange mood for an allegro; melancholy, like a great orator reciting the life of a hero." She leant on the gallery rail. "You make the organ sound clean, alive."

"Thank you," Kate replied. "That's a nice way of describing the piece."

The older woman looked at the girl silently for a second, smiled, and asked, "How are you?"

"I'm well," Kate replied.

"We were all worried about you. I missed you."

Kate returned Clara's smile and gave a small sound in her throat, a tiny laugh, acknowledging the sentiment. "Hmm. No harm done. I'm back to normal."

"Hollis said it was a miracle."

"I think he's exaggerating," said Kate. When Clara offered no reply, Kate pointed at the keyboards and asked, "Do you play?"

Clara raised her eyebrows. "The organ? No. To be honest, it's not something that's ever appealed to me. It always struck me as an overcomplicated, oafish thing. But it comes to life in *your* hands. I suppose if you're a fine enough musician it's possible to make even this... device sing." She paused, gestured at the instrument with her head, and said, "I saw this organ under construction in London."

"Really?" Kate was surprised.

"Yes, a few years ago, before I came here. My cousin Peter was one of the builders." She waved her hand as if to dismiss her own comment. "But I'm holding you up. Will you go on?"

Kate replied, "There are three more pieces. Shall I play through those? Do you mind?"

"Mind? It's a privilege to hear you. Do *you* mind if I watch? I could listen for hours. It's the first time I've heard an organ actually make *music*."

Kate snorted. "I don't think I'm *that* good, Clara." She suddenly realised how much she was enjoying the woman's attention. "But I'd like to play for you. It's nice that you listen." Clara sat down. Kate motioned to Babs, who was next on blower duty, drew the stops, and began.

After the sixth and final piece, Clara clapped and stood. "That was something!" she said. "So that's full organ, yes?"

"That's right," Kate said. "That's all the power there is. I love the sound."

"Power," Clara echoed in two distinct syllables, then slid onto the bench next to Kate. She looked at the three tiered keyboards. "It's amazing," she said. "I can see now why you need so many keys."

She fell silent. Kate was looking straight ahead at the music rack but knew that Clara's eyes were on her – and was acutely aware of the pressure of Clara's thigh against her own. She looked up, met the older woman's gaze, and the attraction between them ignited. Clara turned her lips inwards and moistened them. It looked both thoughtful and predatory, as if she were wondering how best to eat the girl.

Barbara and May remained nearby, fascinated by the tension that had developed. Kate sent them away, "Go!" They exited quickly through the gallery door, allowing it to bang shut behind them.

"Kate," said Clara, but Kate's arms were already around Clara's neck, and Clara's hands were on Kate, drawing the girl closer, lifting her skirt. Their lips met – tongues. Kate's heart was pounding.

"Let me undress you," Clara muttered.

Kate didn't reply, but adjusted her body so the other could pull up her skirt and shift. Her hands were on Clara's breasts.

Jacob was standing in the gallery. Kate saw him over Clara's shoulder. The shock produced a physical response as if she would burst, and embarrassment filled the space previously occupied by the carnal charge. She pulled her skirt back into place, slapping Clara's hand away. Clara realised someone was standing behind them, disengaged from Kate, stood hurriedly and faced the invader.

Jacob was just as embarrassed as they were. "I'm sorry," he said. "Please forgive me – I didn't intend to interrupt."

Kate shook her head. She was coming down from the height of her excitement and couldn't think coherently. She rubbed her eyes and tried to calm her breathing. Clara was speaking. "It's alright," she said. "Just two girls overcome with music."

Jacob nodded, although his attention was not on the woman's explanation. Kate's clawings had exposed even more of Clara's flesh than was usual, and he found it difficult to tear his gaze away. Clara noticed, looked down at herself and adjusted her clothing.

"Sorry," she said.

Jacob swallowed. "No apology necessary."

She continued to stand quietly, immobile, acutely conscious of Jacob's attention (*he's staring at me. He's interested – after all these years*). She listened to Kate's breathing as the girl continued to calm down.

"I need to speak with Kate," said Jacob. "Alone, Clara, if you don't mind."

"Of course," she said and hurried past him through the gallery door.

Kate remained on the organ bench, eyes cast down, unfocused.

"Is it convenient to talk?" Jacob asked. "We'll set another time if this is difficult."

"No," said Kate. "It's alright. I'm sorry you saw that."

He waved her apology away. "Don't concern yourself – I was the intruder."

Kate's face was hot, red with humiliation. She felt her cheeks.

"I've upset you," said Jacob, the girl's discomfort being obvious.

"No," Kate replied. "I'll be alright. Don't worry – go on."

He paused for a few seconds, allowing her emotions to quieten further. Something cracked sharply down in the chapel – wood expanding or contracting.

"You play this instrument extraordinarily well," he said.

"Thank you. Did you hear much?"

"I was sitting downstairs for about twenty minutes. You really are remarkable. You play as well as anyone I've ever heard."

"Thank you, that's nice," she said, thinking, *Calm down, calm down, calm down – it's only new to you – he's seen it all before.*

Jacob sighed, swallowed, preparing to move on to what he'd really come to speak to her about. He looked at the floor and began. "I've been very troubled since what happened."

"You did everything I asked," she replied, "and it all worked."

He looked up. "You achieved what you wanted?"

"Yes," she said.

"You could have died."

"I came back," she said, without hesitation.

Jacob was silent, watching her. "Doctor Wayland thinks I tried to kill you."

There was something flowing from him, something he was trying to hide, some concern, something he wanted to keep secret. It puzzled her and began to take shape in her mind. It was all around him – a darkness. He stood in front of it, but Kate knew it was there. She frowned and said, "Have you killed?"

Her unexpected question speared him between *yes* and *no*, and he found himself completely unable to respond. He knit his brow and slowly filled his lungs, opening his mouth narrowly to complete the action, then held the air briefly before gradually releasing it through his nose, looking at her the whole time.

"What can you see of me?" he asked. There was concern in his voice.

"Not enough," she replied. "Not yet. But we'll have a long association, you and I. I can feel that."

He allowed her words to sink in. "Someone I travelled with not too long ago – a strange woman, blind – warned me about you in a dream. She told me about a young woman with flaming red hair. It terrified her. I think that's you." He paused, bit his lip, then said quietly, "*Is* it you?"

She didn't answer immediately, but watched his eyes, gauged her response. "Probably."

Jacob looked aside, shook his head, and thought, *This is one of the strangest conversations I've ever had. I came here to seek assurance that I'd done you no harm. Instead, it feels as if I'm looking into the pit of my own fate.* He heard someone ask, "Am I ill?" – then realised it had been his own voice.

"You're well," she said. "There's nothing wrong with you."

He shook his head as if to clear it. "You must think me a fool. I shouldn't be speaking like this with a fourteen-year-old girl."

"Thirteen," she said.

He tried to hold on to his tumbling thoughts. "I needed to hear from your own mouth that you don't consider me responsible for what happened in the tower."

"You're not responsible at all, Jacob. You can rest easy. I'm happy."

He suddenly thought he'd feel much easier if Kate were not here. Her presence made him very uncomfortable. He instinctively took a half step towards her, unsure of his own intention, but found that he couldn't approach any further. The air felt oddly thick.

"I'm glad we're friends, Kate," he said. "I admire you. I want to support you – and I'm always at your disposal." He raised his palms in a gesture of openness.

"Thank you," she replied, and smiled. "And if I can help you,

you must tell me."

"You mean it?" he asked.

"I do," she replied. "Of course."

"Thank you. Then I'll bid you good day." He gave a half bow and withdrew.

Clara was seated in the corridor waiting for him, and stood as he emerged. Jacob voiced her name in greeting accompanied by a curt nod, then moved to walk past her – but she blocked his way. It was as if they were engaged in a dance. Kate appeared at the gallery door, and Clara caught sight of her over Jacob's shoulder. The dance went on, he trying to get past, she blocking him, her eyes on his. Her intention was obvious. Kate observed, fascinated. It was a mating ritual between two tigers. They looked at each other coldly. He reached out his hand and slid it along her left flank, sampling her. Clara continued to gaze boldly at him beneath lowered brows, permitting his possessive touch.

"Alright," he muttered. "Come to my room." She stood aside and let him go, fixing Kate with her eyes as he left. Clara lifted her right hand and pointed at the girl. "You and me," she whispered. "Soon." She turned and followed Jacob. Kate watched her as she walked away.

73. KATE'S DORMITORY
– THE SHELTER
Saturday November 13, 1762

"So, Clara's after you," said Mabel. They sat in Kate's dormitory by themselves, Mabel having arrived to change the bedclothes while Kate was reading.

"Yes, that's probably a fair assessment," Kate replied.

"And how do you feel about that?"

Kate thought. "To be honest, I'm excited."

"Hmmm..."

"Tell me what you think."

"I think you're still quite young."

"My mother was married at fifteen."

"And it worked?" asked Mabel.

"Yes," Kate replied. "They were very happy. She died when I was seven. It broke my dad's heart."

"I know," said Mabel. "I remember you telling me before." She sat on Kate's bed and gave her a hug. "What do you want to do?"

Kate was quiet for a moment, then said, "I can't stop thinking about her."

"It's infatuation. You'll grow out of it."

"Maybe," said Kate. Mabel kissed her head. "Have you ever been in love, Mabel?"

"I was...once...years ago."

"What happened?"

"He got bored." She raised her eyebrows. "I loved him. I was shattered when he left."

"I'm sorry," said Kate.

Mabel pressed her lips together, shook her head. "There won't be another...not now."

"Do you wish there were?"

"I wish things had been different."

Kate nodded.

"Kate," said Mabel. "Never let anybody own you. Whatever you do, make sure you're in control. Never be used. If you do go to Clara, see that she doesn't treat you like a toy. Make sure it's equal, you and her. My advice, if you want to hear it, is that you should wait for a while. I know you're nearly fourteen, and your ma was married at fifteen – and it isn't as if there's some arbitrary law that prohibits such things until you're a certain age, as if everyone were the same, like ants in a nest – but I would not wish to see you hurt...like I was..."

"I know," Kate interjected. "Of course, you're right."

"People use each other, Kate. Every day one half of the world uses the other half. Look at all those poor African slaves. They're people, just like us. I don't mean to say there aren't leaders – of course there are. There are people who lead, and people who are led, and that's natural; everybody understands that. There'd be chaos in the world if it were any other way. All I'm saying is that people should treat each other with respect; no-one should ever feel unwanted or valueless. That's what I fear for you – that you'll wind up as just another of Clara's cast-offs. Because if you really fall in love with her, you'll probably get hurt – and that may damage the wonderful person you are. There's love, Kate – and there's...swiving... clipping... treading... fadoodling... jig-a-jog..."

"Yes," said Kate, "I understand that. I know what you mean."

"...grinding... touzling..."

"Yes, yes..."

"You're embarrassed," said Mabel. "Those words make you think of her. But that thing that people do – that's not love. Love is deeper. Love can include that thing – and that thing can be an expression of love. But there's lust as well. Lust can lead to love – but it can also lead to boredom – like it did with my man. And then you get hurt. You have to be strong enough to ride over the top of disappointment, rejection...because life goes on, and you may meet others – after Clara. And once you have real love – that is precious."

"But how would you recognise it," Kate asked, "if you haven't experienced what love *isn't*?"

Mabel smiled, looked away for a moment and sighed. "You're more than a match for me, girl." She looked at Kate with affection. "Just be careful," she said, "be aware, be sensible, be in control. Whatever she gives you, give her back. If it's love, affection, respect – that's fine. If it's scorn, ridicule, abuse – walk away. Don't wait for it to inflate. You'll know when she's bored."

"Suppose I just want the fadoodling?"

A long pause. "Is that it? Is that all you want?"

"I don't know. But suppose it were?"

Mabel thought. "Then it would just be a game, something to amuse yourself with."

"Is that wrong?"

"No," said Mabel. "Perhaps not. I couldn't be that detached. Could you?"

"Yes, I think I probably could," Kate replied.

"Hmm. Am I overthinking the whole thing then? If it's nothing more than a kind of recreation – and you both understand that..." She paused for a long time. "...Then I suppose...there's no reason why not..."

"Am I callous?" asked Kate.

"Callous?" Mabel replied. "No, you're just...growing up. Look, Kate, I'm a fat old maid. Don't listen to me. I've been talking rot. You're a much better judge of what you want than I am. Just remember, whatever happens, I'm always here."

Kate hugged her. "Thank you, Mabel. I love you."

Tuesday November 16

Kate went to her next harp lesson, fully expecting her prospective affair with Clara to be consummated, but she was disappointed. Clara was alert enough to the music but showed little interest in Kate herself. Back in her room, the girl's disappointment quickly turned to frustration. She put on her cape and marched out into the rain, intending to walk off the irritation. Speck was working in the pigpen with Tranter Tickle and John Eldenshaw.

"Speck," she called, voice raised over the downpour. All three men looked up and saw her there, hand raised, seeking attention. Speck said something to the other two and walked through the muck towards her.

"Kate," he said. "What's up?"

"Smoke," she said, monosyllabically. Speck turned, held up ten fingers to the other men and hopped over the gate.

"Come on then," he said.

They walked to a wooden shelter between two of the fields. It was open to the elements on two sides, designed to allow a good view of the livestock while simultaneously keeping the rain off. Kate pulled out her pipe and tobacco, and Speck lit it for her before firing up his own. She took a huge pull and held the smoke for as long as she could before exhaling it.

"Oh, that's good," she sighed, closing her eyes and drawing out the words.

Speck took a more modest draw on his own pipe and said, "Want to talk about it?"

She paused. "Probably not."

"Just want company then?"

"That's about it. Sorry – I thought of you. It was instinctive."

"Well – I'm honoured."

"Where's Bastard?"

"Under the weather. Spending the day with Pixie."

She took a second pull on her pipe, let out the smoke and

said, "You ever been in love, Speck?"

"Ah," he said, "that's it…"

"Have you?"

"Yes Kate, I have."

She paused. For some reason, it wasn't the answer she'd expected. "You never told me before."

"You never asked before."

"But you do talk though. All those hours you spend standing still for me. You talk then. But you never told me you were in love."

He withdrew his pipe and looked at her. "Is it any wonder, Kate?"

She paused. "Who was she?"

"She was my wife – Jenny."

"What happened?"

"She died. More than twenty years ago."

"I'm sorry."

"Not your fault. She was twenty-one. My Jenny."

"Children?"

"No. But there would have been. Something happened a month short of full-term, and she died."

Kate was suddenly aware how paltry and selfish her own anger was. She was disappointed with herself but grateful that she hadn't vented it to anyone else. She remembered her own mother, and her little brother who never was.

"That's bad," she said. "Poor Speck." She rested her hand on his knee, and he covered it with his own. The rain spattered into the earth about them.

"What would we do without tobacco, eh?" he joked, his voice subdued.

"I feel calmer already," she said. "See how good you are for me."

He put his arm round her and hugged her to him. She rested her head on his shoulder.

"You're my favourite girl," he said softly.

"And you're my favourite Speck."

74. SPECK BECKWITH

The Beckwiths had been shepherds for generations, working for the farmers around Jedburgh. They were well-respected, knowledgeable men who devoured the printed word while they "studied" their sheep, each passing his learning down the family line. They were thoughtful people, kind, honest.

Eric Beckwith handfasted seventeen-year-old Linda in 1709. He was ten years older than she, and they'd been courting for two years. Three daughters and a son issued from the marriage: Mary in 1710, Hilda two years later, Marina in 1715, and Speck – the surprise – in 1719. Eric chose his son's name; it had been the name of his own grandfather, and he'd always liked it. Speck grew up in a happy, loving environment; there was never a cross word in the house, and he learnt shepherding as naturally as all the Beckwith men.

But Eric had an exploratory streak. He loved his profession but had heard that fortunes were to be found in the New World. He'd read about it and was drawn to the thrill of travel. The family had been fixed in place for hundreds of years – perhaps it was time for a change. He read more extensively, researched and talked about it as the years went by, but no-one thought he'd ever really act on his fantasy.

Speck's three sisters all found husbands: Marina, aged just eighteen and already pregnant, married shepherd Stephen Alford in 1733; Mary and Hilda were wed within a year of each other, in 1735 and 1736. The family had become a sizeable band, and little children began to issue forth.

Speck met Jenny Clifton in 1737 and fell in love with her at first sight. She was seventeen, and he thought her the most beautiful creature he'd ever seen – blonde hair, blue eyes, soft skin. He wanted to marry her, but her parents said that she must wait for a while, until both she and Speck were really sure. Jenny's parents were weavers and worked at home in Bonchester. She was their precious only child, and they wanted to be sure she'd be happy.

Early in 1739, Eric Beckwith proposed that his extended family cross the Atlantic to New England. He'd built up a substantial list of acquaintances there with whom he'd been corresponding for several years. Work could easily be found for them all, and if they were going to do it, they should do it now while Eric, already aged fifty-seven, could get them settled safely. His enthusiasm fired their imaginations, and after some months of discussion, the family decided to embrace the adventure.

But Speck was in love with Jenny. They planned to marry the following year. Her parents didn't want to emigrate, and Jenny didn't want to leave them. Speck had to choose between his love and a new life with his family. He chose Jenny.

They were handfasted on a bright, happy day in the summer of 1740. Speck had never seen his girl look so lovely, and despite the imminent departure of his parents, siblings, nephews and nieces (by that time Mary, Hilda and Marina had seven children between them), he was confident that his decision to remain in England was the right one.

Nevertheless, the family's departure two months later was tearful and full of promises to write. Speck and Jenny would still be part of the family even though they were separated by such a vast distance. At least, that was the plan.

Jenny saw the sorrow in Speck's face and felt sad for him. "It needn't be forever, my love. We're both young. We can follow later if you want. Give it a little time."

They were happy together, and by Christmas Jenny told him she was expecting his child. Speck was overjoyed –

and Jenny's parents were thrilled at the prospect of becoming grandparents.

But it wasn't to be. Something went badly wrong in Jenny's pregnancy, and she died in April 1741, leaving Speck alone and heartbroken.

He thought briefly about joining his parents and sisters in the New World but felt that he had a duty to Jenny's mother and father, so he remained with them and nursed them in their sad final years. Jenny's father died in 1742, his wife five years later.

During that time he received news that his own parents had died – first Linda, then Eric. His sisters' husbands fell out with each other, arguing about money, and the families went their separate ways. Mary's moved to Delaware and Hilda's to New York. Speck lost touch with Marina's family altogether. According to Mary, they'd left their home, fearing the ongoing military conflicts might close in on them, and travelled south, but she didn't know where they'd gone.

By 1747 Speck was entirely alone. He became a drover, taking livestock all the way to London from various places in the north. The work kept him busy and required concentration and a sharp eye. In some ways it felt like an extension of shepherding. In the warmer weather he slept in fields, in hedgerows, under trees. The companionship was good, and the inns along the way were welcoming. Jenny was always there in his mind, but he grew used to his own company and never looked for another partner.

The advertisement for the job at the Lookout caught his eye in the autumn of 1754. The place sounded idyllic. He had a few weeks of rest, so he wrote to enquire and was invited to visit in February the following year. By the summer he was installed in his little cottage.

Speck had been used to keeping a dog for the shepherding but had ceased to do so in his droving years, relying instead on the animals owned by the other men. But now he

710

was settled, and the companionship of a dog attracted him once more. He asked around and found a litter of puppies on a farm near Harwood Dale. Their mother was a long-haired, shaggy animal – black and white; the father was a herding dog. Speck took a liking to a particularly lively puppy. The farmer was surprised.

"That one? That little bastard?"

"I think so," said Speck, smiling. "Good boy!"

"He's just a little bastard, that one. Yappy, aggressive little bastard."

"What's his name?"

"He don't have a name – little bastard!"

So Speck had a companion. The dog quickly learned what was required of him and performed his tasks efficiently, although he seemed to possess a sense of humour too, and sometimes deliberately feigned stupidity, running around out of control. At those times, his master could be heard shouting his name with exasperation.

Speck had a job, a cosy house and a shaggy friend. He thought the rest of his life would be quiet, easy, solitary. How wrong he was...

75. ANNABELLE'S PARTY
Friday November 26, 1762, 8.15pm

Golda Dryden put her heart and soul into the performance. She sang with eyes closed and fists clenched, heel digging out the rhythm on the floor. Annabelle Trollope, Pearl Huxley and Portia Packard clapped along and joined in the choruses. When the song came to an end they applauded and laughed with the joy of it.

"I love that song!" cried Annabelle.

"The Spanish Lady in Dublin city," said Pearl, looking at her ankles and feet. "I wonder if anyone ever thought that about *my* feet."

"You've got lovely feet, Pearl," said Annabelle. "Who couldn't love your feet? I love your feet."

They were in high spirits – and the two bottles of wine open on the table between them fanned their enjoyment.

Golda sat down and took a long draught. They were in Annabelle's rooms on the first floor of the staff building. It was warm, cosy, with a roaring fire in the grate.

"I wish I could sing like you," said Portia. "I never learned anything about music. My parents weren't interested in it. Oh, but hearing you sing – bringing it all to life – it's so joyful…"

"Glad you like," said Golda. "I'm lucky, I suppose. My parents were both actors – they both had to sing and dance on stage. I picked it up from them."

"You make it really exciting, Golda. And you look so… alive when you're singing. Where's your man? You should have a circle of men on their knees around you, all with their tongues hanging out." The four women laughed at the image.

"There've been a few," said Golda, "but none was quite interested enough. And now there's nobody – not at the moment anyway."

Annabelle reached across the table and covered Golda's hand. "Ah, Golda. *We* love you."

Portia added her hand on top of Annabelle's, and Pearl's hand completed the stack of four.

Pearl said, "What about you, Belle?"

"Me?"

"You and Hollis," said Pearl.

Annabelle shook her head. "We're just friends. We've always been just friends. I'm too old for him anyway."

Golda looked surprised and said, "Go on! You're not forty yet."

"I'm six years older than Hollis."

"Everybody thinks of you as a couple," said Portia.

Annabelle raised her eyebrows. "I suppose they do, but it's never been that way. We both grew up in Lincoln. Hollis's father was a surgeon; mine was a tailor. I used to work in the shop – that's where I learned my craft. My mother and Hollis's were best friends, and I used to look after him. He knew me from his earliest days. I'm his older sister – that's the way he thinks about me. We have a lot in common, but it's because we grew up together."

"But you love him, I think," said Portia.

Annabelle dropped her gaze. "I suppose I do. I don't know what I'd do if he wasn't there."

"He must think the same about you," said Golda.

"Hollis is in love with Clara," Annabelle answered. "He's loved her ever since she arrived four years ago."

"Clara..." said Pearl.

Annabelle shook her head. "Clara's young, barely in her middle twenties. She's... unusual, tempting, attractive. Willing... hungry..."

"Isn't she with Jacob now?" asked Golda.

"Yes, apparently so," said Annabelle. "Hasn't been going on

for long."

"It's strange, how she likes men and women the same," said Pearl. "I can't imagine that..."

Annabelle steered the subject back round to Hollis. "She takes advantage of Hollis. I wish she'd be a bit less selfish. They had a significant liaison a few years ago, but Clara gets bored quickly. She gets about quite a bit. I think she's had an affair with Kipp too, and there are rumours of others. She comes back to Hollis for a few days now and then – and that always gets his hopes up, of course. But it never lasts. I think she just uses him as a place to pause until the next one comes along."

"That's cruel," said Pearl.

"It's the way she is," Annabelle answered. "I do like her, though. Maybe it's just the way she needs to be. But it's a pity that Hollis gets bruised."

Portia opened another bottle of wine and replenished all their glasses. Annabelle's tabby cat Tilly came purring round their feet. Golda reached down and stroked the animal, drawing an immediate and audible purr. "Hello, pussycat!"

"What about you, Pearl?" said Annabelle. "Is it ever going to be you and Egerton?"

"Me and Ben?" Pearl replied.

(The girls all called him Mr Badger, but everyone else knew him as Ben – a name he'd awarded himself, disliking the label his parents had bestowed upon him. Annabelle persisted in calling him Egerton because she liked the sensation of the word in her mouth.)

"He's very keen on you," said Annabelle. "Makes no secret of it."

"It'll never happen," Pearl replied, scratching her chin. "I mean, it's not that I don't like him. It's just... well, can you imagine spending your life with someone who goes around all the time sounding like a trumpet with a nail in it?" They laughed while she went on. "He's sweet enough, I suppose, but honestly… I like my own company."

There was a knock at the door, and Annabelle got up to answer it. Etta Lynn stood there, uncharacteristically dressed in a modest dark blue gown and plain earrings. She held up a bottle of wine. "Did I hear singing?"

Annabelle said, "Anyone who carries a bottle may enter," and opened the door wide.

Etta walked in, saw the others and said, "You don't mind oldies joining you then?" Tilly ran forward and curled herself round Etta's feet. She reached down, tickled the cat and whispered, "Hello darling," followed by a string of kissing sounds.

"You're not an oldie, Etta. Come on in," called Portia.

"Oswald not here?" asked Etta, joining them at the table.

"He might appear later. I think he might have Hornsby with him," Portia replied.

"Dear Hornsby," said Etta, her eyes following the red liquid as Annabelle poured it for her. "How he yearns for me."

They all smiled. Portia and Golda laughed.

"And shall you be his?" asked Pearl.

"No," Etta replied. "I really can't see that happening."

"Time for another song, Golda?" asked Annabelle.

Golda rose. "What shall it be? Um, um, um… The Knight and the Shepherd's Daughter?"

"Good idea," said Pearl. "We can all listen and be thankful that we're not going to be led astray…"

76. ROMANTIC DEVELOPMENTS
December 1762 to March 30, 1763

Sylvie kept Kate behind after her last lesson before Christmas. She sat down, her student opposite her, and said, in French, "Kate, Clara knows how you feel. She likes you very much."

Kate waited, listening, not knowing where this might lead.

"Be patient. For the moment, she is with Jacob. Even I don't see her very much. Let it play out, and she will come back to you. Sorry – she's impulsive, as you know."

"But aren't the two of you...?"

"Yes, yes, of course. I love her. But Clara's leash needs to be long."

Kate spent that Christmas and New Year at home once more, feeling restless, unsettled. She felt she'd been set up by Clara, then passed over; as if she were a meal ordered by a hungry customer but rejected in favour of something tastier.

It's worse still, she thought. *I'd actually arrived at the table and was ready – ready to be eaten.*

She felt inadequate – just not good enough.

To make matters worse, Grace seemed preoccupied, and they met only three times during the holiday.

"What's going on, Grace? You're quieter than usual?"

"I can't tell you. Not yet. In case it comes to nothing."

"Is it Alan?"

"Yes. Look, I've already said too much."

"Have you been to bed with him?" Kate was excited and wanted the details.

"No. Kate, stop digging."

Kate paused. "Alright. But he's interested in you?"

"Yes, he is."

"Is he touching you?"

She thought that Grace was going to answer. There were several seconds of silence, and she could see that her friend was teetering on the brink – but the cork didn't quite come out.

"I'll tell you next time. I promise."

Kate walked down to the bridge several times and looked at the watermill. She wanted to step over the wall and run down to the buildings and the millpond but never quite summoned the courage to do so. Her memories of the place were fragile and precious, and she didn't want to risk disturbing them.

She kept her bedroom door locked when she was at home, and spent a lot of time remembering, and imagining Clara. *Perhaps she's waiting for me, hungry. I'll get back to the school, and she'll want me.*

But Kate returned to the Lookout in January to find Clara still wrapped up in Jacob.

Crispin Stafford finally wed his long-time love Winnie Warwick in the school chapel on Saturday, February 5th. At the couple's request, the ceremony itself was plain, but the chapel was full, and the reception was extravagant. It was the first "below-stairs" staff marriage at the Lookout, so Alvina produced a mighty feast in celebration.

Kate watched Clara throughout the day but received not a single glance.

Anne Pringle (Bip)

Bip's earliest memories were of life in the workhouse in Halifax. She had no recollection of her parents, although she'd picked up whisperings of closely-kept secrets. Her father was some prominent local figure, apparently. Someone once said they believed her mother had committed suicide, but the rumour was suppressed, and she never heard it again despite all her questioning.

She'd always been slender and attractive, and it was her silky, dark brown hair that had gained the attention of the school scouts and resulted in her arrival at the Lookout in 1759 at the age of ten. There'd been two of them – she and Pamela Heron – brought from Halifax simultaneously. Other hopeful girls had been rejected and sent back to their cramped dormitories, twelve to a room. Bip recalled very well the relief she'd felt, the excitement. To have the opportunity to build a new life; it was like a blessing from heaven.

"Bip" was a name she'd been given in the workhouse, apparently the result of a habit she'd had as a very young child, constantly popping her lips and producing her characteristic sound: bipbipbipbipbipbipbipbip... She picked up an extensive vocabulary of colourful language from the older workhouse residents and learned to make friends easily. At the age of thirteen, she was still unsure in which direction her affections lay. She thought about boys frequently (although she'd never had a boyfriend) but was aware that she found girls attractive, particularly Kate. She was concerned that her friend had become so withdrawn, and cornered her about it as they were nibbling cake at Crispin and Winnie's wedding reception in the ballroom.

"You're ogling Clara all the time, you know," she said.

Kate sighed. "Am I? I suppose I am. Sorry. It's pitiful, I know."

"You're only thirteen, like me. What's the hurry?"

Kate was clearly irritated. "The hurry? I wasn't the one in pursuit – *she* was!"

"Clara's like that – you know she is. I think she runs through a list. Getting a girl is easy here – if you want one. Getting a boy – that's much harder."

Kate was genuinely annoyed. "It's not that!"

"Don't snap! God, Kate! You need a drink."

Kate sighed again and reached for her friend's hand. "I'm

sorry. Maybe I'm ill."

"You're not ill," Bip replied. "You're just lovelorn. Maybe you need a jangle."

Kate frowned. "A jangle?"

"Jangle. Go on! You know what a jangle is. It's what Cady used to do to the girls in the bath."

"Ah," Kate replied, smiling. "I might have known." She was quiet for a moment, then said, "Did she ever jangle you?"

"Once," Bip smiled. "Long time ago, when I first got here. She was always on bath duty, always on the jangle."

Kate gave a snort of a laugh, and Bip echoed the sound, relieved to see her unwind at last.

"*You* never got jangled then?" Bip inquired.

"No. I just missed that. She was already with Sarah Alston by the time I got here."

"Yep," said Bip. "Pity about that. Bath time's not as popular as it used to be." She looked at the two maids, sitting next to each other some distance away. "They've been together more than three years now, Cady and Sarah. They make a nice couple, I think. Bet they'd marry each other if they could."

Kate looked at Cady Weston and Sarah Alston, visibly wrapped up in one another – and pictured herself with Clara.

Bip leaned forward and peered at the bridal couple, arm-in-arm at the top table. "And now our Winnie, married at last."

"You're a love, trying to make me feel better," said Kate.

"I'm glad you're smiling again. Love'll find you; you don't have to go chasing it. Look at Winnie. She's five years older than him."

"Is she?" said Kate. "I thought they were the same age."

"You're just not nosey enough, Kate," said Bip, shaking her head. "I can tell you with authority that he's twenty-four, and she's nearly twenty-nine."

"And what about Cady and Sarah?"

"You know how old they are, surely," said Bip. "Cady's nearly twenty-eight, Sarah's birthday's next week. She'll be twenty-six."

"Thirteen sounds pretty stupid, then," said Kate.

"It does, a bit," Bip agreed. "Anyway, I love you. I'll do anything you want."

Kate almost choked on the piece of cake she was eating.

Her fourteenth birthday came around with the usual celebrations. But the big news for Kate was that the two impending love affairs at the farm had been consummated. Grace excitedly admitted to Kate that she was sleeping with Alan Flathers.

"Was that what you couldn't tell me last time?"

"Yes," said Grace. "I'm sorry. I didn't want to sound silly."

"He's twenty-one," said Kate.

"Yes, but I'm sixteen. It's old enough."

"Does your ma know?"

Grace paused. "No, I haven't told her yet. Don't say anything..."

Kate looked intently at her friend, wanting to know. "What's it like?" she asked.

Previously it had always been Kate teaching Grace, but now their places were reversed, and Grace was delighted to be able to give Kate a detailed account of something she hadn't yet experienced for herself.

"Does it hurt?" asked Kate.

"No," said Grace. "Well, only a little the first time. After that it's nice – really nice..."

Inevitably Grace spent a lot of her time with Alan, and Kate often found herself alone, although she now understood why.

It seemed to Kate that everyone was in love. Amy and Walter, long-time sweethearts, had allowed their relationship to come to fruition, although no-one was supposed to know. Even Kate's uncles Adam and William, established bachelors, were both involved with women in the nearby villages. Kate felt left out, forgotten. Seventeen-year-old Beatrice Swift seemed to be the only girl nearby who remained unattached, so she became the centre of Kate's attention in the little time she spent at home on the farm.

On the morning after her birthday party, Kate gathered up some dishes that had to be returned to the Buckleys' house, put them in a basket and began to walk up the hill. Just after she passed the forge she saw a figure coming downhill towards her and realised it was Henry Flesher. Kate had rarely thought about him before; he'd always been cold and aloof, but as he approached, she noticed how handsome he was, and their eyes met.

"Hello Kate," he said, stopping to greet her.

"Hello Henry," she replied, trying to recall if he'd ever spoken to her before.

He looked her up and down appreciatively. "You look good. Older than fourteen."

She felt a flush of pleasure. He liked her. She played along. "So do you. You look nice."

How old is he? she thought. *Middle twenties. Older than Alan Flathers anyway. Probably ten years or so older than me. But he likes me...*

They stood a moment longer, exchanging meaningless small-talk, then he began to walk away down the road towards Watermill Lane and Vine Cottage. She watched him for a moment, smiling inside, before turning to resume her journey. After a few seconds she turned to see how far he'd gone. He was standing still, looking at her. Her heart leapt. *He's looking at me! He wants me!* Immediately she pictured herself with him, in that way that Grace described herself with Alan. Her heart was beating fast. Without thinking, she blew him a kiss, which he caught before blowing it back to her. She almost burst with excitement, turned and ran all the way to Beatrice, eager to tell her what had just happened.

77. THE WHITE BULL, RIBCHESTER
Easter Sunday, April 3, 1763

Helen lay in bed, Francis by her side, both ill. Alex was worried. There was a sickness sweeping the area, and the doctor – recently departed to visit other sufferers in the village – told him that the symptoms displayed by Alex's family looked familiar. The mortality rate was high. He could suggest no more than rest and clean water. Bloodletting seemed useless. "Patience and prayer," he'd said when he left, his hand on Alex's shoulder.

"You didn't go to church, love," said Helen weakly, her face slick with sweat.

Alex was keeping vigil at her bedside. "I didn't want to leave you. I'm sure the Lord will understand."

"You need to busy yourself," she said. "You're just worrying."

"I'm where I want to be," he replied.

"You're not ill?"

"No," he said. "I'm fine."

"How many people are sick in the village?"

"The doctor says eighteen...so far."

"Are there any deaths here yet, Alex? Tell me, please."

"None, love." Actually, there had been three the previous day, but he didn't want to tell her that.

"John and Sarah?"

"They're both good." Neither had been to see Helen and her son that day. Alex had suggested it might be safer if they kept out of the room. The inn itself was closed to all except the very few travellers who arrived on the coach.

Alex continued to sit and watch as the sun went round

the sky. Following the doctor's instructions, he made sure they both drank plenty of water. Twice he took Francis to the privy; Helen made her own way there once. It was good to see her moving about, but she was clearly frail, and Alex was frightened. He touched their foreheads now and then and was not reassured by how clammy they felt. *My God*, he thought. *Please...*

John tapped on the door in the early evening.

"They should eat something if they can, Alex," he whispered. "I've brought you a tray of things."

"Thank you," Alex replied, taking the food from him. "How are you and Sarah?"

"We're both fine so far."

"Any more news from the village?"

"Dilly Sollett and her little girl..."

"Oh no...".

"I'm afraid so."

Alex felt his eyes fill with tears, and John tried to comfort him, laying his hand on his friend's arm.

"We're all praying for you," he said, "for all of you. You yourself, Alex – how do you feel?"

"I feel well, John. I just want my family to be well too."

"Be positive, Alex. People do recover from this."

Alex patted John's shoulder. "God bless you. Give my love to Sarah."

78. JACOB'S BEDROOM
Thursday June 9, 1763, 3.30am

Clara watched him as he sat at the window, motionless, his back to her, staring out at the grey dawn. He was deep in thought, as always, but what he thought about, she didn't know.

The birds were singing. Now and then they'd balance in the window frames and peck out a few of the spiders in the stonework, wings and beaks banging on the glass.

Jacob was a good lover, but Clara's liaisons with men tended to be short-lived. For long-term relationships, she preferred women, occasionally students. Viv Stamper had been one of the earliest – brilliant, fiercely intellectual – passionate, but she'd demanded more commitment than Clara was prepared to give. Kate would be the next.

Her relationship with Jacob was the longest she'd ever had with a man. She'd always kept a small supply of powders but had been forced to send for a much larger quantity to sustain the previous few months, Jacob's bed being where she spent most of her nights. Despite her vigilance, Clara believed she was pregnant. She hadn't bled since March and was becoming increasingly worried about telling Jacob. He didn't strike her as a man who would want children of his own.

She found Jacob fascinating – enigmatic. He was very confident physically, but she was never sure where his thoughts were. His body worked with the efficiency of a mill when they had sex together, but his eyes told her he was a world away.

Occasionally he'd speak as if he were addressing someone else – as if another person were in the room.

"Did you say something?"

"No, no. I was talking to myself. Ignore me."

Three times she'd woken in the dark of night, Jacob asleep next to her, and had been sure someone else was there – a third person, watching in the stillness. She'd convinced herself she could hear their breathing. Once or twice she'd caught movement, dark shapes in the blackness, the soft pad of footsteps. She'd reach out and touch Jacob, the reassuring warmth of his body easing her fear.

The sun had risen higher; the light in the room was a little stronger. Jacob rose from his seat and turned.

"You're awake," he said quietly.

"I was watching you," she replied.

"It's early."

She held open the bedclothes. Jacob yawned and stretched, then climbed in with her, settled on his back and took her in the crook of his left arm. Clara kissed his chest, rested her head there. A moment later she was asleep.

Jacob lay awake, staring, far away.

79. LONDON
Monday to Thursday, July 25 to 28, 1763

Monday

Stella sat again at her annual spyhole and watched as each girl underwent the procedure that marked the end of one stage of her life and the beginning of the next. Elizabeth, Zoe, Yvette, Veronica... Miss Shadow was due for a night out tomorrow, and on Wednesday Stella would attend the sale of Sara Collingwood. Was there anyone in the whole world who drew so much pleasure from their work?

In the room on the opposite side of the chamber sat Jacob, watching only occasionally. He'd become increasingly detached from what had been the central meaning of his existence. He sat here because it was expected of him, but he tried to shut out the sounds that escaped from the room next door. That night two years ago with Vivianne had profoundly changed him, and his days and nights were filled with the memory of her, and of that journey home with Maria and Lucas. It wasn't that he'd come to question himself; it was more as if the self that he'd been – that he'd thought permanent – had drained away. For months now, every night he'd been with Clara, he'd closed his eyes and thought of Vivianne. He had to do something. Something must change. He'd decided to take control.

Tuesday

"You want to take Vivianne out?" said Margaret, surprised.
"Yes, for old times' sake," said Jacob.
Foxley and Margaret looked at each other.
"You'll watch her, of course, won't you?" asked Foxley. "She's a bright one. Wouldn't want her running off."

"Don't worry," replied Jacob. "Do you think she'll agree to it?"

"She'll do as she's told, Jacob. Of course."

"Well, this is a surprise," said Vivianne coldly.

"It's good to see you," he replied. She looked breathtaking, dressed in a striking scarlet gown, embroidered with black.

Viv breathed out audibly through her nose, scoffing at him. "Foxley says you want to take me out. I'm to be a good girl."

"Humour me," he said. "I want to talk to you."

"What about? Marriage? Ha!" She laughed derisively.

"Possibly," he said.

"I'm going to finish you," she said, razor-sharp. "All of you."

"Perhaps I can help."

"You?" she smiled scornfully. "Help?"

"Will you come or won't you. I shan't make you if you'd rather not."

"Where are we going?" she asked.

"Wherever you like. A walk...a meal...the theatre...?"

"I might run."

"I won't stop you."

She paused, watching him; then held up her arms. "Will I do?"

"Emphatically, yes," he said.

It felt strange to be alone with her in the open air. They took a leisurely stroll along Bedford Street, she receiving the usual appreciative glances from passing men.

"How have you been?" he asked.

She snorted at the foolishness of his enquiry. "I'm a prostitute Jacob. Of your making."

"It hurts to hear you say that."

"Why are we here?"

"Do you remember that night, two years ago?"

She was quiet for a long time. He thought she wasn't going

728

to answer. "Of course."

"I think of it all the time," he said.

She shook her head in dismissal of his statement. "It was nothing. It wasn't real."

He was about to reply, thinking she'd stopped, but she continued, speaking with some intensity. "I was between two lives – a dream and a nightmare. The darkness in the room was like a chrysalis. It felt as if that moment was cut off from everything else – as if it could have gone on forever." He listened intently to her words. She went on. "Neither the past nor the future was real. There was only that... sanctuary, that bed, like an island in the night." She paused. "And there you were – where I'd always wanted you to be, before I knew you were a monster. It felt safe." She ceased for two or three seconds, then finished, "It was only an illusion."

"I want you to be with me."

"What?"

"You heard me clearly enough."

She stopped walking. They'd come to a bench by St Paul's Church. He sat down and motioned that she should do the same. A few people passed, glanced at them, thinking them lovers perhaps.

"What do you mean exactly?"

"I've thought of little but you since that night." He'd meant to look into her eyes when he said it but found he was unable to do so.

"So you want me to come away with you and be your little wifey?"

He felt ridiculous, ashamed.

"You? Who've set in motion the suffering of so many?" She paused, shaking her head. "You deserve to be hanged, Jacob."

He was downcast. She hated him. The situation felt absurd, but he was ready to sacrifice himself.

"You're right," he said quietly. "Then let me help you do it,

Vivianne. Let me help you stop it all."

She looked at him for a while, curious, then said, "What happened to you?"

"*You* happened to me, Vivianne."

"It was only one night, Jacob."

"It was a bend in the river," he said. "It set me going in the opposite direction."

"How will you atone for all the suffering you've caused?"

"With my death, if need be," he said.

She watched him, unsure whether to believe him or not.

"This is a trick," she said.

He shook his head. "What do you mean?"

"You know there's more than one copy of my manuscript, but you don't know how many, or where they are."

"The novel you said you'd write?"

"Of course," she replied.

"It's finished?"

"Yes, it's finished – and copied several times."

"But what can you do with it?"

"I know how to bring you down – all of you. And if you try to silence me you'll hit the ground even harder."

He waited a moment, looking at her, beautiful in her determination. He wanted to hold her, kiss her. "This isn't a trick," he said. "Foxley hasn't mentioned your writing to me. I think he has no knowledge of it. Believe me, I want to help. Surely, if I take you away from here it'll be easier for you to achieve your objective."

She shook her head. "How can I possibly trust you, Jacob – of all people?"

"Give me a chance. At least let me try."

"How? I mean, how can you get me? I expect you have some money, but it certainly won't be enough to buy me out. In any case, they'll find your desire for me as incredible as I find your sudden about-turn."

"I'll take you away, today, tomorrow. We'll run – hide. You'll publish your manuscript, or whatever it is you plan to do with it; we'll watch the tower fall… Then perhaps you won't think quite so badly of me."

"You mean it?"

"I do, with all my heart."

She turned aside and said no more. Jacob watched her. She was thinking hard.

"What would you like to do now?" he asked.

"Gin. Buy me a gin."

They sat together in an alehouse for half an hour or so, during which Vivianne drank two large gins and Jacob a pint of strong ale. There was a production of King Lear in the Theatre Royal, and he suggested they might get a box and watch the play.

It was an engrossing performance, with David Garrick taking the title role. Partway through Act 3, Scene 4, at Edgar's "The prince of darkness is a gentleman", Jacob was surprised to find Vivianne's hand on his. He looked at her, and she whispered, "And is that you? The prince of darkness?"

"I think it probably was," he answered.

"You'll stay with me tonight," she said. "We'll discuss things."

Some of the weight lifted from his heart, and a ray of light penetrated his soul.

"Thank you," he said.

They left the theatre and walked hand in hand through the crowds of people. It was difficult to hold a conversation in the hubbub, but he heard her say, "This has to work for everyone. Not just you and me, but for all the girls here – and all those still at the school."

"I know," he said.

There was a commotion some distance behind them. Someone was crying for help, but Jacob and Vivianne were concentrating too hard on each other to notice.

"I have it worked out," she said. "Every detail."

He looked at her, squeezed her hand, then stopped and faced her. "Vivianne. I..."

He was trying to say something – she saw it in his face. *My God*, she thought. *He really loves me. It's true.* But it was too soon; she didn't know what she felt – everything seemed hurried and confused.

"Don't say it," she said. "Not yet."

Jacob nodded, and they walked on.

Someone bustled past Vivianne, and Jacob caught sight of a figure he vaguely recognised – perhaps someone from the old days? He thought briefly of John Noon and Margaret Southwell, working in his father's shop. The figure was quickly swallowed in the crowds ahead, disappeared from sight.

Vivianne stopped walking. Jacob turned and looked at her, still clutching her hand. She was swaying, her mouth open, eyes on his.

"Jacob...?" she muttered, dropped her bag on the ground, pressed her left hand to her side and held up the palm, covered in blood. She looked at it in disbelief, then collapsed.

"Vivianne?" said Jacob in confusion. "What...?"

She got to her knees and supported herself for a moment on her clenched fists, then fell forward, unconscious. A dark pool of blood spread quickly around her.

He knelt and tried to turn her over, horrified, shouting her name. Others came to help, laid Vivianne on her back, spoke to her, trying to find if life remained.

No, no, no, thought Jacob. *It's not happening. Please no...*

Someone listened for her heart, felt her pulse. Her mouth was open, her eyelids half lifted. There was no breath, no breath...

Someone in the crowd produced a large blanket from a basket of washing and handed it to Jacob, presumably with the intention that he should cover the body. He took it, spread it out on the ground, and enlisted the aid of a horrified young man to help him lift Vivianne onto it. The two wrapped the body in the blanket, took it up by the ends, and carried it to King's Place, Jacob hoping that some miracle might be achieved by the convent surgeon.

But it was no good. The doctor examined her less than twenty minutes after the assault, found a single deep stab wound, and pronounced her dead. Foxley sent one of the guards running for the undertaker.

Jacob was stunned, in denial. Edgar was shocked by Vivianne's death, but was even more troubled at the force of Jacob's reaction to it. The two men sat down together by the body, and Foxley put his arm around the other's shoulders.

"Look, Jacob, it's a dreadful thing, but it wasn't your fault."

"I loved her."

Edgar paused, brows knit.

"You're overreacting. You mustn't feel responsible."

The door opened. Margaret stepped into the room and saw the girl on the floor.

"Oh, no…"

"Yes," said Foxley, his arm still draped around Jacob. "The Vampyre, almost certainly."

"Oh, you poor dear," breathed Margaret, kneeling and brushing back Viv's hair. "How…?"

"She was out walking with Jacob in the street."

There was a commotion of footsteps on the stairs beyond the door. Foxley looked over and said, "Keep the girls out. Don't let them see her like this."

But it was too late. The door opened and Harriet Dixon, Midge Fenwick and Nana Hall ran into the room. Holly Graham and Kim Hurley appeared in their wake.

"Viv?" cried Nana in horror.

"I'm afraid she's dead," said Foxley. "Margaret, shut the door, please. Don't let any more in."

Nana knelt down by Vivianne and touched her cheek. She

733

looked up and saw Jacob, his face sticky with tears, shaking his head.

"You bastard!" she cried. Distraught and outraged, she flew across the room and attacked him with her fists. Jacob cowered back, covered his head with his hands and arms, but made no other attempt to deflect her blows. Foxley stood, braced his arms around the girl from behind and forced her back towards Margaret and the others.

"We're all upset, Nana. This had nothing to do with Jacob." Sensing the likelihood of further trouble, he addressed them all. "You have to leave. The undertaker is on his way. There'll be time for grief and goodbyes when his work is done." He turned to Margaret. "Margaret, go with them, please. They'll need you."

Margaret, struggling to control her own tears, shooed the girls through the door despite their protests. "Please, little ones. I'm just as upset as any of you. Let's allow things to settle, and we'll all come back later. I promise."

Foxley listened to the sound of their footsteps mounting the staircase, then turned and looked at Crowan. They were alone with the body again. Edgar had always thought of Jacob as someone who could remain calm, dignified, in any situation; but now he appeared crushed, withdrawn to some dark, interior place. His eyes were glazed, his jaw grimly set. He seemed to be beyond the reach of words. Foxley sat silently with him and waited.

The room was still for about three minutes except for the soft ticking of the wall clock. There was something indecent about the mindless mechanical sound, blindly counting the seconds while this lovely young woman lay dead on the floor.

Movement on the stairs indicated that someone else was coming. *Not more trouble*, thought Foxley. Stella entered the room.

"I heard..." she began. Then she saw Jacob staring vacantly into space – and realised. She grinned inwardly. *What a bit of luck! He was fond of her. Look at him, sitting there snivelling. Not so strong and 'King of the Castle' now are we? Ha!*

She hadn't set out to kill Vivianne; the girl's death had been nothing more than a fortuitous accident. Miss Shadow never looked about her as she cut swathes through the multitude. Wherever her blade dealt death, that was mere fate. She hadn't even seen Vivianne in the throng – but what a delicious fluke. *A game pullet on a plate, sent to the everlasting buttock-ball. How sweet!*

"Oh, my…!" she said. "How did it happen?"

"In the street," said Foxley. "I imagine it's the work of the Vampyre."

"The Vampyre!" she echoed, her spirit delighting in the utterance of her own epithet.

"Yes," said Foxley. "A single thrust, like all the other victims. The bastard! Why can't they track him down?"

"You needn't stay, Stella," Jacob managed. "We're waiting for the undertaker. I'll make the funeral arrangements."

"Very sad," Stella replied. "She was a bright girl. I suppose we should be thankful that the Vampyre took only this Drury Lane vestal, and not someone of greater import."

Crowan looked at her in disgust but didn't immediately answer.

"There'll have been others," said Foxley. "The Vampyre never takes just one. We'll read about more unfortunates in the newspapers, no doubt."

"Go, Stella," said Jacob. "I find your comments tasteless." Was she laughing at him?

"I meant nothing," she said, "other than to point out how fortunate it was that the individual expended was only a piper's wife, and not a person of importance."

Jacob was on his feet in fury. Foxley rose instantly, compelled to restrain him, while Stella stood smiling at Crowan's impotence.

"Sit down, Jacob," said Foxley. "You're distressed – in shock. Calm yourself. I'm sure Stella meant nothing." He looked at her. "Tell him, please."

But their discourse was interrupted by a knock at the door. Margaret entered, and Stella took the opportunity to leave.

"The undertakers are here," said Margaret, and ushered three men into the room, two of them carrying a coffin in which the body could be stored overnight.

"Let me make the arrangements please," said Jacob to Foxley. "I'd like her to have the best. A fine casket..."

"Anything you wish," Foxley replied quietly. "You were obviously fond of her."

"I was. There'll be a proper burial..."

"Of course."

"And a prominent monument."

"Yes Jacob. Anything you wish for the girl, you shall have. It's the least we can do."

Wednesday

The convent closed down for the next few days, and the sale of Sara Collingwood was postponed.

On Wednesday morning early, Holly Graham and Nana Hall visited the market to purchase things for the burial. The undertaker and his assistants returned soon after eight o'clock and helped Nana and Holly wash Vivianne and dress her in a new nightgown, while Margaret Siddon looked on, tutting and wiping away her tears with a handkerchief that quickly became sodden. The body was then laid out on its shroud while the girls sprinkled it with flowers and herbs, still fresh from the morning. Finally, the shroud was wrapped around the body, and the undertakers lifted Vivianne into her casket. All day she was surrounded by weeping girls. Jacob stayed away, not wishing to make himself a target for their anger, fully aware that they needed time to grieve amongst themselves.

Instead, he walked to St Paul's church and made arrangements for the funeral. The rector told him that he was not in the habit of interring draggle-tails in his churchyard, but a banknote for fifty pounds, together with a close inspection of the muzzle of Jacob's pistol, quickly changed his mind. A second banknote for fifty pounds had him agree to all of Jacob's requirements for the service, including a promise that he would keep quiet about the details. The burial was set for twelve noon the next day.

From the church, he walked to the stagecoach terminus in Holborn and enquired into the possibility of hiring a carriage for a long journey. It wasn't an easy thing to arrange at such short notice, but Jacob again noted the ease with which money knocked down obstacles. When all his plans had been finalised he made his way back to King's Place and informed Foxley of the arrangements for the following day.

In the early evening he tried to get into Viv's room with the intention of recovering her manuscript, but found the door locked. His assertion that he'd inadvertently left his spectacles within had Margaret open the door for him, but she stood in the frame while he went about supposedly looking for them, and he wasn't able to hunt for what he genuinely wanted.

Jacob declined Edgar's invitation to dinner. "It's thoughtful of you. Thank you. But I'd rather be alone if it's all the same to you. I'll go for a walk – perhaps work off some of the shock."

"I quite understand, Crowan. Have a good evening. And thanks for undertaking all the necessary for poor Vivianne. Much appreciated. It's good to see you care about them so much."

"It's the least I could do," Jacob replied. "I'll watch the procession move off tomorrow, then I'll go if you don't mind. The girls won't want to see me, so there's no point in upsetting things by appearing at the graveside."

"Of course, Jacob. Very sensible. Very thoughtful, as always."

He ate a solitary meal, she on his mind the whole time, before wandering around. Out of curiosity, he walked past his childhood home, his father's business on Ludgate Hill. It had become a barber's shop. He looked up at the west front of St Paul's Cathedral, bathed in evening sunlight, and remembered with affection his stepmother, Alison. He'd completely lost touch with them after they'd moved to Venice. For all he knew, both she and his father were dead. She'd be fifty-six now, his father seventy-five. Jacob was acutely aware of the depth of lost time – of wastage in his life, of the past, and now also of the future. His dream of an ongoing association with Viv had been literally punctured. She was gone forever. His continued existence seemed pointless, the opportunity for some kind of self-redemption snatched away. The hope of being able to spend a lifetime aspiring to her love had, in the last two years, become a beacon, a lighthouse, for him. But now, the lantern extinguished, he was adrift in darkness; directionless, in an unnavigable ocean of loss, with no known haven, no destination.

He had to get the manuscript. It was the only thing left that gave him any purpose at all. Without it, he may as well fling himself into the Thames.

Jacob walked past Fleet Prison and up through the market on his way back to Covent Garden. Twice he was approached by prostitutes, but thankfully he knew neither of them. He let himself in through the convent's courtyard door and made his way up the stairs towards his room. Stella passed him on her way down, and they paused for a moment, looking at each other. His gaze invited her to explain her vileness, but she met it boldly, saying nothing. She was going out to kill, her blade secured in her sleeve. She imagined how good it would feel to bring it swiftly into play, to slide its length through his ribcage and into his heart. If she wished she could make this the last minute of his life. Their mutual dislike had hardened into cold hatred. Neither moved for a moment. Then she turned her face towards the blood of the evening, made her way swiftly downstairs and out of the door. Jacob watched her go, and wondered if slitting her throat might assuage some of his despair.

Thursday

The undertaker arrived at half past eleven the next morning, and the girls, all dressed in black, stood quietly as four of his men lifted the coffin from the house to the wheeled bier waiting in the courtyard.

Jacob watched from his window as the procession moved away towards the church. When it was out of sight, he followed the maze of corridors and stairs that led to Vivianne's room. The door was still sealed, but his determination got him inside. A single well-focused kick cracked the wood around the lock, weakening it sufficiently for him to shoulder his way in.

He searched the room quickly, coolly, with eyes as keen as a hawk's. Viv's manuscript was concealed in a cavity at the bottom of her wardrobe, accessed from underneath. It took fifteen minutes to locate. Extending to almost two hundred pages in her typical neat hand, it was called, *Deception – Innocent Lives Corrupted by the Lust of Liars*. She hadn't identified herself as the author or used a pseudonym. Instead, she'd written, *by one of the Abused Women, with the consent of all the others*. He carefully flicked through the pages, ensuring that it was all there.

Jacob took the papers with him and returned to his room, put on his cape and packed the manuscript in his bag. Then he walked to the church through the day's grey drizzle and watched the burial service from a distance. The coffin was being lowered into the grave by the time he got there, the girls comforting each other, weeping. Foxley and Margaret stood nearby. Jacob saw the rector mouthing the words of the service, but the distance was too great, and the noise from the street too loud, for him to hear them.

It was all over several minutes before the half-hour, and he stood silently, out of sight, as the girls threaded their way back towards the convent. The rector disappeared into the church. The labourers stood ready to fill in the hole.

Jacob stepped forward and motioned to the coach waiting about fifty yards away, summoning its approach; then he walked into the churchyard and nodded to the two grave-diggers. They hauled the coffin out of the ground, carried it to the vehicle, and lifted it inside. Jacob presented each of them with the agreed ten gold sovereigns, then turned, climbed into the carriage, shut the door behind him and tapped his signal to the driver. The workmen began to fill in the empty grave as the coach moved off.

Jacob looked at his bag and at the casket lying on the seat opposite. The road north would be a long one, but he had something to read.

CHARACTERS ASSOCIATED WITH CAPPLEMAN FARM

The year of birth is given in each case to enable identification of parentage or peer groups.
The year of death is given in some instances where the disclosure does not undermine the unfolding of the story.

The Line of Kate Swithenbank

James White – 1609-1671. Husband of Anne White; father of Daisy.

Anne White – 1621-1646. Witch; wife of James; mother of Daisy.

Slade Marshall – 1636-1701. Husband of Daisy Marshall (née White); father of Scarlet.

Daisy Marshall (née White) – 1641-1712. Daughter of James and Anne White; wife of Slade Marshall; mother of Scarlet.

John Sykes – 1657-1733. Husband of Scarlet (née Marshall); father of Hazel.

Scarlet Sykes (née Marshall) – 1670-1719. Daughter of Slade and Daisy Marshall; wife of John Sykes; mother of Hazel.

Oswin Priestly – 1690-1741. Husband of Hazel (née Sykes); father of Adam, William and Nara; grandfather of Kate Swithenbank.

Hazel Priestly (née Sykes) – 1695. Daughter of John and Scarlet; wife of Oswin; mother of Adam, William and Nara; grandmother of Kate Swithenbank.

Adam Priestly – 1720. Worker at Cappleman Farm; son of Oswin and Hazel; brother of William and Nara; Kate Swithenbank's uncle.

William Priestly – 1724. Worker at Cappleman Farm; son

of Oswin and hazel; brother of Adam and Nara; Kate Swithenbank's uncle.

Nara Swithenbank (née Priestly) – May 18, 1733. Daughter of Oswin and Hazel; sister of Adam and William Priestly; wife of Alder Swithenbank; mother of Kate.

Alder Swithenbank – April 2, 1703. Labourer at Cappleman Farm; son of William and Heather; husband of Nara Priestly, later of Meadow Reid; father of Kate Swithenbank; in his youth, fathered at least eight other children; friend of Tozer Robinson.

Catherine (Kate) Swithenbank – March 29, 1749. Principal character of this story; daughter of Alder and Nara Swithenbank; granddaughter of Hazel Priestly; pupil at the Lookout.

Sally Priestly (née Burton) – 1728. Wife of William Priestly.

Mel Priestly (née Tate) – 1739. Wife of Adam Priestly; mother of Dora.

Dora Priestly – 1764. Daughter of Adam and Mel Priestly.

Fleshers

Benjamin Flesher – 1663-1744. Owner of Cappleman Farm at the commencement of this story. Son of Timothy Flesher; husband of Emmeline Flesher (née Carrol); father of Hugh.

Emmeline Flesher (née Carrol) – 1678-December 1757. Wife of Benjamin; mother of Hugh.

Hugh Flesher – 1701. Owner of Cappleman Farm; son of Benjamin and Emmeline; father of Louise and Henry.

Amelia Flesher (née Barker) – 1713. Wife of Hugh; mother of Louise and Henry.

Louise Flesher – 1737. Daughter of Hugh and Amelia; sister of Henry.

Henry Flesher – 1739. Son of Hugh and Amelia; brother of Louise.

Swifts

Lucinda Swift – 1665-1742. Matriarch; wife of Lawrence Swift; mother of Bernard; rival to Martha Wheatley.

Lawrence Swift – 1658-1726. Husband of Lucinda; father of Bernard.

Martha Wheatley – 1679-1742. Matriarch; wife of Laurence Wheatley; mother of Florence Swift; rival to Lucinda Swift.

Laurence Wheatley – 1673-1732. Husband of Martha Wheatley; father of Florence Swift.

Bernard Swift – 1697-1762. In service to the Fleshers at Cappleman Farm; son of Lucinda and Lawrence; husband of Florence (née Wheatley); father of Richard.

Florence Swift (née Wheatley) – 1705. In service to the Fleshers at Cappleman Farm; daughter of Martha and Laurence; wife of Bernard; mother of Richard.

Richard Swift – 1724. In service to the Fleshers at Cappleman Farm; son of Bernard and Florence; husband of Emma; mother of Amy and Beatrice.

Emma Swift (née Barnaby) – 1721. In service to the Fleshers at Cappleman Farm; wife of Richard Swift; mother of Amy and Beatrice.

Amy Swift – 1744. Daughter of Richard and Emma; sister of Beatrice.

Beatrice Swift – 1746. Daughter of Richard and Emma; sister of Amy.

Buckleys

Douglas Buckley – 1685-1740. In service to the Fleshers at Cappleman Farm; husband of Maria; father of Elys and Sally.

Maria Buckley (née Cox) – 1694-1756. In service to the Fleshers at Cappleman Farm; wife of Douglas; mother of Elys and Sally.

Elys Buckley – 1716. In service to the Fleshers at Cappleman Farm; son of Douglas and Maria; husband of Alicia (née Hebden); father of Walter and Grace; sister of Sally.

Alicia Buckley (née Hebden) – 1719. In service to the Fleshers at Cappleman Farm; wife of Elys; mother of Walter and Grace.

Sally Buckley – 1718. In service to the Fleshers at Cappleman Farm; daughter of Douglas and Maria; sister of Elys.

Walter Buckley – June, 1745. Son of Elys and Alicia; brother of Grace.

Grace Buckley (later, Grace Flathers) – May, 1747. Daughter of Elys and Alicia; sister of Walter; later, wife of Alan Flathers.

Alan Flathers – 1741. Blacksmith on Cappleman Farm; later, husband of Grace Buckley.

Reids

Sigbert Reid – 1703. Playwright living in Egton near Cappleman Farm; libertine; common law husband of Persephone; father of Meadow.

Persephone Reid (née Sergeant) – 1715. Libertine; common law wife of Sigbert; mother of Meadow.

Meadow Reid (later, Meadow Swithenbank) – February 2, 1737. Daughter of Sigbert and Persephone; later, wife of Alder Swithenbank.

Robinsons

Tozer Robinson – 1705-1779. A labourer on Cappleman Farm; husband of Apple Robinson (née Barrow); father of Willow, Hazel; Cedar and Holly; grandfather of "Young" Tozer Kirby, Margery Kirby and Tudor Green; friend of Alder Swithenbank.

Apple Robinson (née Barrow) – 1708; daughter of Harry and Fiona Barrow; wife of Tozer Robinson; mother of Willow, Hazel, Cedar and Holly; grandmother of "Young" Tozer Kirby, Margery Kirby and Tudor Green.

Willow Kirby (née Robinson) – 1725. Eldest child of Tozer and Apple Robinson; sister of Hazel, Cedar and Holly; mother of "Young" Tozer Kirby and Margery Kirby; wife of Revd James Kirby; aunt of Oak Green.

James Kirby, Revd – 1720. Parson of Roxby, 1745-1764; son of Philip and Margery; brother of Andrew; husband of Willow née Robinson; father of "Young Tozer" and Margery; son-in-law of Tozer and Apple Robinson.

Tozer Kirby ("Young" Tozer) – 1752. Son of Revd James Kirby and Willow Kirby (née Robinson); brother of Margery Kirby; grandson of Tozer and Apple Robinson.

Margery Kirby – 1754. Daughter of Revd James Kirby and Willow Kirby (née Robinson); sister of "Young" Tozer; granddaughter of Tozer and Apple Robinson.

Hazel Green (née Robinson) – 1729. Daughter of Tozer and Apple Robinson; sister of Willow, Cedar and Holly; mother of Oak Green; wife of Tudor Green

Tudor Green – 1719. Husband of Hazel Green (née Robinson); father of Oak Green; son-in-law of Tozer and Apple Robinson.

Oak Green – 1756. Son of Tudor Green and Hazel Green (née Robinson); grandson of Tozer and Apple Robinson.

Cedar Robinson – 1731. Worker on Cappleman Farm; son of Tozer and Apple Robinson; brother of Willow, Hazel and Holly; uncle of "Young Tozer" and Margery Kirby, and of Oak Green.

Holly Robinson – 1736. Youngest daughter of Tozer and Apple Robinson; sister of Willow, Cedar and Hazel; aunt of "Young Tozer" and Margery Kirby, and of Oak Green.

Parsons

Hubert Cromwell – 1699. Son of Samuel and Faith Cromwell; parson of Roxby, 1726-1744; partner of Revd Egbert Trommel.

James Kirby – 1720. Parson of Roxby, 1745-1764; son of Philip and Margery; brother of Andrew; husband of Willow (née Robinson); father of "Young Tozer" and Margery; son-in-law of Tozer and Apple Robinson.

Cornelius East – September 12, 1700. Parson of Glaisdale.

Egbert Trommel – 1658-1751. Parson of Easington, 1722-1751. Partner of Revd Hubert Cromwell.

Robert Forest – 1727. Parson of Easington from 1752.

Medical Doctors

William Clover – 1679-1741. Medical practitioner based in Easington, 1708-1741; husband of Miriam; friend of Oswin and Hazel Priestly.

Neil Levinson – 1710. Medical practitioner at Easington from 1741.

Natty Miller's family

Natty Miller – 1710. Mother of Nicholas and Buffy (Pond Girl), with whom she shares the warrener's cottage.

Nicholas Miller – 1726. Warrener at Cappleman Farm; son of Natty; brother of Buffy (Pond Girl)

Buffy Miller (Pond Girl) – March 7, 1742. Daughter of Natty; sister of Nicholas; courted by Brendan Telford and Rendall Storm.

Brownie – Natty's cat

Exleys

Miriam Exley – 1725. Lives at Cappleman Farm; mother of John, Amos and Peter.

John Exley – 1746. Labourer at Cappleman Farm; son of Miriam; brother of Amos and Peter.

Amos Exley – 1748. Labourer at Cappleman Farm; son of Miriam; brother of John and Peter.

Peter Exley – 1750. Labourer at Cappleman Farm; son of Miriam; brother of John and Amos.

Others

Hugo Ash – 1709. Miller at Egton watermill; son of Walter and Rosa; brother of Cristina.

Jack Morris – 1713. Landlord at the Red Lion, Glaisdale.

THE LOOKOUT STAFF

Headmaster
Jacob Crowan

Headmaster's Personal Assistant
Knox Quinton

Headmistress
Stella Tenley

Headmistress's Personal Assistant
Ruth Marlowe

Servants to the upper staff
Milton York
Janet Illif

Housemistresses
Eve Miller
Lettice Shelley
Eleanor Rodman
Denise Trent (later Denise Nisbet)

Porter
Major Alfred Bentley

Doctor
Hollis Wayland

Librarian
Janet Illif

Teaching Staff
Literature
Egerton (Ben) Badger

Mathematics
Terrel Nisbet

Harpsichord and Organ
Rider Browning
Felix Hadleigh

Singing
Golda Dryden

Harp
Clara Sutherland

Music and Movement (Deportment)
Isabella and Edgar Breedon

Fashion/Presentation
Etta Lynn

French
Sylvie Ardoin

Latin
Litton Hornsby

Elocution
Hastings Rayden

Basic Reading
Pearl Huxley

Geography
Pearl Huxley

Needlepoint
Annabelle Trollope

Servants to the Tutors
Oswald and Portia Packard

Domestic Staff and others

Dressmakers/Seamstresses
Mercy Brereton
Ada Davis

Drivers
Kipp Nibley
Stanley Tanner

Stable Boy
Nolly Arkwright

Horses
Demeter, Athena, Nemesis, Aphrodite, Artemis, Hera

Maids to the Girls
Mary Acker
Sarah Alston
Nellie Brent
Molly Colby
Ethel Coombs
Winnie Warwick (later Winnie Stafford)
Cady Weston

Cleaning Staff
Tillie Haley
Jewel Springfield
Mabel Stanton
Birdie Wade
Margaret York

Kitchen Staff
Alvina Rowland (cook)
Rodney Rowland
Annie Alby
Edie Ashton
Maisie Blythe
Opal Clayden
Kim Kelsey

Dairy Maids
Leafy Crosthwaite
Genevieve (Neva) Hutton
Fanny Kirkbride
Florence (Flossy) Ousby (married to Zachariah)
Delia Tweddle
Susannah (Sukey) Westmoreland (married to Theodore)

Footmen
Newton (Newt) Fallowfield
Eugene (Gene) Fenton
Zachariah (Rye) Ousby (married to Florence)
Theodore (Theo) Westmoreland (married to Susannah)

Laundry Staff
Mary and Michael Stafford
Beryl Stafford
Crispin Stafford
Barbara Stafford
Sylvia Stafford

Carpenters
Chad Sandon
Ferret Colborn
Tom Thorne

Gardeners
Solly Birtwistle
Rabbit Shipley
Ned Silden (married to Pixie)

Farmers
Speck Beckwith
John Eldenshaw
Tranter Tickle (married to Teresa)

Blacksmith
Alan Blake (married to Chastity)

Brewers
Dennis McCallum (Head Brewer)
David Fielding
Donald Fitzroy
Douglas Trivet
Richard (Dick) Brent
Franklyn (Daniel) Egan

Soil Boys
Lucas Dent
Edwin Elvet
Jude Farlam
Slade Stone

Gatehouse
Jack Archer (married to Tessa)

Other Residents
Chastity Blake (married to Alan)
Bartholomew (Barney) Blake (son of Alan and Chastity)
Pixie Silden (married to Ned)
Tessa Archer (married to Jack)
Teresa Tickle (married to Tranter)
Bastard (Speck Beckwith's dog)
Tilly (Annabelle Trollope's cat)

KING'S PLACE AND ASSOCIATES

Birth years are given.

Edgar Foxley – 1720. Manager of several London brothels; business partner of Jacob Crowan and Margaret Siddon.

Margaret Siddon – 1707. Brothel madam; partner of Ivor Bentham; later, business partner of Edgar Foxley.

Holly Graham – 1740. Prostitute; ex-student at the Lookout.

Kim Hurley – 1741. Prostitute; ex-student at the Lookout.

Valentine Parker-Sinden, Sir, Earl Horsforth – 1706. Nobleman and landowner; patron of the King's Place brothels; colleague of Edgar Foxley.

Anthony McNeil – 1731. In the employ of Sir Valentine Parker-Sinden.

Oliver Lee – 1732. In the employ of Sir Valentine Parker-Sinden.

Christopher Scott – 1724. In the employ of Sir Valentine Parker-Sinden.

Thomas Field – 1725. In the employ of Edgar Foxley.

Harry Clarke – 1730. In the employ of Edgar Foxley.

Saul Butcher – 1728. In the employ of Edgar Foxley.

William Jones – 1731. In the employ of Edgar Foxley.

Marcus Lewis – 1727. In the employ of Edgar Foxley.

LIST OF ALL THE CHARACTERS
IN ALPHABETICAL ORDER
OF LAST NAMES

The year of birth is given in each case to enable identification
of parentage or peer groups.
The year of death is given in some instances where the
disclosure does not undermine the unfolding of the story.

The list commences with characters whose surnames
do not appear in the text.

?, Agnes – c. 1700. Companion or maid to Margaret Strapp's mother

?, Albert – c. 1740. A highwayman

?, Angus – 1716-1764. A shepherd in Cumbria and Yorkshire, killed in an accident.

?, Anna – 1734. Lover of William Jones.

?, Ben – 1755. A homeless boy of unknown origin; friend of Fuzzy Craw.

?, Bernie – 1719. Member of the kitchen staff at Horsforth Castle.

?, Celia – 1746. A friend of Fuzzy Craw in the York workhouse.

?, Charlotte – 1705. Daughter of Alder Swithenbank's employer in Helmsley; for one event only, Alder Swithenbank's lover.

?, Ciara – 1730. An alehouse worker in Kilbehenny, Ireland; first lover of Alexander Regan.

?, Clemmo – 1699. Son of Samuel Cromwell's driver; friend of the young Hubert Cromwell.

?, Drew – 1732. Manservant to Sir Valentine Parker-Sinden, Earl Horsforth.

?, Elizabeth – 1711. A Grimsby hotel maid; lover of Peter

753

Tilson.

?, Elsa – 1713. A Grimsby hotel maid; lover of Peter Tilson.

?, Fox – 1722. Servant of Sir Arthur Holywell.

?, Hilda – 1734. Nurse to the children of Valentine and Angela Parker-Sinden at Horsforth Castle.

?, Janet – 1720. Midwife, present at the birth of Francis Regan in the White Bull, Ribchester.

?, Jess (née Blythe) – 1728. Daughter of Maisie Blythe

?, John – 1725. Driver to Sigbert and Persephone Reid.

?, Lilly – 1709. A Grimsby hotel maid; lover of Peter Tilson.

?, Lisa – 1746. Maid at Horsforth Castle.

?, Louise – 1742-1761. Daughter of Baildon basket makers; enforced mistress of Sir Valentine Parker-Sinden, Earl Horsforth. Eventually killed for his entertainment.

?, Margaret – 1708. A Grimsby hotel maid; lover of Peter Tilson.

?, Maria – 1694. A mysterious figure of uncertain origin – a blind woman. Claims to have been married to a clergyman and to have taken Viktor Distler as a lover; poisoner.

?, Michael – 1736. Labourer on Alexander Regan's pig farm.

?, Nick – c.1740. A highwayman

?, Patrick – 1734. Labourer on Alexander Regan's pig farm.

?, Prim – 1733. Maid to the Revd Dr Lemuel and Margaret Strapp.

?, Roz – 1729. A Whitby prostitute; acquaintance of Hugo Ash.

?, Sarah – 1712. A Grimsby hotel maid; lover of Peter Tilson.

?, Tessa – 1711. A Grimsby hotel maid; lover of Peter Tilson.

?, Timon – 1748. A friend of Fuzzy Craw in the York workhouse.

?, Tom – 1752. A chorister at Canterbury Cathedral; organ pumper.

?, Violet – 1738. Giles Ottershaw's nurse.

Acker, Mary – 1717. Maid to the girls at the Lookout.

Ainsworth, Stephen – 1707. A Cumbrian farmer.

Alby, Annie – 1727. Member of the Lookout kitchen staff.

Alford, Stephen – 1710. Husband of Marina Alford (née Beckwith).

Alford, Marina (née Beckwith) – 1715. Daughter of Eric and Linda Beckwith; sister of Mary, Hilda and Speck; wife of Stephen Alford.

Alston, Sarah – February 11, 1737. Maid to the girls at the Lookout; partner of Cady Weston.

Archer, Jack – 1695. Gatekeeper at the Lookout; husband of Tessa.

Archer, Tessa – 1681. Wife of Jack Archer.

Ardoin, Sylvie – 1730. French tutor at the Lookout; long-term lover of Clara Sutherland.

Arkwright, Nolly – 1742. Stable boy at the Lookout; lover of Pamela Heron.

Ash, Walter – 1663-1729. Miller at Egton watermill; husband of Rosa; father of Hugo and Cristina.

Ash, Rosa – 1690-1726. Wife of Walter Ash; mother of Hugo and Cristina.

Ash, Hugo – 1709. Miller at Egton watermill; son of Walter and Rosa; brother of Cristina.

Ash, Cristina (later Cristina Ward) – 1714. Daughter of Walter and Rosa; sister of Hugo; wife of David Ward.

Ashton, Edie – 1740. Member of the Lookout kitchen staff.

Badger, Egerton (Ben) – 1721. Literature tutor at the Lookout.

Barge, Mrs – 1692. Jacob Crowan's landlady in Maiden Lane, London.

Barrow, Robert – 1656-1709. Brother of Harry.

Barrow, Harry – 1658-1730. Labourer on Cappleman Farm; brother of Robert; later, husband of Fiona Lemon; father of Apple Barrow (later Apple Robinson).

Barrow, Fiona (née Lemon) – 1670-1736. Wife of Vincent Lemon, then of Harry Barrow; mother of Apple Barrow (later Apple Robinson).

Barrow, Apple (later Apple Robinson) – 1708; daughter of Harry and Fiona Barrow; wife of Tozer Robinson; mother of Willow, Hazel, Cedar and Holly; grandmother of "Young" Tozer Kirby, Margery Kirby and Tudor Green.

Beckett, Aoife (later Aoife Murphy) – 1735. Alehouse worker in Dublin; friend of Colleen O'Farrell; lover of Neil Murphy – later his wife.

Beckwith, Eric – 1682-1744. Shepherd; husband of Linda; father of Mary, Hilda, Marina and Speck.

Beckwith, Linda – 1692-1742. Wife of Eric Beckwith; mother of Mary, Hilda, Marina and Speck.

Beckwith, Mary (later Mary Jones) – 1710. Daughter of Eric and Linda Beckwith; sister of Hilda, Marina and Speck; wife of Albert Jones.

Beckwith, Hilda (later Hilda Miller) – 1712. Daughter of Eric and Linda Beckwith; sister of Mary, Marina and Speck; wife of Samuel Miller.

Beckwith, Marina (later Marina Alford) – 1715. Daughter of Eric and Linda Beckwith; sister of Mary, Hilda and Speck; wife of Stephen Alford.

Beckwith, Speck – July 7, 1719. Farmer at the Lookout; son of Eric and Linda; brother of Mary, Hilda and Marina.

Beckwith, Jenny (née Clifton) – 1720-April 4, 1741. Wife of Speck Beckwith.

Bennett, John – 1715. Landlord of the White Bull, Ribchester; husband of Sarah; employer and friend of Alexander Regan and Helen Shaw.

Bennett, Sarah – 1717. Landlady of the White Bull, Ribchester; wife of John; friend of Alexander Regan and Helen Shaw.

Bentham, Ivor – 1695-1745. Brothel manager; partner of Margaret Siddon.

Bentley, Alfred (Major) – October 20, 1711. Porter at the Lookout.

Berridge, Tom – 1664. Gardener in Helmsley; colleague of Alder Swithenbank.

Bevington, Sura – December 13, 1748. Pupil at the Lookout.

Birtwistle, Solly – 1737. Gardener at the Lookout.

Black, Luke – 1728. A London actor.

Blackburne, Lancelot – 1658-1743. Pirate; Bishop of Exeter – later Archbishop of York; husband of Catherine Blackburne (née Talbot); friend of Samuel and Hubert Cromwell.

Blackburne, Catherine (née Talbot) – 1646-1726. Wife of Lancelot Blackburne.

Blackford, Mrs Nancy – 1735. Lover of Samuel Trillo.

Blackwood, Dearbhla – July 16, 1743. Pupil at the Lookout.

Blake, Alan – 1719. Blacksmith at the Lookout; husband of Chastity; father of Bartholomew.

Blake, Chastity – 1722. Wife of Alan; mother of Bartholomew (Barney).

Blake, Bartholomew (Barney) – March 10, 1752. Son of Alan and Chastity Blake.

Blake, Mary (Polly) – 1722. A Covent Garden prostitute.

Blythe, Maisie – 1706. Member of the Lookout kitchen staff, wife of David (deceased); mother of Jess; grandmother of Ronald.

Boucher d'Argis, Antoine-Gaspard – 1708-1791. Celebrated French lawyer.

Boyle, Robert – 1627-1691. Renowned scientist; brother of Katherine Jones.

Boyle, Katherine Jones, Lady Ranelagh – 1615-1691. Scientist; sister of Robert Boyle.

Breedon, Edgar – 1699. Dancing tutor at the Lookout; husband of Isabella.

Breedon, Isabella – 1702. Dancing tutor at the Lookout; wife of Edgar.

Brent, Nellie – 1730. Maid to the girls at the Lookout; no relation to Richard Brent.

Brent, Richard (Dick) – 1726. Brewer at the Lookout; no relation to Nellie Brent.

Brereton, Mercy – 1714. Seamstress at the Lookout.

Broadbent, Ada – 1701. Recipient of Alder Swithenbank's virginity.

Bromfield, Alison (Ali) – 1747. Pupil at the Lookout.

Brough, Revd Eric – 1725. Parson of Ellerby.

Browning, Rider – 1727. Keyboard tutor at the Lookout; lover of Orla Stapleton.

Buckley, Douglas – 1685-1740. In service to the Fleshers at Cappleman Farm; husband of Maria; father of Elys and Sally.

Buckley, Maria (née Cox) – 1694-1756. In service to the Fleshers at Cappleman Farm; wife of Douglas; mother of Elys and Sally.

Buckley, Elys – 1716. In service to the Fleshers at Cappleman Farm; son of Douglas and Maria; husband of Alicia (née Hebden); father of Walter and Grace; sister of Sally.

Buckley, Alicia (née Hebden) – 1719. In service to the Fleshers at Cappleman Farm; wife of Elys; mother of Walter and Grace.

Buckley, Sally – 1718. In service to the Fleshers at Cappleman Farm; daughter of Douglas and Maria; sister of Elys.

Buckley, Walter – June, 1745. Son of Elys and Alicia; brother of Grace.

Buckley, Grace (later, Grace Flathers) – May, 1747. Daughter of Elys and Alicia; sister of Walter; later, wife of Alan Flathers.

Butcher, Saul – 1728. In the employ of Edgar Foxley; rapist; murderer.

Byrne, Father Francis – 1712. Priest in Christ Church, Bandon, Ireland.

Cappleman, Geoffrey – 1563-1631. One-time owner of Cappleman Farm; father of Margaret.

Cappleman, Margaret – 1598-1667. Daughter of Geoffrey Cappleman; wife of William Flesher.

Carnaby, Aggie – 1747. Pupil at the Lookout.

Carr, John – 1723-1807. Renowned architect.

Clarke, Sir Charles – 1699. Architect; husband of Lady Belinda Clarke; father of James Clarke; grandfather of Edward Charles Clarke and Rachael Belinda Clarke.

Clarke, Lady Belinda Clarke – 1701. Wife of Sir Charles Clarke; mother of James Clarke; grandmother of Edward Charles Clarke and Rachael Belinda Clarke.

Clarke, James – February 1739. Son of Sir Charles and Lady Belinda Clarke; husband of Anna Clarke; lover of Orla Stapleton.

Clarke, Anna – 1740. Wife of James Clarke.

Clarke, Orla (née Stapleton) – March 13, 1745. Daughter of Martha Stapleton; lover of Rider Browning; pupil at the Lookout.

Clarke, Edward Charles – 1763. Son of James and Orla Clarke (née Stapleton).

Clarke, Rachael Belinda – 1765. Daughter of James and Orla Clarke (née Stapleton).

Clarke, Harry – 1730. In the employ of Edgar Foxley; rapist; murderer; no relation to the other Clarkes in this story.

Clayden, Opal – 1729. Member of the Lookout kitchen staff.

Clifton, Jenny (later Jenny Beckwith) – 1720-April 4th, 1741. Wife of Speck Beckwith.

Clover, William – 1679-1741. Medical practitioner based in Easington, 1708-1741; husband of Miriam; friend of Oswin and Hazel Priestly.

Clover, Miriam – 1679. Wife of Dr William Clover.

Colborn, Ferret – 1720. Carpenter/handyman at the Lookout.

Colby, Molly – 1736. Maid to the girls at the Lookout.

Collingwood, Sara – 1747. Pupil at the Lookout.

Coombs, Ethel – 1723. Maid to the girls at the Lookout.

Craw, Fuzzy – September 28, 1747. Pupil at the Lookout; close friend of Kate Swithenbank.

Creed, Ffion – October 1749. Pupil at the Lookout.

Cromwell, Samuel – 1657-1727. Womaniser; father of Hubert Cromwell; husband of Faith; probable lover of Eliza Melbury.

Cromwell, Faith – 1668. Wife of Samuel; mother of Hubert.

Cromwell, Revd Hubert Cromwell – 1699. Son of Samuel and Faith Cromwell; parson of Roxby, 1726-1744; partner of Revd Egbert Trommel.

Cross, Simeon – 1674-1711. Husband of Ava Cross. Father of Janet Illif.

Cross, Ava – 1676. Mother of Janet Illif.

Cross, John – 1698. Son of Simeon and Ava Cross; brother of Janet Illif.

Cross, Anne – 1700. Daughter of Simeon and Ava Cross; sister of Janet Illif.

Cross, Martha – 1702. Daughter of Simeon and Ava Cross; sister of Janet Illif.

Cross, Janet (later Janet Illif) – 1704. Servant to the higher staff at the Lookout; librarian at the Lookout; daughter of Simeon and Ava Cross; wife of Thomas Illif; friend of John Eldenshaw.

Cross, David – 1709. Youngest son of Simeon and Ava Cross; brother of Janet Illif.

Crosthwaite, Effie – 1701. An early lover of Alder Swithenbank.

Crosthwaite, Leafy – 1731. Dairymaid at the Lookout.

Crowan, William – 1688. A London cobbler; husband of Ruby, then Alison; father of Jacob.

Crowan, Ruby – 1699. First wife of William; mother of Jacob.

Crowan, Alison – 1707. Prostitute; second wife of William; stepmother of Jacob.

Crowan, Jacob – April 20, 1729. Son of William and Ruby; brothel manager; partner of Edgar Foxley; headmaster of the Lookout.

Curwen, Gail – 1748. Pupil at the Lookout.

Dalton, Brandy – September 1749. Pupil at the Lookout.

Dashford, Abel – 1719. A London businessman encountered by Jacob Crowan on a stagecoach journey.

Davis, Ada – 1717. Seamstress at the Lookout.

Delisle, Sébastien – 1722. Proprietor of a café, Rue du Faubourg St. Antoine, Paris.

Dent, Lucas – 1746. Soil boy at the Lookout.

Dessin, Pierre (Quillacq) – 1726-1793. Founder, owner and landlord of the Hotel d'Angleterre (Hotel Dessin), Calais.

Distler, Viktor – 1648-1715. Scientist; colleague of Robert Boyle; lover of Maria ? (last name unknown).

Dixon, Harriet – 1745. Pupil at the Lookout.

Dodds, Hilda – 1750. Pupil at the Lookout.

Donald, Meg – 1748. Pupil at the Lookout.

Dooley, Mary – c. 1730. A Dublin woman known to Liam Doyle.

Dore, Peter – 1708. Manager of Borrowby Farm. The barn and field is used for wedding receptions and festivals.

Doyle, Liam – 1729. A lifter and dray driver for the Anchor Brewery in Dublin; friend of Alexander Regan.

Dryden, Golda – 1729. Singing tutor at the Lookout.

Dyson, Penny – 1742. Ex-pupil at the Lookout. One of the few people able to see the boys in the tower.

East, Revd Cornelius East – September 12, 1700. Parson of Glaisdale.

Egan, Franklyn (Daniel) – 1723. Brewer at the Lookout.

Eldenshaw, Gilbert – 1690-1751. Driver to Christopher Howerd, Earl Carham; husband of Maggie Eldenshaw.

Eldenshaw, Maggie – 1695-1732. Wife of Gilbert Eldenshaw; mistress of Christopher Howerd, Earl Carham; mother of John Eldenshaw.

Eldenshaw, John – 1716. Farmer at the Lookout; illegitimate son of Christopher Howerd (Earl Carham) and Maggie Eldenshaw; friend of Janet Illif.

Elliot, Betty – 1745. Pupil at the Lookout. Ex-lover of Jude Farlam.

Elvet, Edwin – 1750. Soil boy at the Lookout.

Exley, Miriam – 1725. Lives at Cappleman Farm; mother of

John, Amos and Peter.

Exley, John – 1746. Labourer at Cappleman Farm; son of Miriam; brother of Amos and Peter.

Exley, Amos – 1748. Labourer at Cappleman Farm; son of Miriam; brother of John and Peter.

Exley, Peter – 1750. Labourer at Cappleman Farm; son of Miriam; brother of John and Amos.

Exmouth, Revd Peter – c. 1690. Retired clergyman, late of Littlebeck – conducts occasional services at the Lookout.

Fallowfield, Newton (Newt) – 1736. Footman at the Lookout.

Farlam, Jude – 1745. Soil boy at the Lookout. Ex-lover of Betty Elliot.

Fellowes, Sybil – 1685. Resident of Glaisdale; friend of Betty Oxby.

Fenton, Eugene (Gene) – 1734. Footman at the Lookout.

Fenwick, Midge – 1746. Pupil at the Lookout.

Field, Thomas – 1725. In the employ of Edgar Foxley; murderer.

Fielding, David – 1728. Brewer at the Lookout.

Fielding, Elizabeth – ?-1774. Wife of Sir John Fielding.

Fielding, Sir John – 1721-1780. Magistrate – the renowned "Blind Beak of Bow Street"; husband of Elizabeth.

Fisher, Kitty – 1741-1767. A celebrated Covent Garden prostitute, the subject of several paintings by Sir Joshua Reynolds, Nathaniel Hone, Francis Cotes, etc.

Fitzroy, Donald – 1719. Brewer at the Lookout.

Flathers, Stephen – 1710. Blacksmith on Cappleman Farm; father of Alan.

Flathers, Alan – 1741. Blacksmith on Cappleman Farm; son of Stephen; later, husband of Grace Buckley.

Flathers, Grace (née Buckley) – May, 1747. Daughter of Elys and Alicia; sister of Walter; later, wife of Alan Flathers.

Flesher, William – 1584-1650. Inheritor of Cappleman Farm; son-in-law of Geoffrey Cappleman; husband of Margaret Cappleman; father of Timothy Flesher.

Flesher, Timothy – 1628-1699. Owner of Cappleman Farm; son of William Flesher and Margaret Cappleman; father of Benjamin.

Flesher, Benjamin – 1663-1744. Owner of Cappleman Farm at the commencement of this story. Son of Timothy Flesher; husband of Emmeline Flesher (née Carrol); father of Hugh.

Flesher, Emmeline (née Carrol) – 1678-December 1757. Wife of Benjamin; mother of Hugh.

Flesher, Hugh – 1701.Owner of Cappleman Farm; son of Benjamin and Emmeline; father of Louise and Henry.

Flesher, Amelia (née Barker) – 1713. Wife of Hugh; mother of Louise and Henry.

Flesher, Louise – 1737. Daughter of Hugh and Amelia; sister of Henry.

Flesher, Henry – 1739. Son of Hugh and Amelia; brother of Louise.

Forest, Revd Robert – 1727. Parson of Easington from 1752.

Foxley, Edgar – 1720. Manager of several London brothels; rapist; partner of Jacob Crowan and Margaret Siddon.

Gent, Thomas – 1693-1778. Celebrated Scarborough publisher.

Glass, Lilith – 1750. Pupil at the Lookout.

Graham, Holly – 1740. Prostitute. Ex-pupil at the Lookout.

Glanville, Drusilla – 1711. Lover of Charles Sutherland.

Gray, Tully – 1748. Pupil at the Lookout.

Green, Tudor – 1719. Husband of Hazel Green (née Robinson); father of Oak Green; son-in-law of Tozer and Apple Robinson.

Green, Hazel (née Robinson) – 1729. Daughter of Tozer and Apple Robinson; sister of Willow, Cedar and Holly; mother of Oak Green; wife of Tudor Green.

Green, Oak – 1756. Son of Tudor Green and Hazel Green (née Robinson); grandson of Tozer and Apple Robinson.

Hadleigh, Felix – 1723. Keyboard tutor at the Lookout.

Haley, Tillie – 1738. Member of the Lookout cleaning staff.

Hall, Nana – 1744. Pupil at the Lookout.

Harris, Revd David – 1742. Parson of Roxby from 1765.

Harrison, Paul – 1690-1763. Husband of Ellen; father of Leah and Miriam.

Harrison, Ellen – 1701. Wife of Paul; mother of Leah and Miriam.

Harrison, Leah – 1735. Daughter of Paul and Ellen; sister of Miriam.

Harrison, Miriam – 1736-1763. Daughter of Paul and Ellen; sister of Leah.

Hebden, Alicia (later Alicia Buckley) – 1719. In service to the Fleshers at Cappleman Farm; wife of Elys; mother of Walter and Grace.

Heron, Pamela (Pammy) – 1749. Pupil at the Lookout.

Holywell, Sir Arthur – 1697. Resident of Adwick le Street. Patron of Edgar Foxley; husband of Lady Dora Holywell.

Holywell, Lady Dora – 1700. Wife of Sir Arthur Holywell.

Horn, Cordelia – 1748. Pupil at the Lookout.

Hornsby, Litton – 1705. Latin tutor at the Lookout.

Howells, Carys – 1747. Pupil at the school at Aberystwyth.

Howells, Hollis William – January 22, 1766. Son of Carys Howells; twin brother of Nana Margaret Howells.

Howells, Nana Margaret – January 22, 1766. Daughter of Carys Howells; twin sister of Hollis William Howells.

Howerd, Christopher, Earl Carham – 1661-1733. A landowner in Northumberland; father of John Eldenshaw.

Hudson, Captain William – 1713. Captain of the sailing ship, *Hastings*.

Huntley, Veronica – 1746. Pupil at the Lookout.

Hurley, Kim – 1741. Prostitute. Ex-pupil at the Lookout.

Hurndall, Mercy – 1740. Nurse to Edward Charles Clarke and Rachael Belinda Clarke.

Hutton, Genevieve (Neva) – 1736. Dairymaid at the Lookout.

Huxley, Pearl – 1726. Tutor of basic reading and geography at the Lookout.

Illif, Thomas – 1656-1727. Undertaker in Whitehaven; husband of Janet Illif.

Illif, Janet (née Cross) – 1704. Servant to the higher staff at the Lookout; librarian at the Lookout; daughter of Simeon and Ava Cross; wife of Thomas Illif; friend of John Eldenshaw.

Illif, Thomas – 1656-1727. Husband of Janet Illif.

Jackson, Charles – 1706. A Justice of the Peace; friend of Sigbert Reid.

Jackson, Robert – 1706-1755. Nancy Sherborne's second husband

Jamieson, Shelagh – October 25, 1748. Pupil at the Lookout.

Joe (Old Joe) – c. 1665. Flamborough head lighthouse keeper

Jones Boyle, Katherine, Lady Ranelagh – 1615-1691. Scientist; sister of Robert Boyle.

Jones, Albert – 1712. Husband of Mary Jones (née Beckwith).

Jones, Mary (née Beckwith) – 1710. Daughter of Eric and Linda Beckwith; sister of Hilda, Marina and Speck; wife of Albert Jones.

Jones, William – 1731. In the employ of Edgar Foxley; lover of Anna ? (surname unknown).

Kelly, Bridget – 1736. Alehouse worker in the King's Arms, Bandon, Ireland.

Kelsey, Kim – 1734. Member of the Lookout kitchen staff.

Kirby, Philip – 1688. Husband of Margery; father of Revd James Kirby and Andrew; grandfather of "Young" Tozer and Margery.

Kirby, Margery – 1693. Wife of Philip; mother of Revd James Kirby and Andrew; grandmother of "Young" Tozer and Margery.

Kirby, Andrew – 1729. Son of Philip and Margery; younger brother of James; uncle of "Young" Tozer and Margery.

Kirby, Revd James – 1720. Parson of Roxby, 1745-1764; son of Philip and Margery; elder brother of Andrew; husband of Willow née Robinson; father of "Young Tozer" and Margery; son-in-law of Tozer and Apple Robinson.

Kirby, Willow (née Robinson) – 1725. Eldest child of Tozer and Apple Robinson; sister of Hazel, Cedar and Holly; mother of "Young" Tozer Kirby and Margery Kirby; wife of Revd James Kirby; aunt of Oak Green.

Kirby, "Young" Tozer – 1752. Son of Revd James Kirby and Willow Kirby (née Robinson); brother of Margery Kirby; grandson of Tozer and Apple Robinson.

Kirby, Margery – 1754. Daughter of Revd James Kirby and Willow Kirby (née Robinson); sister of "Young" Tozer; granddaughter of Tozer and Apple Robinson.

Kirkbride, Fanny – 1738. Dairymaid at the Lookout.

Langton, Norman – 1728. A labourer on a farm west of Easington; husband of Carol; father of Susan and Deborah.

Langton, Carol – 1734. Wife of Norman; mother of Susan and Deborah.

Langton, Susan – 1753. Daughter of Norman and Carol; sister of Deborah.

Langton, Deborah – 1756-60. Daughter of Norma and Carol; sister of Susan.

Last, Mary – 1749. Pupil at the Lookout.

Lea, Barbara – 1751. Pupil at the Lookout.

Lee, Oliver – 1732. In the employ of Sir Valentine Parker-Sinden, Earl Horsforth; murderer.

Leighton, Iris – 1751. Pupil at the Lookout.

Lemon, Vincent – 1667-1705. Husband of Fiona Lemon (later Fiona Barrow).

Lemon, Fiona (later Fiona Barrow) – 1670-1736. Wife of Vincent Lemon, then of Harry Barrow; mother of Apple Barrow (later Apple Robinson).

Leveritt, Alfred – 1707. Captain of a whaling vessel; chief constable of Whitby.

Levinson, William – 1647-1726. Medical practitioner;

Angus Levinson's father; Neil Levinson's grandfather.

Levinson, Angus – 1681-1745. Medical practitioner in Wigton; son of William Levinson; Neil Levinson's father.

Levinson, Neil – 1710. Medical practitioner at Easington from 1741.

Lewis, Marcus – 1727. In the employ of Edgar Foxley; murderer.

Lewis, Linda – 1735. Wife of Marcus; mother of Jack.

Lewis, Jack – 1759. Son of Marcus and Linda.

Little, Iris – 1745. Pupil at the Lookout.

Long Ron – 1701. Member of the taproom staff at Peter Tilson's Grimsby hotel; supposed
father of several children actually sired by Peter Tilson himself.

Lyle, Bridie – 1697. Landlady of a rooming house on Cappleman Farm. Alder Swithenbank and Rendall Storm both rented accommodation from her.

Lynn, Etta – 1717. Fashion/Presentation tutor at the Lookout.

Lynton, Martha – 1751. Pupil at the Lookout.

McBride, Vanessa – 1750. Pupil at the Lookout.

McCallum, Dennis – 1715. Head brewer at the Lookout; would-be lover of Chastity Blake.

McNeil, Anthony – 1731. In the employ of Sir Valentine Parker-Sinden, Earl Horsforth; murderer.

Marlowe, Ruth (later, Ruth Rayden) – 1727. Assistant to Stella Tenley at the Lookout; later, wife of Hastings Rayden.

Marshall, Slade – 1636-1701. Husband of Daisy Marshall (née White); father of Scarlet.

Marshall, Daisy (née White) – 1641-1712. Daughter of James and Anne White; wife of Slade Marshall; mother of Scarlet.

Maxwell, Yvette – 1746. Pupil at the Lookout.

Melbury, Eliza – 1690. Tutor of Hubert Cromwell; probable lover of Samuel Cromwell.

Merrick, Eleanor – 1740. Prostitute; ex-pupil at the Lookout.

Miller, Eve – 1732. Housemistress at the Lookout.

Miller, Samuel – 1700. Husband of Hilda Miller (née Beckwith).

Miller, Hilda (née Beckwith) – 1712. Daughter of Eric and Linda Beckwith; sister of Mary, Marina and Speck; wife of Samuel Miller.

Miller, Natty – 1710. Mother of Nicholas and Buffy (Pond Girl), with whom she shares the warrener's cottage.

Miller, Nicholas – 1726. Warrener at Cappleman Farm; son of Natty; brother of Buffy (Pond Girl)

Miller, Buffy (Pond Girl) – early March, 1742. Daughter of Natty; sister of Nicholas; courted by Brendan Telford and Rendall Storm.

Morfitt, Revd John – ?-1782. Rector of St. John's Church, Scarborough.

Morfitt Junior, John – 1757-1809. Son of Revd John Morfitt.

Morris, Jack – 1713. Landlord at the Red Lion, Glaisdale.

Mortimer, Peter – 1735. Organ builder; son of Peter Mortimer; nephew of Juno Sutherland; cousin, and lover, of Clara Sutherland.

Mortimer, Vincent – 1710. A London violin maker; Juno Sutherland's elder brother; father of Peter Mortimer; uncle of Clara Sutherland.

Mulgrave, Revd Arthur – 1701. Retired clergyman – conducts occasional services at the Lookout.

Murphy, Brian – 1707. Owner and manager of several Dublin alehouses; father of Neil; employer of Alexander Regan, Colleen O'Farrell and Aoife Beckett.

Murphy, Neil – 1731. Son of Brian Murphy; lover of Aoife Beckett – later her husband.

Murphy, Aoife (née Beckett) – 1735. Alehouse worker in Dublin; friend of Colleen O'Farrell; lover of Neil Murphy – later his wife.

Nares, James – 1715-1783. Organist of York Minster; friend of Revd James Kirby.

Nares, Jane (née Pease) – ?-?. Wife of James Nares.

Newce, Archibald – 1697. Landlord of the Kings Arms, Bandon, Ireland; husband of Mary.

Newce, Mary – 1699. Wife of Archibald.

Nibley, Kipp – 1725. Driver at the Lookout.

Nile, Muffy – 1751. Pupil at the Lookout; one time lover of Jude Farlam.

Nisbet, Terrel – 1730. Mathematics tutor at the Lookout.

Nisbet, Denise (née Trent) – 1734. Housemistress at the Lookout; wife of Terrel Nisbet; mother of Elizabeth Ruth Nisbet (Libby Ruthlet).

Nisbet, Elizabeth Ruth (Libby Ruthlet) – May 9, 1762. Daughter of Terrel and Denise Nisbet.

Noon, John – 1709. Assistant cobbler to William Crowan; tutor of Jacob.

Norris, Revd Douglas – c. 1690. Retired clergyman – conducts occasional services at the Lookout.

Norris, Ian – 1724. Deputy Constable from Scarborough.

O'Farrell, Colleen (later Colleen Regan) – 1737. Staff member at the Unicorn alehouse, Dublin; later, wife of Alexander Regan.

O'Rourke, Fintan – 1717. A Dublin docker.

Ogilvie, Flora – November 19, 1746. Pupil at the Lookout.

Ottershaw, Revd Jerome – 1711. Rector of St. John's Church, Halifax; husband of Celia; father of Giles.

Ottershaw, Celia – 1720. Wife of Revd. Jerome Ottershaw; mother of Giles.

Ottershaw, Giles – May 10, 1762. Son of Revd Jerome and Cecilia Ottershaw.

Ousby, Florence (Flossie) – 1736. Dairymaid at the Lookout; wife of Zachariah (Rye) Ousby.

Ousby, Zachariah (Rye) – 1734. Footman at the Lookout; husband of Florence (Flossie) Ousby.

Oxby, Betty – 1674. Oldest resident of Glaisdale.

Packard, Oswald – 1721. Husband to Portia Packard. Tutors' servant at the Lookout.

Packard, Portia – 1726. Wife of Oswald Packard. Tutors' servant at the Lookout.

Parker, Thomas – 1724. A Yorkshire farmer; womaniser.

Parker-Sinden, Sir Valentine, Earl Horsforth – 1706. Nobleman and landowner; husband of Countess Angela Parker-Sinden; father of Philip, Jane and Sarah; patron of the King's Place brothels; colleague of Edgar Foxley; rapist; torturer; murderer.

Parker-Sinden, Countess Angela – 1735. Wife of Sir Valentine Parker-Sinden (Earl Horsforth); mother of Philip, Jane and Sarah.

Parker-Sinden, Philip – May, 1759. Son of Valentine and Angela; brother of Jane and Sarah.

Parker-Sinden, Jane – October, 1760. Daughter of Valentine and Angela; sister of Philip; twin sister of Sarah.

Parker-Sinden, Sarah – October, 1760. Daughter of Valentine and Angela; sister of Philip; twin sister of Jane.

Pebble, Jemima – 1724. Neil Levinson's maid; wife of Brendan; mother of eight children.

Pebble, Brendan – 1720. Husband of Jemima; father of eight children.

Penrose, Morwenna – 1746. Pupil at the school in Tavistock.

Pierson, Doctor ? – 1732. A medical practitioner in Cawood, near Selby, Yorkshire.

Pink, Bonnie – 1749. Pupil at the Lookout; lover of Nolly Arkwright.

Porter, Samuel – 1733-1810. Organist of Canterbury Cathedral, 1757-1803.

Priestly, Oswin – 1690-1741. Husband of Hazel (née Sykes); father of Adam, William and Nara; grandfather of Kate Swithenbank.

Priestly, Hazel (née Sykes) – 1695. Daughter of John and Scarlet; wife of Oswin; mother of Adam, William and Nara; grandmother of Kate Swithenbank.

Priestly, Adam – 1720. Worker at Cappleman Farm; son of Oswin and Hazel; brother of William and Nara; Kate Swithenbank's uncle.

Priestly, William – 1724. Worker at Cappleman Farm; son of Oswin and hazel; brother of Adam and Nara; Kate Swithenbank's uncle.

Priestly, Nara (later Nara Swithenbank) – May 18, 1733. Daughter of Oswin and Hazel; sister of Adam and William Priestly; later wife of Alder Swithenbank; mother of Kate.

Priestly, Sally (née Burton) – 1728. Wife of William Priestly.

Priestly, Mel (née Tate) – 1739. Wife of Adam Priestly; mother of Dora.

Priestly, Dora – 1764. Daughter of Adam and Mel Priestly.

Pringle, Anne (Bip) – 1749. Pupil at the Lookout; friend of Kate Swithenbank.

Quillacq, Pierre (Pierre Dessin) – 1726-1793. Founder, owner and landlord of the Hotel d'Angleterre (Hotel Dessin), Calais.

Quinton, Knox – December 25, 1718. Jacob Crowan's assistant at the Lookout; prizefighter; murderer.

Quinton, Silas – 1691-1727. Worker at the Whitechapel bell foundry; robber; uncle of Knox Quinton.

Ray, Gretchen – 1751. Pupil at the Lookout; lover of Jude Farlam.

Rayden, Hastings – 1707. Elocution teacher at the Lookout; later, husband of Ruth Marlow.

Rayden, Ruth (née Marlowe) – 1727. Assistant to Stella Tenley at the Lookout; later, wife of Hastings Rayden.

Redesdale, Elizabeth – 1746. Pupil at the Lookout.

Regan, Richard – 1708-? Missing. Irishman; drunk; womaniser; pig farmer; husband of Ellen; father of Alexander.

Regan, Ellen – 1712-1751. Wife of Richard; mother of Alexander.

Regan, Alexander – January 10, 1735. Irishman; pig farmer; alehouse worker; shepherd; son of Richard and Ellen; later, husband of Colleen O'Farrell, then Helen Shaw.

Regan, Colleen (née O'Farrell) – 1737. Staff member at the Unicorn alehouse, Dublin; later, first wife of Alexander Regan.

Regan, Helen (née Shaw) – 1736. Staff member at the White Bull Inn, Ribchester; Daughter of Isaac and Maureen Shaw; second wife of Alexander Regan.

Regan, Francis – May 18, 1761. Son of Alexander Regan and Helen Shaw.

Reid, Sigbert – 1703. Playwright living in Egton near Cappleman Farm; libertine; common law husband of Persephone; father of Meadow.

Reid, Persephone (née Sergeant) – 1715. Libertine; common law wife of Sigbert; mother of Meadow.

Reid, Meadow (later, Meadow Swithenbank) – February 2, 1737. Daughter of Sigbert and Persephone; later, wife of Alder Swithenbank.

Ridgley-Lewes, Bernard, Lord Aveland – 1711. A Lincolnshire landowner; patron of the King's Place brothels.

Ridley, Edie – 1746. Pupil at the Lookout.

Roberts, May – 1751. Pupil at the Lookout.

Robinson, Tozer – 1705-1779. A labourer on Cappleman Farm; husband of Apple Robinson (née Barrow); father of Willow, Hazel; Cedar and Holly; grandfather of "Young" Tozer Kirby, Margery Kirby and Tudor Green; friend of Alder Swithenbank.

Robinson, Apple (née Barrow) – 1708; daughter of Harry and Fiona Barrow; wife of Tozer Robinson; mother of Willow, Hazel, Cedar and Holly; grandmother of "Young" Tozer Kirby, Margery Kirby and Tudor Green.

Robinson, Willow (later Willow Kirby) – 1725. Eldest child of Tozer and Apple Robinson; sister of Hazel, Cedar and Holly; mother of "Young" Tozer Kirby and Margery Kirby; wife of Revd James Kirby; aunt of Oak Green.

Robinson, Hazel (later Hazel Green) – 1729. Daughter of Tozer and Apple Robinson; sister of Willow, Cedar and

Holly; mother of Oak Green; wife of Tudor Green.

Robinson, Cedar – 1731. Worker on Cappleman Farm; son of Tozer and Apple Robinson; brother of Willow, Hazel and Holly; uncle of "Young Tozer" and Margery Kirby, and of Oak Green.

Robinson, Holly – 1736. Youngest daughter of Tozer and Apple Robinson; sister of Willow, Cedar and Hazel; aunt of "Young Tozer" and Margery Kirby, and of Oak Green.

Robson, Lilith – 1746. Pupil at the Lookout.

Rodman, Eleanor – 1735. Housemistress at the Lookout.

Rowley, Alvina – 1711. Chief cook at the Lookout; wife of Rodney Rowley.

Rowley, Rodney – 1708. Husband of Alvina Rowley.

Sandon, Chad – 1719. Carpenter/handyman at the Lookout.

Scott, Christopher – 1724. In the employ of Sir Valentine Parker-Sinden, Earl Horsforth; rapist; murderer.

Scott, Zoe – 1746. Pupil at the Lookout.

Shaw, Isaac – 1716. A tanner in Blackburn; husband of Maureen; father of Helen.

Shaw, Maureen – 1715. Wife of Isaac; mother of Helen.

Shaw, Helen (later Helen Regan) – 1736. Staff member at the White Bull Inn, Ribchester; Daughter of Isaac and Maureen Shaw; wife of Alexander Regan.

Shelley, Lettice – 1733. Housemistress at the Lookout.

Sherborne, Gerald – 1694-1763. Nancy Sherborne's third husband

Sherborne, Nancy – 1705. Resident of Easington; widowed three times; later, lover of Neil Levinson.

Shipley, Rabbit – 1695. Gardener at the Lookout.

Siddon, Christopher – 1679-1724. Essex fisherman; husband of Isobel; father of Margaret.

Siddon, Isobel – 1688-1724. Wife of Christopher; mother of Margaret.

Siddon, Margaret – 1707. Daughter of Christopher and Isobel; brothel madam; partner of Ivor Bentham; later, business partner of Edgar Foxley.

Silden, Ned – 1730. Gardener at the Lookout; husband of Pixie Silden.

Silden, Pixie – 1733. Wife of Ned Silden.

Simpson, Laura – 1749. Pupil at the Lookout.

Slate, Revd William (Bill) – 1678. Rector of St. Mary's Church, Chipping Norton; father of Alison.

Slate, Alison – 1704. Daughter of Revd. William Slate; lover of Alder Swithenbank.

Slater, Ryan – 1726. A Hull stable boy; lover of Janet Illif.

Slieve, Brendan – 1733. Landlord of the Strangeway Arms, Welburn

Smart, Frank – 1715. A Hull stable boy; lover of Janet Illif.

Smith, Peter – 1718. Kitty Smith's father.

Smith, Mary – 1718. Kitty Smith's mother.

Smith, Kitty – 1737. Maid to Orla Stapleton (Orla Clarke).

Smith, John – 1739. Kitty Smith's brother.

Smyth, Anne – 1739. Ex-pupil at the Lookout; one time lover of Alan Blake.

Sollett, Dilly – 1743-1763. A Ribchester woman, victim of a contagious illness.

Solomon, Revd – 1684-1761. Husband of Maria ? (last name unknown).

Southwell, Margaret – 1711. Assistant cobbler to William Crowan.

Spooner, Gwendolyn – 1751. Pupil at the Lookout.

Springfield, Jewel – 1739. Member of the Lookout cleaning staff.

Stanton, Hilda – 1701-1754. Mabel Stanton's mother.

Stanton, Mabel – 1724. Member of the Lookout cleaning staff; daughter of Hilda; close friend of Kate Swithenbank.

Stapleton, Martha – 1726-1754. Mother of Orla Stapleton.

Stapleton, Orla (later Orla Clarke) – 1745. Daughter of Martha Stapleton; lover of Rider Browning; pupil at the Lookout.

Stafford, Michael – 1716. Works in the Lookout laundry;

husband of Mary; father of Beryl, Crispin, Barbara and Sylvia; later, father-in-law of Winnie Stafford (née Warwick).

Stafford, Mary – 1719. Runs the Lookout laundry; wife of Michael; mother of Beryl, Crispin, Barbara and Sylvia; later, mother-in-law of Winnie Stafford (née Warwick).

Stafford, Beryl – 1738. Works in the Lookout laundry. Daughter of Michael and Mary; sister of Crispin, Barbara and Sylvia; later, sister-in-law of Winnie Stafford (née Warwick).

Stafford, Crispin – January 1739. Works in the Lookout laundry. Son of Michael and Mary; brother of Beryl, Barbara and Sylvia; later, husband of Winnie Warwick.

Stafford, Barbara – 1741. Works in the Lookout laundry. Daughter of Michael and Mary; sister of Beryl, Crispin and Sylvia; later, sister-in-law of Winnie Stafford (née Warwick).

Stafford, Sylvia – 1743. Works in the Lookout laundry. Daughter of Michael and Mary; sister of Beryl, Crispin and Barbara; later, sister-in-law of Winnie Stafford (née Warwick).

Stafford, Winnie (née Warwick) – May 1734. Maid to the girls at the Lookout; wife of Crispin Stafford; daughter-in-law of Michael and Mary Stafford.

Stamper, Vivianne (Viv) – April 15, 1743. Pupil at the Lookout.

Stone, Slade – 1745. Soil boy at the Lookout.

Storm, Rendall – 1741. Labourer at Cappleman Farm; tenant of Bridie Lyle; lover of Buffy Miller (Pond Girl).

Strapp, Revd Dr Lemuel – 1699. Vicar of All Saints Church, Cawood, Yorkshire; husband of Margaret.

Strapp, Margaret – 1705. Wife of Revd Dr Lemuel Strapp.

Surbiton, Revd Will – 1688. Retired clergyman, late of Harwood Dale – conducts occasional services at the Lookout.

Sutherland, Charles – 1708. Husband of Juno; father of Clara; lover of Drusilla Glanville.

Sutherland, Juno – 1713. London harpist; wife of Charles;

mother of Clara; younger sister of Vincent Mortimer; aunt of Peter Mortimer.

Sutherland, Clara – April 27, 1738. Harp tutor at the Lookout; daughter of Charles and Juno; long-term lover of Sylvie Ardoin.

Swift, Lawrence – 1658-1726. Husband of Lucinda; father of Bernard.

Swift, Lucinda – 1665-1742. Matriarch; wife of Lawrence Swift; mother of Bernard; rival to Martha Wheatley.

Swift, Bernard – 1697-February, 1762. In service to the Fleshers at Cappleman Farm; son of Lucinda and Lawrence; husband of Florence (née Wheatley); father of Richard.

Swift, Florence (née Wheatley) – 1705. In service to the Fleshers at Cappleman Farm; daughter of Martha and Laurence; wife of Bernard; mother of Richard.

Swift, Richard – 1724. In service to the Fleshers at Cappleman Farm; son of Bernard and Florence; husband of Emma; mother of Amy and Beatrice.

Swift, Emma (née Barnaby) – 1721. In service to the Fleshers at Cappleman Farm; wife of Richard Swift; mother of Amy and Beatrice.

Swift, Amy – 1744. Daughter of Richard and Emma; sister of Beatrice.

Swift, Beatrice – 1746. Daughter of Richard and Emma; sister of Amy.

Swithenbank, William – 1680. Labourer on a farm near Burford, Oxfordshire; husband of Heather; father of Alder.

Swithenbank, Heather – 1682. Wife of William; mother of Alder.

Swithenbank, Alder – April 2, 1703. Labourer at Cappleman Farm; son of William and Heather; husband of Nara Priestly, later of Meadow Reid; father of Kate Swithenbank; in his youth, fathered at least eight other children; friend of Tozer Robinson.

Swithenbank, Nara (née Priestly) – May 18, 1733. Daughter of Oswin and Hazel; sister of Adam and William Priestly;

wife of Alder Swithenbank; mother of Kate.

Swithenbank, Catherine (Kate) – March 29, 1749. Principal character of this story; daughter of Alder and Nara Swithenbank; granddaughter of Hazel Priestly; pupil at the Lookout.

Swithenbank, Meadow (née Reid) – February 2, 1737. Daughter of Sigbert and Persephone; later, wife of Alder Swithenbank.

Sykes, John – 1657-1733. Husband of Scarlet (née Marshall); father of Hazel.

Sykes, Scarlet (née Marshall) – 1670-1719. Daughter of Slade and Daisy Marshall; wife of John Sykes; mother of Hazel.

Tanner, Stanley – 1727. Driver at the Lookout; one time lover of Sybil Crockett.

Telford, Brendan – 1738. Labourer at Cappleman Farm. Lover of a very young Buffy Miller (Pond Girl).

Templeton, Esther – December 1749. Pupil at the Lookout.

Tenley, Peter – 1708-1752. Husband of Stella Tenley.

Tenley, Stella (née Seagrove) – 1718. Headmistress at the Lookout; wife of Peter Tenley (deceased); murderess.

Thorne, Tom – 1726. Carpenter/handyman at the Lookout.

Tickle, Tranter – 1708. Farmer at the Lookout; husband of Teresa.

Tickle, Teresa – 1710. Wife of Tranter Tickle.

Tilshead, Edward Lord Tilshead – 1694. A landowner from Wiltshire; patron of the King's Place brothels; would-be rapist of Fuzzy Craw.

Tilson, Peter – 1692. Manager of a Grimsby hotel; husband of Cecilia Tilson; lover of Lilly, Elizabeth, Margaret, Elsa, Sarah, Tessa and numerous others; lover of Janet Illif.

Tilson, Cecilia – 1696. Wife of Peter Tilson.

Trent, Denise (later, Denise Nisbet) – 1734. Housemistress at the Lookout; wife of Terrel Nisbet; mother of Elizabeth Ruth Nisbet (Libby Ruthlet).

Tretheway, Erin – 1748. Pupil at the school in Tavistock.

Trillo, Samuel – 1716. Landlord of The Silver Sea inn, Whitby; second constable of Whitby; lover of Nancy Blackford (Mrs).

Trivet, Douglas – 1735. Brewer at the Lookout; Fuzzy Craw's favourite man.

Trollope, Annabelle – 1723. Needlepoint tutor at the Lookout.

Trommel, Revd Egbert – 1658-1751. Parson of Easington, 1722-1751. Partner of Revd Hubert Cromwell.

Tweddle, Delia – 1739. Dairymaid at the Lookout.

Wade, Birdie – 1703. Member of the Lookout cleaning staff.

Wakeford, Susan – 1747. Pupil at the Lookout.

Walsh, John – 1708. An alehouse manager in Kilbehenny, Ireland; guardian of Ciara.

Ward, David – 1721. Husband of Cristina Ward (née Ash).

Ward, Cristina (née Ash) – 1714. Daughter of Walter and Rosa; sister of Hugo; wife of David Ward.

Warwick, Winnie (later Winnie Stafford) – May 1734. Maid to the girls at the Lookout; later, wife of Crispin Stafford; daughter-in-law of Michael and Mary Stafford.

Wayland, Hollis – June 27, 1729. Medical practitioner at the Lookout.

Westmoreland, Susannah (Sukey) – 1740. Wife of Theo Westmoreland; Dairymaid at the Lookout.

Westmoreland, Theodore (Theo) – 1738. Husband of Sukey Westmoreland; Footman at the Lookout.

Weston, Cady – July 1735. Maid to the girls at the Lookout; daughter of Molly Weston; partner of Sarah Alston.

Weston, Molly – 1706. In service as cook in a house in York; Cady Weston's mother.

Wheatley, Laurence – 1673-1732. Husband of Martha Wheatley; father of Florence Swift.

Wheatley, Martha – 1679-1742. Matriarch; wife of Laurence Wheatley; mother of Florence Swift; rival to Lucinda Swift.

White, James – 1609-1671. Husband of Anne White; father of Daisy.

White, Anne – 1621-1646. Witch; wife of James; mother of Daisy.

Witherington, Carol – 1744. Pupil at the Lookout.

Wynter, William – 1585-1668. Builder of the Lookout; husband of Agnes; father of Tobias.

Wynter, Agnes – 1625-1648. Wife of William; mother of Tobias.

Wynter, Tobias – 1643-1704. Insane son of William and Agnes; husband of Rosalind, father of Lawrence and Robin; murderer.

Wynter, Rosalind – 1675-1704. Wife of Tobias; mother of Lawrence and Robin.

Wynter, Lawrence – 1697-1704. Son of Tobias and Rosalind; twin brother of Robin.

Wynter, Robin – 1697-1704. Son of Tobias and Rosalind; twin brother of Lawrence.

York, Margaret – 1739. Member of the Lookout cleaning staff.

York, Milton – 1702. Servant to the higher staff at the Lookout.

Young, Jane – 1746. Pupil at the Lookout.

Animals named in the text

Bastard – 1755. Speck Beckwith's dog – a shaggy, herding dog.

Tilly – Annabelle Trollope's tabby cat.

Athena, Demeter, Hera, Artemis, Aphrodite, Nemesis – Horses at the Lookout.

Merry and Fiddler – The two spaniels at the King's Place convent.

Brownie – Natty Miller's cat.

Hercules and Goliath – Winch horses, used at the Barnsley mine where Alder Swithenbank worked in early life.

A list of characters arranged by first name appears in Volume 2

TRANSLATION OF FRENCH TEXT IN CHAPTER 68

"Where is Kate?" asked Clara

"I don't know. Away for a few days I think," Sylvie replied.

"She's a sweet girl. I love her so much."

"Not too much I hope. Unless we can share…"

"I think Jacob is fucking her."

"No! I don't believe it! She's too young for him." She thought, then added, "Anyway, Jacob doesn't fuck."

"No?"

"No."

"Just because he hasn't fucked you doesn't mean he doesn't fuck."

"Jacob hasn't fucked you…"

"No, not yet. Anyway, Kate isn't too young for me…"

ABOUT THE AUTHOR

Kevin Corby Bowyer was born in Southend-on-Sea in 1961. He spent most of his life as a professional musician, travelling the world, playing solo concerts, making commercial recordings and trying to teach others how to play. He always thought of his musical performances as acts of story-telling.

Kevin lives in Seamill, Scotland, within sight of the Firth of Clyde and the Isle of Arran. He is the author of *The House on Boulby Cliff* (2020) and *Close to the Silence* (2021).

Photo: Tommy Ga-Ken Wan